THE VIENNA
MELODY

Ernst Lothar

THE VIENNA MELODY

*Translated from the German
by Elizabeth Reynolds Hapgood*

Europa
editions

Europa Editions
214 West 29th Street
New York, N.Y. 10001
www.europaeditions.com
info@europaeditions.com

Copyright © Paul Zsolnay Verlag, Wien 1963
First Publication 2015 by Europa Editions

Translation by Elizabeth Reynolds Hapgood
Original title: *Der Engel mit der Posaune*
Translation copyright © 2015 by Europa Editions

Library of Congress Cataloging in Publication Data is available
ISBN 978-1- 60945-272-8

Lothar, Ernst
The Vienna Melody

Book design by Emanuele Ragnisco
www.mekkanografici.com
Cover photo © LiliGraphie/Shutterstock

Printed in the USA

To Adrienne, once more

CONTENTS

Part Three
THE CELLAR

Part Four
THE YELLOW DRAWING ROOM

THE VIENNA
MELODY

Prologue
THE FOUNDATIONS

Turn in by the church of the Teutonic Order and a short two minutes' walk will bring you to the house on the corner of Seilerstätte and Annagasse. It stands in the middle of the First District, and the First District is the heart of Vienna.

For nearly a hundred years, and up to the present moment of May 9, 1888, this house had consisted of three stories above the ground floor and mezzanine; no substantial burgess in Vienna had a house any higher. With its six windows on narrow Annagasse and seven on broader Seilerstätte, with its dull, yellowish-gray painted exterior and its façade in the pristine style of the Maria Theresa epoch, it made an impression of stateliness and well-being. Were it not for the stationery store prosily ensconced on the ground floor of Number 10 Seilerstätte (the main entrance was on Seilerstätte), one would have taken it for the town residence of an aristocrat.

This impression was strengthened by a coat of arms carved in stone over the Annagasse entrance. To be sure, it did not consist of crowns, banners, or gauntlets, as did those on the houses of various titled neighbors. It consisted of a naked, fat baroque angel. The angel, however, was blowing a trumpet, a rather remarkable instrument. With its long, thin shaft—which the stonecutter had made too long—supported by a naked arm—which he had made too short—it pointed upward like a spear, and the narrow bell at its end did little or nothing to make it look like a trumpet; it was more like a weapon.

To assert that this coat of arms was intended to cloak the middle-class character of the house and give it an aristocratic air would be absurd. It did no more than follow the style of the times, which found pleasure in ornamenting façades and revealing to passers-by the rank or occupation of the owners. The staff entwined with a serpent of Asclepius indicated the house of a physician or apothecary; the scales, a judicial personage; the wheel, a cart-wright; the long-bearded Gutenberg, a printer. As for the angel with the trumpet, the indication was more dubious. To judge by the length and strength of the trumpet, he might have been considered a summoner to doomsday were it not that any such suggestion of final accounting was most distasteful to the Viennese. On the other hand, if he were taken as a symbol of music it would be difficult to perceive why a manufacturer of pianos chose a trumpet as his emblem.

The house had stood for ninety-seven years when Franz Alt, a grandson of the original builder, began to have thoughts of marriage and of a fourth story. The idea was a bold one, since the inhabitants of Number 10 were good Viennese, which means that they were against change; and nothing more revolutionary than building an extra story on top of an old house could possibly have been imagined. The ground floor rose in opposition.

Intricate as it may seem, we shall have to concern ourselves for just a brief spell with the topography of the house and the genealogy of its tenants.

In Apartment 2 on the ground floor, which was occupied mostly by the stationery shop, Miss Sophie Alt, the only surviving daughter of the founder, lived. Her three-room flat was reached by the entrance from Annagasse. A low, square oak door led into a stone-paved entry. The air was always cool here, refreshing on a hot day, and it was so dark that it was lighted summer and winter by a gas lamp hanging from the high vaulted ceiling. Sophie had chosen the ground-floor apartment because she did not care to climb stairs and also because the walnut tree in the courtyard stretched its fragrant leaves into her bedroom windows.

The former Miss Kubelka, from a small Czech town, lived on the mezzanine, directly over Sophie's head, so that one could hear her eternal hacking cough, and when decent folk were in their beds she, God knows why, was still rambling around and stamping overhead. The former Miss Kubelka (that was what Sophie called the widow of her eldest brother) was an "inane creature." As for Anna, the daughter of that Czechish woman, Sophie's uncompromising estimate was: "Anna? She inherited her stupidity from her mother. Otherwise she would never have married the owner of a racing stable!" For that was what Anna had done. At twenty-one she had fallen head over heels in love with Count Hegéssy, owner of a Hungarian stud farm. After he had won the Royal prize in Budapest he had immediately disposed of Anna. Since then she had lived with her mother in the mezzanine Apartment 3, neither married nor divorced—just deserted. The adjoining mezzanine apartments, 4 and 5, housed the Drauffers—father, mother, twin sons, and a dog.

Apartment 6, on the first floor, belonged to Sophie's eldest nephew, her favorite of all the inhabitants of the house. As far as the elderly spinster was concerned, Otto Eberhard was possessed of exclusively good characteristics. His upward career had been rapid and impressive; at forty-nine he was already the Public Prosecutor. Besides, his wife Elsa, the former Baroness Uiberacker, was a dear. Too bad that their ideal marriage had produced only one son, Peter, eight years old and perhaps a bit on the heavy side, but nevertheless a magnificent specimen. One had only to compare him with his cousins on the mezzanine floor, those eternally dirty, howling, unmannerly twins (just as unmannerly as their father, that rarely sober and always brazen painter, Drauffer), and the choice between them was easy to make. Moreover, those terrible mezzanine boys had an equally fearsome dog—Rex, a Doberman—who was Sophie's personal enemy because he barked whenever he saw her. By contrast the quiet little boy on the first floor played, as children in a fine house should, with an always immaculate white poodle on wheels.

The tenant of Apartment 7 on the first floor was another person who did not stand very high in Sophie's favor. This flat belonged to Otto Eberhard's younger sister, Gretl. Her choice of a life companion had fallen on a colonel of Dragoons by the name of Paskiewicz. He was dashingly handsome, yet he had not only humiliated her repeatedly but had also squandered her dowry and her patrimony to the last penny. Since he was a Pole, Sophie found it easy to put him on her list of those—like the Czechish Kubelka woman and Hungarian Count Hegéssy—on whom she freely poured out the bile generated by her rooted nationalistic prejudices.

On the second floor (Apartments 8 and 9) the founder of the house, Christopher Alt, had lived. It remained uninhabited after his death and that of his widow, due to the terms of his will, in which he also stipulated that only members of the family were allowed to live in the house and renting to outsiders was strictly forbidden. Out of his twelve rooms, partitions were removed to make a total of seven: the yellow drawing-room, the large and small sitting rooms, the large and small dining rooms, the conservatory, and the music room. They were available to all members of the family and were used on festive occasions, although much more rarely than old Christopher, with his strong family sense, intended. The reason for this was simple. These unused rooms were freezing cold in winter and could have been made comfortable only through the installation of a new heating system—an expense which no one was willing to undertake.

Franz lived on the third floor, in Apartment 10; he was thir-

teen years younger than his brother, Otto, the lawyer. The contrast between them, which Sophie often remarked on to the
detriment of the younger brother, was striking. Otto Eberhard
was tall and lithe and dressed with care and marked elegance.
Because of the streaks of gray in his moustache and short
pointed beard, at forty-nine he looked older. Whereas Franz,
just turned thirty-six, looked twenty-eight; he was a less refined
type than his brother, ruddier and almost as tall. "Looks like a
peasant," said Sophie, for he spent a great deal less care on his
clothes; one would have found it difficult to believe that his
roomy trousers had ever boasted a crease. He had followed his
father and grandfather in the piano factory, and there was only
one thing Sophie gave him credit for: "When it comes to business he has a good head on his shoulders."

Whatever else reached her ears about the third floor (in
addition to Franz, that Drauffer man had his studio up there)
filled her with disgust. Presumably it was part of a painter's
profession, especially when he paraded the title of professor, to
have a lot of women coming to his studio, but what she could
not understand was why he did not at last take his work seriously and paint the portraits of some men! His Eminence the
Cardinal and Archbishop, she read in her Catholic daily, had
sat for his portrait to a painter named Koch, and our esteemed
Lord Mayor had done as much for Pausinger. That kind of
painting was worth the name, but not the frivolous mess that
this man smeared on canvas and then was brazen enough to
exhibit! She had, to be sure, gone to only one of his exhibitions, in the Künstlerhaus, but that was enough to last her a
lifetime. Coquettish, empty faces, bare arms, yes, and bare
backs too—it was enough to make one blush for the models
and for the painter. Be that as it may, Drauffer had at least the
excuse of his profession. But what pretext could Franz offer
for having women climb up to his third floor to see him, always
different ones, and at night too? That they did come Sophie

knew, because they preferred to use the side entrance from Annagasse rather than the main entrance on Seilerstätte. With rage she listened to their light, quick, and guilty-sounding steps. Franz was really not so young any more that it was still necessary for him to get such things out of his system; or at least that is what she thought. At his age other men had long since given up their wild ways, settled down, and founded proper families. Besides, Franz did not look in the least like that sort of person.

"Good morning, sir," was old Poldi's greeting to this frowned-upon nephew as he rang at Apartment 2 on the ground floor that morning of May 9. "Please wait a moment; the mistress is just dressing her hair."

Franz waited in the vestibule. As usual it was black as night there and smelled of moth balls. Beyond the door Cora, the parrot, was making her high-pitched noises.

"The mistress says please come in," announced the elderly maid, and Franz entered.

"Am I disturbing you?" he asked.

"You can see very well that you are," answered Sophie. She had hastily covered her bed with a dark blue velvet spread which screened it from public view during the daytime. Not that she had just got up. She left her bed every morning on the stroke of seven. Consequently she had already said her rosary on the prayer stool before her private altar and had finished the greater part of her toilet. She had been on the point of arranging her coiffure when her nephew was announced.

"Don't stand. Sit down!" she said firmly.

"How wonderful! How wonderful! Thank you!" croaked the parrot from the dining room—once, twice, and then over again.

"Shut up, Cora!" ordered the old lady. Then to her nephew: "Have some coffee? Or a glass of cherry brandy?"

She was sitting at her absurdly narrow dressing table, which was littered to such an extent with tiny pincushions, glass and porcelain jars that not another thing could possibly be crowded on to it. Beside her, on an even smaller table, lay a copy of the Catholic daily newspaper, her reticule, and a box of thin green peppermint pastilles, which she, with her taste for all sweets, adored. From time to time she slipped one into her mouth, after first coughing slightly and thereby giving herself a medicinal excuse for its enjoyment. It was rather cold in the room. One of the windows, framed in a blue velvet curtain, stood half open, letting in the sunless air. The walnut tree in the courtyard had not yet begun to bloom.

Franz chose the cherry brandy. From where he sat he could see Sophie's face in the mirror. Her back was turned to him as she continued to work on her coiffure with two long-handled tortoise-shell brushes. Her white hair, beautifully soft and completely silvered, was her best feature. Her cheeks and mouth were so withered by age, so thin, pinched, and flesh-less, that they barely existed any more.

"What's on your mind?" She spoke without expression, without the usual caressing smile which she liked to lavish on her elder nephew, Otto Eberhard.

Franz was not in the habit of beating about the bush. Diplomacy (and imagination too, alas!) was a sealed book to him. With him things had to proceed in a straightforward, simple way; anything else he considered fuss. Yet today he hesitated. He felt a chill.

"Don't you have the heat on any longer, Aunt Sophie?" he inquired.

"Is that what you came down at this hour in the morning to find out?" she retorted, in the loud tone of a person hard of hearing, as she shook her head over her nephew (as well as at a strand of silver hair pulled out by her vigorous brushing).

"We don't have the heat on any longer. We don't use heat after Easter. Do you know what coal costs? One florin and eleven coppers! Do you still heat your apartment upstairs?"

"No—that is to say, yes," he continued, increasingly disconcerted. How silly, he said to himself; I am almost afraid.

"Of course! The women up at your place must be kept warm, mustn't they? Drink your brandy if you're chilly," she suggested dryly.

His uneasiness vanished as quickly as it had come. "That's why I'm here," he admitted, "on account of the women."

It was difficult to tell when the old lady's hearing was good and when it was not. There were times when she did not choose to hear.

"What's that?" she asked.

"I said that I came on account of the women," he repeated.

"I already heard that nonsense," she declared. "Only I don't think it's so amusing. At your age—"

"A man should marry. And that's just what I intend to do."

"What?" she said again. She even forgot to slip a peppermint drop into her mouth, although she had prepared the excuse for it by a short cough.

"Imagine," said Franz, "you've been urging it on me for so long, and at last I've brought myself to the point. I'm engaged." There, he thought, I've said it, and how simple it was! He even believed he could detect the joyful effect of his news on the old lady, and he rubbed his hands together.

Sophie had laid down her brushes. She turned quickly around on her stool, looked him straight in the face, and said: "This is a surprise! When did it happen?"

"Oh … not long ago."

"Well, I never! Do I know her?"

"Of course. It's Henriette."

If it was joy that had brightened her face a moment ago there was no doubt that now something else darkened it. There was no disguising the fact, and Franz saw it. His anger flared, as it did so easily with him.

"Is there anything you are not pleased with?" he put in quickly.

Sophie sat bolt upright. "Henriette? You mean Henriette Stein?" she asked, this time almost in a whisper.

"I know only one Henriette."

"The daughter of—" She did not finish her question. She was not even looking at her nephew now; her eyes had dropped to her white dressing gown, which was much too thin for such a cool morning.

"The daughter of Professor Stein of the University," Franz went on in a sharp tone. His usual good humor had vanished. "The daughter of one of our greatest jurists, in case you don't happen to be aware of that fact," he added aggressively.

"I'm quite aware of it."

"The daughter of one of the finest men," Franz continued in the same laudatory strain.

"Thank you! Thank you! Thank you!" croaked the parrot in the silence that fell.

"What does your brother say to this?" asked the old lady, and again her thin lips framed the words so softly.

"He doesn't know about it yet."

"Doesn't know! Why not?"

"Because I wanted to tell you first." Franz was not clever at lying. The flattery sounded insincere.

"He doesn't know about it yet," Sophie repeated stubbornly. "Professor Stein is Jewish, isn't he?"

"He's been baptized. Why do you ask?"

"And who was her mother?" countered Sophie.

"Her maiden name was Aufreiter. She was more Catholic than you, Auntie."

"Aufreiter," said Sophie, and nodded deprecatingly. "Actress, wasn't she?"

"From the opera," answered her nephew, with an effort at self-control. "She was an excellent singer. She died when Henriette was seven years old. You probably never knew her. You were living in Brünn in those days."

Now the old lady was looking straight at him. "Oh, yes—I knew her. That is to say, I knew of her. One heard a lot about her."

"That goes with being on the stage."

"There was more to it than just that," she insisted.

"Her daughter speaks of her with admiration. So does her husband. That should be enough. In any case, it's enough for me," Franz flared up.

That was no way to appease the old lady. She turned abruptly around, snatched up a comb, parted her beautiful thin hair with trembling fingers, and said with a tone of finality: "Of Jewish blood on her father's side. Her mother—but I'd rather not say the word. Listen to me! You say that I'm the first to learn of your engagement. Then let me be the first to warn you. You're no child. This is no schoolboy infatuation. You're nearly forty, and your children will be the ones to take over the firm made great by your father and grandfather. Never forget that!"

Quiet, now, said Franz to himself, clasping and unclasping his hands. What the old lady thinks of Henriette means nothing to me. But unfortunately half of the house belongs to her. "Have you had some bad experiences with Jewesses?" he asked in a suppressed voice. "Mother was Jewish when Father married her. Had you forgotten that?"

Although he did not speak in a loud tone, she heard every word. No, she had not forgotten. That was the point. Who had encouraged Gretl's marriage, with that scamp Paskiewicz? Julie. And why? Because he was a handsome creature. And who had pestered Franz's dear dead-and-gone father until he gave his consent to Pauline's marriage with the insufferable painter Drauffer? Julie. And for the same reason. If girls like Gretl and Pauline chased after men it was because of their mother's blood in their veins. The trouble with Franz was that he also had too much of that blood in him. What luck that Otto Eberhard took after his father!

"I'm aware of that," the elderly spinster replied at length, "and I have no intention of belittling the memory of your dear mother. In her own way she was a good wife to your father."

"In every way."

"It was just that she had strange ideas about bringing up children. I can't say that results have justified her. Look at your sisters!"

"My sisters are getting along splendidly."

"That's a matter of opinion."

"My opinion, Auntie."

"Tell me, Franz. In all Vienna is there no other woman besides Henriette Stein fit to be the wife of the head of the Alt Firm? Have you waited so long only in the end to find no one but her?"

Her nephew answered with such conviction that his rather coarse face lost its expression of displeasure and became almost radiant.

"If there's one thing I'm sure of, it's this! I've waited for Henriette, yes. But I don't want anyone else. No!"

The old lady had finished dressing her hair and put away her brushes and comb. "Then I must congratulate you," she said after a moment of silence. And then, after another pause, she added, "When will you bring her to see me?"

"When would you like me to?"

"You know I'm always at home."

"We'll come very soon," he promised.

"I shall be very pleased," was her reply.

"Thank you," he said, and felt a little touched. Then, with his eyes on the window, he remarked: "Oh, yes, there's another little thing. I'd like to build a fourth story on our house. The plans have been drawn, and it can be done very simply while you're all away in the country. You've no objection, have you?"

"What?" she asked.

He repeated what he had said.

"What do you want a fourth floor for, Franz?"

"Because we want to live there."

"Haven't you enough room on the third floor? Just the two of you?"

"The third doesn't suit us, Aunt Sophie."

Now her voice rose. "Is that so? Why?"

"You know perfectly well. The rooms are either too small or too huge. You can't heat it. There are no bathrooms. Besides, the Annagasse is dark as pitch all winter long."

"Please get my cane from over there."

He handed her the ivory-handled cane. When he offered to help her get up she refused, took hold of her small dressing table, and pulled herself to her feet. It was only when she stood up that one could see how tall she really was.

In her thin dressing gown she walked a few steps beside the bed, past her prayer stool, up to the half-open window and back. Her steps were noiseless, they carried so little weight. Only the cane, which she set down firmly, made a sound. "Miss Stein must be very spoiled!" she exclaimed, and then repeated, "Very spoiled indeed!"

Franz laughed. "In any case, I'd like very much to spoil her," he admitted.

Then the old lady stood still. "Your brother, Otto Eberhard, has often made me feel that I took the place of both your father and mother. You never have. But at least someone must say to you: 'Franz, you are headed for disaster!'"

Her words were not severe. Fear and a slight, very slight, trace of suppressed tenderness were contained in them.

"It's sweet of you to be concerned about me," he answered,

"but it's quite unnecessary. I can assure you that there are no two people in all Vienna who will be happier than Henriette and I."

"As you say," replied Sophie. "You're in no hurry for my approval about the building, I suppose. As for the other, you don't care anyway."

"But I do want your approval now!" he urged. "I have to apply to the City Building Commission for a permit. It will take them a long time to get through with all their fuss."

"But this does not depend on me alone. Your brother and sisters have to give their consent. Each of them is a co-owner of your half of the property."

"Naturally. But when you've agreed, the majority will be in favor," he said, laying his cards on the table with his usual lack of diplomacy.

"I want first to talk the matter over with Otto Eberhard," she concluded.

At that, Franz's sorely tried patience gave way. "You can talk to him as much as you like. You can decide anything you choose, for all I care," he said, with a snap of his fingers. "As you mentioned a moment ago, I shall be forty in a few years. It's simply absurd that a thirty-six-year-old man should have to ask whether or not he can do this or that! The fourth story will be built. You can bank on that. Good-bye!"

With those final words he strode through the dining room, through the sitting room, where Cora sat with ruffled feathers on her brass rod, and on out into the vestibule.

"Thank you! Thank you!" the parrot screeched anxiously after him.

That much he heard. Of what the old lady said only the beginning reached his ears: "There is absolutely nothing absurd about discussing important matters with the few people who belong to you." But when she raised her voice and called after him, "Grownups too make catastrophic mistakes," he was already halfway down three steps leading into the cold passageway.

There were obstacles to be overcome before the fourth story could be built. The remarkable part of it was that they were presented by the people in the house than by outsiders. With his keen of actuality and advantages, Otto Eberhard realized at once he would do better to promote his brother's marriage than to oppose it. He weighed Aunt Sophie's objections, and as one of the most loyal adherents of the Christian Socialist party, he could hardly have been accused of being fascinated by Franz's choice. On the other hand, the fiancée's father, Professor Stein, was a man of importance, who would sooner or later be sure to take his place the Upper Chamber. His influence on the Minister of Justice was considerable, and the Public Prosecutor was subordinate to Minister. All in all, therefore, Otto Eberhard's objections were worth mentioning; so, after Franz had agreed that the equities in the property would not be disturbed and that he would bear all the costs of the construction himself, the family said amen.

But the City Building Commission, on the contrary, introduced formalities which drove impetuous Franz to distraction. They maintained that the equities in the house were by no means clearly established and demanded proper documents from each and every one of the co-owners which not only would include consent to the additional structure but would also offer incontrovertible and properly notarized proof of ownership. Subsequently the family lawyer, on his side, insisted on being provided with all the documents pertaining to the matter, either in original form or in notarized copies.

Thus Franz, who loathed official papers and official bureaus, was obliged to take up his abode for a full day in the Hall of Records while looking up all entries and deeds having a bearing on Number 10. And there was a plethora of them; the reason being that a building law established by Empress Maria Theresa required that any Viennese who built, bought, or inherited a house should produce "proof of eligibility." This meant that all vital facts in the case had to be submitted to a so-called Housing Tribunal, a kind of supervisory organization which interfered in all matters and insisted on knowing everything.

At first with curses, then with resignation, and finally with amusement, Franz studied the "eligibility" documents and learned the history of the house which no longer met his needs.

I, the undersigned, Christopher Alt, respectfully petition the esteemed Housing Tribunal for its consent to the construction of a house on Seilerstätte; the same to stand on the presently unimproved property of Count Harrach, between numbers 8 and 12. The ground plan is herewith submitted; also estimates for the construction in the amount of 9,290 silver florins and 24 coppers. Further enclosure, consisting of extract from the accounts of the Vienna Citizens Savings Institution, showing that I am in possession of a fortune amounting to the sum of 74,366 florins and 19 coppers, and am in consequence well able and prepared to undertake the costs of construction and other consequent expenses as well as personal and real estate taxes without having recourse to any borrowing of funds.

I was born on April 29, 1758, in Vienna, of Roman Catholic faith, the second son of Johann Peter Alt, who, as court organist for thirty-four years of his law-abiding life, played the organ in the chapel of Her Majesty our most illustrious Empress Maria Theresa to her gracious satisfaction. I live in the happiest wedlock with Margaret Ann Ludovica née Landl, of Mürzsteg, Styria, daughter of the chief forester in charge of administration of the Imperial Hunting Preserves, and niece of the priest at the Maria Zell shrine. After passing through the grammar school I finished the course at the Trade School on Hoher Markt. As my sainted father destined me to succeed him in his business and desired me to receive the most excellent training, he sent me, at the age of sixteen, to Pleyel, the world-famous piano manufacturer in Paris, in whose factory I worked for three years as an apprentice. In said circumstances I amassed a store of specialized knowledge which stood me in good stead and which I further enlarged when I worked in a similar capacity in London and St Petersburg. On my father's demise I returned to Vienna, as I had often longed to do while abroad, and with my inheritance I founded, in 1780, the firm of Christopher Alt, Piano Maker, at 194 Wiedner Hauptstrasse.

Through the grace of Divine Providence and my own industry I was enabled to keep pace with international competition and to win for my products a reputation repeatedly attested to in flattering terms by such outstanding virtuosos as Messrs. Lambert, Gustave Schneider, Sr.; the organist to the archbishop at St. Stephen's, and Mr. Haydn, chapel organist to Prince Palffy. I trust the praiseworthy Building Commission will not impute to me too great a lack of modesty if I quote from a letter of the composer and piano virtuoso, Wolfgang A. Mozart: "Each time I have the feeling that it is not ivory and wood under my fingers when I strike the keys, but something quite different. When I touch your instrument it is as though these solid materials evanesced into some floating intangible, revealing that secret quality we so deeply yearn for in tones and in human hearts." Shortly before her demise, Her Majesty the Empress graciously consented that I dedicate to her an Alt grand piano, on which her artistically inclined son and successor, Emperor Joseph II, had deigned to play with his own hands.

The reason for my entering my petition to build is, in my humble estimate, urgent. It arises from the circumstance that with the increase of my family the limited housing facilities of the Wiedner Hauptstrasse are no longer sufficient to meet the demands both of manufacturing activity and private domesticity. It is a permanent family home that I seek to prepare, in the hope that the favor of our Lord will continue to bless the efforts of me and my descendants and insure more firmly the patriarchal bonds uniting these latter.

In the ardent hope of a speedy and favorable action on this my request, I beg to remain, honorable gentlemen of the Building Commission,

Your most humble servant,

CHRISOPHER ALT, *piano-maker*

This entry bore the official note: "Applicant wealthy and reputable. Permit granted. Vienna, July 23, 1790."

Under date of September 2, 1791, an unsigned communication read:

WORTHY GENTLEMEN OF THE TRIBUNAL:

Any decent citizen's sense of order and propriety must be grossly offended if, thanks to an erroneous interpretation of the liberal attitude of our most magnanimous and philanthropic monarch, Joseph II, such things are tolerated as the house-warming celebration of yesterday, September 1, 1791, in the newly constructed building at Number 10 Seilerstätte. Your honors may be aware of the fact that this building is directly opposite Number 5 on Annagasse, where the Futura Lodge of the Masons is housed. But you may not be cognizant of the fact that this celebration and the house itself is nothing more than a clever mask to conceal the inauguration of a new Masonic branch. Of the guests gathered on the second, or living room, floor two-thirds were members of the Futura Lodge. Moreover, the grand master of the Grand Lodge of Vienna and other deputy grand masters, that wanton band who bow neither to Emperor nor Pope, also appeared there.

The pretext used was a piano recital by a lodge member,

Brother Mozart, who gave the first public rendering of an opera composed by him. It is entitled *The Magic Flute*, and it is to be produced in a very few days at the Theater an der Wien. As far as the writer of these lines, who was present in person, could judge of the contents of the libretto, to which we were treated by the librettist himself, one Schikaneder, it consisted of nothing more nor less than a panegyric of freemasonry disguised in fairy tale form, and although the extremely unmelodious music is most unlikely to achieve any success, nevertheless the unpalatable evidence of a fresh extension of freemasonry proselytizing must be noted.

Whether the proprietor of the newly built house, one Christopher Alt, is himself a freemason is as yet to be determined. It was, in any event, a sorry spectacle to perceive the delight, which could not possibly have been genuine, with which he listened to the vain efforts of Lodge Brother Mozart, who in a physical way too was a picture of penury and disarray. Carelessly clothed, his face of a deep yellow pallor, his forehead beaded with sweat, his movements repulsively unsteady, croaking rather than singing the dissonant notes of the arias in his opus—particularly the high part of a so-called Queen of the Night, written for his disreputable sister-in-law, the singer Josefa Weber—he made the impression of a man intoxicated. He and his wildly applauding clique of fellow Masons succeeded in so disturbing the nocturnal peace of the neighborhood that it is to be presumed you have been duly notified about it from other quarters as well. In any case, it can surely not be the purpose of the esteemed Tribunal to allow a newly built house from the very first day of its existence to become a multiple source of public disturbance and its owner to dance to a tune piped over the way at 5 Annagasse.

[*signed*] A FRIEND OF THE ORDER

An official comment read: "Referred to the police authorities for investigation." Accompanying this was a note by the chief of police:

> According to a report by the city authorities, the above complaint is unfounded on both counts. Court Composer Mozart on said evening did not cause a disturbance, either through drunken behaviour or in any other way. Moreover, according to the common testimony of his wife Constance and his family doctor, Dr. Schimmler, he has suffered for some time from atrophy of the kidneys, a chronic illness which in recent weeks has become acute and which on the evening of September 1 caused the symptoms noted by the complainant. Herr Mozart's condition has since become so aggravated that his end must be expected hourly. As concerns the other guests, among them were numbered high-ranking members of the clergy, headed by His Grace the Suffragan Bishop, two major-generals, and one major. There was no indication of Freemason activity, and the implication that the owner of the house, Christopher Alt, was acting as agent for the Freemasons, or is himself a Freemason, is not confirmed by any of the evidence produced.

With a final note by the Tribunal—"filed"—the document ended.

In the next thirteen years there were no additions to the file that seemed worthy of interest to Franz. There was only one, dated December 4, 1804, which struck him. In it the "overjoyed parents" announced the birth of a healthy daughter, christened Sophie. In this manner he discovered her age, which she so carefully concealed: she was eighty-four.

Then followed two death notices:

> The deeply bereaved undersigned [ran the first document] duly announce to the Honorable Tribunal the death of Christopher Alt, respectively our beloved husband, father,

father-in-law, and grandfather, founder and proprietor of the firm C. Alt, owner of the house at Number 10 Seilerstätte. On May 1, 1839, in his eighty-first year, after a God-fearing, laborious life, having partaken of the last sacraments of the Church, he fell peacefully asleep in the Lord.

[*signed*] MARGARET ALT, *née* LANDL, *wife and sole legatee*
KARL LUDWIG ALT
EMIL ALT
HUGO ALT, *sons*
SOPHIE ALT, *daughter*
BETTY ALT, *née* KUBELKA
JULIE ALT, *née* BERGHEIMSTEIN, *daughters-in-law*
OTTO EBERHARD, ANNA, GRETL, PAULINE, *grandchildren*

On May 9, 1843, according to the second death notice, a beloved son and respectively brother, brother-in-law, and uncle, Hugo Alt, had died, having borne his sufferings with gentleness and patience. As Franz remembered, his sufferings came from an illness not mentioned in society.

Next Franz took up a sheet containing the notice of his own birth:

We hereby announce to the Honorable Tribunal the birth, on August 9, 1852, of a healthy son, christened Franz Sebastian. Respectfully submitted,
EMIL ALT, *proprietor of the firm of C. Alt, Piano-maker*
JULIE ALT, *his wife*.

The words "overjoyed parents," Franz noted, did not occur in this announcement.

On the other hand, Franz read the next document with growing pleasure:

It is with a sense of deepest shame and parental indignation [it began, and after a lengthy introduction went on to report] … On Sunday last, April 25, 1854, I, in company with my spouse, my fifteen-year-old son Otto Eberhard, my thirteen-year-old daughter Gretl, and my five-year-old daughter Pauline, was among those citizens of Vienna whose lot it was to be possessed of the inestimable privilege of witnessing the marriage of the Imperial couple in the Augustine Church. The officials of the Diocesan Administration, who issued to me the entrance permits, informed me that the ceremony would commence at half-past four in the afternoon. By three o'clock we were already in our places so that the children might be so situated as to have a nearby view of this memorable rite. The places we obtained were in the benches along the central aisle. As a result, however, of the fact that it was half-past six before the ceremony began to take its due course, the children became hungry, which may to a certain degree be pardonable as they had not partaken of food since their noonday meal. And I naturally preserved all due decorum by not permitting a so awe-inspiring edifice as a cathedral to be profaned by the bringing into it and the consumption there of food. My spouse and I were of one mind: namely, to direct the children's attention to the impending august event and to impress its importance on them in suitable terms. At first we were rewarded in accomplishing this desired end, and had the delay not been quite so protracted all would have passed off satisfactorily and this unhappy, distressful incident have been averted. But the longer we waited the more difficult it became to keep the children patient. On the other hand, and this is perhaps not entirely inexcusable, neither my wife nor I were willing to give up the places secured at the cost of such effort or indeed to sacrifice that on which we had so ardently set our hearts. Alas, had we but done it! For as the procession of the most exalted bridal couple made its entry we deemed it permissible to turn our attention from the children and with all our hearts address ourselves to the magnificent spectacle that must enthral every eye. Yet in the instant when His Eminence the Prince-Archbishop began to enumerate the names and titles of His Majesty the Emperor, Francis Joseph I, the disaster occurred. I shall make no attempt to mitigate what in its very nature was inexcusable; I shall do no more than suggest that possibly the children, in their ignorance and in their above-described state, may have thought that the enumeration would continue indefinitely in that fashion. His Eminence had already pronounced the titles "Emperor of Austria, Apostolic King of Hungary, King of Bohemia, King of Dalmatia, King of Croatia, King of Slavonia, King of Jerusalem, Duke of Lorraine, Duke of Modena, Duke of Parma, Piacenza, and Guastalla, Margrave of Moravia, Count of Hapsburg and Kyburg," and was on the point of continuing his enumeration, when a cry of "I want something to eat!" was heard through the devoutly intent congregation in the cathedral.

It came, I must admit with deepest shame, from the mouth of my five-year-old daughter Pauline.

There were, to be sure, a number of indulgent persons who took the incident humorously, and I am almost inclined to believe that His Eminence was one of them. He paused an instant in amazement, then continued with a smile on his lips. A glance too from the most illustrious bride kneeling before the altar inferred forgiveness. But in the eyes of our most gracious Sovereign and Emperor there was a clear expression of displeasure over such a culpable disturbance at such a supremely solemn moment.

It goes without saying that we withdrew without delay and with as little confusion as possible. At the same time that I do my duty in reporting this all-too-regrettable occurrence to your exalted Tribunal, dare I express the hope that their majesties may be apprized of the fact of how distressed and disgraced we

all feel, including the chief culprit, our minor child, and that
we hereby implore the pardon of their most gracious persons.
I beg to remain your most respectful servant,
EMIL ALT, *piano-maker*
10 Seilerstätte

The official comment of the Tribunal said that the matter
"would be dutifully submitted for the consideration of the
Privy Chancellery of His Apostolic Majesty the gracious
Emperor." Beneath this was a further note dated Ischl. July 12,
1854, from the Privy Chancellery: "His Majesty has deigned to
take cognizance of the above-mentioned matters." And the
Tribunal's usual: "filed." My sister Pauline! thought Franz.
What a devil of a girl—and to find this out only thirty-four
years later. Why, she is practically a historic personage!

Signed by the same members of the family who announced
the death of the head of the firm (except that the name of the
now defunct Hugo was missing and that of the new addition to
the family, Franz, was added) was the notice of the demise, on
December 3, 1854, of Margaret Alt, née Landl, sole owner of
the house. According to an accompanying copy of her will, she
left the house in equal shares to her children, Karl Ludwig,
Emil, and Sophie, this transfer being recorded in the register
of deeds at page seventy-one of the folio.

A notice of the death of Karl Ludwig Alt, councillor in the
Imperial and Royal Ministry of Finance, bore a date six weeks
later. On page seventy-one of the folio was recorded the transfer of his equity in the house to his widow Betty, née Kubelka.

This same widow, in 1859, announced with "pride and joy"
the marriage of her only daughter Anna to Count Elemér
Hegéssy.

In the same year, and likewise with "pride and joy," Emil
Alt recorded the marriage of his son Otto Eberhard with the
highborn Baroness Elsa von Uiberacker, and in 1863 that of his

daughter Gretl with Nicholas Anton Paskiewicz, first lieutenant in the Imperial Army.

The next notice concerned the Imperial Dragoons captain,
Nicholas Paskiewicz: it was the printed War Ministry casualty
list with the names of those killed in the Austrian Army in the
unsuccessful campaign against Prussia, and his name was
underlined with red ink.

This printed list remained in the file, although it was proved
false by another announcement under date of July 19, 1866:

> I am happy to announce that my beloved husband did not, as
> was originally believed, die of wounds received during the
> battle of Koenigrätz, but is convalescing in a hospital for offi-
> cers in Olmütz.
> [*signed*] GRETL PASKIEWICZ, *née* ALT

With "pride and joy" Major Nicholas and Gretl Paskiewicz,
née Alt, on March 13, 1878, notified the esteemed Tribunal of
the birth of a healthy daughter, christened Christine Anna Maria.

This concluded the file of documents, for in 1879 Emperor
Francis Joseph abrogated the Maria Theresa building injunc-
tions and thereby deprived the Housing Tribunal of its much
resented jurisdictions.

Only the transfers of property effected since that date were
available for inspection on page seventy-two of the folio.

> Emil Alt, died March 18, 1880. His half interest in the house
> transferred by will to his widow, Julie Alt.
> Julie Alt, died August 17, 1881. Her half interest in the house
> transferred by will in four equal parts to her children, Otto
> Eberhard Alt, Gred Paskiewicz, Pauline Drauffer, Franz Alt.

The equities, Franz found, were established with absolute
clarity, and only "paid troublemongers" (his term for govern-

ment officials) could possibly stir up any difficulties on the legal side. Even on the personal side these dry documents had clarified for him things that he had not rightly been aware of before. They were a long-lived family, these Alts. They had married late for the most part. And they were not all so virtuous, so lamb-like (take Uncle Hugo, for example, or Sister Pauline and brothers-in-law Hegéssy and Paskiewicz). They had had their share of luck, a goodly share; he wished he could feel that that too was amply proven. Yet these papers, in their official gray bindings, for a reason he would find difficult to define, somehow gave him the opposite impression. Underneath all their submissive announcements of marriages, births, deaths, and disturbed ceremonies so much was left unsaid.

His meagre imagination failed him. Were they happy, those predecessors at Number 10? He had never thought of this before. But now he was wondering about it.

Long after he had gone out into the May evening he kept asking himself: What in those papers has made such a sinister impression on me? And again, as he sat in a carriage and drove to fetch Henriette, the stiff, impersonal words with their elaborate lettering, adorning joy and death with impartial hand, were still before his eyes.

Part One
THE FOURTH FLOOR

CHAPTER 1
Ride in the Prater

The rubber wheels of the cab rolled rapidly down the noble avenue of the Prater. They made no noise; all one heard was the hoofbeats of the quick-trotting horses. The open carriage swung smoothly along. The coachman had only to click his tongue now and then or artfully curl his whip over the manes of his pair of blacks to keep them at their brisk pace.

Henriette loved to drive along at a smart clip; it enhanced her enjoyment of life to overtake everyone, pedestrians and carriages alike. At this hour there were, to be sure, not many people on foot and even fewer carriages. She and Franz were almost alone under the tall chestnut trees, with their white candlelike blossoms, which lined both sides of the broad, straight roadway. For fully half an hour they drove along the avenue in the shade of this shimmering beauty, from the Praterstern to the Lusthaus.

The air was laden with the fragrance of May. The violets, growing wild in the neighboring meadows, added their sweetness. The breeze blowing from the Danube added a mild freshness like a caress.

As he gazed at her with that worshipping expression which she found quite repugnant, she said, "The chestnut trees are beautiful, aren't they?"

"Very. By the way, are you superstitious, Hetti?"

"I? Frightfully. Why?"

"Of course, it's all nonsense. But as I sat there this morning and read what you might call our prehistory—" He did not know exactly how to explain this to her. Then he thought of something which was at least possible to tell her, although it was not what mainly preoccupied him. "I can't get it out of my head that Mozart, when he played *The Magic Flute* at my grandfather's housewarming, was already mortally ill. He died a few weeks later."

"Really?" she said, but her thoughts were elsewhere.

"Oh, it's absurd." He laughed at his own remark. Then he changed the subject. "What were you doing all day?" he asked, and took her hand.

So like a soldier with his sweetheart, she thought, and replied: "Nothing in particular. First I went to my milliner's, then Papa took me with him to the University. The oral examinations are being held today."

"Then you will be free longer today?"

"Until nine."

"Wonderful!"

The horses raced on. When they reached the Lusthaus—a kind of casino at the end of the main drive, beyond which lay the meadows and the Freudenau race track—the coachman drew up. He let his passengers get out, for that was the proper thing to do on a drive to the Prater. You always rode as far as the casino and then had the coachman walk the horses behind you while you went on foot under the chestnut trees to the Second Rondeau.

"You look so adorable again," he said admiringly. In her presence he lost all naturalness. He was so conscious of his none-too-impressive appearance that he attempted to compensate for his lack of personal charm with a kind of conventional chivalry. In so doing he quite overlooked the banality of his flattering remarks.

She looked at him out of the corner of her eye. No, he was not fascinating. Not even well-dressed. How was it possible that one single overcoat could contain quite such a mess of wrinkles? If one compared him to—Well, better not! But he had one quality: you could see right through him like a glass; there was nothing opaque about him, nor was there any pretence. He would never leave you suddenly in the lurch. Not he! "I'm glad that at least you like me," she answered.

He found this remark so encouraging that he lost no time in slipping his arm around her waist.

She tried to pull away. "Franz! Will you never learn that there are such things as unwritten laws? You don't hold hands in an open carriage and you do not walk *bras dessus, bras dessous* on a public thoroughfare."

"Where did you hear that?" His tone was matter-of-fact.

"I was told," she replied, laughing.

"And you believe in unwritten laws?"

"I even obey them."

"Really? And what about the written ones? I've also had things told to me."

He was so transparent that she could see there was something behind his words. She hesitated before she asked: "And what have you been told?" Meantime she picked up the skirt of her dark blue velvet suit, although it was not dragging on the ground.

He was obviously enjoying his advantage, a situation which did not often arise between them. "Aha! Now you'd like to know, wouldn't you?"

"Not in the least."

"Then I shan't tell you!"

"That suits me."

"They say you were very much in love," he nevertheless declared.

Her face did not change. It was a fascinating face. Deep-set black eyes, which had an extraordinary way of looking up and then slant-wise from under very long lashes, a gleaming skin, and a sensuous, beautiful mouth made it soft and womanly. How much does he know? she wondered. He cannot know anything, or he would act quite differently.

"Is this in the prehistory of your house?" she managed to ask, with a careless laugh.

This or something else made him laugh too. He looked at her sideways with an expression more ironic than adoring. "Then you were in love with the Crown Prince?"

She realized that it was both stupid and inapt to choose this moment to smell the bunch of violets he had brought her, but she did. "Whoever put such ideas in your head?" she asked in a tone of such alarm that she noticed it herself.

Evidently he was not aware of anything. "Why not? Rudolf chases after women like a crazy man. And you, my dear young lady, are a snob, if I may say so." He laughed again.

Obviously his good humor was not affected. But she must find out how she stood. "Who told you that about me?"

"Someone."

"When?"

"Some time or other. I don't remember. A few weeks ago."

"And you mention it only today?"

"Why not?"

"In all that time you weren't interested?"

"Oh, yes. I was interested enough. But I thought to myself, I'll save it up for the right moment. In speaking of unwritten laws it came into my head. Well—is it yes or no? Is it true?" He was standing still now.

She walked on, her heart beating so fast that she had to struggle for breath. "Of course not. Or do you believe that a girl with the name of Stein would have the ghost of a chance with a crown prince?"

"It would be enough if he had had any chance with you. Did he?" He was speaking a shade more insistently now.

"Now I absolutely insist on knowing who the idiot is who put such ideas into your head! Or is it a secret?"

"Not in the least. It was Otto Eberhard. And in Vienna Public Prosecutors have informers when matters concern a member of the Imperial family."

"You can give my regards to your brother and tell him he has execrable informers. There's not a word of truth in the whole story."

All the while he was watching her. "Didn't you realize that I was just leading you on?"

This she had certainly not realized. It was possible that he was not entirely in earnest. But she was prepared to swear that he had not spoken out of sheer sport. She pulled herself together. "And don't you believe that I would have told you all about it—if only to make myself appear interesting?" she asked.

"It really wouldn't have occurred to me!" Again he looked at her sideways. Again he laughed. "Where shall we eat? In the Third Coffee House or at the Brown Stag?"

After they were seated in the Third Coffee House at a round table with a white cloth, the light from the gas lamps falling on his face, she laid her hand on his arm. "All right, Franz. I did have a crush on him for a while."

He had been studying the menu. He laid the elaborate hand-written sheet on the table and replied: "You see. That's exactly what I said to Otto Eberhard. 'It might well be she had a crush on him the way all the silly young girls in the Burgtheater galleries have on the actor Sonnenthal.' Would you rather have fried chicken or a schnitzel?"

"I also was infatuated by Sonnenthal. That is, I still am."

"But no longer on the Crown Prince?"

With irresistible frankness she shook her head and with it her velvet toque trimmed with a slim blue feather.

"Strawberry or May wine? And crayfish, of course. Where did you meet him?"

"May wine. At a party at the Szeps', the editor's. Papa took me along."

Franz was on the point of saying something, but the waiter had come up to the table, so he told him exactly what they wanted.

"How the Crown Prince gets around!" he ventured when the waiter had left. "Did you talk to him?"

"A lot."

"Was it fun?"

"Yes."

"Did he pay his addresses to you?"

"Rather"

"Did he kiss you?"

"Are you crazy? At a dinner party at which Papa was present!" Her exclamation sounded positively convincing.

"It needn't have been at the dinner party," he said, but she did not doubt that he believed her.

When the May wine came he poured out two glasses. The green springs of herbs in it smelled refreshing. "*Prosit!*" he said, raising his glass to her.

She clinked her glass with his. "Confession over?" she asked after draining her glass.

He nodded.

"Absolution?"

"A rosary."

"Thanks, Padre."

"And a kiss!"

"Unwritten laws!"

"I don't care a straw for them."

"But I do."

"So, you are for the Hapsburg ritual!"

She offered him her lips for a fleeting second.

In an open pavilion on the main side of the garden a brass band had begun to play. It was the army band of the Vienna regiment, the Fourth Hoch-und-Deutschmeister. The men in blue uniforms sat there stiffly behind trumpets, cymbals, and drums, led by a band-master whose left hand, with out-stretched ring finger, rested on his hip. The polished surfaces of the instruments reflected the light of the gas lamps, and the lyre-shaped program stand in front of the balustrade displayed a number one. Number one was the "Double Eagle March."

She held out her empty glass.

"That's what I like. *Prosit!*" he said rapturously.

"*Prosit.*"

Then the crayfish were brought in a tureen reeking with caraway; on the lid was a red crayfish in porcelain.

"Why aren't you eating?"

She had emptied a second glass. "But I am," she said, taking up a pair of claw crackers with deft fingers. In the light numbness induced by the wine everything seemed easier. It might be possible to forget that it was not for love she had chosen this man who was gazing at her so ecstatically, but for another reason, one she could not confide to anyone—not anyone in the world. Not even to him who, despite all, was in her thoughts night and day—to him least of all! In her romantic little head all doubts disappeared, and in their stead arose a boundless conviction that what one desires one can have. And enjoy. And hold fast to. Even him! Oh, if only she could have held him fast! It required only a mite more courage, such a ridiculously tiny mite! And that Greek girl, a sixteen-year-old child, would not now have been in her place! The child was not "afraid of conventions"—that was all. Good God, when she reflected how much she had turned her back on! She struggled with the thoughts which the wine and the military music brought back so powerfully to her mind. It was while listening to this same music that they had made their plans, plans more dazzling than anything else in the world!

Franz spoke her name, and she looked up.

"Are you lost in a daze? What were you thinking about just then?"

"I was listening to the music. They play well. Pour me another glass!"

"Won't you get tipsy?"

"I'd like to."

The herbs gave a dry tang to the cold white wine which seemed to grow lighter the more one drank of it. The guests at the various tables applauded, and the bandmaster bowed. His dark moustache was turned up in twirled points. A color sergeant laid the notes for the next piece on the stand in front of him, and a corporal turned the program placard so that now number two was displayed. Number two was a potpourri from the *Fledermaus* operetta: "'Tis here with us a custom, *chacun à son goût*." The guests at the tables hummed their favorite verses.

"Look out for the sauce; sauce coming," warned the waiters, darting about with high-stacked trays. Appetites seemed insatiable; people ordered dishes with their cheeks already stuffed full, and when those dishes came they sent for more. The May evening was still young enough for the glow from the gas lamps to create a twilight in which one could distinctly glimpse the crests of the chestnut trees with their luxuriant pink and white blossoms; the sky between them was deep and cloudless. "'Tis here with us a custom, *chacun à son goût!*" blared the band, and every one seemed to have had a particularly good day today, or, if it was bad, to have forgotten it. A wave of well-being engulfed the garden.

When they had finished dinner Franz told their driver that they were going over to the fairgrounds of the Wurstelprater for an hour or so and would meet him at a quarter of nine at the Jantschtheater to drive home.

"Very good, Herr Baron," answered the driver.

If only there were not this eternal comparison! He too had said to his coachman: "Bratfisch, follow us." And Bratfisch had tipped his small-brimmed top hat and had answered, "Very good, Your Imperial Highness!" And then he had given her his arm, and it had been heaven on earth.

Now she was walking arm in arm with her fiancé past the merry-go-rounds and the shooting-galleries, with their ear-splitting noise. With the other man she had gone on to the still meadows where there were violets.

In front of the booths the barkers yelled hoarsely, "Roll up! We're just beginning! Good evening, sir! Good evening, madame! Six shots for two coppers! Will the lady have a try? She is surely a fine shot; you can see that right off!" They said that to every female being who passed by, whether cook or countess. And although Henriette was no shot at all, she believed them literally. She was in a state in which the word 'impossible' (a word she rarely used, even when in a completely sober state) became superfluous. What does anyone know? Everything is possible. Perhaps he will give up the Greek girl and come back to me. Why not? He was utterly ruthless. Franz was considerate. Perhaps she would come to love Franz. Why not? People do say that you can come to love a person even when you don't love him at first.

She laid the light rifle to her cheek and aimed at a harlequin holding a drum in front of himself. He had a black heart on his breast, and in the center of the heart was a red circle. That was what one had to hit, and she did. The harlequin rattled his drum, and Franz shouted, "That's marvellous! I had no idea what a good shot you are!"

She nodded. She had not known it herself. Next she aimed at an eggshell bobbing up and down on a jet of water, and the egg splintered.

"A third try for the lady!" bawled the owner of the booth. "Three hits and you get a butter dish! What is the lady's target?"

The lady's target was the door of a tiny house. She aimed and missed. She did not win the butter dish but was given a lead medal instead.

Arm in arm, they wandered on. Now it was already night and the stars were out. A woman with a basket of lilies-of-the-valley stood by the path. He bought her a bunch and she stuck them, with her violets and her medal, in her belt. Then they went to a merry-go-round called "Kalafatti," after a gigantic Chinese figure made of wood. The Chinaman stood in the center surrounded by black and white horses and gaily painted carts which swung up and down. She swung herself up on a white horse, and he mounted a black one. As she rode sidesaddle on her toy horse, he thought she looked like a child despite her long velvet skirt. It occurred to him that he should never forget that. He did not mean by this that he was too old for her, but rather that she had a perfect right to the unrestricted fun of her youth which had been denied him in his. It was remarkable how seldom she let him see this side, he could not help thinking, for she always acted so grown up.

"Do you like to ride on a merry-go-round?" he inquired tenderly.

"I adore it!" she replied.

Next he took her to a flea circus, a small wooden shed with a table on which was a glass case. An elderly woman stood behind it and overhead an oil lamp hung. It was all just as he had remembered it when as a boy he had longed in vain to be allowed to see it.

"Your Excellencies have come just in time for the races," the woman said, and pointed to the glass case with a knitting needle as she introduced the fleas: "This is Pepi. This one Marie. This Rudi, Laura, Maxie."

Five tiny dots were visible to the naked eye.

"Go!" the woman ordered, and rang a tiny silver bell. The five dots on the floor of the case began to move.

"All five got away to a good start!" the woman explained, and then, urging them on, she said: "Maxie, don't be lazy! Laura, look sharp!"

Pointing with her knitting needle, she added quickly: "Pepi will make it! Pepi is a whirlwind!"

That Pepi, the flea, was quick as a whirlwind made Henriette laugh. She might just as well have cried, for at this moment either would have been easy.

She was still laughing when they sat together in a small compartment the Giant Wheel, that delight of the Viennese. It rose from the ground imperceptibly, slowly, very slowly going up until it was way above the whole city. The soft outlines of the hills and the bordering woods were to be sensed rather than seen, though the Danube glistened under the bridges and through the districts, and both the flickering lights below and the restless stars above were swallowed up in the same glow along the horizon.

"I wish I could always ride like this! It should not go down," she said.

"It shan't! In a month at the latest we'll begin to build. I'll build you a room way up high, shall I?" His words were like a promise to a child.

A warm breeze, carrying the confused sounds from below, came through the open windows of their compartment. The higher the wheel turned the quieter it grew.

"Yes," she answered, but in the dark he could not see whether she was still laughing.

When they reached the ground again it was striking nine. But the coachman knew a short cut. At a sharp trot they left the Prater through the Augarten gate. "To All Men from a Friend of Mankind" read the Emperor Joseph's century-old dedication inscription over it.

CHAPTER 2
Betrothal Calls

They made family calls; that was part of being engaged and was considered good manners. He should have introduced her to his family long ago! But Franz was aware that the inhabitants of Number 10 were almost unanimously opposed to the match, and in monuments of pessimism he also realized with what small degree of enthusiasm Henriette herself must look upon their marriage. Here was beautiful daughter of a famous father marrying an older man, who was no Adonis although he was nice and respectable (Franz in no way underestimated himself). However, he was no count, no virtuoso, no millionaire. Under the circumstances he rather hesitated to make calls on people from whom he could not expect the slightest evidence of enthusiasm! But now he could no longer delay, for his sister-in-law Elsa, Otto Eberhard's wife, had surprised him by asking: "Is your engagement broken?" To his perplexed "How so?" she had replied tartly: "I only thought it must be because you've waited so long to bring your fiancée to call on us."

Whereupon he dressed himself, as was customary, in a long black coat, cursing as he put on a top hat and even took a pair of gloves. Then he drove to fetch Henriette at her home in Karolinengasse. She was dressed for the occasion in a new spring suit of shimmering green moiré which he found irresistible the moment he laid eyes on it, although the next instant he realized that the extremely tight bodice would not increase her chances with his family; not to mention her huge straw hat, laden with artificial flowers and velvet ribbons, which sat on her luxuriant chestnut braids and which anyone could see from afar was beyond the means of any ordinary mortal. I should have prepared her in advance, he thought.

They entered the old house through the main entrance on Seilerstätte. Henriette had never been there before, as no young girl of good family could visit her fiancé in his apartment. As the heavy oaken door swung open and Pawlik, the janitor, tipped his cap, she felt a rush of coolness which seemed to have been stored up there for a hundred years. She regretted having brought her fan.

They rang first at Apartment 7 on the first floor.

"Well, I've brought her to see you!" Franz said, after they had been taken into the living room. Then he performed the introductions. "This is my brother, Otto Eberhard. And this is my sister-in-law, Elsa."

"Very pleased," returned the Public Prosecutor, bowed to his future sister-in-law, and waited until she held out her hand, which he took.

"We are delighted," said his wife, the former Baroness Uiberacker, and stretched three fingers out towards the young girl. Then she pointed to the sofa on one side of the room, which looked so dark with its golden-brown walls. The gentlemen seated themselves in armchairs.

Silence.

Really someone ought to say something, thought Henriette.

"I hear you are going to live on the fourth floor," remarked the lawyer's wife. "That is, when it is built."

Henriette nodded. "I hope you won't be disturbed by the building," she said as primly as she knew how.

"Not a bit! Otto's family will have gone to the country long before then," observed Franz, who longed to light a cigar but did not think the time was yet ripe for it.

"My brother is always generous," ventured Otto Eberhard, and then, with an engaging smile, he added, "at the expense of others." Henriette, who was still young enough to take instantaneous likes or dislikes, began to hate the Public Prosecutor for that remark.

He went on smoothly: "It's of no consequence at all. We shall just have to breathe in a little more dust."

"I shall be sorry," answered Henriette, opening and closing the fan she held in her hand.

"There's no occasion for that," said the lawyer.

So he was the one who denounced me to Franz, she thought as she looked into his cold blue eyes. She resolved that the subject of Rudolf should under no circumstances be raised.

More silence.

"Where is Peter?" Franz finally brought out. "Henriette would so much like to see him."

"Oh, yes, very much indeed," she repeated, although she had no idea whom they were talking about. There were so many names in this house!

A bell was rung three times, whereupon a fat little boy was led in by a straitlaced woman whose carriage was a model of erectness,

"*Dites bonjour*, Pierre!" she suggested. The little boy said, "*Bonjour*," and was given a piece of candy obviously brought along for the purpose by his uncle Franz.

"You see, this is your new aunt," he said, as he gave him the bonbon. The boy took the candy and put it immediately into his mouth; his new aunt did not interest him.

"Pierre!" the Frenchwoman said in a reminding tone. She herself had not been introduced.

Henriette asked Pierre his age in French and received the answer that he was *huit ans*. She did not inquire whether he was already going to school and could read and write, because when she was a child she had hated such questions. As soon as the candy give signs of disappearing, Peter's mother exchanged looks with his governess, and after he had once more made the rounds, with "*Bonjour, mademoiselle*" to Henriette, and "*Bonjour, Papa; bonjour, Maman; bonjour, mon oncle*" to the others, he was led away.

"You speak beautiful French," Elsa said, with a glance of recognition.

The lawyer inquired: "How is your distinguished father, Miss Henriette? I had the privilege of studying under him at one time. But he would scarcely remember me."

At this Franz's patience wore thin. "Really, I can't stand this any longer! Miss Henriette! Your distinguished father! Give each other a kiss and begin using your first names!"

"You think every one is as free and easy as you are! How do you know she would like it?" asked Otto Eberhard, turning to his brother.

That he meant to imply that it was distasteful to him did not reach her at all. She was far too spoiled even to suspect that she might be unwelcome to them as a sister-in-law; in her eyes there was certainly no overwhelming social cleavage between the daughter of Professor Stein of the University and the grandson of Alt, a piano manufacturer.

"Why not? Of course," was her answer to the Public Prosecutor's query.

Nevertheless, Elsa brought the conversation around to the impending unveiling of the Maria Theresa monument and the difficulty of obtaining tickets for the special stand. It was a problem they discussed at length, after which the engaged couple left.

"Well," Franz said after they were out in the hall, "how did you like them?"

"Very much," she replied. "He's good-looking." She did not mention Otto Eberhard's wife.

"So much the better!" he said, somewhat amazed. "Now pull yourself together for Number 8!"

His elder sister Gretl, a faded, worn creature, opened the door for them herself. "My maid's out today," she explained, and added, "Won't you sit down a moment? I'll go and call my husband. But, Franz, and you too, Miss Stein, don't tell him he doesn't look well! He's had another attack."

When she had disappeared Henriette gave her fiancé a look

which seemed to him so dejected that the rage he felt against his family rose violently, despite his laborious efforts to restrain it. In the first quarter of an hour they had succeeded in completely intimidating the girl!

The girl was not intimidated. It was something else. When Frau Paskiewicz had opened the door into the next room a terrifying odor of artificial oxygen had issued from it.

"My sister is a panicmonger," Franz said in excusing her.

The terrifying odor was noticeable again when a man in the dress uniform of a colonel in the Dragoons came in on Gretl's arm.

"Infinitely delighted to make your acquaintance," was his greeting to Henriette. He spoke with a soft Polish accent, catching his breath between every word and smiling with lips marked by death. His good looks were striking.

"Oh, but do sit down," he begged. And again they were all seated according to custom, with the two ladies on the sofa and the two gentlemen in armchairs. "You have brought a ray of sunshine into our house, Franz!" said the colonel.

"You mustn't talk so much, Niki," warned Frau Paskiewicz. "How do you think he looks, Franz?"

"Splendid!" was her brother's curt reply.

Henriette added impulsively, "The colonel looks very well."

There was a spark in the sick man's look which gave life to his depressed features. His wife noticed it. She had always feared that expression more than anything else. Before this, when he was well, that was how it had started each time—with this flash in his eyes. Afterwards had come the lies, the waiting up at night, the quarrels, the humiliation, and the pitiful reconciliation. The faded woman turned against her future sister-in-law.

"My dear, you are sweet to an invalid! You are definitely to be congratulated, Franz, and the whole family too! They've been urgently in need of just such a glorious bit of springtime!"

"Thanks, Niki. But we shall not detain you any longer,"

answered the prospective bridegroom, fuming at his sister who had not as yet said a single pleasant word to Henriette. The crazy, hysterical creature!

"Nothing of the sort," objected the colonel. "First we must pledge each other in wine. Gretl, be good enough to give us some Tokay."

"But you shouldn't drink anything, Niki," his wife said imploringly.

Then, just as in the old days, she heard his threatening words, "Did you understand me?" It was said in the same old deadly tone. Turning to the others, he added, "She thinks it harms me. But that's a superstition. Good wine never harms, only bad."

At this moment the door opened slowly and softly and a child came in. She was a tall, overgrown, pallid girl with the colonel's profile.

"Who called you?" asked Frau Paskiewicz.

"No one," replied the child.

"Then you can go," said her mother.

But the colonel said, "Come here, old lady."

The child came over to the grown-ups. Her large dark eyes moved anxiously from one to the other.

"Can't you at least say how do you do?" asked her mother.

"How do you do?" said the child. She had come in because her parents' voices had caused her so much anxiety. When Mama had come in to fetch Papa she had heard her say to him, "At most just a moment, Niki! Will you promise? You know Dr. Herz does not like you to move about!"

And Papa had given his word to Mama, but the moment was long since past and her parents' voices were so disturbing. Everything she could ever remember was disturbing.

"Sit down, Christine," Franz said to her. But he had no candy for her.

"Thank you," the child replied, and sat down on the edge of a chair.

Meanwhile her mother had poured out wine for the guests, and in doing it her hand trembled so that she spilled some.

"Anyone can see that you are out of practice," remarked her husband. "No glass for you?"

"You know I don't drink," she replied softly.

Earlier in the day young Dr. Herz had told her that if the colonel's "asthma" (as he euphemistically called it) did not subside he would have to remain absolutely motionless, without saying a word. Any motion might do him harm. But Niki had insisted on getting up, shaving himself, putting on his dress uniform, and doing the honors to this preposterously bedecked little Jewess!

"You will pour some for yourself and clink glasses with us," she heard him say.

The child stared at her with a pale face. She poured out the wine.

The colonel stood up. He held himself straight as a die, clicked the heels of his patent-leather boots, on which light silver spurs jingled, and said in his best cavalry manner: "I raise my glass to the new party of the newly-to-be-constructed fourth floor, to the charming young lady who is doing us the honor of joining our family. *Hoch soll sie leben, hoch soll sie leben, dreimal hoch*!" There he stood as in the old days, a full glass in his hand, and sang the last words.

"Thank you," said Henriette.

"Thank you, Niki," said Franz, who had also joined in the singing.

"You permit me?" asked the colonel, and walked four steps, erect and unassisted, over to Henriette. A trace of color passed over his cheeks. With easy grace he crooked his arm through hers and they drank together. Then he drew her to him and touched her lips. "Henriette," he said, and she heard how hard he was breathing.

"Niki," she replied.

"Well, and you ladies now?"

"We do it without ceremony," Henriette put in quickly.

The faded wife touched her glass with her lips. "Your health, Henriette," she whispered.

"Yours, Gretl," said the bride-to-be.

The child, who up to this point had not moved, now smiled with relief.

"I envy you," the colonel confided to Franz as he shook his hand when they were leaving.

While they climbed up to the second story, Henriette thought to herself that this man with the narrow, grizzled temples, whose veins stood out with every word he said, would lie there exactly as her mother had done. And his wife would reproach herself bitterly for not having been kinder to him, exactly as she had reproached herself bitterly for having opposed her mother in the last hour of her life. "You are a wicked girl," her mother had said in that last hour.

They were standing now in the corridor of the second floor and Franz was searching his key ring for the key to the "party rooms."

"Neither your sister nor your sister-in-law was really nice to me, were they?" she asked.

He was still looking for the key. "Most probably they're jealous of you."

"Oh, nonsense! What for?"

"Because you're young. Because you're beautiful. Because you're—"

"Because I am…?" she asked with a sort of laugh, for it was funny to see him struggling with both keys and compliments.

"Besides, they were naturally jealous."

"The Public Prosecutor's wife too? Isn't the Public Prosecutor altogether law-abiding?"

The key was found at last. He took her trough the conservatory, past the potted palms and laurels, and into the yellow drawing room, a six-sided chamber with faded yellow damask on the walls and furniture.

"This was where Mozart played," he remarked, with a touch of pride. As she said nothing he went back to her earlier question: "In that way all men are alike. On this point the colonel, incidentally only a lieutenant."

He had expected her to admire the yellow drawing room.

But all she said was: "I'm sorry for the colonel."

"For him? He has more on his conscience than any priest can absolve!"

"But he'll die soon."

"What of it? Are you sorry for every one who must die?"

"Yes!" Her reply came from the depths of her conviction.

He did not like that. In other women he would have called it fuss. In her he excused it by saying: "You have a kind heart."

She did not tell him what it was, for she would have had to explain that 'being sorry' was a disease like any other, and he would not have understood, yet with her this was a fact. She could be so painfully 'sorry' for people that she would do the most foolish things. And the most foolish things made her 'sorry.' An old woman sitting in the sun. People coming home on a Sunday evening from an excursion, with six hard days ahead of them. A child in the park begging his mother, "Buy me a pinwheel too!" A man studying the prices in a delicatessen shop window and then walking on. "He must be very poor," she would insist.

"That anyone should sympathize with Niki Paskiewicz is something new to me!" Franz's tone was almost impatient. "You had better look at this. This is the family relic!"

He pointed to a low piano made of yellow pearwood. It had three legs, two of which were solidly connected by a handsomely carved crossbar. There were no pedals, nor any cover for the board with yellowed keys. "Christofori Pianoforte, Leipzig, 1726. Improved by Christopher Alt, Vienna,

1777" read the inscription inlaid in mother-of-pearl above the keys.

"This is the first instrument that my grandfather brought out under his own name," he explained to her. "Do you see this hammer? Grandfather was the one to hit on the idea of percussion action. That is to say, improved percussion action. He made use of the hammer pivoted within this sheath here. He fixed it to the key in such a way that its head points towards the front of the instrument. See? Its butt he had introduced into this beak here, known as the 'hammer butt,' for the purpose of engaging what was later called the 'escapement.'"

As an expert, to whom all this was a matter of course, he could not imagine that anyone else could not take it in. She played the piano—very nicely too—and that was enough for him. He went on throwing technical expressions around and enjoyed showing himself off in his own field. She was spared no detail.

While he was busily talking and demonstrating, she thought: *I hope he won't ask me any questions afterwards. I haven't the vaguest notion about anything!* And it flashed through her head this man knew as little about herself as she did about "escapement."

"You see what I mean?" he asked, concluding his lecture.

The tone of her "yes" passed unnoticed because, now that he had proved to her that he was no less capable than the other men in the house, he felt more sure of himself. They had titles and decorations, yes, but what would remain of their accomplishments? The product he made was world-famous. "Piano maker" was what his grandfather modestly called himself, not a manufacturer. His son and grandson took pride in following his example. Franz pointed out to her the oil portrait of old Christopher, smiling down on the pearwood instrument. It showed a serene, red-cheeked, clean-shaven gentleman with his white hair brushed forward from his temples, a high-standing black neckcloth, and one hand thrust between the buttons on his long double-breasted blue morning coat.

"Nice picture, isn't it?"

"Very."

Once more they were standing by the chill, moldy-smelling staircase. "Shall I quickly show you where I live before we go down?" he suggested.

"Of course."

Is it possible that one person can be so little aware of what is going on in another? He let her see his bachelor quarters, on which the taste of the Makart era had left its imprint. There were peacock fathers, blades of dried grass and palm leaves in tall vases; Moorish pages holding torches; bronze busts of Beethoven and Mozart on the tiled stoves; photograph albums with stiff covers; pictures in ornate frames, "Piazza San Marco," "Leda and the Swan," a girl with a rose between her lips, "Susanna in Her Bath," a copy of the Adam portrait of Empress Elizabeth on horseback; plush, china, skin rugs.

They came to his bedroom.

"Perhaps I really shouldn't bring you in here?" he suggested, following close on her heels. "Do you like it?"

She was ready to scream with nervousness.

"Oh, yes," she said.

This time he seemed to sense something. He walked rapidly to the window. "Look how far you can see," he said shyly. And when she made no response he went on, "On the fourth floor we have an even better outlook. Our bedroom will be exactly over this one."

She knew it was not the right moment: nevertheless she decided to ask the question. "Didn't you say something about two rooms?" She did not look at him as she spoke. Beside the polar bear skin on the floor there was a leopard rug; she fastened her attention on counting the spots on it.

"Two bedrooms?" he asked.

Fourteen spots. "Yes," she replied, "or did I misunderstand what you said recently when we went up on the Giant Wheel?"

"We must go," he said. "It's getting late."

Apartments 4 and 5 on the mezzanine were next on their list. They found a jolly apple-cheeked woman, a man with a beard like Saint Peter's, a pair of freckled twins, and a Doberman pinscher—the household of the painter Drauffer and his wife Pauline, Franz's younger sister, the one who, when she was five years old, grew so hungry at the Emperor's wedding. They were all inquisitive people and wanted to find out a great many things.

"What do you think of our house? It's a sort of monkey house, isn't it?" "Do you think you'll have such a pair of rascals as these two here?" "And what do you think of Brother Franz?" "Is it true your father is going to be named to the Upper Chamber?"

All well-meant questions, but hard to answer.

Next came Franz's widowed aunt, the former Miss Kubelka, in Apartment 3 on the mezzanine, where it smelled of burned milk. They waited for a long time to see the daughter of the house, Anna, who had just taken their pug out. On the point of leaving, and indeed already at the door, the couple met her. She was dressed all in black, as though she had just come from a funeral, and her attention was centered entirely on the dog. As she removed his leash and muzzle she said, "Good little doggie. Such a good little doggie. Strulli did all his business."

The pug, who must have been quite aged, because he waddled so and every movement made him pant, did not allow himself to be petted. But the former Miss Kubelka, an old woman going, on eighty, who was tiny and not quite clear in her head, made every effort to retain her visitors. First she attempted to do so by giving them coffee, but the milk was scorched. Then there was Anna, who did not come for so long.

Now she turned to the dog, trying to make him interesting, but he refused to be petted. In the back of her mind there was only one thought: *These two will go downstairs to Sophie, and Sophie will say mean things about me!*

"Allow me to introduce you to my fiancée," Franz had said to his cousin Anna. The erstwhile Countess Hegéssy nodded with a stony expression. What her face may have looked like earlier in her history was hardly to be guessed at. Now it was completely blank. "I trust you will be happy," was all she said.

To live one's life out in this house! The thought was like a cord around Henriette's throat as they went downstairs to make their last call. She was not used to a family, for she had lived alone with her father for years. Professor Stein had no family, or at least he acted that way. In any case, she could not remember ever hearing of grandparents, of an uncle or an aunt on her father's side. As for her mother, she had always been told that her maiden name was Aufreiter, that she came from Goricia, and that she was the daughter of a landowner. But no one had even so much as seen this landowner or his relatives.

"Anna has had a lot of bad luck," Franz explained.

"You can see that from her appearance. She has behind her what is now confronting your sister Gretl, hasn't she?"

Franz shrugged his shoulders. "I haven't seen Cousin Hegéssy in an age. But if you ask me, Gretl has been through more. The count at least ticked Anna right off, nearly twenty-five years ago. But Gretl has been obliged, for at least that time, to watch the colonel, whom you are so sorry for, carry on with all his rascality. That is much worse."

"Extraordinary!" Henriette said. "And all under the same roof."

At which old Poldi opened the door to them at Apartment Number 2 on the ground floor.

Sophie was arrayed in her best finery that day. From the parting in her white hair to the tips of her shoes she gave an impression of impeccable neatness, and one could offer her no more pleasing compliment than to remark on a certain likeness which undoubtedly existed.

Henriette gave her this pleasure. "You are the image of Countess Festetics!" she exclaimed, thereby comparing her to the first lady-in-waiting to the Empress.

"Did he tell you that I like to be told that?" the old lady asked as she extended her hand for the girl to kiss. "Where does it come from—Paris?" was her immediate inquiry as soon as they were settled in the tapestry armchairs which commanded a view of the green walnut tree. "Don't hesitate to say yes, because I too believe that Paris is the only place to buy clothes."

So Henriette confessed that her dress was a French model from the Spitzer Salon. If only these visits were over, she thought.

"Charming," Sophie admitted, and asked if they had made all the calls in the house and whether they had seen every one. "Even the—" She was itching to say something about her arch-enemy, the former Kubelka woman, but decided it would be improper to initiate her new relative into such delicate matters too abruptly, so she desisted. On the other hand, she had no scruples about putting a question which so horrified Franz that his mouth fell open and he started out of his chair.

"You know that I was opposed to your marriage?" she said bluntly to Henriette.

Despite the experience of the last hour the girl looked at the old lady helplessly. "No," she replied.

"What's that?" Sophie asked, suddenly turned deaf.

"Aunt Sophie," Franz roared, "we came to make a call on you!"

"Don't you think he's a silly fellow?" Sophie said, devoting herself to Henriette. "Of course you've come to make a call, and the last one in the house, at that. You have been to see that—that Kubelka woman first. And if you had had it your way you wouldn't have come calling at all. I mean Franz—I don't know about you," she added to Henriette.

At this point old Poldi came in with some cherry brandy and Sacher cake.

Sophie shook her head as she watched her elderly servant pass the refreshments, and after Poldi had left she said, "You must be sure, my child, to get good maids. So much in life depends on the Poldis and the Maries. How many servants will you keep?"

This question being somewhat difficult to relate to the preceding one, a break in the conversation occurred, during which the parrot repeatedly offered thanks for nothing and Sophie, with firm fingers, cut the thin layers of the cake with chocolate icing. "I can well believe that you have had to eat your way through a lot of stuff," she suggested as she passed the cake. "You can leave what you don't want." She herself tasted a little piece. "Well, how many servants will you keep?"

"We don't know yet," her nephew answered curtly.

"Miserable stuff, this icing," Sophie objected. "You're not angry with me for what I said a few minutes ago, are you, my child?"

"Frankly I am, a little."

Sophie nodded. "That's just what I like. I mean frankness. I never have liked to play hide-and-seek. I told Franz—"

"Auntie!" her nephew interrupted.

"Oh, shut up! Do you think the girl can't take the truth? I did my best to talk him out of this marriage, I daresay you can guess why."

"Here I am! Here I am!" the parrot croaked from the next room.

"Yes, there you are! " the old lady replied. She pushed away her painted porcelain plate with the slice of cake. "Or aren't you interested?"

"I'm afraid it wouldn't alter things even if I knew what you have against me," said Henriette, mustering her last forces of self-control.

"That's the first nonsense I've heard you talk," Sophie said decidedly. "Now if you two had let me have my say—it is advisable, my child, to let other people have their say, especially if they have had a little more experience—I should have told you that I had revised my opinion about you. Not only because of your appearance, which to be sure is not against you—it's a good sign that you are capable of blushing! You're clever too. Not too clever, I trust—it's never good for a wife to be too clever. You could probably be a good wife for that foolish man there if only you were a little less conceited. Tell me, what are you conceited of, anyway? You can't help being pretty or being clever either. And one may only be conceited about things one can do something about. Take, for instance, the things one denies oneself. Come here. Give me a kiss."

Henriette had listened to her in a state of wounded feelings and confusion which increased with every word the old lady said. Yet she obeyed and went over and kissed her on her thin cheek. She also received the ghost of a kiss.

"Will you promise me something?" Sophie asked. "With you young people one can never tell when it will occur to you to call again on us old people. Did you go to school at the Sacré Coeur?"

"Yes."

"Stand over there under that picture. Don't look so idiotic, Franz. By the time you have built your fourth story—one of your most foolish ideas; you would have had plenty of room on the third floor—it may well be that I shall have left this apartment. Consequently I now want her to promise me something. Does she know that I stand in the place of a parent to you?" Then, turning to Henriette: "He has, of course, never taken advantage of that and has always followed his own pig-headed way. But never mind that. Will you promise me something, my dear?"

On either side of the ikon over the private altar under which Henriette was standing two small oil lamps of ruby-colored glass were burning. The image was one of St. Jude. The whole proceeding suddenly struck her as so unbearably absurd that she would rather have run away.

"Yes," she said.

The old lady rose, took her ivory-headed cane, and walked across the room. When she stood before her prayer stool she towered over Henriette. "That is right," she declared, laying her cool thin hand on Henriette's. "Now repeat after me: I shall be a good wife to Franz!"

"I shall be a good wife to Franz."

"I shall make sacrifices if need be."

"I shall make sacrifices if need be."

Sophie nodded. "Thank you, my child. I feel much easier in my mind now."

A moment later the engaged couple stepped out of the Annagasse entrance into the open. Outside it was warm and bright.

"Now at least you know about the house," Franz said as though pleading for forgiveness. "You can see why we need a fourth story?"

She looked at the angel with the trumpet without seeing him. "Yes, now I know the house," she answered mechanically. *Absurd! Absurd! Absurd!* The word kept running through her head.

CHAPTER 3
Audience in Broad Daylight

"His Imperial Highness requests your presence."

The doorman had let her in through the iron door on the Albrecht terrace of the palace and then had led her through the so-called 'kitchen wing' to the adjutant's apartment. There she was taken in charge by an Imperial groom of the chambers, who brought her as far as the high gold-and-white double doors.

From the very instant when she had received the note with these words: "I must speak to you and beg you to give me five minutes. You cannot refuse! All depends on these five minutes!" everything had happened in feverish haste. By a stroke of luck Papa was still at the University, and Theresa, the factotum who as a rule accompanied her on most occasions, was going to have a birthday in four days; so she had been able to say to her: "I cannot take you with me today. I must go and buy you a birthday present." She had not had time even to change her clothes.

It was the afternoon of the Flower Parade, an occasion when those Viennese who had money drove in flower-decked carriages down the main avenue of the Prater. Those who had none lined the sidewalks and watched them. Consequently the city was empty.

"What has happened, Bratfisch?" she asked in her excitement. But the coachman said he knew nothing except that he had been ordered to fetch the young lady immediately. To her question: "Where to? You know that at least," he only replied: "To the palace."

In broad daylight to the palace?

He noted her expression. "Shall we wager a bottle of wine that no one will so much as lay eyes on our young lady?" he declared, "Or do you think I am taking you to the Amaliastairs? At the Opera Cross Drive Your Grace will get out. You will go a few steps up towards the Albrecht Palace to a small iron door and wait in front of it. Someone will open it. That will be Herr Loschek."

The carriage smelled of his Turkish tobacco. On the back seat lay the black-and-white-checked robe, the same one he had wrapped her in once when they were on their way home from Mayerling. On the coach box sat Bratfisch, in his narrowbrimmed top hat, his brown velvet coat bound in black and his flowing black tie, just as he used to when he fetched her day after day without her ever being quite sure where he was taking her. It all came back.

Heugasse. Schwarzenberg Square. Schwarzenberg Street. To the right she could see Seilerstätte; a corner house there was surrounded by a high scaffolding; they were adding a fourth story. Was the elderly spinster still there, or had she already gone to the country? If she was still there the little ruby oil lamps were burning on either side of the image of a saint.

I shan't go! Henriette said to herself. The words, however, meant nothing. She might just as well have said, "Today is the Flower Parade." It would have made more sense, for Franz had wanted to drive her in the Flower Parade and they had even settled how their carriage would be trimmed: with pink La France roses. But an unexpected meeting of the Chamber of Commerce had interfered. "You understand," Franz had said. She had understood. Franz was a member of the board of the Chamber of Commerce.

She wanted to think about him as she sat in the closed carriage, about how attentive he had been all these last weeks, how touching his efforts had been; but she was unable even to recall his looks. The face of another she could recall with terrifying clarity, every feature: this was how he looked when he laughed, and this how he looked when he was serious, but he laughed more often. That all was over between them—a more ridiculous lie could not be imagined! On the contrary, since she had held those few scribbled lines in her hand it was all as overwhelming as it had been on that first day. She tried to pray, but she could not do that either.

Kruger Street. He need not think that time had made her more pliant. He probably had thought to himself: *Keep her waiting long enough and she will give in*. Error! What she had always said to him she would say again today. *I am not Mitzi*

Kasper who will go off on overnight trips. I am not the little Greek Baroness Vetsera who throws herself on your neck because you are the Crown Prince. Nor am I the Countess Larisch, who hates your wife and wants to see you divorced at all costs because she wants to become empress herself. They all want that. But I want you, and since I cannot have you, you cannot have me. Yes, I know that I am what you call "afraid of conventions" and have the "morals of a middle-class girl." I'm sorry, but I am a middle-class girl!

Kaerntner Street. *What if I cannot keep up my resistance?* She thought to herself, and hurriedly reached for the rubber tube to call to the coachman to stop. *Why do I fool myself? Franz is nothing to me, nothing at all. He is all that counts. A thousand times since it all ended I have wished: If only he would send me word again! And now he has sent word! Dear Lord in heaven, I'm going to see him!*

She spoke into the tube.

"Your Grace wishes…?" the coachman asked, half turning his head.

"I wish to get out!"

"One moment, Your Grace. We shall be there immediately."

"But I'm not going there, Bratfisch!"

The man on the box seemed to hear nothing. The Opera Cross Drive. To the left Café Scheidl. To the right Hotel Sacher. The gentleman who is staring into the carriage so rudely is called Armbruster. *If you knew where I am going you would stare even more impudently, Herr Armbruster!*

What is the matter with me? Am I so far gone that after months of silence he can suddenly send me a command, just because he is in the mood, and say: "Now you are to come to the palace because promptly at three o'clock His Imperial Highness wants you for his mistress"?

"Let me get out, Bratfisch!" she almost screamed.

"We are already there," the coachman replied, pulling up the horses. He let her get out, cracked his whip, and with the customary "I kiss your hand" drove rapidly away. She stood there bewildered and watched him go.

On the other side of Augustiner Street someone was waving. It was Kitty, with that horrid friend of hers. What was her name, anyhow? They crossed over to her. And Bratfisch had said no one would see her!

"How is it you're not at the Flower Parade?" Kitty asked. Could anyone be more tactless? Rosie Blum was her friend's name.

"You aren't there either!" Henriette retorted.

"I'm not engaged either!" Kitty said.

Then the little Blum girl asked, "When is it you're getting married?"

"Not until the fourth story is built. You know we're adding on a fourth story. You must excuse me. I have to go to the Graben," Henriette explained. She could not stand either of them. Nevertheless, it was an extraordinary piece of luck that she had met them. They were the two people to whom she was to be eternally grateful.

She went down Augustiner Street, past the Augustiner Church, in the direction of the Joseph Square. Grateful for what? Because she was going to marry Franz? Kitty was having a flirtation with that awfully handsome young Baron Stoeger, and the other girl was crazy about young Waldstetter, who was a lieutenant in a Uhlan regiment. But she would marry a member of the board of the Chamber of Commerce.

She looked back. The two girls had disappeared. No one would open the gate to her now anyway. It was already eight minutes past three by the Augustiner Church clock.

She retraced her steps. There was the little iron gate. She would neither knock nor ring but simply stand in front of it for a moment. In the first place it was too late, and in the second place no one could see through an iron door. Consequently no one would open it and she would immediately go away again and yet have done what was requested of her.

She stepped up to the door, and it opened.

"Follow me, please," said the voice of the doorman, Loschek. A few minutes later the voice of the groom of the chambers, Puechel, said: "His Imperial Highness requests your presence."

The gold-and-white double doors had opened, and now she was standing before him. Her heart pounded so that she could neither speak nor see.

His voice said: "Thank you for coming. Sit down. Have you a few minutes to spare?"

He looked so changed, or was that due to a mist before her eyes which disappeared when she sat down? Yes, he was changed. There were deep shadows under his eyes which had not been there before. He was very pale, and his mouth twitched slighdy even when he was not speaking. There was no sign of that ironic smile which she had found so captivating and he moved his lower lip in the manner of someone who is trying not to cry.

"How are you?" he asked. His tone was the same. His voice was the same, an irresistible voice. How wonderful it was to see him again after all this time!

"Thank you, very well," she answered. "And you?"

"Thank you, not well." He was sitting at his desk, and she was in an armchair facing him.

It was not until later that she became aware that the gold-and-white room had an extraordinarily high ceiling and gigantic windows, or that she saw the antlers, the stuffed animals, the arms on the walls and in glass cases, the mass of papers and manuscripts strewn over the desk, and a table in the background.

"You do look a bit tired," she said. She loved him so much she could hardly speak. "I hope you're not sick."

He leaned back, crossed his arms, and looked at her. In

addition to his shooting jacket he wore the green necktie that she had given him.

"The last news I had of you I read in the *Fremdenblatt*," he said. "You became engaged?"

"Yes."

"Are you happy?"

She nodded.

"Forgive my wretched memory: I've forgotten who your fiancé is."

"Franz Alt. Of the piano firm."

"Right. Hasn't he a brother who's a lawyer?"

"Yes, that's his brother."

"And he's young and handsome? Of course!" he answered his own question.

The original of the Adam portrait of the Empress Elizabeth on horseback, of which Franz had a copy, hung opposite Hentiette. With her eyes on his mother's perfectly lovely features, which danced up and down and then blurred, she said, "Neither young nor handsome."

"But in love?"

"He likes me."

"And you?" He hunted for something among his papers, could not find it, and threw them all into a basket on his right.

She could not say any more, so was silent.

Jumping up, he began to stride around the room without coming near her chair. On the contrary, he paced up and down in a diagonal between a stuffed bear which bore the inscription "Munkács. September 17, 1883," and a collection of tropical birds.

"How much time have you?" His excitement was so obvious that did not dare remind him of the five minutes for which he had asked.

"A little while longer," she replied. He had grown much thinner. He looked younger, fascinating.

He checked his nervous pacing and stood by one of the two windows facing on the Francis Court. On the opposite wall was an old sundial, on which the shadow fell at twenty minutes past three.

"I've something to ask of you," he said with his face turned away from her. "It's a lot. A frightful lot!"

She did not move, for she knew what was coming. "This is no love," he would tell her again. "This isn't anything. If you really love me you must prove it to me!"

Looking across to the sundial and to the bronze monument of Emperor Francis, whom the Viennese nicknamed "Good Emperor Franz", he spoke quickly, in snatches, and very softly: "The point is that I—But you're not angry with me? We spoke of it once. Do you remember? That I foresaw the day when I should have enough. You said then that you didn't care either. Don't say anything. For God's sake, listen to me! The point is—I shall try to explain it to you. If it's cowardice, all right. Cowardice, terrible egotism, irresponsibility—what you will. But I am afraid. Not of doing it—in our family only my mother is perhaps a better shot. But you can never tell how it will turn out. Ferdie Pállfy will be a cripple all his life. I don't want that. Besides, I know it's idiotic, but can't help thinking all the time—what happens afterwards? The churchmen say there's nothing but purgatory for suicides. Idiotic! There's nothing afterwards. Absolutely nothing! Nevertheless, it might happen that at the decisive moment I might be taken in by this Church fraud. Recently I haven't been sure of myself. 'It's nerves,' says Dr. Widerhofer. My hand might be unsteady—that's what I fear. And—if one—I mean—if the two of us—I mean if one isn't alone—it's easier. What comes first—and what comes afterwards—if anything comes—"

He turned round. Beads of perspiration were on his brow, and he was so exhausted that he supported himself on the windowsill. "You're the only one who understands me," he added.

All she understood was that he wanted to die. Perhaps they had spoken of it some time before, between a sip of wine and a joke. But in this instant she had no memory of it, and she was stunned. That he was also asking her to die was swallowed up in the incomprehensibility of the fact that this man, who to her meant life itself, wanted to die.

"So it is no?" he asked in despair.

He must be helped! she thought to herself in her benumbed state. "You mustn't do this!" she said.

He gave her an unbearable look.

You can ask what you like of me and I shall do it! was the answer in her eyes. She was prepared to break the vow she had given under the ruby oil lamps. What madness it was to be afraid of conventions when his very life was at stake!

"Spare me what you're on the point of saying," he implored. "That I'm not just any man, that I have a mission in life, et cetera, et cetera. Save yourself the trouble! That this is going to happen is decided, and no one in the world can help me—only you. Do you understand?"

There was a gentle knock on the double doors.

"Good God!" burst from him. "Can't I have ten minutes of peace? Come in!"

Someone announced, "Your Highness's aide-de-camp, Count Bombelles, begs for a moment's audience. It's very important, says the count."

Henriette had risen.

"Sit still!" he said. "There's only one thing of importance— the answer you're going to give me!" He had started to light a cigarette, but his hand trembled so that he had to strike a second match.

A gentleman in the uniform of a vice-admiral entered the room with a deep bow.

"What's so urgently important now?" he was asked. The aide-de-camp looked at Henriette and hesitated.

"Speak without reserve; the lady is at least as trustworthy as I am."

"His Majesty's Adjutant-General begs leave to recall to Your Imperial Highness that His Majesty is going to the Burgtheater to the opening performance this evening of *Promise Behind the Hearth* and will await Your Imperial Highness at seven in the incognito box."

He threw away his cigarette. "And is that so important?" he asked with passion. "Tell Count Paar I regret that I cannot come this evening!"

"Your Imperial Highness will recall that His Majesty already expressed his wishes a week ago, and that Your Imperial Highness at that time accepted. Her Imperial Highness the Crown Princess will also be present."

He had sat down at the narrow end of his desk, one of his hunting-boots tapping at intervals against the wood.

"I've altered my arrangements! Tonight is impossible! I shall avail myself in the near future of the immense pleasure of seeing the Schratt lady in a new role."

"At your service, Your Imperial Highness."

"And something else! Tell Count Paar next time he wants anything he'll have to take the trouble to come down to me himself!"

"At your service, Your Imperial Highness."

"And invent some excuse why I can't come tonight. Say I have my old neuralgia again. A thousand thanks, Bombelles."

The gold-and-white door opened and closed again.

"There, he doesn't object! There, he thinks it's quite in order! To the Burgtheater! Tonight!" Again he paced round the room, always faster, lighting one cigarette after another, throwing the half-smoked ones away and stamping them out with the heel of his foot.

"That's the sort of thing he patronizes! Of course—if Miss Schratt is involved—she is sacrosanct! Mediocrity—that's

what he worships! Keep in line! Preserve appearances! Have a
little friend to chat with, nothing more—of course not! How
he adores art! And he gives his approval so impartially to inter-
course regardless of rank! And has never, never, never had a
mistress. What an irreproachable, God-fearing man! It's
laughable! To think that the whole world is still taken in by this
play for propriety and popularity on the part of a man no one
can bear. His wife can't—she runs away from him—nor his
children, for whom he hasn't a vestige of feeling; nor his
Ministers, who fear him; nor his subjects, whom he never sees!
He is a blind man, a deaf man, and, moreover, proud of lagging
behind the times! Those who want to make him see and hear
he forbids to speak—not with passion, mind you, but with a
kind of scornful arrogance that makes your blood run cold!
He's a man from whom everything glances off, like a rock! A
terrifying man by the side of whom life is impossible!"

Gasping, he stood still. The hatred which broke from him
was so savage that Henriette gazed at him speechless. Was this
the same man who was capable of such gentle and enthralling
charm?

Had anyone told her he had lost his reason she would have
been prepared to believe it. The twitching around his mouth
was incessant now; he could barely hold a cigarette.

She was so frightened she did not dare to move. Reared,
like all the Viennese of her generation, in unreserved respect
for Francis Joseph, his words were blackest treason to her.

Having calmed himself slightly, he exclaimed: "Forgive me!
But sometimes it carries me away." He threw himself into the
chair at his desk.

"I fear you are really ill," was all she could say.

He smiled sarcastically. "Alas, not ill enough, my dear!
With their united forces they have made me ill—*viribus uni-
tis*—according to the exalted motto of our house! But, as bad
luck will have it, I'm still well enough to realize what is meant

by it. On the twenty-first of August I shall be thirty-one. Do you think I've ever, even once in my life, been allowed to discuss politics with my father? Do you think he has ever so much as asked me, 'What are your plans?' Never! He asks me, 'How is your good wife; does she still play Chopin so charmingly?' and sometimes for months on end he does not ask me anything at all. To him I am, at thirty, a very young, untalented boy, with liberal leanings at that, who must be kept in check. That I'm the Crown Prince does not enter his consciousness. That I could do better than he—incomparably better—would never occur to him and his Taaffes and Kalnokys. The idea that he is dooming us all with his dynastic policies is as unknown to him as a person who might tell him the truth!"

"Don't say any more!" she implored.

"Must you go?" His tone was hostile now. Again he searched through his papers.

"Soon."

"Soon. I see. Tell me—when was that thing about you published in the papers? Four weeks ago, wasn't it?" Now he found what he had been looking for. It was a copy of the semi-official *Fremdenblatt* for May 2, in which the engagement of Miss Henriette Stein was announced in the Personal Notices.

"Four weeks ago," he went on as he reached for another paper, "or, to be more precise, on the second of May, I sent a communication to Rome. You're in a hurry, I know, but I think this will interest you. I asked the Holy Father to annul my marriage. Here is a copy of the letter carried personally to Rome by my friend Pepi Hoyos. If you have the time may I read it to you?"

He held the sheet of paper with trembling fingers and, without waiting for her reply, read:

"To use the time-worn word 'unhappy' to describe my marriage would be senseless. From the hour of its inception up to this very day it has been a sequence of incessant torment. I have no intention of blaming anyone, least of all my wife, to whom they bound me for what are known as reasons of State in the case of heirs to the throne.

"Procurement is punished only in the case of bourgeois people," he said scornfully as he looked up from the letter.

"If there have been cases in which the differences between two individuals joined together by force have not led to catastrophic results, [he continued] mine is not one of them. My wife, affianced when was fifteen because of her Catholic faith and the fact that she was a member of the Belgian royal family, has nothing in common with me. Our one daughter is devoted to me but not to her mother. Loth as I am to state this, it is nevertheless the truth that we are to such a degree intolerable to one another that our being together is absurd and undignified. Neither time nor circumstances can effect any change in this."

He interrupted himself: "Are you listening?"

"Yes," she said. Absurd. That our being together is absurd.

He went on:

"Any who possesses, as does Your Holiness, an insight into human relations deeper than that of ordinary mortals will not find this question too bold: What is it that can prevent a man from abandoning his innate and inalienable claim to happiness and human dignity? His duty? I have no faith in any such duty, whether it falls on sovereigns citizens, for I believe no good can be based on any duty which creates good. But if such a duty is laid on crowned heads, then I hereby submit to Your Holiness my solemn declaration that I am prepared to renounce unconditionally my right to the succession to the throne of Austro-Hungarian monarchy and to disappear in the masses as a private citizen if this will enable me to find the path to the freedom of my own personal life. I lay my fate in your hands. It is that of a man who has been taught to believe that he was born with greater rights than most men and who has learned that he must live with fewer than any. Your Holiness can see into my heart, and you will not refuse me your support, on which everything depends. If anyone can have influence over my father's inflexible will it is Your Holiness. As a faithful son of the Church he will accept your decision with submission."

He threw the paper down.

"His decision! Do you know what he did? He sent the original of my letter on to my father and recommended him to return to my 'peace of soul.' It happened today. At one o'clock my sent down for me; my great-uncle Albrecht was upstairs. Uncle Karl Ludwig, and Archbishop Rauscher. At the same time as peace was being returned to my soul my father's luncheon was served, for it was one o'clock, and at the stroke of one he eats his boiled beef. Five minutes later he was finished with his boiled beef and my existence. 'You should be old enough to abandon such childish undertakings,' was the opinion he expressed in a tone only he can use—that frigid, distant, impersonal tone. That was all he had to say." He kicked back the chair and jumped up. "Did you note the date of my letter?" he asked brusquely.

She did. The letter had been written on the day when her engagement was announced in the newspaper.

"And do you know now why I sent for you today as soon as my audience was over?"

With the last remnant of reason she could still command she struggled against the impelling connection. It was so terrifying to believe! So heavenly! Her thoughts swayed between horror, fear, sympathy, and a passion beyond her reach. She was so stirred that the overwhelmingness of it all paralysed her, and it almost seemed as if she took no part in it.

"Apparently it's not quite clear to you even yet?" he queried bitterly. "Then may I make it so clear that no shadow of doubt will remain?"

No! He must not say it!

"It was because of you that I wanted to get a divorce," he said.

No! she remonstrated in silence as he went on. *It was*

because you were unhappy with your wife! It was not on my account!

"It was for you that I was willing to renounce everything," he said.

No! she thought. *It was because you were not in accord with your father, because you couldn't wait for him to make way for you—or some other reason, but not on my account! I am only a simple bourgeois girl; isn't that what you have often called me? An Austrian Crown Prince does not give up a throne for a simple bourgeois girl! It is not true!* She struggled with all her might against such an incredible thought.

"I wanted to marry you," he said.

She closed her eyes.

"Why did you never say this to me before?" she asked, opening her eyes again.

"Is that a reproach?"

If only he had told me that, she thought, *I should never have become engaged. But he didn't tell me, because it wasn't true! Frantically she clung to that thought. He said good-bye to me because I would not be the sort of girl the Kasper girl was. That was the truth!*

"Perhaps I didn't say it," he admitted, "but you must have known it!"

God was her witness, she had not known it. It was only a flirtation, a heavenly flirtation, yes, and she had never been so unhappy as she was when it ended. But it had never been anything more, so how could he say such a fantastic thing?

"Why have you never made a sign since then?" she asked.

"Because I could come to you only with a torn-up marriage certificate," he retorted almost scornfully, and his excitement, which seemed to have abated for a few moments, again carried him away.

"You were not willing to become my mistress—that I understood. And I respected it."

"By falling in love with that little Vetsera!" she threw back in self-defense.

"The little Vetsera! Yes!" he admitted almost with a scream. It was obvious that he was again on the verge of losing all control over himself.

"If you fell in love with Mary Vetsera immediately after me it couldn't have been such a great love!"

"But you too fell in love. Even became engaged."

Where did the discrepancy lie? She felt a rift in the overwhelming arguments he was forcing on her.

"So you do love her?" she said, asking the only logical question that came to her mind.

"Are you changing places with my wife? No—if you must know! I don't love her! Shall I call in as witness Miguel Braganza, whom I have often tried to persuade to marry that girl? Do put an end to these disgusting questions! Mary is a little love-crazy youngster! No one takes her seriously!"

"Is that what you said about me when anyone inquired?"

He took both her hands. "Don't pretend to be worse than you are! Look at me!"

But she had been looking at him all the time and had seen something she had never seen before. It was not pleasant, yet it helped her. "Tell me," she begged, "have you asked Mary the same thing you have asked me today?"

"Present arms!" came the rolling command from the palace courtyard. He had gone over to the window and saw his father drive out of the gate. In the open coach with black-and-yellow wheels Francis Joseph sat on the right side, and on the left, Count Paar, his adjutant-general. The rumble of the military drums, the hoofbeats on the pavement, the cheers of passersby all died away.

"There he goes!" said his son. "Off to inspect something or other. Or to open an exhibition. The sacred routine as ever! At one o'clock boiled beef; at seven Miss Schratt. That he did away my existence at one o'clock has vanished from his mind!"

Then, turning back to her with an expression of glowering bitterness, he answered her question:

"Did I ask Mary? No. I asked you. Because you know—or at least I thought you knew—what goes on inside a human being! If I've made a mistake it won't be the first. But you may be sure at least that I'm convinced it's my last! Now you must probably be going?"

The shadow on the sundial fell across ten minutes before four.

"Rudolf," she begged, "give me your hand."

Without moving he looked at her. Then he nodded vehemently, biting his lips, and said, "Adieu."

All expression left his face: the bitterness, hate, scorn, disappointment. He looked once more as he had in those days when he had been her joy, except that he seemed far, far away and dreadfully lonely.

She was so unspeakably sorry for him that she could not say what she would have liked to. All she could say was, "You will let me know when you need me?"

He made an abrupt gesture. "You're an angel!" he answered, deeply moved. "Thank you."

The high-ceilinged room was no longer so large. The gold in it no longer shone.

"Mouche!" she heard him whisper.

It was so long since he had called her Mouche! "Adieu," she said quickly. Then she left.

Once more she went down the 'back stairs,' once more through the little iron doorway out on to the Albrecht terrace; yet it seemed to her that between her arrival and departure not an hour had elapsed, but years. Everything looked different.

It was past four when she met Franz, who was walking up and down impatiently in front of the Chamber of Commerce.

It had been an endless session, he told her, and the only ray of comfort was the clock in the assembly hall, which showed how long it was until four o'clock. At first everything had dragged unbearably, and then, thank goodness, the time began to pass more quickly. Why so silent today? The time, too, until the fourth story will be ready will pass; it will be still three months, or at the most four. Three or four months can seem short when one knows what is coming afterwards, can't they?

If one isn't alone—it is easier. What comes first—and what comes afterwards—if anything comes—

"You're not even listening! What are you thinking about?"

"Nothing. Forgive me."

CHAPTER 4
The House of Austria

The four children sat at the 'kittens' table.' It was laid with damask, silver, and crystal, and decorated with mimosa and violets every bit as handsomely as the banquet table of the grown-up guests; even inscribed cards were laid at each place. On one long side were Christine and Peter, and on the two short sides (to put at least a table's length between them) were Fritz and Otto. On the second long side sat Mademoiselle Leblanc. Both the table for the grown-ups and the 'kittens' table' stood in the large dining room on the second floor, at last pressed into service again and earning its title of 'party room,' which the children had never been able to understand. All the maids in the house were present; they wore with gloves and special white caps. Great-aunt Sophie's old Poldi kept wiping her eyes, although her mistress had been dead at least two months. And there were three real waiters in tails who looked exactly as they did in restaurants. In the small dining room there were four more men in tails who provided music.

The dishes just passed to the children consisted of venison trimmed with orange slices, on each of which was a pile of berry conserve; with this were served potato croquettes and a sweet red sauce, which was so thick that one's knife stuck in it. Yet the French governess, who was not really concerned with anything except Cousin Peter, insisted that one must not eat it with a knife. She was the only fly in the ointment for the twins.

At the grown-ups' table someone tapped on a glass, and Mlle Leblanc cautioned, "*Soyez tranquilles!*"

"Will you shut up!" Christine whispered to her twin cousins. She was certainly putting on airs, and she was a year younger than they, not even eleven yet! One of them, Fritz, kicked her on the shin under the table.

Meanwhile at the grown-ups' table a gentleman had risen to his feet. He looked like an actor, for his face was clean-shaven.

"*C'est un* toast!" explained the Frenchwoman.

"What's his name?" inquired the other twin, Otto, who thought toast was a person. Whereupon the little eight-year-old toad of a Peter had the impertinence to explode with laughter at the expense of his cousin, who was four years his senior! Otto squashed his foot for him so accurately that the fat boy yelped with pain. Christine, before, had not moved an eyelash.

"*Taisez-vous!*" cried Mademoiselle with horror.

The orator at the other table had begun his speech, which the twins found very boring. First he spoke of the house, said that it was a corner house overlooking two streets (which everybody knew anyhow), one of which was very old, very narrow, leading out into the open, and the other, which was quite new, very broad and open on all sides. A dozen steps from here, in a narrow alley, in the Government Archives Building, was where a great man of old Austria had worked, a man whose difficult name so often appeared in the boring German literature textbooks, that of the poet Grillparzer. And over

there in the Ring Boulevard the architects were at work building a new Austria. Yes, the inhabitants of this house—every
one of them—were to be congratulated on this double oudook
because it had taught them how to cling fast and unchanged to
the great tradition of the centuries and at the same time how to
give full credit to the new epoch which called for reconstruc-
tion, additions, and new constructions. The new fourth story
was the best demonstration of this.

The twins felt that they were receiving congratulations
without having understood a word the clean-shaven gentleman
had said. Now he bowed to Uncle Otto Eberhard, and Uncle
Paskiewicz, to Father and Uncle Franz. "Inhabited by representatives of the law and our glorious army, of art and artistic
handicraft, the home of people with the varied blood of so
many nations, this house is not only a true Austrian house, but
even, if I may use the term, the very house of Austria. And if
an artist like Maestro Drauffer undertook to paint its portrait,
I am convinced that it would provide him with a symbolic
background."

To hear their father's name mentioned, the twins found, was
a point in favor of the speech. Thereupon the orator lifted his
glass and drank to this Austrian house, to its inhabitants, and to
the unclouded happiness of those whose new home was to be on
the fourth story. The glasses clinked. "To your health!" "*Prosit!*"
"A beautiful speech, Professor," were the exclamations heard on
all sides. "*Magnifique!*" was the opinion of the Frenchwoman,
who explained that the speaker was Professor Stein.

The next to rise was Uncle Otto Eberhard, who, in a rather
long address, spoke of the bride as a young lady reared by her
father in the spirit of liberalism, in a most progressive way. On
his lips these terms sounded almost like a reproach. Even
Uncle Paskiewicz contributed something, but thank goodness
he was briefer, for all he did was to propose a toast to the reign-
ing house:

"That we can be gathered here together on this joyous occasion is due the protection and wisdom of our most gracious rulers. To Their Apostolic Majesties Emperor Francis Joseph the First and Empress Elizabeth, Their Imperial Highnesses Crown Prince Rudolf and Crown Princess Stephanie—long may they live!"

In the next room the four men in tail coats played the national anthem, and every one, including the children, had to rise and sing, "God preserve…"; but when they came to "our Emperor, our land," one of the twins noticed that their new aunt looked as if she were going to faint. He whispered this immediately to Mademoiselle, who was singing, "Mighty through the might of faith," and she whispered back, "*C'est idiot! Chantez!*"

True, the new aunt did not actually collapse, but Fritz was right in noticing that she suddenly clutched the back of her chair for support. Nevertheless his attention was diverted by old Poldi, who lighted the gas lamps. It still grew absolutely dark towards four in the afternoon, although it was already January 29 and the worst of the winter was really supposed to be over.

The bridegroom, Uncle Franz, looked quite changed in a long frock Coat with a sprig of myrtle in his huttonhole. He really not look like the bridegroom at all, but more like the father of the new aunt, didn't he? This comment Fritz also confided to the Frenchwoman, because he was sitting so far from his brother Otto and couldn't get any satisfaction out of talking to either of his. "*Pas du tout,*" was her reaction, for she found that "*votre oncle*" was "*très bien,*" and if he did have a more settled appearance, "*voyons!*" that was as it should be. She always knew better! Fortunately at this point they served the dessert—ices built up in the form of flowers and fruits, crowned by a tiny piano on top of which stood an angel blowing a trumpet. It was now possible deliver to oneself up to its enjoyment unimpeded by Uncle Otto Eberhard's monotonous reading of the congrat-

ulatory telegrams piled on a silver tray in front of him. He read
the texts and signatures, but he emphasized the senders more
than their messages and the names of titled senders more than
those without titles. For a long time the names and titles of dig-
nitaries were read aloud above the clamor of voices and spoons
without receiving any attention. Fritz was the more surprised
(although this time he kept his thoughts to himself) that the
new aunt showed such particular interest. When Uncle Otto
Eberhard finished she even said "Is that all?" as though it were
not enough!

Then all the grown-ups rose and moved into the yellow
drawing room to have their coffee. The four children, however,
were told to take their leave of Uncle Franz and Aunt Henriette
and go back to their apartments.

But, to the boundless astonishment of the twins, their
cousin Christine announced that she did not want to go and
please couldn't she stay. She spoke so excitedly that the new
aunt turned round, startled.

"Of course! You carried my train in church so beautifully.
Of course you may stay here," she said.

To which Christine replied, "I want to stay with you
always!"

And the twins were compelled to witness with their own
eyes the shocking occurrence of their very own cousin being
taken on to the lap of their new aunt! A girl of almost eleven!
And what was worse, while she sat there as though she were in
seventh heaven, they all missed their chance of getting away.
For their mother went on to announce, "Herr Alfred Grünreld
is going to be kind enough to play for us."

They had already had to sit still for two whole hours!

Someone had seated himself at the piano, and what he
played was nice enough, but it puzzled the twins why all the
grown-ups suddenly sat there looking as though there were
nothing better in the world.

"*C'est* 'La Truite' *de* Schubert," whispered the French-woman, quite carried away by it, although she pronounced it Schoebéer instead of Schubert. And did they hear how the water gurgled and the trout sprang around? The trout sprang around for quite a while, and then there was applause.

"Auntie," the twins overheard Christine whispering, "will you always be with us now?"

The new aunt replied, "After a few weeks."

"Not after today?" Christine asked.

Again the new aunt answered: "We are going away this evening for a few weeks, then we shall come back to stay, Christl. Shall I call you Christl?"

The silly goose said, "Why are you going away?"

With the same strange expression on her face that she had had while the telegrams were being read the new aunt replied: "When people marry they go off on a journey after the wedding."

The gentleman at the piano began to play again, but the twins' father, the painter Drauffer, came over and commanded, "Off with you!" and off they went. At the door they looked round; a few couples were already dancing, and Christine sat rooted to the spot watching the new aunt dance.

CHAPTER 5
The View from Above

The three groomsmen danced with the three bridesmaids. The three groomsmen were very young. Of the bridesmaids the oldest was twenty-one. The best man, Otto Eberhard, danced too, and Professor Stein insisted on dancing with Otto's wife. Altogether there were fourteen couples, and the non-dancers sat watching them from their gilt chairs: the former Miss Kubelka, her daughter Anna, dressed in black, the family physician, Dr. Herz, Frau Paskiewicz and her daughter, the little Christine.

Frau Paskiewicz did not notice the child until later, when the dance had been in progress some time, for her attention was riveted on her husband. He was dancing! His eyes shining from the champagne, he held a coquettish young woman in his arms; with his right arm he encircled her waist, and with his outstretched left arm he piloted her with supreme skill over the floor. "Each step may his last—isn't that so, Dr. Herz?" Frau Paskiewicz inquired. The doctor smiled philosophically. Naturally any second might bring a coronary thrombosis which he, to be quite frank, had been expecting in this patient for some nine months now. According to science he should have been dead at least as long as that. Nevertheless, he was dancing. Consequently, not science but Colonel Paskiewicz was right. "Why not let him dance!" answered the doctor, grimly chewing his cigar.

"But if anything should happen to him!" exclaimed Frau Paskiewicz in a voice that was quite loud enough for little Christine to hear.

The child had lived in a state of fear about her father ever since she could remember. At first she was afraid that he would come late or not at all. She had lain awake night after night listening for his key in the lock and for his light step. Even then she never knew whether that would be the end of the night's torment, because sometimes after the light step there were sounds of a subdued quarrel, of which the sleepless child could hear an occasional curse. She would lie there with her thumbs pressed to her ears, praying to God not to let Papa beat Mama again as on Easter Thursday. He had not stayed at home in the evenings until he fell ill. Christine had been happy over his illness until a conversation not meant for her ears had revealed to her that her father's death might be expected any moment. "If he dies, I'll kill myself!" her mother had said to Aunt Elsa.

Every prospect seemed so hopeless! But then Aunt Hetti came. Christine had never seen anyone more fascinating, no one who transformed everything when she came into the room. The child had counted the days until the wedding, because after that her new aunt would be coming, not for a brief half-hour, but for always. And now she was leaving for weeks!

"The Danube so blue," played Herr Grünfeld, and Henriette danced with her bridegroom. The music was irresistible under the wooing touch of the virtuoso pianist. Franz was an excellent dancer, and he set himself to prove it. His face, so very easy to read, beamed, and his hand held her as though he would never let her go again. The Danube so blue, so blue, so blue. When you waltz and whirl everything slips out of your mind.

Then her father came up to her. If only he would not make that face, as if to say, "Yes, yes, she's leaving me all alone!" I took a husband for your sake, Papa! I shall never tell you this and I do not reproach you. I only wish you would not make that face! It drives me wild, she thought.

Professor Stein said, "Wouldn't it be a good idea to have a little rest before you leave? You've been on the go since six this morning. Come and have tea with me, you and your husband. When does your train leave?"

"You and your husband" sounded so strange. The train left the South Station at eight forty-five. Franz did not object to making the call, on condition that he could show her the almost completed fourth story beforehand. As they left the yellow drawing room the Schoenbrunn waltz was being played. Someone ran after them to the door and asked with consternation, "Are you leaving already?" It was Christine.

Henriette kissed the child. "What's the matter?" she asked in a whisper.

"I'm so afraid, Aunt Hetti!"

The bride patted her thin little cheeks. "Nonsense! Who's

afraid? In a few weeks I'll be back and we can play shops together. And I'll send you some picture postcards from our journey. Shall I?

"Where are you going now?"

The child shrugged her shoulders, as though it did not matter where she went. But then she drew herself together and said, "Downstairs. To our apartment. *Bon voyage*, Auntie. *Bon voyage*, Uncle," and ran down the staircase.

The bridal couple walked upstairs.

"What a crazy little monkey," Franz said.

When they reached the top landing he drew a new key from his pocket and unlocked a shining brown door with a highly polished brass plate inscribed with the name "F. Alt." In the public hallway an uncovered gas jet was burning, and it smelled of plaster and paint.

"Wait!" he said. "Let me go in and light up. Think of something beautiful before you cross the threshold for the first time! Have you done it? Now come in!"

The last touches were still to be given to the rooms because the couple would not return from their honeymoon for quite a while. It had taken long enough to build; all calculations had been thrown out, first by the bricklayers' strike, and then because the walls had dried out so slowly in the winter cold. But now at least the walls were up, and they made a home.

As they walked through the seven rooms, some of which were already papered and furnished and had pictures on the walls, and where stoves were humming day and night, he watched her in suspense.

"Magnificent!" was her comment.

"Isn't it?" he asked proudly. "And did you notice your triple pier glass? I sent especially to Paris for it."

"Wonderful! It really is."

"Now you must look at the books. I can't be sure of having suited your taste. Goethe, Schiller, Lessing—Wait a second;

what's this? This is Grillparzer. And that other red book is Lenau, whom I have never read, but probably you have. These are the poems of your beloved Heine, and this is Stifter. And down there is an encyclopedia, complete with three supplements. You'll have enough to read?"

"Of course."

He was standing in front of the glass doors of the ebony bookcase just a step from her. Yet he seemed so far away that she could not imagine if possible ever to call this stranger "husband." It unimaginable, too, that she should ever speak of these rooms as "home."

"Which room do you like best?"

"Perhaps the sitting room?" she suggested.

"Let's look at your room once more."

They went back again to the room designated as hers. He stood at the foot of the narrow bed and said, "I didn't forget it!"

"That was sweet of you."

"Is that all?" he asked, coming closer. There was a smell of wine.

"May I use the new mirror?" she asked quickly. She had long since taken off her trailing veil, yet she still felt the pressure on her temples which had hurt her so in church, and now her own face seemed strange to her as she looked in the Paris mirror. She loosened her hair, which was dressed in heavy braids low on the nape of her neck.

Perhaps she would like to see the view? He led her to the corner window in the sitting room. But outside all they could see was snow. It was falling in thick flakes. The carriages in the streets must have been replaced by sleighs, for they heard the jingle of bells.

"Funny. I hadn't even noticed it was snowing," she said.

"When one is happy one doesn't notice such things," he replied, then corrected himself by saying: "I mean when one's head is full of a thousand things."

I'm being horrid to him, she thought. *I should say something nice*. What she said was: "If we are to have time to see Papa mustn't we go soon?" Home! Only to go home!

"Why you have to go there I don't see. In any case, don't forget that we're having supper at Otto Eberhard's at half-past seven."

"Aren't you coming with me?" She tried to add "Franz."

"I'd rather not. Honestly, your father always makes me feel as though he were examining me. And I've always failed! So now you go down to Pauline's and change your clothes and then drive to Karolinengasse. I shall be waiting for you promptly at seven. Our train leaves at eight forty-five, which means we must leave here at eight-fifteen at the latest." As he went through the rooms, turning out the lamps everywhere, he said: "Tell me, when Otto Eberhard was reading the telegrams aloud why did you ask, 'Is that all?' There was such a pile of them!"

"What ideas you get!"

It was several minutes before he came back to her. "I don't want to get any ideas about you," he said. His tone had changed. "Do you hear me?" It did not sound like a threat; it was more like a plea.

"You won't," she answered.

"I'm counting on that," he said slowly. "It's confoundedly dark in here. Be careful!

They walked downstairs, first the new flight and then the old ones with their worn treads.

"I kiss your hand, madam."

"Poldi spoke to you! Why don't you answer her?"

"Excuse me, Poldi; it's the first time anyone has called me madam. I'm not used to it yet."

"Of course, madam. Madam will soon get used to it."

CHAPTER 6
The Bells

Father and daughter sat opposite each other in the library, just as they always had done. She was in her going-away clothes now. "I feel like a caller," she said, looking down at the bunch of violets pinned on her gray muff.

Except for a few summer trips she had spent the whole of her twenty-two years here. She was part of every piece of furniture, of every shadow on the wall. Here she had experienced the light of morning and the falling of darkness at night. Here she had learned that words exist and also people to whom you speak them. When people smiled you liked them. Her father had nearly always smiled when he came to her; she could not remember any other expression on his face, from the time when he leaned down to her and was thrilled because she had already learned to talk, to walk, to read. But when he looked as he did now it was hard to bear. It was like the time when Mama lay over there on the sofa and they had told her she must say good-bye because Mama was going on a little journey. She had refused to say good-bye to her, and Mama had complained: "You are a wicked girl." Now she too was going on a little journey and would not return. Probably that was what Papa had on his mind.

They sat there and did not speak. It occurred to her how often she had pictured to herself what her wedding would be like. Her wedding dress, the church, the breakfast, the going away. Would she be married in the summertime? Her bridegroom would look like her Professor of the History of Art. No, like the actor Emmerich Robert. No, like the Crown Prince. There was scarcely a room in the apartment that had not been associated for a long time with these happy thoughts.

"It was a pretty wedding, wasn't it, Papa?" she asked. Professor Stein nodded vigorously. It was more than that: it was beautiful and dignified; it was quite an exceptional wedding.

The discourse of the priest in the cathedral, Otto Eberhard's speech at the wedding breakfast, Alfred Grünfeld's playing. He almost overpraised it all.

"And now," she said, "how will you get along, Papa?"

"Oh," he replied, and the smile reminiscent of sad days grew deeper around his lips, "I'll find ways of entertaining myself! I have my lecture before the Academy on February sixth—"

"On the fifth!"

"On the fifth, and on the sixteenth the half-year ends, and I shan't know what I'm doing during the examination period."

"Pass them all, won't you?"

"I can't promise."

"Who was elected at the meeting about the candidacy for the chair of criminal law?"

"Julius Glaser."

"That was what you wanted, wasn't it?"

"Of course—that was the only possible solution. Won't you take a little, tea?"

In the old days he would have said: "Drink your tea!"

He is treating me like a guest, she thought, and the tea stuck in her throat.

The clock on the wall ticked on. What an untold number of times she had sat in that very chair watching it and wishing: Tick faster! First, because she did not want to be a baby any longer. Then because she did not want to go to school any more. Then because morning or evening or any other time didn't arrive quickly enough. The pendulum had always swung too slowly. Today it was going too fast.

"So you've decided on the Hotel Danieli?"

"Yes."

"A splendid hotel. You'll send me a wire when you get there?"

"Of course."

"And you won't be too stingy about writing?"

"Every day!"

"Ridiculous. At most every three or four days."

"No, every day."

He saw that the saucer in her hand trembled and went on: "Don't forget the Palazzo Vendramin! You remember who lived there?"

Now she had to smile. "Candidate Stein, please tell me who lived in the Palazzo Vendramin?"

"Well, who?"

"Richard Wagner, Professor."

"Very good. Sit down."

The pendulum rushed madly to and fro. In ten minutes she would have to leave.

"Papa?"

"Yes?"

"I should like—"

"Don't make any new discoveries! A few people before us have been in this same situation. Why, it's even in the Bible."

Teresa had come into the room. "Oh, Miss Hetti looks very smart! Oh, excuse me—Mrs. Hetti. May I clear the tea-things away, Professor?"

"Will you keep a good eye on Papa, Theresa?"

"I'll do my best, Miss Hetti—excuse me, Mrs. Hetti," said their factotum, and walked stiffly out with the tray.

"Papa, you know I'm no speechmaker. So all I can say now is thank you. For everything. It was so wonderful here with you." That was all she could bring out. She felt for her gloves inside her muff, although they were lying in plain sight on her lap.

"Now, now Hetti, please. Let's talk of something more senisible. When will you be back—approximately, I mean?"

"In exactly three weeks."

Professor Stein took out his pocket calendar and ran through the leaves. "Today is Tuesday, January 29, so that

would make it Tuesday, February 19. But perhaps you can persuade that husband of yours to take you on down to Rome?"

The shy, thin man with the delicately formed, nervous face
rose paced up and down in front of the bookshelves which
filled the walls almost to the ceiling. As he walked he said:
"Don't forget your mother. Think of her in everything you do."
While he spoke his eyes turned to the gold-framed portrait of
a strikingly pretty, somewhat overdressed and slightly coarse-
looking woman. "You didn't have a chance to know her. But
whatever good qualities you possess come from her. Your heritage from the Steins, on the other hand, you must take only
cum beneficio inventarii, as the Roman jurists put it, which
means only after you have made up your mind what you don't
want out of it. You know, I sometimes think that talent—yes,
and even genius—means less than we think. They exist for the
supreme moments, but life is made up of everyday hours.
Comradeship—we need that—and then there is a great art I
have not yet acquired: to measure up to life—I mean to meet
it with readiness, optimism, and capability. Your mother was
mistress of that art." He broke off and walked to the opposite
end of the library with his eyes on the floor.

The time was up. "Good-bye, Papa," she said. "We shall
see each other soon!"

"Bless you, child. Have you your warm clothes? It can be
disgustingly cold in Italy at this time of year."

"I have my fur jacket." An embrace, a kiss, and already the
horses were carrying her off in a sleigh. It was still snowing, but
she noticed neither the snow nor the cold. She sat bolt upright
in the small two-seated open sleigh and repeated to herself:
"Think of your mother!" It was because she had thought of her
mother that her name was now Frau Franz Alt. What things you
can make men believe during your lifetime and even after death!
Papa was so convinced that Mama was a splendid wife that it
would take all of Herr Jarescu's proofs to force him to believe

the contrary. It almost eased her heart to think of that man Jarescu. Were it not for him, and had it not been necessary that she at all costs prevent her father from learning how ridiculous his blind faith in his wife was, she would not have been obliged to take this journey now ahead of her. But Herr Jarescu did exist; he even had the audacity to send them a congratulatory telegram, and brother-in-law Otto Eberhard had read it aloud.

With a vehement gesture she shook the snow off her cheeks and hair. *He* had sent no telegram to the wedding!

If it were a question of an outing, or a plan for them to die together, then he could send her messages! To die together! To this day she blushed and felt ashamed when she thought of the scene he had staged for her, which she was silly enough to believe. Obviously you can hoodwink women as well as men; you can make them believe all sorts of things, as, for example, that one is a charming, tactful, devastating person. But he was only a heartless, ambitious poseur, who craved either the Kasper girl's lack of restraint or Mary Vetsera's blind infatuation. Wrong. He needed both! That was why no one but the little Greek existed for him now. The day before yesterday, at the ball of the German Ambassador, Prince Reuss, she had behaved so outrageously that the whole city was talking about it!

They drove past the flower shop in front of which his coachman Bratfisch had so often picked her up. In those days there had always been a bunch of violets in the carriage for her. Now that other girl had them. At the ball in the German Embassy she had worn violets in her hair and on her low-cut evening dress, the newspaper said. I am glad of it, Henriette thought. There are things you think are impossible, but when they happen they help. It is easier for me that he did not send me any violets today.

The snow blanketed all sounds of traffic in the street. How wonderful to be going to Venice! When I come back I shall have my clothes made in me Spitzer Salon and my hats at

Passecker's. I shall have a box at the opera. I shall send out nicely printed cards: Mrs. Franz Alt. *At home—Tuesdays and Fridays, from 5 to 7.* Wonderful, wasn't it? she persuaded herself. And now in her thoughts she saw the husband who was a part of all this wonderful life, and suddenly she was more frightened than she had ever been.

When she stepped into the house at 10 Seilerstätte, she felt as though she were opening the door to a prison. *I must be crazy*, she said to herself. *For I am really very lucky. Most people would envy me. Tomorrow morning I shall be in Venice. I have never been to Italy.*

"Three cheers for the bride—hip, hip, hooray!" came a chorus voices to greet her as she entered the vestibule of Otto Eberhard's appartment. With raised glasses in their hands seven or eight gentlemen, with Colonel Paskiewicz as their commander, came out to meet her: "Private Franz! Rightabout turn!" And Private Franz, obeying the colonel's order, took his place beside his bride. Through an archway formed by these enthusiastic friends of the family the couple made their entry into the living room. The apartment was filled with cigar smoke and a great deal of noise. The wedding guests who had remained after the wedding breakfast appeared to have used the time during Henriette's absence to advantage; they were flushed, talkative, and inclined to rather racy remarks. One saw a wink here or a knowing grin there.

> *"Oh, the R's all three were never for me;*
> *Since I was but nine I've lived with swine.*
> *The joy of my life, in lieu of a wife,*
> *Or wearing good togs, was to raise fine hogs!"*

This well-kdown verse, from the popular new operetta, *The Gypsy Baron*, was being sung, somewhat off key, by one of the family friends. Had Henriette seen the marvellous production?

"Oh, pardon me," the gentleman excused himself in the same breath. "I quite forgot that it is only today you reach the age for operettas!" And he insisted that she must not miss the pleasure of seeing it when she returned from her "moonlight nights in Venice." Why, it was only round the corner! He referred to the fact that operetta, which had been enthralling Vienna for weeks, was being played across the way on Seilerstätte in the Stadttheater, and even the lawyer Otto, who had now grown expansive under the influence of all the good things he had enjoyed, confirmed the Minister of Justice's laudatory opinion that the music and production were excellent. Nothing was said, however, of the plot.

Here was a chance to get away from all the winking and grinning!

"How about going over now?" Henriette suggested impulsively. "We can probably see most of it before our train leaves. What do you say, Franz?" For the soup had just been served.

Frau Elsa, the hostess, gave a look that spoke volumes. Otto Eberhard said coolly: "Won't you have plenty of time for that after your return from Venice?"

But he was overruled right in his own house by Drauffer the painter—who was on fire with delight for the suggestion and who had already gone by himself twice to see the play—and also, most emphatically, by Colonel Paskiewicz. Yet Franz, all his life under the influence of his elder brother, would have preferred to say "no." On the other hand, he did not like to refuse Henriette her first wish on her wedding day. "Do you really mean it?" he asked hesitatingly.

She did mean it, and the party broke up—-an incredible breach of conduct, according to the conventional Otto and his wife and two or three others to whom it would never in the wide world have occurred to get up and leave a supper on the point of being served (not to mention the sentiments of Countess Hegéssy and the colonel's wife!). But the triumphant gentlemen hastily filled their glasses once more, lighted fresh cigars, threw their coats over their shoulders, and, with their top hats set at rakish angles, started off with the bride in the center, like a guard of honor.

"I wonder if there's any sense in our doing this?" Franz asked as he crossed the street in the snow with Henriette on his arm.

"Must everything have sense to it?" she retorted. The later it grew the more frightened she became. Perhaps she could still run away from him? She had taken a glass of Otto Eberhard's Tokay wine. "From the Imperial cellars," he had told her. But the Imperial cellars had not improved her state of mind.

Soon they were all sitting in two red-and-gold boxes, in the already darkened theater, watching the conductor wield his baton with passionate gestures. It was Johann Strauss, the composer, who was leading his operetta in person. The Overture had just begun, but the curtain, adorned with rose-veiled divinities and naked nymphs, was still down. At the conclusion of the Overture the crowded house broke into a storm of applause. "Bravo, Strauss!" yelled the Viennese until he turned, smiled, acknowledged the applause by laying hand on his heart, and then, suddenly facing the orchestra again, raised both hands to give the signal for the first act to begin.

The curtain rose on a Hungarian village, and the bright lights the stage also dimly illuminated the red, white, and gold auditorium. The faces of the spectators became visible. Henriette saw not only the frivolous stage, forbidden to the sight of young, but also every feature of the man who was her husband. In two hours she would be alone with him. "My God!" Involuntarily the words broke from her.

"Did you want something?" asked her brother-in-law Drauffer, who was sitting directly behind her.

She shook her head. "Girardi is marvellous," was her reply.

The comedian Girardi was marvellous: He played the gypsy who was called Zsupan on the program; with unique charm he imitated the Hungarian accent, and in every word and gesture he really was the shrewd, illiterate person who would later sing that about the three R's.

Henriette tried to fix her attention on the stage, on the music, whose magic she heard but did not enjoy; all that remained was vague, tumultuous, crass jumble. *I've never been afraid*, she told herself. *And I'm not afraid now!* Sitting bolt upright in her red velvet and gilt chair, she forced herself to laugh and appear as gay as the others who watched Girardi with beaming faces. He had sung the couplet about the three R's, and the public was wild with excitement. He had already repeated it once, but they were clamoring to hear it a third time. Applause showered from the orchestra, the boxes, the galleries. Flowers fell near the prompter's box, and Johann Strauss raised his baton to acquiesce to the wishes of the public. With languid grace the actor stepped from the wings, his shoulders bowed, a wry smile on his lips, as much as to say: "Man's wishes make his paradise." But at the same instant another man, dressed in street clothes, with no make-up on—indeed, he was very pale—emerged from the wings, and he too walked towards the middle of the stage, but with much quicker steps. A few of the audience looked at their programs to see who he might be. With a voice he could not control he began to speak, and in less than a fraction of a minute the general atmosphere of pleasure gave way to complete consternation. People looked at him with horror. For he had announced that His Imperial and Royal Highness Crown Prince Rudolf had died very suddenly of a heart ailment. As a sign of mourning the theater would be closed at once, and the public was asked to withdraw in the quiet manner consonant with the tragic event. The pale man disappeared into the wings, but it was some time before anyone stirred.

The house lights and the lamps in the boxes were turned up; the curtain with its divinities and nymphs was lowered; the musicians put away their instruments; the performance was over. People stood up in front of their seats. Many looked as though they were bereft of sight. Someone in the gallery cried, "Oh, God!" and as though that were a signal, a sound of sobbing swept through the theater. Someone else exclaimed, "It was only the day before yesterday that he was dancing at the German Embassy!" This revived a bit of Viennese optimism. Perhaps it was only a false rumor? But while they were getting their wraps they heard the dull, unceasing toll of the bells of St. Stephen and St. Augustine. It was true.

In front of Number 10 Seilerstätte they said good-bye to their friends and relatives. The brothers-in-law went into the house; the friends drove off in sleighs.

"Shall we go upstairs for a while?" Franz asked when Henriette made no move in that direction. "Our luggage is all up there, and perhaps you would like a little coffee before we leave?"

"Then we're leaving?" she asked.

"Why not? You mean on account of the Crown Prince?"

She meant on account of the man she had worshipped. He was dead. "Yes," she said.

He grew slightly impatient. "Naturally it's a terrible calamity, which every Austrian must deeply deplore—but, after all, it doesn't affect us personally."

"It affects me!"

"Pardon me," he said, "I quite forgot that you had a crush on him."

Her despair was so great that it overshadowed everything else, even this remark. "Do you think this is the time to undertake a pleasure trip?" she asked.

He stepped backward. "Do you mean by that that we should postpone our wedding journey?"

"I should like to go to the funeral. Don't you want to go too?"

"Never mind what I want or don't want! I refuse to make

myself ridiculous. I'm no archduke and you're no archduchess. We have nothing to do with that funeral!"

The snow fell without ceasing.

"I shall go to the funeral," she said. "I shall go to the funeral."

"You're not going to the funeral, but with me to Venice tonight! Do you understand me?" The bells tolled in muffled tones. Those of St. Michael were now added to the bells of St. Stephen and St. Augustine.

The young wife turned suddenly and fled. She had no realization of what she was doing. Something impelled her, and she gave way to it. In her temples pounded a refrain: He is dead. The only human being for whom there was any reason to live or to die was dead.

In Annagasse, in front of the door with the angel and the the trumpet, he caught up with her. "Are you out of your mind?" he said breathlessly.

She pushed him away and ran on.

Then she lost her footing in the slippery snow and fell. He helped her up. There was devastation in his face as he leaned over her. "So you want to get away?" he asked.

She looked into his face. "Forgive me," she said. "I think I mst have had too much Tokay."

"Of course!" His voice echoed his relief. "That was it!"

CHAPTER 7
Ride in a Gondola

The gondola slipped along without a sound. Only the gondolier's oar made a rhythmic gurgling noise. How cloudless the sky! Had it really snowed yesterday? In the Public Gardens the wistaria hung in lavender clusters. The water smelled of fish. The soft blue air quivered.

If one lay back on the black cushions of the black gondola

the hot sun shone in one's face. Could it be that there was only a single night between winter and all this warmth? Henriette revelled in it. Everything had changed. Nothing was as she had imagined it. She did not like the fishy smell, but she was fascinated by the colors A the splashing of the water against the palazzo walls. This was her first big journey.

"Eh" came the warning cry from the gondolier as he turned once more into the Grand Canal. "*Guardi, signora?*" There again was the church she had admired so enthusiastically, Santa Maria della Salute, much more beautiful than Vienna's somewhat similar

Karlskirche. And over there the Campanile, San Marco, and the Doge's Palace, from where they had started. And farther on the Bridge of Sighs. "*Guardi?*"

Franz told her the story of the Bridge of Sighs. She would have preferred to hear the gondolier go on talking, although she understood very little Italian. Everything the man said enraptured her. He spoke so melodiously and with such an abundance of persuasive gestures.

"We are almost back at the Hotel Danieli," Franz explained.

"Already?" There was regret in her voice.

"Already? We've been riding in this gondola for at least two hours! Aren't you hungry? I must say I'm looking forward to some *scampi* and a *risotto!*"

"Can't we ride a few minutes more?" she begged. "It's so beautiful!"

He looked at her lovingly. "All right then. Ten minutes longer!" And to the gondolier he said in the frightful Italian he mustered for her edification: "*Allora, diece minuti. Capisce?*"

"*Va bene, signore,*" the gondolier replied, suppressing a smile as he turned his boat towards the lagoon.

Franz moved nearer to her along the black upholstered seat and laid his arm across her shoulders. She did not move. With injured feelings he reached for the *Neues Wiener Tagblatt* he had bought earlier on the San Marco Square. "I might as well read the newspaper!"

A deep lassitude had come over her. Just to close her eyes, feel the sun, listen to the splash of water. Nothing mattered. Nothing was real. She was not the wife of Franz Alt. Rudolf was not dead. Her conviction that life will give you what you want from it came back to her.

"I declare!" Franz exclaimed. "What do you say to this?"

The water gurgled softly around the keel of the gondola. The cupolas of San Marco gleamed like purest gold. If one closed one's eyes one could imagine being way out there where the red sails tacked back and forth.

"What do you say to this, Hetti? It was suicide!"

She blinked, leaning back in her black seat, and went on listening to the wonderful, soothing sound of the water. What had he said? No matter! Nothing mattered. "Eh!" cried the gondolier to another gondola which should have yielded the right of way to them and didn't. What a remarkably provocative cry! And to think that the gondoliers always stand as they row! They glided on. Was it over the Bridge of Sighs they took prisoners condemned to death?

She had never been good at history. Fortunately the only task her father had set her was the Palazzo Vendramin.

"... that he died as a result of a heart attack in his hunting lodge Mayerling near Baden is not in accordance with the facts. On the contrary, His Imperial and Royal Highness our most illustrious Crown Prince, so we learn on highest authority, is said to have taken his own life in a moment of sudden mental aberration.' Are you listening? And I can tell you that's not the whole truth either! All you have to do is compare the telegrams sent by our Emperor to Kaiser Wilhelm and the Pope. To Kaiser Wilhelm he wired: 'In deepest sorrow I beg to inform you that while on a hunting trip in Mayerling the

Crown Prince suddenly passed away. Presumably heart failure.' And that of the Pope—my French is not so good as yours: '*C'est avec la plus profonde douleur que je viens annoncer à Votre Sainteté la mort subite de mon fils Rodolphe. Je suis sûr de la part sincère qu'elle prendra à cette perte cruelle; j'en fais ce sacrifice à Dieu, auquel je rends sans murmure ce que j'ai reçu de Lui. J'implore pour moi et ma famille la bénédiction apostolique.*' No mention of heart failure! Evidently you cannot deceive the Pope!"

The words had gone into her ears; she had heard them, but they had had no more meaning than the splash of water against the keel of the gondola. Suddenly they acquired such an overwhelming meaning that she roused herself from unreality and tore the newspaper out of his hands. "On the contrary… is said to have taken his own life. The dispatch printed yesterday in these columns, giving the reason for the demise of His Imperial and Royal Highness the Crown Prince, is not in accordance with the facts. On the contrary, his Imperial and Royal Highness our most illustrious Crown Prince … in a moment of sudden mental aberration …" She read it through twice.

"Let's go back!" she said.

"But it's only seven minutes! Don't you think that he was murdered? Why would he take his own life? If there was one person in the world who had no grounds for suicide, it was he. Don't you agree?"

"I'm not so sure," she said.

"But you knew him. Didn't he give you the impression of enjoying life as few do?"

On my wedding day! she thought to herself. "I'm not so sure," she repeated.

"Well, I suppose one can never see inside another person," he said.

They had arrived at the mooring posts rising from the water

in front of the Hotel Danieli. The gondolier looked scornfully at the money in his palm, demanded more, was given it, and then, with a *"Grazie tanto!"* helped the signora out of the gondola.

It took some time to choose a table in the dining room, to which she had accompanied her husband without knowing where she was going. As a typical Viennese Franz spurned the proposals of the head-waiter, who recommended two different tables on the shady side, and consequently chose one on the sunny side. With Viennese dislike of a fixed course, he also brushed aside the regular menu and gave the waiter not only precise instructions as to what he wished but also how he wished it prepared. His tone with such people had already irritated her on the journey down. With porters, conductors, drivers, or waiters her father had always been meticulously polite, and Rudolf had treated them as personal friends.

"Don't drink until you've had something to eat!" Franz warned.

If she just pretended to eat but principally drank the cool red Chianti, soon nothing would matter. Her father would have her telegram by now: "Wonderful trip, safe arrival." He would show it to Theresa, who would say in an injured tone: "That's fine." She could picture them both and could have cried. For if Franz was a typical Viennese, Henriette was a creature of her time in her complete sense of security, which bred a yearning for danger and even for suffering. *Weltschmerz* was what it was called a century earlier, and although that name no longer existed, the romantic sentimentality of Goethe's Werther still haunted the minds of every young generation living in seclusion and protection from the rough winds of realities. To those who willingly indulged in this romanticism it never occurred that it had grown threadbare, that it overestimated emotions and exaggerated individualism. In Henriette's mind a trivial incident was capable of becoming an event instantaneously and anything romantic reached immense proportions. She felt that her destiny had raised her to dizzy heights and that she had been painfully unequal to it. Her thoughts were laden with self-reproach as they kept turning back to the man who had gone to his death on her wedding day. Did he despise her now that he knew what came afterwards?

"*Signora* Alt?"

"*Si?*"

"*Un telegramma.*"

A page in a red uniform handed her a telegram.

"It is a reply from Papa," she conjectured. "Do you know that this is the first wire I've ever received?" She laid it on the table beside her.

He laughed. "Did I ever tell you what I like best about you? It's that you're such a child yet. Aren't you going to open it?"

Picking up the narrow gray envelope, he read aloud the address: "'The Honorable Frau Henriette Alt, née Stein, Hotel Danieli, Venice, Italy.' Your father is indeed polite with you!"

"Is all that really on the envelope?" she asked. Then she read the address herself. It was funny that her father should put all that on his telegram. Then she opened it.

YOUR IMMEDIATE RETURN AND EARLIEST POSSIBLE APPEARANCE AT THIS OFFICE REQUESTED.
(*signed*) PRIVY CHANCELLERY OF HIS MAJESTY THE EMPEROR AND KING.

"From your father?"

She nodded.

"Anything new?"

"He thanks me for my wire."

"May I see it?"

"Of course. Aren't these shrimps delicious? Would you order few more?"

"Waiter!" he called delightedly. "At last I've found something which suits your taste. Waiter! Those people are never here when want them! *Cammeriere! Ancora una porzione scampi.*"

"*Pronto, signore!*"

With his usual unconcern for public notice, which she detested, Franz laid his hand on hers. She not only did not repulse his gesture but pressed his fingers in return.

"Now see what you've done! One can't read it any more!" she said. The paper she held in her hand was all crumpled. She tore it into bits and gave it to the waiter to take away.

"No great harm done," he remarked guiltily. "Or did you want keep it as a souvenir?"

"Perhaps."

Her thoughts were working feverishly. It must, of course, be something connected with Rudolf. She would have to leave that very evening. Franz must not, under any condition, find out the reason. Otherwise she could never make any request of him in the Jarescu matter, and all, all would have been in vain!

"Actually, how could a telegram from your father reach here so quickly? When did you wire him?" Franz inquired.

"Before we went out in the gondola."

"One hour to go, and one to get back? The Royal Italian Postal and Telegraph Service is certainly improving. Otherwise they run things in a *non plus ultra* filthy way!"

She had to bring him to the point of letting her leave for Vienna that evening without his discovering why. It was an impossible thing to do, and yet she had to make it possible. All during the rest of the meal she racked her brains.

After they had gone up to their rooms and he had sat down beside the chaise longue on which she had thrown herself she asked, "How long did you really intend to be away?"

Although he had eyes only for her, he pretended to look out of the window. "You know as well as I—three weeks. Why?"

"Because we must go back tonight."

"That's a rather poor joke."

"But I'm serious. We must go. At least I must. You can, of course, stay here if you choose."

"Is this some new torment you've invented for me?"

"I'm frightfully sorry. But the telegram said—" She had no notion of what she was going to say.

"I thought right away it wasn't from your father," he declared reproachfully.

"But it was from him. I mean—it concerned him."

"What does that mean?"

"It's on Papa's account that I have to go back at once," she decided to say.

His expression, which until now had wavered between unbelief and amusement, grew serious. "Something unpleasant?"

"Rather."

"Is he ill?"

"No, thank goodness."

"Well, then? Have you so little confidence in me?"

"You saw that I wanted to show you the telegram! It said that I must be in Vienna early tomorrow."

"What!" He started. "How do you know it's on account of your father?"

"Because he told me yesterday, when I went home, that I might receive such a telegram."

"I don't understand anything! What did the telegram say?"

"Look, there's no use in cross-questioning me. It's something which concerns only my father, and for that reason I can't tell you what it is. But it's nothing so serious. Let me go this evening and I'll be back here with you the day after tomorrow. Will you?" Once the lie was invented it fell from her lips with such naturalness that she was amazed herself.

"You must be crazy! Do you think I'd let you make two such long trips alone? You were travelling yesterday; you want to do it again today, and then the day after?"

"All right. Then I'll come on Saturday."

"All I see is how little you care about me! Everything else counts. But not I!"

She had to risk all or nothing. "You know that's not true," she said, and kissed him.

Immediately disarmed by her first spontaneous kiss, he replied, "I know nothing. Are you trying to bribe me?" he added promptly, with a touch of suspicion. "Unfortunately I belong to those who let themselves be bribed!" With clumsy tenderness he took her in his arms, fearing all the while that she would again show how little he meant to her.

CHAPTER 8
The Metternich Tradition

In tarvis they bought the Vienna evening papers, were they found twelve lines printed in small type, in an obscure column, under the heading "A Letter from the Crown Prince":

In the following letter, the late Crown Prince Rudolf named Count Ladislaus von Szoegyényi-Marich, Chief of Division in the Ministry of Foreign Affairs, as the executor of his will:
Dear Szoegyényi! Enclosed you will find a codicil to the will I made two years ago. The most important of my papers are in my study in the palace, and I, leave it to you to decide which ones you think should be made available for publication. I enclose the key to the small table by the sofa. When you receive these lines I shall no longer be alive. Take care of my dogs. Black, my hunting partner, goes to Latour, who is to treat him well in memory of me. Let Bombelles have Kastor and Schlieferl; the former is a good and loyal beast, while the latter laughs beautifully. I send my warmest greetings to all my friends. God bless our land.
                                                              RUDOLF

"That looks more like suicide," was Franz's opinion after he had read it aloud to Henriette from his upper berth. "But I wonder why he didn't make his father his executor?"

"What was the date of the letter?" she inquired.

"It doesn't say. Why?"

"The train joggles frightfully!"

"And you wanted to take it again tomorrow! ... Shall I put out the light?"

No, she did not want him to put out the light.

"Try to sleep. You've been awake so long."

"Yes. And thank you again for coming with me. It was awfully sweet of you."

"You baby! Did you think I'd let you go alone? ... Hadn't I better turn out the light?"

Since the train had crossed into Austria its speed had doubled. An occasional flash from a passing light came through the blue curtains. She lay there with closed eyes. Everything was so strange: the narrow compartment, travelling at night, being with someone at night. Marriage was really a kind of imprisonment.

"Are you still awake?" he asked.

She was still awake.

"Tell me, do you still feel so badly over his death?"

"What do you mean?"

"I mean—the day before yesterday you were ready to run away from me. Do you still want to run away from me?"

"No."

"That doesn't sound very enthusiastic."

"Then don't ask me such questions."

The train rattled on. When she was a little girl she always said a rhyme to herself in the train that seemed to fit the throb of the engine: *I am gay, all the way. I am gay, all the way.*

"Hetti?"

"Yes, what is it?"

"Nothing. Good night."

The sound of snoring was now added to the rattle of the train. "When you marry, your husband must neither smoke cigars nor snore," her father had often said jokingly. But tomorrow he would ask her whether she was happy. "Take care of my dogs." "Immediate return and earliest possible appearance at this office requested." "Take care of my dogs." Should she go directly froth the station? Yet the Chancellery would probably not be open at eight o'clock. Perhaps Franz would take less notice if she went straight home from the South Station. She would get out in Karolinengasse and wait downstairs until he had driven on, and then she could take a sleigh herself. If she were lucky she would not meet anyone ...

She was lucky. It was not yet eight o'clock as she sat in a closed carriage. The snow of two days earlier had disappeared, and a black flag fluttered from every house in all the streets through which she drove. At eight o'clock she was at her destination.

In the vestibule into which she was ushered a charwoman with pail, duster, and broom was busy with the morning cleaning.

"Calling on the chief or the assistant chief?" the woman inquired. Henriette did not know on whom she was calling. On the Privy Chancellery of His Majesty the Emperor and King. Until now she had not taken into consideration whether it was a chief or assistant chief. "I don't know," she said. "I have an appointment."

"But you're too early! The assistant to the chief does not come until nine. And the chief much later," the charwoman explained.

Henriette said she would wait. On each of the two high doors coved with green felt she saw a plate with a printed name. Prepared with her replies to the questions which would be put to her behind those doors, she once more went over the answers she had repeated to herself in the sleeping car until she knew them by heart.

At the same time she recalled some other words which she thought sadder than any she had ever heard: "While the latter laughs beautifully."

At nine a man appeared, hung his coat and hat in a wardrobe in the waiting-room, put on a gold-braided official cap, took out his paper and a buttered bun, and sat down behind a table. "Have you an appointment?" he inquired of the waiting Henriette, and began once to munch his bun and read. A quarter of an hour later a gentleman in an astrakhan fur coat, whom he greeted obsequiously, came in. Then for half an hour nothing at all happened.

"I have an appointment," Henriette reminded the man with the official cap. He made a backward gesture with his thumb and on reading. On the wall behind him hung a printed sign: *Office hours 10-12.*

Henriette said: "Would you be good enough to announce that Frau Alt is here? I was sent for from Venice." As she spoke she laid a coin on the table. The man picked up the coin, looked her suspiciously, but ushered her immediately through the door labelled "Dr. Karl Zsismar, *Assistant Chief of the Imperial and Royal Privy Chancellery.*"

The gentleman of this name rose behind his desk. "I am infinitely sorry that you should be kept waiting. The chief should be any moment," he said.

"Can't you attend to the matter yourself?" Henriette asked. She had promised to stop for Franz at his office at eleven, and she began to fear that he would get in touch with her father if she were delayed.

"Unfortunately, that is not possible," was the official's negative reaction. "Did you have a good journey up?"

"Yes, thank you."

"Is it warm down there now?"

"Rather."

"Magnificent city, Venice."

"Magnificent,"

From outside came sounds of obsequious greetings coupled with the name of the departmental chief, and immediately afterwards Henriette was ushered into another room and introduced to an extremely small-statured, gray-haired gentleman who appeared to be chilled, for he stood warming his back and hands in front of a white-tiled stove.

"Please be seated," he said briefly, gave Henriette an unmistakable look, then asked, "You were the mistress of the Crown Prince?"

She jumped up.

"Please remain seated. Well?"

"I knew the Crown Prince. But I was not his mistress!" she said indignantly.

"No? But you had secret meetings with him? You went to Baden, Voeslau, Alland, and Mayerling with him?"

She admitted this.

"How long did you know him?"

"For about a year and a half."

"You married recently?"

"Yes."

"Is your husband aware of your—well, your relationship to the Crown Prince?"

"He knows that I was acquainted with him."

"He knows nothing of the more intimate circumstances? Nothing about the night drives, the rendezvous in more or less secret places?"

"No."

"Why not, if it was all so innocent?"

"He never asked. If he does I shall tell him." Henriette had never hated anyone so much before.

The small gentleman left the stove and sat down at his desk.

"Frau Alt, you had a meeting with His Imperial Highness here in the palace. When?"

"In May."

"Why did he insist on seeing you here rather than at some other place where you usually met?"

"That I don't know."

"You don't know. Do you recall the subject of your conversation on that occasion?"

"Definitely."

"What was it?" the Privy Chancellery chief asked after a second's pause. Her tone had made him hesitate.

"He told me he had requested the Pope to annul his marriage."

"Continue. Did he relate that request to you?"

Thinking with the speed she could command in decisive moments, she gave the negative reply.

"That's not altogether logical. If he really sent for you to tell that, he must have had some purpose in mind. Try to remember, Frau Alt! Your deposition may be of the highest significance in exploring the question of whether or not His Imperial Highness had any motive for suicide."

"Since he did commit suicide he must have had such a motive," was her hostile reply.

Her questioner blew into the palms of his hands. "Have you some definite conjecture in this regard?"

"The marriage of His Imperial Highness was very unhappy. Moreover, there was deep opposition between him and His Majesty," she said.

"Did he mention this explicitly to you?"

"Yes, explicitly."

"Also this latter—I mean the opposition which you mentioned?"

"Yes. That especially."

"Can you recall his words?"

"Exactly."

The small gentleman appeared to be so chilled that he went back the stove and, leaning against it, continued, "You said a moment ago that the Crown Prince committed suicide. Do you exclude any other possibility?"

"Such as?"

"You knew Baroness Mary Vetsera?"

"Yes. Why?"

"What impression did you have of her?"

"I met her only three or four times. She's very attractive."

"You don't know that Baroness Vetsera is no longer alive?"

"No!" she screamed.

"What excites you so? You said you knew her only casually."

The Greek girl was dead! "How did she die?" Henriette asked in a voice scarcely audible.

Exuding his own chilliness until everything in the room seemed to freeze, the small gentleman countered with another question, "What do you think, Frau Alt?"

"Did she die with him?"

Abandoning his fruitless efforts to warm himself, the chief of His Majesty's Privy Chancellery came over to the chair where Henriette was sitting, her eyes staring blankly. He studied her for a moment before he asked, "What put that thought into your mind?"

"Please, Excellency, tell me—did Mary Vetsera die with him?"

"That appears to be the case."

Not she. She was not so cowardly as I, thought Henriette. She trembled so that he said to her, "Aren't you well? Is there anything you wish?"

She did not wish anything.

Without transition he put the next question, "Would you like to be involved in a criminal case, Frau Alt?"

Terrified, she shook her head.

"Then tell me the truth. Beyond me no one shall hear it. That much I promise you."

"I've told you all I know."

The small gentleman began to jot down notes. "Kindly recapitulate. You believe the Crown Prince committed suicide?" She did believe in the Crown Prince's suicide.

"And you believe the motive was—What did you believe the motive to be?"

She believed it was his marriage and—

"His marriage," he interrupted.

"And his breach with his father," she went on.

"Quite so. In this regard you're able to recall certain of his expressions."

"Yes. He said—"

"That's sufficient. For your consideration I may add that we're in possession of valid reasons for casting doubt on the theory of suicide. It's indeed all but certain that His Imperial Highness was the victim of Baroness Vetsera."

Incapable of speech, she stared at him.

"A glass containing suspect substances was found on the night table. It's almost positively a case of murder, Frau Alt. Not suicide."

"That's madness!" she cried. "I never liked Mary Vetsera, but you're doing her a monstrous injustice! She simply went with him because no one else would go with him!"

"I thought you knew more. What is it that you know, Frau Alt?"

She was trembling so violently that she had to hold fast to the armchair in which she was seated. "Nothing."

"Pray calm yourself," the small man said, and gave her a look different from the first one he had given her. "You are very much upset."

"May I go now?"

"I have one more thing to say to you, and I recommend it

to your particular attention. Up to now you have seen these matters in the light put on them by the deceased and perhaps by your father, who also affects extremely liberal views. It's not my office to express any judgment of the qualities of statesmanship possessed by His Imperial Highness the Crown Prince. But one thing is sure: What he strove to bring about, under the influence of his Anglophile tendency and of certain circles—he called it democratic progress—was a Utopia not only not reconcilable with the best understanding of the interest of our country but even fatal to it. There is only one authoritative judge of what is necessary and beneficial to this land, which differs so from every other land and therefore must be handled differently, and that judge is His Majesty the Emperor. In a reign of over forty years he has determined on the course he must steer if this land is to continue to exist. How superhumanly difficult this has been, what unspeakable sacrifices of personal welfare it has entailed, is known to him and the very few who have had the privilege of accompanying him along this hard path. It may be that the deceased, in a moment of depression or regrettable nervous disorder and lack of self-control, to which he was subject, misunderstood some action or expression on the part of His Majesty. But not one of these actions or expressions—not one!—was dictated by anything except a deep-rooted, irreproachable sense of duty and responsibility. Of this I can say that I, an old man and one rather experienced, know of no comparable example in the history of the world." Red spots burned on the cheeks of the small gentleman. "Frau Alt," he went on in a lowered voice, "these are catastrophic days for every loyal Austrian, and I appeal to your loyalty. The rumors to the effect that what you mentioned earlier as a breach between father and son might have driven the Crown Prince to his death have reached even His Majesty's ears. And they have cut deeper than anything else. If he is obliged to admit that that was actually the case it would be a blow which even his iron constitution could not withstand. We must prevent that. At all costs! Do you understand me?"

"Not entirely, Excellency. You did say that you don't believe he committed suicide?"

"Certainly. But it would be much more decisive if His Majesty believed it. And you can be of material assistance in this."

"I?"

"Yes, you. His Majesty has expressed a wish to see you. You will render him and your country an extremely important service if on that occasion you leave certain things unsaid."

"But what am I to say?"

"You have a ready tongue. You'll know what to say. But in order that you know what you're not to say, I must ask you to sign this declaration." He took a prepared statement from his desk and handed it to her.

The elaborately lettered text danced for a while in front of her eyes before she could distinguish any words and before those words took on any meaning:

I, the undersigned, hereby solemnly do swear that I shall maintain under all circumstances an absolutely unbroken silence on everything said to me by his late Imperial and Royal Highness, the august Crown Prince Rudolf, concerning any personages of the supreme Imperial and Royal House. I have been instructed to the effect that any breach of this oath would constitute an act of high treason.

Vienna,
February 1, 1889

"I shan't sign that," she said, and laid the paper back on the desk. The little man stared at her as though he had misheard. "I beg your pardon?"

"No," she repeated.

"And why not, if I may inquire?"

She looked off into space. "I've been cowardly enough."

He coughed. "This heroic attitude in which you fancy your-self is not only stupid, but dangerous. Do you grasp that?"

"I've been cowardly enough," she said again, more to her-self than to him.

"In any case, you'll never be in a position to assert that you were not warned. Good morning, Frau Alt."

"Good morning, Excellency."

CHAPTER 9
There are No Miracles

Black flags. Black draperies. Everywhere his picture swathed in black. "When is the funeral?" she asked a policeman in the Michael Square. It had taken place the day before, she learned. Yesterday she had ridden in a gondola, while he rode in a hearse. "You were the mistress of the Crown Prince?" "I knew him, but I was not his mistress." What was I to him really? she asked her-self in the storm of thoughts driving her without her knowing where she was going or what she was doing. *If I were say to any-one, "I have lost the Crown Prince," I should be considered crazy.* "His Majesty has expressed a wish to see you. You will render him and your country an extremely important service…" Can one go crazy without ever having been ill before? "What did you believe the motive to be?" *You will think me crazy, Excellency, but perhaps I was the motive! Perhaps he wanted to send word to me: Come, I need you. And then did not dare because I sent him a marriage announcement. It was to Mary Vetsera he said it. On my wedding day. On my wedding day he did it. Do you realize what that means, Your Excellency?*

She was seized with a fit of crying in the middle of

Augustiner Street. She went into the church where two days earlier she had been married and sat down in the last row of pews. She was so racked with sobs that a woman saying her beads laid her hand gently on her shoulder and said, "Have you lost someone?"

She nodded.

"Then you mustn't cry," the woman said. "It hurts the dead."

She nodded again and went out. For she could not tell anyone that she had promised to die with the man who was now dead, and that her still being alive was a betrayal. What could she say, anyway? Nothing!

Everything around her seemed to swim. Strange, all that is a matter of course takes its toll. If you do not eat your breakfast you are punished. If you are called Henriette Stein and fall in love with the Crown Prince you are punished. There are no miracles, Papa used to say. Yet she was so irrevocably convinced of the opposite! There were miracles. You had only to wish for them! You could love the Crown Prince. You could become Empress. You could buy off Jarescu. If that was all untrue life would not be worth living.

Jarescu forced her confused thoughts to focus themselves on him for an instant. She must give him an answer. But if Franz discovered anything …? Why was it suddenly so hard to think? Every single thought caused pain.

She reached the piano factory in Wiedner Hauptstrasse almost in time. Foedermayer, the head clerk, told her that Herr Alt had been called away on urgent business and had left word for her ladyship to wait. When Franz finally crossed the threshold of the glass door which divided his private office from the showroom his excitement and the change in him were immediately obvious. "Where have you been?" he asked before he had walked into the room. "You weren't at your father's! He doesn't even know you're in town!"

How exhausted she was by all this questioning! She was unspeakably exhausted. If only she did not have to be questioned! If only she need not think! Once more she made an effort to find at all cost some alibi, but how long could this go on? One cannot think up alibis indefinitely! "I was taken up all morning by the matter I told you about," she answered when nothing else occurred to her.

"I want you to realize that there's no point in trying to hoodwink me!" he retorted threateningly. "Do you know where I've just been? With Otto Eberhard at his office. He sent for me. He is conducting the investigation concerning the death of the Crown Prince."

All right. One more threat. When you are so deadly tired it makes little difference. "Really?" she said apathetically.

"Yes! I know everything! That telegram was from the Privy Chancellery. So you did see the Crown Prince in the palace? Answer me at least!"

If it were not for Jarescu it would have made no vestige of difference what she answered now. Indeed, she would not have needed to answer at all. And not Mary Vetsera, but she herself, would be with him now. It wasn't really cowardice. It was Jarescu. "Yes, I went there," she admitted.

"And you kept that from me!"

If she lost her nerve now the Jarescu matter would be hopeless. "I wasn't able to tell you," she declared. How many pianos could she see in there beyond the glass door? She counted two boudoir grands, three drawing-room grands, two concert grands. Seven. A lucky number.

"It must have been something extraordinary that you weren't able to confide to your husband!"

Now would he go on to say, "You were the mistress of the Crown Prince?" Her ears rang. All she knew was that she answered, "I have nothing to conceal from you," but she did not hear her own words.

He made some reply, but she did not hear that either, and then the glass door went black and her wish not to have to think was fulfilled for a quarter of an hour.

CHAPTER 10
The Dossier of a Love

"Nothing but romantic sentimentalities! Sentimental considerations are of no consequence here! I understand perfectly what's going on inside you, but you simply owe it to our name!"

"You mean I owe it to your position as a lawyer?"

"What I mean is we are good Austrians! I am. You are. Every one in our house has been, since it was built. That is why our sainted grandfather allowed only members of the family to live there. It is unthinkable that we should include anyone in our family has aroused displeasure in the highest circles!"

"Oh, shut up! Our sister Pauline aroused displeasure in the highest circles when she was only five years old."

"I'm really in no mood for jokes, Franz. Yours is no private matter. It doesn't depend on you. One can't entertain relations subversive elements!"

"What then?"

"One politely arranges for an absolute and final severance of ties."

"As politely as they treated the Vetseras? Under cover of night girl was dumped into the ground like a dog in Heiligenkreuz Covent and her family chased across the frontier like gypsies!"

"Considerations of State sometimes impose hardships. In the case of your wife, however, you can't possibly assert that there is the slightest ground for clemency. Self-aggrandizement, coquetry, and frivolity were her only motives. And you have no choice but to draw your own conclusions. And do it immediately."

"But we've only been married six days!"

"Then the divorce will have even less significance later on, when sentiment will no longer be in the picture."

Franz stood up. "Don't give yourself any trouble. I shall not get a divorce," he said curtly.

His brother followed him to the door and laid a hand on his shoulder. "In all the thirty-seven years you have known me have I ever done you a bad turn, Franzl?"

The question was without sentiment, yet Franz could not ignore it. "No," he answered. "I'm convinced that no one could mean better by me. Nevertheless, you must leave to me my choice of the person with whom I want to spend my life."

Otto Eberhard made a gesture of regret. "I really have no right to show you this," he said, returning to his desk and handing Franz an official file. "It's a breach of state secrecy. But in this case I take full responsibility for my act."

On the official gray cover of the file were the words: "Imperial and Royal Police Headquarters, Vienna. Inquiry Proceedings re: Henriette Stein." The "Henriette Stein" had been corrected to read "Henriette Alt, née Stein." Inside the covers were reports, each of which was stamped "Strictly confidential."

"Henriette Stein," read the first report, "21, Roman Catholic, daughter of Ludwig Stein, professor at the University, address, Fourth District, Number 9 Karolinerigasse, accompanied His Imperial Highness the Crown Prince yesterday, November 8, 1887, on a drive to Baden, near Vienna. The couple left Vienna at 11 A.M., arrived at their destination at 12:45 P.M., lunched at the Gasthof Zur Stadt Wien, and returned to Vienna at 3 P.M." A second report revealed that Henriette Stein had gone on another drive with the Crown Prince up the Helenental—"total time elapsed, there and back, 2 hours and 40 minutes." A third report mentioned a *"dejeuner dinatoîre"* at Mayerling, on November 19, at which the Crown Prince, "the aforesaid Stein," Prince Philip of Coburg, Count Joseph Hoyos, and Count Leopold Traun were present. And, pedantically enough, it included the menu: *"Consommé en tasse, truite bleue, viande froide assortie, salade verte, petits fours, vin de Tokaye,* 1848, Grinzinger Auslese, 1876, Pomméry *extra sec,* 1861," and added the time of the departures and arrivals: Dep. Vienna, South Station 10:05 A.M. Arr. Mayerling 12:15 P.M. Dep. Mayerling 1:40 P.M. Arr. Vienna, South Station, 3:50 P.M." A number of sheets contained brief notes such as: "Meeting at the Second Rondeau in the Prater: the Stein woman was waiting there. His Imperial Highness, however, did not get out but waved to her from the carriage and drove on immediately because Herr Andor von Péchy came into sight at that moment from the direction of the Krieau Restaurant." Or: "H.I.H. waited in vain for the Stein from 2:30 to 4:15 in the afternoon in front of the Passecker millinery shop on the Kohlmarkt, where she was trying on spring hats." Or: "At the opening of the Hans Makart Exhibition His Imperial Highness engaged the Stein woman in conversation at such that Her Imperial Highness the Crown Princess stamped her foot with impatience and displeasure." The informer's report on the "visit in the palace" took up more space. After an exact statement of time and the route taken, it went on: "The Stein woman's one-hour visit with the Crown Prince was interrupted only once, for five minutes, by Vice-Admiral Count Bombelles. According to the depositions of Captain of the Guard Ferdinand Kirschner, who during the entire time was stationed in the antechamber, the voice the Crown Prince was constantly audible and sounded excited and extremely angry, as though he were violently reproaching the Stein woman. Captain Kirschner recalled having distinctly heard such words as 'torture' and 'anyone who is so absolutely devoid of understanding!' Puechel, groom of the chambers, made a deposition to the effect that for many minutes after the departure of the Stein woman His Imperial Highness remained seated motionless at his desk with a distorted expression on his face."

Besides all this the gray file contained the following official entry: "Henriette Stein married to Franz Alt, member of the board of the Chamber of Commerce, owner of the C. Alt piano factory," and concluded with a "comment" from the Privy Chancellery addressed to Police Headquarters under date of February 1, 1889: "Frau Alt, née Stein, conforming to telegraph request, called at this office this morning. She gave rise to the impression that she belongs to certain circles which, under cover of liberal views, harbour anti-dynastic, unpatriotic, and revolutionary sentiments. She remained inaccessible to the representations made to her in this connection. Since the aforesaid Stein woman, through her relationship to His Imperial Highness the late Crown Prince, has come into possession of knowledge of certain circumstances which, if made known, would have most regrettable political repercussions, and since above all it might put the tragic demise of his said Highness in a light calculated to cause unrest among the people, consequently it is respectfully recommended that appropriate measures to deal with this matter be weighed." To this comment the chief of police had added a note his own handwriting: "To be laid before the first district attorney for consideration of official inquiry along lines of Paragraph 58 of the Penal Code."

Franz handed the file of documents back to his brother. "What is Paragraph 58?" he asked.

"High treason," Otto Eberhard explained in the same suave tone he used to such effect when scoring some deadly point in a drawing room or in court.

"And what do you propose to do, Mr. Public Prosecutor?"

"That's what I should like to hear first from you," said the elder brother. "But I can't believe you can have any remaining doubts after reading that file!"

"Quite right," replied the younger one, and his face, so clouded with the cares of the last few days, now brightened for the first time. "I feel now there's no doubt at all."

"Go to Dr. Winiwarter. He is the best lawyer for divorces."

"I have no need of him," Franz said. "The one thing I don't understand is how you have built up your reputation as a lawyer. In that whole filthy little file there's nothing except that Hetti is a wonderful girl! Thanks for the proof. So long!"

He closed the office door firmly behind him, and once in the long stone-paved corridor of the County Criminal Courthouse, his face grew even brighter, until he began to whistle. It was a tune from *The Gypsy Baron*.

CHAPTER 11
The Mistake

The remarkable thing about Herr Jarescu was that he did not consider himself an ordinary blackmailer, and at that a rather coarse and stupid one, but a writer of some stature. Yet he was a regular blackmail journalist, whose paper, *Vienna Signals*, which he published weekly himself, was a typical scandal sheet, obtaining readers by what it printed and money by what it left unprinted.

Jarescu, according to his own assertions, came from Romania—from Bucharest, the capital. He had been a resident of Vienna for nearly twenty years, and whoever considered himself in society there read his paper, which devoted its attention more to private lives than to politics and provided both with flowery comments—which was why Daniel Spitzer, the witty journalist, spoke of it in his "Vienna Strolls" as the "hotbed of Vienna journalism."

Nevertheless, Jarescu's sources were splendid. He scorned denials, and his "honor as a journalist," which he maintained he possessed, he based on the literal exactitude of all that was disparaging, spiteful, and detrimental in his little weekly. His column was called "The Reverse of the Medal," and every Friday fresh victims looked forward with terror to its appearance.

When, ten months earlier, a person who remained anonymous called to Henriette's attention an impending article in which her mother's life and death were dragged in the mud she had not been clearly aware of Jarescu's motives. Yet they were so simple. His eldest son, a law student, had had the bad luck to be failed by Professor Stein in his oral examinations for his doctor's degree. As soon as the Romanian gentleman began to look round he always found things, and in the case of this unaccommodating professor he had discovered enough to break his very backbone—five letters. These proved that his wife—whom, as every one in Vienna knew, he had put on a pedestal of adoration—had been the mistress of the director of the opera throughout her married life. A few quotations from a few love letters, and the professor's life illusion would fall about his head like a house of cards, and with such finality that there could be no restoration.

At least, that was what Jarescu had explained to Henriette. "You understand, my dear young lady," he had said to her in his affected Viennese dialect, from which he was still unable to exclude his original habits of speech, "that all this is extremely painful for me. But put yourself in my place. I came into possession of certain documents by purest chance, as I emphasized to you earlier. If your father were a private individual, well and good; we should draw a veil over the whole matter. But alas, he's not that. An entire younger generation is studying civil law under him, marriage laws! Now it's important, as you will admit, Miss Henriette, that the public should be properly informed about such a man. I have that authentic information, and consequently my honor as a journalist requires that I should publish it."

It was because of this conversation that Henriette's life had taken such an extreme and dangerous turn and had continued so since then. Thanks to her conviction that with sufficient will one can achieve any end, she had simply said: "Those letters may not be published." This had also been discussed, and it became apparent what an accommodating gentleman Jarescu was. In return for a certain sum—shall we say ten thousand florins? (he was the one who suggested it)—he would abstain from publicity. Anyone else would have seen through Jarescu's scheme, and would have told himself: "In the first place, those five letters don't mean much; in the second place, it can't be altogether difficult to dispose of a blackmailer. A simple call on the chief of police will do." It would not have occurred to anyone else even to consider buying off a Jarescu for ten thousand florins. Henriette, however, who was "the most unpractical creature in the world" (her father's indulgent way of describing her definite inability to take things at their proper value), delighted to find a path out of this horrible labyrinth, said: "Agreed." Now all she had to solve was the mere trifle of the problem: who would pay the ten thousand florins? She would do it, she maintained. Meanwhile, easy as Jarescu was to talk to, it was extremely difficult to make him believe anything.

"What guarantee shall I have?" he demanded to know. There was none. Her father was not rich; Henriette herself had three hundred and eleven florins in her account, all of which the Romanian gentleman unfortunately seemed to know already. "Perhaps someone else would step into the breach?" he suggested suddenly, and somehow it did not seem as though he were making such a proposal for the first time in his life, for it dropped so fluently from his bluish, smooth-shaven lips. One thing led to another, and as an expat he soon saw how easy it was to throw this young lady into a state of panic, so he quickly tightened the noose as soon as he had both ends in his hands. Wasn't there a Herr Alt whom the young lady had mentioned several times? To be sure, the publisher of the *Signals* had not the privilege of a personal acquaintance with him, but the Alt pianos were among the most exquisite in the world. And when would the wedding take place? At that time the engagement had not even taken place. But to Henriette it appeared to be the only way to get rid of this man with whom she was so utterly unable to cope, and so she named a day. Thereupon all that remained to be done was the signing of a small document. At times since then, when his splendid sources of information gave him occasion to do so, Jarescu recalled himself to her consciousness. In such cases he had sent warning messages and had received written assurances that everything was proceeding in the best possible way and that he must only have a little more patience.

But today he appeared in person and rang the bell on the fourth story shortly after Henriette had decided to engage the manservant sent to her by an employment agency. With a butler in the house she felt even more unsure of herself. She had never had one and therefore was quite uncertain how to deal with him. But what had she been sure of in those first unearthly days? At first she woke up weeping and was frightened by the new rooms. They were cold.

Life in them was all compulsion and menace. Something was going behind her back, and no one told her what it was. Her brother-in-law Otto Eberhard was scarcely civil; her father treated her like an invalid; she hardly knew even Franz, he had suddenly become so reserved. "Why did you really come back so soon from your wedding journey?" her girl friends asked. Others asked: "Tell me, is it wonderful?" She never had girl friends she liked. Little Christine from the first floor was the only one who put no questions and understood everything. You could sit with her for hours and sob your heart out, without having to hide from her, as from others, that you had lost someone.

"A gentleman to call, your ladyship," announced the new butler. On the visiting card he handed her she read:

FERDINAND MICHAEL ALEXANDER JARESCU
Publicist and Editor-in-Chief of *Vienna Signals*

"Ask him to come in," Henriette said. She had almost lost her capacity to be afraid.

The presence of little Christine seemed to annoy the publicist, but Henriette said to her: "Please stay!" And to the gentleman with the highly pomaded shining black part in his hair: "This is my new relative. You can speak freely before her. We have no secrets from one another, have we, Christl?"

"No!" replied the child, who had changed amazingly since Henriette had moved into the house. She was no longer sad. She had blossomed out.

"Frau Alt," her caller began, "has it perhaps escaped your attention that today is already February 4 in the calendar?"

"I know, it's really terrible! But I shall speak to my husband this very day," she promised. It still cost her an effort to say "my husband."

"It's high time, I must say," Jarescu declared, and then, after looking at the little girl, he added a remark deriving from some of his splendid fund of information. "Especially as you're not likely to have much more time in which to do it."

Henriette, thinking that here was the man who was the cause of all that had happened to her, did not grasp the implication of his remark. She was surprised that she saw him more as a source of wonder than of hatred. She realized that there were bad people, but she looked on him more as a freak.

Meanwhile little Christine had taken her firmly by the arm.

"What does this gentleman want from you? " she asked softly, and in her large dark eyes there glowed the hatred Henriette did not feel.

"Nothing, Christl," she replied.

"What we have to discuss is perhaps not entirely suited to the ears of children," Jarescu suggested.

"Why not?" said Henriette, still rapt in her thoughts. "I prefer to have someone with me who is on my side. Two against one. That gives me a chance."

The publisher of the *Signals* altered his velvety conversational tone a shade. "If you're counting on your possible arrest to liberate you from your responsibility in regard to me you're mistaken!"

Was he threatening to have her arrested? In such matters she was utterly unsuspecting and less like the daughter of an eminent jurist than like that of the opera singer Madame Aufreiter, who to the day of her death looked upon laws and everything that went with them as an impenetrable mystery. It was only in the Romanian's following remark that she found a clue to what he meant by arrest, but that she understood even less. It was impossible to be arrested because one had refused to give a signature to a document as required by a Chancellery chief!

"Don't be ridiculous!" she said.

Now that was something Jarescu never had any intention of being. "Frau Alt," he protested, "it may fascinate certain highly or less highly placed persons to watch your display of naïveté. But you will be kind enough to spare me. Today is Wednesday. I'll give you until tomorrow. If you haven't settled my affair promptly by tomorrow noon, I'll not allow you to make a fool of me any longer, and the article will appear the day after tomorrow. Moreover, I'm convinced that its readers will look forward to a little story about the daughter of so romantic a mother who has shown herself quite inclined to romance too!"

"Hello, darling," said Franz, who had entered the room while the publicist was still speaking. He had hurried straight back from the County Criminal Courthouse, whistling all the way. With every step he had realized more clearly that he could not have asked for better proof than that gray file.

"My husband—Herr Jarescu." Henriette performed the introduction. The moment which she had feared and delayed so long had come. It could hardly have come less favorably, without any preparation and at the very time when Franz was so different. *I always used to have so much luck*, she thought to herself.

"How do you do?" Franz said. "What were you two saying about romance? I came home too soon, I know. But today I was particularly anxious to get home."

Jarescu, on the other hand, found the time most favorable. Here was a husband fresh from his honeymoon, head over heels in love—that much was obvious to a blind man—and all unsuspecting that this coquettish little person did not care anything about him and wasn't even depressed by the prospect of having the secret police brutally intrude on the idyll the next day or even more probably that day! "I can quite understand your feelings," was his approving remark, and he prepared to take hold of this husband in the way his experience had taught him. "A chivalrous gentleman like you," he would say to him, "would not care whether you gave your lovely wife a beautiful string of pearls or an even more costly present if it would return her peace of mind to her!" That would untie his purse strings. Men are so vain!

"Herr Jarescu has come," Henriette began, pressing the finger tips of both hands to her temples, a gesture characteristic of her in moments of extreme perplexity, "to get me—" She stammered. The long-awaited occasion found her unprepared. "You see, he is—"

The instant he had entered the room Franz had sensed that this fellow, who exuded such a penetrating barber-shop odor, was unpleasing to Henriette. I must have seen him before somewhere was the thought that crossed his mind.

"Herr Jarescu happens to be the publisher of *Vienna Signals*," Henriette ventured.

Something clicked in Franz's memory. This was the man who, at performances of various virtuosos in the Musikverein concert hall, always pushed his way into the green room, although someone else the music critic on his filthy paper. However, it was an established fact that it was a filthy paper. The *Presse*, too, was a filthy paper. All liberal papers were 'filthy rags.' Although. Franz was convinced he was no anti-Semite, nevertheless he shared the general opinion with regard to newspapers—namely, that liberal-minded Jews wrote for and financed them, and all liberalism was a filthy bussiness.

"Aha," he said, "and to what may we attribute the pleasure of this call?"

"Perhaps you and I could discuss this privately?" the Romanian proposed. That was the last thing Henriette desired. But Franz was already on his feet, and with a "This way, please," he showed him into the next room and followed him.

Little Christine asked, "Why are you so afraid of that man, Aunt Hetti?"

Because what was going on in there now was the worst that could happen! Franz would hear all about Mama's dreadful past and that Henriette herself had married him on material grounds. Under the influence of phrases current in her day, she had built her world on foundations already laid without its ever occurring to her to test them. Mama's 'dreadful past ' could be boiled down to an affair with the man to whom she owed her position as a singer. But to marry a person on 'material grounds,' according to the novels she had been brought up on, was a crime. On the other hand, to put someone on a pedestal, as Papa had done with Mama, was such a wonderful-sounding phrase that it must be true.

An undertone of voices came from the next room. At this very moment her future was being decided.

"Don't make a face like that!" Christine pleaded. "Shall I play a hand of marriage with you?"

She had the cards ready and dealt them out. Six for Henriette, six for herself. And to make the game more enticing she exclaimed: "It seems to me I have very bad cards!"

Diamonds were trumps. They had not yet taken the mourning draperies off the Coburg Palace.

"Your turn. Aunt Hetti!"

What are trumps?

Diamonds.

King, queen, ace of clubs. "Marriage! Auntie!"

At any moment the voices must grow louder. Could she have believed that Franz would pay such an enormous sum of money for something which really did not mean anything to him? While she listened with bated breath for sounds from the next room she somehow could not grasp how she had talked herself into it all. Her towering hopes, when faced with reality, fell in a heap like the cards before her. She might just as well not have married at all! She might just as well have screwed up the little mite of courage that Greek girl had had! She would have ruined everything as far as Franz was concerned anyhow. A tremendous mistake, the whole thing!

"But, Auntie, diamonds are trumps!"

Henriette jumped up because the door of the next rootii opened suddenly and the two men appeared. Franz was smoking a cigar. "We have talked the matter out." He nodded smilingly to Henriette.

"Really?" she said, bewildered.

"Completely," he answered, and blew a huge smoke ring into the air. I think we must not detain our editor any longer."

He opened the door into the vestibule. "By the way, what's the name of the man you engaged?" he inquired as he did so.

"Johann." Her voice trembled. "But he asked to be called by his surname, Simmerl."

"Simmerl!" Franz called in a loud tone.

"Yes, Your Grace!" echoed a voice from outside.

"Show this gentleman out. He's in a hurry!"

Jarescu's carefully shaven cheeks had taken on a sickly hue. "Thanks, I can find the way by myself," he declared.

"Simmerl, show the gentleman out!" Franz repeated with emphasis.

The new butler appeared in the doorway of the living room and walked up behind the caller. "This way, if you please, sir."

A second later the apartment door slammed behind the publicist.

"Bravo!" Franz exclaimed with appreciation. "You seem to be experienced in throwing people out, Simmerl!"

"Thank you, Your Grace. I have my method!" replied the recipient of the praise.

When Franz left the vestibule and came back into the living room he went straight over to Henriette and took her into his arms. Pride was written all over his easily readable face. "Do you know what, Hetti? You're really a marvellous girl!"

"What did he tell you, Franz?" She decided to risk the question.

"He? We're rid of him! I gave him the address of where to go. The same place from which I have just come. By the way, at that place—and from that filthy rat just now too—I discovered something I've known for a long time but which it's always fun to hear again, and that is: I'm the luckiest husband in the world! Frau Alt, allow me to congratulate myself on you!" He passed his hand tenderly over her hair. The smug self-satisfaction which she had found so distasteful in him had almost vanished. She had never had a brother, and now it seemed to her as if she had one.

"Uncle Franz, you are wonderful!" cried little Christine, full of delight.

"'Out of the mouths of babes,'" he quoted, laughing. "Does that man think Simmerl is such a beautiful name? Simmerl! Will dinner be ready soon?"

It was a long time since there had been nothing to fear.

CHAPTER 12
Audience at Dawn

The young chambermaid helped Henriette to dress. It seemed almost certain that dark blue was an appropriate color, although perhaps black would be more suitable for the occasion? Should she wear a hat? And if so, which one? What about gloves? Every one knew that Frau Schratt never appeared at court without the fan which the Empress had made fashionable.

The chambermaid unfortunately had no experience to draw on, even if Henriette had dared to ask her, because in her only other place she had served an unfriendly, inelegant elderly lady, and therefore her admiration for her new mistress was boundless. She slowed things up instead of expediting them, because she was so enchanted with everything and gaped at each object before she handed it over. Yet speed was urgently necessary; the cab was already waiting downstairs, for the possibility of arriving late for an appointment, with Francis Joseph was beyond the realm of the conceivable. The audience had been announced half an hour earlier by a palace guardsman; it was due to begin in twelve minutes' time. Meanwhile she had to finish dressing and reach the appointed place.

Franz, who had run downstairs to get the cab, was waiting impatiently outside the Annagasse entrance. It was past six, but the February day was as dark as one in December. The gas streetlamps were still lighted. Franz had had the cab drive up to the Annagasse entrance because he thought it would be less noticeable there. Pulling his watch out and looking past the angel with the trumpet up to the lighted windows of the fourth story, he realized with despair how late she was.

Meanwhile she was standing in front of the mirror from Paris, putting on the hat she had decided to wear, the one trimmed with marten. She asked the chambermaid to tie her veil under the knot of her hair because her own fingers were stiff with cold. She had been hauled out of her bed like some criminal, it seemed to her. Her rebellious coiffure would not stay brushed smoothly enough at her temples, and her lips were too pale. She bit them with her teeth, but still there was no color in them. She drew on her gloves as she went down the staircase.

The house, which must not learn about all this, was still wrapped in slumber. The milk bottles and morning papers lay before the doors of the various apartments. Nearly all the members of the family read the Catholic daily. Only in front of the Drauffers' door lay a copy of the liberal *Presse*. She had left her fan upstairs after all!

"Hurry! Hurry!" Franz called from downstairs. "We have just five minutes!" He helped her into the closed carriage and then stepped in himself, for he had insisted on accompanying her.

"Our Emperor is an early riser!" he said reassuringly as they drove along, but it was obvious that he was worried. "And, of course, we were prepared for this," he repeated twice over, as though that meant anything. But that did not fit in either. After she had refused to sign the declaration she was convinced that the Privy Chancellery chief would never let her go to this audience, and Franz agreed with her view.

"Am I very dishevelled?" she asked.

"Not in the least. You look as though you had just come out of a bandbox," he declared. In the same breath he added nervously: "You're not too excited?" To be called to the Emperor, who except to his Ministers and generals was not accessible to any ordinary mortal, was an occasion of incomparable significance to any patriotic Viennese and a former officer in the reserve such as Franz. "And be sure not to speak unless he asks a question! You know no one is allowed to speak unless he asks a question. And back out when you leave him!" were his last instructions.

Yes, she knew that.

In the Franzenshof the gas streetlights were just being extinguished.

"All right then, I'll wait here for you," he said as she passed the two huge guardsmen standing in their sentry boxes and entered the gray baroque portal. Inside she was taken in charge by the captain of the guard, who wrote down her name, after inquiring, "Frau Henriette Alt?"

"Yes."

She was conducted up a staircase as cold as the one at 10 Seilerstatte and almost as dark. A few gas jets flickered here and there on the walls. On the first floor both wings of a high gold-and-white door flew open the instant Henriette and her escort stood before it. Then she reached an endless hall in which a general, holding his green-befeathered hat on his left hip and dragging the tip of his saber after him, was walking up and down with a gentleman in tails and white tie. As the hall was not carpeted but had a smooth parquet floor, one could hear the gentlemen as they walked, step by step. And the trailing saber, too. The general turned round stood still, and then, with a slight bow, inquired, "Frau Henriette Alt?"

"Yes."

She recognized him from the pictures of his remarkable slanting mouth: it was the Adjutant-General, Count Paar. She did not recognize the gentleman in civilian clothing.

"Tell Count Paar next time he wants anything he'll have to

take the trouble to come down to me himself!" the man whose voice no one would ever hear again had said. She heard that voice. And the gold-and-white door had opened just as noiselessly on that day too.

"I must beg you to be patient for a moment," said the general with the green-befeathered hat, and resumed his promenade up and down the endless hall. The gentleman in tails walked beside him. Neither of them spoke.

Then another door opened and a black-bearded gentleman, also in tails, a top hat, and kid gloves in his hand, emerged. He joined the other two, and Henriette heard the Hungarian greeting, "*Jonapot kivánok!*" Whereupon she was signalled to enter the same door through which the black-bearded gentleman had just come. She found herself in a hall, quite alone. From there she came to the Emperor.

Francis Joseph stood in his small study beside an upright desk, his right arm resting lightly on it. He wore a blue tunic with a gold collar, the Golden Fleece and two other medals, the black trousers with the red stripes of a general—the uniform in which the Viennese were invariably accustomed to seeing him. The Viennese saying that he never changed and that, except for a few white hairs in his moustache and sideboards, at fifty-eight he looked as he did at forty was no longer true. In the last few days he had aged years.

The small room was lighted by a central chandelier with three frosted globes. Against the long wall was a chest of drawers covered with photographs, a writing table beside the one high arched window, and the upright desk above which hung a portrait of the Empress; an officer's cap, a saber with a gold sword knot, and a pair of white kid gloves lay on a little table.

At the door Henriette made the low curtsey every Viennese girl learned at her dancing class.

"Please come nearer," were the words she heard while her head was still bowed. It was a businesslike, even gray tone which in no way reminded her of that other wild one. "Frau Alt, I presume?"

"Yes, Your Majesty."

He made an inviting gesture in the direction of the only seat in the room besides the armchair at his desk. When she hesitated he said: "Please seat yourself."

He himself remained standing at his desk, studying her. "You know my son?" he asked after a while.

"Yes, Your Majesty."

"How long?"

"About a year and a half."

"In the course of that time did you see him often?"

"Yes, Your Majesty."

His fingers tightened their hold on the desk. "Did he discuss any things with you?"

"Yes, Your Majesty."

"What things?"

"He had many interests."

"Did he also discuss politics with you?"

She weighed her words and then said, "Almost never." The pale light of the February morning began to fall through the high window that faced the Franzenshof, the Emperor Francis monument, and the sundial—which told no time, for it cast no shadow.

"I asked you to come here, Frau Alt, in order to get some information from you," said the Emperor. His voice was unchanged, his words dry as straw. But she could see how tightly his fingers grasped the desk. "Do you prefer to have me question you? Or would you rather tell me what you know?"

"I beg Your Majesty to question me." She suddenly had the impression that he thought the veil she was wearing over her face was inappropriate, so she tried to raise it. But her hands would not obey her, and it took some time before she succeeded in throwing it back over her hat. His face was unmoved. She seemed to have been mistaken.

"You believe my son committed suicide. You said so to the head of the Privy Chancellery, did you not?"

"Yes, Your Majesty."

"And you have formed an opinion as to what the reason for it was?" He was now holding fast to his desk with both hands. A look which she was barely able to stand accompanied his unchanging, routine tone of voice.

"No, Your Majesty."

For the first time he faced her squarely. "No?" He cleared his throat, and when she did not speak he repeated, "No?"

"No, Your Majesty."

In his stony face not a muscle moved. "Did my son ever communicate to you his feelings of lack of harmony between——him and me? You may speak quite frankly. I promise you that not a word of what you say will go beyond these walls." For a brief second his darkly encircled eyes sought hers, and then they fixed themselves on the threadbare red Smyrna carpet on the floor.

"His Imperial Highness never mentioned Your Majesty except with the deepest devotion and respect," was her answer.

Francis Joseph again cleared his throat, then he drew a deep breath and studied his visitor for what seemed like an eternity to her. "Is that the truth, Frau Alt?"

"Yes, Your Majesty."

"You are a Catholic, I suppose?"

"Yes, Your Majesty."

"Would you be willing to take an oath on what you have just told me?"

"Yes, Your Majesty."

The pallid light in the small room grew stronger. The lamps were superfluous now. "It's already growing light earlier," commented Francis Joseph. His gray voice rang with a shade more of warmth. "You married recently?"

"Yes, Your Majesty."

"I trust you are very happy."

"Your Majesty is too gracious."

He was silent. Then he drew a telegram out of his desk. "Before you leave I should like to show you something," he said, and brought it over to her.

It was sent from Mayerling on January the twenty-eighth and read:

TO HIS MAJESTY THE EMPEROR, THE PALACE, VIENNA.

ENGEDELMET KYREK, HA LEM GYUVEK. KEVESET BETEG VAGYOK.

TISZTELEMA FOEHERZEPNE.

RUDOLF

"Do you know Hungarian?" he asked as she read it.

"A little, Your Majesty."

"Then you will have seen that on the day before his death my son felt so ill that he was obliged to cancel an appointment with me. Do you not envisage the possibility that it was fear of illness which might have driven him to his fatal decision? You're young yourself; you must know that it's not always in their parents that children confide?" His tired, restless eyes demanded that she might answer yes.

She did.

He extended the finger tips of his icy hand. "You have given me valuable information, Fraü Alt. I thank you."

She bowed low in a curtsey, then backed out of the room. The gold-and-white doors opened for her. Someone was there to escort her down the icy stairs, which she descended one after another without knowing what she did. Below stood Franz.

The sun had begun to shine, but the dial in the Franzenshof

still cast no shadows. The walls were too high. It was so chill that one had a fierce yearning for some warmth.

"Let's go home," she begged, and it was the first time she had spoken of the fourth story in that way.

CHAPTER 13
The Fruit of Ignorance

Professor Stein had been there, as always on Thursday forenoons, between his lecture and his seminar. He had come and gone again with his usual punctuality and had sipped a glass of sherry which Simmerl had brought him with some thin slices of Westphalian ham in the guise of a light lunch. He had looked a bit worried, as he had a way of doing when he came to visit Henriette. Ever since her marriage all essential things had remained unsaid between father and daughter, except for an occasional fleeting look on his delicate, nervous face and a smile on hers. This meant: Are you beginning to grow accustomed to it? and: Yes. Always he treated her like a child, asked if she were clad warmly enough or ate enough, and, now that her confinement was approaching, he inquired what the doctor had said. "Your mother used to …" he would remind her, and constantly recommend to her, as an example, what her mother had done or found indispensable.

Today he had been in fine form, for he had expiated on his favorite political theme. According to him, Francis Joseph, since death two years before of both German Emperors William and Frederick, was now not only the senior partner of the Triple Alliance but its very head—"*primus inter non pares*," as he expressed it. With his characteristic eloquence, which so enthralled his students in the lecture hall, he had expounded the special mission in European culture that he attributed to "*homo Austriacus*," because he embodied in himself the ideal mixture of soul, grace, and proficiency, whereas "*homo Germanicus*" possessed mostly the latter, "*homo Italicus*" only the former, in the shape of art. And he considered Francis Joseph—with whom "the idea of the ruler overpowered that of the man, making his personal individuality its servant"—"the most underestimated monarch of modern times," and Henriette was obliged to think: Can he be mistaken in that too? Yet she knew no one as gifted as he in raising you up into a higher, purer sphere. Where he had his being problems ceased to be physical and became intellectual.

"Your Herr Papa was looking splendid today," Simmerl remarked as he cleared the table. Henriette nodded and sighed softly. During his visit she had not wanted to let herself go because he would immediately have worried so. "Are you coming in to clean the brass?" she asked the butler. For before her father had come Simmerl had been regaling her with his endless store of experiences in the Königswarter household, which she enjoyed listening to. He told such a lot of gossip with such a dignified expression, and curiosity was something she did not even attempt to combat. She simply did not understand people who knitted their brows over such things. Human beings were so immensely interesting!

Simmerl (who had finally succeeded in having himself called "Herr" Simmerl) went on from the point where he had been interrupted by Professor Stein's Thursday call. As he polished the brass fittings on the dining room door he came to the dramatic moment. "Said the baron to me, 'Herr Simmerl,' he said, 'if you ever see that captain again face to face, you must let me know immediately!' For you must know that the baron never talked much, and as for the baroness, he had a kind of admiration—Does your ladyship not feel well?"

"I'm not sure," she said. "Please go on, Herr Simmerl."

The tall man with the long face, on which there were scarcely any eyebrows, so that its expression was one of constant wonder, proceeded with his task of story-telling and cleaning the door brasses, for which he used a chamois cloth and some white polish. But Henriette had let a sound of pain escape, so he stopped a second time.

"Perhaps it were better to notify Dr. Herz?" he asked, as usual speaking in the subjunctive and thereby implying that his suggestion was only tentative.

When Dr. Herz came he maintained—as usual when he came to visit one of his patients at Number 10—that everything was exactly as it should be. A little later, as Henriette lay in her bed, the thought came to her that she would die.

"What nonsense!" said Dr. Herz, who seemed to have arranged for a protracted stay. "Everything is absolutely normal!"

Normal that one should have such pain and afterwards such a sense of passing away? Why had no one ever told her that it was so frightful?

"Why should they have discouraged you? A first birth is always a little more strenuous," the doctor explained with a gentleness which aroused only bitterness in her. "You must surely have known that."

"I don't think I can stand it!" she replied. She had known nothing of the sort! Up to this very second she had not even known what would happen.

"Now, now! They all stand it," Dr. Herz said. "To do a good job takes time. We can't alter nature. You can understand that, can't you, my dear little lady?"

The pains and deathly terror never abated now. Towards three o'clock they fetched Franz home from his office. Towards seven a man whom she was barely able to distinguish came into the room of pain-wracked woman. He was a consulting specialist—not an ordinary physician, but a professor of gynaecology—whom Dr. Herz had sent for. He, Dr. Herz, was only a general practitioner, and you couldn't afford to take chances at a house like Number 10. Dr. Herz not only was no specialist, but was also young and poor. He couldn't risk losing patients who paid five florins for each visit. The professor first examined the case, then declared to Franz, when he joined him in the next room, that perhaps the case was not quite so normal as his esteemed colleague had supposed. "I don't wish to alarm you in any way," he said, "but the labour pains have ceased."

"Does that occur sometimes?" Franz asked.

"Oh, certainly! We see it repeatedly."

"Is she in danger?"

"Not at the moment."

Whereupon Franz, who had sat there motionless for four hours, fists pressed together, rose slowly from his seat. He slipped a small silver cross he had been holding into his vest pocket. "She must not die!" he said to the professor.

"Everything that lies in my power will be done." The professor did not include the power of Dr. Herz.

"She must not die!" repeated Franz. "Do you understand me?" The attitude of this husband, whom the professor had known in his chess club and whom he considered a rather unemotional fellow, was so unexpected that he regaled the other club members with his story at the next occasion. "Lots of things have happened to me in life," he told them, "but never anything like this. I've seen relatives of patients who beseech me as though I were a saviour or bribe me as though I were a highwayman. But never one who wanted to murder me! I swear to you that man would have strangled me with his own hands!"

However that may have been, and although Franz, for the four hours since he had come home, had been strictly forbidden to do so, he now tore open the door to his wife's bedroom and stood on the threshold staring at the bed like one bereft of his senses until he was forcibly led away.

Henriette was not aware of this either. The storm of pain

had passed, but her body felt like lead. Her thoughts, too, were blunted and consisted mostly of a vague consciousness of being dead. She tried, without success, to remember when it had happened. Nor could she fathom where she was. But the roaring sound in her ears and the putrid, sweetish smell of lagoons was something she recognized. Then they both passed; she was swallowed up in complete blankness and darkness. That, too, disappeared for a few seconds at a time and then returned for a few seconds.

"Tampons! Quick!"

The lagoon smelled so sickeningly sweet.

"How is the pulse?"

"All right, Professor."

"You call such a weak pulse all right! I knew it! If only I hadn't let myself be pushed into this by you! You can't operate in a private home! I need oxygen, by God!"

All black. Empty. Ugh, that smell!

"How is her respiration now?"

"I'd call it all right, Professor."

A harsh glare of light in front of her closed eyelids.

"Tampons! Quickly! She's bleeding!"

I'm bleeding, she thought, without picturing to herself what it meant. Then there was a metallic roar and she plunged into deepest darkness.

"Hetti! Do you hear me? Hetti!"

Oh, yes. She heard him. The engine rushed along. They were in a sleeping-car. There is a rhyme to go with the throb of the engine.

"Herr Alt! If you remain here I refuse to take any responsibility!"

"Don't you see that she's not moving at all? God in heaven!" It was such a soul-rending cry that it penetrated the leaden apathy of Henriette's consciousness. She opened her eyes.

"Don't go back to sleep again right away, please, my dear little lady. Otherwise we shall never get your nervous husband out of the room!"

The glaring light was painful.

"Are you convinced now that your wife's all right, Herr Alt? We'll let you know when the time comes! Won't we, Frau Alt?" The engine roared on. *I am dead, all the way. I am dead, all the way.*

"The pulse is much better, Professor!"

"Give her another intravenous injection of caffeine, Dr. Herz."

"I don't think she needs it any more. The whole trouble was she made no effort herself."

"My dear colleague, you're mistaken again! The trouble is all stupid secretiveness. If you don't know anything about life you can't stand it!"

"I can stand it," she said.

Later that night of October 21, 1890, she gave life to a son and preserved her own.

Part Two
THE ROOF ON FIRE

CHAPTER 14
A Child is Silent

From the very first instant he saw her Hans loved his mother above everything. "Mammi!" was his first spoken word, and even before he could frame it with his lips he said it with his eyes.

His whole little round face was wreathed in smiles as long as she was near him; it was only when she left him that he learned to cry. Indeed, he seemed born to laughter, for even when he still lay on his carrying pillow he hummed softly and pulled his mouth into jolly grimaces; he was the happiest child ever seen at Number 10. Not even the former Baroness Uiberacker, who kept sharp track of sister-in-law on the fourth floor, could assert that Henriette was a bad mother. Two years after Hans, Franziska was born, and a year after Franziska, Hermann came along. Although they did so with reluctance, the first floor was obliged to concede that the extravagant, flirtatious, and thoroughly undisciplined person on the floor was a better wife than they had expected her to be. In any case, it would have been hard to find a more contented husband than Franz. He was, to be sure, no pillar of the church, and it was quite ridiculous how he worshipped Henriette. Heaven only knows whether she was not perhaps leading him around by the nose and hiding things from him and the rest of the house.

When Hans learned to walk and talk he exercised the first of these faculties incessantly but made hardly any use of the second. On his sturdy little legs he slipped up and down the smooth old steps and the new stairs like a squirrel; in the nursery he squatted on the floor and studied with equal fascination the animal pictures in his cloth storybooks, with which he surrounded himself as with a circus, and the insides of his dolls. For hours on end he would stand in front of the cage of Cora, Sophie's parrot, now an inhabitant of the fourth floor, listening to her monologues. When the parrot spoke he nodded enthusiastically. But he himself hardly ever spoke.

Agnes the nurse, called Neni, found this so disturbing that she worried Henriette with her fear that he might end up with some speech defect. A child of almost four who did not talk! In Neni's rich experience such a thing had never occurred before. The family's physician, Dr. Herz, however, declared that the nurse was an alarmist and that Hans's power of speech was absolutely normal. There are quiet and noisy children. Hans belonged to the quiet group.

Nevertheless, the more Hans made a habit of using gestures instead of words to express what he wanted or thought, the more disturbed Henriette became. Sometimes one could think that the child, except for the one word "Mammi," really was mute, for he no longer even sang or hummed as he used to. Moreover, his eyes, which had remained as blue as they were immediately after his birth, took on the searching, penetrating look of a deaf-mute.

As Henriette reached the climax of her worry the inexplicable inhibition was suddenly removed. It was Christine, the little daughter of Colonel Paskiewicz, who brought it about. She was fourteen now, taller, and promising to be as beautiful as her father, who, according to the laws of science, should long since have died but who nevertheless lived on. Anxiety about him still dominated Christine's home, since the colonel, between his inevitable attacks, challenged death with the same insouciance as he used to challenge his opponent in a duel. For Christine, going up to the fourth floor meant an escape into a better world. Up there everything was heavenly. The girl's adoration of Henriette took on dimensions which the rest of the house viewed with disapproval. It was not only the twins, but the grown-ups as well, who called her a "hysterical ninny." But it was the colonel himself who annoyed his sister-in-law Elsa, the wife of the Public Prosecutor, by saying: "In this Godforsaken house she has sought out the only interesting person!"

As usual, Christine rushed upstairs after school, two steps at a time, and inquired breathlessly of the maid whether Aunt Hetti was in. No, Madame had gone out upon an errand. Disappointed, Christine, for whom this question was the event of each day, knocked nursery door. Neni, the nurse, was ironing innumerable tiny shirts on a long board underneath which Hans had cosily installed himself. He liked a roof over his head—just like a dog, Neni had often said to him by way of reproach, but this did not disturb him; he sat happily beneath the ironing-board, surrounded by his picture books and engaged in dismembering a woolly bear. At the window two-year-old Franziska sat in her high chair and rattled a little bell with persistence. Hermann, born one year after, lay sleeping in his cradle, his fists tightly balled. Except for the tinkle of the bell all was quiet.

"I thought maybe I might come in for a while," Christine said, apologetically.

The nurse sprinkled a shirt with water and whispered: "But mind you don't wake my baby!" There was a secret rivalry between these two, for Hans worshipped his cousin. After Henriette, she was the one he liked best in the house. The others did not exist for him. And now his eyes brightened as he pointed to the floor, meaning: "Sit down by me."

Christine was familiar with his gestures, and not just with them, for she also knew the speech of children in general, whether explicit or implied. She knew so well what children say and what they keep to themselves. Of this latter perhaps she knew even more. Without a word she sat down next to Hans on the floor.

"You shouldn't always give in to him," the nurse declared in a low tone over their heads. "The boy does nothing except what he pleases. In every way people spoil him!"

But Hans had shown his big cousin the lion who was rampant page one of his cloth picture book and was pointing to it with his index finger. "Tell me about the lion!" was what he meant, and Christine told him. She did not tell him as a grown-up would, but in the way she had always wished stories might be told to her, with an answer to every question, so that one could tell what happened afterwards. "And then they live happy and contented for ever more," was the way the fairy tales of the grown-ups were accustomed to end, but, according to Christine, that was no end but a beginning. Up to the moment when they lived happily they had existed in a state of terror or frightful adventures, and you really wanted to find out at last what a life of happiness and contentment was like. In a subdued voice, so as not to waken the baby, Christine told her story with one eye on the door to watch for Aunt Hetti's arrival home. Hans listened with rapt interest. When it reached the most exciting climax the nurse announced that she had finished ironing and that it was time to go for a walk in the Stadtpark. But Hans shook his head passionately. Stay here! Find out what happens next! Since she knew he was in safe hands, Neni dressed little Franziska, tucked the soundly sleeping Hermann into his carriage, and went off with the two of them. You could hear her say to Herr Simmerl, who helped her downstairs with the baby carriage. "That dumb boy is getting more headstrong every day! He's being brought up all wrong!" After which the dumb boy and Christine were left alone.

Hans sat under the ironing board and was delighted to learn that the wild lion grew tame and no one in the world had cause to fear him any longer, neither the king, nor the queen, nor the five princes. So he stroked the lion in the picture book, turned to the next page, where a peacock preened himself, and pointed to it, as much as to say: "Tell me about the peacock." But Christine shook her head, for her opportunity had come. If she succeeded where every one else had failed, would Aunt Hetti perhaps love her a little more?

"Do you want to do something to please Christl very, very much?" she asked the boy.

He nodded eagerly.

"You know, I'm always alone and have no one to tell me any stories. Would you like to tell me one now? No one can hear us. One about the peacock? Yes?"

His face was thoughtful.

"You know, if you tell me a story I'll be happy again at once!" she declared.

"Are you unhappy?" he asked with the first words anyone had heard him say for a long time.

She admitted it.

Whereupon he looked at her and at the cloth picture in his peculiarly penetrating way, hesitated a little, laughed, grew serious again, and began: "Once upon a time there lived a peacock ..." That his tale about the peacock repeated what she had just told him about the lion did not bother either of them, for all he wanted to do was to comfort her, and all she wanted was to hear him speak. The happier she grew, the prouder and more loquacious he became, and the words he had so long scorned to use now came tumbling from his lips: "Then the peacock roared so frightfully that his yellow mane shook!" he was saying as Aunt Hetti entered.

She remained standing at the door, listening to the tongue-tied child, who in the heat of his narrative paid not the slightest attention to her, as he used words applicable to a lion in describing a peacock.

No one could look more rapturously happy at that moment

than she did, thought Christine. If only she loved me that much too! Went through her mind. And both Henriette and Christine listened until the story ended and the peacock was tamed, whereupon they praised the story-teller highly. But what he wanted to know was whether Christine was still unhappy. This she denied. Henriette said no word of thanks to her.

From then on Hans talked.

CHAPTER 15
Humanistic Education

How often had it been said to him, as though it were the best thing that could happen to anyone, "Wait until you get into the Upper School!" To reach that stage increased one's standing from a schoolboy to a student, and Hans had even seen visiting cards on which "*Stud, gym.,*" standing for "*Studiosus gymnasii,*" was neatly printed under the name. The school was the Francis Joseph Gymnasium at Number 3 Hegelgasse, two streets from Seilerstätte.

Until the day in July when his father led him by the hand along that short distance to take his entrance examinations he had not known fear. The first ten years of his existence had been clouded once by measles and once by his mother's absence on a trip to Abbazia, during which the children remained alone with Neni nine weeks in all. Now, as the door of the great gray building in which they promised to equip him with a "humanistic education," closed behind him, everything in his life suddenly began to change. He entered a classroom on the door of which the following inscription was pencilled: "Entrance Examinations for the School Year 1900-1." It was only much later that he realized the meaning of what his grandfather Stein said to him after his examinations: "You will hardly come to know the new century in there." On the broad, raised

platform which occupied a third of the room stood a broad
brown and green table, a chair, and an even broader blackboard. Above the table, on the gray plaster wall, hung a cruci-
fix, and over the blackboard a framed lithograph of Francis
Joseph; it represented him in his red velvet, ermine-trimmed
coronation robes, a sceptre in his hand, a crown on his head.
Behind the table, dominating the eleven rows of low, rigid
benches with their erstwhile green desks, now devoid of color
as a result of ink spots and penknife carvings indicted on them
by generations of scholars, sat Professor Alwin Miklau. He was
the master of the class to be formed by the boys passing their
tests on this day. He was over sixty and had been on the faculty
of this school for more than thirty years. Latin and Greek were
his subjects; he had gall-bladder trouble; his face was yellowish,
and his round shoulders were bowed. The salary of an Imperial
and Royal high school teacher enabled him to take the cure at
Karlsbad every fourth year and to buy in turn a suit or an overcoat about every third year. He came from Styria; consequently
he spoke the dialect of the Ausseer region and hated cities and
city people. Whether he was married or single, where he lived,
what he did in his free time not one of his thousands of students
had ever known and not a single one of them had ever been
interested enough to find out. They feared or hated him,
whereas to him they were a matter of indifference. Their task
was to execute the curriculum endorsed by the Imperial and
Royal Ministry of Education and to follow the rules prescribed
by the Municipal School Council. The curriculum subjected
them to almost daily tests for a term of eight years, and the rules
for the same period: forbade them to smoke, imbibe alcoholic
drinks, join societies, or publish any of their own writings. The
strict observance of these commands and prohibitions consti-
tuted the whole of Professor Miklau's (and of his associates')
relations to his class.

This was the man who taught Hans the meaning of fear, Hans

was afraid of him from the very first hour. It began when the professor said: "You will now say the Lord's Prayer with me. Cross yourselves." Then the prayer was said in chorus, whereupon he repeated: "Cross yourselves! And now," he went on, after he had given the examination contestants a sign with the palm of his hand indicating they were to sit down, for he had had them stand during the prayer, "I shall dictate seven sentences. You are to write these sentences on the left side of your copybooks, and the analysis, which you will undertake to make of them, on the right-hand side. Plan the spacing so that you have a margin of three finger-breadths to the right and two to the left." He pronounced these words as though he were translating from the Latin, and he did not address the boys in the familiar second person singular to which they had been accustomed in elementary school, nor did he greet them at all. The fact that they were new there did not penetrate his consciousness.

He then dictated in his Styrian dialect, which not all of them could understand, and so rapidly that not all of them could follow. So Hans put up his hand and asked about the words he had not understood; he thought he was allowed to do that.

"What is your name?" was the question he received instead of a reply, to which he answered: "Hans Alt."

"Alt, Hans," he was informed, "you will impress on your mind once and for all: you are to keep silent except when you are questioned! *Si tacuisses, philosophus mansisses*! You should have paid better attention! You have twenty minutes left. Anyone who does not finish will not pass. Alt, Hans, and every other one of you will bear that in mind."

In Hans's short life this was the first time that anyone had threatened him.

According to the regulations of the entrance examinations in the upper schools of Austria, the morning was devoted to written tests and the afternoon to oral tests, although the 'oral' was given only to the candidates who had not passed the 'written.' Consequently, to be called up for the 'oral' was in the nature of a disgrace.

Professor Mildau was followed by Professor Rusetter, teacher of natural history and mathematics. He was somewhat older than Miklau; his eyes were weak, and no one had ever seen him without dark glasses. He too gave dictation; his dialect was Tyrolean, his manner of speech military (he had served as a captain in the Bosnian Campaign), and his graying side-whiskers originally must have been red. He had a habit of stroking them stiffly with both hands.

"You there in the second row!" he said to Hans. "You are improperly clad! Tell your parents that no one is allowed here with uncovered [he avoided the word 'naked'] legs!" While the boys were struggling to solve the arithmetic examples he had given them he stood by the window, with his back turned, and examined his inflamed eyes in a small pocket mirror. It was good he did that at least, Hans thought. But he was mistaken, for the mirror served as a means of detecting credulous boys who dared to copy their comrades' problems. The former captain stalked them like a hunter until the mirror exposed them, then he would suddenly turn and, despite his heavy weight, rush over and pounce on the evildoer. "Caught!" he would cry gleefully, snatch away the boy's exercise book, and then lie in wait for his next victim.

After Professor Rusetter came the catechist, Professor Haberl. The snuffbox which he was constantly pulling out of the pocket in his cassock was made of horn. He had cotton-wool in his ears and sneezed resonantly after every pinch of snuff. Hans was relieved to find that at least he could laugh.

When the written test was over the students could, go home, but they had to return at two o'clock to find out who was obliged to take the 'oral' and who was not. Mammi was as adorable as ever; Papa even found time to ask some questions, and there was Hans's favorite dish for luncheon—schnitzel with cucumber salad. Until now he had believed that the rest of the world depended on his parents, this home, this house. But now it appeared that they had no influence on the school. Perhaps he would fail? He was ashamed, too, of his bare legs.

At two o'clock, dressed in long black cotton stockings, he stood once more before Professor Miklau, who read their names out of a large stiff book with black covers. "The following candidates have not passed their written examinations: Alt, Hans …"

Until now he had not known ambition or envy either. As he saw the successful scholars who did not have to undergo any more tests leave, and found himself among the poor scholars who had to remain, he learned to know those emotions. "Alt, Hans," said Professor, Miklau (for he came first alphabetically), "you handed in a fairly satisfactory paper in mathematics but a lamentable one in grammar. What goes on in your mind—if you have one? Do you think this school is here for illiterates?"

Hans did not know what illiterates were, for he had only just turned ten last October. But Professor Miklau was obliged by the Imperial and Royal Ministry of Education to use the formal third person plural in addressing ten-year-olds, and that, in his eyes, obliged them to be grown-ups. Besides, one could not begin too soon to root out the frivolous Viennese notion that to live is to enjoy!

"Alt, Hans, write on the blackboard: Life is a serious—comma—hard—comma—lasting struggle—period. Analyse the sentence!"

Hans said it was a "simple sentence," "life" was the subject, "is a struggle" the predicate, and "serious, hard, and lasting" were adjectives modifying "struggle."

"Well, then, make a note of it!" Professor Miklau said.

With that and his answer to the next question, to the effect that Vienna was the one-time Celtic Vindobona and had been in existence for two thousand years, he had passed. He was a little proud and a little embarrassed. He might have saved himself the oral test. In his sleep that night he was frightened by a vision of the ex-captain watching him in his mirror.

"I didn't copy anything!" he shrieked in terror, and Neni called sleepily and mechanically from the nursery (for Hans now slept across the hall in the study): "Hush! Go to sleep! Be a good child."

With all her experience she might have known that his childhood had been taken away that day—but grown-ups sometimes are unaware of even the simplest things.

CHAPTER 16
The Metternich Ball

The rumor that Colonel Paskiewicz was dying spread once more through the house as it had so often before, but no one look it seriously. The colonel, they said, will outlive us all! Nevertheless, he died at the very moment when his wife was on the point of fetching a priest. She had waited for this moment for fully twenty years, and when it came it found her unprepared. Deprived of everything that had kept her strength and patience in a state of tension for so long, she collapsed.

When Christine returned from the kindergarten on the Stubenbastei, where she had been teaching since the previous autumn, she found her father lying rigid and dead and her mother stretched motionless over him. At first she thought them both dead, and it was her cry for help that Hans heard when he came home from school.

He knocked until she let him in, and then he saw his first corpse, for he remembered nothing about the death of his great-aunt, the former Miss Kubelka, except the black horses who drew her hearse.

The dead man lay in the bed, and he had the slightly altered features of Uncle Paskiewicz. Nor did Aunt Gretl move, yet one could see her breathe. Christl's teeth were chattering so much that she was unable to speak.

"Does Mammi know?" Hans asked.

She shook her head.

"Shall I go and fetch her?"

She nodded.

"Right away!" he promised, then took his school bag, and ran up to the fourth floor.

He had forgotten that Henriette had left the house in the early afternoon: "As a patroness, your mother had to help with the arrangements," Herr Simmerl explained to him. Could she be reached? Hans wanted to know. "Whatever is the young master thinking of? Madame cannot be disturbed now! Does not the young master realize that it is a great distinction to be a patroness for the Metternich Redoute? It is the first great social event since the end of the court mourning for our poor Empress," explained the butler, who took a personal interest in everything that concerned Vienna. Would his mother at least come home to change her clothes? No, Madame had taken her things along with her in the carriage.

The boy waited for nearly half an hour before he went downstairs again. He was embarrassed because his mother was not there. Of course she could not know that Uncle Paskiewicz would die, but should he tell Christl that she was away making preparations for a masquerade ball? If Papa at least were there ... But he had left a few days earlier on a business trip.

"Mammi is out just now," he said to the girl whom he loved best after his own mother. Meanwhile Aunt Gretl had recovered consciousness and was lying in her own room; Dr. Herz had given her a sedative. Christl told him that and added only, "I think you had better go back upstairs now."

He would have liked to do that. First of all he was frightened by the dead man, and besides, he had to learn his Latin vocabulary for the next day. But Christl was so sad. "I'll go in a minute," he said, but stayed on. After a bit he added, "Mammi will surely be coming very soon!" At that her poor pale face lightened. Now you could see for the first time how much she looked like Uncle Paskiewicz.

He wanted to talk to her, to get her to think about other things, but since she tiptoed around all the time it was evidently necessary to keep quiet. So he seated himself aimlessly on the windowsill and looked at the walnut tree in the yard and at the green blinds which year in and year out covered the windows of the ground-floor apartment where old Sophie, whom he had never known, had died. With a face which he avoided looking at, Christl came and went, doing all sorts of things for Uncle Paskiewicz. She lighted candles on either side of the bed. She closed his eyes. She folded his hands over the coverlet. She laid a small cross in them. She handled him like a doll. Hans did not hear her cry, and that consoled him. When you are dreadfully sad you weep.

When she had finished she drew up a chair beside the bed and sat down. What had become of Uncle now? When a man dies he goes to heaven or to hell. But Uncle was still lying there. He looked as though he were asleep, and sound asleep too, for the longer you looked at him the more clearly you saw that he was smiling. "Look at him," said the boy. "He will surely wake up again!" Christl shook her head. "He won't ever wake up!" she whispered. If that were so then the dead would not go either to heaven or to hell, for there they did wake up. After he had sat by the window for almost an hour and watched carefully to see if his uncle were breathing, Hans realized that he was not. It was only yesterday afternoon on the staircase that he had called to him, "Hello, Hans! Can you conjugate *amo* yet?" And tonight he could not say anything to him although he had the same mouth.

A little later Christl began to cry. That bewildered the boy even more. "Perhaps Mammi has come home by now. I'll go and take a look," he said. She nodded disconsolately through her tears.

Once more he climbed the stairs, and again only Herr Simmerl, Neni, the chambermaid, the cook, and his brother and sister were home. It was time for the children's supper, so they were seated in the nursery and given their food.

"Why are you so excited about your uncle?" Neni asked. "He was always sick. It is a release for him."

Franziska, who was already in the third class, and Hermann, who was going to be in the second next year, giggled as usual about everything. After supper Hans went into his study to work on his vocabulary for the next day.

He took his exercise book, labelled "Alt, Hans, Class Ia," out of his school-bag and laid one hand over the half of the page with the translation of the words. "*Jucundus*—gay. *Pulcher*—beautiful. *Amoenus*—agreeable. *Jucundus*—gay. *Pulcher*—" If he made of mess of his Latin test next day Professor Miklau would give him a black mark in his monthly report. "*Aureus*—golden. *Aureus*—golden. *Aureus*—golden." Memorizing the words, he paced up and down the small room, which was situated between his mother's bedroom and the big nursery. Across the way in Seilerstätte blazed the lights of the Ronacher Theater. It was less than four weeks now the end of the first term. "*Aetas*—age. *Jucundus*—gay." I hope she isn't crying any longer. "*Bellum*—war. *Castrum*—armed camp." Christl would never have left him by himself! She had always come to him when he was sad. "*Aureus*—" Will those silly creatures in the next room never get to sleep? Elementary-school children should be in bed!

Up and down paced the student, the little blue exercise book in his hand. He tried not to think about anything except the foreign words written in his own stiff, vertical handwriting, which Professor Miklau would probably use in tomorrow's Latin test. Was she still sitting by the bedside of the dead man? Perhaps Aunt Gretl was with her now. But that would not help. That was why Christl loved Mammi so, for Aunt Gretl cared only for Uncle and never for her. And just today Mammi had to be away! "*Castrum*—armed camp." Was she still crying?

Her tear-stained, helpless face gave him no peace. When the familiar noises next door indicated that Neni had put the other children to bed and the chambermaid had cleared the table, he softly opened the door into the vestibule. An instant later he was on the staircase and in no time stood before the door of Christine's apartment.

He rang; no one answered. He rang again. Then he knocked with his fingers and then with his fist. No one stirred. He laid his ear to the door and was startled. Weeping! Perfectly distinct! "Christl!" he cried. "It's me!"

No answer. Only sobs.

"Christl? Christl!"

Was she angry with him? He had promised to bring his mother and had not done it. They had left her all alone, he and Mammi!

"Christl—do listen to me!" he begged through the keyhole. "Mammi will soon be here! Please! Say something!" Now she will surely answer!

He waited. When there was no reply he rushed downstairs. As it was almost nine o'clock Pawlik, the janitor, was standing in his dressing gown and slippers at the Seilerstätte door, preparing to lock up. "Where to so late?" he asked. "To buy an exercise book!" Hans fibbed, and was already outside. "At this hour—an exercise book?" the janitor grumbled after him.

Hans had neither jacket nor cap on, but since he was running he did not feel the cold. All he could think of was: Hurry! The sooner I bring her the less I shall have cheated Christl! Then she will realize at least that it was not my fault!

As he ran his soft blond hair fell over his forehead, behind which his thoughts were pounding pell-mell. The dead man. Aunt Gretl who didn't stir. Christl's bloodless face. The flickering candles—the cry—the dreadful sobbing—Oh, hurry! Perhaps she would do something to herself. He had heard that people did something, although he had no exact idea of what it meant. If he did not run fast enough perhaps they would not get there in time.

Never had he been in the streets so late as this. But the bright gas streetlamps showed him the way. In the Schwarzenberg Square a policeman stopped him. "Where are you running to, laddie?" Fortunately a tram was coming up to a stop and he could appear to be running towards it. When the policeman turned away he ran on; he had no money for a tram fare.

In the Rennweg he had to ask the way, and in the Ungargasse he lost his direction. But in not much over half an hour he had reached the Marxergasse. The endless line of an endless number of carriages hacks showed him where the Sophia Hall was.

He had imagined that he would simply say, "I want to see Frau. She has something to do with this ball." The word "patroness" had slipped his mind. But when he mentioned it to the huge doorman the latter looked at him as though he were speaking a foreign language. There he stood, with his gold-and-black cocked hat, fur collar, and gilt pouch belt, between two placards: "January 17, 1901. Black and Gold Ball. Under the patronage of Her Serene Highness Princess Pauline Metternich-Sándor. Proceeds to the Polyclinic Hospital. Bands under the direction of C. M. Ziehrer, Karl Komzak, Franz Lehár." The doorman, his hands now full opening the doors of the carriages of the late-comers said: "Why, dear child, how in the world could I find your mother among these thousands of guests? Do you know what? Be a good boy; go home and wait till she comes. Your servant, Herr Graf! I kiss your hand, Frau Gräfin! To the right, to the right, please, for the gentlemen!

Ladies to the left! Your servant, Herr Hofrat! To the left, please, to the left for the ladies!"

Hans did not budge. He felt that it was cold. "At least step into vestibule," the tall man said. "Is it really so important?" Frightfully important, Hans replied. He wanted to explain why, but the doorman had no time; he turned him over to another attendant in gold-and-black livery with the words: "It seems lad's mother is a patroness. See that he finds her." The lad thanked him and smiled. He did not want the tall man to see how near he was to crying. Then the other one took him by the hand, and they went into the hall where the dance was being held.

In the first few seconds the boy forgot his errand, for everything before him seemed so fairylike. The immense ballrooms, three in number, were one blaze of light, dancing, flowers, and music. The whole background was like a scene in the theater: a colossal frame of gold and black, reaching from floor to ceiling, enclosed a gigantic picture of Castle Schönbrunn, the green Kahlenberg Mountain, the Danube, and Vienna with St Stephen's steeple and the City Hall, and from all the windows of the painted houses, as well as from all bridges across the painted Danube, real lights glittered like diamonds. On a platform which looked like a garden musicians dressed in yellow satin evening clothes were playing. And how they played! It was as though they wanted the dancers never to stop: they kindled their excitement; they flattered them; they played low; they played furiously. And the roses! All the yellow roses in the world must be here: they grew on trellises the length of the rooms, covering the gilt pillars and arches; the trellises were artificial, but the roses were real, for their fragrance was bewitching. Among them black tulips bloomed. The chandeliers, too, were immense, gorgeous bouquets of roses and tulips, and yellow and black were the colors worn by the dancing ladies. But all their faces were covered! They wore black masks over their eyes and almost down to their mouths and were terrifying to see. The gentlemen wore none. They were in evening dress, with yellow roses in their buttonholes, and the officers wore yellow roses under the shoulder straps of their decoration-studded uniforms. There was no pause in the dancing. The couples for whom there was no room in the large ballroom danced in the smaller ones opposite, and there, too, orchestras were playing and it was a fairyland full of roses, tulips, and brilliance.

The boy gazed speechless all round him. It was only when the man beside him said impatiently, "Well, have you found her? I can't stand about here with you for ever!" that he remembered that he was searching for his mother and that it was frightfully urgent. But how could he find her here? He did not dare ask the man, so he replied: "I haven't looked for her yet." Then he would have to do it by himself, for there was too much to attend to downstairs with the new arrivals, the man said, and, showing Hans the places where he might and might not stand, he left him alone.

So there he stood. The orchestra in the large ballroom played "Vienna Blood," and he decided it would be best for him to place himself right out in front until his mother should dance by. The mask might make it difficult for him to recognize her, but he knew the way she dressed her hair. Dazzled and a little tired, he stood there and carefully examined each one of the ladies as she danced by. Most of them had a blissful expression around the little bit of mouth left uncovered by the mask. And the gentlemen held them so tight. In the intensity of his observation Hans sometimes took a step beyond the limit prescribed, and then he would be carried along by the dancers until he was standing in quite another place. At times the stream of light began to go dark before his eyes.

"Well, little man, what are you doing here?" he heard an old lady ask. She leaned down to him from a laurel-wreathed stand. She had the face of a bulldog and was as ugly as could be.

"Nothing," he answered, looking up at her. But he was

standing before the one woman in Austria who would not accept an excuse.

"A little chap like you ought to have been in bed long ago," she declared. Then she said something to a gentleman behind her who shrugged his shoulders, stepped down, took Hans, who was alarmed by her ugliness, and together they led him through the dancer to the exit. "Since when are you letting children in here?" she asked the two lackeys standing there bowing obsequiously.

"The doorman sent the youngster up, Your Serene Highness! He's looking for his mother," was the contrite excuse offered by one of them.

"Really?" the old lady asked. "Is that so?"

Hans nodded.

"And why must you see your mamma *à tout prix*?"

Hans felt that the time had come to tell the thruth to this old lady with the pearls wound around her short neck and with a diamond-encrusted decoration just like an officer's on the left side of her low-cut dress.

"It's because of Christl," he answered. "Her father, my uncle, has died, and Christl is waiting for my mother to come to her!"

"Aha!" the lady said. "That's all not very clear. Kindly tell us now who your uncle is and who your mamma."

"Uncle Paskiewicz," Hans told her.

"Paskiewicz? Wasn't he in the Dragoons?" And when she herd that he had been a colonel in the Dragoons she remembered. "A good-looking man! Magnificent cotillion dancer! And what is your mamma's name?"

When he told her a change of expression went over her bulldog. "So? Is she your mamma? Very good-looking too." Hans took it as an inquiry and nodded so vigorously that the old lady laughed. "So you like her! Do you see that corridor opposite us? Go down there to the pillar. Tell the gentleman with a list in his hand that Princess Metternich sent you and that he is to take you Frau Alt. Can you remember all that?"

The perfume of the roses was stupefying. But Hans clearly saw corridor running between the large and small ballrooms, with its red doors on either side, and the fat man in evening clothes in front of the middle column. He went up to him and gave him the message.

The man looked at his sheet of paper. "Number nine, on the left," he checked, pointing to one of the red doors. "Wait, wait!" he called as Hans ran on. "I must announce you first!" He didn't need to be announced to his Mammi, the child thought, and dashed in.

It was a very small red-papered room, in which there was a table, laid for supper, in front of a red brocade sofa. Above the sofa hung a half-blank mirror in a gilt frame; beside it stood a champagne cooler, and on the sofa sat Mammi. She still had her black half-mask on. Close beside her sat a gentleman, and he had his arm around her waist. At first Hans thought his father had come back from his trip.

"Hans!" cried Henriette. The gentleman beside her let his arm fall and turned round. It wasn't Papa. "This is a funny way to act!" he said crossly. But Mammi explained: "This is my little boy, Count Poldo." Then the gentleman said: "You don't tell me! Why, he's quite a little man! Glad to see you! And what is your name?"

"Hans," the boy replied sullenly. He couldn't bear the gentleman. Then he explained to his mother why he was there and that it was frightfully urgent. But all she wanted to know was how he had found his way there and whether anything had happened to him in the street. And the gentleman said: "There's no such hurry! Good old Niki took his time about pushing off! I'll order a cup of chocolate and whipped cream for the young gentleman. Or shall we give him a glass of champagne, just to break him in?"

Mammi looked so strange, as though she wanted to laugh all the time. She was lovely to look at, with her brown hair parted in the middle and dressed low, with yellow roses at her temples and on her décolleté gold velvet dress with a train. She was so like the picture Papa had of the Empress Elizabeth. But her eyes had a changed look. It wasn't just the mask.

"I really should be grateful to this little intruder. Now I'll at least find out, finally, who my beautiful unknown of this evening is," the gentleman declared. It sounded like a phrase learned by heart. If he knew who Uncle Paskiewicz was, must he not also be acquainted with Mammi? Her eyes glistened disturbingly.

"Gome along, Mammi," the child urged.

"Directly," she said. "Don't you like it here? It's so wonderful here!"

From the next room came sounds of giggling. Someone sang, to the tune of the waltz, "*Wiener Blut, das ist gut!*" Someone else called, "I have been waiting half an hour for my champagne!" To which the reply came, "One little moment, Herr Baron." Someone whispered, "Sweetheart! Do take that silly mask off at last!" The music, the air, in which smoke, perfume from the flowers, and wine were sweetly mixed, the constant, insistent sound of dancing, all had a bewildering and exciting effect. "Have some cake," Mammi said. Hans didn't want any cake. And he didn't think it was wonderful there.

"Please, come along," he begged again.

"Well, he is very persistent!" the gentleman said. He was tall and good-looking, and he pleased Hans less and less.

"Yes, I'll come," Mammi told him. "Don't you want to listen to the military band? As you go out it's playing on the left. The Lehár military band. Ask one of the waiters. You like military bands."

"Thank you, no," Hans answered. It was the first time he had not done what she asked.

"When your mamma asks you to do something you should obey!" the gentleman declared, and smiled, although his face was filled with anger.

What right had he to give orders? Fatigue and bewilderment fell from the boy. "Don't you love Christl any more?" he asked his mother.

At this Mammi made an apologetic gesture and said to the gentleman, "You see, Count Poldo, my son is very severe with me!" She took her black velvet coat trimmed with chinchilla from the rack and gave it to gentleman to hold for her as she pulled on her long kid gloves. He put the coat slowly around her bare shoulders, ridiculously slowly, thought Hans, who never took his eyes off him.

"Get your overcoat and cap," Mammi said. "We're going now."

Hans answered he had brought nothing with him.

"What!" Mammi cried with horror. "You came here bareheaded? In January?"

"This young man seems to have his own ideas of obedience," the gentleman remarked.

"There was no time," Hans explained.

"Good-bye, Count Poldo," Mammi said. "I'm sorry it's all over so soon."

"I'm awfully sorry!" the gentleman replied. "When shall I hear from you?"

"Will you telephone me?" Mammi asked.

"Tomorrow?" the gentleman asked.

"Very well."

If he didn't know who Mammi was how could he telephone? Would she tell him her telephone number?

But she did not tell him, and she did hot take off her mask.

"I kiss your hand," the gentleman said, and bowed over Mammi's right hand. Did he need to take so long just to kiss her glove?

Mammi's eyes had that terrifying glitter in them. And her voice was suddenly very low when she said, "Good night, Count Poldo. Pleasant dreams!"

"I know what I shall dream about," he answered. "A thousand thanks for the charming evening." Then they left the overheated little red room. The music throbbed on, the couples danced on, and the roses had not yet faded.

The tall doorman called a cab. "So you found your mother?" he asked with a grin. "Yes," Hans said.

In the carriage he sat beside her. "If you're cold cover yourself with my coat," she suggested, wrapping him in her perfumed soft cloak and drawing him so close to her that he could hear how her heart was pounding. Otherwise she paid no attention to him; she did not stroke his hair, as she usually did, and she did not ask him anything. He imagined she was so silent because she was thinking of his dead uncle. But then he heard her hum softly, "*Wiener Blut, das is gut.*" When a street lamp threw some light into the carriage he saw how her eyes still glittered.

"Mammi?" he asked.

"Yes?"

"Aren't you at all sorry that Uncle has died?" He could not understand why she took so long to answer.

But she had remembered something. That was how Franz had questioned her a long time ago, a long, long time ago, "Aren't you at all sorry that Auntie has died?" "Of course I'm sorry," she said. Then she lapsed into silence again ...

It was after half-past ten when they rang the bell on the first floor, and as they went upstairs the child's terror returned with every step. In the adventure and excitement earlier he had almost forgotten it. "I wonder whether she's still alive?" he whispered.

"What bad things you've inherited from me," was her astonishing comment. Then she went on to comfort him:

"Don't be afraid. Believe me, fear is the most superfluous thing in the world!"

She was right, for when they went into the apartment Christine was alive and did not seem to have been weeping at all. Nor was she alone. Strangely enough, she suddenly reminded Hans of his Aunt Hegéssy, because she looked with such a fixed stare at all the people in the death chamber—Aunt Gretl, Aunt and Uncle Otto Eberhard, Aunt and Uncle Drauffer, Aunt Hegéssy, the twins, and Cousin Peter. How they were all there Hans could not understand, but their presence embarrassed him. Needn't he have fetched Mammi? The other relatives looked at Mammi as though they had never seen her. The twins, now twenty-four years old and both university students, exchanged remarks in a low tone.

The candles were still burning in the room, and in addition they had lit two corner lamps and draped them with crepe. Christl and Aunt Gretl were in black. On the carpet beside the bed, bouquets of flowers, arranged in long sheaves with wire and laurel, gave off an austere perfume. The dead man was now dressed in a uniform with a pale blue tunic, a half-black, half-gold collar, and the coverlet reached up to the point on his chest where his Signum Laudis hung. Hans knew he had received that medal for a charge he had made on horseback in the Battle of Koeniggraetz.

His folded hands still held the cross, but he no longer had the same face. It had become that of some strange, aged man, and seemed made of wax or wood.

The relatives, all clad in dark clothing, were silent or talked in subdued tones to Aunt Gretl and suddenly appeared to have a feeling of great respect for Uncle Paskiewicz such as they had never showed before.

"Celebrating!" Aunt Elsa said to Mammi in a repressed voice. Out of haste, or for some other reason, Mammi had forgotten to remove her mask and did so only now. There she stood in her golden-yellow dress, with yellow roses in the point of the heart-shaped neckline and in her hair. Her shoulders and arms were bare; in her obvious embarrassment she had pulled off her long kid gloves. As she went over to Aunt Gretl Hans noticed, too, that she wore high-heeled black silk evening slippers which made walking difficult. "My deepest sympathy," she said to her. Then she went up to Christine and kissed her twice. Then she wanted to kneel at the deathbed, but along one side were the flowers, and along the other Aunt Hegéssy, Uncle Otto Eberhard, and Cousin Peter were kneeling, and they did not make room for her. Uncle Otto Eberhard even said, in a tone loud enough for every one to hear: "Don't desecrate the dead with your masquerade!"

Again the twins exchanged whispers. Otherwise no one stirred. Only Christl said, "Wait, Aunt Hetti, I'll make room for you. I know Father was very fond of you."

"That's true!" someone said. It was Uncle Drauffer. Aunt Pauline nodded.

Under the disapproving eyes of the others Christl removed two bouquets from the floor and Uncle Drauffer two others, so that Mammi could kneel at the bedside and say a prayer.

"Why is the boy still up?" Aunt Elsa asked.

"Because he wanted to help me! He was the first to come to me. That was terribly sweet of you, Hans," Christl answered, although the question was directed to Mammi.

Christl did not speak of his having fetched Mammi. She went to the door with him and laid a cold hand in his. Had he been of help to her?

Her hand was too cold. It almost seemed to him as though he had only made everything worse by bringing his mother there.

"Come along, Mammi," he said almost angrily.

This time she went with him at once.

CHAPTER 17
The Violet Meadow

Henriette's love for this man so overwhelmed her that she had room for nothing else in her life. It was an obsession, come suddenly upon her after a decade of conventionality and daily routine. Whoever said that you grow accustomed to another person lied. Whoever said you can grow fond of someone you have never loved did not know life. She believed that she knew it now. Ten years wasted was what she felt.

The children had been born, and people said, A happy marriage. Franz even declared he had never been happier. Even that she questioned. Oh, he loved her with a dependable kind of affection which was slightly warming but never, never, never set one on fire. He fussed over her, but that was not what she wanted. She wanted someone who could raise her to the heights. Anything but the commonplace!

The children were handsome, and thoughts of Herr Jarescu had faded to a pale shadow. Papa was a member of the Upper Chamber, and she herself was a respected member of society. Even the bachelors in the chess club, to which Franz went regularly every evening after dinner, respected her. At thirty-two Henrietta was inclined to a distrust which at twenty-two had been foreign to her nature. She ceased to have illusions about herself.

When she met Count Poldo Traun she knew that resistance was useless. She did not even attempt it. Memories crowded overpoweringly into her mind—his fascinating eyes, his inimitable, careless grace of gait. His speech was like *his* had been, with many foreign words and a contempt for the commonplace. He even dressed as Rudolf had. She had never seen English-cut suits on anyone else. She did not think him either clever or even dazzlingly handsome. Rudolf was incomparably cleverer. She saw all of his faults before she capitulated to his charm. But she capitulated completely.

In the past ten years, which had been so uniform that she could not distinguish one from another, with childbearing, parties in the yellow drawing-room, summer holidays in Ischl, there had been no lack of occasions when she had said to herself: This protected and safe life is the right one. For a while she had expected that her conversation with the Emperor would lift her out of her rut of uniformity. But Francis Joseph appeared to have forgotten her existence. When she was compelled to admit that the house and its atmosphere lay like a pall over her and that she no longer called it anything but a prison to herself, she decided that it was foolish to make such an effort to remain merely with jailers and fellow prisoners. The slogan of wasted life was going around Vienna in those days, after the publication of Arthur Schnitzer's story *To Die*. In an impulsive moment she wrote to him how enthusiastic she, an unknown reader, was about the book and that it had taught her to see life in its true colors. "I fear you overestimate my insignificant contribution to the knowledge of men. Such as we can teach only those who already know the answers," was the ironical author's reply.

Conveniently enough, Franz had to leave on a two-week trip to Trieste and Agram. After that she met Count Traun every day. At the Metternich Ball they met for the fourth time, and it was only then that he reminded her that they had dined together, many years earlier, at Mayerling. She had forgotten that, for Mayerling was associated in her mind with only one person. This abruptly reawakened memory swept all her scruples. Her superstitions did the rest, and all fear of conventions vanished.

The day after the ball she went to his apartment, and from then on lived in a state of ecstasy such as astonished even her experienced lover: he had never known such passion combined with such innocence. When he said as much to her she grew angry, because she thought he did not understand her.

One might assert she was a bad wife and a bad mother, but not talk such sheer nonsense of someone who knew life as she did! Yet he insisted on it. He went so far as to swear that it was her greatest charm.

Even before Martha Monica was born rumors were rife in the house. They reached Franz's ears without his believing them even for an instant. His self-respect prevented his doing so. Besides, he was unflinchingly certain that Henriette was not deceiving him. She had her peculiar ways, not all of them comprehensible to him (or, the longer their marriage lasted, attractive), but they all derived, and on this he was ready to take an oath, from her hypersensitivity and aversion to commonplace things. What could a stiff-necked person like Otto Eberhard know about such matters? He counted up the eight years between the birth of little Hermann and Martha Monica and based his trifling doubts on that. And how impossible it was for a faded creature like Gretl or a well-behaved stay-at-home like his sister-in-law Elsa, with whom no one had ever flirted, not to envy Henriette. Franz found it beneath him and his dignity to make even the slightest suggestion on this score to his wife.

Nevertheless, when Martha Monica was barely a week old he and Count Traun fought a duel. It was not the duel, however, but the fact that it was witnessed by two eleven-year-old schoolboys, that brought forth the most violent censure from Number 10 (as well as of all Vienna Society). Moreover, the grounds which led Franz to act as he did were described as "frivolous," "sadistic," and "incomprehensible," although from his point of view they were clear enough.

Hans had told the boys in his class about his new little sister, brought to him by the stork. During the following Latin lesson the boy who sat next to him, von Blaas, whispered that there was no stork. There was, Hans contradicted, for who else would have bitten his Mammi in the leg and made it necessary for her to be in bed? *Laudo*, I praise, was the verb given by

Professor Miklau to be conjugated; as he was calling on boys whose names began with the letter Z, Hans, who came first in the alphabet, and his comrade, who came next, felt safe. Yet young von Blaas persisted and whispered to Hans why there were no storks. "'I have praised,' Alt?" Professor Miklau asked triumphantly, having caught the whisperer. Hans jumped up and replied, on a chance, "*Laudo*" which cost him a black mark in Miklau's notebook. That, however, did not disturb Hans nearly so much as the drawing that his neighbor scrawled in his copybook; it burned before his eyes, and he felt compelled to keep looking at it until the teacher noticed it and confiscated the exercise book with a cry of horror.

An interview after class elicited the fact of who drew the picture. Von Blaas was punished with four hours of confinement, while Hans escaped with the task of copying the conjugation of *laudo* twenty-five times. The next day young von Blaas, who was furious, said, "Don't you know what stork bit your mother? It was Count Traun!" All the other boys heard that too, and although Hans was utterly at a loss to understand the remark or the general grinning and giggling that went on, he boxed von Blaas's ears soundly. In the ensuing wild scramble Hans was the victor, but all he got out of it were bruises and a torturing uncertainty. He could not ask his parents; that much his sense of tact, a quality developed early in him, told him. Christl was equally unavailable, for since the night of Uncle Paskiewicz's death she was noticeably absent from the fourth floor, and it was rumored around the house that she was entertaining strange intentions. Nor could Hans even discover what those intentions were. Perhaps she would marry someone, he thought. His only informant, when all other sources failed, was Herr Simmerl, to whom he confided his conjecture. Herr Simmerl drew his longest face, and said, "Perhaps you could put it that way." Everything was full of insoluble riddles; you were haunted by them day and night.

Therefore when Hans met Count Traun not long after the squabble in the school (Neni had taken the children for their usual afternoon walk in the Stadtpark) he turned and looked at him so markedly that the count, who was with another gentleman, noticed it. Recognizing Henriette's boy, he called, "Hello! How are you, son?" and started to go on. But Hans ran after him and, when he overtook him, asked breathlessly, "Is it true that you bit my Mammi?" The gentleman with the count gave a loud laugh, whereat Traun remarked angrily to Neni, who by this time had caught up with her charge, "You should keep a better eye on that youngster! He's getting impertinent!" With that the two gentlemen started to walk away.

But Hans, with an instinctive feeling that it was this man and none other who had brought the riddles into his home where everything had changed so sadly, said obstinately, "I am not impertinent! I only asked you if it is true."

Purple in the face, the nurse, who had not missed any of the incident, could hardly believe her ears. "You will apologize instantly!" she demanded.

Hans did not apologize.

"Then I shall tell your father!" Neni threatened.

"All right," Hans said. Another trait in his character, one that also developed early, was a sense of justice. Everything in him protested against an apology.

"He's just a little savage," the count told his companion, looking around with an expression of assumed indifference as they walked away.

"I'm not a savage!" Hans yelled after him, in broad daylight in the Stadtpark, only a few steps from the Kursalon, where all the best Society was sitting at afternoon coffee.

This is the end of everything! Neni thought. All her life she had piqued herself on bringing up the children confided to her care with the manners of the highest class, and here was an example of an opposition (already in undesirable evidence on former occasions) that must be broken.

That very evening she reported the incident to Herr Alt, since the lady of the house, still confined to her bed, could not be disturbed.

"Send the boy in to me!" Franz demanded.

For the first time there was a serious encounter between father and son. Until now Hans had never felt that his father was an authority. He had always taken him for a playmate who never had much time, who was often in a good humor, although never as tenderly affectionate as his mother, and who was never severe. Tonight all this had changed.

"Well, what happened?" Papa asked, and all at once there was no difference between him and Professor Miklau. Were children always in the wrong in the eyes of grown-ups, just because they were children? Hans had often wondered. Or was it because the grown-ups, set over the children, were too old? Neni was almost seventy. Of his teachers, the most youthful was over sixty. Papa would soon be fifty. Hans recounted what had happened in school.

"The cheek of that young von Blaas!" his father said. It seemed to Hans as though he blanched.

"I was right, wasn't I, Papa?" he insisted.

"What? Yes. Of course you were right! That is … with regard to that other boy. As for the count, you were, of course, in the wrong," he was told.

"Why? If Mammi had to stay in bed on his account?"

Papa made an impatient gesture. "Do stop that nonsense. You're no longer such an infant that you can be made to believe such—such things. Your mother doesn't even know Count Traun. Incidentally, how do you happen to be acquainted with him?"

Had it not been quite out of the question, Hans would have thought that his father was looking at him rather fearfully. But grown-ups cannot be afraid of children! "Through von Blaas," he answered. Something warned him against mentioning the ball.

"I never did like any of that family. Inflated idiots, who think they are something because they have a *von* in front of their name!" Papa's face was almost normal now, "Don't let anything like this happen again!" was his final order, then he added, "Go to sleep!"

But the boy lay in his bed and could not sleep. If the count really had not done anything bad, then surely Papa would have demanded that he apologize to him. He thought that over. Then he heard talking, and his heart pounded so that for a while he could not follow it clearly. It was Papa talking with Mammi; Hans could distinguish the voices, for her bedroom was next to his. Since his little sister's arrival, the light in that room was put out at nine o'clock in the evening and complete silence was imposed. But now a light was visible under the door and Papa's excited voice was saying:

"You can't reproach me for ever having paid attention to gossip. Think how people have always gossiped about you! But there's a limit to everything. Sometimes you can pretend not to hear what you really have heard. But when it comes to the point where schoolboys begin to talk my good nature gives out!"

Mammi's voice replied, "Do you put more faith in schoolboys than in me?"

"I ask nothing better than to believe you," Papa's voice said, and, thank goodness, it did not sound so angry. "That's why I put the question to you. Hetti, do you remember what you promised Aunt Sophie that time?"

For an instant there was silence. Dear God, do make her say yes, longed the child sitting up in his bed, not even knowing what it was all about.

"Yes," came Mammi's voice.

"Really?" Papa asked after a pause. Then there was another

pause, as though he were going to ask something else, but he said, "If you only knew how I loathe all this gossip! Well, have a good night. I'm sorry I woke you."

"You didn't wake me," Mammi told him.

Then a door closed and everything was dark. It was a long time before Hans could bring himself to lie down. Once he heard Mammi sigh.

Two days later, very early in the morning, Papa, Hans, and young von Blaas drove out to the Prater in a cab. The evening before Papa had told Hans to invite his school friend for an excursion; it was violet time, and they could do some botany for their natural-science class; they would be back punctually in time for school. So the two boys rode on the back seat of the hired carriage, von Blaas delighted over the reconciliation with his school chum, on whose friendship he depended for copying his Latin tests, and Hans, on the contrary, puzzled as to why no one, neither Mammi nor Neni, nor even Herr Simmerl, was allowed to know about the excursion. "You know your mother should sleep late these days!" was the explanation offered, but Hans did not believe it.

The nearer they came to the meadows where the violets were, the more remarkable Papa's face became. During the ride he had not uttered a word, but now he said, "Boys, I want you to listen to me. I've something to say to you. To each one of you. Not long ago you told Hans something which was false from beginning to end. If you make an assertion which you can't prove you are either a tattler, a liar, or a slanderer. In any case, a scoundrel!" Never had Hans seen his father so angry. He was talking to von Blaas, whose beaming face now clouded, but it sounded as though he were addressing not him but someone entirely different. "Do you know what's going to happen as the result of your gossiping?" Papa asked von Blaas.

"No," the boy said dejectedly.

"The events of the next half-hour. After that I trust you'll neither indulge in nor believe slander!"

Hans felt that these last words were aimed at him, and he said anxiously, "But I didn't believe it, Papa!"

"Then why did you insult Count Traun so childishly?"

"I don't know," the boy said. He sensed that Papa was right.

"Your mother," Papa continued, "is above any suspicion. You might have known that!"

Hans did not grasp exactly what it was to be above suspicion, but he thought of the masquerade ball. *That* was why he had believed the accusations against Count Traun. *That*, however, was something he could not possibly tell. For a moment no one spoke.

"I've called Count Traun to account," Papa said suddenly.

Why, thought Hans, if it was all untrue?

Again silence fell.

"That's why we are here now," Papa went on. "When we reach the spot you'll get out with me and place yourselves somewhere so that you'll be able to watch the duel without being seen. People are bound to say that I should have left you at home. I care nothing for what people say!"

If he cared so little for what people said why was he so angry with von Blaas? Hans looked at his father.

"What are you looking at? Don't you know what a duel is? Two enemies shoot at each other. I'm an enemy and Count Traun is an enemy."

"But, Papa, you said that he had done nothing to you!"

"That's just it! That's why he considered it an insult when I demanded an explanation from him and challenged me to a duel!"

"Why?"

"Why? Because he is chivalrous from the crown of his head to the soles of his feet!"

"Will you shoot him, Herr Alt?" asked von Blaas with shining eyes.

"He's supposed to be a good shot," was Papa's rather too matter-of-fact reply.

"Better than you, Papa?"

"I haven't as much time to keep up my pistol practice as these gentlemen. I sometimes go out to shoot deer or rabbits. These gentlemen spend their lives hunting all sorts of game."

Hans, who had been routed out of bed so early and faced with problems that far exceeded his powers of comprehension, began to be frightened. So he asked, "Papa, are you afraid?"

"That's why I brought you along, because one mustn't be afraid," was the answer he received, "and because one mustn't stand for anything! Not from anyone! Not from an archduke and not from any paltry count!" Something had completely transformed Papa. Even his face was different.

"Well, here we are," he said.

The sun had not yet risen, but the finches were already twittering in the fresh foliage of the chestnut and oak trees. The small clearing where they had drawn up was blue with tiny violets; one could have told that by their perfume even without seeing them. Two men in uniform and an elderly one in mufti, who were walking up and down the meadow, turned towards them when they arrived. Hans recognized his grown-up cousins, the twins Fritz and Otto, who were both stationed with a Dragoon regiment in Enns during their one-year term of voluntary military service. He did not know the older man in civilian clothing. "What are the boys doing here?" Cousin Fritz asked with consternation.

"Studying botany!" Papa replied curtly, and Hans ran off, hid himself behind a bush, and picked some violets. He overheard Fritz ask, "Are you crazy?" To which Papa made a reply in a low voice, and Fritz said, "I see. That's different. But I'm afraid Hetti won't take it the right way, aren't you?"

"What do I care?" was Papa's violent rejoinder. "At least she'll be impressed by it."

"What do you think will happen?" Hans asked von Blaas, who stuck close to his side.

In the pale light of dawn Hans strained his eyes to look as far as possible in all directions, but nowhere could he discover Count Traun. Papa, the twins, and the man in civilian clothing walked up and down together. Hans could hear them talking but could not distinguish the words.

"I'm scared," said von Blaas instead of answering Hans's question.

"Go on! You should be ashamed!" Hans told him. His one hope was that Count Traun would not come.

It grew lighter, but the sky remained overcast. There was a soft haze in the air, and a breeze sprang up among the trees, shaking the dew from the leaves so that it seemed almost like rain.

"Perhaps he won't come," Hans said.

Suddenly a private carriage, with a coachman and footman in livery on the box, appeared along the highway. It drew nearer at a fast trot and pulled up beside the two cabs already standing there. The footman jumped down and opened the door. Four men stepped out: an officer in the uniform of the Hussars, one in that of the Imperial Life Guards, and two civilians. One of these latter was Count Traun. He wore a black bowler, a short dun-colored overcoat, gloves, a rose in his buttonhole, and he was laughing. Hans hated him. The other civilian remained standing beside him while the officers joined the group in the meadow. The twins saluted them stiffly, while the officers negligently touched their caps, saying, "Good morning."

So they weren't enemies?

Papa and the elderly man came over to the bush where Hans had hidden himself. "Are you there, boys?" he asked. He still had that completely changed, almost distorted look on his face.

"Yes, Papa," Hans said. Von Blaas said nothing.

Papa nodded. "Watch everything carefully," he said. "You may have to describe it to someone." Then he walked away, but turned back again immediately and said: "In any case, I hope everything will go well with you!"

The man in civilian clothing took his arm. "This is the worst possible time to get yourself so wrought up, Franz!"

Papa answered, "I'm not in the least excited, Doctor. If you took my pulse now it wouldn't be over seventy." Then he went away.

Meanwhile the twins were measuring something; they were taking long steps in the middle of the meadow, from an oak to a chestnut tree, counting from one to ten as they did so. Thereupon the officers counted from one to ten in the opposite direction, from the chestnut to the oak, taking the same long steps. Then one of them, the hussar, brought a long black case from the carriage, which he gave to the guard officer, who took two pistols from it. Apparently Papa and Count Traun had not seen each other yet.

Cousin Fritz took one pistol and then the other into the palm of his hand, seeming to weigh or compare them. The pistols had mother-of-pearl handles. Cousin Otto repeated Fritz's procedure immediately after him. Then they both saluted and handed the pistols back to the officers.

Then they both saluted and handed the pistols back to the officers. It seemed to Hans, whose eyes were fixed steadily on them, that this cousin, especially Otto, conducted themselves with as much subservience as the footman who was standing, hat in hand, beside the coach waiting for further orders.

"Private Drauffer," the officer of the guards now said to Cousin Fritz, "is your principal prepared to proffer a public apology to His Excellency Count Traun?"

"No!" Hans replied under his breath for Cousin Fritz.

"No, Lieutenant," Cousin Fritz answered in a loud voice. "My principal believes—"

"That is sufficient," the officer interrupted brusquely. He wore a tunic gold buttons and a gold collar, and red trousers. To Traun he said, "Are you ready, Poldo?" now Count Traun had walked up and down continually, smoking and talking. He had not so much as glanced in Papa's direction. "I was just telling our good doctor here the story of the Trail Stakes," he called to the lieutenant, and then added to the man in civilian clothing, "Remind me afterwards to tell you the climax, Doctor!" After which he walked to the officers,

The two civilians had hurried over to the carriage, on the step of which ley laid two long cases. With a strange air of languor Count removed his right-hand glove and threw it to the footman, who caught it. He kept the left one on. Then he made a movement with his right hand. It looked like a fish mouth opening and closing. He repeated the gesture. Then he took the pistol from the officer of the guards. Meantime Papa, too, had received a pistol from Cousin Fritz. He examined it carefully.

"The seconds for His Excellency Count Leopold Traun," announced the officer of the guards, and gave his own name, "First Lietenant Count Khuen."

"First Lieutenant Prince Schwarzenberg," said the hussar, giving his name.

"The seconds for Herr Franz Alt," said Cousin Fritz. "Volunteer Private in the Dragoons Fritz Drauffer," added Cousin Otto, and clicked his heels.

"Inasmuch as the offender, Herr Franz Alt, has refused to proffer an apology," the guards officer said with a matter-of-course manner, as though he were reading it off, "he is therefore obliged to give His Excellency Count Traun satisfaction by arms. The conditions agreed upon yesterday between the seconds of both parties are as follows: two exchanges of shots at ten paces. His Excellency, as the offended party, was given the choice of weapons and the first shot. May I ask you to proceed, Poldo?"

Count Traun laughed. "*Merci*," he said, "*Merci*, Alexandre. Am I properly placed?"

The spot where he had taken his stand was checked, whereupon the two officers stepped aside to the right and left, leaving him alone.

Opposite him Papa and the twins had done precisely the same thing. It seemed to Hans that they merely aped the others.

"They're going to win!" whispered von Blaas, meaning the other side.

"Shut up!" Hans answered tremblingly.

As the adversaries had their faces turned to him and Papa and the twins were standing with their backs to him, he could see only what was happening on the other side. He wished that he could see his father's face. The sun had not yet come out, but the breeze was stronger now.

"You fire on the count of three, Poldo!" said the officer of the guards.

"Excellent!" Count Traun replied. He had not yet looked at Papa.

"One!" barked the second in the white tunic. "Two!"

At "two" Count Traun raised his pistol with an abrupt gesture and aimed. As he did so he closed his left eye. His right arm, in which he held his weapon, was stretched out straight as a piece of wood, aiming at Papa. The laughter had vanished from his face.

"Dear God in heaven!" breathed Hans.

A gust of wind. A few raindrops fell.

"Three!" ordered the second.

A flash, a crack, a whistling rush of sound. Otherwise nothing changed. Papa stood there as before. His right shoulder was now raised, for he was taking aim.

Count Traun began to whistle, "She is a sweet, sweet maiden," from the operetta *The Sweet Girl.*

"One," commanded Cousin Fritz. At "three" Papa fired. There was a report and some smoke. Count Traun took a quick step forward, then another. Then he fell to the ground. The civilian and both officers ran to him.

Papa looked round. His face was terrible to see. "It's raining," he said.

Hans hardly dared to breathe. What would happen if Count Traun stood up again? But he remained lying on the ground. Presently the man in civilian dress made a remark which Hans did not catch. It was then repeated by someone else. It was in Latin.

A little later they drove back as they had come. Papa was in the front seat, the boys in the rear. The only difference was that Hans had some violets in his hand and the carriage was closed on account of the rain.

"What has happened to Count Traun?" Hans asked.

Papa's face was still distorted. "He's dead," was his reply. Otherwise no word was spoken on the return trip.

As they came into Prater Avenue the city was just coming to life. The red electric trams, which had almost entirely replaced the green horse-drawn trams, passed jangling by; milk wagons were stopping in front of houses; the bakery boys and news-women were delivering fresh rolls and morning papers from house to house. Hans could not see enough of these signs of life. He did not take in the fact that Count Traun was dead. Since he had learned from Uncle Paskiewicz what being dead meant, he understood it even less. He had hated the count. Nevertheless, it was unthinkable that Papa had shot him. He avoided looking at him, for it made him feel strange.

At half-past seven they drew up at the corner of the

Hegelgasse. The doors of the school had just been opened. "Now, then," Papa said "learn your lessons properly." Yet one could see that he was thinking of something else.

Hans could think of nothing else than the morning's events. He lived it over again and again. The officers pacing off the distance. The counting. Taking aim. The pistol report. "Be of good cheer; springtime is here. Autumn and winter passed away, comes the spring with flowers gay. Be of good cheer; springtime is here," sang the class, for it was the singing lesson. "Fox, where is the goose you've stolen? Give it back again, give it back again. Else you'll see the hunter coming—with his great big gun," they sang next. To Hans—who until now had been the most childish of the ten-year-old boys in his class ("Either you are really so childish still or else all too clever already!" Professor Miklau had said)—it seemed unspeakably childish. In the last lesson he had joined enthusiastically in the singing. In this one he was asked whether he could not open his mouth. He could, but he found it so silly. Spring had come, and in the meadow with the violets there lay someone whom Papa had shot with his gun. "Else you'll see the hunter coming—with his great big gun—oh, gun," the class sang.

After the singing lesson came German, and they read Wilhelm Hauff's "Story of the Lopped-off Hand." Hans was struck by the lowing phrase: "Life is the most precious possession. Therefore, from the first instant to the last, everything is concentrated on the preservation of life." All untrue! If what he had seen with his own eyes was possible, that you can aim at a man and kill him when you count one, two, three, how could they print such lies in books?

In the recess he was amazed at the appetite with which von Blaas ate his sandwich. Hans could not choke down a morsel, although he had had his breakfast very early.

In the botany class Professor Rusetter had rejected the violets. The class had gone only as far as the *Pulsatilla vulgaris*, the common pasque-flower, and the violet came much later on. "Get this into your head once and for all, Alt. Everything in nature is based on a fixed order of precedence," said the former captain, who gave a military cast to all his instruction. "Out of the lower orders the higher are developed, and from them the supreme. None can be jumped over without doing violence to creation. Think of it approximately in terms of the army. You know, I trust, what a one-year volunteer private is? A private cannot immediately become a first lieutenant; he must previously go through the grades of corporal, sergeant, and second lieutenant. It is exactly the same with plants. Before we come to the violet we must have studied the anemone and considered its lowest form, the *Anemona nemorosa*, after which we shall have had the next in order, the hepatica or liverwort, and so on. The violet is, as you might say, a second lieutenant. Can you see that? Take your violets home."

Hans could see that. He saw the volunteer privates and the lieutenants. He saw nothing else. When he took the violets home they were withered. Mammi lay in bed, her eyes swollen. Martha Monica, his new little sister, lay in the bassinet beside her.

"Go to your room, Hans," Mammi said. Since Martha Monica had come she cared for no one but the baby ...

During the night he heard voices again and there was a light under the door. This time the voices were much louder, but they did not waken Hans, for he had not been able to get to sleep.

Papa said, "So you complained about me to your father!" Mammi replied, "I wanted my father to tell me how one can go on living after such a thing."

"What your father says is of no consequence to me!" raged Papa. "He never told you the truth! That you became what you have become is largely his fault!"

Mammi's words were just as fiery and even more bitter. "This time he has told me the truth! Marriage can be an agony like nothing else on earth. His own marriage was such an agony, he said, from beginning to end! And to me and all the world he acted as though it were pure harmony! That's what I must do, he told me. I have children."

"To think you're not ashamed!"

"I am ashamed. No one ought to be as stupid as I am."

"That's all the thanks I get!"

"For what?"

"Do you ask that seriously?"

"In my life there have been two men. You have murdered them both."

"If you say that word once more—"

"You are a murderer. Perhaps you don't know it."

Then the door slammed. Hans tried to think. He was so exhausted he could not; he knew only that it had been a frightful day and that someone kept yelling, "One! Two! Three!" He counted and counted and finally fell asleep.

CHAPTER 18
The Vows

Beautiful and poignant came the sound of the *Veni, Creator*, over the swelling tones of the organ. Amid the clouds of incense swung by the acolytes and between rows of chanting nuns kneeled the candidate who was taking the veil before the high altar of the church of the Salesian order and before the aged suffragan bishop of Vienna.

It was only a few blocks away from the house where she had been born. Yet those few blocks had put an unbridgeable distance between her and her birthplace.

A billowing white dress had made a bride of her. The white

veil and the ring, which the bishop consecrated on the epistle side of the high altar, were to make her the bride of the Saviour.

The silver bells of the altar boys rang out. The nuns sang as they kneeled to receive the holy communion to be offered by them to their future sister. The young voice of the candidate in their midst soared above the choir, "*Veni, Creator Spiritus— mentes tuorum visita. Imple superna gratia—quae tu creasti pectora—*"

The suffragan bishop had sprinkled the veil and the ring with holy water and perfumed them with incense. The mother superior had risen from her knees and gone over to the candidate, to whom she had said, "Offer to God the sacrifice of praise. Candidate Christine Anna Maria Paskiewicz."

To this the nuns had added, "And pay thy vows to the Most High."

Whereupon the candidate had risen to her feet, looking so slim, tall, and erect in her white dress, and had taken a step towards the bishop, saying: "I will pay my vows to the Lord in the sight of all His people, in the courts of the house of the Lord."

The singing died away. The organ ceased. A great silence fell, during which the odour of incense was suffocating.

"If thou art prepared to pay thy vows say yes," the suffragan bishop addressed the bride.

The listening congregation heard the word 'yes.'

"Pay thy vows," the suffragan bishop said.

The candidate took a second step in his direction, and said with a voice which towards the end was barely perceptible, "In the name of our Lord and Saviour Jesus Christ, and under the protection of His Immaculate Mother Mary, ever Virgin, I, called in religion Sister Agatha, do vow and promise to God, poverty, chastity, and obedience, and the service of the poor, sick, and ignorant, and to persevere until death in this congregation."

The aged man raised his right arm high over her head. "What God hath commenced in thee may He Himself perfect, and may the body of our Lord Jesus Christ preserve thy soul unto everlasting life."

Those who were seated on the first rows of benches were all inhabitants of 10 Seilerstätte. For the first time the house took cognizance of the young girl on whom they had heretofore wasted no attention, not to speak of sympathy, and whom they had always considered highly strung.

Otto Eberhard had taken the first seats in the first row of the central nave reserved for the family; his wife Elsa and his son Peter sat beside him. The Public Prosecutor was now an Aulic Councillor, and his hair was almost white; his wife still had her pompous manner and arrogant look, and the fat boy Peter had grown up into a portly Korps-student, member of the "Ostmark" fraternity; the bandage under his left eye testified to the fact that in addition to the scar he already had on his face, as a result of duelling, a second had now been added. The Dragoon Regiment twins, Fritz and Otto Drauffer, who had made a special journey from Enns, declared later that they preferred the incense to the smell of carbolic exuded by their cousin. Their father still looked like Saint Peter, except that he gave somewhat freer rein to his hair and beard, in which he seemed to be following the example of the composer Brahms and the writer Hermann Bahr. He had made successful portraits of these two and had exhibited them in the Künstlerhaus (unfortunately Sophie had not lived to see him do this 'real' painting). His wife Pauline had kept her jolly eyes, but her apple-cheeked plumpness was gone. The women in the house withered early. Pauline's older sister, Gretl Paskiewicz, mother of the novice, might have been taken for an old crone. Only Countess Hegéssy showed scarcely any signs of change. Dressed in her customary black, she attended this family event, too, as though it were a funeral.

Hans, with his sister and brother, Franziska and Hermann, and his mother and father, sat in the second row of reserved seats. Although it was an ordinary Thursday, he had been let out of school, and tomorrow he would carry with him an 'excuse' signed by his father to the effect that "due to a festive family event he had unfortunately been prevented from attending his classes." To Hans that was the one good thing in the whole matter. As for the solemn occasion itself, the suggestions forwarded by Herr Simmerl (he was present together with the other servants from Number 10, and Hanni, the chambermaid, sat beside him) did not please Hans at all. The incense made him feel sick, and he could not see why Christl had to become a nun. The habit of a nun was connected in his mind with illness, because as soon as anyone fell ill a nun appeared; but you called her "Sister" instead of nun.

Why? How incomprehensible that Christl should have chosen that! Yet since the incomprehensible had gained such prevalence in Hans's life he had given up asking "Why?"; one never could get the truth out of grown-ups in any case. So he would not see Christl again? For Herr Simmerl, who was as well informed in ecclesiastical matters as in mundane ones, had told him that the order which she was entering was one of the strictest and that there could be no question for the present of a novice's going out into the world. In a year or so one might occasionally be allowed to visit her in the convent. After a year! Hans was still so young that a year to him was an eternity.

Yet for Henriette, towards whom the curious and watchful looks of the family were directed on this occasion, as on every other in the twelve years of her life under their roof, the time of puzzles was past. Everything had become crystal clear. "The only mistake is life itself," Rudolf had asserted. How right he had been! For when one understood life, as she believed she did, and knew it so well that she was no longer capable of any illusions, it was not worth living. Henriette could not forgive

Franz. No matter if her reason told her a hundred times that he had had nothing at all to do with Rudolf's death, that his suicide on her wedding day had been a pure coincidence, still her feelings whispered to her a thousand times the opposite. In any case, he had murdered Count Traun—out of hatred, out of jealousy for the tiny bit of happiness which at last had fallen to her lot. "Where the house, which thou inhabitest, knows no rejoicing except that which comes from duty, and no joy except that from grace," the suffragan bishop had said in his first address. That much Christl could have had at Number 10 too. Number 10 Seilerstätte knew no rejoicing, and it murdered happiness.

As her eyes rested on the girl who had renounced happiness, she knew that there was a connection between them. Some took the veil; others married men like Franz. Christl, too, had felt herself betrayed and bartered, and why? Because she simply could not forgive her, Henriette, the happiness she had sensed in her at the time of her own distress, when Hans had brought her from the ball to the colonel's deathbed. "I was frivolous enough to be happy at the wrong time," Henriette thought. And during the "Veni, Creator Spiritus," it occurred to her, How remarkable is the love human beings bear to one another! If Christl's love for me had been really great then must she not have said to herself: "I do not begrudge her this bit of rejoicing?"

The tenderness she had felt for the novice since the Jarescu days was now submerged by her conviction that the ceremony before the high altar was nothing else than a demonstration against her. "I believed in you and you destroyed my faith in human beings!" the girl in her white veil kept crying to her. Oh, she heard it well!

Henriette's bitterness had assumed proportions which to her were not a persecution mania but perfectly simple—yes, even self-evident. She had lost not only the power but also even the desire to be just. Feeling herself to be in the vortex of disfavor in the house, her resistance to it waxed with every hour. But the worst of it was that she saw no way out. "Condemned for life to Seilerstätte," she had written in her diary shortly after the duel.

Many voices were singing "*Gloria Patri et Filio et Spiritu Sancto.*" When that had died away the ceremony was concluded. Sister Agatha, dead to the world, bride of eternity, without turning round, without seeing anything, joined the ranks of the other nuns at the high altar.

"Christl!" cried Hans.

"Will you keep still!" came the angry reprimand of his mother.

But the novice looked directly at the spot where he and his mother were sitting. With a gesture of final renunciation she raised her hand a little way and then let it fall again. Then the companion of his wonderful, wordless, carefree years vanished.

"Mammi!" Hans said, beside himself.

"She is happier than we are," Papa told him, and put on his narrow-brimmed silk hat, for now they were out in the street. All the rest of the family was gathered there too, so that they walked back together through Salesianergasse to Annagasse and home.

"There's no end to these family celebrations," Otto Eberhard declared as he parted from his brother at the angel-with-the-trumpet entrance. "Will it be a big party? I'm only asking on Elsa's account. She's teasing me about getting a new dress."

"I don't think that I've teased you much," objected the councillor's wife. "In any case, Franz will have only one fiftieth-birthday celebration in his lifetime."

"You see how she favors you, although you don't deserve it," Otto Eberhard remarked to his younger brother, who had cost him many a sleepless night; it had been no child's play to avert an investigation into the duel.

When, eight days later, it was being celebrated in the 'party rooms' of the second floor, all the ladies of the family appeared in new dresses, all but Henriette. She had on the yellow velvet gown she had worn to the Metternich Ball.

After dinner little Hermann recited to his father a poem which Neni had composed, and of which the first verse ran:

In this little heart of mine,
See, for you, my father dear,
There is nought but love, and it
Grows from year to year.

Papa and the uncles and aunts said, "Charming!" Mammi said nothing. Hans thought the verses were silly.

He searched everywhere for Christl, now called Sister Agatha, although he was quite aware that she could not be there.

Mammi looked lovely, but he could not stand that dress, that disastrous dress, and it was terrifying to see how strangely she looked at Papa.

Being for the first time at a 'party,' he did not know that these rooms, where her wedding reception had been celebrated, filled his mother with aversion. He still had much to learn.

The family and guests were gathered in the yellow drawing-room when a telegram from the Imperial Privy Chancellery arrived. His Apostolic Majesty had been gracious enough to honor Franz Alt, commercial councillor, with an appointment as Imperial and Royal Purveyor to the Court.

"Congratulations!" said Otto Eberhard, who felt that this appointment removed a load from his mind. So the affair of the duel was now finally shelved.

"Congratulations!" said the other relatives and guests.

"Congratulations!" said Professor Stein, member of the Upper Chamber, to his son-in-law. "His Majesty has always know how to appreciate true merit."

"Congratulations!" Hans heard his mother say to his father. "His Majesty wipes out old scores."

CHAPTER 19
Unveiling the Secret

Hans was almost seventeen when Mrs. Einried began to appear at the tutoring lessons her son was giving him in crystallography. Crystallography was a hobby of the natural science professor, the ex-captain, and the whole class trembled whenever he had the tray with the paper models on it carried in. Then he would finger his notebook, call a name, and begin in honeyed tones to say: "Some nice boy will now trot up and tell me. There would be an anxious pause, during which the teacher, with agonizing slowness, chose a model, which he thrust with an abrupt gesture into the pupil's hand: "What is this?" (the three last words being hurled out like the blast of a trumpet), whereupon the nice boy had exactly one minute in which to study the model. "Don't turn it!" the examiner would yell, his watch in hand, if the examinee in his anxiety turned the model in his fingers. If in the next thirty seconds he did not succeed in identifying it correctly as a rhombododecagon, icositetradon, or whatever it might be, the ex-captain would snatch the model disgustedly away from him, throw it down with the others on a tray, enter a minus score in his notebook, and give the order, "About turn!" This proceeding upset the youngsters' nerves every time it was repeated.

Einried was the best student at crystallography, and the retired captain had recommended that Alt, as a poor scholar, should take some tutoring lessons from his competent comrade. For that purpose Hans went to his house three afternoons a week. In the beginning he never laid eyes on Mrs. Einried, but when the tutoring lessons had been in progress some time she used to make a practice of coming in for a moment or two and saying, "Don't let me disturb you." She would smoke a cigarette in one corner of the room, disappear, come back with a plate of fruit or cakes, stroke her son's hair, and then leave. She was about forty, and Hans imagined she was much younger. He admired her red hair. Her perfume disconcerted him. It became increasingly difficult for him not to feel disturbed when she was in the room.

She stayed longer, as the lessons went on, for she was interested, so she said, in natural science. That was lucky, thought Hans, who had never considered crystallography as a natural science, and hated it as he did everything connected with precision. Nor did he like his brilliant schoolmate. He had never met the boy's father, who was a chief of division in the Finance Ministry.

When he arrived one Saturday afternoon as usual at three o'clock Mrs. Einried told him that her son had at the last minute got a ticket, for the matinee at the Burgtheater and there had not been any time to cancel the lesson. The play was *Emilia Galotti*, by Lessing. She hoped Hans was not angry. "Not in the least," he declared, bowed, and wanted to leave. Mrs. Einried asked him if he would not like a piece of *Gugelhupf*. "Thank you, yes," Hans answered, although he did not particularly care for crumb cake.

He took the piece Mrs. Einried brought him, and she sat down opposite him while he ate it. The telephone rang. "I shall be going in about a quarter of an hour," she said in reply to a question.

"Do you find that the lessons with my son are helpful?" she asked Hans.

"Oh, yes," he replied. He had to cough and clear his throat, for he had swallowed a bit of cake the wrong way. "Excuse me," he said apologetically.

"You're sweet," she said. "Do you know that?"

"I beg your pardon?" he asked, embarrassed.

"Has no one ever told you that?"

She took a cigarette from her ease. "Do you smoke?" she said, offering him one. "Of course you smoke," she answered for him, and handed him a light. He swallowed the smoke and coughed again, much to his annoyance. Now she would believe it was his first cigarette! He inhaled, which was the most difficult thing to do, and he succeeded perfectly.

"Has no one really ever said that to you?" she asked with a laugh. "Here is an ashtray."

Now he had knocked the ashes off on the cake! "I don't think so," he stammered.

"Another little piece?"

"No, thank you very much, Mrs. Einried."

"Do you like to go to the theater?"

"Very much."

"Too bad! Had I known that I should have got two tickets for this afternoon."

"Oh, no, thank you so much." Wrong again. He wanted to say he liked it this way better. How do you say things like that? They smoked.

"Have you a sweetheart?" she asked.

"I beg your pardon?"

"Don't make such a hypocritical face! Surely you are in love with someone. Does she love you too?"

She had come close to him and was stroking his hair the way she did her son's. She stood so near that her disconcerting perfume enveloped him. His heart pounded madly. Would he dare do what he had often dreamed of: take her hand, hold it for a second, and kiss her fingertips? He suddenly blushed deeply, for he feared she had guessed what was in his mind.

She would box his ears, he thought. "Thanks for the cake. I must go now," he decided to say.

"That's not true," she told him. "If my son had been here you wouldn't have left for another hour."

"But you're going out yourself. You just said so on the telephone, didn't you, Mrs. Einried?"

"Don't call me Mrs. Einried. Do you think I am as old as all that? How old do you think I am?"

"Thirty?" he ventured.

"You *are* sweet! A little older than that! In any case, I'm not going out."

Her hand still rested on his head. Now she slipped the other over his cheek, held his face fast between them, leaned over, and kissed him lightly on the mouth.

His heart beat so that for a second he saw nothing.

"Did you like that?"

He nodded with bated breath. Looking up to her, he gathered courage. He took her hand and touched it with his lips.

She laughed. "How gallant we are!"

Now she's making fun of me, he suspected with horror.

But she had gently raised him from his seat. Her mouth was in front of his mouth, "Kiss me," she said. She did say it. There was no mistake. Never in his life had he been so proud.

Except for his mother, he had never kissed a woman. When she discovers this she will laugh at me, he thought, swaying between ecstasy and fear.

He kissed her.

"We can be seen here," she said, and went into the next room. The door was open.

Embarrassment overwhelmed him. He was to discover the secret towards which he had been impelled by an unspeakable curiosity, by an impulse growing more excited and restless with every day and every night, the more impenetrably it was guarded by grown-ups.

*

With eyes sharpened by disillusion Henriette saw instantly what had happened. In this regard too she and Franz had disagreed when she had told him it was madness to let a boy remain so innocent. But with persistent stubbornness, and apparently backed up by Otto Eberhard, he had maintained that in questions of education he would once and for all not allow himself to be influenced. It was bad enough that he had let her talk him into sending Hans to the liberal Francis Joseph Gymnasium instead of the Kalksburg Institute where little Hermann was; there at least boys were trained in strict Catholic and loyal monarchist traditions to be good Austrians and not the nervous, sophisticated weaklings of the Hegelgasse School. The fruits of a liberal upbringing were in raw enough evidence in her case! It had done no good for her to try to prove to him that she had been brought up not in the liberal way but much more in the grotesque secretiveness which had left her unequipped with any knowledge right up to her marriage and had almost cost her her life. But Franz's mind was no longer open to arguments. Since he had found out that she had betrayed him, all his confidence in her had been destroyed. Every other word was a hidden reproach. And every third was: "Don't think I am going to let you make a laughing stock of me any longer!" Nevertheless, he shied away from the idea of a divorce. The spirit of the house, she realized only too clearly, had triumphed over her own.

"Where have you been so long?" she asked her eldest child. She was in the same room where he was born. But since that time she had refurbished with Secession Era furniture, which had followed the Makart fashion and seemed more modern to her. But the mirror was the same, and she sat for hours before it, gazing into it and manipulating her heavy chestnut hair with two long-handled tortoiseshell brushes. Sophie had done the same years earlier down in her ground floor apartment, and even she was only following the example of Empress Elizabeth. Along Hentiette's parting there was a narrow streak of gray. She knew that it was becoming, yet, with her undiminished predilection for romantic expressions, she called it the beginning of the end. "You are fifteen minutes late!" she said to Hans.

She saw him in her mirror. The overgrown youth, who resembled her except for his father's long upper lip on which a fuzzy growth had begun to appear, smiled uncertainly. "We did a few algebra problems," he explained. "We have mathematics on Monday."

"Don't lie!" she said. "Why don't you come near me?"

She sensed the embarrassment with which he took a few steps towards her. Then she noticed the strange perfume. "You have been with a woman. Shame!" *Why do I say "Shame!"? she thought. I did not expect anything different. And I had promised myself that I would make it easy for him.*

Hans looked at his mother. She was no older than Eugenie. Perhaps even younger. He flushed.

"Don't look at me like that! Who is she?"

"I was at Einried's, Mother."

"Sit down. There's no sense in lying. Who was she? A woman from the street?

"No!" he denied, giving himself away so that there was no longer any retreat possible. "I can't tell you!" he added.

How strange that nothing helps even when you see it coming. When it comes it hurts just the same. "Very well, then don't tell me," she said with an effort.

"Are you angry?" he asked.

She shook her head. It was hard to speak. If she had let herself go she would have said, "Yes! Angry! Until now you have belonged to me. You are the boy who for so long never said a word. You are the boy who for so long was fond of me." You cannot count on your children, her father had said recently, although he was the last person to have any cause to make such remarks. *You cannot count on your children*, she repeated to herself. *After this person someone else will steal you, for an hour or for a night. And in three or four years someone will steal you for life. What shall I be to you then? To the thief you will say: Just a moment! I must rush over and say hello to my mother! And you really will do it in a rush, in five minutes in and out of the door, and your conscience will be as light as a feather after-wards! She brushed away violently. That is why one's hair gets white!*

"No, I'm not angry," she said. "I only want you to remain decent." She broke off. What is the use? she thought. Children don't do what you tell them.

"Watch out that your father—I mean, it would be better if your father doesn't ask you any questions. He would not take it as easily is I do." With a tired gesture she laid the brushes down. "Run along now," she said.

He leaned over her hand to kiss it. "There's no one like you," he said. He knew that even that was not expressed as it should be, hut he hoped that she would feel what he meant to say.

"Who knows?" she answered, snatching her hand away brusquely and pressing her fingertips to her temples.

Why is it wrong? he thought.

CHAPTER 20
Entrance Examination for Painters

"Herr Hoflieferant!" was the greeting of the senior master, Professor Miklau, to Franz, whom he had asked to come for a consultation. "I am afraid that your son Hans will not come to any very good end. There is no doubt *(non dubitandum quin)* that he has always been a poor scholar. But he is also an enemy of good morals, a fact which, as his final examinations draw near, opens up more serious prospects. From the very first day of school, when my colleague Herr Rusetter was obliged to reprimand him for being improperly clothed, your son has been an element of lack of discipline. He has tendencies to exaggerated outbursts of feelings, yes, and as soon as any opposition is shown him he flares up in the most headstrong way. Now, in addition to his unenviable school record, he has developed an almost more deplorable private way of life. Every step he takes is in violation of our code of discipline. He smokes; he frequents, according to positive evidence, various coffee houses. He reads ghastly books; one of them, an indecent piece of obscenity by a local writer, Schnitzler, which he was reading recently in class, I confiscated. His other private reading is equally unsatisfactory. He reads unsuitable plays by Ibsen, and the even coarser plays of a certain Strindberg. Nor is that all. *Quousque tandem abutere, Catilina, patientia nostra*! The young creature has a mistress! Here is the proof of that, which I found in the confiscated book, and, God knows, that is where it belongs! She must be some woman from the dregs of the people who is not ashamed to use such expressions, and to misspell them too!"

He handed Franz a blue note. It was signed with the letter E, smelled vaguely of lilies-of-the-valley, thanked him for some flowers, and fixed a rendezvous. She addressed him as, "My young squire!" The last line said, "I know it is madness to love you and you will make me suffer for it. But I do love you!"

Franz's rage, which flared instantly when the senior master began to speak, was now turned from the teacher to his son. First it was the teacher he found insufferable. Having been a poor scholar himself, he had never been able to abide the whole profession. Also he was annoyed at being given unsolicited advice. Had Hans been weak in Latin or mathematics he could have forgiven him. But that he was involved in obscenities roused his ire. "I'll settle the boy," he said with decision. "May I keep the letter?" It was given to him.

As he did not want Henriette to find out anything about it—she only magnified things, and the boy got it from her anyway—he made an appointment for Hans to come to his private office in the Wiedner Hauptstrasse.

"You've got yourself in a pretty state!" he began as Hans stood before him.

Just as at the time of the Count Traun affair, Hans had the feeling that there was no difference between his father and Professor Miklau except that, in the meantime, he had learned to look at his father with other eyes. In the infinite number of occasions when he had witnessed differences of opinion between his parents he was always blindly partisan on his mother's side. His mother was the superior one; a hundred times cleverer than his father, a thousand times more interesting. To her, the children meant a great deal; to him, practically nothing. He had put Franziska and Hermann into boarding schools from which they came home at Christmas, Easter, Whitsuntide, and the long vacation. Moreover, Franziska even spent most of her long summer vacation at Sacre Coeur. As for Martha Monica, the youngest of them, whom Hans absolutely adored, he seemed to hate her. To his own questions his father answered regularly, "You don't understand that yet." The very mention of "progress" made him see red. Hans had never seen him read a book. When a Christian Socialist by the name of Bielohlawek called Tolstoy "an old nincompoop" in the Vienna Town Council, Papa had said, "He's absolutely right. It's all humanitarian slop." He had no respect for anything under one hundred years old, and what he called "education" was training for extreme old age. Papa was no friend. He was a superior officer.

"What do you mean?" Hans asked. His very tone should

have indicated to his father that he no longer had a boy with whom to deal.

But Franz had an application before him in which the C. Alt firm was requesting a patent from the Vienna Patent Office "for a new set of pedal keys applied to grand pianofortes for sounding certain bass notes with the feet." The typewriter had left the middle bar in each letter *f* unclear, so that it looked almost like a *t*. Confound these typewriters, anyway! How much more impressive, personal, and finer the old type of elaborate handwriting had been. The Emperor was quite right in requiring that all public papers were to be written as usual in longhand.

Having reinforced the middle bar in the *f*'s with his pen, Franz reread the sheet. It dealt with an invention of his own, no epoch-making one, to be sure, but one of solid worth and importance to the tradition of the firm and following on in their march of improvements. He had improved on an invention of Pierre Erard, as his grandfather had on one of Christofori.

"Don't beat about the bush," he said, throwing down his pen. Opening his crocodile leather wallet, he drew out the blue note.

Hans had been ready to kick himself for having taken the letter with him to school. But he had done it in one of those moments of absent-mindedness into which he sometimes allowed himself to sink.

"Please give the letter back to me, Papa," he said, and his voice expressed all the irritation stored up in him.

"Not until you tell me who it's from," his father replied.

"That I can't do," the son explained.

"Don't play the knight. Who is she?"

"Forgive me, Papa. I've already said that I can't tell you her name."

In the sales room, beyond the glass door, someone was playing a C-major scale.

Franz had jumped up in his rage. "If you talk to me like that you'll catch it! Idling around, learning nothing, and being impertinent to boot! You'll tell me her name this instant!" Arpeggios were being played next door. "No!" retorted his son.

"No?" And with that Franz slapped him in the face.

Sinnce that hand had shot at someone who lay dead in a meadow violets Hans had never been able to look at it dispassionately. Now he shook it off. "I won't have you hit me!" he said.

"You dare oppose your own father, do you?" Again a violent blow.

His son, mastering himself by an effort of all his young strength, asked, "Are you my enemy, Papa?"

Foedermayer, the head clerk, appeared at the glass door and laid finger on his lips.

"Clear out of here!" Franz said in a low tone to his eldest son.

In the sales room stood a lady who could not make up her mind whether she wanted a concert or a baby-grand. The salesman was urging a concert-grand, "Madame has such a wonderful touch!"

Had he arrived at that conclusion from her playing the C-major scale or the arpeggios? People lie so to one another, it is scandalous! His face stinging from the slaps, his forehead on fire with rage, Hans ran down the Wiedner Hauptstrasse. A passionate hatred took possession of him more and more with every step, and when he realized that it was his father whom he hated he was frightened by his own emotions.

He stopped short, then he went on. He did not even notice that he was going in the wrong direction until he reached the Matzleinsdorfer Church; he rarely had been in this section. To think that some time soon he would have to come every day into this part of town! Papa wanted him to go into the factory as soon as he finished school.

"No!" he said.

"Are you talking to yourself?" asked a girl who had been trailing him for some distance. "Are you coming my way, *junger Herr?*" she added quickly in a whisper, and gave him a visiting card.

"Thanks. Excuse me!" he answered, turned, and ran in the opposite direction. His classmate Ebeseder had been spoken to by a prostitute, and he looked at least nineteen. Do I already look so grown-up? he thought to himself. This consoled him a little. Then he thought of Eugenie and that he had a rendezvous with her for the next day.

A numbing thought occurred to him. If Papa does not give me back that letter Eugenie's husband will find out about it! For every afternoon Mr. Einried played tarot with Papa from five to seven in the Cafe Matschakerhof, Eugenie had told him in imploring him to be careful.

What time is it? If I go to the Panorama I can kill time for three-quarters of an hour and be at the café to meet Papa. I shall tell him the letter is from "Mizzi Stepanek, District IV, Rotmuehlgasse 3, 2nd Floor, Apartment 6," he read from the card he was still holding in his hand. Should I go back to his office and apologize? he thought; but immediately rejected the idea. In the first place his father would not allow him to be admitted, and secondly he had no desire to apologize.

In the Panorama he sat on a stool in front of a stereopticon box, turning the knob and looking at the "Waterworks at Castle Hellbrunn near Salzburg." As the pictures of the rose garden, the deer park, and the lodge passed in plastic review before him to the tinkle of a bell at each change, the injustice to which he had been subjected was thrown into bold relief to his eyes. It was his father who should apologize. As though they had all been saints in their youth! Yes, all of them! Papa. His teachers. Grandfather Stein. Neni. His uncles at Number 10. And Mother? Not she. You could see that least she understood what was going on inside you. Christl had been right.

She had drawn the proper conclusions! No one understood you. No one wanted to recall that they had once been young. His rage swept over him again and made him leave before he had had his pennyworth of pictures.

Even so, Eugenie's timetable proved to be inexact, for Papa was already engaged in his game of cards while Hans was still pacing up and down in the street before the café. Looking by accident through the big glass window, he saw him sitting there with his back turned to him. Which of the other two men was Eugenie's husband he not know.

He stood outside for a while thinking things over. Papa would probably not show the letter; the three of them were too absorbed in their game. Having reached this conclusion, he was on the point of going home. Then his father put his hand in his inside pocket and drew out his wallet.

An instant later Hans stood beside the card table. Papa had merely taken out a five-crown note to pay the waiter for some Virginia cigars he had brought.

"Never mind," he said to Hans. He was thinking: The boy wants to apologize after all. It's some extravagance and fuss he has inherited from his mother. He might have restrained himself till I reached home! That he had slapped his son in the face only a short time before had vanished from his consciousness; in any case he had no qualms. If young scamps get impertinent, that is the only language you can use to them, and Hans, unfortunately, was in the most annoying period of his fledgling years.

"Go on home," he said to him. Then, sorting his cards, he addressed: the other players: "A three-spot! Have you left me anything worth while in the stock, Herr Sektionschef?" Evidently the old gentleman with the bald spot was Eugenie's husband. He looked at Papa, absorbed in his cards, then at the small bronze plate over the card table inscribed with the words: "At this table Franz Grillparzer created his *Medea*," and finally answered Papa's question with a cautious,

"Double!" Papa apparently had excepted something different, for when he picked up and glanced through the six cards lying on the table and added three of them to his hand he declared, "I certainly have a run of bad luck today! Did you ever see such a stock! Not a single tarot in it!"

The game went on; the men smoked their cigars and accompanied each trick with strange ejaculations such as "Meet me with a club," or "The black widow." Hans said good-bye and left.

The letter was retrieved for him the following day by his mother, and so that worry was removed. But the relation between father and son was not bettered at all. The intolerable prospect of being obliged to enter his father's factory never left Hans's mind. "Aren't you fond of music?" Eugenie had asked him when he let drop some remark about it. Oh, yes, he loved to sit in the fourth balcony in the opera, or in Bosendorfer Hall, and hear the Rose Quartet play; he played not too badly himself; that was something his mother had taught him. But to manufacture pianos! Oh, worse than that, to sell pianos! What had that to do with music? At most it was related to physics and figures, and he hated both. And it had to do with compulsion, with being under his father's supervision from morning to night—unthinkable! Why did he not tell his father so quite frankly? Eugenie had inquired. A lot she knew! Who could explain anything to Papa? For him there existed only one point of view—his own. "Then what you must do is to find the right approach. Then he'll begin to see things your way a little," was Eugenie's opinion. Good God! "Diversions of fantasy which are often more noxious than beneficent," the Emperor had asserted recently at the opening of a Hunting Exhibition, and Papa had read it aloud exultingly in the *Reichspost* at dinner. Since he had become Purveyor to the Court he apparently had taken the Emperor more than ever as his model.

But it was Hans's schoolmate Ebeseder who had a better idea. The son of an ironworker, who played a considerable part in the Social Democratic party as reorganized by Victor Adler, he had for years been reserved in his manner towards Hans. A mother's pet, a scion of capitalism, spoiled, petted, soft, and innocent, so Hans seemed to one coming up from below. But from the moment when Hans had praised a rebellious retort he made to their militaristic natural-science teacher, a kind of rapprochement had been effected. Ebeseder, with his cheap suits that he was always in the state of outgrowing with too-short sleeves and trousers, read into Hans's enthusiasm something more than enjoyment over the discomfiture of an unpopular professor. Subsequent conversations, which led constantly farther afield, confirmed this. In their next-to-last year the youth with the outgrown trousers had a violent clash with Miklau, the senior master, an incident which threatened to result in his being expelled from the school. While the matter was being weighed by the authorities he said to Hans with a shrug of the shoulders, "Chances for the University are gone now anyway. You can do me a favor. In a month I'm taking the entrance examinations for the Academy of Art. Your uncle teaches there. Put in a word for me!"

This Hans did, and he had even taken him drawings prepared by Ebeseder, which, frankly, he disliked. Some of them were indecent and others distorted. There was one of an emaciated woman with a hydrocephalic child at her breast and leading by the hand another, who looked half starved, which Hans thought was revolting. But Uncle Drauffer, presumably out of a spirit of contradiction, declared that it was that particular drawing which gave promise of "great talent" and said he would do what lay in his power. When Hans gave that message to his friend this latter remarked, "Now at least I have some patronage, and in Austria that's all one needs! By the way, why don't you make a try too? You've been daubing around for years, and if you really are set against going into your father's factory why don't you consider getting into the Academy? If you pass then your father can have nothing to say. And if you fail—well, he needn't know anything about it."

With Hans's sudden and uncontrollable yearning for independence, these words fell on fertile ground. In his early years in school he had played with water colors for his own amusement and his product had been considered not too bad. The idea of becoming an artist now inflamed him. He could not imagine why he had never hit on this himself. An artist, of course! The only possible profession for him. But when the first wave of enthusiasm had passed and given way to cooler reason he thought doubtfully: "Uncle Drauffer is on the jury. Won't Papa hear about it through him?"

But Ebeseder was not to be upset. "The only thing is for him to find out in advance," was his advice. "Once he sees you sitting there he won't wring your neck. Besides, I shall be there."

That settled the matter, and a few weeks later, on October 19, 1907, at eight o'clock in the morning, the young people who in that Vienna autumn considered themselves artists entered the Art Academy building to take their entrance examinations. They were divided alphabetically, and a jury was assigned to each group of seven. Hans, as his family name began with A, was in the first. The aspirants with whom he was to compete were: Christ, Alois; Ebeseder, Heinrich; Gamillschegg, Kurt; Goldschmied, Emil; Hitler, Adolf; Hutterer, Heinrich. The rector himself presided, Professor Alfred Roller, a man of about fifty, lean, with a nonchalant manner, full beard, and glasses. There were innumerable anecdotes current about his unvarnished Viennese manner of speech, and every one knew that he drove Gustav Mahler, the head of the opera, to despair whenever he entrusted him with the staging of a production. The other bearded member of the jury was Uncle Drauffer. In addition to them it consisted of the landscape painter Poell and the water-colorist Isidor Levi, who was also an art critic.

"Are you out of your mind?" was Uncle Drauffer's only remark to his nephew. Then he laughed a great deal and pretended not to know him.

The entrants could choose among three projects: the façade of the Vienna Opera House or Burgtheater from memory, the head of an Academy model by the name of Zajiczek, a drawing of Raphael's Expulsion from Paradise. The medium, whether oils, water colors, or pencil, was also left to their choice, and they were given four hours. "It couldn't be easier!" said the landscape painter Poell.

Hans chose to do the head of old Zajiczek. The old man, a model for generations of Vienna art students, sat in a beautiful pose on a platform, his shining white locks hung low on his neck, his nose aquiline, his mouth nobly cut. He had been a singer and lost his voice. Full of repose, he sat up there, with his eyes so cleverly directed towards the candidates that he could at the same time see his Crown Journal, conveniently laid out before him on a stool. When he turned the pages he did it so adroitly that no one noticed the slightest change of position.

There was a deep furrow between Ebeseder's eyes. He was the only one who had chosen the Expulsion. On the other hand, there were three competitors besides Hans sitting in front of the model. The two remaining candidates had each taken up a post at a window of the hall from which they could see, not the facade, but at least the roof of the Opera House.

Hans felt that he was getting along swimmingly. He would hardly need the full four hours; long before that everything would have been accomplished according to his desires. He would come home as a full-fledged artist, rid of the Francis Joseph Gymnasium, relieved of the dread of final examinations. And, best of all, he would not need to have any traffic with the piano factory. Tomorrow he would be able to say to Eugenie: "That's no way to handle an artist!" He winked happily at Uncle Drauffer, who was busy with something at the green center table. But his uncle did not see him.

His left-hand neighbor was constantly erasing, having elected to make his drawing in pencil. Hans was surprised at this choice; a character sketch of the kind called for oils.

The model moved slightly, and the candidate to the left said something impatiently under his breath. His teeth were noticeably bad. He picked up his eraser, examined it, then threw it aside as useless. He turned restless eyes in Hans's direction. "Would you lend me yours?" he whispered. "That idiot! Why doesn't he sit still?"

Hans had been thinking that the old man posed like a statue of marble. He made no comment, however, as he handed over his morsel of rubber.

"Should he be reading that paper?" grumbled the other, moving his big, pale, round head brusquely.

For a while no sound was heard but that of brushes and pencils. Hans was becoming more and more pleased with his own handiwork. He threw an inquiring glance in the direction of Ebeseder to see if he were having as satisfactory a time with his "Paradise." A shrug of the shoulders and a wry smile were the only answer.

The moody candidate to his left seemed to be content with his pencil.

After two hours the members of the jury began to make their rounds, going from one candidate to another. They would stand behind the easel or drawing-board, watch for a minute or two, make notes on a sheet of paper, and then pass on. None of them said a word. Even Uncle Drauffer was noncommittal in his manner, and Hans found this rather discouraging.

"Swine!" muttered the restless neighbor on his left. The sketch. It was bad, Hans had to admit.

At this point the examiner Levi looked directly at the whisperer.

"Is there anything you wish, Herr"—his eyes skimmed the list of entrants for the right name. "Herr Hitler?"

"No, Professor." The tone was suddenly respectful. "I took the liberty of asking the loan of an eraser. Thank you very much, Professor."

Isidor Levi nodded, jotted down a note, and passed on.

"A good enough fellow, that one," said Hans's neighbor in a low tone. "Do you read his criticisms? He writes well, brilliantly in fact."

"Quiet!" demanded the professor in charge. It was the first word he had spoken since the test began. "Perhaps you young gentlemen have heard the name of Goethe?" he went on from where he was sitting behind a drawing-board. "Goethe said, 'Above the trees there is quiet.' Please bear that in mind."

"Swine!" whispered the pale young man.

When the time allotted to them was up they were told to hand in their drawings and wait out in the corridor for the results of their test.

"Well?" Ebeseder said to Hans.

"I think mine turned out pretty well," he replied. "And yours?"

"A mess!" exclaimed the other. "I just haven't any talent!"

Then they heard someone in the entry below say, "The candidates are waiting on the first floor. It may be quite a while. Will you be good enough to go on up?"

It was the attendant sending up two ladies and a gentleman. The ladies appeared to be the mothers of two of the candidates. They had brought along ham sandwiches and oranges and asked at once, "Well, what was it like?" The gentleman introduced himself to every one present with the words, "My name is Imperial Councillor Hutterer." Then he inquired, "Do you think you got through, Heini?"

Then an elderly woman of humble appearance arrived, who gazed about her with an uncertain and apologetic air. When her eyes fell on the pale young man she seemed relieved and hurried over to his side. He saw her coming and, turning his back with a show of embarrassment, looked out of the window. Her steps slowed.

"Did you—did you get through all right?" she whispered.

He gave a quick and sullen response in so low a tone that no one could hear what he said. Immediately afterwards the old woman retraced her steps and went down the stairs again, with a hurt expression on her face.

Before even the oranges had been consumed Uncle Drauffer opened the doors of the examination hall and said laughingly, "Come on in, you bandits!"

Behind the green baize table stood Professor Roller, who announced, "Accepted: Christ, Alois; Ebeseder, Heinrich; Gamillschegg, Kurt; Goldschmied, Emil. The following gentlemen performed their test drawings unsatisfactorily and were rejected: Alt, Hans; Hitler, Adolf; Hutterer, Heinrich."

Hans thought he must have misheard.

"Let us draw the veil of brotherly love over it," Uncle Drauffer told him without being overheard by anyone else. "Did I ever in all your life say that you had any talent? In any case, it was never I who told you. And I shall never tell anyone!"

Meanwhile the pale young man with the bad teeth pushed his way through the successful candidates, who were being congratulated in turn by the chairman of the jury. "You wish?" Professor Roller asked him.

"I request an explanation of why I was failed," said Hitler, Adolf.

"Because of lack of talent," Professor Roller replied, shaking hands with the next successful candidate.

"And what do you understand that term to mean?" persisted the unsuccessful one. Hans, having suffered the same fate, felt some sympathy with him.

"Absolute lack of talent," repeated Professor Roller dryly.

The third of the unsuccessful ones—Hutterer, Heinrich— was so upset that he kept muttering to himself, "I never!"

"Sorry I gave you bad advice," Ebeseder said apologetically as they went down the marble steps of the Academy.

Absolute lack of talent. Now Hans knew.

CHAPTER 21
A Child Speaks

Little Martha Monica was so beautiful that people stopped to look at her when she went walking with Neni in the Stadtpark. She had Henriette's gorgeous hair, only a shade lighter, to her soft, lovely face in corkscrew curls. The same dark sheen was deeply reflected in the large, long-lashed eyes of the child; she even had her mother's strange look. In addition she had a natural grace of motion, an unconsciousness and ease which was reminiscent neither of Henriette's shyness nor even less of Franz. There was nothing coarse-grained about the little girl; her hands in her gloves were slim; her legs were long and slender; her bones were fashioned with absolute delicacy. Only her voice left something to be desired; it was almost shrill, but in time that would wear off.

Everyone spoiled the child. Her mother did it to excess; her brothers and sister, Neni the nurse, even Herr Simmerl. And in chambermaid, who had come into the service of the fourth floor so young and had now been there for seven years, she had a particularly fierce partisan. This chambermaid (Hanni Kern was her name) had from the beginning been on Henriette's side and against Franz. As for the rest of the house, they were all agreed that Martha Monica was charming, but restrained themselves from any expression of affection. However, as that was the rule in Number 10, no one took any notice, least of all the child.

This was changed when the weddings took place which Uncle Drauffer called the "marriage epidemic of Seilerstätte." Otto Eberhard's son Peter led off. This former member of a duelling fraternity had become an official in the Ministry of the Interior, and although it was difficult for an ordinary middle-class citizen to obtain such a post, it was facilitated for Otto Eberhard's son. The girl he married came from Potsdam, near Berlin; her maiden name was Annemarie von Stumm, and Peter had met her during a holiday on the North Sea. She was a flaxen blonde and wore her hair in round braided coils over her ears. She raved about Vienna, found the house "charming" and its inhabitants "heavenly."

According to Uncle Drauffer, who hated everything Prussian, this marriage was the cause of the "epidemic." For not long afterwards his own son Fritz, who had abandoned a legal career to become an unsuccessful composer, had married Liesl Schoenwieser. Liesl was a member of the ballet at the Court Opera House. Number 10, however, expressed its derogatory attitude by saying merely that she was "from the ballet." On top of that she was not even a "Coriphée" but only a member of the ensemble, and appeared in the background as the eleventh hussar in *Puppenfee* and as a moonbeam in *Sun and Earth*. But in *Coppélia* she was a "carnation" and stood on her toes. For years Fritz had had the kind of 'affair' with her that decent Viennese burghers' sons had with less decent female beings before they made up their minds to marriage and propriety. "There was probably a reason," was the opinion of the other twin Otto, who had managed to worm his way into the circle of the all-powerful Burgermeister Lueger and was in the process of becoming a politician. But this spiteful remark proved to be pure malice, for Fräulein Schoenwieser continued to dance as the tightly corseted hussar even after she became Frau Drauffer. Such people, according to Number 10, were not the ones to marry. "After the daughter of a singer, this is a step even lower down!" It was the Widow Paskiewicz who coined that phrase. Her pride over her daughter's holy state had made her, in regard to moral questions, intransigent.

The pendulum of favor at Number 10 swung emphatically in the direction of Peter's young wife, as if to say: "This is what happens when we don't have to force ourselves to take in a new member." As a natural corollary to this was a retort made by Countess Hegéssy (the very one who at times appeared to have tongue at all) when the ballet dancer made an extravagant remark about Martha Monica's beauty: "That's because she is Count Poldo's child!" Countess Hegéssy had possessed her titled husband only half a year. But since then she had always looked upon herself as belonging to the aristocracy.

The young Frau Drauffer, however, was a typical Viennese, and discretion was not her strong point. She found the remark all the more interesting because it provided grist for her mill against the hypocritical impertinence of her newly acquired relatives; so she repeated it to various and sundry until Cousin Hegéssy's words finaly reached Franz's ears. That his fiercely fought and, in his eyes, chivalrous battle through the years to maintain an appearance in which even he did not believe, should end in this disastrous way, drove him to despair. He had never admitted it. Not even to himself. His passionate love for Henriette had always smothered his disillusion in her. When that passion waned with his years, and his nature gave way to her instinctive reticence, there was still affection enough in him for Henriette. There was even more personal pride to protect her name, and consequently his own, from the blight of scandal.

He called his taciturn cousin to account. But she, with a brutality to Sophie's frankness and yet raised to a more callous degree, said without a flicker, "Don't be absurd! You need only look at the child to see it is of aristocratic blood!"

That evening, when the little girl wanted to kiss him good night usual, he turned his back on her.

"Mono wants to kiss you," Henriette said.

"She can kiss the photograph on your desk," blurted out Franz in the presence of his elder son, and left the room. He had tolerated photograph on Henriette's desk. Whenever he saw it he felt a pang, but he let it stay there year in and year out. On the Empress's desk, as all Vienna knew, there stood a photograph of Frau Schratt, and it had choked all scandalous rumors. He had attempted to do same. But without success.

That same night Hans stood by the open window in his study by the court, letting the autumn breeze cool his brow and listening to the familiar sound of the ripe nuts as they fell from Sophie's old tree on the pavement below. The crest of the tree now reached his window and the wind blew a branch stubbornly against it. "I must, mistaken," the young man said to himself. "It's absolutely finable that anyone should be so brutal."

He had ceased to be childish for his years. The moustache on his upper lip had not made his face seem much older; he still looked exactly like many others of his kind, nice-looking boys of good families, well dressed, well fed, well cared for, with no reason to worry; no distinguishing mark in all that. Nevertheless (and Henriette noticed it), a decided change had come over him, which was constantly growing more unmistakable. Where others, and even Henriette herself, were unquestioning, he was filled with doubts. Things which as she grew older tended in her to breed distrust and almost misanthropy, in him very early grew into an urgent need of clarity. As a small child, sitting on the floor surrounded by his picture books and toys, he had loved to take apart anything that was not tightly joined. Now he was doing the same with life. Perhaps he should be a doctor, Henriette came to think. He thumped things, looked at them from every angle in order to diagnose them. At least, that is what it seemed to her. That precision was not one of his qualities, and that dissection rather than integration was his forte, she overlooked. She encouraged his attitude, for she felt that her undoing came from having asked too few questions and from taking too much for granted.

Standing at the window, Hans tried to clear his mind about his father. The first opponent to cross his path in life had been his father. The others, Professor Miklau and the natural science captain, were chance opponents. That Papa in contrast was an opponent by destiny, he felt was clear. And not just Papa, for it had been the same in every other family he had been in. The sons of good families were afraid of their fathers, who seemed determined to handle them as 'black-sheep sons'—a term taken from novels, and one which enraged him because it cast the blame on the sons. The fathers were the ones to blame. They were the ones to make impossible demands on the sons. Yes, one might have been a better student. But could one want to sell pianos? Papa said: "Yes, of course," and that was the trouble. If he had only said: "Of course, selling pianos cannot be fascinating, but we have the factory and I need your help—get that into your mind," then things would be different. The intolerable part of it was to stand things upside down and then insist that they were right side up. Or did Papa believe what he said?

Out of the night came the sound of a gramophone:

"Georgie boy, buy me an automobile.
Georgie boy, then you'll *see* how I feel!"

No. Papa did hot believe it! He had had a lot of affairs before he married Mother: Aunt Pauline could tell stories on that score. He had even wanted to be a painter, so Uncle Drauffer had confided to Hans to comfort him. But now he said: "Ridiculous, one just doesn't become a painter!" when Hans was in question. So he was lying. So he was not on his side.

At this point Hans went off on a false trail, but precision was not his forte. "Inaccuracy is the curse of Austrians," Grandfather Stein used to say, particularly in regard to this grandson. The longer Hans thought about it, the more indisputable it seemed to him that there were only two possibilities: either Papa had no conception of what goes on inside a young person, or he knew and didn't care. Finally he discovered a third possibility. Papa was old, fifty-six, and even so he was younger than most Vienna fathers. They married late (after they had had their fling, as Hermann Bahr said in his book about Vienna), and it was only late in their lives that they achieved worthwhile positions. Wasn't Vienna really run by graybeards? Anyone at forty was still "much too young" for any use. To become a Minister of State, a general, a councillor, or anybody who had a voice in affairs, one had to be at least sixty. To be young was decidedly a dreadful mistake. Perhaps all this was connected with the fact that the Emperor was so old he wished every one who governed with him, whether as fathers or otherwise, to be old too?

Ebeseder had declared that the Crown Prince had committed suicide because he could not get on with his father. Hans was inclined to believe that on the face of it.

His thoughts strayed off without probing to the bottom of the possibility. He thought of Ebeseder whom he no longer saw. Too bad. He had been the only one in school who said things that opened one's eyes. Of course Mother did too at times. Yet with all her captivating qualities she possessed neither logic nor consistency, Hans had to admit. She would say one thing one day and contradict it the next. He realized that everything depended with her on her sympathies and antipathies, by which she always allowed herself to be led.

"Georgie boy, the car isn't dear!"

Eugenie sang that idiotic song too. Sometimes her pretence at being so young was quite embarrassing.

Mother is the only person to whom I cannot make a single reproach, he reflected. *Unless perhaps it was that she had been too hard on Christl? There are an untold number of things with which I can reproach Papa. "She can kiss the photograph on your desk!" How hateful!*

With impetuous steps he crossed his narrow room. Next door in Mother's bedroom all was dark and still. Probably she was across the hall sitting by Mono's bed. And Papa, of course, was at his chess club.

That his mother had not been guilty of doing anything wrong with Count Traun he was prepared to swear. The scene of years ago, in the tiny red room at the Sophia Hall, rose vividly before his eyes. "Chambre séparée" was what they called such a place. The scenes in *Anatol* were laid in *chambres séparées*, he had learned since then. But Mother was no woman out of *Anatol*. When they drove out that time to the violet meadow Papa had said: "Your mother is above all suspicion." Why then did he act so horridly now and cloud her with suspicion?

But what if he were right?

If Mother really had deceived Papa then?

If Mono was not Papa's child?

Then Papa would be right? And Mother wrong?

Each one of these thoughts choked him. He reflected, then he tore open the door into the next room, intending to run through to the nursery beyond, where he imagined his mother was. He simply must talk to her!

"Is that you, Hans?" her voice came out of the dark.

"Are you there, Mother?"

"Yes, I'm already in bed. Wait a moment, I'll turn on the light."

"No, don't," he begged. "I'd rather you didn't. May I stay a moment with you? Or are you too tired?"

The mull curtains, drawn over the half-open window, billowed in the breeze. The arc light on the corner of Seilerstätte and Annagasse threw an occasional flash on them.

"No, sit down by me."

He seated himself by the narrow little bed where she had borne him.

"I heard you pacing up and down," she said. "Can't you get to sleep?"

"It's that awful gramophone. Can't people be stopped from playing the same song for ever? It's enough to drive you crazy!"

"I'm afraid it can't be done," she answered. "One can't forbid anyone anything—of that sort, I mean. Besides, it's a nice song, isn't it? I was just thinking perhaps you should ask Papa to buy an automobile. It would stir up a hornet's nest of talk in the house, but we are used to that. Then at least we could drive out somewhere every evening. To Laxenburg. Or to Baden. Or to—Couldn't we?"

"Mother," Hans said, "would you be angry if I asked you something?"

I am used to that, she thought to herself. *All this questioning has made me so tired, unutterably tired, less questions?* "What is it?" she replied.

If she knew what I want to ask! Hans thought, and he was so excited he could not speak.

But she knew.

"Don't think I want to butt into anything which doesn't concern me," he began.

Quite right, she thought, *it does not concern you. That is the reason why you ask.*

"But it is so important to me," he went on, and then hesitated because it was hard to put into words.

It is not in the least important to you, she thought. *If I was happy for a few hours in my life, of what did I rob you? I might have been happy all my life, do you know that? Then you would not have born, here in this dreadful house, and would not, at your birth, nearly have cost me my life.* "What is it that's so important to?" she asked.

He took heart. "I mean—what Papa said this evening. It isn't true, is it, Mother?"

She could not see his face.

Out of the darkness she answered, "It isn't true." *In this room*, she thought, *there have always been lies told, from the very day when the walls were still damp, yes, from the day when the walls had not even been built.* What was one lie more or less? One charge more or less made no difference. *In this house I have been a defendant since I first crossed the threshold.* She remembered the ruby glass lamps down on the ground floor burning on either side of the sacred image. First it was Franz's relatives by whom she was accused. Then it was Franz himself. Now it was his son. That she loved the son she now forgot. She was too deeply wounded.

"Thank you!" he exclaimed with relief. He had jumped up and ted to kiss her.

"Not so impetuously!" she said, turning away. "Keep that for—others."

Nevertheless he kissed her: "Are you crying, Mother?" he asked as his lips sensed that she was.

"No. But I'm very tired."

CHAPTER 22
The Victory that Counts

The derby box holders met in the grandstand at the Freudenau race track. On this Sunday in June an unheard-of event had taken place; some of them, a growing minority, had come not in their private carriages or hired coaches, but in automobiles.

Henriette was jubilant. Until now she had not been able to get Franz to buy an automobile. "The Emperor always drives in a carriage," he said, rejecting her extravagant proposal. People who didn't allow themselves to be taken in by every modern contraption, he declared, could get along without this new instrument of torture with its stinking smell and explosive noises. Bicycles? Well, all right, he would cede that point because they induced healthy physical exercise, and Hans could have one if he passed his second half-yearly exams. But as for gramophones, motor-cars, and all that modern rubbish, they would please be kind enough not to expect him to provide them. Music was to be made with hands or throat, and motion could be achieved by means of your own or horses' legs. What was good enough for the Emperor would not be too poor for Henriette! The time had gone by when he made every effort to gratify her least wish. Since that day in the violet-strewn meadow he had had the upper hand and he let it be felt.

It was near the Heustadlwasser, in the main avenue, however, that they witnessed the event: Princess Pauline Metternich and Priricess Croy were each riding at a whirlwind pace in a new, high, and mysteriously propelled vehicle.

"You see!" Henriette said to Franz. He merely shrugged his shoulders, "You can't take those two as an example. They always were crazy!"

Another thing she had never been able to wring from him was a season box for the races. He said it was a swindle. The Alts were no idlers. Or, if Henriette was really so interested in horse racing, would she like to watch it from the public stands? That would be in keeping for a simple citizen, and he had no objections to it. In this respect he was not so narrow-minded as his cousin Anna, the former Miss Kubelka's daughter and the deserted wife of Count Hegéssy.

They met her on the staircase as they were leaving Number 10 to go to the Derby, and as the deserted wife was in her black Sunday wearing even a brand-new hat, Franz jokingly asked her her she too was going to the Derby. She did not so much as answer, but turned pale with indignation. *How silly of that strange woman!* Franz thought.

But the other extreme was also against his nature, as was any extreme. Henriette wanted to sit in the grandstand, divided by only a glass partition from the highly aristocratic Jockey Club enclosure.

That was not where average people belonged, Franz had told her not once but many times. It did not and would not occur to him that every face in there brought back memories to her and that was the very reason why she came.

She wore a champagne-colored dress. It was in the latest French style, with a high neck, lace sleeves puffed at the shoulders, a long not pinched bodice, and a skirt reaching down below her shoes. Her hat was wide, with waving white ostrich plumes, and held in place by hatpins with broad, round heads of tortoiseshell and opals.

Her champagne-colored parasol had an ivory handle. Henriette was beautiful, and her gleaming white skin, thanks to the Paris powder she had begun to use, was whiter than ever, and her lips more red. She had learned to use cosmetics. Ever and again, even when it seemed most foolish and surprising, she felt herself overwhelmed by a desire she supposed she had long since suppressed. It was the desire to be seen. And at such times she wanted to be beautiful.

She stood by Franz in his regulation morning coat and narrowbrimmed, old-fashioned top hat, to which he clung even in everyday life out of a defiant attitude. They were in the upper-most tier of the granstand. That their places were so high up, directly beneath the tea room of the court caterer Demel, was what distinguished them from the holders of season boxes, who now began to fill the more desirable seats in the first, second, and third tiers. This was the first time for years that the Derby was not threatened with bad weather; the sky was gleaming blue, and new clothes and hats could be paraded without fear of rain. Besides, there were two derby favorites promising big returns from the heavy bets placed them; they were the three-year-old Heracles, from the stable of the Barons Springer, and the three-year-old mare Vilja, from the Rothschild stable. People were streaming in in droves.

The Springer stable was Jewish, and the owners of it, the two equally stout and eternally cigar-smoking brothers, Gustav and Heinrich, were just as popular as Gyulyas, their jockey. The Rothschild stable was Jewish, too, and on this Sunday their blue and yellow colors were being worn by three other candidates: two for a maiden handicap, one for a steeplechase. "The Judaization of the Vienna turf" had, on the previous Friday, been the subject of complaint in an article in the *Vienna Signals*. This in turn had called forth, on the Saturday before the races, an interpellation in the City Council; the author of which was Otto Drauffer and the mouthpiece was that city councillor Bielohlawek (who had said: "Tolstoy is an old nincompoop!"). The question in the interpellation was: "Is the burgermeister aware of the fact that one of the ornaments of Viennese public life, the sport of horse racing, is in danger of succumbing to Jewish influence and Jewish capital?"

Whereupon "our Wotan-bearded Burgermeister Lueger" had, as the liberal *Neue Freie Presse* pointed out with approval in its leading article of this morning, "given the answer of a *bon juge* who held to the policy that the middle course is the only right one," when he said: "I am the one to decide who is a

Jew!" To be sure the next item mentioned with commendation in the paper was a notice of the suspension of civil rights in Prague and Brünn. The Young Czech hotheads apparently had gone too far again in their unfounded claims for equal rights. "Since the unhappy cry of 'Away from Rome!' has been set up by the fanatic Herr von Schoenerer," said the liberal newspaper, "Austria has become an arena of national conflicts in the mixed language areas. Pan-Slavism, with its athletic clubs and youth organizations, has stirred up as much trouble as the ultramontane movement has in Catholic circles and Pan-Germanism has in the German nationalist and clerical quarters." Having forgotten the middle way praised above, the liberal paper went on to state lower down, "The hotheads in all the camps are in need of a thorough cooling off."

Henriette saw the two Springer brothers sitting in wicker armchairs on the lawn in the Jockey Club enclosure. She saw the tall figure of the very youthful Baroness Clarice Rothschild, née Montefiore, from London, as she took her place in her box in the front row under a shower of greetings from her neighbors on either side, the old Princess Croy and Prince Thassilo Festetics, while her husband and brothers-in-law sat behind the glass partition among the highest of the court-ranking nobility. They themselves, according to Henriette's conviction, looked like nobles of the best blood. Wherever the barriers raised by origin were broken down she had a sense of personal triumph. Down there too a captain in the Imperial Life Guards was greeting the owner of a third Jewish racing stable, Herr Horace Ritter von Landau. Henriette recalled that captain of the Imperial Life Guards. "Frau Henriette Alt?" he had inquired early one dark morning in a tone of unsurpassable disdain.

"Look!" she said, pointing the incident out to Franz. It was too bad that Otto Eberhard and his narrow-minded wife could not be there; at least they would have seen that Vienna no longer held any prejudices and no one took seriously such epithets as Jew or Christian. No one but a blind person could escape the fact that they had merged to a degree which made them indistinguishable. There stood the knighted actor from the Court Theater, Adolf von Sonnenthal, a Jewish tailor by origin, surrounded by an adoring throng of countesses and counts whom he, from the stage of the Burgtheater, instructed in model manners. And yonder the tyrant of the stamping foot, which he exercised even in leading the orchestra, the director of the Court Opera, Gustav Mahler, was evading the efforts of Countess Kinsky to speak to him.

"Do you see? Anton Dreher is greeting us from below," said Franz, bowing to the tall, thin brewer who was also the owner of a stable and represented the solid middle class in the racing world.

Henriette acknowledged the greeting briefly. Everything that Franz did rubbed her the wrong way. He had not even noticed her dress. For whom had she ever put it on! They never went out anywhere, except in the house. Tea at Elsa's, supper at the Drauffers', a supper for Franz's friends from the chess club, a box party at the An der Wien Theater or Ronacher's, together with the Drauffers or the Otto Eberhards—that was the extent of their sociability. With a sense of bitterness she took up her mother-of-pearl opera glasses. Almost to a man the owners of the grandstand boxes were now in their customary places. When old Princess Metternich looked up in her direction Henriette turned aside. In the old days, after the Metternich ball, she could easily have played the same kind of role in Vienna society as the young Baroness Rothschild. But no, Franz would not hear of it. Her world was and would remain 10 Seilerstätte.

The introductory races had gone by almost unnoticed. The trials the Derby were now due.

In the glass-shielded stand of the Jockey Club the gentlemen rose their feet. Word was passed that the Emperor had come. But it turned out that it was the heir to the throne, Francis Ferdinand and his consort. They were led to the gilt chairs in the center of the stand, where they sat down. Then the heir to the throne spoke to Prince Montenuovo, Imperial Chief Steward. This was the signal for a hum of conversation in the grandstand, because every one knew that it was Montenuovo who had made an intransigent fight against Francis Ferdinand's marriage with a simple court lady, Countess Chotek, and had finally agreed not to a ceremony implying equal birth but to a "morganatic" one. Neither in the face of the white-bearded old prince nor in that of the heir to the throne was there the slightest trace of amiability. To look at them one could forget that such a thing as a smile existed in the world. The present "Duchess of Hohenberg" turned red, then pale. Henriette's eyes did not leave the morganatic couple. They were sitting in a place which should have been filled by another.

Her thoughts did not soar quite so high that she said to herself: "That might have been my place." Nevertheless she felt deep down that it was only because of her own will that she was not now sitting there. Probably Prince Montenuovo would have been even harder on her. But she too would have achieved in the end what that woman down there had achieved, she who was appearing for the first time in public and before whom, despite all, the court people had to bow their heads.

That she alone in all the world knew this fact caused her an almost unbearable sensation. "If you but knew!" she thought, and the mother-of-pearl opera glasses trembled in her gloved hands.

"I kiss your hand, dear lady! How are you? But it's an age since we met!" said someone who had come up the grandstand and was now in front of her box. "Do you still remember me? Hoyos is my name."

"I sent Pepi Hoyos to Rome," Rudolf had said. In the meantime Pepi Hoyos had become an old man.

"Of course! A thousand thanks for coming up!" she answered, and grew as pale as a debutante. When she spoke with aristocrats she involuntarily imitated their speech. "My husband—Count Hoyos." She performed the introduction. Of the four men with whom she had had that *déjeuner* in Mayerling only two were still alive. One had committed suicide; the other had been killed by Franz.

"Your servant, sir," Franz said.

"I recognized you the minute you arrived, and I thought to myself, I'll go over and say how do you do. You're looking splendid, dear lady! *Hors concours!*" declared the man who on her account had journeyed to the Pope. On the tunic of his Uhlan major's uniform glinted two small buttons bound in silver cord, the symbol of his rank as Imperial Chamberlain. "Well, now! How shall we bet?" He turned to Franz, stuck his monocle in his eye, fingered the green program, began to mark with his pencil the starters just posted, and showed every sign of watching the Derby from the box of Mr. Alt.

But Franz did not invite him to stay, and as Henriette made a move to do so he anticipated her words with the remark, "The race will start immediately! I think you will reach the Jockey Club stand more easily down the center aisle."

Then Henriette said, "Won't you join us, Count Hoyos? We are *à deux.*" Quite naturally she fell back into a way of speech she had had for only such a short time.

"A thousand thanks," said the count, and took a seat behind her. Henriette noticed with satisfaction that this had already struck the attention of the lower rows in the grandstand. "Perhaps you will exchanges places with the count?" she suggested to Franz. Countess Goluchowski glared at her, as did Countess Wydenbruck through her pince-nez.

"A thousand thanks. This seat is excellent!" answered their

guest, and drew his chair a shade nearer to Henriette's. "It looks as though things were beginning to break loose again in Prague, doesn't it?" he said, turning again to Franz. And again Franz did not say anything.

"How have you bet, Count Pepi?" asked Henriette, who had quite blossomed out since his arrival. How fortunate that she had sprinkled some Violette de Parme on her handkerchief just before she left home.

"Heracles and Vilja, to win and to place. As a matter of fact, I have more faith in good old Vilja. She ran marvellously in Alag. Just a moment ago I said to Alphonse [he meant the owner of the horse, Baron Rothschild], 'Your Vilja is so chic that even you bet on her!' You know, don't you, that the Rothschilds never bet their own horses?"

"Of course," Henriette told him, although she did not know. She too was strongly in favor of Vilja's winning. Or Heracles. She was for the Rothschild and Springer stables. She was for martial law. She was for anything and everything except Franz. Prince Festetics' son, Georgie, had bowed to her. Life could still be beautiful.

The starting bell rang; the starting tape was lifted. "They all got away to a good start," Count Hoyos said approvingly. Who had used those same words? As the horses began to run she racked her brains. But she could not recall.

In the lead from the start was a wiry brown whose jockey wore black and red colors. "Heracles!" yelled the betters from the public stands. Heracles was a full three lengths ahead. The two Barons Springer, down in the wicker armchairs, puffed furiously at their cigars.

On the turn at the 1600-metre line (they were to go round the course twice) Vilja moved up. The blue and yellow colors of the Rothschild stable gleamed in the sun. "I told you!" cried Count Hoyos. Princess Lubomirska, to the right below in Box 2, was hard of hearing and yelled at the Lord Chief

Chamberlain, Count Lanckoronski, who sat as close behind her as Count Hoyos behind Henriette, "What horse is that?" (She said "hoss" in the affectedly slipshod way of all aristocrats.) The Lord Chief Chamberlain, who had the most penetrating voice of anyone at court, answered in an equally loud tone, into the ear-trumpet she held out to him: "Vilja." "Just like in the operetta—is that her name?" screamed the elderly princess. "*Exactement*, just as in *The Merry Widow*," trumpeted Lanckoronski. And over the three intervening boxes, with complete disregard of whether he was disturbing anyone, he called in his shrill voice to Clarice Rothschild: "Vilja is in marvellous form, Baroness!"

From then on the people in the grandstand crossed their fingers for Vilja.

"I trust you've laid a bet, dear lady?" the guest asked.

"Alas, no," she answered.

"What a shame!" the count said. Franz had not yet uttered a word, but he had listened with irritation to every word spoken by his wife and his guest. Now, to every one's surprise, he exclaimed, looking out over the track, "Anna!"

When the field, in a compact group, reached the starting posts on the first round, Heracles and Vilja fell back. The blue-and-white-dotted colors of the Uechtritz stable pulled ahead, and Madame des Renaudes, a lady in the second tier of boxes, was overcome with excitement.

Vilja was now in the lead. Suddenly, quite from the outside, under the lashing and spurring of a jockey who rose in his stirrups, leaned over, lashed again, there emerged a horse which until now had escaped all notice. It had not been in the running at all, but by long strides it gained the lead. One heard the deaf princess screaming: "Why, what's that?" It was some time before she received the answer: "Number 9, Erzébet." Meanwhile the whole grandstand had followed the Lord High Chamberlain's example and hunted up the outsider's name in the program. "Count Elemer Hegéssy's three-year-old mare, Erzébet. Up, Jockey G. Janek," said the program.

"Do you see Anna?" Franz asked his wife, and grabbed her by the arm. With his other arm he pointed excitedly, "Over there!"

By a white balustrade, at a point where the public and the judges' stands were closest together, stood a woman in black. She had rushed over there from the cheaper seats to a place where no one was supposed to stand because the clods of earth, torn up by the hoofs of the racing horses, fell like hail all around. But this woman stood there clinging to the white balustrade.

"Erzébet!" she screamed, so passionately and so piercingly that the whole race-track heard her. It was Anna, who grew indignant if anyone went to the races. It was Anna, who had never raised her voice.

"Erzébet!" yelled the public stands a moment later.

"Vilja! Vilja! Vilja!" urged the grandstand in competition.

"Erzébet!" screamed the woman in black to Franz's unspeakable surprise.

"Erzébet!" The cry now came from the stand of the Jockey Club, which on this Derby Sunday had made a great exception and allowed a lady in. The man beside the lady, the heir to the throne, Francis Ferdinand, was the one who first took up the cry of "Erzébet!" For Erzébet belonged to a blue-blooded count, and a Vilja belonged only to the house of Rothschild.

Erzébet beat Vilja by half a length, as well as the crack mounts of the Springer and Uechtritz stables, who came in neck and neck. The finish was so close that the results remained in doubt until the numbers were posted: 9, 4, 2. The odds on Number 9 had been 34 to 1. The race-track was in an uproar. The noonday news that irrepressible "Young Czechs" had been fired on in Prague no longer interested anyone. Erzébet's victory for the court and the nobility was the only thing that counted. But the middle class, which had lost, was thinking about its money.

When the owner of the winning horse, an old and bowed gentleman, led it by the reins to the scales, according to custom, an incident occurred which appeared in the paper next day under the heading "Tragedy at the Derby." According to a brief account, a lady dressed in mourning crossed the path of Count Hegéssy. In the public stands they called her the Baroness of the Turf because she hardly ever missed a race. Beaming with joy over his victory, the count accepted the congratulations of the lady and with true Magyar cordiality embraced and kissed her and then went on to the scales. But the Baroness of the Turf, presumably out of excitement caused by the victory of an outsider, on whom she may have bet, was overcome by an indisposition and succumbed to it on the spot.

"It is incomprehensible that she should have gone to every race!" was the obituary comment of Number 10. How can one lead a double life? was what Franz could not understand. Henriette understood. Moreover, this was the only thing she ever had understood about Anna Hegéssy. One who has lost something goes on seeking everywhere and forever. Human beings are unreasonable, she knew. They do not believe in their loss.

CHAPTER 23
Social Education

Hans was arranging the testimonials given to the firm of G. Alt in the course of the years, for the one hundred and fiftieth anniversary of the house was at hand and Papa wished to get out a jubilee publication. Liszt had written, " ... *grâce aux prodigieux pianos à queue que vous avez eu l'extrême amabilité d'envoyer ici ...*" and: "*La perfection d'un Alt surpasse l'idéal de*

mes espérances." Richard Wagner's praise took this form: "*Mes répétitions aux fêtes musicales de Bayreuth, auxquelles les pianos, sortant de votre éminente fabrique, ont grandement aide …*"
And Paderewski: "*Le piano était tout à fait merveilleux, en beaucoup de choses idéal, et c'est pour moi un grand plaisir de vous le faire savoir.*"

Sitting there in the little compartment partitioned off for him between the turners and the cabinet-makers, surrounded by the racket of saws and lathes, he had translated it, for better or for worse, into French. But why the devil into French, when the letters were written in German? Why did Papa insist on getting out his jubilee pamphlet in French?

The translation for Beethoven's words of praises—"A jewel of piano construction"—did not come to his mind, and he stalked angrily around his square little cubbyhole where it reeked of glue and where in broad daylight you had to use artificial light, as everywhere in his father's factory. It faced a court, or rather a blind wall, and stood in the constant shadow of the parish church of the holy Nepomuk. Hans put his fingers in his ears, for the tuning had begun again. Next beyond the turnery was the tuning-room, where tuning 'by ear' was still held preferable to tuning 'by sight.' The tuning-forks and wrest-pins tested the same G string for hours on end, until you were nervous enough to jump out of your skin.

Fortunately the other earsplitting noises, from the metal casting and wire drawing, were confined to a lower story—namely, the cellar. It was so damp there that water ran from the walls. These dripping blotches, which kept appearing in different places, were the only decoration in the three elongated, crypt-like vaults; they were still lighted in part by unshielded gas jets, together with the smallest, cheapest electric light bulbs suspended from unprotected wires, producing a most inharmonious light. If your foot came in contact with any soft object the chances were that it would almost certainly be a rat.

But why in French? Hans protested furiously, and again could comprehend why a factory of harmonious instruments produced such horrible noises. "The Austrian has a fatherland and loves it, and has reason, too, to love it!" The quotation, from Schiller's *Wallenstein's Death*, which was the theme he had had to write on for his final examinations, occurred to him. "If the Austrian had a fatherland why did he prefer all other countries to it? If he had cause to love it, why this deference and reverence towards everything foreign? If Austria had classic writers like Grillparzer, Raimund, Nestroy, Lenau, Stifter, Schnitzer, and Hofmannsthal, why did it make sheep's eyes at Maupassant, Dotoevsky, and Hauptmann? If it was true that Austria dominated the world of music with its Mozart, Haydn, Schubert, Beethoven, Brahms, Johann Strauss, and Bruckner, why the courting of Richard Strauss? If it was not lack of riches it must be a poverty of self-confidence that makes love of country a rare phenomenon in Austria."

Hans remembered every word of what he had written and also the criticism in red ink at the end: "Not unlaudable in train of tought. But delight in contradiction for the sake of contradiction leads to faulty judgment and to a cynical presumptuousness which is alien to Austrian character. From such eulogists may a kindly providence preserve us! The theme is unsatisfactory."

He still went hot and cold when he thought of the disgrace of his final oral examinations. When Professor Miklau, the jailer of his eight years in jail, gave him the passage he was to translate from the Latin, the description of the death of Agrippina from Tacitus, he had remarked, "Alt, Hans, the passage is not easy. But one must have some conscience about sending people like you out into life. I cannot prevent your one day becoming a journalist or engaging in some other frivolous occupation in which to dish up some so-called modern literature. But, by God, I can delay that time!" With this blank cheque of prospective failure, Hans had stood there, dressed in a long, buttoned-up black dress coat and white kid gloves on a painfully hot morning in July in the public hall of the Francis Joseph Gymnasium. It was not any knowledge of the Latin tongue, but the deadly enmity he felt for the slave driver Miklau, which prompted him to succeed in his translation. Afterwards his new dress suit was so permeated with the sweat of his agony that he could never wear it again. The only occasion, however, on which he might have used it would have been at the examinations of the University where attendance was denied to him. Although he had now been declared 'mature' enough to attend it, and although he had implored his father most urgently to let him go there, and had been backed up in this by his mother, it was forbidden him. "You barely scraped through," Papa had declared. "You have no head for science. As soon as possible we must make a useful member of society out of you." Whereupon a cubbyhole was walled off for him next to the cabinet-making in the factory.

As for Papa, Hans now had to admit his superiority in a field he had never been aware of before—that of an expert. He ran his business with minutely detailed practicality and besides had a gift for tonal effects which bordered on creativeness. If Papa had looked on the production of musical instruments a little more from the musician's standpoint and not principally as a turner, wire-drawer, metal-caster, and salesman, Hans could have been on more understanding terms with him. But everywhere he looked he was discouraged. At home it was like living on a volcano; his parents hardly spoke to each other. His affair with Eugenie was dragging along listlessly, the more so as the jealous and ageing woman clung to Hans's youth. As to friends, he was like his mother in this—he had none. When his mother's proposal that his brother Hermann, three years his junior, be put sooner or later in his place in the factory was finally turned down (that Hermann was a vastly better student than Hans was given as the reason for the refusal), he saw the last avenue of escape barred. Nothing now stood between him and the drudgery of a hateful occupation under his father's constant supervision. Finally he was threatened with military service, before which he quailed as he did before any compulsion. He toyed with ideas of suicide, a not unusual game at his age and in his circle.

At this point help came to him from a quarter where he least expected it: from Number 10. Fritz Drauffer, his much older cousin, had engaged him in casual conversation as they walked upstairs together. The subject was Stifter's *Indian Summer*, which Fritz asserted was the most beautiful piece of German prose since Goethe, whereas Hans had preferred Grillparzer's *The Poor Fiddler*. Other conversations followed, and Hans found to his amazement that a delightful man lived under the roof of Number 10. With the enthusiasm he was capable of giving to anything creative, became devoted to his musician cousin; what his prickly pride would not allow him to take from others he accepted from Fritz. He let him call him an idiot, and Fritz apparently had no objection to bring called one himself. In Hans's lifetime Fritz was the first 'grown-up' who had not treated him with arrogance, and consequently his influence was all the greater.

Fritz, for his part, had not yet freed himself from the influence which his idolized Gustav Mahler exercised on him and all young Viennese musicians. He wore his hair like Mahler; in speaking he used the same flowing gestures and the abrupt jerk of the bespectacled head. No wonder, then, that in his opinion he was a mouthpiece for the maestro who had taken him in to play for the rehearsals of the singers. When Vienna let this opera director fall from favor Fritz Drauffer took it as a personal affront and was through with Vienna. He refused to serve under Mahler's successors and preferred to sit at home and fume, to give piano lessons, and to compose an opera for which a young Austrian lyrical poet, Anton Wildgans, wrote the libretto.

Consequently he was quite in the mood to sympathize with another malcontent. "Get it into your head once and for all," he had said encouragingly to Hans, "that you never disturb me. What I am composing is a mess anyhow. The oftener you interrupt me, the better." So they sat together in the congenial atmosphere of the music room, when Hans came home from the factory, at first occasionally and later on nearly every day. Fritz sat on the revolving piano stool, but Hans walked up and down because his restlessness kept him from staying in one place; there were so many questions which as a rule began with the house and wound up far away outside. Fritz would not tolerate the idea that it was a "catastrophe" to work in a famous piano factory, and he emphatically declared that it was the height of nonsense and the arrogance of an imbecile to believe that the "free professions" were preferable to manual labour. He did not even like to hear criticism of the family; in that respect he was surprisingly prejudiced. If Hans pinned a particularly ill-natured remark on Otto Eberhard, then Fritz would look at him over his glasses, twirl around on the piano stool, stop short, and say, "Look here, you are an idiot. You forget that you and I are making other demands on life. What you and I want is to be alone! What your uncle and your father want is to be together!"

"But I don't want to be alone," Hans would contradict. "On the contrary, I want—"

"I know," Fritz would promptly interrupt. "That's why we're talking. Uncle Otto Eberhard—who, by the way, has his merits, although I doubt if you have discovered them yet; after all, absolute propriety is something—is convinced that being together, once you are together, has a higher significance. You either separate at once, or never. Anywhere else than in Austria that would be considered madness. But in Austria there's a method in it. Did it never occur to you that Austria is a compulsory bringing together of people?—of a lot of inhabitants who do not belong together? The Czechs cannot stand the Germans. Nor the Poles the Czechs. Nor the Italians the Germans. Nor the Slovaks the Czechs. Nor the Slovenes the Slovaks. Nor the Ruthenians the Slovenes. Nor the Serbs the Italians. Nor the Romanians the Ruthenians. And of course the Hungarians cannot stand anyone else in the world—'*extra Hungariam non est vita et si est vita, non est ita!*' What you scrambled together in your final examination theme and were so proud of is arrant nonsense. What is an Austrian anyway? There's no such animal! It is a designation thought up by the Hapsburgs to excuse the power of their house. The Austrians are no nation. They are twelve odd nations—that is, none at all. If an Austrian speaks German as you and I do he considers himself the Austrian and imagines meanwhile that the Czech or the Italian or the Pole feels just the way he does, proud of Vienna, the Imperial City, of Mozart, of the waltzes and the local wine. Ridiculous! The Pole in Przemysl or the Italian in Trient or the Bohemian in Budweis has no other thought in his head but the one: How am I to get out of this infernal prison where my own language is not the 'official language' but a second-rate Hindu dialect, where I have it dinned into me from morning to night that I am a third-rate creature, and yet where they force me to serve for three years in the army and to pay taxes all my life for the first-class creatures, the Viennese? What is a Frenchman? A man who speaks French and feels French. What is an Austrian? A man who speaks Ruthenian or Slovak and is supposed to feel Viennese! And for what reason, I ask you, you mature Austrian? Because at some remote time—I am weak on dates—the Turks threatened us, and it seemed reasonable to gather together any nations that were handy and throw them in for our defence. The Turkish peril— you learned that, and I learned that. It was the 'Mission of

Austria,' and the Italian and the Czech agreed to it. It was better to be Hapsburg than Turkish. But what, pray tell me, is going to convince him in this day and generation that it is better for him to be governed by Francis Joseph, to have unpleasant neighbors living unpleasantly with him, instead of being independent in his own house or at least on his own floor people of his own choosing? That is what I mean by being let alone. You can interpret it, incidentally, in terms of the spirit as Well as in those of a nation."

Thereupon Hans would be shocked into reflection and then say, "Then you don't want to be an Austrian?"

And with an indignant toss of his head Fritz would reply, "Haven't you any ear, you unmusical wretch? I never even breathed such a thing. I never under any circumstances whatsoever want to be anything but an Austrian. When my train pulls into the Anhalter station in Berlin exactly on time, and I am offered the first fruits of German thoroughness, my stomach turns, and I long for our own sloppiness. When I go to the opera in Paris I bless every Viennese box usher. I thumb my nose at American civilization where they shoot into the sky in an 'elevator' and with their skyscraping civilization smother culture. But I am an Austrian who realizes that Austria exists only for the House of Hapsburg and the Viennese. Perhaps for Salzburgers too."

Or he would say, "Don't you believe your grandfather Stein! He is a very shrewd man, but alas, he is a liberal patriot of the stamp of the historian Friedjung, and consequently confuses Francis Joseph with Joseph II. In all seriousness! He thinks Francis Joseph is an underestimated monarch! But our Emperor is a disgrace. He actually said to an American President, 'You see in me the last monarch of the old school,' and was proud of the disgrace! For that old school of monarchy was firmly convinced that it was the duty of subjects to sacrifice themselves for the dynasty instead of the other way round. It also believed, because it upheld the impersonal conception of empire or kingdom, that the emperor or king stood above every one and was unimpeachable, even when he was a nonentity. Take Queen Victoria, the feminine counterpart of Francis Joseph, only cleverer. In all his life the fact has never penetrated Francis Joseph's skull that there could exist any Austrian patriotism which is not bound up with devotion to his person. And in this fixed belief that it is the dynasty which stands above national interest he has completely forgotten what Joseph II knew a hundred years ago: that a dynasty is a unifying idea only so long as its subjects prosper. But to take and not to give in return is a fatal error. To rule is to give!"

Hans was beginning to see things and people from this point of view now and had ceased to demand that thistles produce roses (a phrase favored by Fritz), when events transpired in the Wiedner Hauptstrasse factory which the liberal *Press of Vienna* at first completely ignored and later covered with a few lines in smallest type.

It was only *The Workers' Journal*, the organ of the Socialist movement developing in the train of the industrialization of Austria, which featured the occurrence. *The London Times* sent a special reporter to Vienna, and a New York paper had their correspondent cable a report to which they put the heading "A Historic Day for the World." A special article in the Paris *Figaro* seemed, however, to link the happenings of Monday, September 17, 1910, with a demonstration on the previous Sunday which led thousands of Viennese to go out to the Vienna Woods.

These Viennese, wrote the French journalist M. Mercier, had gone out there as harmless holidaymakers, taking their wives and children and picnic baskets as on any ordinary Sunday, and had come back as rebels. Their excursion was undertaken in connection with the tenth anniversary of the death of a certain Joseph Schoeffel, who, in the 1870's, had succeeded in blocking a capitalistic enterprise to cut down the Vienna Woods. That the loveliest woods in the world still provide cool green refreshment to a world capital, the only one which lies as it were in a forest, is to the immortal credit of that same Schoieffel: so said the poetic Frenchman. Yet the modern-day generation of Viennese do not even know his name. They accept the millions of beech trees, elms, and oaks covering the gentle hills in front of their very doors as a matter of course. Wherefore, then, this sudden decision to honor this forgotten man, to whom, to be sure, a monument was erected somewhere, although not two Viennese put of a hundred could say where?

M. Mercier's question was logical. But his report left the answer in the air. He confirmed the fact that on Sunday evening thousands of lanterns and flaming torches were carried by people on the Kahlenberg Heights overlooking Vienna and they sang and yelled all sorts of things. Among others, "Hurrah for Schoeffel! Long live the Second Internationale!" The first cry had seldom been heard and the second never before in Vienna, and neither apparently had the slightest relation to the other. The police, arriving too late on the scene, found, in any event, no reason to interfere, except in the case of three particularly vociferous young men whose names the Parisian columnist rescued from oblivion. They were Berg, Ebeseder, and Oppenheim. Berg and Oppenheim were University students; Ebeseder was at the Academy of Painting.

Whether by coincidence or not, on the following Monday there were four instances of unrest in Vienna factories. They occurred in the Urban and Brévillier screw factory, the two hardware factories, Felton-Guillaume and Brand and Lhuillier, and the C. Alt piano factory.

When Hans, on this morning, appeared in the Wiedner Hauptstrasse building shortly after the hateful reminder emitted by the factory whistle, it struck him that the workday noises were not as much in evidence as usual. But blue

Mondays were not an exception. Yet at seven forty-five (Papa arrived on the dot of eight o'clock) it was obvious that no work was being done either in the wire-drawing or metal-casting departments; the hammering of the cabinetmakers was the only customary sound. Hans's head was full of more important things, for he had evolved the idea of suggesting to his father that he should allow him to take an evening course at the University. He could hardly refuse him, since the classes began only after factory hours. Uneasy at last over the quiet, he left his bleak task of compiling export statistics to go down to the cellar and investigate what the matter was.

He was not popular with the workers. Papa's insincere efforts to make him so upset him, and the inhibitions he succumbed to whenever he was unsure of himself contributed to this unpopularity. To the workers, as he well knew, he was nothing but the owner's son and the future proprietor, and therefore his father's pretence that he was just another worker seemed quite false. To be sure, after he finished school, he had skimmed through the various factory departments as an apprentice. But only skimmed through—and now he had a little office of his own where he engaged in writing but no manual labour. He attempted to conceal his feeling that he was an intruder and that he had neither fondness for nor interest in the enterprise of his forbears, because he considered it tactless to demand work of others which you do not like to do yourself. And he was equally determined not to inveigle himself into their good graces. Since he felt that they despised him, he was as reserved with the workers as he had been with his schoolmates for eight years.

Four of them came towards him. They were still in their street clothes, and started to pass him without any greeting to go upstairs to the first floor.

"What's going on here, Czerny?" he asked, for it seemed to him they might have said "Good morning."

"That's just it. Not a thing," was the reply of the man he had addressed; and his three companions laughed, as did the others in the vaulted cellar. The casemates echoed.

"Is your father upstairs yet?" asked the same man, a foreman of the wire-drawers.

"I don't know," Hans answered. "Do you want to see him?" The man admitted that they were on their way to the boss. "Come on. Let's get going," he said, turning to the other three in whom Hans recognized the foremen of the metal-casters. And to the others, standing idly around in their work clothes in the cellar, which was artificially lighted despite the fact that it was a sunny day, he added: "Now, fellows, watch out! Don't stir till we get back. And don't listen to anyone. Not even to the young master here!" With that the four men went on up the stairs.

Hans lingered irresolutely in the subterranean workshops. He felt that the workers' eyes were on his face, and he was ashamed of blushing. His position seemed to him so ridiculous that, because of his inner dread of derision, he made himself ask, "You gentlemen apparently are in a bad humor?" It sounded arrogant.

No one answered him.

He sensed that he must assert himself. "I spoke to you," he said sharply.

"We have nothing to say to you," came the retort. Hans noticed that it was made by Bochner, a metal-caster, but he acted as though he did not know who spoke. With the same presence of mind which his mother could produce in critical moments he said, in the silence which had fallen: "That is too bad. I don't know what you have on your minds, but it might not have been a bad idea on your part to take me into your confidence." Whereupon he went back to his ground-floor cubbyhole, on either side of which the turners and the cabinet-makers were busily at work.

His grandfather Stein used to introduce his lecture on the philosophy of law with these words: "The fate of the world may ever and again be determined according to whether some individual or other at a given moment has dined, digested, or slept well or badly." At this moment it was determined by the fact that the apprentice and heir of the C. Alt Piano-maker Firm felt himself to be despised. His being looked upon as a fifth wheel to the coach had been carried too far. This was rather illogical, however; for he did not have any exaggerated opinion of himself. He settled down to adding up the number of grand pianos and concert grands which had been exported to Belgium in February. Then the sound of voices suddenly struck his ears with such force that he gave up his figuring. He knew his father's flaring temper. After a while he went upstairs to the first floor.

It was on the first floor, where Great-grandfather Christopher's own apartments had been, that the offices of the firm were situated. Until recently Papa had had his private office next to the salesroom on the ground floor, immediately beyond the glass door, and this was where Great-grandfather and Grandfather Alt had sat until their deaths. The chief clerk, Mr. Foedermayer, however, had convinced that this was no longer a suitable place for the head of such an important enterprise. Every Tom, Dick, and Harry should not be able to step from the street right into the sanctum of a purveyor to the Imperial and Royal Court.

When Hans entered his father was sitting at his desk. Mr. Foedermayer, with his face even more drawn than usual, stood beside him, and the four workmen faced them. Papa was saying to Czerny, "Anyone who does not like it here can go. I'm not obliging any one to stay. That is my final word!" To his son he said with equal violence, "What do you want here?"

"I thought," Hans began shyly, and wanted to add, "that I might be of help to you." If Franz had let him finish his sentence

Professor Stein's theory about the trivial causes precipitating world events would have had one less confirmation. But in his present state of indignation the head of the firm imagined that his ever-recalcitrant son was against him and intended to take up the cudgels for the opposing side. If for no other reason he must make an example of him. The boy should see what authority was.

"You can think less and work more!" he yelled at him. "That goes for you too, you men! And now clear out—the whole lot of you!"

The foreman Czerny said to Hans, "Thank you, sir. That was very decent of you. But we'll be able to settle with your father without your help." And the four of them went on out.

"What are you still standing there for?" Papa roared. And with that the spark of understanding, kindled in Hans by his sense of being scorned by the workers earlier and by Fritz's influence over him, was promptly smothered. His only reaction to this yelling at one another, and the implication that the louder voice carried the better argument, was opposition. Without a word he left the room.

Meanwhile the turners and cabinet-makers had laid down their tools. From his nook, to which he had returned, Hans heard them all go down together to the cellar. Then for a while silence reigned. Fritz's saying, that of two people who disagree both are right, did not apply to Papa's case, thought Hans. Papa was always wrong. Even if he were to say that twice two is four it would not be so.

Then he heard a loud voice from below which he took to be that of Czerny, the foreman: " … lacking in all understanding and appreciation for other classes or other people … rigid … unbending … sticks to the letter of the contract when the basis for it has completely changed with the passing of time … He says he is our friend. No one who distrusts you is your friend. He is our enemy, and so are all of his kind." And constantly interlarded was the expression "Comrades!"

This man was saying almost word for word what Hans was thinking. No one who distrusts you is your friend. No one who lacks not only the power but also the will to understand you. He hurried down into the cellar. There stood Czerny, on a platform improvised out of two wooden cases, haranguing away with large gestures. When Hans appeared they ostentatiously made way for him.

"In the presence of the future owner of the factory, who has more social consciousness than his father, I call on you to vote on our motion," said the speaker, and as they were crying, "Hooray for Alt Junior," Hans said:

"I want to tell you that I feel exactly as you do."

"Hear! Hear!" called Bochner, the metal-caster.

"I hope you won't think that I came here to seek your applause," Hans went on, instinctively uncomfortable at being in the foreground. "I came because I feel that I have to do what I can to convince my father that you are right." He was on the point of saying that his father was a person who meant well but from whom you could get nothing by force, when the police appeared at the entrances to the cellar shops. "No one move!" came the order.

One man yelled, "Shame!" Then every voice took up the cry, "Shame!" Had there been but one man among them all— the police put the count at ninety-two—who might have been willing to go back to work, the fact that the police had been called in now made them all irreconcilable.

The police officer in charge, a lieutenant, acted as though he were preparing an army roll call, and began to take down Christian and surnames, dates of birth, religion, and home addresses.

But before he had finished with the first one Czerny, the foreman, asked, "Just what are you doing here? We were quietly discussing a weekly pay increase of fifty hellers. We had a perfect right to do that."

"We were informed that you were planning a strike," replied the police lieutenant.

"We have a perfect right to do that too," declared Czerny.

"No," answered the lieutenant. "That would have been a criminal extortion."

"I'd like to see you prove that!" Czerny said. "Now in the textile strike in Glasgow—"

"We're not in Britain," the lieutenant cut him short. "According to our criminal code, a strike is a crime of extortion, and inciting to strike is inciting to a crime of extortion. Which of you is called Anton Czerny?"

The foreman acknowledged that that was his name. The three other foremen, also called up, acknowledged theirs. They were declared under arrest.

"And what is your name?" Hans was asked.

"He had nothing to do with it," explained Czerny.

For the second time Hans blushed. The first time it was at the unbelievable cowardice of his father's calling the police. Now it was because of the protection offered him for nothing.

"He was making a speech when we came in," contradicted the lieutenant. "How was it that he was making a speech if he had nothing to do with it!"

It was only now Hans learned that the whole incident was caused by a difference in wages amounting to fifty hellers a week. On the other hand, the fact was known to him that the export balance of the firm of C. Alt had shown a net profit of seventy-four thousand crowns for the last six months.

He said nothing, but went with the others. That Papa had not even put in an appearance made him most indignant of all.

As they were being escorted into the waiting green patrol wagon a shot was fired which wounded the lieutenant in the arm. Immediately afterwards Bochner, the metal-caster, was thrown into the wan with the others.

Towards three in the afternoon the workers of the metal-shops of Urban and Brévillier, Felton-Guillaume, Brand and Lhuillier, the Floridsdorf Locomotive Works, the United Machine Shops, the Wiener Neustaedter Machine Shops, left and walked four abreast down the Ring Boulevard. When they reached Schwarzenberg Square they were joined by more than a thousand workers from the Landstrasse and Ottakring districts, from the Dreher, Mautner von Markhof, and Kuffner breweries. They carried placards, inscribed by hand, with the words; "A strike is not extortion!" "Working Vienna, awake!" "Long live the Second Internationale!" and "Down with Reaction!" Before the demonstrators reached the Parliament building they were met by two squadrons of mounted police, who drove a wedge in them and forced them off into the outlying districts. One hundred and twelve participants in the demonstration were ridden down by the police, of whom ninety-five men and four women died. By evening order was restored.

Hans, spending the night in the Elizabeth Promenade Police Prison, knew nothing of all this. The prison was a new structure, and it still smelled of paint and plaster in the immense hall into which the new arrivals were put, but Hans preferred that odour to those of the drunks who lay on benches along the walls, sleeping off their sprees. The society of beggars, vagrants, pickpockets, and prostitutes, with whom he now found himself and in whose company he was obliged to remain until the regular morning hearing in court, was less frightening to him than it was repulsive. It was less a sense of fear, too, that possessed him than one of fresh bewilderment. That others too were in conflict with his father did not make his own conflict easier, and the fact that their conflict was vastly more important than his was something he was unwilling to admit, nor could he see any solution.

Huddled in a corner, his legs drawn up, his hat pulled low

over his forehead so that the light and the evil smells would not be too annoying, he told himself that he had nothing to do with the people here nor they with him. Not with Czerny, not with any of the others. They were common, coarse, smelly, and had no use for the things that were important to him. Moreover, they were his born enemies. It was ridiculous that he was sitting there as though he belonged to them.

But Fritz said once (or was it Ebeseder?): man is innocent of one thing only, and guilty of everything else. That one thing is his birth. The longer Hans sat there and tried to sleep, the more that saying, which earlier had never meant much to him, stuck in his mind. "We too should have preferred to be born rich," Czerny had said to Papa. That was clear. That fellow over there, who reeked a yard away of cheap liquor, could not help that he had not come into the world as the son of a piano-maker, or as an archduke, or as a young Baron Rothschild. Consequently …

The "consequently" opened such an immeasurable train of corollaries that the perplexed youth made renewed efforts to get to sleep. Would Papa have told Mother where he was? It was incomprehensible that he had called the police to his aid! He might have discharged the men. He could have given them time to think things over …

His thoughts blurred, he fell asleep. But something awakened him at once; at least it seemed to him that it was at once. In any case, he now remained awake. Recalling the thought that was in his mind before he fell asleep, he pursued it. His head was clear now. There was one question of responsibility to be answered. Did the fact that these ragged and drunken creatures were not responsible for having been born make others responsible? Whom? Their parents, of course. And who was to blame for them? Their parents, of course. He realized that this was a shabby solution, and he decided to state the question differently. Since these creatures had been born into the world as beggars through no fault of their own, was the world responsible for letting them go on being beggars? Since they could not help their parents being poor and I cannot help my parents being rich—Hans hesitated before reaching the conclusion he felt impelled to accept—then they have a claim. On whom? On me?

In the twilight of early morning which cast a pallid light over these pitiful beings this new problem presented itself to him with such harshness and trenchancy that again he closed his eyes on it. Until now no one had made him see it or even guess that it existed. Neither at home nor in school had there ever been any talk of it. It was not to be found in his favorite books. Schnitzer's heroes were well-to-do middle-class burghers. Hofmannsthal's heroes were classic Greeks or modern princes. Thomas Mann told the stories of problem sons of patricians. To have the problems which arose in popular novels their heroes were obliged to have money. People who had no money did not appear either in books or in polite conversation. One simply did not associate with them. It was a sort of Stigma. Mother called poor persons just "the people." The inscription over the main entrance to the Liechtenstein Gallery, which he often saw in passing, was couched in these words: "To Art, to Artists—I, Prince of Liechtenstein."

"I'd like to know what you are doing in this mess!" exploded Uncle Otto Eberhard, to whose office Hans had been taken after being put through an inconclusive police hearing early in the morning. "It's a disgrace and a scandal!"

He laid the morning edition of the *Catholic Reichspost* in front of Hans, having marked with a blue pencil the following lines: "An old and renowned manufactory of musical instruments in the Fourth District was the source of the lamentable disturbances of yesterday."

"That it's a disgrace and a scandal not to give those poor

devils fifty hellers more a week and that instead the police were called in, yes!" boldly retorted Hans, tense and feverish from being rushed at thus.

Otto Eberhard had recently celebrated his seventieth birthday. With all the honor due to a man of his merit, proper notice had been taken of the occasion; there were brief articles in the newspapers, a eulogy by the Minister of Justice, and the cross of a commander of the Order of Francis Joseph was graciously conferred on him. His whiskers, trimmed with painful precision on either side of his shapely and slightly wrinkled face, no longer had a single dark hair in them. The carefully parted hair on his head was also quite white now, and its silvery sheen was reminiscent of his dead aunt Sophie. In general his likeness to her was emerging as Otto Eberhard's cheeks grew thinner and his always erect body grew lighter.

"You look a sight," he said to his nephew, whose appearance had suffered from the night spent in the lock-up. After a pause, in which he drew a handkerchief from an inside pocket, unfolded it, touched his lips to it, and then carefully restored it to its resting-place, he leaned across to where his nephew sat opposite him. The scent of Eau de Cologne, which he liked to diffuse, grew stronger. "In other words you admit a connection with these people!" he now concluded.

"It's so mean!" his nephew declared.

"What do you consider so mean?" Otto Eberhard asked.

"Papa makes hundreds of thousands out of his factory! He could have agreed to the fifty hellers for them and felt the loss of it less than that!" Hans said, flicking off a blade of straw which had clung to his sleeve from the previous night.

The uncle followed the wisp of straw with his eyes. "Then you think it's only a question of fifty hellers?"

"But that is absolutely clear, Uncle!"

Then, with a tone of finality which greatly impressed the excited youth, the Public Prosecutor declared: "In that assumption you are fundamentally wrong. It is neither a question of fifty hellers nor of five thousand crowns. It is not even a question of money, but of something beyond all price, the loss of which one would feel not as little as that dirt you have not yet fully removed from your disordered clothing, but would suffer from even more painfully than a deadly illness. It is a question of the principle of justice in making a demand. Since life consists of making demands, it is a question of life itself."

"Yet they had justice on their side in asking for an increase in wages," Hans put in rather uncertainly. "They say that meat and bread prices have risen 25 percent, and they ask for a 16 percent, rise!"

"That is their version. But you overlook something. Since Herr Victor Adler abstracts from their wages as much as he thinks he needs to run his Social Democratic party machine and thereby enable himself to play his part, this is already the third increase in wages which they have demanded. The third in two years. Did your informants tell you that?"

Hans began to have a sense of inferiority in the face of this impeccably dressed man who had not a speck of dust about him nor a grain of doubt about the order of things. One never could prove one's point to Uncle Otto Eberhard. It had always been that way. "I know that one can't live on such wages," Hans insisted.

"Really? And how do you know that?" His questioner appeared determined not to tolerate any emotion, and to maintain the rarefied atmosphere of a supreme court in which humanity is fanned to make way for principles. "If the workers did not have to make the payments required of them, not by their employers but by Herr Adler, they would at all times have abundant means. They may not, as they say in their jargon, 'have enough to gorge,' but they have more than enough even now, as proved by police statistics, to get drunk on."

"The party dues are to their advantage!" Hans said.

"Possibly. That's not entirely out of the question. At least those benefactors of humanity, Messrs. Adler, Ebeseder, and Oppenheim, maintain that is the case. You went to school, if I'm not mistaken, with young Ebeseder, the son of the secretary to the party?"

"Yes. Why do you ask?"

"It crossed my mind. He's under indictment for *lèse-majesté* and rioting."

"He's the decentest sort of man."

"He'll be given every opportunity to prove himself one. But let us stick to the subject. We were speaking of the justice of making demands. There are—and this is something I wish you would bear clearly in mind—limits to the means employed in making demands.

"Whoever cloaks his demand with extortion puts himself in the wrong, even if his demand were justified. For any demand, even an unjust one, could be extorted by a strike. Do you grasp that?"

Hans hesitated to express himself when confronted with so much accumulated logic even though to him it seemed to contain a rift. He made an effort to discover that rift.

"I see that you're thinking it over," his uncle said. "I shall help you. Is it clear to you that it is not the workers in your father's factory who are fomenting a strike but Messrs. Victor Adler, Ebeseder and Oppenheim? That it's not your foreman Czerny who thinks that wages should be raised but these other gentlemen? Have you understood that?"

"Naturally," Hans said.

"It is less natural than you imagine. In fact, it is absolutely unnatural. Nature creates degrees. An oak is higher than a bush. The lion is bigger than a worm. Messrs. Adler and comrades—who since yesterday arrogate to themselves the right to rule in Austria—are, to put it in exaggeratedly polite terms, inferior to His Majesty the Emperor. His Majesty the Emperor governs in Austria. Not Herr Adler."

"I thought that Parliament governed in Austria," Hans contradicted. The infinite arrogance in his uncle's every word so embittered him that he could not find the demolishing retort he sought.

"I congratulate you on the results of your association with our home-grown Beethoven Fritz!" Otto Eberhard remarked scornfully. "Yes, Parliament governs. But it is a callow Parliament which carries Parliamentarianism to absurdity because its conduct reminds one of nothing so much as the antics of a lot of young scamps during recess at school. Therefore His Majesty keeps finding himself obliged to pack these scamps, who call themselves representatives, off home and to take the measures which are dictated to him by his wisdom. Do you propose to say that Herr Adler should prescribe to His Majesty?"

"If he knows better," said Hans, who thought he at last had his answer ready. "What makes you think the Emperor knows better than Herr Adler?"

Whereupon a deathly silence fell. Otto Eberhard, who was in the process of lighting a Virginia, had to lay the long, thin black cigar aside for a moment, his hand trembled so. "That exceeds all comprehension!" he exclaimed.

Meanwhile in the next room an exchange of words became audible, and immediately afterwards Henriette entered the lawyer's office, into which the morning sun was now throwing its full rays.

"I beg your pardon!" the old gentleman said indignantly. "I am in conference!"

But the mother had rushed over to her son and now held him close in her arms.

"Henriette," Otto Eberhard said to his sister-in-law, "I must urgently insist that you leave me alone with this young man. We're not through yet."

"He has done nothing!" answered the frandc mother. "I shall not leave until you promise me that nothing will happen to him!" Otto Eberhard nodded. "It's a matter of form," he said with disgust. That was all.

"It really would be better, Mother, if you waited outside for a little," Hans put in. It made him shy for her to embrace him and plead for him. This was no family matter, and he was no longer a baby.

But Henriette thought differently. With flashing eyes she measured her old adversary. "I don't see why I should leave the room! I am his mother. I know him better than you. He has done nothing wrong!"

"Victor Adler, David Oppenheim, and Company," remarked the elderly gentleman, omitting Ebeseder, the one Christian, from the list. "All that has its natural reasons," he added, in case anyone might doubt his meaning.

Here, however, he had taken a step beyond what was favorable for the purpose he was pursuing. Hans's opposition, which had died down with his embarrassment, now flared up violently and, hot with anger, he said: "Just when you sent for me, Uncle, the police official was saying that all I had to do was to explain that I only spoke to the workers on Papa's behalf and that I was on the point of offering them to mediate, when the police arrived. If I do that then the incident would be closed and my arrest was made in error."

"And you will make that statement forthwith," assumed Otto. Eberhard, his mouth drawn down in the corners with exasperation.

"I refuse to make it!" Hans contradicted.

"Don't be crazy!" his mother warned. She had been through a similar situation in her own life. An old and inimical man had demanded a statement from her and she had refused to make it. She was twenty-two then. Now she was forty-five. Twenty-three years make a difference.

Otto Eberhard rose. He was almost taller than his late aunt Sophie and stood just as erect. "I am not interested in your statements," he said to Hans, laying a world of distance between himself and the other two. It was the same world he had disapproved of when his brother first let himself be taken in by this pretty face. Not even the face was pretty any more. The unmerciful morning light brought out lines and shadows, emphasizing them unnecessarily. *Jewesses age early*, the lawyer reflected. "Take your offspring along with you," he said. "He does you absolute credit." And to Hans he remarked, in a tone of finality: "You are not going to do any play-acting for me. If your unfortunate father allows anything of the kind, that's his affair."

"You're neglecting your duty, Uncle!" countered the emboldened boy, now stung to the quick. "I declare—and you, Mother, are a witness—that what I said to the workers was that they were in the right!"

"It is eight-thirty," called the Aulic Councillor and Public Prosecutor through a speaking tube, which put him in direct communication with his associate in the next room without his being obliged to have recourse to that distasteful instrument— a telephone. "And I must go to the Minister of Justice. Will you kindly look after this lady and gentleman for as long as they care to remain?" He took up his stiff felt hat, gloves, and brief case and left. He was on his way to present to the Minister of Justice a projected law entitled "A Supplementary Statute to Paragraph 98 of the Penal Code," which ran as follows: "In accordance with Paragraph 14 of the Fundamental Law of December 21, 1867, I hereby order: In amendment of Paragraph 98 of the Penal Code strikes are to be considered a crime of extortion. Strikes, interruptions of work, slowing up of work, which serve as a violent means to obtain demands, shall henceforth be classed as crimes *sui generis*. Such crimes and incitement to them will be punished by death and attempted crimes with up to twenty years of imprisonment with hard labour." Francis Joseph's signature to this document, to be countersigned by the Minister of Justice, would, such was Otto Eberhard's hope, finally restore the criminally impaired limits of decency. And although the Imperial signature was not forthcoming, the rumor of the Minister's having signed it, which spread like wildfire, was sufficient to precipitate a train of development which became known as the "Battle of Vienna for the human rights of the Proletariat" and which spread from Vienna to the rest of the world.

"Do you know what the worst of it all is?" Henriette asked when she and Hans were out in that same Court Boulevard where no signs remained of the fact that on the day before people had been ridden down and *killed* here under the hooves of horses. "That everything turns out to be exactly what it seemed in the very first instant. No one is mistaken!" She was thinking of Franz and of her own life.

"I am not so sure," her son answered doubtfully. A red spot on the hoarding near which they stood as they waited for the tram might just as well be color as blood. In any case, it was in keeping that the advertisement announcing the two hundred and fiftieth celebration performance of *The Merry Widow* should be printed in red letters. "Isn't it perhaps worse that every one is convinced he is right?" he asked.

He was thinking of his father, of Fritz, of Otto Eberhard, of the drunks in the lock-up, of himself, and of his schoolmate Ebeseder. If he had a spark of decency he would try to do something about him at once. But he had to go at once to the factory where he would see his father. What if he couldn't 'mediate'? What if he couldn't convince his father, who was so convinced of being right, that he was in the wrong? What if he used his authority to compel him to give in? What if everything went on unchanged as before? "No," Hans said, correcting himself, "the worst of all is that in spite of everything, everything is allowed to go on as if nothing had happened. What should really be done to stop this terrible state of affairs?" He put the question more to himself than to her.

She replied, "Nothing. It always goes on." She was thinking of Rudolf and of death.

CHAPTER 24
The Origin of All

Contrary to all expectations, Franz took a conciliatory attitude towards his eldest son. Perhaps the fact that he was responsible for Hans's having been arrested accounted for it; perhaps it was an attempt on his part, obviously in evidence since the Monday strike, to appear impartial and strictly fair. The threatened dismissals had been rescinded. When Vienna industry, after various sanguinary incidents in the provinces, resumed its course he even declared that he was ready "of his own free will" to raise wages. The rise consisted, not of fifty, but of twenty-five hellers per hand a week.

Not satisfied with that, he went on, in this sudden and remarkable display of tolerance, to sign a petition Hans was sending to the district recruiting office with the request for a postponement of his military service until he had finished his studies. That amounted to giving his consent to Hans's taking afternoon and evening courses at the University. What Papa's reason was for this unexpected attitude, Hans could not guess. It did not occur to him that it might simply be the way, the way of Franz Alt the man, to show remorse without admtting it. And he was too happy over the postponement of his military service, which had always filled him with terror since hearing Fritz's stories of barracks life, to go on cudgelling his brains about Papa. Postponed for four whole years! Any price was worth paying for that, even sitting on school benches again.

And if his luck held then his younger brother Hermann, who in his last years the Kalksburg Institute fortunately was turning out to be a mediocre scholar, might be slipped into his stead in the factory. As it developed, when things went wrong Papa gave in. So Hans registred for a course (under Professor Guido Adler) in the history of music, since that was vaguely related to piano-making; moreover, in order to fill the requisite number of academic hours, he took three courses open as electives to Austrian students of philosophy: Ethics (under Professor Jodl), Philosophy of Religion (under the world preacher Laurence Muellner), and Analysis of Dream Life (under Professor Sigmund Freud). To forestall any change of heart on Papa's part he went through the matriculation formalities with utmost speed, so that barely two weeks after the strike he found himself in possession of the gray 'index' booklet which made him a student of the Universitas Literaris Vindobonensis.

The thing he had not dared to hope for happened. His university studies, which he had undertaken to avoid the army and the factory, made another person of him. What a contrast between this and high school! Of course there were dark spots. Guido Adler was full of bombast, and Jodi was dry. And the duelling fraternity students were simply intolerable. With their scars on their faces, ridiculous little caps on their heads, black, red, and gold ribbons across their chests, they rioted around, attacking in turn the Czechs, the Jews, the Italians, swinging their knobby canes until blood flowed. If you could not avoid sitting at one of their *Kommers*, as they called their evening gatherings in restaurants, you were literally made sick by it. They obliged you to drink an immense mug of beer down to the last drop in one draught, and not just one, but one after another, something which to them seemed German and manly. On the other hand, how fascinating it was to attend the Muellner lectures, where none of the hard-drinking rowdies ever strayed, and to discover that there is no such thing as chance, but that everything which had been created or had occurred is obeying the law of necessity! When Hans had time free to do so he went to the lectures of his grandfather, who taught constitutional law with peerless wit; he assigned to the state the part of service and to the people in the state the part of governing. In the lectures of Freud, however, he experienced at first an almost physical revulsion; the very theme of them seemed to him to be a constant infringement of his sense of modesty. Later he succumbed to the personality of the lecturer, whose whole teaching radiated the inner purity of his diagnostic fantasy and lucidity.

This was the first time in Hans's life when the intellect talked to him. Until now the things that had held appeal for him were personal experience or routine or prejudice, or the cynicism of that peculiarly Viennese trick of justifying a witticism in order to be able to express one. Suddenly, in this engaging city of Vienna, where the saying "We shall never stand in need of any judge" was as current as an act of compromise, he found himself face to face with spirit pure and simple, which was incapable of concessions because it did not know them. He had been drawn to Fritz earlier because he sensed in him talent and opposition; but here he felt strongly that the same thing was raised to a much higher degree—to genius and conviction. It was an entirely different world. For the first time he was not obliged to accept teachings as something already proved, but he could be a helper and a witness in the process of their creation. This was what he, who as a child had loved to take things apart, had longed for all his life. But he had never dreamed that reintegration could be so absorbing or learning such a source of enjoyment. His attention was drawn to a girl who sat in front of him in Professor Muellner's classes and on the same bench with him in Professor Freud's. She was one of the few women students at the University at that time, and he was struck by the fact that she evinced equal enthusiasm for Muellner the preacher and Freud the sceptic, even before he was aware that she was pretty.

A few days later he had to admit that he had been mistaken in his estimate of her looks. She was not pretty, she was beautiful; but only, he realized, at certain times. Her beauty was like a light which she could turn on and off almost at will. There were days when her gray eyes—her quite remarkable eyes, the source of her curious power and the mirror of all her moods—seemed restive and unhappy. At such times she could seem even plain; at any rate, lacking in that radiance which made such an impression on him. A smile, however, could change her appearance completely. It lit her face up, beginning with her rather lofty brow, taking all suggestion of sharpness from her thin but finely chiselled nose, softening the line of her cheeks.

Her incandescence was not due solely to her eyes or her great warmth of smile. She had traits making it impossible for him to his eyes away from her: a way of tossing her head back to free her brow of the reddish-brown hair which made a careless fringe above it; a constant grace of pose which gave her thin and almost boyish body an attraction far above the healthy curves of most of the girls he knew; a light manner of walking, as though she moved without conscious effort. He was constantly surprised at the daring which had prompted her to wear her hair short, an almost unheardof thing; so short, in fact, that it revealed the shape of her head.

Once day the truth flashed on him: She was like an actress; a natural actress, however, still unaware of this power to project herself and her moods, but the more successful on that account.

Her name was Selma Rosner, and she was not yet nineteen. He found in a very few days that he had fallen passionately in love with her. There now began for him a time when he could not imagine that he had ever despised or cursed a single hour a single hour of this life. For him now life was magnificent. Vienna was like a perfect dream. To study was enchantment. Selma Rosner had done this for him; she had come into his life like a miracle.

She spoke to no one except the professors, and to them, in class, she gave irritatingly independent answers. She seemed to be constantly on the defensive, to assert herself and guard against the ridicule to which she was subject as a woman student among men. The first time Hans spoke to her for the purpose of asking her for a formula by Muellner that he had missed, she dictated it to him by memory and made further conversation impossible by her almost offensive curtness. This was repeated on a second attempt. Finally, though, they did get into a debate over the formula theory.

Hans maintained that Muellner's philosophy had a touch of genius. Selma thought that amount of praise was an "overdose." She would call it at best, so she explained, a system but not a philosophy, then she interrupted herself quickly and said: "We are playing Goethe and Schiller!" He did not know at once what she meant until she reminded him that the first conversation between Goethe and Schiller, on the subject of the plant prototype, was initiated in almost the same fashion. With the girls of his acquaintance he could talk about nothing but tennis or society chitchat. And even his mother was no exception to the rule; and Eugenie only said, "I'm too old for you!" in order to have him reply, "No, you're young!" So he was all the more impressed with Selma. Without betraying it, however, he answered, "I trust our conversation will bear the same fruits in friendship."

"Do you say that because it also grew out of aversion?"

"Certainly not on my side," he told her bluntly.

"Thanks. Do you find it incredible that I should have thought so? I don't enjoy too much sympathy around here."

Was this now real or ironical again? "I should feel sorry if you took the ragging here to heart," he said stiffly. After all, a man had his pride.

"I don't," she answered lightly. "Thanks just the same."

That brought the conversation to a close.

It was shortly resumed when Selma, in reply to a question by Professor Muellner concerning basic motives for human reactions, gave fear as the origin of all; whereas the professor wished fear, love, joy, hunger, and revenge to be considered as reasons of equal validity. But Selma's position was that the four others were only "derivative," having their origin in the one primary feeling of fear. The argument that arose in class on this point was carried on after the lecture was over.

"That's nonsense!" Hans declared. "Do you intend by that to make fear the father of all things?"

"That's what it is," Selma told him and smiled in her surprisingly transforming way.

They were standing by a window in the high marble hall of the University, which led into the vaulted court containing the marble busts of dead men of learning.

Her smile and the change it brought about in her bewildered him. He was still easily upset. He would have given anything to have the brain behind that fine high brow finally take cognizance of his existence. She must at last—and despite her so-called "inferiority complex," which Professor Freud was always bringing up and which she obviously over-compensated for with her brightness—realize that she had made an impression on him. More than any other girl he had ever met. He was discovering to his delight that she was marvellously clever, that he could talk to her on any subject. Why he could even ask her for advice, a man of a mere girl! To be loved by such a person—He decided to give up this silly beating about the bush. If he went on in this fashion she would be right and fear really was at the base of everything.

"How do you explain love?" he asked. "You can't possibly

assert that love derives from fear? Revenge—well, I'll concede that point. But love certainly not. Nor hunger!" he added quickly.

"I most certainly do assert it," she said, with her usual outrageous self-confidence. "The first sound that a human being utters is a cry. He cries because the light hurts him. In any case he doesn't cry because of love, joy, hunger, or revenge. When man is one second old he has no desire for revenge, and presumably no appetite. He cries because he's afraid of life. Similarly, fear is the cause of his last sound, his last gesture. Because man is afraid of death. In between lies existence. As for love, it derives in the first instance from the fear of not pleasing. Think it over."

If only she had not said, "Think it over," with that outrageous superiority! She had no conception of how deeply he had been stirred by her fear hypothesis. Yet he could not tell her that, or she would be more conceited than ever. In his life he had had to face so much fear. It was because of that and because his fears were now swept away for all time that he was seized with such an insatiable hunger for life, and to be alive seemed so wonderful to him!

"Thanks for the kind permission," he replied out of fear of making her more conceited and losing his chances with her. "And what about hunger? Does that also arise, according to your enlightened theory, from fear or just from the contraction of the nerves of the stomach?"

She did not answer but smiled her absolutely enthralling smile.

Don't argue with her, kiss her! was what went through his mind. But with her that was out of the question. She would only make a person painfully ridiculous.

"Oh, Fräulein Rosner, you belong to those people who want to be different at any price. That's why you wear your hair short, no doubt."

"If you must know I cut my hair because it's comfortable and hygienic."

"And because you know it's becoming to you!"

"Do you think it is?"

He was pleased to find in her this first trace of coquetry. But she immediately wiped it out with her assertion: "As for hunger, you can't deny that it belongs to the impulses. Recendy I took out a book by a certain Nietzsche. It's called *Beyond Good and Evil*, and in it is this sentence: 'Without exception impulses are begotten by fear, born by fear, and buried by fear.' I'll bring it to show you if you're interested?"

He begged her to do it, for it was at least a point of contact. How absurd! Here she was discussing impulses with him without the slightest embarrassment, whereas the girls and women of his acquaintance blushed at the very mention of the word "naked." And even more strange was the fact that he would have made no bones at all about kissing one of these society girls, whereas he felt that it was quite unthinkable even to call Selma by her first name. Besides, if he did she would not bring the book.

But she did bring it to him, and it had been a long time since he had been made as happy by anything as by that black-bound volume from the lending library, which he read through in one single night and returned the next afternoon. He longed to discuss it with her. As there was no time for that at the University, he accompanied her home. She lived in the Landstrasse District, a good three-quarters of an hour away, and fortunately seemed to prefer walking to taking the tram. That she was anxious to save the fare never entered his head. Who in the world would ever think about those few pennies! But Sechs-Krügelgasse, the narrow street where she lived behind St. Roch's, was in a part of town he never visited, and it impressed him as rather dreary. When he inquired about her parents she said that only her mother was living. Her mother had a tobacco shop and was ailing, so that Selma had to help her sell cigars, cigarettes, and newspapers. That was why she could take only the afternoon and evening courses at the University. All this, however, he learned later.

For the time being Nietzsche was the subject of discussion, and after him came Karl Kraus, writer and publisher of the satiric periodical *The Torch*, and Peter Altenberg, a Viennese devotee un-Viennese things. After that the painters were taken up. Selma lauded Klimt, the Secessionists, the insurgent "Wiener Werkstaette" with their "true fabric" art handicrafts, and she inveighed violently against the "calcified baroque angels" among painters still painting as in the days of Watteau. After they had walked up and down the narrow, poverty-stricken Sechs-Krügelgasse three times a thought occurred to her and she said, "I had quite forgotten that I really shouldn't have said that! You have a painter uncle, haven't you?"

What he had drawn from her words was less the disparagement of Uncle Drauffer than the fact that she must have made inquiries about him, Hans. Consequently she must be interested in him! "My uncle does quite nice things," he said jubilantly. He was careful not to admit that on one October day he had cherished the dream of being a painter and had drawn the portrait of a broken-down singer with silvery hair, but it seemed appropriate to him to dampem her all-knowing attitude with the remark: "Anyhow, that's a matter of taste. The person who still enjoys Watteau will find beauty in the painting of calcified baroque angels, although I don't find your expression particularly apt. If you'll pardon my saying so."

"Why not?" she asked. "We no longer travel by post horses or light our homes with oil lamps. Art should mirror its epoch or interpret it. Otherwise it is trash."

How simple that was. And yet no one had ever stated it to him in such striking terms. Not even Fritz.

"It must be wonderful to be so clever," he said innocently.

She did not believe in innocence (something he also found out later). Consequently she took it for derision and was ready, with one toss of her lofty-browed head, to annihilate the small degree which they had moved towards one another. This he prevented her from doing. "Selma," he said, making an effort to overcome his shyness, and taking her hand in his, "why do you instinctively always think the worst of a person? And why do you keep feeling that you must assert yourself when that is no longer necessary?"

She tolerated the use of her first name and did not take away her hand. "Do I do that?" was her astonished reply.

Thus began their love.

CHAPTER 25
The Bells

Henriette gave the last family party this summer. It was a double holiday, with Sunday and the festival of Peter and Paul, and although the expression "week-end" had not yet been heard in Vienna, many Viennese had already left town on Friday evening to go to nearby Semmering or even nearer Bruehl. Franz spent the holiday out hunting. His old inclinations came back more freely as he took fewer pains to appear to Henriette to be anything except himself. He had finally abandoned all attempts to make her like him, which did not mean he did not love her any more. But he was reconciled now to his own inability to please her. Hunting was obnoxious to her and had been since the Mayerling days. Yet he had always been an impassioned hunter, although for her sake there had been a time when he pretended not to be. Now there was no longer any reason for his self-denial. And since he had come to that sober realization he had gone out more often to Lobau to shoot deer.

The Sunday afternoon parties on the fourth floor were a standing event, frequented also by many who were not members of the family. On this occasion, however, the gathering was focused exclusively on the Baiers, newly returned from their wedding journey, for Dr. Baier's wife was Henriette's daughter Franziska. Having finished at Sacré Coeur, she had lost no time in falling in love with the young assistant to the Emperor's personal physician. After a brief two-month engagement they were married and visited Venice and Rome. Their obvious happiness made Henriette melancholy. Sooner or later the prospect was that she would be a grandmother. How life rushed by!

She never seemed old to herself, although a woman of forty-nine was positively aged. Why did one observe it only in the mirror or in others but never in oneself? Inwardly she felt not the slightest change; she still hated some people the very instant she laid eyes on them and took violent dislikes. For example, there was her close-lipped son-in-law, who might at least have brought back an Italian sunburn from Italy instead of remaining so freckled and pale. To think that anyone could fall in love with such a creature! She herself might have fallen in love any day if she hadn't known she was forty-nine. Between today and the time when Henriette had come back from Venice there lay a lifetime. The interval of resignation, when she had made herself believe that all was ended and that she must limit herself to being a mother, that period had come and gone, as everything else came and went. It had now made way for the present epoch, in which she preferred to dress herself like a woman of thirty. She would in any case dress herself better than Franziska, whose reseda-green dress she found was horribly insipid; that girl inherited her taste from Franz.

Professor Stein was also present at the party because he had been prevented from making his usual call the previous Thursday morning; he had had to deliver a speech in the

Upper Chamber for an understanding with the South Slavs. There was Hermann, too, finishing his year of voluntary military service with the local Vienna regiment, the Fourth Hoch-und-Deutschmeister, and he was causing quite a stir with his yellow stripes of an acting cadet officer. Who could have persuaded him to grow that silly little moustache? And without question he was using pomade on his hair. When he opened his mouth he poured out pure nonsense.

Henriette, in a blue-and-white-striped dress which was short enough to reveal the silk stockings on her slenderly perfect legs, was astonished that these were her children. Perhaps in both cases it was the eight years when they were away at boarding school, and against which she had argued with Franz so violently, that were the cause of this. In any event she felt like a complete stranger to this homely and ridiculously enamoured young bride and this rather comical and certainly not clever young man in uniform. When she compared this with her feeling for Hans (who was late again because he was running around with that highbrow girl) or for Martha Monica, who sat beside her and at thirteen was a striking beauty, she was almost convinced that she had just two children; not four.

The bride and groom were waited on by another pair of newlyweds. Herr Simmerl had married Hanni Kern the chambermaid, the same who from the very first had admired Henriette so extravagantly and was also so devoted to Herr Simmerl that moral Franz had called the butler to his office one day. As a result of the interview a wedding had taken place in the church of St. Anna, where only a month later the Baiers had been pronounced man and wife. The feeling of being bound more than ever to the family relaxed the butler's sedate features each time he poured the coffee for Dr. Baier or passed the whipped cream for his wife's. He too had taken Hanni on a wedding journey, not of four weeks but of one, to the pilgrimage center of Mariazell in Styria; and although Mariazell naturally did not compare with Italy, still they went there in apple blossom time. As for Hanni, she grew red in the face as she passed the traditional *Sachertorte*, served in the house since the days of Sophie. For a person of her age, and the recent date of her marriage, her figure was indecorously large; yet instead of sending her away somewhere until she became presentable again (that was Henriette's suggestion), Franz, a stickler for principles like the others in Number 10, had insisted on the religious ceremony.

As so often under this roof, Sophie's shadow slipped in, and, strangely enough, it was Henriette who took over her role. Without her having suspected or wanted it, the house had left its mark on her. In Sophie's stead she was now the one to deprecate the Sacher cake and the middle-aged newlywed who was serving it. At Hanni's age, according to her, one should not have children or blush like a schoolgirl.

"Well, when are you leaving?" Professor Stein asked. He did not mention the destination, as that was understood. Since Francis Joseph had made Ischl, that green little hill town in Upper Austria, his summer residence, the patricians of Vienna went there for their summer holidays. Sophie had done it; Otto Eberhard had his own villa there; Franz rented one; and the Paskiewicz family, as long as the colonel was alive, spent several weeks regularly in the Hotel Kaiserin Elisabeth. It was only the Drauffers who preferred the seashore.

"On the fifteenth. When Mono's school is out," Henriette replied.

The living room in which they were gathered already showed signs of the summer dismantling which always began three weeks to the day before they took the train from the Western Station. Then curtains were taken down and laid in camphor; carpets were cleaned with sauerkraut; the floors were washed, refinished, and waxed; the furniture and chandeliers were covered with newspapers and gray calico slips; the windows were blocked with brown cardboard, and everywhere man-high packing cases filled with shavings were stacked up to such a degree that living in the apartment grew to be quite a problem. For the present all this was still in the preliminary stage, yet it reeked so of camphor that all the windows had to be opened despite the hot sun.

"Lavender to buy, two penny worth a bunch; buy lavender!" came the melodious cry that had rung through Vienna's streets for centuries in summer. It was the women who had come in from the country to go from house to house with their baskets full of fragrant blue bunches of lavender, offering them for sale.

"Why don't you use lavender instead of camphor, Mother?" asked Martha Monica, who did not even remotely realize the outrageousness of such a question. She had made it with the complete unself-consciousness with which she did everything, and meanwhile went on eating her piece of cake. Yet Henriette knew Number 10 well enough not to be surprised that Herr Simnjerl had his breath so taken away by this question from her youngest daughter that for a moment he could not go on serving.

"Camphor is what is used," she said evasively.

"But it smells so," Martha Monica said.

"That is why it is used," her mother told her. "A long time from now you will discover that the art of perfect housekeeping means that you make your days as difficult and burdensome as possible. To be a good *Hausfrau* means to lead a miserable life, and care for things instead of for people." A remark like that she dared to make only when Franz was not at home. But with the protecting presence of her father and under the shocked expression of her son-in-law, who was positively goggle-eyed, she took a fiendish delight in saying them. It was her retort to the spirit of tradition and perfection against which she had raged in vain since the very beginning, until, although she did not admit it, she had somewhat succumbed to it.

"You must not take everything your mother says at its face value," was the instructive advice given to Mono by her grandfather, who was always ready to make concessions in Parliament or in life although not in his classroom.

"Oh, but I love it!" answered the lovely young girl. "It's so entertaining when Mummy says things like that!"

Henriette beamed. This child spoke her language. It was not exactly that of Number 10 and rather more suited, let's say, to the Palais Coburg across the street.

"And so you did not see the Palazzo Vendramin," she turned to her elder daughter, in order not to reveal her partiality for Martha Monica too much. "What do you say to that, Papa?"

Professor Stein looked at his daughter. His "jubilee year" at the University was imminent, but to look at him no one would have guessed it. His refined and sensitive face was as taut as ever. Between his look and its object he put, as always, a clarifying and intellectualizing perspective. As always, his daughter read what was behind her father's look. The "Have you grown accustomed to it?" of twenty-seven years earlier was now: "So you have not yet grown accustomed to it. But you must still do it." Between these two, who never put the essentials into words, this had never been said.

"Of course, that was an oversight," the professor admitted. "In her day I gave your mother the Palazzo Vendramin as a special assignment."

"Extra edition of the *Neue Freie Presse*!" they heard the newsboys calling in Seilerstätte. "Extra!"

"The *Neue Freie Presse* is issuing an extra edition?" exclaimed Professor Stein with surprise. "There must be some extraordinary reason."

"It is probably the racing results," was the opinion of the

acting cadet officer, although the leading liberal paper only reluctantly concerned itself with such vanities as racing, or, indeed, such crudities as sports.

"Get the Herr Hofrat a copy of the extra," Henriette ordered. She hated the way Simmerl never did such matter-of-course things on his own initiative but always had to be asked to do them.

"Right away, madam," he said, and disappeared.

"And how were the scampi at the Hotel Danieli?" Henriette inquired of her son-in-law. She found it just as difficult to call him by his first name as to feel like a mother-in-law.

"Did we have scampi?" Dr. Baier asked his young wife who was gazing at him with adoring eyes.

"I hope so," put in Henriette in her daughter's stead. And to Simmerl who had come in with the extra: "You look like Cassandra!" This family gathering was getting on her nerves the longer Hans delayed coming home. Out of consideration for the bride and groom he might have come on time. But no! He must not lose one precious minute with that Fraulein Rosner! Henriette decided to have it out with him that very day.

"Well, give it here," she said to the butler, who was still standing at the door with the newspaper in his hand.

He gave it to her, stiffly and solemnly.

"The Heir to the Throne and the Duchess of Hohenberg," read the heavy headlines, and beside them was printed a large black cross under which were the words:

SARAJEVO, June 28, 1914: His Imperial and Royal Highness, the Heir to the Throne Archduke Francis Ferdinand, and his Noble Consort, Her Highness the Duchess of Hohenberg, were today the victims of an infamous assault. As Their Highnesses, who were on an inspection tour of the recently annexed provinces of Bosnia and Herzegovina, were driving to the government building, the Konak, an assassin hidden in the crowds of cheering spectators fired into the imperial vehicle. The bullets struck the archduke and his wife and they succumbed soon afterwards. The murderer is a twenty-year-old Serbian student by the name of Gavrilo Princip. He was arrested on the scene of the crime and confessed that he had committed the deed as an act of revenge because of the annexation ...

From the right wing of the Ronacher Theater stage came the actor Girardi with hesitating steps. Johann Strauss lifted his baton. From the left wing hurried an unknown gentleman who said: "His Imperial and Royal Highness, the most august Crown Prince Archduke Rudolf ..." Henriette had closed her eyes. The past had loomed before her.

"Extra edition of the *Neue Freie Presse*!"

"Extra edition of the *Neues Wiener Tagblatt*!"

"Extra edition of the *Reichspost*!" came the cries from below. In the living room on the fourth floor no one spoke. The paper passed from hand to hand. The bells of St. Stephen had begun to toll. Henriette knew that those of St. Augustine would follow. And then those of St. Michael.

"Does Your Grace need anything?" It was Simmerl who asked the question.

That too had been said to her in exactly the same words. Everything came back. "No," she said. Now the bells of St. Augustine were ringing.

"I'll be going along," said the acting-cadet officer, "I must be back at barracks by six."

"Do that, Hermann," Professor Stein agreed. Henriette had never seen her father struggle so to maintain his self-control.

"How frightful for His Majesty," said the new son-in-law and assistant to the Emperor's personal physician.

Professor Stein again agreed, "Frightful." As a historian, he was thinking back to the last extra edition of the *Neue Freie Presse.* Then its heavily leaded headlines read, "Empress

Elizabeth," and beside her name was a large black cross, and underneath it ran the statement:

GENEVA, September 10, 1898: Her Majesty, the Empress and Queen, while on her way from the Hotel Beau Rivage to the steamship landing, fell a victim to an infamous assault carried out by an Italian anarchist called Luigi Lucheni, who stabbed the most exalted lady to the heart with a pointed file. The criminal was seized on the spot and confessed his crime, although he was unable to give any reason for it.

"Frightful," Professor Stein repeated. "Three times in one generation!"

"The poor woman," said the thirteen-year-old girl. Henriette nodded silently and ignored what her father went on to say. As usual, he was speaking of politics.

What did they know! To her it all proved that one does not forget anything, not the smallest atom. No matter how one tried to delude oneself, it was there, it was not allayed, it cut, it pained, it bled as on that first day. The bells! How pitilessly they tolled it all back to her. Now she was running away; now she fell in the snow; now she was in the sleeping-car on her way back to be examined …

"Thank you a thousand times," the bride and groom were saying. "It was delightful." They lived in the young physician's official apartment in the Schönbrunn Palace and had a long way to go.

Henriette did not detain them. It was perfect that they had broken away from the habits of the house and, for reasons of the Emperor's health, were unable to take up their residence in Seilerstätte. Besides, Henriette would not have known what to do with them.

She also bade good-bye to her son Hermann. "Come again soon," she said to him, as to the bridal couple.

"Not before next Sunday," he told her. "I have to cram for my officer's commission exam."

"That is really most important," Professor Stein declared, once more in agreement.

But then all examinations were important to him, for that was his profession, so Henriette's attention strayed off. The bells boomed. St Michael's had joined in, and others too, for they were terrifyingly loud now. They hammered at her head and her heart. She longed to be alone. When her father left he said, "Good-bye, my child. In the case of an elemental event one should maintain an impersonal attitude." In their fashion of communicating with each other, she interpreted that to mean: "You are thinking too much about yourself."

Magnanimity! General considerations! Anyone who had not suffered could easily afford to be magnanimous and indulge in general considerations! The child here understood her. She did not offer her any wise precepts, asked no questions, she simply loved her. That is what one craved. Not blame. Not perpetual supervision. Blame and supervision produced no good. One did not even grow up under them. One was always twenty-one, even at forty-nine.

Nevertheless, Henriette blamed her eldest child when he came home. "Your sister and brother-in-law have left long since. The others too. I must say that you show little consideration."

She noticed an unfamiliar expression around his mouth. "Where were you?" she asked, although she hated to be questioned herself and although she knew only too well how unsympathetic one made oneself by doing it. She no longer cared. Very well, she would make herself unsympathetic. She had done it long before. The people who made themselves sympathetic, grinned at everything, accepted everything, pretending to be likeable, were hypocrites or stupid. You were sympathetic in any case to those who liked you. As for the rest—you paid no attention.

"Where were you?" she repeated when Hans did not answer. "I mean, where were you both? Were you with that person again?"

"Please don't call her 'that person,'" Hans said, and went over to one of the windows from which there was a view across to the king Boulevard.

"Oh, excuse me," she replied ironically. "Mono, be an angel and run down to Aunt Pauline's. Ask her to lend me some brown darning silk."

"Yes, Mummy," the girl answered. Hugging her big brother, she comforted him with the words, "Don't be so sad, Hans. Everything will turn out all right."

"Of course," he said, and kissed her as she left the room.

"Where were you?" Henriette insisted. She was sitting in her favorite tapestry armchair, darning some silk stockings.

"Walking," he answered curtly. "In Dornbach."

"Did you have dinner at the Woodcock?"

"Yes."

"Did the music stop? I mean, when the news came?"

The music had stopped.

"Don't pull such a long face," she said. "It is quite proper that you should feel patriotic, but after all, it does not concern you. You have often said that you were not enthusiastic about Francis Ferdinand."

Years ago someone had said the same thing to her on a similar occasion: "After all, it does not concern us. We are no archdukes." She was unaware that she was now speaking with the accents of Number 10; if anyone had pointed this out to her she would have denied it.

Hans thought it might concern him. Besides, he had decided, in view of the other occurrences of that Sunday, finally to settle the question of Selma with his mother.

As he stood at the window, staring down at the crowds now excitedly thronging the thoroughfares, usually so deserted on a

Sunday evening, the day just past came back to him, from its bright beginning to its bitter conclusion. "Well, young man, aren't you happy? This may well mean war! I envy you. If you're lucky you'll be wearing our Emperor's colors and marching against the Serb bandits within a very few days!"

Early that Sunday he had fetched Selma. They had ridden out to Heiligenstadt and from there had strolled for hours along the roads they both enjoyed so much. It had been lovelier than ever. Each time it seemed to them exciting and wonderful that Beethoven had walked there, that those very linden trees had afforded him shade. He had kissed her; she had let him do it; he had told her how deeply he loved her, and she had returned his kiss. But when she had suggested going to Nussdorf he had had the unhappy idea of celebrating her kiss by suggesting "something better" the Golden Woodcock at Dornbach, a society rendezvous, then the height of fashion. To be sure, his only intention was to take her somewhere else than to one of the cheap small restaurants in which they usually concealed themselves. But she had remarked, "Is that the place where smart young men go with their lady-loves?"

That had made him indignant. "I don't see why we should always be in hiding," he had replied.

"I was not the one to begin this game of hiding," she had said. "All these months no place was sufficiently out of sight for you." Again it had been that tone of reproach which enraged him. *I, the poor girl. You, the patrician.*

"Selma," he had insisted, "you must finally give up that sort of thing. You know exactly how much you mean to me."

"How should I?" she had asked. "Because you have made me declarations of love? How often had you done that before me? How often will you do it after me? I'll tell you. One day after I have done what you want of me. Or perhaps three months? I am generous."

"That is disgusting of you!" he had said.

"But right. Why should two people like us go on indefinitely lying to one another? You're a dear, but you are like all of your kind. ["Well, young man, if you are lucky you will be marching within a very few days!"] I mean as much to you as any liaison means to any fashionable young man," Selma had told him. "In all this time you have never even introduced me to your parents. Whenever we come into the neighborhood of Seilerstätte you grow nervous. The very mention of your father's name or even that of your pompous lawyer uncle is something you carefully avoid. Do you think I'm deaf?" "You're infinitely unjust," he had replied. "You don't know Seilerstätte."

"I can imagine it," she had said. "I trust you have not for a single second inferred that I'm interested in your family out of regard for my future? You don't know me! We've been having a flirtation. If you had your way it would be more than that, but naturally never anything more than an affair. I don't deny that I sometimes have inclinations that way myself. Why the emphasis? How is it that Schnitzer puts it: 'Who in May ever thinks of August?' We are in June. Let's stick to today." ["Well, young man, within a very few days."]

This was not the first time that there had been this bitter resignation underneath her cynical superiority. But this time he had lost his patience. "And you don't know me!" he had hurled back her own words. "When I'm convinced that someone is wrong I refuse to give in. Not a single syllable of yours is true! Between your future and mine there is no difference. It's our future. And you know it!" ["Well, young man, aren't you happy?"]

"Consequently we are going to the Golden Woodcock and exhibit ourselves," Selma had replied with her ironic logic. "It will raise the prestige of the junior Alt when society hears that he has a girl."

The only thing to do would have been to give in, to remain

under the spell of simple, green Heiligenstadt or quiet, lovable little Nussdorf instead of exchanging them for a sophisticated place, especially on a double holiday week-end. But Hans had his father's flaring temper as well as his mother's obstinacy. "Yes, we're going to the Woodcock," he had insisted.

They had gone there. The headwaiter had sized up this excursion couple with a disparaging glance. Selma was in a sports blouse, a checked skirt, green suède cap, and her shoes were dusty. After an endless wait they were given a small table on the extreme edge of the farthest terrace. That was the one good thing about it, for there, at least, they no longer had to run the gauntlet of the eyes of the dining bourgeoisie, who loved nothing so much as to devour a reputation with every morsel of food.

There was a shady linden tree overhead, but alas, there was a band almost at their side, a string orchestra led by Herr Hügel with plaintive, languorous lightness, which every one found so charming.

Nevertheless they had had food, and the band had been playing "Girlie, You're Dancing Just Like My Wife" with honeyed tones, when Selma noticed that she was being stared at by a lady. It was Eugenie. She was dining with her husband at a table only a short distance from them, and she stared so noticeably that Hans, who had seen her some time before, could not help blushing. "Oh, I see!" Selma had said without his knowing what she meant.

But then she had gone on to ask, "Isn't that a certain lady whom you have always represented to me as *à quantité négligeable*? Did you want to keep up her devotion by a visual lesson? In any case your efforts seem to have met with success. Handsome of you."

Had it not been for the sudden stopping of the music and the rumor that sped from table to table of some terrible occurrence, Hans would not have known what to do under the cross

298 · ERNST LOTHAR

fire of the two women's looks. In a way the terrible news had come to his rescue, for the questions, exclamations, and horror of the guests who were hurrying away had concealed his dilemma. When finally he and Selma had been passing the Einrieds' table Eugenie had detained him.

"Mr. Alt!" she had called. "I'd like to introduce you to my husband. You know, Mr. Alt was a classmate of our boy," she had explained to her husband.

"Very pleased, I'm sure," had been the comment of the baldheaded gentleman whom Hans remembered from that memorable game of tarot in the Café Matschakerhof. "Well, young man," he had added, "aren't you happy? This may well mean war. I envy you. If you're lucky you'll be wearing our Emperor's colors and marching against the Serb bandits within a very few days! Waiter! The bill!"

For the first time in Hans's life someone had used the word 'war' not as a textbook expression of the past but as a possibility and even a probability of today. Coming from the mouth of this bald-headed, malicious high official, it sounded to Hans like something obscene. He took it for the belated threat of a jealous husband rather than for anything else. People didn't wage war any more. And why should there be war? Because some fanatic had killed an archduke? When Papa killed a count no one so much as lifted a finger, and it had been just as horrible.

"It's a catastrophe," Eugenie had said to Hans while the waiter was adding up two orders of roast veal with spinach. Hans had realized that she meant Selma, but pretended that she was speaking of the assassination. "Yes, horrible," he had said.

Then he and Selma had ridden back to town, jammed close together in a tram that was so overcrowded they had had to stand on the steps. And she had looked at him with eyes from which every trace of reproach had vanished, almost as though she were frightened. He knew she was thinking of young men lucky enough to be marching off in a very few days.

There were people in the tramcar who said, "This means war! We can't tolerate it any longer!" What language did they speak? War was a medieval, fiendish word. It had no place in a living language. And what was it they would not tolerate? Papa had shot a man in a violet meadow as nowadays he shot deer. Hans had thought then that it should not be tolerated. Yet they had tolerated it. What was the difference?

Selma and he had parted as usual on the corner, far enough away from Number 10 not to be seen. It was then that Hans had made his decision.

As he stood with his back to his mother and looked down at the excited crowds below, it all had passed in review before his eyes, from start to end. Now he turned abruptly round to her and said: 'Mother, I want to marry Selma."

The bells were still booming and reverberating. "I don't think that this is the right moment," Henriette said slowly.

"I know, Mother. But I have already put it off too long!"

She knew that nothing she might say to him now would change anything. She would lose him. To a girl named Selma. Nevertheless she said: "I've already indicated on many occasions that I'm not in favor of this relationship."

"You have no reasons," he replied.

She had the best reason there was. She did not want to lose him. Besides, she had discovered all sorts of things about this Selma. She was vain, egotistical, much too clever. It was not a good idea to marry a girl who is vain, egotistical, and clever. They don't make their husbands happy. Yet this boy should be happy! He should have a better wife than his father had! A thousand times better one! Henriette knew it was in vain. So all she asked of him was: "We'll speak of this another time, Hans. It really isn't the moment now."

"Oh, yes, Mother," he said. "They say there may be war."

"No!" she cried. "No!" Then, controlling herself: "Do you believe that?"

They heard Mono coming back.

"No," he said. "I can't imagine human beings waging war in 1914."

The bells grew louder, drowning out the steps and voices outside.

"Nor I," Henriette said, her eyes open wide.

CHAPTER 26
Letters from the Field

Henriette sat on a bench in the garden of her Ischl villa and read her letters while she waited for a long-distance call from Vienna. Through the trees it was possible to glimpse the green heights of Mount Jainzen, the green waters of the Traun, and a bit of the yellow Imperial villa. She had sat there a year earlier, after the war had broken out, when Franz, despite his age, had resumed his old rank of first lieutenant in the reserve and gone to headquarters in Teschen, and Hermann, newly commissioned as a second lieutenant, had left for Serbia, and Hans, as a volunteer in the Hoch-und-Deutschmeister Fourth Regiment, had been sent to the Rennweg Barracks to be trained.

Exactly a year ago the air had been filled day and night with triumphant singing: "Prince Eugene, of men most knightly, laid a bridge across the river, led his men victorious ever, to the fortress Belgerad"; "Staunch stands and true the watch, the watch on the Rhine"; "In our homeland, in our homeland, you and I will meet again!" Singing, strewn with flowers, with oak-leaves on the shakos of their dress uniforms, the enthusiastic troops marched away between lines of enthusiastic crowds. "See you at Christmas!" and they had yelled back: "In September!"

In September, before the leaves fell, the general staff had published the communiqué: "Lemberg is still in our hands."

In September, when school opened, Henriette and Martha Monica had returned to Vienna. It was war. They were obliged to adapt themselves to that obsolete word which to their generations of security had had so little meaning. It was an adjustment even more difficult for Henriette than for many others, brought up as she had been in the atmosphere of Professor Stein's steadfast faith in the humane powers of liberalism, tolerance, and progress. But it was war, and it was not over in three weeks like the campaign of 1866. The house in Seilerstätte grew emptier. Fritz and Otto Drauffer too were called up. The men left in the house were Otto Eberhard, his son Peter, brother-in-law Drauffer, Herr Simmerl, the janitor Pawlik, and the stationer. From time to time Hans came over from the barracks. He grew constantly thinner, the Emperor's colors did not suit him. Once Selma came with him. They were engaged. Before Hans, now a corporal, went to Serbia he had insisted on getting married. His father had refused his consent, for Hans was not quite twenty-four, and any soldier who was not of legal age in Austria was obliged to have the consent of his father or his mother. His mother gave hers, but his father knew nothing about that.

Henriette's mail consisted really of just one card from the field. For the two letters she held in her hand had already arrived some days earlier. Yet she read them over and over.

On the card was written:

Teschen, August 17, 1915

DEAR HETTI,

On this first anniversary of our separation I am thinking of you with especial affection. I am extremely well and trust you are the same. I sent you a basket of eggs and four kilograms of butter. I trust you will receive the same safely. I am glad

Martha Monica gets such good reports in school. Please tell her that from me. The splendid news from the front must help us through this time of separation. Tomorrow, on the occasion of His Majesty's birthday, I shall drink to your health. Write soon.

Love and greetings.
YOUR FRANZ

She pressed her lips together. He still wrote in the style of business letters. Still with the copybook precise up-and-down strokes differentiating the Gothic letters and the elaborate loop with the signature "Franz" exactly in the center. Once upon a time when she was young and still nourished the absurd hope of moulding Franz a little she had plucked up the courage to speak to him about the dryness of his personal letters. His reply had been "Nonsense!" But shortly afterwards he had brought her—goodness only knows where he procured it—a copy of a letter from a certain Count Hohenembs to the Empress Elizabeth in Corfu, on the subject of the roses in the private gardens of the Schönbrunn Palace, and it was couched in the style of a bookkeeper. She could still recall one sentence from it: "And I cut the same as soon as they bloom profusely." Count Hohenembs, however, was the pseudonym under which Francis Joseph corresponded with his wife when she was travelling abroad, and Franz's opinion was, "What is good enough for the Empress should not be too bad for you!" To which she had replied, "But you are not the Emperor."

She looked down to the yellow wall of the Imperial villa with the green wooden shutters, whence the one word "yes" could have freed her from her painful unrest. This summer, as every year, Francis Joseph had arrived there before his birthday. "And you are not the Empress," Franz had said to her. With a sigh she laid the card down beside her. How absurd of

Franz to take as usual for his pattern a person who never had the slightest care for human beings! Her freckled son-in-law had recently told her how His Majesty had had the "greatness" not to pause even for a second in his daily round of obligations when Franz Ferdinand died. The same was said of him when his brother Maximilian was shot in Mexico, when his son committed suicide, and when his wife was murdered. How could anyone call that greatness? He was simply a man without a heart. Otherwise he never could have borne it all. Such men had no reason to be surprised when they received no happiness. They gave none.

As if to confirm this, Henriette took up one of the two letters. It was dated August 4, carried a field-post-office-stamp number, without further identification of origin, and read:

DEAR MOTHER,

Just a few lines to thank you for your sweet letter and to let you know that I am in grand shape. You probably know directly from Hans that he has now been assigned to my company since he says he wrote you. It is really funny to have my "elder brother" under me. If you do not hear from me in the near future the reason will be only that we are going to be somewhat busier shooting up these Serbian swine. No one can imagine what a tricky, filthy, lousy lot they are! But shoulder to shoulder with our German brothers in arms we shall soon clean up this mess! Best regards to all.

YOUR HERMANN, Lieutenant

Your Hermann, Lieutenant!

"Miss Mono on the telephone," Herr Simmerl announced. "She sends word that the mixed doubles will not begin until one and to please not wait luncheon for her. Is that all right?"

"I'll go myself," Henriette said. "Is she phoning from Strobl?" "She did phone," replied the tall butler.

"You drive me crazy with your way of speech, Simmerl. Why didn't you say in the first place that she had telephoned?"

"Sorry, Your Grace," Simmerl, deprived of the "Herr," excused himself. "Miss Mono had said she was telephoning from Strobl and it costs money if you have to wait on a long-distance call. But on the next occasion I shall not fail to advise Your Ladyship."

"That will be kind of you, Simmerl," Henriette told him. "I happen to be waiting for a call."

"Very good, madam," responded the butler with injured feelings, and withdrew.

For a moment she reflected about whether she ought to leave Martha Monica alone over in Strobl at the tournament. Then she noticed that it was already almost noon. How long it took to get a call through from Vienna today!

Nervously she read the second letter which she knew by heart, syllable for syllable. It carried the same army-post-office-stamp number, was not dated, and had been cancelled a week earlier. The square stamp of the "Imperial and Royal Supreme Military Command Censor" was below the address.

My dear Mother [it ran], I am now here, bag and baggage, but I may not tell you where. It is more refreshing and instructive than I had ever imagined. You see and experience a lot. On the march down here, for instance, I saw my first dead horses. They whinny so strangely before they die. As though they knew. I have also seen people hanging on gallows; it makes quite an impression when they sway in the wind. They were all criminals, Serbs of course, who had met with their just deserts. The first gunfire is also an experience which I should not like to have missed. When you suddenly hear the whizzing sound in the air, made by the bullets, which Hermann so aptly calls "blue beans," as they fly at you, at least you know why you were born! Partly to serve as a target for these whistling beans, and partly to plant them in someone else. That it is in a human body you are supposed to plant them is perhaps the greatest experience of all in these great days, for which Hermann has another apt expression: he calls them a steel shower. You aim at men whose faces you hardly ever see, and, unless you are a criminally poor shot, you have the incomparable satisfaction of seeing their bodies tumble like so many sacks on the faces you never saw. My one regret is that I still do not shoot well enough.

That I am serving under Hermann naturally also contributes to my well-being. We need men like him in these times. Not pitiful weaklings who drool about humanity.

Do you see Selma? Please, be good to her!

I long for you all, for you, for her, for Mono. When you get a chance, send me some books.

YOUR HANS

In this letter the censor had inserted the word "not" before the phrase "to serve as a target for these whistling beans."

Since the arrival of this letter Henriette had not slept. His helpless cry for rescue had reverberated in the sweet green quiet of this summer holiday resort where people were holding tennis tournaments, going on afternoon outings, dancing in the Zauner restaurant in the Pfarrgasse, or else playing tarot on the terrace at the Café Walter. She had racked her brains until the idea came to her of sending the telegram, the answer to which she was now awaiting by a long-distance call from Vienna.

At last it came. Herr Simmerl announced that someone was calling madam, and Henriette heard the old man's voice of Count Hoyos, who, when he was young, had travelled on her account to Pope Leo XIII: "Now then, lovely lady, everything has been set in motion in the right direction." But when in a wave of joy she wanted to find out more about it, all he would say was, "Don't be too impatient, lovely lady; a few days more or less are of no consequence. You will hear from me again! I kiss your hands!"

With that the telephone conversation and her wave of joy were summarily ended. In the few days which were of no consequence the word "not," which the censor had so stupidly inserted in Hans's letter, might long since have lost its meaning.

How does one bear it? she thought to herself once again. She went back to her bench in the garden and looked across to the modest yellow summer home with the green blinds. There lived the man on whom it depended. For a moment the thought flashed through her mind: What if I went to him myself? I gave him back his son. Perhaps he will give me mine? But as swiftly as it had come it vanished again. That man down in the Imperial villa had not lifted a finger when little Pauline, who had disturbed his marriage ceremony, begged humbly for forgiveness; the chronicles of the house revealed that. He had not moved a muscle when he had put the question of his life to her; Henriette recalled that. He had maintained his impeccable attitude when the coffin of his murdered wife was sunk into the Capuchin crypt; she was there and saw it. He was not human.

CHAPTER 27
A Service comes to an End

In one of the fourteen hundred and forty-one rooms of the yellow baroque castle of Schönbrunn Francis Joseph was preparing to die. His apartments were in the left wing of the low, two-winged building, in the extreme right end of which he had been born eighty-six years earlier.

The doctors had left him at three-forty-five in the afternoon. Out in the corridor (because of the coal shortage the Emperor occupied only two tiny rooms, in either one of which you could hear every word spoken in the other) Dr. Ortner had given his instructions to Ketterl, His Majesty's valet: continuous steaming, to the extent possible on an alcohol burner; every two hours a powder compounded of phenacetin and caffeine; in case of paroxysms of coughing, lukewarm marshmallow root tea; at 7 P.M. temperature to be taken. In the event of any alarming change in His Majesty's condition Dr. Kerzl or his assistant, Dr. Baier, to be notified at once. And the patient was not to be left alone even for a second.

"Very well, Herr Hofrat," the valet had said.

Then the doctors had withdrawn, and Ketterl had gone back to his master.

The Emperor lay with closed eyes on the narrow iron army cot on which he had spent most of the nights of his life.

"Your Majesty must take this powder," said the Imperial valet.

Francis Joseph shook his head.

"But Herr Hofrat Ortner insists on it," the servant ventured to say to the man on the army cot whom he had served for forty-seven years and whose every expression and gesture he knew. That he was desperately ill was no secret to the valet. That he would die was known only to the dying man. He refused to take the powder, and so it was left. A little later he fell asleep.

Sitting at the foot of the iron bedstead, Ketterl watched every breath of the sleeping man. He rasped now and then, but that was nothing unusual for him. In this cursed huge and unheatable castle, with its icy corridors and staircases, he had caught bronchitis one time after another. But would he exchange this place for a healthier one? Nothing of the kind! Hadn't that intelligent young assistant to the Imperial physician suggested only the day before yesterday that His Majesty should go to Semmering for a few days of recreation? "Tell the young man not to try any such foolishness on me," had been the response given Ketterl to convey to Dr. Baier from his master.

No dog would want to live as he did! In two tiny rooms, up at four in the morning, at work by four-thirty, and with no pause until his evening meal. His breakfast and lunch were served on a tray on his desk; he did not even look at what he ate. Nothing but official papers. Nothing but audiences. Yet of all the people who came to him year in and year out, and who all wanted something from him, there was not one who would so much as ask: "How is Your Majesty? Did Your Majesty have a good night?" Of course no one was supposed to put questions to an emperor. But not even the Imperial family bothered about him! Archduchess Marie Valerie, his daughter, came sometimes but left almost immediately. Or Princess Windischgrätz, his granddaughter, and she too went away immediately. Dear God in heaven, there was not a more neglected person in the whole world. If it were not for Frau Schratt, who now and then saw to it that he had some proper food or took him out for a half-hour drive, he would not have had a soul near him. Except for me, thought the servant.

His Majesty seemed to benefit by his slumber. His cheeks, which had been the color of parchment, were now tinged with a healthy pink. He had a marvellous constitution indeed!

How early it grew dark! In the palace courtyard the arc lights were already burning. Ketterl tiptoed to the windows and drew the heavy brown velvet curtains and fastened them together with a pin he carried under the lapel of his livery. At least those annoying outside lamps would not throw any light on to the bed.

The Emperor murmured.

"Yes, Your Majesty?" said Ketterl, thinking he was speaking to him.

The sick man's lips, barely visible in the' dark, were moving. Sometimes they formed an incomprehensible word, again and again. His breath was more rapid now.

"Your Majesty!" said the servant, who felt it was his duty to interrupt these uneasy dreams.

Francis Joseph awoke and pointed to his old gold pocket watch on the night stand.

"Gone four-thirty, Your Majesty," answered the servant, who understood the gesture. "Does Your Majesty feel better?"

"Has anyone been here?" asked the Emperor, pausing between each word.

"Not just now. Before Herr Hofrat Ortner came Prince Montenuovo and Baron Bolfras were here."

A questioning movement of the head, concerning Baron Bolfras.

"He wanted to submit a telegram from the front, Your Majesty. It was from General von Falkenhayn, so His Excellency said."

A gesture with the index finger.

"But Your Majesty must not have any light! That is bad for the eyes."

Francis Joseph said, "Carry on,"

So the servant lit a candle on the nightstand, for His Majesty did not like electric lights. When he handed him his glasses along with the telegram he noticed how hot the invalid's hand was.

"Krakow, in Wallachia, has been taken," the Emperor said with difficulty.

"That is good news, Your Majesty, isn't it?"

A gesture for the candle to be put out.

It was done. For a while there was no sound except of rough, rapid breathing. Then Ketterl heard his master say: "Fetch Bishop Seydl."

That frightened the servant so that he could not answer at once. Only that very morning, when Archduchess Marie Valerie had brought a special blessing from His Holiness the Pope, His Majesty had been angry that His Holiness had been disturbed because of an ordinary attack of bronchitis.

"Immediately," replied Ketterl, as soon as he was able to

speak. Half an hour later the bishop of the Court Chapel, Dr. Seydl, was sitting in the dark room at the Emperor's bedside. A movement of the head had sent Ketterl into the next room, from which one overheard everything, even when one did not wish to do so.

"I desire to make my confession," Francis Joseph said to the priest, who for untold years bad received his confessions and who, like all the other functionaries of the court, had grown old with him.

Ketterl considered going out into the corridor. But he did not dare to. Dr. Ortner had ordered him not to leave the invalid alone for a second. So he stayed.

The bishop spoke. His Majesty replied, pausing between words, "I no longer have any time for that."

"But, Your Majesty" the bishop said, "tomorrow or the day after you will be quite restored to health!"

"I believe that you are mistaken," the Emperor said. Then for a long time they whispered.

"*Et cum spiritu tuo*," came His Majesty's voice. A pause. Then His Majesty apparently asked a question, for Dr. Seydl said: "Neither from the religious nor the human standpoint. It would have been quite incompatible with the exalted duty of the Emperor to favor the divorce of the Crown Prince."

"I thought so," the Emperor replied. "But he did not." Further whispering. Again Dr. Seydl replied, "For that too Your Majesty need not reproach, yourself. Her Majesty the Empress's turn of mind was not endowed for matters of State. All her interests were directed to fields which Your Majesty lacked not the will but the time to cultivate."

"The will, too," His Majesty said. Ketterl heard him repeat, "The will, too." He continued murmuring. The bishop's voice said, "If Your Majesty will permit I shall lean a little closer. Then Your Majesty will not have to make such an effort. Now I hear every word."

The servant heard no sound for so long that he grew stiff with fear. Finally the bishop said: "I know what Your Majesty has in mind, and it makes me sad to see that you doubt the unquestionable greatness of your services to Austria. The care to maintain in undiminished form the possessions and position of the Imperial House, a care never absent during an entire reign, is not open to the slightest reproach of personal ambition. Your Majesty never had anything in mind except the welfare of your lands and subjects, which in turn depended entirely on the undiminished power of their ruling house to protect them."

Now His Majesty's answer came in a clear tone, "I thank you, my Lord Bishop."

"I wish Your Majesty a good recovery."

"I thank you," again came His Majesty's reply.

Then the bishop felt his way to the door and the Imperial valet returned to his post in the dark room.

"Are you there, Ketterl?" His Majesty asked.

"At Your Majesty's service," the servant answered.

"I feel better. Light a candle and give me the documents on my desk and my glasses," was his request. "I want to catch up the amount I fell behind today."

"Your Majesty should know that when Your Majesty is well again, Your Majesty should let these documents be, and allow himself a bit of a holiday and happiness," suggested the servant, overjoyed that the sick man was so much better and vexed that his mind was already on the pile of papers.

"Holidays and happiness?" was the astonished answer of the man who had become Emperor at eighteen. "Then it would be the first time in my life."

As Ketterl was straightening his pillows and helping him to sit up he was seized with a paroxysm of coughing.

"A deep breath!" the valet told him as he always did on such occasions. "A nice breath of damp steam, Your Majesty!"

Struggling for breath, Francis Joseph made his usual retort, "Nonsense!" But when he saw the injured expression on his servant's face he smiled slightly and added, "Thank you, Ketterl."

Ketterl smiled too. We get along perfectly, he thought. You just have to know him, then you get along with him perfectly. And as if to reward his master for his thoughtfulness, he carried a very small part of the documents asked for to his bedside!

"Here are the papers," he said, and allowed himself to admonish the man who refused to fall behind his schedule even for one day. "Don't work too hard, Your Majesty."

But this time the Emperor took neither the papers nor the pen offered him.

Young Dr. Baier told them this story of the Emperor's death. He told it in the words of the valet, who had come for him a few minutes after the Emperor's death. Since Schönbrunn Castle could no longer be heated on account of the coal shortage, Dr. Baier and his bride were now living at Number 10. He repeated what Ketterl, between constant sobs, had confided to him. Henriette, Franziska, and Martha Monica listened.

The "few days" that Henriette had been told over a year ago to be patient had still not passed, and Hans was lying in the field hospital of Kragujevac, ill with spotted typhus, but had not yet had any leave. Even after he was well Count Hoyos had again promised to obtain a leave for him "at once"; for unknown reasons, however, it had not been of the slightest avail, and he had been transferred from Serbia to Poland. Hermann, on the other hand, had come home for a fortnight's leave, was the possessor of the cross of military merit with swords, and had returned long since to Serbia. Franz, at headquarters, had been promoted to the rank of captain; Mr. Foedermayer received instructions from him for the factory regularly once a week.

"Don't you too think that the war will be over sooner now

that the Emperor has died?" Martha Monica asked through the door of the little room with a single window which she occupied in Hans's stead. It was almost midnight, but she knew it was never too late to talk to her mother.

Henriette was not sleeping any better on this night of November 21, 1916, than on any other, and she answered, "I don't know." It seemed beyond all doubt to her that the man who had died that day, even by his death, could not bring happiness. "Go to bed," she said to her daughter.

"Right away," Martha Monica promised. But her head was still so full of thoughts requiring attention, and not one of them was depressing or frightening. In all her fifteen years of life she had had a wonderful time. She could not understand why her mother worried so. While the lovely young girl blew the smoke of a forbidden cigarette out of the window her mother called: "You aren't still standing at that open window, are you, Mono? It is frightfully cold!"

Yes, she was standing at the window, and she was thinking of the army post office letter she had received that day from her tennis partner, in which he wrote: "I love you madly!" Life was so wonderful. The bells which boomed with such irresistible metallic vibration were ringing in better times; of this she was sure.

"Those bells will be the death of me!" her mother said. And since Martha Monica thought she heard her coming she quickly hid her cigarette and jumped back into bed. But her mother did not come. In the dark the girl dreamed on with open eyes, finished her cigarette, threw it away, and went to sleep.

An hour later the fire engines were summoned to Number 10 by Otto Eberhard, himself. Sleepless with grief over his Emperor's death, he wandered about his rooms and thought he smelled smoke coming down from the upper floor. He investigated at once. The fourth floor, of course! That constant source of disorder and disquiet! That fourth floor which had to be built to become the center of disturbance! Now it was on the point of destroying itself, and with it Number 10, the hearth of tradition and decency!

But the fire, started in Martha Monica's little room by the cigarette she threw away, caused comparatively little damage. Apart from some slight shock, Martha Monica, who had been awakened by her mother, suffered only from inconsiderable burns. Henriette carried her down the staircase. Most of Hans's books and his sister's bed were destroyed; the velvet curtains, irreplaceable because of the existing shortage of materials, were charred, and through the open window the flames spread to the rafters which overhung Annagasse.

From below, the inhabitants of Number 10 watched the fire. "Already!" said Otto Eberhard to himself while the mourning bells for Francis Joseph still tolled. "Already! Disorder is quick to start!"

When the fire was brought under control and the red glow in an otherwise completely black sky had vanished, the Public Prosecutor's thoughts immediately went back to the greater misfortune of that night. To think that at this very hour the man who for almost seven decades had given life and honor, foundation and roof, to his Empire lay without life on his Spartan bedstead in Schönbrunn. Francis Joseph dead! Before Otto Eberhard's eyes appeared the venerable and familiar figure after whom, he, and innumerable others of his kind, had modelled their own lives, appearance, views, iron principles. Francis Joseph no more! The old man's eyes grew moist.

Martha Monica saw it. "I am so sorry," she said: "Please, Uncle, don't take it so seriously! Nothing much has happened."

"What do you mean?" the lawyer asked sternly.

"I thought you were weeping," replied the bewildered girl.

"Nonsense! It is only that awful smoke."

While the Alts were returning to their rescued home the mourning bells still had not ceased.

Part Three
THE CELLAR

CHAPTER 28
Homecoming of an Austrian

The day Franz came home he was past sixty-six and Austria had lost the war. It was November 17, 1918. The 'final victory' had been one of those dogmas never subject to doubt even up to the last minute. He had felt disgraced because his years prevented him from doing active duty at the front, a feeling mitigated only by the fact of his having two sons in the field. The older one, Hans, was a prisoner of war and only a sergeant, whereas Hermann, the younger one, was a hero with several medals.

When his train pulled into the North Station a lady was standing on the platform. She waved to him, and she was still beautiful. He struggled against the tears that came and against the fact that he still loved her so much. For a moment he forgot that Austria had been defeated.

As the elderly gentleman in a captain's uniform, with gleaming patent-leather boots, fresh-shaven despite the early morning hour, with two bags in his hands, came towards her, Henriette could not repress the warm rush of sympathy rising in her. For more than four years they had not lived under the same roof.

He put his bags down and kissed her hand. She kissed his cheek.

"It's good to be home again," he said, brief as ever.

"I'm glad you have come," she said. "Didn't you bring your orderly?"

"No," he said. "The scamp deserted."

They did not mention the revolution.

There were neither porters, nor taxis, nor cabs at the North Station, and they had to walk with the bags as far as the Praterstern to get a tram. It was so crowded that Franz had great difficulty in pushing his luggage on to the open platform of the back car and then forced his way into the closed part where Henriette stood. The passengers were mostly factory workmen on their way to work.

"You're looking splendid," Franz told her, and glanced around the car. Those sitting down were practically all men. They might have given a seat to a lady, he thought.

"So are you," she said, returning the compliment.

The critical way in which he inspected the sitting passengers had not gone unnoticed.

"Anything wrong?" asked a youngish man who sat beside a still younger one at the window reading a newspaper.

"Did you receive my express letter in time?" Henriette put in quickly.

But Franz answered the newspaper reader instead. "Don't you see there is a lady standing up?"

"I like to stand. It's just a few streets more," Henriette said, hoping to head him off.

But from the other end of the car somebody had already yelled, "Brass-hat swine!"

That was the insult with which the angry and disillusioned mob gave vent to their feelings when they saw men who had 'wangled' themselves jobs away from the front lines and put their skins in safety, in the rear. This officer of the Dragoons, so scrupulously clean-shaven, with gleaming buttons and boots, looked like one of them. Moreover, he was an officer, and it had been the officers who for four years had ordered them out to die.

The man who had yelled was a common soldier. He wore the field uniform of the Vienna home regiment, the Fourth

Hoch-und-Deutschmeister, but the erstwhile blue of his collar could hardly be distinguished, so dirty was it with the blood and filth of the trenches.

"Private!" Franz said. "You will report to your superior officer. I shall see to it that you—"

"Like hell!" interrupted the man. "You've finished giving orders!"

Henriette, who in the five days since the revolution started had witnessed similar incidents, leaned over to Franz and whispered:

"It's no use!"

"No use!" he said angrily, "As long as a fellow like that wears His Majesty's uniform he's subject to discipline!"

Before the words were out of his mouth the man who was reading the newspaper had jumped up and made a sign with his head to the one next to him. Now they pushed their way up behind Franz; one of them grabbed his arms and held them in a vice-like grip, while the other tore the insignia from his officer's cap and the gold stars from his collar.

"There!" he said as he did it. "Now you have finished commanding!"

Henriette saw the veins stand out on Franz's temples, grown so gray, the sign of his flaring temper that she had so feared and hated in the past. Now, standing close by his side, she felt nothing but sympathy. He had hardly ever made her feel sorry for him, but in this instant she felt more sorry for him than for anyone ever before. She knew what was going on inside him. What she had gone through thirty years earlier, when her world crumbled for her, he was now feeling himself.

In an attempt to extricate himself with his hands and feet from the vice in which he was held, Franz said in a tone of infinite contempt, "You rabble!"

To a man all the passengers sided against him.

"Who's rabble?" yelled a woman with a stack of morning

papers for delivery under her arm. "Two of my lads they shot, they did—and for what? Your Goddamn discipline!"

"That's right!" someone else yelled. "No food! No heat! And why? 'Cause we had to stand around, and click our heels, and say 'Yes, sir' while you fine gentlemen in shiny boots ordered us out to be killed!"

"Throw him out!" suggested the newspaper reader.

Someone on the platform had already shoved Franz's bags off; they crashed on the pavement. The conductor stopped the car.

"The gentleman had better see to his luggage," he told Henriette. His aversion to the officer was as obvious as that of the others.

"Come," Henriette begged. For a moment she felt like saying to the people, "I also have two sons at the front." But she only looked at them and they made way for her. As she stood in the street with Franz he grew dizzy, and she had to steady him. He recovered quickly, straightened his disordered uniform, picked up his bags, and refused to let her help him. He managed to struggle along with them until they found a taxi to drive them home.

During the ride he looked at her from time to time but said nothing. It was only when the angel with the trumpet came in sight that he said in a low voice, "What do you think of that?"

"You mustn't take it so hard," she replied. "It's just that those people are having a miserable time of it." She thought he meant the people in the tram.

But he meant a poster they had passed: "The reckoning with the Hapsburg Criminals. Read today's *Workers' Journal*."

Herr Simmerl was standing at the entrance under the angel with the trumpet. "Welcome back, Captain," he greeted his master, and gave no sign of noticing the defaced collar on the uniform and the cap on which the cockade of the Imperial house was missing.

Franz held out his hand to him. "Well, what do you say to all this, Herr Simmerl?"

"It is just a catastrophe, Captain," answered the tall man in the Styrian jacket and spotless white cravat. It was impossible to say whether he was making excuses or complaining.

"You may well say that!" Franz declared, having decided he meant the latter. Then he expressed the request, "Get me today's *Workers' Journal*."

It was only now that the tall man, who had been waiting at the door for two hours because his mistress would not allow him to go to the station, lost his composure. "Sir?" he asked, hoping that he had misheard, But the order was repeated.

As the couple went up the few steps from the entrance to the main floor Henriette noticed how heavily Franz was breathing.

"Don't you feel well?" she asked.

"Thank you. I'm quite well," he answered gratefully. They had passed the door of Sophie's former apartment, and he thought. Who would have believed that Austria could go down to defeat? But that Henriette would be a bad wife they would all have sworn. Sophie, Otto Eberhard. He even admitted that for a while he was one of them. But Henriette was a good wife! She had made mistakes, as every one does. But she was a fine, good wife. The icy band around his heart, which had robbed him of his breath as he came into his home, now relaxed. "Is Otto Eberhard still unrelenting?" he asked, to please her, as they reached his doorway.

"Don't you want to see him?" she offered.

"Let's go in for a moment."

"You too?"

"Why not?"

"That's really very friendly of you. Thank you ever so much. But I think it's a bit early. Otto Eberhard is no longer so young as he might be either. Excuse me; I meant myself, of course. You have remained marvellously young."

As they went on upstairs he was tempted to offer her his arm out of that sense of somewhat exaggerated chivalry that belonged to bygone days. They all came back now, with the joys and with the griefs that followed them. "Do you remember the betrothal calls we made when we were engaged?" he asked.

"I was thinking of them too."

They were now in front of the apartment where the Paskiewiczs had lived, now inhabited by Peter and his Prussian wife. Peter was indispensable to the Ministry of Instruction, so he had not seen active service.

"Is she still convinced that our German brothers protected us so wonderfully?" asked Franz, pointing to the apartment door. "Do you know who really got us into such a hole?" he added softly. "It was our German brothers! I've come to know them in the last four years! What intolerable arrogance! I'll tell you what. We Austrians would never have had the whole world against us if we had not had the worst man in the world, Kaiser Wilhelm, for us!" Again he was so overcome with excitement that his breath gave out.

"Let's stand here a bit," she suggested. "There's no hurry."

He did as she bade. "You are very sweet to me," he said.

If such a slight thing makes an impression on him now, what must I have been like? she thought. As they climbed from the first to the second story she said, "Come. Take my arm."

With a round, embracing gesture, which long ago had been so distasteful to her, he accepted her suggestion. A remarkable man, she thought, taking the arm he held out to her, ignoring the fact that he was obviously reluctant to lean on her and preferred her to lean on him. Incorrigibly old-fashioned! He denies that the world has changed. He insists on a world that no longer exists.

As she was thinking of that and of what this man had done to her she instinctively drew away. "Am I too heavy for you?"

he asked instantly. "Not at all," she answered, pressing his arm closer. A man through whom you can see. Even now, as he is growing old, he still has the same traits of candour and simplicity of his earlier years. Not even old age can change a man so set against all change!

They climbed with extreme slowness. With an optimism which only she could muster when everything looked black ("an inopportune optimist" was what her father sometimes called her), she laid it to the after-effects of the shock he had received in the tramcar.

"It's all over for people of our kind," he said suddenly and unexpectedly. His words echoed through the dark, cold staircase like a verdict.

Before he spoke she had been thinking: *If he had not been of such small caliber things might have been different between us.* But when he had uttered his judgment she not only was moved again by sympathy for him, but thought: *Since I have known this man he has never taken a step that was devious or disgraceful. He has always gone straight. He has never concealed anything. He has been as punctual as clockwork. His reliability has been matchless. He has conducted his business on strict principles. Whether he acts rightly or wrongly, he does it out of conviction.*

"You must allow yourself a few days of absolute rest, Franz," she said in a warmer tone.

"Impossible," was his firm reply. "I must be in my office not later than nine o'clock. Foedermayer is expecting, me. Even so, everything will be topsy-turvy. Thanks just the same for your thoughtfulness."

His gratitude put her to shame, and that he should call it thoughtfulness was almost unbearable. How thoughtless she must have been in the past!

The walls from the entrance up to the 'party rooms' on the uninhabited second story were so full of cracks that Franz shook his head. And when they passed the door on the third floor which led to his former bachelor quarters, and which were now occupied by Otto Drauffer, he commented: "Not growing any younger either!" He might be referring to the disrepair of the door or to his recurrent breathlessness. He held fast to the banister, looking down the three stories he used to climb so lightly as a young man at night, alone or (to Sophie's annoyance) in company. *Men like me have had so much to enjoy in the past*, came into his mind as he glanced at the woman by his side with tenderness. *One can't very easily ask others to be satisfied with so little!*

"I am afraid I haven't made things easy for you," he said as they reached the fourth story he had built for her.

This confession, which she had waited for from him for heaven knows how long but had never heard, so upset her that it was several moments before she could answer, in the best manner of Number 10, "Surely you haven't grown sentimental! First you shall have some nice hot coffee. I can't guarantee that it will taste exactly like coffee, but there will be eight real coffee beans in it!"

He laughed. "That's four more than we brass-hat swine have been accustomed to for the last year." Then he cleared his throat and asked, "And how are you, Martha Monica?"

The girl was standing in the open door of the apartment and held her arms out to the homecomer. "Papa!" she cried with delight. He stroked her hair and said: "You've grown into a real beauty." She was so beautiful and radiated such joyousness that she seemed to light up the darkness of the staircase.

Hanni, the former chambermaid who had become Frau Simmerl and was the mother of a daughter, immediately appeared on the scene. She greeted, in her usual manner, the man for whom her mistress was much too good, "Welcome home, sir."

These were the present occupants of the fourth story. For

Hans was a prisoner of war, and Hermann was still with his regiment, waiting for his release from the Isonzo front. Neni was dead; the cook had been dismissed, and the Simmerl child was being brought up in the country. After Francis Joseph's death Franziska and her husband, Dr. Baier, had moved to Salzburg, where there were not so many Reds and people still went to mass.

With Henriette on his right and Martha Monica on his left Franz crossed the threshold of his home. "At last!" he said. Some trace of comfort and protection enfolded him. The rooms were heated as well as possible. In the dining room the table was laid for breakfast; the tall silver coffee pot, with its chicory content, and the smaller jug, with bluish, watery milk, gleamed brightly. The maize bread, modified with bran, had been toasted so that the gray flecks in it were not noticeable, and the jam made of carrots and turnips, when put in a crystal container, looked deceptively like the best marmalade.

"What in the world has happened to the master's—"

But before Hanni could finish her question about what her master had done with the three gold stars on his collar, Henriette's glance and the return of Herr Simmerl checked her. Her words stuck in her throat. But her eyes, which had never looked with favor on her master, remained glued on his torn collar with its aspect of infinite disorder. He had always been so meticulous, so uncomfortable in the order he exacted.

Herr Simmerl conducted himself less objectionably. The newspaper he had been ordered to fetch he had dutifully obtained at the tobacconist's at Number 7, for even in times like the present it would never have occurred to him to refuse to do anything he was told. There were masters and servants in the world; it had been that way and it would always be that way, because it was right, no matter what the loud-mouthed people in the street bellowed. And even when an order verged on insanity, such as bringing a Red sheet into the house of highborn people, where the members of the family were spoken to with respectful titles and letters bore special modes of address, an order was an order. At best one could lay the filthy rag away somewhere out of sight. This is what the tall man proceeded to do and thereby hoped to spare himself the spectacle of an imperial and royal officer and a court purveyor reading the words of Messrs. Victor Adler, Friedrich Austerlitz, and Company, who had turned our magnificent imperial city into the capital of a poverty-stricken, miserable, shabby little republic!

"The coffee—excellent," praised Franz. He also took a bit of margarine on a slice of suspiciously dark-colored toast, spread it with the questionable sweet concoction, and asked, "Did you get me that paper, Simmerl?"

What could the tall man do except answer "Yes, sir," and hand over the disgusting sheet with a bow.

"Thanks, Simmerl," replied his master, and proceeded to do with the *Workers' Journal* what he had done for years with the *Reichspost*. He propped it up against his glass while he ate.

"Oh, don't read that stuff," Henriette said. "You'll only get all excited."

"I'll be finished in a moment," he answered. He was ready to admit that justifiable bitterness could make people blind. To be sure, reproaches could be made to the Prussians. Probably to the generals too. But there were certain limits beyond which even the best-founded bitterness must not go. These limits included the Imperial House, to whom every Austrian, and above all every Viennese, owed everything he had and was.

With a pair of horn-rimmed glasses on his nose, a piece of toast in his hand, he read the leading article by the editor, Karl Leuthner, published that morning:

Of the fifty-five million people who were condemned to form the grandeur of the Hapsburgs, at least thirty-five million wanted the defeat of Austria-Hungary and placed their hopes on the victory of the Entente. To think that a state in which the overwhelming majority want to have nothing to do with it, who actually hate and abhor it, should be able to endure! Moreover, this state had the criminal audacity to provoke a war. A handful of unscrupulous scoundrels—Berchtold and two or three of his henchmen, Hoetzendorf, Stuergkh, Tisza—had the power to unchain this wanton war out of bravado and plunge mankind into misery. Yet those who started it and those who prolonged it still think they were in the right!

You see them swarming together like vermin—the court parasites, the officers, the officials of the entire one-time Empire, who lacked every attribute to help man rise above his lowest instincts. In the service of their employer they were mere mercenaries both by outlook and by morals. At present, however, these counter-revolutionary criminals bow before the storm of our November the twelfth revolution. But they are ready to pounce! They congregate at the apartment of some fallen prince. The apartment of a fallen prince, be it ever so small, is a court—and what has a court and what have court parasites to do in a republic? Who would not be ready to pay a reasonable sum to be rid at last of our beloved dynasty? We deplore, of course, the irreparable losses and devastation of the war. Yet its outcome affords us pleasure, and we esteem the collapse of the Hapsburg Empire as compensation for all we have suffered and lost.

Franz's hand dropped the piece of grayish bread. Henriette, who was accustomed to his old habit of reading his paper at meal-time, had taken the opportunity of describing in low tones to Martha Monica what had happened in the tram. It was the grating sound of the falling bread that caused her to look up.

"That is beyond anything!" Franz exclaimed, and pointed

to the place in the paper on which his eyes rested. "That is" he repeated, and then his mouth made some inarticulate, babbling sounds. Then he was unable to say any more.

Dr. Herz, still the family physician, and still against speaking the ruthless truth, did not say the court purveyor had lost his speech, but stated that it was a "nervous derangement," which with proper rest and in time would, he hoped, be overcome. And as Henriette sat by the bed in which Franz had been obliged to rest, and saw how helplessly he moved his lips, she thought of Hans, who also had been unable to speak. One of her fantastic, superstitious ideas flashed through her mind: Christl had by some miracle brought Hans to speak. Christl must come!

Without reflecting for even a minute, she told Martha Monica what to do for Papa and instantly left the house. It was only when she was on her way to Salesianergasse that she admitted to herself that for several years she had neither seen nor wished to see the woman to whom she was hurrying.

"It is inexcusable of me," she said when they stood face to face. "I can't justify it. But if you knew what my life has been, perhaps you would understand why I have felt shy about coming to see you."

"I know your life," said the nun, who, when she had walked into the bare reception room, had grown as white as her starched collar. Her forty years lay lightly on her. She still had the charm and slimness of her youth; it was only a deep-set line around her mouth and the look in her eyes that betrayed her loneliness and renunciation.

Henriette asked in surprise: "How can you know about my life?"

"I have always asked about you," the nun answered simply.

"But your informants have no doubt had a lot to criticize in me?" Henriette asked of the woman who once so idolized her, and who now stood before her like a judge.

"You've been a very good mother," the nun said.

"Thank you," Henriette said. It was incomprehensible to her how completely their roles had been exchanged and that she now was in the position of an inferior. Was it because of the stiff headgear and the white cord on which there hung a cross? Surely I am not going to capitulate to a costume! she thought. Christl had grown arrogant!

But the nun did not need to ask, "How have things gone with you?" in the unchanged tone of the past in order to put her in the wrong. "Thank you, well," answered Henriette, with a feeling of shame she had already experienced so often that morning. "And how have things gone with you, Christl? Excuse me, I should say, Sister Agatha."

"It makes no difference. Call me Christl. I like to have you do it. Thank you, things have gone well with me."

Then they talked about Hans, for Henriette could not bring herself to say why she had come. It seemed to her that Christl thought she had come because at last she wished to see her again.

"Did you want me to do something for you?" the nun asked. "I should be so happy if I could be of help to you."

"You can help me. Only you can do it," was Henriette's instant reply. Then she asked, "Are you really not angry with me any more?"

Sister Agatha gazed at the worldly woman. It was a look of such deep affection that Henriette dropped her eyes. "I was never angry with you," said the nun.

"But you came here because of me? I mean into the convent?" Henriette dared at last to stand the trial she had never faced and make her defence, of which she had graver doubts as time went by.

"Yes," admitted the nun freely. "I thought you needed someone to pray for you."

That was the second verdict Henriette had heard that morning. She asked, "Do you still hold it against me?"

The nun reflected for an instant. "I never did. I wanted you to be happy."

Henriette was silent. When she finally decided to tell her, a smile flitted across Sister Agatha's face and vanished. "How lovely that you still believe in miracles," she said. "In other ways, too, you have hardly changed." Then she grew more serious. "I didn't know that Uncle Franz is ill."

"He isn't ill. He got too excited and had a shock. Dr. Herz—you remember him?—does not consider it a stroke, but a temporary derangement."

The nun recalled Dr. Herz's tactful diagnosis of Colonel Paskiewicz's attacks as "asthma." Again the terrifying odour of oxygen seemed to enfold her as she left the bare reception room and went to the mother superior to ask for permission to visit a sickbed, her first request since she had been there and had had her training in the convent hospital. Receiving the necessary permission, she and Henriette started off.

"I remember so well that time when Hans began to talk. He did it quite by himself," she said as they walked along the street; it made her feel dizzy, so unused had she grown to the outside air and to people. She had resolved to stay away from both for the rest of her life. Her feet moved with such difficulty that she could not keep up with her hurrying companion.

"But you wanted to help him," Henriette contradicted. "Why do you walk so slowly?"

Two schoolboys ran towards them from the direction of the skating rink. "Spit three times!" they called out laughingly. "A nun!" They spat and ran on.

For the previous six days it had been the fashion in Catholic Vienna to drag everything Catholic in the dust.

"Yes, I did want to," Sister Agatha confirmed. But that this was her first excursion into the outside world since she took the veil, that she had resolved to remain cut off from all other human beings for the rest of her life, and that she would have broken that resolve for no one in the world except Henriette, all that she kept to herself.

"If you could do it then, when you were not even a nun, you must be much better able to do it now!" Henriette answered in her always naively illogical way.

The Salesian sister did not respond. Everything along their short way seemed to her to have changed. There stood the same houses, but they looked unfamiliar. Their size was all wrong. What used to be broad was narrow now.

"Please don't tell him I came to fetch you," begged Henriette as they entered the angel doorway.

"No, I shan't," the nun promised.

Franz was sleeping. It was an uneasy sleep that brought beads of sweat to his forehead. Sometimes one could hear him babbling. Martha Monica sat by his bed. The curtains were drawn.

"This is your cousin, Sister Agatha," Henriette said softly to her daughter.

"My saintly cousin?" asked the girl with a smile. She showed no signs of embarrassment either at the nun's religious garb or at the odour of carbolic that she exuded. She kissed her.

"Yes. I think she is saintly," Henriette answered.

The nun's pale cheeks tinged with color. "How lovely she is!" she said to Henriette. This young creature was so like her mother that she seemed to bring back the past with irresistible force. "Perfectly lovely!" she repeated, and looked at Mono with the admiration she had had for Henriette and which Number 10, disapprovingly, called worship.

"You're terribly sweet," Martha Monica said to her new relative, who now was spoken of as a saint in Number 10.

When the invalid woke up he made a gesture in Henriette's direction. "Do you want to be alone with me?" she asked. He nodded and tried to speak. As she leaned over to hear him better it seemed to her that his mouth had become twisted. But it was hard to see in the darkened room.

She made a sign to Martha Monica to leave, then said: "Christl is here. She wanted to pay you a visit."

An incomprehensible answer came from Franz's lips.

"Good morning, Uncle Franz," Sister Agatha greeted him, with the steady tone of someone accustomed to reeling at home beside a sickbed. "You have overdone things. A little rest will be good for you."

Her uncle made a contemptuous gesture and then indicated that he wanted to write. Henriette brought him a pad and a pencil, drew the curtains, and, with Christl's help, propped him up on his pillows. Now his twisted mouth was so visible that Henriette threw a look of horror at her niece. The nun nodded reassuringly to her from behind the sick man.

"Ask Mr. Foedermayer to come to me as soon as possible," Franz had written in his precise handwriting.

Henriette promised to notify the head clerk of the Alt Firm at once. When she came back from the telephone she heard Sister Agatha say, "It's best not to talk, Uncle Franz."

He raised his hand and let it fall again, as much as to say, "Nonsense!"

Yet, with a firmness which contrasted with her soft voice, Sister Agatha insisted, "Believe me, Uncle Franz. The person who has not learned to be silent knows nothing. I haven't spoken out for seventeen years."

The words were addressed to the sick man, but Henriette knew they were meant for her. On hearing that dreadful reproach she said imploringly, "Christl!"

The nun understood. Do a miracle, was what she meant.

Her firmness belied her gentleness. She rose. "I hope you will soon feel better, Uncle Franz," she said firmly and softly. "I shall pray for you." And she left the room.

Henriette followed her into the vestibule. "Don't go," she said.

"But, Aunt Hetti—" answered the nun, calling her for the

first time by that name, just as she did when they were playing 'marriage' together and Uncle Franz was dealing with a dangerous adversary in the next room. Now he fought against one who was more dangerous. In her innermost heart Sister Agatha envied him. Uncle Franz would fight, be conquered, and conquer.

"Why won't you help him?" Henriette asked.

"Because I cannot," was the answer.

"Because you will not!"

"Do you still believe everything depends on will?"

"I need your help!"

"Uncle Franz will be helped," the nun told her. "Say goodbye to Martha Monica for me. She must come to see me some time, if she has the leisure. I may have callers every Monday and every Friday from three to four." With that she left.

Henriette heard her steps going down as far as the first floor, where, presumably before her former home, they stopped, but became immediately audible again and finally faded away.

For seventeen years she has waited for me every Monday and Friday, thought Henriette, shaken and ashamed. Then she went back to the sickroom, saying to herself, "I will help him! It does depend on will!"

As if Franz wished to put to the test what was in her mind, when she sat down beside him, took his hand and stroked it, his twisted mouth took on an expression which she thought was a smile. Time passed. Otto Eberhard came, but was refused admittance. Down in the streets there were piercing cries, "Extra! The Hapsburg crime expiated! Parliament exiles Emperor Charles, Empress Zita, and the Imperial Family from Austria!"

Henriette stroked the burning brow of the sick man. Yes. He was smiling.

CHAPTER 29
Letter from a Better World

This is the letter which reached Hans before his return journey from his prison camp:

Hans! It makes me indescribably happy to know that you are coming back. If words could only convey some conception of it! How many others before me have said they were happy. I am happier than they are, but there are no words for it.

When you get back you will see all the calendars hanging on the wall of my room, on which I crossed off the days, keeping the old calendars. It was the only thing that showed me time was passing. The day you were taken ill, the day you were wounded, the day you were taken prisoner, the day I learned you were one of those most unfortunate ones 'without documents'—each has a star. They were all Sundays, and Sunday always used to be my unlucky day. The casualty-list Thursdays are marked with a half-moon. Did you know that the lists of casualties were published every Thursday at the State Printing House in the Rennweg? Each half-moon meant: Not on the casualty list! This is just so as to help you understand my signs. Perhaps they will convey more to you than my words.

This is the first letter I have written you free from fear. Hence it is my first perfectly honest letter. The time has come for you to have a clear picture of everything.

The innumerable days and nights which I counted and crossed off, were a ghost-ridden interlude. In a mechanical way you continue to live even then, to be ambitious (see later), to work, to be subject to appetite and desire (Freud: "The uninhibited frankness of Fräulein Rosner"—remember?). But the whole thing is absolutely unreal. You are kept constantly running by a motor, presumably hope, you are constantly held back, and the brake is undoubtedly fear. And something always is telling you: this is infinitely unimportant. The one important thing is that Hans Alt is alive and is coming home.

So immeasurable has been my egotism. Or should I say my love? No, egotism is the more correct word. The people here, who turned anti-dynastic overnight, declared that the downfall of the house of Hapsburg was the downfall of egotism because the Hapsburgs never cared for anything except their house. You will remember what I thought of the house of Hapsburg. But I find the people who are complaining about egotism much more unbearable. Do you know anyone who is not egotistic? I don't.

By which I only mean to tell you how infinitely puny my conduct has been in these 'great days' and since. Alas, you cannot be proud of me. All I ever wanted was to have it over. A thousand times better that we should lose the war than that I should lose you. I did not work in the Silver Cross or railway station canteens or in any of the other places you might have liked to have me work, although you were tactful enough not to say so. I loathed the war like the plague. And also the people who organized benefit balls, teas, exhibitions. If a woman wants to go into war service she should be a nurse in a front-line hospital. Nothing else counts. But I could not stand the smell of a hospital. No, you really can't be proud of me.

That is also why I have paid so little attention to your family. Theoretically they should perhaps have paid some attention to me, for "after all I am your wife (if only a war bride). But all these years they have preferred to have nothing to do with me, and your noble uncle, who grows more and more like the Duke of Alba in Don Carlos, even turned his face ostentatiously the other way recently when I passed him in Karntnerstrasse. That your mother cannot stand me is, of course, a 'historic fact, and as for your father, the expression 'cannot stand' is probably much too mild. I think he looks on me as the offspring of all that is evil. How this will turn out when we all shall be living under the same roof is difficult for me to imagine.

Now, Hans, brace yourself. Here comes the real thing. The introduction has been long enough (perhaps Freud's remark on my 'uninhibitedness' is only ninety percent true?). But I do so want him to be one hundred percent, right! Because it was through him, thanks to him, that I have been for four weeks now—a member of the Burgtheater!

Joking aside, it's true.

I could send you a notice from the *Neue Freie Presse* in which Raoul Auernheimer wrote about me as follows: "The Grillparzer 'Hero' of Fraülein Rosner is full of promise; indeed, it is already full of accomplishment." I could enclose the notice of Felix Salten, which begins, "Heavens, but this little Selma Rosner has a great talent!" I could even quote Alfred Polgar to you; "Fraülein Rosner takes a definite step away round from the pretty to the positive. She adds an earthy and convincing grain of salt to the pallid, baby-blue part of a sweet, naïve young thing, by means of a charm that is clever enough to appear to be naïve. She plays, as it were, from her head to her heart, instead of the other way round." I could add other chapters and verses to prove to you what a real success I had, but if I know you it would only irritate you more. You do not enjoy being faced with faits accomplis, and I am bringing you face to face with something which will remain one.

This is the chronological development of the remarkable happening. In the interlude condition I was in, my academic achievements left much to be desired. Jodi and Muellner had the patience of angels with me, but Freud lost his. One day he said, "Why don't you go on the stage, Fraülein Rosner? You will never become a practitioner of psycho-analysis. But I believe you are already a noteworthy actress." (You see, I had made some excuses about not having my thesis ready because I had to help my mother in the store—incidentally that was the truth.) You know the complacent tone with which he says things like that and the deprecatory shrug of the shoulders which follows, making one feel like more of an idiot than ever. In any case, I was ready to murder him, and you can well imagine how my sweet fellow students enjoyed it. In my rage I asked right out of the blue whether he was intimating that he was preparing to fail me. But he explained in a quite matter-of-fact way that he had meant it in all seriousness. That I was wasting my time. If he were in my place he would let the seminars go and take lessons in acting.

That day, when I came home, I found the news that you had been taken prisoner. The slip from the Ministry of War gave no indication of your whereabouts. I did not know where to write you. I did not know how you were. My state of mind led to one of those scenes with my mother in which I behave so intolerably. She had chosen that particular moment as appropriate in which to tell me that your family is under obligation to do something for me if you no longer can. She, in any case, had reached the end of her rope. I regret to say I grew violent, too much so, took my belongings, and spent the night in the Golden Pear (the place you maintain is not a hotel. Nor is it.) To a certain extent my mother was right. A woman of my age should not be dependent. Even if I had received my Ph.D. summa cum laude it would have taken, as you know, at least three more years to get a paid job as a teacher.

So the next morning I went to the Berggasse to see Freud. He made me sit in the famous green armchair for more than an hour, talking in a frank and friendly way. Finally he sent me off with a letter in which he stated that he looked upon himself as an undiscovered dramatic critic and asked his esteemed friend, Hermann Bahr, elected head of the Burgtheater by the Reds, to give the bearer a trial. Mr. Bahr, whose beard is even longer than your unde Drauffer's, is fascinatingly clever. He received me and said, "All anyone needs to ruin his chances

with me is a letter of recommendation. In your case the recommendation comes from the most distinguished living
Viennese. Therefore I promise I shall not let it influence me
against you. Recite something for me."

I could have recited Muellner's formula theories or Jodi's
value theory of ethics, but he wanted the Maid of Orleans or
at any rate Viola in *Twelfth Night*. He finally agreed to let me
do two scenes from Shaw's *Cleopatra*, which I had played in
that charity performance in the Baden Arena, after which you
and I argued so passionately and you were (rightly) so displeased. As I recited I had before me your angry face and I
undertook to prove to you, not Mr. Bahr, that I was better
than I had been in Baden. In any case, the director of the
Burgtheater approved a scholarship for me at the Academy of
Acting, I received instruction from Albert Heine, and four
weeks ago I made my debut.

On the morning of the dress rehearsal a rumor was going
round that the Austrian prisoners of war would be exchanged
witnin the next two weeks. I was in such a state of bliss that I
was a quarter of an hour late, for I had been waiting at the
Ministry of War for confirmation. An unknown actress by the
name of Selma Rosner, daughter of a tobacconist, about to
make her debut, and she arrives late at a dress rehearsal in the
former Imperial and Royal Burgtheater—you can imagine!
The court actors and court actresses who had been looking
askance at me now looked clean through me as though I were
air. Before the curtain went up the stage-hands were saying that
the news about the prisoners had been officially confirmed. I
was so good that the honorable die-hards all around me grew
stiffer than ever. The stage-hands—in general I was considered
a Red—applauded me from the wings. Hermann Bahr came to
me in the interval and whispered, "For God's sake, don't tell
anyone that I congratulated you. You will have the biggest success anyone can achieve in Vienna. People will fight over you!"

On the opening night I was feeling terrible because the news about the prisoners didn't mean those 'without documents.' But it was probably on account of my frightful shyness that I made a hit. Reimers (handsome George!) said to me in his pompous manner and with his resounding vowels, "My che-ild, you are the che-arming!" And gorgeous Otto Tressler wanted me to drive out to Grinzing for supper with him.

Hans! I am an actress of the Burgtheater! With a five-year contract! How often have we ridiculed the outmoded way of acting of the court theater. Nevertheless, I am tremendously proud. (I know you won't be—see above—and your family most certainly are not, for they have shown no signs of life.) My next part is Viola, with Tressler as Malvolio. Now you know.

When you arrive my marks on the calendars must plead for me with you. (Other marks, even those I might want to conceal from you, there are none.) Forgive me for presenting you with this fait accompli, and especially one which will in addition make trouble for you with your family. First a dancer and now an actress. And a Red, at that! Well, I am just an egotist who loves you. Do you know a better expression for that certainty than that you cling to a person as you do to your own breath?

SELMA

P.S. I was almost tempted to rent an enchanting place, which has just been vacated out at Grinzing, for us to live in. It is an adorable little house with an old garden, right opposite the vineyard slopes. Must it be Seilerstätte for us, irrevocably and for ever? Is there no such thing as vis major? Do endless years of separation, a lost war, and the incontrovertible evidence that the wrong people made it for the wrong reason not add up to one? Think about this and do not jump to the conclusion that it is *lèse-majesti*. In a crashing world even the will of a great-grandfather can perhaps eventually lose its validity.

CHAPTER 30
Homecoming of a Son

The return of the two brothers occurred with a long and unexpected interval between. Hermann came first.

When he appeared before Henriette she looked in vain for any familiar trait in this young man whom she had not seen for so long. The war had transformed him. He had grown much stockier; his face, with its small eyes and unusually low forehead which he wrinkled up when he was serious, was surmounted by hair parted on the side, and he wore a jauntily upturned moustache. The wrist of his left hand was ornamented with a gold bracelet. He was in civilian clothes, and as he spoke he shot his shirt-cuffs forward. Henriette, who no longer allowed herself the luxury of illusions, thought he looked rather comic.

Their greeting was formal. His mother had not forgotten that of the four children Hermann was the only one who had always, no matter how seldom he was in her vicinity, preferred being with his father. Now too he immediately asked to see his father.

"For only a moment," his mother said. "And don't tell him anything that might excite him." (Old Dr. Herz meanwhile had modified his protective tactics and admitted "a slight stroke," warning against excitement because of "certain fluctuations of blood pressure.")

"Self-evidently," remarked the son, using an expression he had picked up in army communications.

"He is a hero," she reasoned. The ribbon of the Military Merit Cross was in his buttonhole.

As they went into the sickroom, Henriette, who was on the lookout for things that would speak in favor of this son, noticed that he was frightened by the sight of his father.

Franz no longer lay in bed. He was allowed to walk around

in the house, but no farther, for Dr. Herz thought the staircase too steep. Constant confinement indoors had robbed his face of its customary ruddiness; its mouth remained twisted. But it was one of his unnoticed achievements that he had overcome the babbling sounds with which he had accompanied his gestures during the early weeks of his illness. What he had to say he wrote down. He had acquired the habit of stroking his upper lip with his hand, thus concealing the mouth.

Hermann kissed the hand of his father, who nodded to him repeatedly. That meant, I am proud of you. Then he wrote: "What are your plans?"

"To tell the truth, Father, what I should like to do most would be to enter the factory."

Franz seemed pleased. He was saying what Hans had never said! "Are you no longer interested in lithography?" he wrote.

"No," Hermann answered. "I was only interested in that as long as I thought it would be possible to found a large publishing house in Vienna. But that's impossible now. Our Austrian writers will prefer German publishers more than ever, and my idea of publishing German authors in Vienna is completely out of the question now. The gentlemen in St. Germain have seen to that too. The scoundrels!" he added, and pulled out his shirt-cuffs.

Again Franz nodded. His son was speaking his own inmost thoughts.

"Where do you intend to live?" he wrote.

"Here, of course. Or should I bother you?"

Henriette liked him less than ever. "Certainly not," she said. "Would you like to fix up the little study?"

"Where will Hans live when he comes home?" Hermann asked.

"In Aunt Sophie's former apartment," his mother told him.

"Too bad. I should have liked that ground-floor apartment," Hermann said.

"That unfortunately is out of the question," Henriette said firmly.

"Why, if I may make so bold as to ask?" Hermann said.

"Because Hans, as you know, is married, and two people need more room than one."

"Is that still intact? I thought that had blown up long ago! What's the little Jewess called?"

Franz reprimanded this lack of tact with a shake of his head. He did not care for the daughter-in-law who had been forced on him by a war marriage. But she was Hans's wife. It was bad enough that they had left her to live at home with her mother instead of having her in the house.

Henriette, on the other hand, found herself in the remarkable position of defending her daughter-in-law, about whom she was probably even less enthusiastic than Franz. "The little Jewess is called Selma Rosner, and she has had a great success at die Burgtheater," she said. "I haven't had time yet to see her, but the consensus of opinion was that she was quite excellent."

"Really. The Burgtheater is now under a departmental chief called Vetter," the young man said, "and isn't he a violent Social Democrat?"

"That I don't know," Henriette answered evasively. "The director of the theater is Hermann Bahr."

But Franz had nodded. Vetter was really a Red.

"Then I'm not surprised that this Fraulein Rosner is suddenly able to get into the Burgtheater," Hermann said to his father. "She's a member of the Social Democratic party. But you knew that anyhow."

No! No one in the house knew that. There had been talk of the peculiar political views the actress was supposed to hold. But a party member? Franz's face clouded.

"That is probably just gossip," Henriette suggested. All this concerned Hans, and there was nothing to do except stand up for the much too clever know-it-all girl. If only he were back! "It's quite authentic, Mother," Hermann told her with a glibness characteristic of all he did and said. "Incidentally, that explains Hans's conduct. He was under my command, as you know. I tell you, a real Sozi would not have behaved differently."

"Getting typhus! And a wound—"

"In his right arm!"

"What are you implying?" Henriette asked indignantly.

"A shot in the right arm," explained Hermann, "is what we called a thousand-gulden shot. That was what it was worth to the man who was wounded. There were even those who perpetrated them on themselves."

Franz pointed at him violently with his index finger. "You go too far!" this indicated.

"Naturally I was not referring to Hans," said Hermann, hastily retracting his words. "I merely meant that his attitude struck me. After all, he let himself be taken prisoner by the Russians."

"And what is that intended to imply?" Henriette asked.

"There were people who refused to let themselves be taken prisoner. Especially by the Russians. You don't have to let yourself be taken if you don't want to, Mother."

"I suppose you would like to have a bath?" Henriette said.

"I really should have liked that ground floor apartment for myself," repeated Hermann. "Where is our master composer Fritz living?"

"In his old apartment in the mezzanine."

"Really, these gentlemen who sat around composing operas while the rest of us were at the front should make room for men like us. Don't you find, Father, that there's a certain claim there?"

Franz's face, usually so easy to read, was bereft of all expression. Yet Henriette could have sworn that he was on the side of this son who was making such upsetting claims.

"Fritz was at the front for five months," she said. "Then he was ordered home on account of his defective eyesight."

"Four months," her son corrected. "And his twin brother Otto spent three years at Press Headquarters where other fine gentlemen like Rilke, Stefan Zweig, and God knows what other heroic minds fattened and battened. And Cousin Peter was safely stowed in the Ministry of Education. I have the impression sometimes you think those four and a half years out there were just a lark!"

Franz shook his head as if to say, "No one believes that!" But Hermann shrugged his shoulders. At this point he looked bewildered. For the first time since he came home Henriette felt sorry for him. "No one believes that," she also said. "We did our full share of trembling for you."

"You? For me?" he asked.

Then Martha Monica came in. "You have been here for ages, and Simmerl has only just told me," she said, running over to her brother, and kissing him soundly. "Let's look at you! Do you realize I've never seen you in civvies? You're positively fetching! Isn't he, Mama?"

Since she had come into it the usually darkened sickroom seemed to be lighter.

"I can return the compliment," her brother said. "You've grown into a real beauty, Mono."

"Really?" she asked, delighted. "As a matter of fact, I know terribly little about you. I'll tell you what. You take the small study for your room. That is next to mine. Then we can chat all night through the door. Yes?"

To Henriette's astonishment, he answered without hesitation, "Yes."

Franz tried to smile. Then he pointed to Martha Monica's evening dress.

"I am going to a dinner party at Liesl's, and I am supposed to help her with laying the table," she explained, accustomed to interpreting her father's sign language. Franz, for his part, was accustomed to forget that she was not his child. "Do I please you?" she asked, with a touch of flattery. "Gracious! It's almost seven! Good night, Papa; get well quick! Good night, Mama! Good night, Hermann! We'll begin our chats this very night! I'll tell you what the party was like, and you can tell me about your deeds of heroism!" And she ran out as quickly as she had come in. Martha Monica was always in a hurry, always leaving for or coming from parties. No one had seen her yet in a bad mood. She liked every minute of everything. It was not that she didn't realize what life was like. It was just that she found it so wonderful to be alive.

Franz nodded after her. She pleased him.

"Come," Henriette said to Hermann. "I'll show you where everything is."

Later, in the study, when he was taking his treasured, meagre old belongings out of his battered bag, she again felt sorry for him.

"You'll have to get some clothing, it's so long since you've worn mufti," she ventured, taking from, him various things he had wrapped in newspapers: stiff collars, much too high; a double breasted pearl-gray waistcoat in the style of 1914; ties with ghastly patterns. "Have you enough money?"

He had emptied the bag in which his civilian stuff had been stored and had begun to unpack a second one containing his military effects. "For the time being," he rejected her implied offer. "Thanks just the same." The headlines on the newspaper which had served to wrap his belongings announced great Austrian victories.

Having laid the small amount of linen he possessed in the bureau, she turned round to him. It seemed wiser to her to clear up the situation between them right in the beginning. "What have you against me?" she asked. "Do you imagine that I'm not aware of your preference for your father? As far as I know, I have never done you an ill turn."

He was holding his tunic in both hands. "Nor yet a good one," he said, flicking the dust off it. As he did it the medals and decorations attached to it tinkled.

"Do you know what you are saying, Hermann?"

"Definitely. Do you think I never noticed, when I was only home for those few holiday weeks each year, how you could hardly wait for me to go away again?" He gave his tunic a more violent shake. "Or are you of the opinion that I had a happy time of it for eight years at the Institute and four and a half at the front? A dog's life is what I've had. But what did you care? In the eight years I was at Kalksburg you visited me twice. I wasn't Hans, that's all!"

"You're only imagining things," she said, deeply struck by his words.

"Perhaps," he answered. "Perhaps we only imagined everything. That we were being educated for something great. That we were fighting for something great. That we were brave. All imagination." He had finished cleaning his tunic, and he thrust one the newspapers on the floor aside with his foot. "Let's forget it, Mother. I'm going out to look for a place to live. You've never wanted me to live at home."

She could not restrain him. He packed his few belongings and left.

CHAPTER 31
Life is Beautiful

Martha Monica and her cousin Fritz took their places, in the orchestra seats of the Burgtheater. Each member of the opera had the right to two passes for the Burgtheater once a week, and Fritz's wife, Liesl Schoenwieser, had given hers to her husband to see their new cousin-in-law in Grillparzer's *Des Meeres und der Liebe Wellen*. To tell the truth, the ballet dancer did not care much for the classics. But she promised to be backstage after the performance to tell Hans's wife how good she was. For Number 10 was to attend the performance for that purpose tonight.

Obviously Fritz was somewhat smitten with Martha Monica—as much or as little as it lay in his nature to be. He still patterned himself on Gustav Mahler, but the effect he produced with his enormous glasses, his ascetic face, his sloppy dress, and his wild, nervous movements was anything but enticing. It was not just Martha Monica's beauty which appealed to Fritz; it was rather the warmth she radiated, the cheerful readiness to take part in everything, to enjoy or to lighten it. "Uncomplicated" was what he called her; as his own wife proved, that was what he liked in women. That was also the reason why he was not particularly drawn to his new cousin-in-law, Selma. "Women," he said dogmatically, "should be one thing, but completely that: womanly. That is the purpose of their existence." And he did not intend to be taken in by Selma's acting ability either. The critics had indeed raved about her. But every one knows what those people are! Always in a discovering mood whenever a new face turned up; so immensely proud of their infallibility in seeing through things at the first glance. Fritz was determined to form his own opinion. He didn't care a damn about reviews.

Martha Monica's pleasure at being taken to the theater by her much older and cleverer artist cousin knew no bounds. She was prepared to like Selma's acting even before the curtain rose. She knew it would be great. And how thrilling to sit here and be related to the girl playing the leading part! The building itself filled her with enthusiasm. As soon as she came into the high oval auditorium with its four tiers of boxes, ivory pillars and balconies, deep-red silk walls and seats, she was seized with a festive mood. There also was that suggestive aroma as in the Opera House, sweet, cool, and exciting; it enveloped you as soon as you came in. Fritz, the destroyer of illusions, had told her that it was a mixture of smells from glue, scenery, rank perfume, and the chocolate tarts hawked up in the gallery buffet by Gerstner, the court confectioner. She believed this, as she believed everything that was told her. Nevertheless, she sensed that it was an aroma which defied definition. To her it was almost the aroma of fairyland.

The performance would begin any moment now, and there was barely time to glance around the auditorium. Martha Monica waved excitedly to box 12, where her mother was sitting. She did not at first remember the lady next to Mama and to whom she was talking. She looked somewhat pale and weary. But Mama looked wonderful. No one dressed as beautifully as she did. She wore a hat of purple velvet to match her purple dress, because in the boxes of the former Imperial Theaters ladies had to wear hats. Almost no one else did it, though, for Vienna of the revolution no longer 'dressed' for the theater. This did not diminish Martha Monica's delight. Fritz, however, spoke of it caustically. "You don't prove you have a better sense of freedom by indulging in worse manners," he said. Yet he himself never wore evening dress, and his suit had certainly not been pressed for months. "Yes, Fritz," the girl said.

It was always a fresh sensation to her, and her heart beat faster when they began to tune the instruments for the brief musical prelude that preceded all performances at the Burgtheater. The conductor raised his baton, the lights faded, and the music began; the real world vanished. Martha Monica closed her eyes for a second and was completely happy.

She opened them, and her joy was enhanced. On the enormous stage there was a Greek temple, built in the characteristic style of Alfred Roller, the scene designer. At first glance it gave the illusion which people like Martha Monica craved for their life, because they took it to be life. The clear and convincing outlines of this stage temple did not deceive. They did not pretend to be Corinthian columns or made of marble. Yet they produced the effect of both and more. In the instant when the curtain went up this structure of cloth and laths made one believe in an ancient Greece which, as in all the Greek plays of Grillparzer, Vienna's classic writer, possessed Greek greatness and Viennese charm.

That was also what the young actress playing the part of Hero was able to produce in amazing degree. Who had taught her, where she had learned how to do it, remained a puzzle. At all events it was not the former court actors who stood beside her on the stage. With every step she took she brushed aside conventions and robbed the classic style of its stilts. She spoke iambics in a casual way. She did not make the verses resound; she made them vibrate like a tautly drawn string of an instrument. When she loosed it one believed one heard her soul. Yet her revolutionary naturalness was not free of inhibitions, and tonight she was probably more inhibited than usual, for she knew that Number 10 was watching her. In any ease, it added a touching quality to her appearance, already so fragile under the spotlight and in her costume.

She had not finished her first monologue and started to adorn the pillars of the Greek temple with wreaths when Fritz changed his position. He leaned forward, his right elbow on his knee and his chin propped in his hand. Martha Monica recognized this position from the times when they had gone to the opera together. When he sat like that he was entranced.

Martha Monica knew a hundred times less about art than her artist cousin. But to her there was no doubt that Selma was magnificent. How proud she was of her! She would have loved to tell every one that she was her sister-in-law. Slim, with an almost austere grace, the actress came forward, like a being from some higher sphere moving among earthly mortals, and spoke her first words of love to Leander. That was how love should be spoken, Martha Monica felt. That was how love should come to you, in a tidal wave. Oh, what a joyous feeling it was to be lifted out of the here and now of times that were growing grimmer with every day! She squeezed Fritz's hand, and whispered, "It's divine!"

In the orchestra box 12, on the right, Henriette was wrestling with her emotions. She was no longer able to use the excuse of not leaving Franz alone and therefore of not being able to go to the theater. Since Hermann had come home and his irritable mood had worn off—it had been possible to arrange for him to have the ground-floor apartment because Hans's return, despite all intervention on his behalf, was mysteriously delayed—Franz now had company in the evening. And Franz himself had written on one of his conversation slips that the girl had a right to be judged impartially also as an actress by the family. "Her impossible political views" so he had written, "belong in a different category and will be taken up if, after his return, Hans should still feel himself bound to her."

Should he still feel himself bound to her Henriette knew Hans better. It would never have entered her head to think that he would give up this wife, as apparently Franz did and as Hermann was convinced that he would. Her yearning for her favorite son did not confuse her estimate of him. Hans was slow to reach decisions, but, once made, he stuck to them. He would never give up this Selma. If only she had something to offer him! A wife without glamour. A wife with a critical faculty—Henriette knew exactly how harmful that was as a dowry. A wife without family background, whose dead father evidently had had an obscure past. Her mother ran a tobacco shop, and since their war marriage had never put in an appearance although she had repeatedly been invited to the house.

It was this mother who now sat beside Henriette in the box. For when Selma learned of the family's intention to appear in force in order to see her act, she had put a box at Henriette's disposal. Originally it was planned that Martha Monica and Hermann should use it too, but Martha Monica had accepted Fritz's invitation and Hermann refused to leave his father. So Selma had asked whether Henriette would object if her mother sat in the box with her, as no other seats were available. Henriette had said it would be a particular pleasure to have her. Rarely had she gone to the theater so reluctantly.

Widowed Frau Rosner, however, did not displease Henriette. She was an excited mother, proud of her daughter, and anxious to break down the resistance to her which existed in the Alt family. Henriette even suspected that Frau Rosner had wanted to sit next to her in order to put her daughter in the right light. Perhaps she would have done the same for Hans, she thought, as she studied this woman's intelligent face marked with illness. She had heart disease, Henriette learned, and excitement was not the best thing for her. But Frau Rosner loved excitement. Was there anything more beautiful than to sit here, in Europe's most beautiful playhouse, waiting for the curtain to go up and then to see your daughter standing on the stage, acting simply magnificently? But Frau Alt must excuse her; she really had no intention of influencing her opinion.

The curtain went up, and it took Henriette no longer than it had Fritz to see that Selma was quite exceptional. She had seen others in the part of Hero, actresses who had more charm, more warmth.

For the first quarter of an hour she tried to resist. Then she caught the quick, inquiring glance of the woman beside her and began to be ashamed of herself.

She had come there intent on finding Selma mediocre if not actually bad. She had wanted to be able to say to the others and to Hans: "More ambition than talent. Anyone who has so much ambition that others take it for talent thinks of no one but herself. She'll make a poor wife."

It was true about Selma's ambition. It flamed in the eyes of that slim little figure on the stage! But it was equally true as to her talent. When Frau Rosner again glanced at her inquiringly, the one mother said to the other mother, "Selma is extraordinary."

The ill woman was as delighted as if everything had depended on that praise. She too knew her child.

In the intermission Fritz and Martha Monica went out into the marble foyer in search of a cigarette and lemonade. "Fantastic!" Fritz said. "That girl is unique!" The buffet was meagrely stocked with tinned food, displayed on silver platters. "Isn't she?" Martha Monica agreed enthusiastically.

"*Benissimo!*" someone beside Martha Monica exclaimed in vibrant Italian. She looked round, because it sounded so lovely and she thought it was meant for her. But it was an officer talking to a gentleman. He wore a foreign uniform that contrasted noticeably with the prevailing civilian clothing of a public from which military figures had disappeared. In addition it was bright scarlet. "*Scusi,*" he said to her, as if having taken the glass of lemonade for which she had been waiting.

"*Niente,*" she replied.

"You speak Italian?" he asked with an excruciating pronunciation.

"*Un poco,*" she laughed.

"We must be going," Fritz told her. He had been attempting to capture one of the sandwiches sold there as containing ham, although it was really corned beef.

The Italian offered Martha Monica his plate. Three of the precious products lay on it. Fritz gesticulated to her to refuse, but she had already, with a "*Tante grazie,*" bitten into one of them. Then she exclaimed, "It's real ham!"

"Not quite real," said the Italian, mispronouncing three words out of three. Then, bowing to Fritz, he introduced himself, "Conte Gaetano Corbellini, of the Italian Military Mission."

"Delighted," the composer said, jerking his head back nervously.

"May I be favored with an introduction to your daughter?" the officer asked.

A memory flashed through Fritz's mind. A man like this in red trousers, and with a white instead of a red tunic, stood in a meadow full of violets, and, with an arrogance he had never forgotten, called the command, "One, two, three!" Fritz had never cared much for red trousers.

"May I introduce Conte—"

"Corbellini."

"—to you?" he said to his cousin. He did not mention the relationship.

With a glass of lemonade in one hand and a sandwich in the other, Martha Monica indicated in pantomime that she had no hand free to offer to the gentleman thus introduced. "*Scusi*," she added. But since she felt that that was not enough, she went on, "A magnificent performance, don't you think?"

The officer expressed himself in a torrent of superlatives, and the gentleman to whom earlier he had said "*benissimo*" moved off. The curtain-call bell now rang shrilly, and every one, including Fritz and his cousin, went back into the auditorium. The Italian was swallowed up in the crowd.

"The idiot," Fritz remarked.

"Who?" she asked.

"That red monkey."

"But he was so good-looking!"

"Ridiculous idiot," Fritz insisted. They found their seats, and the enchantment was renewed.

The great love scene between Hero and Leander had hardly begun when Martha Monica became aware that someone was staring at her. She would have liked to turn round but did not dare. She distinctly felt something behind her. Someone was sitting at her back and staring at her. It was a remarkable sensation. Like a physical touch.

As unobtrusively as possible, so that Fritz would not notice, she looked round. Beside her and behind sat people with ecstatic and intent expressions on their faces. For most or them a visit to the Burgtheater had been until now beyond their means; only since the revolution had things changed.

I must have been mistaken, thought the girl, turning her eyes back towards the stage. As she did that they swept over both sides of the auditorium. In the box on her right sat her mother, smiling, enchanted, and enchanting. On the left in the first tier was a scarlet uniform. A hand held an opera glass. It was directed at Martha Monica.

From where she sat no one could notice that her attention was divided between the love scene and the opera glass. There was no doubt about it—it was pointed at her. Not for a fraction of a minute did it alter its direction. Its lenses glinted in the dark.

Why won't he look away? Martha Monica thought.

She considered changing her position quietly, so that he could not see her face.

But then wouldn't he know that she had noticed him?

Impertinent creature!

I mustn't so much as glance in his direction, she thought. If I don't take my eyes off the stage he will stop. When she had stood it long enough she looked again. The opera glass had not deviated from its position even by an inch.

In one way it was quite sporting of him, she admitted. Too bad that he interfered with one's enjoyment of the performance.

In the High Priest scene at least he will surely look at the stage?

But no, he was still gazing at her.

What did he think, anyhow? He could do it because he was

an Italian? "All Italians are treacherous," Grandfather Stein used to say. But probably only because they had broken the Triple Alliance.

Doesn't he realize that it is awfully noticeable to stare into the auditorium during the performance? And he in the uniform of a former enemy!

The uniform was good-looking. People might say what they pleased, a uniform was more becoming than civilian dress. He himself was rather handsome, and he knew it, of course. Undoubtedly he was very conceited and had had all kinds of love affairs.

Martha Monica would drop her gloves and pick them up so that she could turn round and have her back to him. Thank goodness, up to now he could not possibly have noticed that she was aware of his gaze. Did Mama notice his staring? No. She did not. She seemed to like Selma's performance tremendously.

As unobtrusively as possible Martha Monica shifted her position.

"Why are you squirming around so? Are you bored?" Fritz whispered, annoyed.

"What do you mean? I'm enjoying it hugely!" she whispered back.

"You should!" Fritz said.

Incredible. That man had risen and was now standing and staring at her. She was not going to tolerate that! From someone who had only just been introduced! Not even turning her back on him had had any effect. Now he just stared at her back. Besides, her dress was so décolleté.

Selma was a great actress. Mustn't it be marvellous to be able to act like this? Conte meant "count." To think he took Fritz for her father! She didn't even resemble Fritz. But she did not resemble Papa either. How disgustingly uneasy it made you when someone did not let you out of his sight for an instant!

Gaetano Corbellini. Conte Gaetano Corbellini. Italians had such pretty names. Yet how could he be called Count since titles of nobility had been abolished? But not in Italy, she recalled. His accent was so funny!

The end of the play. No one could be more convincingly and at the same time less theatrically in love than Selma was on the stage. Good for her and Hans. At last the Italian had stopped.

After the performance Fritz went backstage to congratulate Selma and to meet his wife. As outsiders were strictly forbidden admittance there, Martha Monica hurried up to the first floor to her mother's box so that they could all go home together. But neither Mama nor her companion were there.

For the two mothers also had gone backstage. Frau Rosner was already a familiar figure to the staff, and she beamed with pride when the strictly guarded iron door was so quickly opened to her and her companion.

Walking into Selma's dressing-room, Henriette felt the old antagonism with which she had come to the theater return. In her eyes the fact that Selma was undoubtedly a great artist did not improve matters. On the contrary, Selma's fame would make up to Hans for the glamour she did not have. Her fascinating profession would replace for him the charm she lacked. Her erroneous views and prejudices would gain authenticity through the admiration with which the Viennese spoiled actors.

"Frau Alt wanted to tell you how much she liked your performance." Frau Rosner's words betrayed anxiety and excitement.

Henriette looked at the luxurious dressing table and then at the slim figure which jumped up as she came in.

"You were wonderful, Selma," she said.

"Really?" Selma asked doubtfully. "Did you really like me?" It could not be just her make up which made her face so pale.

She must be very fond of Hans, thought Henriette. Otherwise she would not lay so much weight on what I think. Then, on the impulse of the sudden feelings which sometimes came over her without a second's warning, she took the violets she was wearing, handed them to her daughter-in-law, and kissed her.

Martha Monica stood waiting for Mama, Fritz, and Liesl in front of the stage door. This was also where the enthusiasts gathered to see what the actors looked like without make up. The portrayer of the High Priest was the first to come out. "Hooray for Devrient!" called the enthusiasts.

"Good evening," came the muffled reply of the handsome white-haired man, with the collar of his fur coat turned up and a handkerchief over his mouth, as he pushed his way through the crowd of autograph-hunters.

"*Evviva!*" came a belated cheer.

It was the Italian officer who emerged from the stage door. Suddenly he was at Martha Monica's side, in his gold-trimmed hat, long pale-blue cape, and dragging saber. "*Evviva! Evviva, Signorina Ah! Prego, un autogramma!*" he cried.

Although she would rather not have done so, she laughed. It was so easy to make her laugh.

Then he went on in a rapid flow of barbarously mispronounced words: "Please, I am in Vienna only until tomorrow morning. Please come to Sacher's and have supper with me. I know it is impertinent. But I beg of you, do it. I have always wanted to meet a real Viennese girl. Now I know the loveliest Viennese girl in Vienna! Don't say no—please!"

"You are crazy!" she said,

"Perhaps," he admitted. "Beautiful women have a way of making me crazy." As he pronounced it, it sounded like "crazier."

"But I'm not by myself," she explained.

"*Naturalmente!* You bring your cousin and his wife too. Your mother is to take Signorina Rosner and another lady home. I just met her when I told Signorina Rosner she was as great as Duse."

"How do you know suddenly my cousin is my cousin? Didn't you think he was my father?" Martha Monica asked. "And how did you get backstage, anyway?"

"I am a diplomat," he told her with his merry laugh. "Besides, I have made investigations meanwhile."

Here Fritz and Liesl appeared, and with his greeting of "*Buona sera, Signora* Drauffer," he repeated his invitation.

If the dancer had had anything more tempting than warmed-up turnips and rice-pudding awaiting her for supper, Fritz might have been able to forestall her acceptance. Now, however, not only Martha Monica, but Liesl too, was so obviously in favor of it that the Italian simply offered his arm to the dancer, leading her to a taxicab, while Martha Monica was still standing with Fritz, persuading him not to spoil Liesl's pleasure.

The restaurant where the best food in Europe was served had continued unchanged; in fact, the food was still the best. Revolution, poverty, hate, had apparently melted quietly away in the face of this square red room, where there was place for not more than fifteen white-draped tables and where the waiters looked like prebendaries. On the wall, whence it had looked down for so long at the epicurean enjoyments of the archdukes of the house now banned, there still hung unmolested the Koch portrait of Francis Joseph. Frau Anna Sacher, the owner, still came to speak to her favored guests, with many of whom she was on a matriarchal footing. She dressed her hair in the style of the eighties, piled like a tower on her head and with frizzed curls across her forehead; her neck was enclosed in a high dog-collar necklace; she trailed a long skirt, carried a lighted cigar in her hand, and talked to you as she always had done. If under the monarchy she used to say, in her mannish voice: "Don't chatter such nonsense, Imperial Highness!" she was just as cavalier with the people who, having founded the republic, were already running it down.

She noticed at once that the Italian officer would require special attention, and she ordered Jean, head-waiter for generations, to give him a corner table reserved for someone else. "When the gentleman from the National Council comes send him into the Hunting room," she said contemptuously. She had served so many deputies of the Reichsrat that it struck her as ridiculous to have that already superfluous institution now called the National Council. Just now she had been saying to one of her regular guests, Professor Stein, how stupid it was of the Sozis to change all names connected with the past; just as stupid as it had been during the war to tear down signs like "*Magasin de Modes*" and to declare Shakespeare an enemy alien. The Burg Ring Boulevard was now called the November Twelfth Ring, as if one would not remember that horrid day anyhow; Richardgasse was rechristened Jaurèsgasse. These asses believed that a change of name was sufficient to wipe out a tradition!

Of the two ladies and two gentlemen who were given the corner table, she was interested only in the young girl whom the officer put next to him. She was so pretty and thorough-bred! She seemed quite young, and it was obviously her first supper here. Frau Sacher supposed that it would not be her last. As for the Italian, she believed she had seen him before. In any case she looked upon him as one of the foreign parasites who had infested Vienna, since peace was declared, like so many bluebottle flies. They drained the city of what little blood had been left to her and lived here like kings, for the Austrian currency daily was sinking farther into bottomless depths, and they were given incredible amounts of Austrian crowns in exchange for their own trumpery bills. But the idiotic Government kept insisting that these people represented foreign lands with whom, no matter what the cost, it was necessary to be on good terms in order to obtain loans and staple foods. The devil take them!

"I trust you find everything to your taste," was her greeting to her new guests.

As far as Fritz was concerned, this was not the case. On the other hand, Liesl enjoyed the delicious food, and Martha Monica was blissfully happy. For an instant it had struck her as strange that Grandfather Stein had left almost as soon as they had come in, so that she did not have an opportunity to speak to him. In the next instant she argued that he had probably not seen her. She did find, however, that it was horrid of Fritz not to take cognizance of the extravagant pains of their host to please all of them. They were given food the very existence of which was only a memory. And Fritz did not even touch it. Besides, they had champagne—the real French wine, not the German *Sekt*! This was the first French champagne of Martha Monica's career. How untrue it was to say that it was a strong drink. Quite the contrary. It slipped down like lightning, and afterwards you felt as light as a feather.

Everything suddenly made you laugh. Even Fritz, when he said again and again: "We must be going now." Fortunately the gentleman at her side paid not the slightest attention. She really could not call him "the gentleman at her side." He wanted her to call him "Gaetano," but she had known him too short a time for that. He called her "Donna Monica." How wonderful that sounded on his lips! Perhaps she could call him "Conte Gaetano"? She tried it, but that too sounded funny.

"Please, Fritz, let's stay here a little longer! Don't be so difficult. Do you think it's so awfully nice in Seilerstätte? Here it's warm and bright and gay. At home it's cold and dark!" She had intended to keep these thoughts to herself, but suddenly she had expressed them out loud.

"I don't wish to stand in the way of your enjoyment," Fritz replied in an almost sullen manner. "But I fear we've already trespassed too long on the hospitality of Conte Corbellini."

Of course he would! Why had he not taken a drink? If you don't drink champagne you do act like a stick of wood.

The Italian remonstrated energetically, but Fritz insisted on their leaving. Martha Monica would never forgive him as long as she lived! He made a sign to Liesl and she rose; Conte Gaetano made a regretful gesture—they all had to go. As they passed Frau Sacher she said to Martha Monica: "We shall see you here again soon, Fräulein."

If only she might be right! But who would ever take her out into the big world since Conte Gaetano was leaving early tomorrow! "It was heavenly," she said to him as he helped her into her coat in the vestibule.

"Donna Monica," he answered quickly in Italian, "I love you! I'm leaving for Rome tomorrow morning at six. We'll never see each other again. *Dio mio*, do find some way so that we can still be together for a little while! I love you! Do you hear me?"

She heard. This was not the first declaration of love that had been made to her, but it was the first that could be taken quite seriously. This was not just a tennis partner. It was an Italian officer who was a diplomat and was leaving tomorrow at six for Rome. "That will be impossible," she answered, racking her brains how to make it possible.

"You live at Number 10 Seilerstätte," he said. "I shall wait at the corner of Annagasse until you come."

In front of the hotel he said good-bye in formal manner to his guests.

On the way home they were approached at every other step by beggars. One veteran who had lost both legs was selling shoelaces. "Please!" he called. "Please!" One veteran, whose whole body trembled from nervous shock, was selling comic papers.

"A ghastly evening," said Fritz.

"But the food was excellent," commented his wife.

"Among hyenas I have no appetite," he said.

Meanwhile Martha Monica had found the answer to her problem. You could say what you liked against the Sozis, but it was a first-rate thing in their favor that they had done away with janitors and introduced individual door keys. To be sure, she did not possess one of her own yet, but she borrowed one under strictest admonishments from Liesl while Fritz was buying a morning paper. "But watch out!" warned the dancer good-naturedly. "He's dangerous!"

"Didn't you like him, Liesl?" Martha Monica asked.

"Who, I? Enormously!" Liesl admitted.

The angel-with-the-trumpet entrance was unlocked, and good-nights were said. After the Drauffer couple had gone into their apartment Martha Monica waited with pounding heart for some time. Then she slipped downstairs again and unlocked the door. On the corner of Annagasse stood the man whom she did not know what to call.

"Promise me one thing," she said, when he greeted her with a cry of joy.

"Anything!"

"You will not kiss me. If you don't promise me that I shall go back."

He promised.

They walked off together into the night. There was something ghostly about the misery that pushed its way into districts where some remnants of well-being still remained and where night life was provided for foreigners. Between the exhibition of neediness in the streets and the routine of the night clubs there was no bridge. The music of the entertainment business drowned out the whistles of the rescue cars, picking up people collapsing from starvation in front of doors behind which bands played for pleasure-seeking foreigners and for native Viennese who wrung a profit out of misery.

Martha Monica was frightened. But the Italian reassured her. "Don't think of bad people today. Rather think of me," he said in his amusing accent.

Why were these people bad? the girl wanted to know.

Santa Madonna! They were just people who made capital out of their infirmities, so she learned. Besides, some of these infirmities were not even real, but simulated. Would she bet him that that fellow over there in a tattered infantry uniform was artificially producing that chronic trembling in his limbs?

With the unfathomable readiness of human nature to insult the misery of others in order to lull its own conscience, the smooth-speaking Italian piled proof on proof. In its abundance it sounded plausible, and besides, Martha Monica had no possible way of checking it. Foreigners always knew better than the residents.

Soon they were sitting in the Trocadero, to which they had gone on foot the short distance from Seilerstätte along Walfischgasse.

Conte Gaetano regretted that they had had to walk. Tomorrow (for it was not true that he was leaving the next day) he would make it clear to an acquaintance of his in the Police Administration that something must be done about this terrible annoyance. How could a person get into the mood of enjoyment if along the pavement people with amputated limbs and nervous affections were allowed to make themselves so troublesome?

"A small loge, Count?" inquired the head-waiter with obsequious recognition.

This was Martha Monica's first night club. How much she had heard about them and how ardently she had wished to see one! Yet what now met her eyes exceeded her dreams. The colored spotlights on the dancing couples! The flattering music that never stopped! No one had any cares. No one was sad. They danced. They sang. They laughed.

Champagne was brought when they had barely taken their seats, and the head-waiter bowed and asked if the count had any special wishes for the band; Herr Haupt, the leader, would consider it an honor to play anything for him. Conte Gaetano smiled, drew out a ten-thousand-crown note from his purse, handed it to the amiable *chef de salle*, and asked Donna Monica what the band should play. She said "*Wien, Wien nur du allein*," and a second later the bandmaster was leading it just for her, and the musicians were singing it just in her honor, "*Wien, Wien, nur du allein, sollst stets die Stadt meiner Traüme sein …*" As they played and sang a flower-girl brought a basket of long-stemmed yellow roses and held out a few of them, whereupon Conte Gaetano bought them all and laid them beside Martha Monica. Then he led her out on the dance floor, the band played the Strauss "Emperor Waltz." Never had she danced before with such a marvellous partner. He held you so lightly and firmly, led you with the sureness of a sleepwalker, and whirled you till you lost your breath. And every now and then he whispered, "*Io t'amo, Donna Monica!*"

"Why do you have to leave tomorrow?" she asked as they danced, and he answered: "Orders. Don't you want me to go?" She knew she shouldn't say no, but she said it. After the "Emperor Waltz" came a tango, and they danced it. They danced a one-step and the "Rosenkavalier Waltz" they rested for a little, and it was more beautiful than any dream.

"Did you notice that in the theater I had eyes for nothing but you?" he inquired.

She knew she should not say yes, but she said it.

They danced again, and then there was a slight interruption. A man with an appallingly emaciated face had forced his way in and was standing in the midst of the dancing couples. A spotlight fell full on him, on his dry lips, his gray, sunken cheeks, on his infantry uniform which had grown so big for him. He stood there with wide-open eyes and did not move. A couple waltzed past him. The gentleman in evening dress said to his artificially blonde partner, "What strange persons they let stand around here!" Another man put his hand into his pocket, found some small coins, and offered them to him. But the head-waiter had already taken the intruder by both arms; he did not weigh much, so it was not difficult to throw him out.

As he left he was heard to shriek, "They are dancing!"

"It was bananas, bananas she wanted from me," blared the band. Martha Monica had looked inquiringly at her partner. Simply outrageous that beggars were now allowed to get into such exclusive restaurants, was his comment. But Martha Monica had meant the man's cry and the extraordinary way he looked round, as though he were trying to comprehend something and could not.

She soon forgot him, however, for after that dance there was champagne, and after the champagne another dance. Conte Gaetano said that he worshipped her, and the music was more wonderful all the time and if only he didn't have to go away it would be paradise.

When it was time to leave he asked, "What would you do if I stayed?"

He was not going to stay, so she replied, "I should be happy."

"I shall stay," he said. "I love you too much."

Clinging close to him, she walked home. He promised to stay as long as she wished.

"For ever!" she said.

His enthusiastic reply was, "*Va bene!*" It was the loveliest answer of her life.

On the corner of Walfischgasse stood the emaciated man. As they passed they heard him mutter, "They are dancing!" again and again to himself in a bewildered way.

"Do you think he's crazy?" Martha Monica asked.

"Drunk," was his reply.

They walked on and the man vanished. "Tell me once more that you love me."

"I love you."

"How long did it take for you to love me?"

"One second."

"Are you a liar, Gaetano?"

"I love you, Donna Monica."

CHAPTER 32
Life is Ghastly

Hans had hardly reached home when he realized that it could not go on like this.

The thought of 'going home' had kept him alive. He was one of those most unfortunate so-called 'undocumented' military persons whose personal identification papers had, it was alleged, been lost in a prison camp and proved irrecoverable. Such persons, despite the conclusion of peace, were not transferred until the necessary papers were finally produced. According to the findings of the League of Nations, called to the rescue of these unhappy ones, the lack of proper papers served in most cases merely as a pretext to hinder the return home of "displeasing or undesirable elements." The result was that for 78,522 prisoners the war lasted not four but up to eight years. Hans was one of these, and, like the rest, never discovered what the reasons were.

When the bliss of the first meeting, the happiness of speaking his own language, the joy of not having to obey any orders was over, the disenchantment was violent.

In his endless years as a prisoner Hans had given up what Sigmund Freud once had called his "luxury of evasion" and had learned to think things through to the end. While he was still in the trenches Selma had sent him a novel. The title was *The Murdered Man, Not the Murderer, Is Guilty*, and the author's name was Franz Werfel. Hans had taken this book, and especially two words out of it, with him into captivity. They were two remarkable words, which as such displeased him: "social release." In the life of every young person, according to them, comes a day when his individual worthlessness ceases and he must take his place within the frame of existing society. His complete individual worthlessness had been drilled into Hans by the war in all its horror. One had ceased to have a will or a mind of one's own. But what he, on the other hand, did not agree with was the place in an already-existing society. The longer he thought about it, the more he was inclined to believe that social release was the initiation into a part of your life when you should take up your position not in an existing society but against it.

All of his conclusions in life had been reached through the things he had experienced, seen, or felt, before he could think them out. "Herr Hans Alt suffers from incurable empiricism," had been another of Freud's sarcastic remarks. This tendency had reached an acute stage in the time of Hans's utter loneliness. To think that human beings should suffer the things he had suffered and seen others suffer; that the chalked-up inscription on troop trains, originally destined for cattle, "Ten Horses and Forty Men," wiped out the difference between man and animal, he had had to see with his own eyes in order to draw his conclusions about it; that killing was not murder and a crime, as he had been brought up to believe, but heroism, he would not have thought credible had he himself not been required to aim and shoot at unknown men.

When he had the incontrovertible proof that all this was done not for his country but against it, he went through a crisis. His faith in authority, which had been hammered into his very marrow by school and home, had been shaken that morning in the violet meadow. Nevertheless, it remained. His school, his father, his Emperor still had right on their side. But now their unrighteousness cried aloud to heaven, so that his faith in authority was dumb. Every one had been shamelessly betrayed. The sons who came back as despised beggars or, worse still, didn't come back and became names on tiny churchyard crosses or numbers in prison camps. The mothers who had given those sons. The fathers who had given all their money for war loans. The last trace of regard for anything that might go by the name of respectability vanished. Everything was criminally false that had been said, taught, required by authority for ages past.

Revolution, which is in the blood of Parisians, was not in the veins of the Viennese. In Hans's blood there was the Austrian amiability and the good manners learned in his nursery. He was not radical enough to come directly to final conclusions. Day and night, in his desolate prison barracks, while he was almost despairing of his coming home at all, he struggled to find a compromise. He found it in his decision to convince himself with his own eyes, as soon as he came home; the terrible reports reaching the prison camp might be exaggerated and aimed at convincing the prisoners that their camp was better than their home. But when he did see with his own eyes that it was far more terrible than anything he had heard, he did not allow himself any further evasion. Now at last he was ready for the final outcome.

One of the first things to strike him was that people in Vienna did not realize what had happened, and it was like a slap in the face. They went about and expected to continue as usual. But there was nothing to continue! Vienna had been an imperial capital, and an imperial capital cannot do without an empire. But the empire no longer existed. Austria was the concept of a super-national nation uniting nationalities. The concept had been destroyed. "German Austria," the little land with seven million inhabitants, carved out of an empire of fifty-five million, possessed neither money nor friends. Nevertheless, at St. Germain they had been cynical enough to pile the burden of a succession on them that had no basis for existence.

Most incomprehensible of all to this returning prisoner was the attitude of Number 10. They were still calling the people begging in the streets "beggars," because they either did not know or did not want to know that six out of every ten Viennese were compelled to beg and that Austria itself had been assigned a role which was nothing else than that of an international beggar. They carried on their businesses, continued to go to their offices, went on receiving their pensions.

"Of course, if you are suddenly going to expect your family to develop a social consciousness …!" Selma had said.

No, it was not social consciousness that Hans demanded; that smacked too much of politics, which was something that he, like most of his generation, rejected. What he demanded and what he intended absolutely to insist upon was that they open their eyes! They were asleep! Not even his illness was any excuse for Papa's writing the words for him, "No rise in wages!" Otto Eberhard repeated endlessly, "The terrors of the streets." Even Mother had completely distorted ideas and seemed to believe that certain circles were not affected by the present, hers included. No need even to mention that complete ass Hermann, who was offering his war experiences to the *Neue Freie Presse*, while Martha Monica chose this moment as suited to falling passionately in love,

"Open their eyes?" Selma had asked. "Have you ever seen anyone who could? Besides, perhaps the way to learn anything is through happiness. I don't know. But what I do know is that you don't learn from catastrophes. Don't be angry with me if I ask: In what capacity and with what do you intend to open the eyes of people who all their lives have never really had them open?" She was thinking of the vain attempts she had made to get on to some kind of footing with the people called Hans's parents, his brother and sisters and relatives, and who seemed more strangers to her than anyone else on earth.

The answer was so obvious that Hans was surprised at the question. He would do it in the capacity of an eyewitness and with truth.

Thus in their very first talk Selma realized that his case was incomparably more complicated than that of others who had come home a long time before him. Those others had had to grapple only with disillusionment and changes. But at Number 10 you had to battle a family whom neither victory nor defeat had budged an infinitesimal degree from its foundations.

She had had abundant samples of that. The ground-floor apartment, which had been promised her as soon as Hans came home, was not free. Hermann lived there; there had been nothing else to do, as Hans's homecoming was so unexpectedly long delayed. But the former studio of Uncle Drauffer on the third floor was free, for since no one had their portraits painted any longer he had put his painting on the shelf and was selling antiques. Of course it had to be thoroughly cleaned and furnished, and for the moment no one was available to undertake that. In any case there was one bedroom available on the fourth floor until Hans should have reached a decision. For it was Hans who would make the decisions, was it not?

The thought of a bedroom on the fourth floor had put Selma into such a panic that she spent every free minute day and night getting the studio, which it had not been possible to get cleaned for at least six months, in order. For weeks in the evenings, after performances, she had appeared with a bucket and cloths and had done her utmost to remove the traces of a portrait painter's career from the floor and walls. She was complained of, upstairs and downstairs, for making too much noise, but when Hans arrived the apartment was ready. He did not so much as look round properly; his thoughts were frighteningly far away. Selma had prepared the calendars to show him. But she did not show them. She was bent on trying to understand, to help him.

"Where are you going?" he asked as she put on her hat and coat. "To the theater, I have to act."

"You're acting on our first evening together?"

"The repertoire, unfortunately, doesn't depend on me. Won't you come along? I thought you might be interested." No sooner had she said that than she realized she should not have. His eyes were still full of the things he had had to look on. She could almost see them herself in those absent-minded, frightened eyes.

"For the time being I've no taste for the theater. Forgive me," he said.

"Of course. It was awfully stupid of me to suggest it. Will you have supper alone or will you wait for me? I'll be back at a quarter to ten at the latest. I'll hurry like mad."

He looked at her. You could see how hard it was for him, coming from another world, to accustom himself to this one. "You can't believe there's such a profession nowadays as acting," he said.

She had waited until the last moment to put on her hat and coat, and it was getting late. "I understand how you feel," she said. "But, believe me, people have rarely needed two hours of enjoyment as much as they do now."

"Whom are you supplying with these two hours? The people who need them? Or the profiteers who have the money to pay for them? The people who have nothing to eat don't go to the theater!" She saw how it pained him no matter what was said. "Will you wait for me?" she asked. "Yes. I hope you don't take it amiss that I'm not going with you tonight. Naturally I'm keen to see you on the stage—it's just—you must be patient with me. I must adjust myself again. One always imagines things all wrong."

"Yes, Hans. Perhaps you'll go up to your mother? I don't like you to stay alone."

"You're really not angry with me, Selma? My nerves are on edge. I'll get over it."

She kissed him. "If I were you I'd go round all day bellowing or striking people. You're much too self-controlled. Don't you want to box my ears?" She thought of the stars and half-moons on her calendars.

He laughed. Thousands of miles lay between that laughter and her. Death and horror. Deathly loneliness. And hundreds and thousands of thoughts which he had imagined quite differently. His face was still young. Experiences had been powerless to change it. They had made it only more transparent. The high forehead, beneath the soft hair, wrinkled itself into deep-cut furrows when he thought. Beneath these furrows and his light eyebrows, which were lighter than his hair, he looked at you as one suddenly emerging from the darkness into a harsh light; his sensitive mouth, with its long upper lip, inherited from his father, trembled when he was silent, and opened with an effort as it does with people who have kept silent too long. Selma had met Sister Agatha, who sometimes came to visit the invalid, on the fourth floor. When Hans laughed she recognized a resemblance to her.

"Good-bye," she said. "You may get bored but not angry. Think for a bit how unspeakably happy we are that you've come!"

He heard her go down the stairs. He almost ran after her. It was a shame the way they treated her here in the house. And Mother's conduct towards her was worst of all!

He threw open a window and called after her.

"Yes?" she called back. She had just reached the doorway.

"I only wanted to bellow a little. You're wonderful!"

"But you don't want to see me!" Her face was enchantingly transformed.

"Off the stage!" he bellowed. "And you have done marvels with this apartment! And I'm happy to be with you!"

"Thanks," she called. As far as he could see her she was waving to him.

We shall straighten things out at once, he decided, and hurried up to the fourth floor.

The table in the dining room was laid for supper; in front of Papa's beer glass lay the evening paper; the knives and forks rested on little silver holders; the napkins were folded in triangles on each plate. It had always been thus since he could remember.

As always, since he could remember, Mother was standing at the sideboard just before supper, preparing little appetizers to be eaten before the main course. Today it was anchovy rings on toast. She was the only one in the room, for it was a few minutes before half-past seven.

Henriette, too, was disillusioned and deeply hurt. The homecoming of her favorite son had not been much happier than that of her younger one long before. He had spent the entire day with Selma. Men came back from war as strangers, almost as enemies. And how she had trembled for him. Should she tell him that on the day he went to war she had taken a vow? Never to go to parties. Never to touch a drop of wine. Never to read a novel. And that she had kept it all the years until today? No, she would not tell him. With this son it was not the war or being a prisoner which had changed him. It was Selma! Under the guise of getting-out-of-the-way and not-wishing-to-disturb-you she did as she pleased. Under the pretence of understanding him better than anyone else, she estranged him from his mother. She had been doing that methodically through her letters: that was obvious from his answers. How often he had written to her and how seldom to his mother! "Love to all," he had written. "All" meant her. And today he had remained barely an hour with her and then gone straight to Selma. Yes, Selma was an excellent actress. And she was 'intellectual.' Perhaps she was cleverer. She had read more books. She knew how to debate. To discuss problems. *I can't carry on a conversation about Karl Marx or Freud*, thought Henriette. *And when it comes to politics I am an idiot. But I know a thousand times more about feelings than she does! What makes a person happy, what he yearns for, what hurts him—all that I know. What these intellectual women are suddenly trying to make us believe is the only right way, and what they call the new objectivity, is all ridiculously untrue. Whether among emperors or metal-casters, life depends on the emotions and nothing else!*

What was it that had been the magic of Vienna? It was a lack of weighing every step you took. It was a letting-go of yourself, allowing yourself to be swept away by everything that had nothing to do with reason and everything to do with the heart. Try to declare war on charm! And you will lose your life. What a futile thing it is not to wish to show your feelings. If you do not show them you have none to show. If you have none to show you brand them as sentimental. Oh, this Selma was a cold, calculating person! If I did not know people, Henriette thought, *perhaps I might even have been taken in by her sometimes. Talented—yes, she is talented, and she gives herself such an air of propriety. Propriety! Anyone can be proper. You don't need a heart for that. As a matter of fact, she fits very well into this house from which she wants to force me. Dear God in heaven! To be forced out of this house! I never desired anything else. But now it is too late for that. For forty years I have been a prisoner here. My jailers have grown old; Otto Eberhard is senile; Franz is no more than a shadow. I could not oppose them. But I can and will oppose a creature who has come into this house on an entirely different basis from me.*

All day long she had been mulling over these and similar thoughts. "Well, how do you like it downstairs?" she now asked her son. "Where is Selma?"

"At the theater," he answered curtly.

"That's bad luck, on your first evening," she said. "What is she playing in? The new comedy?"

"I don't know."

"Aren't you going?"

"Not tonight."

"Have you ever seen her on the stage?"

"Once in an amateur performance. I hardly remember it."

"She's highly gifted. As Hero and Viola, in any case, she was excellent. I haven't yet seen her in the comedy."

Hans came over to her. "It's no use, Mother," he said. "Don't make such an effort. That is why I came up. Nothing on earth will separate me from Selma. Not even you."

This was the first time he had used such a tone in speaking to her. "I thought you had come up to give me a kiss," she said with a voice that quavered. "We haven't seen each other for so long."

"This is why I came up. During all my absence you were dreadful to Selma. It must stop."

"She has complained to you!"

"Not by a single syllable. She's much too fine for that."

"How can you speak to me like that, Hans? Have you forgotten everything?"

"Nothing, Mother. But I believe you are forgetting that these are frightful times. We'll need every ounce of our strength to get through them. Every one of us. We must make it easier for each other, Mother. Not harder."

She was so hurt that her eyes grew moist. In one short day that person had stolen thirty years. "I don't know what you are hinting at," she said. "I have nothing against Selma. On the contrary, I tried to be fair to her. Probably she has something against me."

"You must understand, Mother, that it's not enough not to have anything against someone. You must try to love Selma."

"Hans, I told you. I've done my best to be fair to her!"

"The only person who had sufficient imagination to realize what it was like out there was Selma. The only one who helped me with her letters and books."

"Because she loves you much more than I do. Of course she does!"

"Not more than you. Just more unselfishly."

Henriette lost control over herself. "Do you think you can teach a mother what unselfish love is? Selma loves only herself. No. Only her profession. You'll discover this when it will be too late."

From the vestibule Simmerl could be heard saying, "Supper is served." In the same instant Franz entered the dining room, Hermann following immediately.

His father waved to Hans and went to the chair at his place, which Simmerl was holding for him. The devastation in the sick man's face was rapidly growing. Henriette and Hermann also seated themselves.

"Won't you have supper with us?" Henriette asked when Hans remained standing.

His father pointed to an empty chair on the long side of the table. Hans obeyed. He still obeyed this man.

When they were all seated Simmerl brought the hors d'oeuvres prepared by Henriette. He was dressed in a gray Styrian jacket with green revers, a white neckcloth, a green waistcoat with silver buttons, long gray trousers with broad green stripes, and the usual white cotton gloves for serving. The only change in him was his bald spot.

"Is Fraülein Martha Monica not home?" asked Henriette, whose hands trembled as she helped herself to the toast;

"Not up to the present," the butler said solemnly.

An instant later the front door was opened and slammed

shut again. With a "Do please forgive me; there was a traffic block near the opera house," in stormed the girl for whom they were waiting. She kissed Franz's and Henriette's hands, nodded to her two brothers, and sat down beside the older one. "I'm so glad you're here!" she said in her thoroughly cordial way. She smelled of jasmine.

Hans thought of the stench of corpses and carbolic in the Carpathian trench where half of his company had been shelled to bits but could not be removed for three days.

"Will the young master not take an appetizer?" asked Simmerl.

No, the young master would not take an appetizer.

"Are you having supper later on with Selma?" inquired Marthai Monica.

"Yes," he replied.

They sat there and had a butler to wait on them! They were aware of nothing! They realized nothing! Someone should have screamed at them, "This cannot go on! Do you hear?"

Hermann said, "Tell us about your prison camp in Russia."

Martha Monica chimed in, "Yes, please do, Hans. It's frightfully interesting!"

Franz ate with an effort. His paralysed mouth made chewing and swallowing infinitely difficult. But he chewed and swallowed. It seemed that he did not care to associate himself with the wishes of Hermann and Martha Monica. Henrietta's hands still trembled.

"It was ghastly," Hans said. Then he was silent.

"Is that all?" Hermann asked. "I should have thought you would like it. I mean—be interested by it. The political point of view and so on?"

Hans looked at him, at his jauntily upturned moustache, his face lacking in all expression.

"Ghastly," he repeated. Before his eyes rose the image of the pigsty in which he and fifty-six others had lived like animals for years on end.

"You poor thing," Martha Monica said, leaning closer to him with her perfume. To him it smelled like the manure in the pigsty and the delousing chemicals.

"And have you any idea why they wouldn't set you free for so long? There must have been a strong reason for it. Was it your conduct? Or your—opinions, maybe?"

"I don't know."

"There's someone on the telephone for you, Fraülein," announced Simmerl.

The girl blushed and said shyly: "It's probably Liesl." She ran into the hall and was overheard to say, "Shortly … Yes … No … I don't think so … Rather the Kruger Cinema."

Hans jumped up.

"I thought you were not going to the theater tonight," Henriette said.

But he said, "Good night," and left. *I must watch myself*, he thought as he walked downstairs. *I can't go on like this either.*

He went up Annagasse. In front of the "Roman Emperor" an assignation rendezvous, there were prostitutes promenading up and down. Across the way, in the church of St. Anna, the organ was pealing. Beside the church the Max and Moritz cabaret, where they played farces, showed a sign "House full." Next beyond that an unending stream of jazz poured from the Kaiser Bar. Near the Kruger Cinema, around the corner, people were standing in line for tickets, and three steps farther on they were doing the same in front of the Frischler Bakery, waiting for leftover stale bread.

The famous "Fenstergucker" coffee house, in Kärntnerstrasse, was turned into a bank. The quotations for foreign exchange read: 1 dollar–90,000 Crowns; 1 Pound Sterling–450,000 Crowns.

On the show window of the Old Bond Street dress shop there was a printed notice posted: "We exchange dresses for food." A woman said to Hans, "Junger Herr! I'll go with you for a million!" In the Koeberl and Pientok delicatessen store the prices were written in chalk on a blackboard: "Eggs–five thousand crowns apiece. Condensed milk–fifteen thousand crowns a tin. Corned beef–twenty thousand crowns a tin." As Hans was going by a hand erased the price of eggs on the board, changing the five to six thousand.

Where am I? thought this man who had come home. *We used to walk along this same Kärntnerstrasse and think we were a cultured nation. When was that?* He realized that a very long space of time had sufficed to bring them back to the point from which they had started. The cave-dwellers had engaged in barter. The Viennese were now bartering, and even advertising the fact. Had anyone said even a ghastly short time ago that eggs would cost one crown, instead of four hellers, he would have been put in an insane asylum. Now they were writing prices in the thousands and revising them upward with every hour that passed. *What has happened to the human brain?* thought Hans. *How can it grow accustomed to the unimaginable? How can it be that people walk apathetically past these placards and signs instead of crying, "Madness!" until the whole world hears it?*

He was in such a degree of excitement that he wanted to cry "Madness!" in the middle of Kärntnerstrasse; it took all his strength to control himself. With both fists pressed against his mouth he stood there as though transfixed; he had no idea for how long. When he dropped his hands his palms had traces of blood on them.

Selma saw him standing at the stage door and for a brief instant was filled with the ardent hope that he had changed his mind and come to see her act. But he had come only to fetch her.

"Was it bad at home?" she asked.

He shook his head.

Two famous associates of Selma's walked out of the stage door. She wanted to introduce him, but he refused.

Even the young people who stood around and asked for

autographs made him bitter. "Have they no other worries?" he asked. She had to restrain him from saying as much to one young man who asked her for her signature.

"These are our most devoted supporters! We cannot afford to offend them," she said.

"We? Who are we?" he asked.

"We actors."

"I see. I thought you meant you and I. Or we Austrians. My mistake."

It was hard for her to repress the answer hovering on her lips. She was still trembling from the excitement of acting. She had been so convinced, after he called to her from the window, that he would come to see her play. She had acted just far him. She would never be so good again. The farewell scene in the third act had come off well for the first time. How she would have liked to discuss it with him! And also the part which had been promised her half an hour ago—St. Joan! She had longed passionately to play this part for which her famous associates had been angling. And she was to be the one to play it! But this did not interest him.

They walked along in silence for a while.

"Don't you want to ride?" she asked.

He wanted to walk. He had been walking for two hours, but the house for him was terrifying. And even the streets which led to it. "Shall we sit down for a bit in the Volksgarten?" he suggested. "Or are you very hungry?"

She was very hungry, but she sat down with him on a bench near the Grillparzer Memorial. "Tell me, what happened at home?" she asked. "You find that they talk a language you no longer understand, don't you?" She took his feverish hand with its wounds from, his finger-nails.

He tried to explain.

"Yes," she said. "But can you reproach people with wanting to live on as usual? Because if they still cling to that they have to make the most neckbreaking efforts."

"Human beings are not clowns," he said.

"Yes, they are," she argued. "When you actually realize how things are you either commit suicide or you deceive yourself. We deceive ourselves. That's Austrian."

"That's just what it isn't," he contradicted. "It would be Austrian if it had a trace of humanity. Or decency. Or modesty. Or human dignity—or whatever you wish to call it. But not that crass, intolerable, grasping egotism!"

"I'm not sure," she said, "but what you overestimate the Austrians." She was not one to say, "Do you really love me so little that our first day should be like this? Have I overestimated you?"

They walked home by way of the Heldenplatz and Ringstrasse, where there was less evidence of hectic night life. There was no light in the staircase of Number 10; it was past ten o'clock.

"Home," she said. "You are home..."

When this first day turned completely into night he entreated her, "Help me. I need you so."

She kissed him.

"Do you really love me, Selma?"

"I'll have to chastise you by going to get all those calendars!" He restrained her. "If you love me then I'll know where I belong," he said softly. "You see, I'm not sure any more."

It sounded so sad that she had to make an effort to keep from crying. "What have they done to you!" she said, deeply affected, and stroked his hair.

"To us all," he answered. "Do you love me?"

"I love you."

For a long time he was silent. "Could you make friends with my mother?" he asked finally. "I'm afraid you underestimate her. Not even you will be a better mother. Why don't you say anything?"

No reply.

"What's the matter, Selma?"

"I shall not be a mother," she said. All day long she had dreaded this.

"What did you say?"

She hesitated over every word. "This is no time. This is no time to bring children into the world. This world isn't right for it. You say so yourself."

He was sitting up now. "You don't want a child from me," he said.

"Do you know how children can be brought up now? I don't. What they are to be brought up for? I don't know. I know only this. They should be spared. Children who haven't enough to eat. Children for whom you can't provide enough childhood."

It was very silent in the room. Now and then strains of jazz from the Kaiser Bar were to be heard.

"It's an excuse," he said. "You don't want to have any children. Look at your cousin Peter's children," she said. "Little Kurt died at three months. Joachim seems very sickly. I've never seen Adelheid and Otto Adolf laugh."

"You mean it would be an obstacle to you in your profession," Hans said with utmost slowness.

She had expected that too. She lacked courage to admit it. She was not cowardly enough to deny it. "Hans," she begged, "you must have patience with me too."

He remembered what his mother had said to him, "You will discover it." *I have discovered it*, he thought. *And with what terrifying speed!*

CHAPTER 33
Res Publica

Life at Gaetano's side was bliss. Martha Monica had never doubted that life was wonderful, but that it could be so entrancing, pure heaven on earth, from the time she woke up until she went to bed again, was something that filled her with a constantly wondering delight and tender gratitude. He had remained here for her sake. She took his word for it, her Gaetano, whom she no longer called Conte, but by his Christian name, which sounded like music. And he not only discussed the most weighty matters with her; he also actually showed her the most important documents, the most incredible State secrets, so great was his trust in his Monica. He had shown her, for example, a letter from someone he called the greatest living man; it began with "*Carissimo Amico*," and was signed "Benito." In it were expressed not only the highest appreciation of the person thus addressed but also tenderest love and admiration for Austria.

Gaetano was an angel! He found nothing too good for her. And how touchingly he protected her good name! In his apartment in Fasangasse, in the vicinity of the Palais Modena, which housed the Italian military mission after the Armistice and now the Legation, he had furnished three rooms for her, completely separated from his own and with a private entrance. No one could criticize it in the least. And the way he had arranged it for her! With its view out over the Botanical Garden, it was a model of luxury and comfort. She did not live there, so long as she was not married, of course, but she often spent some time and occasionally stayed overnight. But it was too bad that Papa had such completely unfounded objections to it, and, strangely enough, Hans had too. Mother, on the other hand, was understanding. As for Hermann, whom Martha Monica had rather underestimated, he turned out to be much nicer than she had thought at first. He came, and went to her apartment, for Gaetano liked him particularly and considered him positively brilliant. In his presence he had said expressly that he would marry Martha Monica the very instant the Italian Government had acted on his application to remain in Vienna. Should he be transferred elsewhere, they would also get married, but in the city of his new assignment, as was the custom in diplomatic life.

Why wouldn't Papa and Hans understand so simple a matter? Everything had changed; even the time when a young girl was not allowed to go out in the streets alone had passed. You no longer wore ankle-length skirts but extremely short ones; you went skiing; you cut your hair like a boy, and if you went swimming you thought nothing of showing yourself as God made you. Martha Monica made excuses for poor sick Papa, who could not keep up with things, as she always excused everything and could never be angry with anyone. But she could not grasp why it was that her favorite brother Hans deserted her. He had always been the most progressive of them all. Except perhaps Fritz, who also was no great admirer of Gaetano; but a bit of jealousy might account for that.

Martha Monica sat beaming in the diplomatic box in Parliament, with Gaetano on one side of her and the Spanish *chargé d'affaires* on the other. This was her first great social triumph. For despite his angelic qualities Gaetano had until now never taken her to any official occasions. Today, however, he had done it without being asked; indeed, he had insisted on it, and there never could be an occasion which would command more eyes and ears.

On the speaker's tribunal stood the Catholic Prelate Seipel, who had followed the Social Democrat Renner, as head of the Government, and who had just returned from a journey abroad. It was said that the question of whether Austria could continue to exist depended on the result of this journey.

"Before I undertook this journey," said the priest with the lean face, sharply protuberant nose, straight upper lip, and thin-lipped mouth which opened so slightly as he spoke dispassionately, with icy calm, monotonous intonation, and in the inflection of the country folk, "Austria was condemned to downfall. Conditions here beggared description, and still beggar description. An undeserved defeat turned our poor land into a mortally stricken cripple, incapable of righting itself again, without support and yet deprived by unscrupulous parasites of every last shred of power and dignity."

"*Benissimo*," Gaetano approved softly.

"Members of the Parliament," continued the speaker, who bore the nickname of Gray Eminence, to have to ask for alms is a task to bow one's pride. I took that task on myself when I journeyed to our neighbors, to Berlin, Prague, and Verona, to convince them that Austria must have credits. It is a source of satisfaction to me to be in a position to report to the House that my arguments met with success. I have returned with credits amounting to five hundred millions of gold crowns."

The hall, which was packed to the roof, had been holding its breath. Now a storm of applause broke from the benches of the Christian Socialists and Greater Germany partisans. "Long live Seipel!" came the enthusiastic cries. But the left side of the hall, where the Social Democrats sat, was silent.

The speaker in the soutane stood there unmoved. His eyes, behind his strong, steel-rimmed glasses, never left his manuscript. When the noise had lasted too long to suit him he made a gesture with one hand to be allowed to go on speaking.

"He looks awfully interesting," Martha Monica whispered.

"*Si*," agreed Gaetano, who had been constantly looking around. Finally he seemed to have found what he was searching for.

"To whom were you waving, darling?" she inquired. Everything here was so awfully interesting.

"An acquaintance," he replied, and told her to be quiet as the prelate was continuing his speech. When he concluded with the request to be authorized to accept the loans, the applause was renewed, and it became demonstrative when a left deputy rose. It was Renner, Seipel's predecessor, "*un porco socialista*" explained Gaetano to the girl; the Social Democrats, who took over the Government in 1918, had proved themselves utterly incapable since then, so he asserted in low tones. But now they were foaming at the mouth with rage and envy because a Catholic priest had succeeded where they had failed so lamentably. He waved again in the direction of the gallery.

"We know," said the speaker for the opposition, "that as things are today, Austria has no future. We can just keep ourselves alive until the hour of liberation strikes; that is, until we as Germans can decide in favor of the state to which we belong by the nature of things. You are bartering the hopes our people have in the future. That's why I say we shall not vote with you. No, no, and again no!"

"What does he mean?" Martha Monica inquired.

"A union with Germany!" explained Gaetano contemptuously. "The criminal!"

Another speaker, for whom the Italian seemed to have an even greater antipathy, now held the floor; he was a certain Otto Bauer, so he told her, the intellectual leader of the Socialists who, after the death of Victor Adler, had decided to take on this "poisonous reptile."

"With high treason we do not enter into discussion!" called this man. "So long as it is harmless we treat it with contempt. But when it becomes a menace we crush it!"

The hot agreement this provoked among the Socialists and the enraged bitterness on the Government benches was a drama Martha Monica drank in. To her it was incomparably more exciting than the most thrilling play. But the tumult which had broken out subsided the instant the man in the soutane rose from his seat.

"In reply to the remarks of the preceding speakers," he said without gesture or emphasis, although his cheeks were tinged a darker hue, "may I offer for the consideration of the House the fact that policy represents concern for the *res publica*, as the Latins called the state"

"*Benissimo!*" Gaetano cried at the mention of the Latins, but immediately covered his diplomatic indiscretion with a slight cough.

"Concern for the *res publica*," repeated the speaker, "and not for *res privata*, the affairs of a clique."

A cry from the left, "Long live the republic, Monsignor Seipel!"

"To give the loudest cheer for the republic, Deputy Leuthner, is not so important as to do more work for it!" countered the prelate. "In these days, when an apocalyptic panorama of decay is unrolling before our horrified gaze, let us speak *sub specie aeternitatis*, under the aspect of eternity. The gentlemen of the opposition impute to me having bartered Austrian freedom abroad—"

"So you did!" someone called.

"That I did not do, Deputy Ebeseder. In fact, that is more likely to be the fate of Austrian freedom if those who hope to see Austria absorbed into another country are given their way. Everywhere I have been assured that our freedom and our territorial integrity would be respected. But"—and here the speaker for the first time gave evidence of impatience— "should our neighbors be led to believe that certain unrest in Austria was constituting a menace to the peace of Europe— then, obviously, no one can say what will happen."

In the silence which followed this warning the speaker sat down.

With unprecedented bitterness one deputy spoke out: "We hoped there would never be a St. Germain again! We don't believe, and never wished to believe, that a man elected from among the German Austrian people would be a party to the betrayal of his own nation. You, Herr Chancellor, are prepared to sell Austria's right to self-determination to our enemies in exchange for a few paltry millions. We Socialists cannot pardon this crime, the crime of high treason to our people and land! A crime committed by a man who calls himself a priest!"

"The beast!" murmured Gaetano, and in his indignation seized Martha Monica by the hand. But she had only been half listening, because she was so pleased with the fact that the wife of the Minister of Commerce had bowed to her first, and that handsome Prince Dietrichstein, who, now that titles were abolished, was called prince only in private, was making signs to her indicating that he was fascinated by her. How far she had risen since the time when Gaetano had stared at her so continuously at the Burgtheater. Now it was not one pair of eyes which were fixed on her but many, and the sensation of being stared at had long since ceased to be frightening and had become pleasant. She had often envied her sister-in-law Selma for being the focal point of attention. Now she could be it too. She smiled gratefully at Gaetano.

"Do you know him?" he asked.

He meant the embittered speaker. Of course she knew him; it was Herr Seitz, the Socialist mayor of Vienna, who rivalled popular Lueger as a man of the people. "He's so nice," was her epithet for him as for most people, and she recalled the jingle made by the ironical Viennese:

Now let us see Bauer, Renner, and Seitz,
Show if they know how to put us to rights.

"A scamp!" Gaetano retorted. This time he spoke so loud that the Spanish diplomat on Martha Monica's left cleared his throat admonishingly and quickly asked his neighbor if she would like to go to the opening in the Raimund Theater this evening. They were giving one of the craziest plays, something they now called "expressionistic" a good friend of his, who had a part in it, had confided in him that in the second act the ladies—The rest he whispered into the girl's ear. For an instant she wondered whether she should be shocked. Then she laughed heartily. Why shouldn't one use risqué words? That was one more prejudice which these times had obliterated, and it was wonderful of these times to do it. Men spoke with you on equal terms; at last you were no longer the 'weaker sex.'

"I should have loved to go," she explained to the Spaniard. "But we are doing the grand tour tonight." By that was meant going to as many night clubs as you could manage between 11 P.M. and 7 A.M. The Spaniard clearly recognized the cogency of her refusal but hoped to meet Martha Monica on her grand tour.

"An abyss is yawning at our feet and we act as though we were standing on firm ground," someone said. "If we want to live we must see the abyss and build a bridge across it. If we want to be destroyed we shall cover our eyes and crash down into it."

Was that the monsignor again? He was getting somewhat tiresome, according to Martha Monica, besides, with his ascetic austerity he made you think of a preacher. And what else did he want, anyway, now that he had so much money and every one would have enough? She no longer paid any attention to Monsignor Seipel. The charm of the novelty had worn off, and in any case she had an appointment at three at the hairdresser's. As her eyes strayed about, her attention was caught by an elegant woman who was watching her from the gallery. Ready to acknowledge one more look directed at her, Martha Monica smiled, but in that same instant the lady looked away. Immediately afterwards she discovered her brother Hans. Although she made every effort to attract his eye, she did not succeed. With his head resting on his hands, he was sitting on the stairs in the gallery. He reminded her of a little boy listening to his favorite story.

"There is Hans over there!" she told Gaetano.

"Where?" he asked in an unusually nervous manner.

She pointed him out.

"Not an agreeable person," remarked Gaetano.

"You don't know each other well enough," declared Hans's sister. "He's a darling."

Later in the foyer she arranged to wait for Hans. It was ridiculous that he and Gaetano avoided each other; they really must make it up. Angel that he was, Gaetano had not the slightest objection to waiting in the crowded corridors. On the contrary, he was entertained by it. How many acquaintances he had! All sorts of fascinating people. He spoke to his colleagues from Sofia and Bucharest. And he chatted for a moment with that elegant woman. An Italian, he said, when Martha Monica asked her name. Then Hans came.

As he had seen the Italian from a distance, he was determined not to speak to Martha Monica. In his opinion this alluring gentleman would bear watching. Hans could not stand his troubadour ways, nor yet his half-comic mispronunciation of the language which appeared to be deliberate.

But Martha Monica would not allow him to get by. She literally took him by the hand. The Italian said, "How did you do?" and Martha Monica laughed somewhat nervously.

He was well, Hans said, but he must hurry. He was on his way to fetch Selma during the noon recess after her rehearsal at the Burgtheater. "Won't you come along?" he suggested to his sister.

The Italian made a negative gesture.

"I'm sorry, I have an appointment at the hairdresser's," she replied. "But I could telephone and cancel it; then perhaps we could come—I mean Conte Corbellini and I. I should so like him to meet Selma. He will be delighted."

"But not Selma," Hans said. It slipped out. "What I mean is," he said, correcting himself at once, "after rehearsals she is always a little nervous."

"Your brother has funny manners," the Italian told her with a perfect pronunciation. He laughed as he said it, and showed his dazzling white teeth.

"I'm sorry if I make that impression," Hans said. "It wasn't my intention to insult you."

"Of course not!" exclaimed Martha Monica. "You see, Gaetano is laughing!"

"Such people cannot possibly slight me," said Conte Corbellini in a burst of sudden vehemence. "Not Herr Otto Bauer, nor Herr Seitz, nor Herr Alt." He made no mistakes, as when he talked with Martha Monica, but spoke with perfect correctness.

Yet that was not what struck Martha Monica. It was the company with which he associated her brother and it led to the explanation, "You know, Hans, he can't stand the Sozis."

"Good-bye, Mono," Hans said. "I must be going now." His meagre stock of patience had already been exhausted by the session of Parliament in which, according to his opinion, both parties left unmentioned the most essential things.

The Italian said loudly enough for Hans to hear, "Naturally his wife cannot possibly be enthusiastic about me. Someone who is so enthusiastic about Otto Bauer!"

Don't listen, said Hans to himself.

When he did not get the reaction he expected Conte Corbellini called after Hans, "I'm accustomed to being treated politely, you Sozi!" His otherwise melodious voice echoed sharply in the marble corridor.

Hans turned instantly round. He had never tolerated scorn. Two strides had brought him back to the Italian, when someone behind him remarked, "This gentleman has unclear ideas about immunity. It's valid in Parliament for deputies but not for diplomats. Why don't you say that to him, Hans? He has already shown by his exclamations that he doesn't clearly grasp where he is."

Despite the rage which had driven the blood into his head, Hans recognized the speaker. It was someone he had not seen for a long time—Ebeseder, his schoolmate, who had, meanwhile, become a deputy.

The Italian turned contemptuously round. "I accept no instructions from Sozis, nor from people whose wives consort with Sozis—"

As Hans's arm shot vehemently forward it was quickly seized and forced down by Ebeseder's hands. "Quiet," he said. "We're not going to give this gentleman the satisfaction of some free political advertisement. But it will afford me a juicy titbit when I question our Minister of Foreign Affairs on the subject of the functions of a military attaché of the Italian Government and ask whether we've already been so far sold out that people who are here to keep their mouths shut can open them so wide."

This last he said to Hans as they approached the main staircase arm-in-arm. "How have you been keeping?" he asked. "I've heard about you indirectly from time to time. You seem to have remained a decent sort of chap."

"What impertinence!"

"He's of no importance," was Ebeseder's view. "We shall get rid of him and all his kind. You were at the session?"

"What does a man like that think he's doing?"

"Chancellor Seipel things he has saved Austria. Incidentally, do you believe that too?"

"A people cannot be saved by money. The insolent fellow!"

"Correct," Ebeseder answered as they reached the entrance of the Social Democratic Club. "Perhaps we can get together some time?"

As Hans went out into the street the City Hall clock struck three. His thoughts were still in confusion. Seipel had not saved Austria. Selma was all for Otto Bauer. One, two, three, he could have stood in a meadow full of violets and shot at a man. For a long time he had held that against his father. But it does not depend on you. When he saw the Burgtheater Square, where he was to meet Selma, he changed again. You must not shoot at a man. It does depend on you.

"Isn't it so, it does depend on you?" he asked as Selma walked towards him, waving her hand.

Accustomed as she was to his skipping premises, she answered, "Of course; on whom should it depend?"

"On others. On the State. On God."

"I'm not informed as to God and State. But as to others—no."

"What if, let us say, they are losing our land for us? Or—or—let us say—one's love for another person?"

She smiled in the way which transfigured her face so beautifully. "The land one has lost one finds again. Love does not get lost."

"Never?"

"Never."

CHAPTER 34
The Failures

One day Selma found she could barely move her left arm. It must have been due to the constant draught she was in on the huge Burgtheater stage; for some time she did not deem it necessary to consult a physician. Old Dr. Herz had given up his practice completely, and ms successor had the reputation, according to Number 10, of "making complications." It was only when her brother-in-law Dr. Baier came up from Salzburg that she asked him casually for advice. By then the troublesome condition had already lasted a number of weeks. It was especially inconvenient on the evenings when she played Saint Joan, because she was obliged to hold Dunois' banner in her left arm while she used her right for her sword.

It was neuralgia, in the opinion of brother-in-law Baier, who had watched over the last hours of Francis Joseph and who since then had preferred to treat the members of the aristocratic and clerical circles of the small town of Salzburg, where people still went to mass. He advised diathermy.

It did not help. The longer Selma subjected herself to this treatment the more stubborn the uncomfortable, albeit painless, ailment became, and it was no longer just the upper arm but her left hand as well which she could barely control.

Obviously no one must know about this or her triumph as Saint Joan would have gone for nothing; she would have had to go on the sick list and someone else would have taken over her part. She kept it a secret even from Hans, who was worried by any kind of illness. Her secret triumph had been to win back his confidence after that night he came home from the war, and it was coincident with the first. Since then Hans had been so proud of her. After the opening he had said to her, "I admit it is more important to be a genius than to be a mother." It was his way of begging her pardon, and with that their conversation of that first night was wiped out.

It was only now, in their daily life together, that she realized completely how lovable he was. There was hardly a trait in him that she would have liked to see changed. He still had his boyish idealism, with its firm conviction that everything can be "made better"—a piano factory, a state, human beings; his easily aroused enthusiasm; his typically Austrian way of swinging from optimism to pessimism, and his un-Austrian, almost touching steadfastness. Never an excuse; tactful to a degree. Were it not for his hot temper and slight conceit, Selma's critical estimate would have pronounced him faultless. What she liked most about him was his adherence to things that were real and his aversion to all pretence. Also he was the handsomest man she knew.

"Hand me the saucers," requested her mother-in-law, for a

tea-table was being festively arranged in celebration of Professor Stein's eightieth birthday. Simmerl and his wife were on their annual pilgrimage to Mariazell, where their daughter performed certain duties in a convent. And Martha Monica, as usual, had not finished dressing. So Selma had been asked to come up to lend a hand.

"You needn't make me feel, with every saucer you hand me, how you look down on this trivial occupation," Henriette said. "It would be lovely, but unfortunately we can't all be geniuses."

For the first time Selma felt pain in her arm, and although she ascribed it to her nervousness, it cost her an effort each time she used her hand. "It's much simpler, Mother," she declared. "I'm a lamentable housekeeper." And she handed her mother-in-law the beautiful old Viennese porcelain with the beehive mark.

"Fuss!" Henriette answered, using the expression of Franz's which, when she was young, had annoyed her. In Selma's presence, however, she unconsciously took the part of the house against an outsider, as had been done by others to her for so long. She had made an effort, as best she could. For Hans's sake she had tried to like her daughter-in-law. Sometimes she had persuaded herself that she did like her. But as time went on she did not succeed. There was no doubt that her daughter-in-law had taken her son away from her. Besides, Selma used every means to belittle and to question what she had done for Hans. "You didn't educate him for life," she had dared to tell her!

"Professor Stein doesn't look his age at all," Selma said.

The fact that the whole house was celebrating her father's birthday was to Henriette a personal triumph. "Be a dear and go and get the whipped cream," she said in a more friendly tone, for she felt she had rather let herself go.

The whipped cream stood ready in the kitchen, and all

Selma had to do was stretch out her right hand for it. Nothing could be simpler. All there was to do was to lift a hand, pick up a small, light silver jug, and carry it into the dining room.

Suddenly this simple act became an insoluble problem. As Selma went to stretch out her right hand it refused to obey.

"Do hurry," Henriette called from the dining room. "They will be here any minute. You know how punctual they are!"

Selma struggled with the silver jug. Then suddenly, as the weakness had come in her right hand, it vanished. With a sense of infinite relief the young woman picked up the jug and hurried back with it. "You're not exactly quick," commented Henriette. "Has Hans not been able to train you? He's coming, isn't he?"

Hans came, but the punctual ones were there ahead of him. Otto Eberhard and his wife Elsa were the first of all. Immediately following came Franz, Professor Stein, Peter, and Annemarie. The Drauffers and their twin sons followed (Fritz's wife, the dancer, had to look after two-year-old Raimund, their son, or at least, that was how Fritz excused her not taking part in the family festivities). The last guests to arrive were the Widow Paskiewicz and Martha Monica. Peter's children were to come after the tea had been served and recite poems. With Hermann, the only person who arrived late, the complement of the grown-up residents was full.

"I haven't yet been able to see *Saint Joan*," said Otto Eberhard, who was sitting on the left of the hostess, to Selma as she poured him some tea. He was five years older than the birthday celebrant, and to him a person of a mere eighty years seemed an inexperienced creature, as to Aunt Sophie, in her day, Poldi, her factotum, had seemed a raw recruit. He scarcely ever encountered the actress. Since one met people who were lacking in all manners everywhere nowadays—ministers who had been shoe merchants in Graz, chiefs of departments who ate with their knives—Otto Eberhard no longer went into society. He sat erect, in his impeccably spotless black coat, which had grown a shade too large for him, his whiskers freshly clipped, and in his buttonhole the rosette of a commander of the Order of Francis Joseph.

"You will see it some time," Selma said. She could not quite bring herself to call this severe old gentleman "Uncle Otto Eberhard."

"But you've missed a great deal," remarked the always gracious guest of honor, seated on his daughter's right, as he unfolded his damask napkin, in the corner of which was pinned a rosebud. He put the rose in the buttonhole of his stylishly cut suit and helped himself to tea. "You are incomparable in this role," he said, complimenting his grandson's wife. "I shall surely go again to sec the play."

"Yes. She was splendid," Henriette admitted.

Every bit of praise directed at Selma, who for the first time was being confronted by the solid majority of the house, was pleasing to Hans. Wasn't it the devil that so much importance was still put on whether the house praised or blamed a person! He sat next to Fritz, who indulged in sarcastic comments.

"I have read the play," remarked Otto Eberhard. "I can't say I like it. Now, Schiller's *Maid of Orleans*—"

"On the other hand," Fritz anticipated softly.

"On the other hand," continued the retired Public Prosecutor, "is incomparably better."

"If I may say so, Papa, I think you're mistaken," said his son Peter. This stout gentleman let one feel, with every word he uttered, the importance of the position he occupied in the Ministry of Instruction. He had survived the Reds there, and his attitude showed that he was determined to survive every one else who did not understand the gentle art of governing. Without him neither the ex–shoe merchants who became Ministers, nor the other questionable political amateurs could take a single step on the slippery parquet of administration without stumbling at every step over paragraphs. "I consider it an outstanding modern play," he added, with the knowing air of a man entrusted with the cultural affairs of his country.

"How can you—"

"Say such a thing," Fritz again anticipated.

Annemarie, who had come from Potsdam, near Berlin, really did not disappoint him. She reproached her husband with his preference for the English play. With the best will in the world she had not been able to discover anything in it but bombast and cynicism. Nor had the production been done to her satisfaction.

Hans's eyes narrowed.

"Keep your mouth shut," warned his former mentor. "Annemarie is undoubtedly one of the stupidest women in five continents."

"All this is only being said on Selma's account!" declared Hans. "Well," Fritz agreed, unmoved, "she will survive it. For her career, what you and I think of her still is more important. And we think she is a genius."

"Who is a genius?" Hermann asked in the midst of his conversation with his cousin Otto, who wore a blond beard in the fashion of the late Lueger, Vienna's most popular burgermeister.

"Selma," Fritz explained defiantly.

"Sure," Hermann agreed. "I must confess it's been a long time since I have been as thrilled by anything in the theater as by her Saint Joan. An absolutely top-notch achievement."

"I'm glad," Selma told her brother-in-law.

Hans, too, was so surprised and pleased by his brother's enthusiasm that he decided not to tell him how offensive he had found the radio program arranged by him the day before; Hermann was no longer employed at the factory, but for some time had been assigned as assistant to Captain Kunsti, head of the program department of the Vienna Radio Station "Ravag."

In this capacity he not only arranged "Austrian Broadcasts," directed against the people who wanted to tamper with Austrian independence, but also he found opportunity to give free rein to his rather suddenly developed literary inclinations. He had recently appeared in print in an article calculated to curry favor with the *Neue Freie Presse*, in which he put forward the assertion that Saphir and Daniel Spitzer, the fathers of the "Vienna *feuilleton*," were "the wittiest minds of Austria."

"Why didn't you invite Selma to participate in your broadcast last night if you admire her so?" asked Fritz, with embarrassing directness. "She would have been an oasis in your desert of mediocrity." Hermann nodded with an expression of resignation. "You know my chief. No relatives! Otherwise it smacks immediately of influence!"

"Well, in the first place, I don't think Selma needed the job," explained the musician, "and secondly, as far as family influence is concerned, you need have no sins of omission on your conscience. Don't you agree, Peter? I don't think you did Hermann much harm when he was trying for a job at Ravag."

"Do you really get so much enjoyment out of always playing the enfant terrible?" asked his cousin. "I should think that some time or another one would outgrow one's short trousers."

Franz had rapped on his glass sharply. He was sitting beside his sister-in-law Elsa, and he pointed to Professor Stein. This is the important person here, was what he meant to indicate. Do think of him at least. His face, with its twisted, paralysed mouth, was hardly more than skin and bones.

The birthday guest had a different point of view. "Let the youngsters argue, Franz!" To him they were still youngsters, and all his life he had encouraged discussion among youngsters.

Henriette shook her head. She was annoyed by the lot of laudatory remarks about Selma. If this went on she would not only dominate Hans but Number 10 as well. "I don't think you have passed the cake to Uncle Otto Eberhard," she said pointedly to her daughter-in-law.

Hans thought that the disfavor apparent in his mother's remark was all but unbearable. She did not dare to say a single word against Martha Monica, who sat there like a guest when she might just as well be helping to pass things. Yet no matter what Selma did she could not overcome Mother's aversion; and witnessing such things made him feel his love for his mother growing cold. On the other hand, surely the remark about the cake could not account for such an alarming change in Selma's expression. He was on the point of getting up and rushing over to his wife, who had grown terrifyingly pale, when she began to smile once more and was going round from guest to guest. Besides, Martha Monica was now helping her at last.

"Anything wrong?" he asked softly when she came to him.

"Why?" she replied, put a piece of cake on his plate, and was already standing by the next person.

"Martha Monica," Otto Eberhard said severely.

"Yes, Uncle?" answered the girl who was following Selma and pouring Malaga into small glasses.

"You have a magnificent string of pearls."

"Gorgeous," Elsa and Annemarie said in admiring unison. But Widow Paskiewicz remarked, "I've been thinking all the time—it really looks almost like tke necklace of Empress Elizabeth."

"So it is," the girl admitted radiantly, and fingered the large pearls which gave off a soft rosy sheen.

"What?" asked the retired Public Prosecutor stiffly.

Henriette threw an expressive glance at her daughter.

"You don't mean to tell me," said the old gentleman, and his hand trembled so that the fork in it rattled, "you don't mean to tell me that you are wearing the pearls of Her Majesty?" He waited for her reply before continuing with his food.

"It's an excellent imitation," said the girl, under the influence of her mother's glance.

"Not real?" asked Widow Paskiewicz, relieved.

"Of course not," Martha Monica explained. "They make such wonderful imitations nowadays." And she went on pouring the Malaga.

"That's good," concluded the old gentleman after an instant of reflection. "There are people now who have no compunction about wearing and doing things which, whether they are real or unreal, are not suitable for them. I hope you don't belong to such people."

"Quite my opinion," agreed Otto Drauffer, who rivalled Widow Paskiewicz for silence. "The profiteers are running around the place and buying up the Hapsburg crown jewels for the price of a sandwich. I have it on good authority that there are diplomats who have come here exclusively for that purpose."

"Surely not a certain Conte Corbellini?" inquired tactless Fritz. Since the Italian had been in Vienna Martha Monica no longer paid any attention to her cousin.

"Conte Corbellini is a military attaché," answered Martha Monica innocently, although Fritz's question had been intended for his twin brother. She did not mention the fact, however, that the necklace was a present from Gaetano.

"Really?" said Otto with the long Lueger beard. "I thought he was attached elsewhere."

Franz looked at Martha Monica with a glance she avoided. But her mother said encouragingly, "Count Corbellini is charming." The fact that Martha Monica was wearing the pearls which had almost been destined for her had filled her with a deep satisfaction ever since she had known it. At last destiny was beginning to give signs of remorse and bestowing on the daughter what it had denied to the mother.

"You're to be married, I hear?" asked the colonel's widow,

who, since her daughter had become the bride of the Saviour, looked upon all marriages as vain.

Only now did the birthday guest exercise his prerogative as chief person by saying to his granddaughter, "Diplomats are birds of passage. If you clip their wings you deprive them of their power to soar." He preferred to express himself in the terms favored by the *feuilleton* writers of the *Neue Freie Presse*. Presumably that was why Hermann nodded at him in such agreement. But he might just as well have said, "If you listen to me you'll not marry this man," Before Martha Monica's eyes rose that supper at Hotel Sacher when Grandfather Stein had taken his leave the instant she had come in with Gaetano: "Yes, Grandfather," she replied, embarrassed. But Otto Eberhard had no desire to let the idea that Mr. Stein could ever have any say or be the principal person in this house gain currency. Even his having an eightieth birthday did not in any way alter matters. "I should be interested to meet this Count Corbellini," he suggested. "Perhaps you'll bring him to sec us. Don't you agree, Elsa?" he asked his wife, who unconditionally agreed to everything he desired. After all, the man in question was an officer and a count.

"Yes, Uncle Otto Eberhard," Martha Monica promised too, and order was re-established; Otto Eberhard ruled the house; the opinion he would form would be the one to count; intruders had no voice in family affairs.

Franz nodded. The nod of this younger brother with his paralysed face was acknowledged by a nod with a trace of a smile by the older brother. Just leave it to me, the smile indicated. In my hands the interests of our grandfather's descendants are still well protected. The index finger of his now bony hand, on which the veins stood out, rapped on his glass of Malaga. Instantly a complete silence fell.

The retired Public Prosecutor rose to his feet. He said: "Ladies and gentlemen, we are celebrating here the birthday of a man whose merits are many. As scholar, as former member of the Upper Chamber, as patriot, and not least as father of our hostess, he has lavished his gifts, on our monarchy and our house. We acknowledge this with gratitude and wish Professor Stein continued good." With that he sat down. It was a birthday congratulation and at the same time an accusation.

A wince passed, over the sensitive face of the guest of honor, whose hearing, at eighty, was as keen as ever. As he clinked his glass with the others raised in his honor it occurred to him that he had been the one at his daughter's wedding under the roof here to propose the toast. A toast to the happiness of the two houses of 10 Seilerstätte and Austria. The house of Austria no longer existed. The house of 10 Seilerstätte was not happy. That old fox was right, he thought; toasts are not worth drinking. In the tone he had used all his life to unteachable students, the professor, emeritus said:

"The honorable gentleman who has just spoken referred to my modest merits. Whether I have accomplished anything in the public domain only time will tell. But in private life, on the other hand, I do have a claim. It is here beside me. I am filled with pride that the achievement of my life should have been my gift to this truly Austrian house, on which she has lavished charm, talent, spirit, and life. I drink to the health of my daughter, Henriette."

He, too, had re-established the order of thing.

Henriette blushed as of old. Her father's words had done her an infinite amount of good. She alone knew what it had cost her to make it possible to say such things about her here.

"Thank you, Papa," she said to the man who had trained her to leave the essentials unsaid. They still clung to the old custom between them.

At the very moment when all eyes were on her, and Franz, holding high the glass of wine he was not allowed to drink, was looking at her with the expression of an unbroken love in a broken life, they heard a crash. A plate had slipped from Selma's hands and had broken to bits. She herself appeared to be unable to stand, and Hans caught her in his arms. There were beads of sweat on her high forehead. Her whole body quivered as though she had a chill.

Hermann rushed to the telephone, but before he could reach the family physician Selma seemed to have recovered. The spasm in her face relaxed and she said apologetically, "I have had a bad headache since this morning. Please don't let me disturb you. It's nothing." And to prove it she took one of the small glasses filled with Malaga and drank it down.

Otto Eberhard's expression, which had turned to stone after Professor Stein's speech, grew a shade more hostile. An actress! Draws attention to herself if she isn't in the limelight all the time! That was the spurious kind of talent that had pushed its way into the house and instead of scorn was received with glory!

"Come," Hans insisted.

"Why?" Henriette asked. "One should not give in to one's body."

"Selma has to act tonight," was Hans's reply to his mother.

"It brings good luck," Martha Monica said comfortingly, as she leaned over to pick up the shattered fragments.

Meantime Peter's children had come in, hand in hand, from the vestibule. Little Adelheid wore a white dress with a blue sash; Joachim and Otto Adolf were in sailor suits. They placed themselves prettily in the middle of the room to recite a birthday poem in unison. Involuntarily the twins, who for many years had had little in common, looked at each other; they remembered. Other generations were now reciting the birthday poems, but they were the same halting, unnatural phrases. As they were saying, "On this the glad day of your birth, we wish you all the joy on earth," Hans took the opportunity to slip away unnoticed with Selma. She made no objection and even let herself be persuaded to lie down for a little while. How sweet it was to hear him say: "You have to act tonight," as that were now important to him as well …

Later he accompanied her to the theater and went with her to her dressing-room. "You mustn't get sick," he pleaded. "I have only you; never forget that."

As she began to put on her make-up for the comedy part she was to play that evening she asked, "Since when?"

"Since the letter about the calendars," he said.

That too was so sweet that she felt all her strength returning. She was almost able to move her left arm.

"Don't be angry with my mother," he begged. And then he left quickly, as though he did not want to say any more.

As he walked home thoughts crowded on him which he again did not want to face. He was relieved, therefore, when he saw his old schoolmate Ebeseder walking ahead of him along Loewelstrasse, or rather hurrying, for Ebeseder preferred the quickest possible gait. Hans called after him until he made himself heard.

"Are you going to visit with me in the street?" Ebeseder asked good-naturedly. "Better in the street than not at all! Will you come and eat with me? I am famished!"

Hans said he would be glad to join him.

They were on the point of entering the Klomsor Restaurant when a shower of leaflets fluttered down on to the pavement. In the narrow street through which they were passing it was impossible to see from where they came. Neatly printed, they carried the words in Gothic script: "Germans of Vienna! Join Hitler! He is your one escape from Red and Black!" Beneath this was a spiderlike emblem Hans had never seen.

"Do you remember the chap with the bad teeth who took the examinations for the Art Academy when we did?" Ebeseder asked.

"Is this the same one?" Hans wanted to know, looking again at one of the leaflets.

"Correct," Deputy Ebeseder said. And after they had ordered their meal he told Hans that their former co-candidate at the examinations had abandoned painting and founded a political party, the emblem of which was that spiderlike design.

"Selma also was on the verge of being failed," said Hans, whose thoughts kept coming back to her. "The failures make their way." And he added, in a tone of resignation, "Perhaps then I, too, can have another chance?"

CHAPTER 35
"I Will Deliver You from Fear"

Whenever Selma Played St. Joan, Hans was in the theater from the first moment to the last. He had not yet missed a single one of the performances which moved him deeply. The play moved him in that it did not reject miracles, and made them all so human and understandable; it comforted him to believe that there were miracles and that the vanquished could become the victors. But he was moved by Selma to a degree which was all but overwhelming. Each time it filled him with fresh astonishment that this being, whom he thought he knew Completely, radiated such unknown, unsuspected, irresistible power the instant she set foot on the stage. He had always thought her eminently clever and gifted. But that she had qualities of genius was something he discovered only now.

Hans was standing in the left wings, watching. This was strictly forbidden to every one "not engaged" in the production, but the stage manager, Mr. Wiesner, made an exception in the case of this enthusiastic husband. To him Hans was a theater maniac, and on top of that in love, so that he was not satisfied to sit in a box and admire his wife from there; he must also breathe in the air of backstage. Well, why not, if his happiness depended on it? Besides, the court actors and actresses were accustomed to seeing Hans Alt tiptoeing into the left wings and standing entranced beside the fire warden as soon as his wife appeared in this part. They took the achievements of their colleague somewhat more coolly. Talented—oh, yes. But, heavens, what a meagre appearance! And what a birdlike voice which could not reach even me fourth gallery! Not to mention a lack of technical equipment. This beginner had no notion of how to stand, or walk, or to sit down effectively. She had been raised to this pinnacle by influence; that was the solution of the whole problem! Her mother was said to be the owner of a tobacco store. And nowadays a person like that could play the main parts on this venerable stage where Wolter had uttered her immortal cry! The handsome, white-haired court actors and the stately, refined court actresses were much too well-mannered to let this amateurish associate of theirs learn their true estimate of her. But in the green room or in aristocratic homes, where they were still called court actors, although there was no longer any court, they let off steam.

No, Prince, it was no longer a distinction to belong to this once outstanding institution! As for Hans, he was rather popular in the wings of the former Imperial Theater. He was a good-looking man, with excellent manners, the future head of the C. Alt firm as soon as the old gentleman, who was said to be very ill, should have paid his tribute to nature. Besides, the firm of C. Alt was a concept like the Burg-theater, a cultural asset of Vienna, which belonged to tradition.

"Well, young man," commented the splendidly handsome portrayer of the archbishop, and contemptuously flicked away a fly that had the audacity to settle on his nose, "back at your post?"

"Yes, Herr Hofrat," Hans answered modestly. The enchantment of this stately institution had caught him up. He recognized that these gentlemen, like his uncle, the Public Prosecutor, also carried the title of Aulic Councillor and were no better than old-fashioned rubber stamps. However, they were part of his youth, and it was fascinating to be near them in all their beauty, with their gold-encrusted costumes, a slight smell of mastic and Eau de Cologne.

"Your wife is in particularly good form," whispered a woman of riper years, with an effort at being pleasant. She was the one who had raised heaven and hell to have the part assigned to her. She was in street clothing and had dropped in unnoticed, for she lived in the neighborhood.

"Yes, Countess," Hans answered. He also thought that Selma was playing better than ever tonight. How wonderfully she said the words, "Do you not know that I bring you better help than ever came to any general or any town?"

"Your own?" asked Dunois, Bastard of France, playing opposite her.

"No," she replied, "the help and counsel of the King of Heaven." Never had she said this more naturally. Hans was delighted. That was how art should be! So simple. So convincing.

She looked enchanting in her light, close-fitting cuirass of silver mail, with the pointed banner of France, three golden lilies embroidered on a field of blue in her left hand, and in her right her sword. Like a young boy, Hans thought.

Her eyes fell on him, as always, before she said the line, "I will deliver you from fear." For it was not said to Dunois, but to him, to him alone, since she believed that fear was his failing and that he must rid himself of it. As she said it she raised the banner, as if in salute.

He nodded, entranced.

"Your wife's voice a bit thin today?" the stage manager remarked as he prepared the wind machine to be used three pages farther on.

"Not a man will follow you," retorted Dunois on the stage, sitting with folded arms before his tent.

"I will not look back to see whether anyone is following

me," answered Joan. Now it seemed even to Hans that her voice was very light.

During the pause artfully introduced by Dunois at this point, Hans made a sign to her from the wings, "Louder!"

Dunois had risen to his feet. He went over to the girl in the silver cuirass, stood looking her over, his hands on his hips, then tapped her briskly on the shoulders and said: "Good. You have the making of a soldier in you."

The triangular blue banner fell from Joan's hand.

"You are in love with war," Dunois went on with his lines as he gave a puzzled look at the banner, picked it up, and handed it to her.

She did not take it.

There was a pause, during which the prompter could be heard whispering the cue, "And the archbishop said I was in love with religion."

Saint Joan did not seem to hear. She did not take the banner; now her sword fell.

Dunois' eyes turned from the banner still in his hand to the sword at his feet.

"And the archbishop said I was in love with religion!" repeated the prompter more loudly.

"What's going on here?" asked the stage manager, his finger on the sentence Selma was supposed to say but did not. He ran round to the other side to prompt her from a nearer angle. These beginners! Once they lose their lines they don't know how to help themselves.

But Dunois had already taken over Joan's lines. "You mean you were in love with religion," he said, helping her along. Then, since "religion" was the cue for his next sentence, he went on, "I, God forgive me, am a little in love with war myself, the ugly devil! I am like a man with two wives. Do you want to be like a woman with two husbands?" As he said this in his most masculine way, he stood the banner, which embarrassed him, against the tent, picked up the sword, and toyed with it as though that were part of his role.

"I will never take a husband," came from Selma's lips, and Hans, who had been holding his breath, gave a sigh of relief. But it sounded as though it came from some enormous distance. "I am a servant of God," the incredibly far-away voice continued. "My sword is sacred." At these words she was in the habit of making a gesture with her sword that Hans particularly liked: she would cradle it tenderly in her arms and then hold it to her breast. Since she must have the sword to do that, Dunois now handed it to her. "Your sword," he improvised as he did it.

She stretched out her hand; it dropped stiffly. Her lips said, "My heart is full of courage, not of anger." Then she paused.

"I will lead," came from the prompter's box.

"I will lead," Selma repeated. At me word "lead" she was supposed to move towards the center of the stage, to the entrance of Dunois' tent. She took the first step and the second. Then she collapsed.

"And your men will follow. That is all I can do," whispered the prompter without raising her eyes from her book.

The girl in the silver armour lay on the floor of the stage. Her lips opened to speak. Her eyes were turned on Hans with a fear he had never seen in any human eyes.

"Selma!" he cried.

The stage manager had had the curtain rung down in the middle of the scene. Since the Imperial and Royal Burgtheater had been in existence no such thing had ever happened.

"What's wrong with the little woman?" asked the portrayer of the archbishop, holding his brocade train around his hips so that he could walk freely. "Send for a physician," he called majestically into the wings. And to the mature lady who had so wanted to play Joan he said softly, "You know the lines, Countess? In your place I'd make a quick change. Now they can see what happens when they give leading parts to little amateurs. It goes to their heads, and they lose them."

Meanwhile Selma had been laid on a sofa backstage. She was no longer conscious. When the theater physician had examined her he appeared to have reached an opinion. Had Frau Alt complained earlier of any such indisposition? Fainting? Early-morning nausea? Hans gave completely confused answers. Something similar, though of a less pronounced order, had occurred before, he said to the doctor. When? Five or six weeks ago. What had happened? It was necessary to be more precise. Frau Alt would have to go back into her part in thirty minutes at the utmost, therefore Hans must realize that everything depended on his furnishing exact information. If the patient did not look so feverish, the doctor said with a smile, he would be inclined to explain the occurrence in the simplest and happiest way.

People were standing about. "Quiet on the stage!" warned the stage manager. What a piece of luck that Joan did not appear in the next, the fourth, scene! Then came the long interval, and surely she would be ready to play in the courtroom scene?

"Presumably so," said the house doctor, and looked at the thermometer he had given the patient. He shook it down immediately, so that Hans had no opportunity to read it. A slight temperature.

"What am I hearing?" asked the stage director on duty, who had been called over from the cafe across the way. "What a piece of luck that the public has not noticed anything!"

The actor playing Dunois came over while the stage was being set for the fourth scene. "Has she come to?" he asked, pressing his moustache, which had come loose with the excitement, with two fingers.

Hans shook his head.

"A little weakness. It happens sometimes," the hero said

ungraciously. In a group of actors, clustering not far away, one could hear him recount the whole incident a moment later, "I see the banner fall from her hand. *All right*, I think, *it's an accident*. Then she drops her sword. Right at my feet. *Isn't she going to pick it up?* I think. Not for anything. She won't pick it up. And she comes down on her line. Old Krischke down below is bellowing like a stuck pig once, twice, three times. She comes down on her lines. I sweat blood. The devil, I think to myself, I'll take the line. Then she collapses on me completely—and just before the wind scene! *I'll be damned*, I think! *She's gone and wrecked the wind scene for me!*"

Oh the sofa where Selma lay, with cheeks so red and respiration too rapid to please Hans, what an untold number of actresses had played illness and death. Perhaps that was why none, except Hans, attributed much significance to her illness. The only point of interest was whether she would be able to go on with the part or whether an understudy must be put in.

"She will under no circumstances act," Hans called to the group of actors.

"Young man," remarked the archbishop, who came over to the sofa as spokesman for the others, "I understand and share your excitement. But the fate of a performance is in the balance. Private considerations have no place here. Our good doctor will give the little woman an injection and put her on her feet again. I played Mephisto on three injections and with a temperature of 104."

"She's not going to act," Hans insisted.

Unexpectedly, the house doctor concurred in this opinion. He recommended that the patient should be taken home.

Hans carried her in his arms down the stairs and out through the entrance usually crowded with autograph seekers, but today the hour was still too early for them.

His arms, which had carried the unconscious form down

the stairs in the theater, now carried her up the stairs at Number 10. The slim figure in the silver armour was light.

He met Otto Eberhard on the first landing, just returning from his evening stroll. "What does this mean?" he asked, catching sight of his nephew with a painted female in his arms.

"Selma is ill," Hans told him, taking two steps at a time.

"Couldn't you at least have wrapped a cape around her?" asked Otto Eberhard, with obvious disgust.

But Hans and his light burden were already on the third floor. A quarter of an hour later Dr. Herz walked in.

"Another alarm?" the physician inquired, with a determined smile which seemed to say: But don't pay any attention to us doctors!

He had long since given up interfering with God's creatures and had retired on a pension. But he let himself be persuaded to come for the sake of that youngster there who had caused him so much trouble on his arrival in the world. He thoughtfully laid his cigar aside on an ashtray, hung up his hat and coat, took his brown wooden stethoscope from his waistcoat pocket, and said: "Now, then, let's take a look at her." Even though one had not practiced for six years and did nothing at present but collect stamps, it was yet in one's blood and bones.

"She's still unconscious," Hans said when they reached the patient.

"So I see," the doctor remarked, with his old trick of calming others by never appearing surprised himself. Nevertheless, he was not able to restrain all signs of uneasiness when he had finished his examination.

"Something serious?" Hans asked.

Let's not change styles now, thought the elderly practitioner; *let's tell him it isn't serious*. So he said it, as he had said it untold times before, in light cases as in serious ones. Nevertheless he insisted on a stomach lavage. He himself was too old to undertake it, but a colleague would do it. He telephoned to a colleague.

With one ear on the breathing of his wife and the other listening to the telephone conversation, Hans caught one foreign word he did not know. When he inquired about it Dr. Herz said, "Nonsense!"

When the colleague arrived they held a consultation; they spent half an hour alone with the patient and then left together. Dr. Herz promised to telephone the results of the chemical analysis. He did not telephone but came himself. It was shortly before midnight when he rang the doorbell. Selma was not wholly conscious yet.

With his cigar in his mouth and his ready smile, Dr. Herz explained: "I wanted to relieve your mind before you went to bed. Tell me, by the way, your wife takes sleeping tablets, doesn't she?"

"Never."

"How can you state that so categorically?"

"Because I know it. Of us two I am the sleepless one. Selma sleeps perfectly."

"Do you take sleeping drafts, Hans?"

"No. Why?"

"Because I do not know how else to explain the presence of veronal in her stomach."

"Veronal? We don't even have any in the house."

"Didn't you tell me that your wife suffered from headaches? What did she take for them?"

"If I'm not mistaken, pyramidon," Hans said, making an effort to be as precise as possible, although his anxiety was increasing with every second. Selma made a movement as though she were in pain. Dr. Herz asked to see where their medicines were kept.

"Does anyone in the house take strychnine?" he inquired, bringing each little bottle and box of tablets up to his short-sighted eyes.

"Papa, I think. Didn't you prescribe it for him yourself?"

"That's why I asked," the old man remarked, and continued his search. "I prescribed a strychnine and quinine combination when I was still coming here. It was the so-called *Wenckebach*—pills. So he's still taking them?"

"I believe so," Hans replied, bewildered.

"And who has the prescription?" the doctor asked, chewing on his cigar.

"Mother, probably. What does all this mean?"

"Your wife, naturally, sees your father quite often?"

"Mother takes care of him almost singlehanded. She never likes to have anyone help."

Closing the door of the small medicine cabinet, the old gentleman remarked, "Don't lay any special significance on my questions. But tell me, Hans, have you two quarrelled? I mean, has your wife on your account or for any other reason—perhaps professionally—had a disappointment?" As he spoke he wandered around the room, examining whatever lay on the table and desk.

"There is no happier marriage than ours! And professionally Selma has recently scored her greatest success!"

"Of course," agreed Dr. Herz, puffing away fiercely. "My memory is like a sieve. What was it now? As the Maid of Orleans?" Hans now barred his way. "Please, Dr. Herz! What is it you're hiding from me?" He could no longer stand the old man's walking around and searching.

"I'm hiding nothing, my boy. But nature seems to be hiding something from me; that is a trick she is unfortunately in the habit of playing on us doctors. Now if I only knew whether your wife had any motives—Good God, don't look at me in such despair! I don't deny that there are symptoms of poison present. Please remember you picked up the word 'poliomyelitis' earlier. That would have been a thousand times worse, for that is infantile paralysis, and I confess that my first suspicions were directed that way. The report on the contents of the stomach fortunately excludes that now, as it admits of a much more logical explanation."

The old man threw himself into an armchair. *My God, how I beat about the bush!* he thought to himself. Instead of asking the boy straight from the shoulder: Why has she attempted to commit suicide? he continued to blow smoke rings. Logic! he raged; where is there any logic? Veronal and strychnine. All right. That explains the symptoms. In any case the shallow breathing and, hypothetically at least, the paralysis. But why did such an amount not have an instant and lethal effect? And how can she have had a similar attack some weeks ago, as the boy asserts?

He sprang suddenly to his feet and, with a speed amazing in so old a man, rushed to Selma's bed, knelt down beside it, and attempted to convince himself of something that Hans could not fathom. He raised her eyelids and lighted matches in front of them. He took great pains to study her gums. He kept testing her reflexes again and again. Finally he said, "Well, good night. I shall be back early tomorrow morning. Meanwhile I'll send in a nurse."

"Is it so serious?" Hans asked, beginning to lose his self-control. Scorning his well-worn tricks, the old doctor replied, "It is an acute condition which must reach a crisis. Tomorrow we shall see."

"Could I ask my cousin to come over?" Hans asked. "If Selma saw a nurse, she would think she was very ill. My cousin visits my father occasionally, and it would be easier to explain." He did not say that he still believed Christl could help where all others failed.

"Of course," approved Dr. Herz. "You mean the little Paskiewicz?" He forgot that the little Paskiewicz was middle-aged, but recalled that her father, the colonel, had fooled him for years on end about dying. The memory of that obviously revived him. In this house anything was possible. You gave these people days or even hours to live and they went on for another twenty years!

"Look, I'll write down what the little Paskiewicz is to do," he said, in a better frame of mind, and filled a prescription page with notes and then left with the words he usually said in severe cases, "Sleep as much as you can. Ask as few questions as possible."

Sister Agatha came about one o'clock. After she arrived things were not so frightening. She read her instructions and had no difficulty in deciphering the old man's scrawl of Dr. Herz, to which she had been accustomed since her childhood. Under her care the patient seemed to breathe more quietly.

"Christl!" Hans said in despair. To her he dared show all his anguish. She had understood him even at a time when he did not wish to speak. Her nun's habit, to be sure, removed the intimacy of those earlier days, but in her eyes lay the same readiness to help. "Dr. Herz thinks it's very serious, doesn't he?" he asked.

"Dr. Herz has left quite simple instructions," she replied. "Don't be afraid, Hans." She still knew him so well that she did not add, "God will help."

The doorbell rang. Henriette had come down from the fourth floor. "Selma is sick?" she asked her son in the vestibule. "Simmerl tells me Dr. Herz has been twice to see her." Then she noticed Christine. "You here too? And I'm not told?"

The nun answered, "You have your hands full already. Hans did not want to disturb you. Please come in."

On the threshold of the bedroom Henriette stopped. Her look fell on the patient and then on the silver cuirass which hung over a chair. The nun followed her look, which suddenly grew disturbed. She knew what Henriette was thinking. One night, in this same house, she had come in costume into a room where it was a question of life and death. Then she had worn a mask, and Christl had looked under her mask.

"Masquerade!" someone had exclaimed reprovingly on that faraway night. Henriette could hear it as though it were today, and she turned cold at the thought. Up on the fourth floor lay Franz, sleepless as on most of the nights these years. She had sat beside him as on most nights, and read to him. Sometimes he looked at her so reproachfully. But here was this nun who was a lifelong reproach. All because of a long-since-expiated tiny scrap of happiness. *It's a wonder people don't go crazy in this house!* thought Henriette. Hans too had noticed his mother's suddenly disturbed expression. "What is wrong with her?" Henriette asked him.

"Dr. Herz says she has taken sleeping tablets."

"How often have I warned her not to take so many powders," said Henriette, picking the costume up with the intention of putting it away.

"What kind of powders?" Hans asked.

"For headaches. She kept coming to me for them when her own gave out."

"To you?"

"She insisted that Algokratin helped her more than anything else."

"Is there veronal in those powders?"

"I don't know. Why?"

"She is awake now," the nun said.

Selma's eyes opened slowly. They fell on Henriette, who was still holding the silver costume in her hands. "No!" she murmured fearfully, as though trying to defend herself.

"Please go away," Hans begged his mother. "She's afraid of you."

"She is afraid of me," Henriette repeated. She put the costume down and left the apartment without looking back.

Selma had closed her eyes again. "Hans," she called distinctly. "I'm just here," he answered. "You're all well again, aren't you?"

She shook her head quickly. "Not well," she murmured. A tense expression came over her face. "Listen to me," she demanded. Then again, "Listen to me."

"I'm listening," Hans said, looking to Christl for help. "Don't you hear me?"

"It's just the fever," the nun told him comfortingly.

"Listen to me, Bastard of France," repeated the patient. Then she was silent. And then, as though she had found at last what she was searching for, she continued in a hesitant voice, "I will deliver you from fear. I will never take a husband. I am a soldier. I do not care for the things women care for. They—"

She stopped. Her expression grew more and more tense. It was obvious that she believed she was on the stage and could not remember her lines.

"They dream of lover." Hans, who could hardly speak, helped her along.

"They dream of lovers," Selma repeated. A trace of her old smile appeared and slowly began to transfigure her face as she went on, "I am a servant of God. My sword is sacred—" She looked for her sword and seemed to find it.

"My heart is full of courage, not of anger," put in Hans, to whom Christl nodded, indicating mat he should help her.

Selma did not repeat it. She smiled ever more enchandngly.

Hans looked at her transfigured face. "She is better? Isn't she, Christl?" he asked imploringly. "Isn't she, Christl?"

"Yes," the nun said after a pause. "No one is better now than she is."

And then, after another pause, Christl, who had helped him as a child, came up behind him and said softly, "Hans. Whom the Lord loves, He makes to suffer. Whom He loves most, He takes to Him."

CHAPTER 36
Brother and Sister

An autopsy was held on Selma's body. Old Dr. Herz, who usually was so philosophic and inclined to let things take their course, had insisted upon it with surprising energy, and Hans was too crushed to offer any resistance. With her death coming out of a clear sky (and it had been thanks only to her life that the sky had been clear), everything to him seemed dark.

The autopsy established the fact of poisoning by veronal and strychnine. As there was no basis for any indication of suicide, the word 'murder' came to the fore. But it was used only tentatively, and naturally appeared first in *Vienna Signals*, called, since Mr. Jarescu had left it to his son, *Vienna Truths* (Mr. Jarescu's son, for his part, now boldly called himself Esk). From thence the news found its way into the daily *Press*. And when the *Neues Wiener Journal* came out with an article entitled "The Murder of a Genius," making the flat assertion that Selma Rosner-Alt had been murdered, her death became a sensation, and Otto Eberhard's successor felt it incumbent on him to consult his predecessor.

The successor was one of those 'upstarts' whom Otto Eberhard could not stand. Moreover, the old gentleman found all the public excitement about the suicide of an actress distressing. When a councillor died after a long life of effort and self-denial, having, God knows, contributed far more than a young undisciplined creature of this sort, he was sent to his grave unhonored and unsung. But the Viennese had always made of every actor a being of some higher order instead of a creature of disorder *per se*, Otto Eberhard did not need his decades of experience to tell his successor that undisciplined people are born suicides. No motive for suicide? People like this Selma were constantly out of control; a cold draft was sufficient to make them bellow or howl or commit suicide. To search for causality here was a waste of effort. The retired Public Prosecutor bowed his successor politely out. He regretted that he was unable to give him any advice or clues, either officially or privately. He had known the deceased only fleetingly. All he had been able to establish was that she was a typical actress.

The successor was equally polite in his thanks, and when he returned to the office, where Otto Eberhard had spent half his life, he ordered an investigation, on grounds of murder, into the death of the actress Selma Rosner-Alt.

Every one of the inhabitants of Number 10 was called to testify. Even Hans, when he was able to summon the strength, appeared before the examining magistrate.

"You suffer so from this death," said the examining magistrate to him, "you should not be so indifferent. On the contrary, shouldn't you have a burning desire to search out the person responsible for destroying your happiness?"

Hans shrugged his shoulders. He had but one desire left.

Only two depositions provided food for thought to Otto Eberhard's successor. One of them came from Johann Simmerl, butler on the fourth floor in 10 Seilerstätte. He testified that Fraulein Martha Monica had copied down a prescription which lay on the medicine table of her invalid father, Herr Franz Alt. To be sure the witness could not identify the prescription. And Martha Monica, also called to testify; did not even recall having copied it. The second remarkable statement was that of the keeper of the stationery shop on the ground floor of the house. (As to this stationer, it was rumored in the house that he was an offspring of the late bachelor Hugo Alt, who had died of some disease not mentioned in polite circles.) He had seen the deceased come home one night in the company of a gentleman who had had to support her. The stationer was of the opinion that she was not sober. As to her companion, all he could say was it had not been Herr Hans Alt but someone of much smaller stature. He was not able to see his face. The deceased and her companion had come through the angel entrance together, had locked the door after them, and he could not recall that the companion left the house that night. He declared under oath that he had listened for him. In answer to the question of what had prompted him to do so, he replied: curiosity.

The depositions of the members of the Burgtheater coincided almost word for word with the opinion of the actor who played the archbishop: Suicide. The ambitious woman, prematurely lauded to the sky, had had enough sense of self-criticism to know that she could never measure up to the over-exaggerated expectations of her future accomplishment.

Rumors, conclusions, and suspicions occupied public opinion until they proved groundless. Then the sensational case was dropped.

When the daily newspaper comments ceased Number 10 breathed more easily. Hans was treated with greatest possible consideration; the house put its best foot forward: the blow to one of them they parried as a whole. Fritz came nearly every evening to discuss one and the same thing with his cousin: Why? To what end? Why did Selma take her life? To what end should one go on living now that she was dead? His father, still the head of the C. Alt Firm, frequently wrote that Hans had done this or that "quite excellently." His brother Hermann gave proof of an understanding for which Hans was particularly grateful; although he had some time before displaced him in the factory, the younger brother did not hold this against the older one, and even helped him in his free time. And Henriette surrounded her favorite son with a tenderness she had withheld from him since Selma had been in the house. Even Otto Eberhard nodded in a conciliatory manner when he met his obviously misguided nephew on the stairs.

For Hans the hardest to bear were the sleepless nights. He rarely lay down any more; he paced the rooms where traces of her still spoke to him on every hand. Her clothes hung in the wardrobes. The books that she had read lay there. On her desk lay the scrapbook in which she had begun to paste newspaper reports. Ever and again he would say to himself, She is in the next room; and would call, "Selma." More often he could not grasp the idea of her death.

He was a person who became attached to others only with difficulty. Once he formed an attachment it was for life, even when his choice proved a disillusion. It was the first time in his life that he knew, in Selma, what confirmation and fulfilment were: She was the first to turn his vague concept of happiness into reality. The first person never to disappoint him. The only one who knew him: the extent of his inhibitions, his devotion to the country in which he lived. She had realized that his ardent "patriotism" was not a case of violated pride which made it impossible for him to live in a country defeated to the point of annihilation and humiliated beyond compare, that it was a question of spiritual survival. The words "Austrian incarnate," which the poet Wildgans had returned to current use, were applicable to Hans as to few others. Selma had never from the first instant doubted that Austria meant more than a country to him; she recognized that to him it was an idea, and she loved him all the more for that.

Since she knew so well what he was, he had no need either to explain or prove himself to her. That did away with his uncertainty. With her he recovered his desire to live and the gaiety which was natural to him but which had been deadened by his long period of isolation.

Nor was that the only reason that he felt her loss so irreparably. It was also because Selma had been destroyed before she could fulfil herself. The very word 'death,' in connection with a life full of such unspent riches, seemed to him incomprehensible. As in everything, he sought the meaning, but could not find it.

"Spiritual monogamy" was the expression used by his

teacher Freud when he wrote him a letter of condolence and spoke of the consequences of a "cult oriented toward the past."

Every evening he would talk to her picture. He told her what had happened that day, what he had thought about, every thought being bound up with her. He begged her pardon for many things, over and over again for that evening he first came home, when he did not want to see her on the stage. The devastating sense that he could never make up for the hurt feelings now left him no peace; he recalled every lacerating word he had ever said. But in the name of God's mercy, surely she would not have gone out of life for that? Sometimes he tortured himself with the thought that there was some basis for the stationer's testimony, some things he did not know; there may have been another man whom she had loved and she had fled from life on his account; at that his heart stood still.

On one of these nights he was reading the last letter she wrote to his prison camp, and which he had always carried with him since that time, when Martha Monica came to see him. Since Selma's death he had had the feeling that his sister had drawn away from him. But as he noticed nothing and, moreover, knew that she did not think of anyone except her lover, he paid no attention to this. Sometimes it occurred to him that people were right who insisted she was not his father's child. Besides, he had reached the point where he no longer expected anything either from fate or from people.

"It's late," she said. "But you were not in bed anyway. I can't sleep either. So I thought I'd come and see what you are doing."

He noticed how badly she looked. Perhaps she expected him to ask why she could not sleep. But he did not do it. His grief had made him taciturn.

He offered her a cigarette, which she threw away half smoked. Her voice and her fingers were restless. "I don't know how to tell you, Hans ..." she began tentatively.

Go ahead and say it, he thought. *You are going to have a child. Or he has deceived you. Or you are in love with someone else. Just say, "I can't bear it." And I'll answer, "You are to be envied! Oh, how I envy you! It is only finality which is unbearable."*

"It is about Mother," Martha Monica said.

"Is she ill?"

"No." Now she looked positively alarming.

"Is it about Mother and—Father?"

She seemed to search for words without finding them.

"With Mother and—you," she said finally.

He was more attentive now. Had not Martha Monica always been one to take things lightly—in any case much more lightly than Father took them?

"Please give me another cigarette," she said. She took a few puffs, then said in an expressionless, jerky voice, as she put match after match to her already lighted cigarette, "At first I thought I shouldn't tell you at all. You have no idea how often I have been on the point of telling you. But then I always said to myself, Why do it? It's hard enough for him as it is. But I can't stand it any longer. I wanted to ask someone what I should do. I didn't know what I ought to do. Yesterday I asked Hermann. He thought I must absolutely tell you, because it depends on you." She was not looking at him.

"What depends on me?"

She opened and closed her hand spasmodically; her cigarette fell from it. "I have a terrible suspicion," she said.

He gazed into her face.

"You understood me, Hans?"

Selma's wrist-watch, which he wound up every night, lay on the desk. It was so still in the room that its ticking could be heard.

"What do you know?" he asked tonelessly.

She had overheard a conversation, she said in a scarcely

audible voice. Selma had reproached Mother with not understanding Hans. He should be treated like a patient. Martha
Monica hesitated.

"Go on!" he urged.

"Because it's a thousand times harder for you," she continued. "You're an idealist, and the people in the house here are
killing you because they demand that you continue with your
life as though there had been no war or revolution or defeat.
And because you have to work in the factory instead of wherever you might achieve what you wish to achieve. This house is
your undoing, and she intended to ask Papa to allow you to
move away."

"What did Mother say to this?"

"Mother answered that she knew you best and would not
allow Selma to raise the question of moving away with Papa,
who must be protected from excitement. She herself had suffered from the house, but she had conquered her feelings, and
Selma would too." Martha Monica stopped to take breath.
"Selma said if Mother insisted that you could not live elsewhere she would not stay with you in Vienna. She would
accept a film contract to go to America."

"When was this?"

"After the opening of *Saint Joan.*"

"What did Mother say? Word for word!"

"She would in no circumstances let you go to America. But
when Selma said that Mother had no authority over you,
Mother answered, 'You're not going to put yourself in my way!
Not you! I'll see to that!'"

In the numbness which gripped him like a vice, and in
which he heard the ticking of Selma's watch ten times more
acutely and painfully, Hans asked, "Have you any more stories
to tell?" He stressed the word 'stories.'

Tears rose to Martha Monica's eyes. "Don't look at me like
that! That's why I haven't wanted to tell you for so long,

because I thought you would be angry with me. I have nothing to do with it!"

"Correct," he said, using Ebeseder's favorite expression. "And what has"—he hesitated to say "Mother;" then he ended—"she to do with it?"

Martha Monica went on with her account. She related facts she had denied before the examining magistrate. She had seen Mother take the little white envelopes out of the box of powders for Papa's heart ailment, empty and dissolve them in a glass of water. This glass, covered with a strip of parchment, had remained untouched for several days on the medicine table in Papa's room and then disappeared. Papa had not touched it. On the day the glass disappeared Mother had asked her to copy the prescription of old Dr. Herz, so that she could have it filled at the St. Anna pharmacy. Why disturb old Dr. Herz, who was no longer practicing? Mother had said. Martha Monica had asked what became of the glass on Papa's table. Then Mother had looked very frightened, had not been able to speak at all at first, and had finally asserted she had had to throw it out because it had stood too long.

The wristwatch ticked on fatefully. Hans stood up and put it away in a drawer in the desk. Still its incessant ticking sounded like a hammer in the silent room. "Is that all?" he asked.

That was all.

"To whom else have you told this nonsense?"

He had gone over to the window. The walnut tree was withered and leafless, although it was only July. The walls, usually veiled by its foliage, were bare. Old gray walls from which bits of mortar were crumbling.

"That's no proof," he said before she could answer.

"Don't you think so?" she asked. "Really? You really think it's no proof?"

"I am convinced of it." His back was turned to her.

"I am so glad to hear you say that!" she exclaimed. And

since he said nothing, "Forgive me for having told you about it at all! Perhaps it wasn't even worth mentioning."

"Thank you," he said. "You meant well, as always. Good night." He did not turn round.

When, infinitely relieved, she had gone away, his small amount of self-control deserted him. He too had had that inexpressible suspicion, but had repressed and overcome it as madness. That night when Selma died, and Mother stood at her bed with such hatred in her, he had had the real proof in front of his very eyes, yet did not want to see it. She had always hated Selma. Even when he first told her he was engaged. Now Hans called it all to mind. The jealousy. The envy. The disfavor. Never a kind look. Never a friendly word. Only the desire to humiliate or to belittle her.

As he stood at the window this son piled up against his mother an accusation of such inescapable force as Public Prosecutor Otto Eberhard could never have formulated. Yet as he did it he seemed to feel the last bit of solid ground cut from beneath his own feet. He heard everything splinter and crash into the abyss. Crushed, his memories fled the time when nothing in the world counted for him but his mother. But he could not rid himself of these memories. Everything that was wonderful in his childhood stemmed from her: the protection, the lightness, all the warmth.

He stood with his forehead pressed against the window, outside which towered the black skeleton of the long-since-withered but not felled walnut tree, and in him something happened that he was unable to prevent. He used all his power to protect himself against it, but to no avail. *Why is it I do not hate her?* he asked himself. He wanted to hate her. He tried to do so. He invoked Selma's last hours, her helpless smile before she died. He saw his mother standing at the bed of his dying wife. With the eyes of a mortal enemy she stood there. She had outwitted her, he told himself, through deceit, jealousy, cruelty, and in cold blood. He knelt beside me bed where murdered Selma had smiled her last smile. He pressed his lips to the pillow on which she had died. He loved her with a tenderness and sadness greater than ever. But he could not hate the woman who had murdered her.

Could not love be undone? Would he love Selma less had he known she had murdered someone? He tried to think about this and clung to the thought. He would love her just as much, he answered himself.

"You suffer so from this death. Therefore should you not have a burning desire to search out the person responsible for destroying your happiness?" the examining magistrate had said to him.

He had searched her out. His mother.

The branches before the window, which for generations had showered thousands of nuts on the ground, now stirred in sterile movements. Mother had cracked his first nut for him. All the first things had been done for him by her. It was she who had taught him how things tasted, how they felt. It was Mother who taught him what people are and what one must be to people.

Mother was Selma's murderess. He had not needed Martha Monica to know this. Unconsciously he had known it all the time, and not wanted to know it; he had sealed it away inside himself and thought it would never come to the surface; he had doubted it a hundred times and believed it a thousand. Never in his life had he struggled as much with anything. Mother was Selma's murderess. Not wanting to see had been of no avail; the not wanting to speak of it was of no avail; the countless ways of defence he had sought and found in his sleepless nights were of no avail. This was not a matter between him and his mother. It lay between him and Selma. He owed it to Selma to hate her murderess. No. He owed it to a murder to hate the murderess.

That much he admitted.

He owed it to Selma to call the murderess to account. If God were merciful she would not prove to be the murderess. But he must call her to account.

That much he admitted.

What did he owe his mother?

He had always stood with his forehead pressed against the windowpane whenever his life was in confusion. And so he stood now. Christl had been mistaken. It was not Selma's death which was hardest for him to bear. It was this hour.

He turned and nodded to her picture.

"I'm going now," he said to the picture, as always before he left.

He walked up the stairs from the third to the fourth floor; there were only twenty-three steps. As an infant he had been carried up them in his baby carriage; as a boy he had bounded up them impatiently; as a man he had never noticed them. Now each step was a mountain, so steep he could hardly tell how to climb it. When he reached the top he hesitated before the door to the apartment of his past. He knew he had come in order to shut it forever behind him.

Simmerl opened to him.

"So late?" asked the tall man whose back had gradually grown bowed with time. He was in a dressing gown and ridiculous pointed nightcap without which he never went to bed.

"I want to speak to my mother," Hans said.

"I think Her Ladyship only went to bed a short while ago," said the butler. "The master has been having a very restless night, and she has been with him all the time." He waited to see whether these words, which more than hinted at protecting people in need of rest, would determine the young master to withdraw. When this did not prove to be the case he nodded, as usual when egoists imposed their orders on him, "I'll call Her Ladyship."

CHAPTER 37
Mother and Son

Henriette came into the room. A hundred times during these nights, with their words of comfort which meant nothing, with their medicines which did not relieve, she had said to herself that it would be a release for both of them. He now led nothing more than a shadowy existence; there was no reality to it; nothing that came near him was alive. One felt unreal oneself in this atmosphere of make-believe, in this maintenance of a world that no longer existed. Nevertheless, she refused to admit the idea of his death. He belonged to her. And she to him. She no longer denied that.

"So late?" she too asked.

"Is Papa not so well?" Hans asked. The words slipped from him, his eyes saw with difficulty. They looked on an exhausted woman, to whom he must say something that might break all ties between them.

"Not particularly well," she answered. "It's dear of you to come up. You need your sleep yourself, my poor boy."

"Mother," he said, and then stopped.

"Do you know, Hans," she said, noticing that he was deeply moved, "sometimes I think it would be a release for Papa. I know one should not say such things. And to you least of all."

She had made it easier for him. "It was no release for Selma. She wanted to live," he replied.

"Who knows what one has been spared? Do you think it's so wonderful to be alive in this world?"

I shall watch her closely, he thought. She has often said not everyone can be an actor. "What did you want to spare her?" he asked.

She sighed. "Unfortunately there was so little I could spare her. I often reproach myself now because of it. I'm glad we have put this into words. I wasn't kind to Selma. I was too jealous of her."

"That is why you murdered her," he said.

Guilty!

Her face underwent a terrifying change. He would have given Selma's life if only her face had not had this expression of guilt.

"What are you saying?" she asked tonelessly.

He repeated his words.

She had risen slowly to her feet. From where she stood she looked into his face. Then she screamed, "Hans!" Simmerl rushed in excitedly. She had stretched her hand out towards her son. Although she stood beside him, she pointed to him as though he were far away.

"Madam," begged Simmerl. "Madam! Master will hear you!"

She no longer screamed. Sobs racked her. After a little her strength was exhausted. Gasping, she sank back into a chair. "Go and see how Herr Alt is," she stammered. When Simmerl had left the room she said, "I swear to you by your father's life."

That was the most terrible of all. She swore by the life of a dying man. She swore by the life of someone she had never loved.

"Is that not enough?" The lips which framed the question were bloodless.

Before Hans could reply Simmerl returned. "The master!" he said.

She nodded. As she rose she had to support herself. "Wait here," she said. "We must talk. I'll come back." Then she went to the invalid.

"Perhaps the young master will fetch a priest?" Simmerl asked. "The young master is still dressed."

"Is Papa so ill?" asked the son to whom his father's life had meant so little.

The old servant's eyes had filled with tears.

"I'll go at once," Hans said, and hurried away.

Meanwhile Henriette sat by Franz's deathbed. For her he did not need to write things down on a slip of paper as he did for others; it sufficed to write them in the air with his forefinger. In the course of years she had learned to decipher it. "Why?" he now wrote.

"Why did you scream?" it meant.

She had never spoken the truth to this man. She had married him by mistake. It was only at the end that this mistake had been converted into a kind of truth, if only a half-truth. Once more she kept the truth from him. "I was frightened by something." She concocted an excuse, as always when obliged to. "I thought there was someone in the room."

And—as all his life, with one exception long since forgiven—he believed her lie. With a look such as he had so often sought her and which she so often had found unbearable, he now gazed at her. To her alone belonged the spark of life still lingering in him.

"Tell," wrote his forefinger in the air.

"I'm to tell you something?" she asked.

He pointed to his own breast.

"You want to tell me something?"

His face nodded. His finger wrote: "Forgive."

"I have nothing to forgive you, Franz." She made an effort to speak as distinctly as she could through her tears.

Then this man, who had always been against 'fuss' and for sober objectivity, shook his head. He realized that he must make himself clearly understood once and for all. So he rested a moment, gathered all his remaining strength, and wrote, "For marrying you."

He wrote it word for word. No letter was missing in his writing in the air, not even the flourishes he used to put on certain letters.

She read it. Stirred to her very depths as she faced a finality beyond which nothing lay, she too made a supreme effort at clarity.

"You were very good to me, and I was unkind to you. I didn't understand things right. Now I do. A love like yours, which trusts even when it suspects, is the best. A love that forgives even when it accuses is a miracle! Forgive me."

In this chamber of death her words sounded like a confession from the wrong lips. But it was the first complete truth she had ever spoken to him in her life.

A smile hovered around his palsied lips. In his eyes there shone the pride that had always filled them when they fell on this woman. He gazed on her at length. For him time could not alter this face. He did not see the ravages of age. He overlooked the traces of suffering, and even those of despair. For him she was still the embodiment of all beauty, as she was on the first day he saw her.

His finger pointed to his mouth.

Henriette leaned over him. The dying man's lips made a great effort. They succeeded in framing a kiss. He sank back exhausted. Then he knew he had one more thing to do, which had not yet been done, so this man, who had never tolerated arrears in his work, wrote in the air, "Thank you."

Soon he fell into a kind of doze which alarmed her, and she went to call Simmerl. But the old servant had long been standing outside the door.

"Monsignor will be here directly," he said.

Henriette thought she caught another smile on Franz's lips. She said to Simmerl, "Call the Public Prosecutor."

But in the quiet which preceded the end the dying man, fully conscious, made a negative gesture. He did not wish to see his brother. And when she, no longer making any pretence of not knowing he was about to die, asked him openly if he wished to see his children he indicated as plainly that he did not, and pointed to her.

"You are the only one," that meant.

She no longer saw anything through her tears. The terrible mistake of her life was now cleared away. It was not that she had married this man. It was that she had looked upon it as a mistake.

And once more, in this night which had added years to Henriette's life, something incomprehensible happened. When the priest arrived and asked Herr Franz Alt to relieve his soul by holy confession Herr Franz Alt refused. He pointed first to himself and then to his wife.

"I have already made my confession," it signified. But as a good Christian he asked for and received the last sacraments.

After the priest had gone he lived on for an hour. During that hour he held Henriette's hand. One last time his hand attempted to write, "Thank you." He succeeded. Then the man who had always hated anything extravagant and who had possessed so infinitely little imagination was no more.

CHAPTER 38
An Austrian is Buried

The dead man's coffin was borne by his sons Hans and Hermann and his nephews Fritz and Otto. They had carried it down from the fourth floor, through the door of the apartment he had built when he married, past the doors where he had lived as a bachelor and where he had been born. It occurred to Fritz, who with his twin brother held the foot of the coffin while the two sons supported the head, that three doors told the story of the dead man's life. Like most of his generation, he had scarcely traveled abroad. He had never moved. In the same house one was born, one lived his life, and died.

On the coffin were laid the wreaths of his widow, his children, and brother, while the untold number of the others were piled high in the two carriages following the hearse, and behind them walked Henriette on Otto Eberhard's arm. Her long widow's veil of black crepe darkened her look. Franz's brother, thirteen years his senior, despite the July day wore the prescribed long black coat, black cravat, and black gloves and carried his high hat, with a broad mourning band, in his left hand. Nothing in his face betrayed his thoughts.

They were followed by the daughters, Franziska and Martha Monica, with Franziska accompanied by her husband, Dr. Baier, and Martha Monica walking alone. There were no grandchildren. The sisters of the deceased joined the others, the elder one, Gretl Paskiewicz, with her daughter, the nun. His younger one, Pauline, followed on the arm of Franz's brother-in-law Drauffer; then came Otto Eberhard's wife Elsa with her son Peter. And Peter's wife, Annemarie, had charge of their three children, Joachim, Adelheid, and Otto Adolf, who walked in a row before her, whereas Fritz's late-born son Raimund, whom his mother Liesl led by the hand, was the last of the family group.

At a slight distance came the servants. Herr Simmerl with his wife, Hanni, and their daughter, sent for from Mariazell, were at the head. Like all the men in the funeral cortege, Herr Simmerl, with his long black coat, black cravat, black gloves, and high hat with a broad mourning band, followed the example of the head of the house. And all the maids were dressed like their mistresses. Even the stationer from the ground floor was in deep mourning.

Everything was as Otto Eberhard had directed, in sequence and appearance. Perhaps, thought Fritz the pallbearer, he looked upon it as a kind of dress rehearsal for the next funeral at Number 10 and wished to see with his own eyes how he himself, in the not too far distant future, would be laid to rest.

At the angel entrance stood the hearse; over its black top rose a knight's head of iron with helmet and open visor; in front of it four black horses were harnessed, and on them sat outriders in black doublets slashed with velvet and high top boots. The pallbearers pushed the casket into the hearse. Then they placed themselves in a row behind the carriages with the flowers. The cortege began to move.

Immediately after the family group there was a space. At the head of the long train of mourners not related to the family came a delegation from the C. Alt piano-maker firm, led by Mr. Foedermayer, foreman Czerny, and metal-caster Bochner.

The muffled bells of St. Anna and St. Augustine were tolling. According to Otto Eberhard's directions, the late Purveyor to the Court had to be buried from St. Augustine's, because the one to whom his title and the prosperity of his forbears was due was accustomed to attend the funerals of reputable citizens there. Since the Hapsburgs had reigned and made distinctions in life and in death, all the members of all good families, though not of the highest rank, which entitled them to burial in the Capuchin crypt, had received their last church blessing here. That these distinctions had been blown away by a revolution was a fact of which the retired Public Prosecutor and Aulic Councillor did not take cognizance. As he had ordained it, it was proper to act; revolutions did not abolish the proprieties for him.

To the droning of the bells Henriette walked by his side. Could she have asked for one favor it would have been to stop those bells. Their muffled tones had accompanied every catastrophe of her life. With a relentlessness against which she was impotent, they now hammered her memories of the past back into her mind. She had not followed the hearse the first time they had tolled so accusingly, the first time she was widowed. Then she had run away, for it was her wedding night. Nor had she followed the coffin of the man to whom she owed that infinitely tiny bit of happiness. She had fled, for it was her shame. Now she walked with head erect, on the arm of a man who had been her lifelong adversary, behind the coffin of a man who was not able to give her either a crown or happiness and who was the cause of so much self-reproach to her. If only the bells would cease!

Two steps behind her walked the one person, perhaps, in all the world on whose account she need not reproach herself. Yet he of all people had made to her the most inhuman reproach and was still making it. She sensed it in his looks. She knew what her enemy, on whose arm she walked, was thinking. An unfaithful, bad, selfish wife! His looks showed it. The bells droned ever louder. Her steps faltered, and she pressed her free hand to her temples.

"Control yourself," said her companion. "No play-acting!"

She walked on to the merciless and menacing hammering of the bells. In the July heat the perfume of the flowers was suffocating. On the left of the funeral train the Albrecht terrace and the old Imperial castle came into sight. As they drew near St. Augustine's a red glow appeared on the horizon and the shrill sound of the fire engines was added to the tolling. They had reached the cathedral where Henriette and Franz were married.

Inside the cathedral the coolness was a relief. It was only the incense that confused the senses. The four pallbearers had carried the casket to the catafalque below the high altar. The incense grew more acrid and stifling the closer they came to the altar.

Henriette knelt in the first row. On her right stood Otto Eberhard. On her left, so near that she could have touched it with her outstretched arm, was the coffin, at the head and foot of which were lighted candles in candelabra. One of the two broad lavender silk streamers hanging from the wreath of roses and violets on the middle of the casket bore her name. "I thank you" were the words on the other. When it was still in her apartment Otto Eberhard had looked on it with disparagement. No new styles! On funeral wreaths the inscriptions should read "Rest in peace" or "Until we meet."

His Eminence the Cardinal Archbishop of Vienna began the mass for the dead. His calm peasant face bore the expression appropriate to the occasion. A well-known patrician had died, one who had contributed to the cultural life of Vienna— not one of the leading figures of the epoch, to be sure, but an upright man and a good Catholic. As to his wife, there had been some unsavoury rumors in the past. But on the other hand his brother, who himself had one foot in the grave, had always enjoyed the confidence of the highest circles because of his outstanding position. This had been duly put to the cardinal, together with the request that he read the mass in person, and for the sake of the elder brother he had acquiesced in manifestly honoring the obsequies of the younger brother.

"*Introibo ad altarem Dei*," they heard him intone the prayer, surrounded by his assistants. Henriette's eyes wandered. Where the deacon of the archbishopric was standing, holding the hem of the archbishop's vestment, she herself had stood and said "Yes" to the question of whether she was willing to become the wife of Franz Alt. Over there, where Simmerl sat, she had sat, and to the woman who asked her if she had lost someone she had said: "Yes." The woman had answered: "You mustn't cry; it hurts the dead."

"Have I hurt you?" she asked the dead man. She knew that he still heard her. Earlier, at the last minute before they left the apartment, she had looked at him through the glass at the head of the coffin, and he had seen her too. "Franz," she now said, and bowed her head towards him as the cardinal moved to the Host, "when I said 'Yes' up there to you I was lying. Ask me now, and I shall answer!"

With bated breath she listened and heard his question.

She answered distinctly, in the presence of the cardinal, who had fallen to his knees before the Host, "Yes."

It was only when she felt that she was now in truth wedded to him that the feverish tension in her relaxed. She could weep.

As often as he had come into the room he had always nodded first. Then he had said, "God greet you." First the nod, then the greeting. Never otherwise. The unimaginativeness of this sequence was something she could never forgive him, and she had never nodded back. It was only now that she realized this nod was the limit of expression to which anyone in Number 10 was trained. "No play-acting!" As long as there was time in which to do it she wanted to make up for her omission. She nodded to the dead man. Again. Again. "Franzl," she said as she did it. That caressing name, too, she had never been willing to give him. When the *saecula sceculorum* was heard the pallbearers raised the coffin in which lay the man who only once had turned against her. The burden trembled for a moment, then rested firmly on the four shoulders. Henriette nodded one last time and said a final farewell aloud, "God greet you."

Otto Eberhard whispered, "Do stop. Acknowledge the condolences!" For as they left, on either side came voices and outstretched hands, "My sympathy! My deepest sympathy!"

While they waited in Augustinerstrasse for the carriages to drive up and take them to the cemetery, an incident occurred which they did not immediately understand. They did not know that during the funeral service the Palace of Justice, only a few blocks away, had been set on fire by some persons acting in revenge for a partisan verdict pronounced against workers. The hearse and the carriages, piled high with the floral tributes, could not move because of the crowds in the streets. Because of them too no one could see the red glow of the fire. Even the sound of the shots fired at the incendiaries was swallowed up by the tolling bells.

Some of the rioters, pushed back into Augustinerstrasse by the police, reached there just in time to see His Eminence, with his exalted entourage, leaving the cathedral, gathering up the skirts of their soutanes to avoid the dust of the streets.

"You'd do better to minister to the innocents being shot down, Cardinal!" yelled someone in the crowd.

The prince of the Church, accustomed to matching his expression to the exigencies of the occasion, raised his hand in benediction. From the Corpus Christi processions he was used to seeing the street mobs sink to their knees on the spot. This time no one kneeled. "You can bring the police to their knees—not us!" came another outcry.

Then someone confronted the man who had shouted. He had sought him out in the crowd and now barred the way to him. It was an aged man in a long black coat, a high hat with a broad mourning band on his head, with black gloves on his hands and the rosette of a commander of the Order of Francis Joseph in his buttonhole. Unconcerned by the threatening attitude of the crowd, he was standing before the rioter, a half-grown youth. "Kneel down!" he commanded with biting contempt.

The youth stared at him. Then he broke into a roar of laughter.

"Leave him alone, Herr Hofrat," begged His Eminence. "He doesn't know any better." And as the mob prepared to fall upon the old gentleman, the cardinal himself stepped from the onlookers and personally escorted Otto Eberhard to his carriage; a nun walked on his left side.

"There are no Imperial Councillors any more!" someone bellowed.

An officer in Italian uniform yelled for the police. Hans said, "Thanks, Conte Corbellini. We need neither your protection nor that of the police."

Before the former Public Prosecutor stepped into the carriage which was to drive him to his younger brother's grave he turned and called in a loud and steady voice, "A people which has forgotten how to kneel is doomed!"

The carriages drove off. The sky had grown redder.

CHAPTER 39
Rehabilitation of an Austrian

Hans received Conte Corbellini only on Martha Monica's urgent request. According to her, he had returned from a journey and at all costs insisted on speaking to her elder brother. She stressed how much Conte Corbellini regretted having exchanged "unfriendly words" with Hans and how sincerely he desired to restore the friendliest of relationships with him.

Hans was under the impression that the Italian intended to ask him for his sister's hand, looking upon him as the head of the family, a role for which he felt absolutely inadequate. Day and night he was absorbed by cares other than marrying off Martha Monica, especially to a man he distrusted. But he had no proof to offer against him.

That was what plagued him constantly: he had no proof. Not the proof that Signor Corbellini was a swindler. It was something else, and on it depended whether he could ever again trust anyone.

On this other point he finally had to express himself to his younger brother. For it was Hermann who, according to Martha Monica, believed in Mother's guilt, and it was he who one day brought up the subject. Hans, however, wouldn't discuss it. It seemed monstrous to him for two sons to discuss their mother's innocence or guilt. But Hermann had insisted, and the brothers had taken a walk together, the first that Hans could remember.

Just as formerly he had piled up the evidence of guilt, Hans had, in the months that followed, attempted to dissipate it. Without her knowing it, he had watched his mother. For nights on end he had conferred with Dr. Herz. Eventually he had worked out a logical explanation.

On this the first walk together in their lives he had given the explanation to his brother as best he could. But Hermann had answered, with a tone of distress which vouched for his sincerity, "I hadn't dreamed that you still had any doubts and for that reason remained passive! Else I should have felt myself obliged to tell you what I saw with my own eyes long ago. Mother, I'm sorry to say, made your poor wife, who came to her with a headache, drink a solution—prepared out of the glass Martha Monica knows about. I had known that for a time, when Martha Monica shared her suspicions with me. All the more reason for her to be the one to speak to you. If I had come to you first you wouldn't even have listened to me. You never were well-disposed towards me—forgive me, this is no time to bring that up. I only wanted to explain why I didn't tell you."

"And what would you do if you were in my place?" Hans had asked his brother.

"There would be no question in my mind," Hermann had answered. As he spoke he leaned over to pick up one of the paper leaflets that for some time had been showered daily on the streets of Vienna and angrily tore it to, bits. "Come to Hitler!" was printed on the slip.

"You never loved Mother," had been Hans's exasperated rejoinder.

"I never sympathized with her particularly," Hermann readily admitted. "That's why I thought it was only fair not to exercise any influence over you. I knew that I was prejudiced against her. However, I kept silent."

"And what makes you break your silence now?"

"Justice."

"In other words, you would institute a suit against your mother?" Hans had asked him.

"I should speak to Uncle Otto Eberhard," had been his advice. "By doing so you avoid taking ultimate steps. On the other hand, you could not find anyone more competent to judge. Uncle Otto Eberhard is not just a famous lawyer and a great jurist; he has always—no matter what you may hold against him—held the reputation of the family above everything else."

"But who has anything to gain from it?" Hans had asked in desperation. "Not Selma; she's dead. Not Mother; she would not survive it. Not the house, which would see its fabulous reputation undermined. I want to keep my silence!"

"I'm surprised," Hermann had answered. "People have always said you're an idealist. But you argue like a lawyer. Guilt cannot be a question of opportunism! Nor can justice. Do you feel Mother led such an impeccable life? Martha Monica, I think, is the proof to the contrary. Or do you still believe in Mother's fairy tales? She lied to you as to anyone else. She——"

"Thank you," Hans had cut him short.

Thereupon he had set himself the limit of one week. The week was up this evening. At nine o'clock he had asked for an interview with his uncle.

At four that afternoon the Italian had called on him, and the thought had crossed Hans's mind: At four I give my sister in marriage to a swindler; at nine I denounce my mother to the Public Prosecutor. "I know what brings you to me," he had said in greeting his visitor.

They were sitting in the office of the head of the piano factory, where a third portrait had been added to the other two; beside the paintings of his great-grandfather and grandfather now hung one of Hans's father in a gold frame, a truly unnerving likeness done by Uncle Drauffer. Whenever the present head of the firm looked at it he had to think of Selma's expression of "baroque angel painting." If she, that fanatical devotee to the truth, could see this revealingly true portrait she would have had to revise her opinion of Uncle Drauffer as he, in the course of time, had revised his own of his father. In that sober look there was clarity. In that shy, frugal smile on the straight mouth of earlier days there was trustworthiness. In the unobtrusive dress and manner lay an unrelenting self-restraint. It was remarkable how, in this picture, the sum of the insignificant became significant.

"*Lei non mi serba rancore, verro?*" asked the Italian, and then acted as if he and Hans had never exchanged an "unfriendly word." He explained at once that his errand was not bound up with Martha Monica, for as far as he and Signorina Alt were concerned, he would still have to have a brief postponement. Hans had no doubt been informed that for a long time he, Corbellini, had been making unceasing efforts to obtain from the Congregation of Rites the annulment of his first marriage. The Virgin be praised, on his recent visit to Rome he finally was given the assurance that he would receive it in the near future. That visit to Rome, on the other hand, was what brought him to Hans today. He had had the honor of being received by Il Duce.

He said "Il Duce" so melodiously, so reverently, as if he were still standing in his presence. He also looked around the office of the head of the firm to see if any listeners were about. Through the door now covered with green felt—the one change Hans had allowed to be made—came the muted noises from the tuning room.

"We can't be overheard?" inquired the Italian, in order to be doubly sure.

Hans said "No." He thought of the interview ahead of him that evening.

Va bene, for the matter to be considered was the anxiety with which Il Duce was following the development of events in Austria. It was a well-known fact that no one was a more cordial friend to Austria and an advocate of her absolute independence than he. Conte Corbellini quoted a note he had made on his conversation with him: "*Può cioè esistere un secondo stato tedesco in Europa, tedesco, ma padrone del suo proprio destino.*" This independence was now being mortally threatened from the right and from the left. The menace might come from the Socialists, under Otto Bauer, of whom Lenin had made a highly personal remark—this too was jotted down on another slip: "This man, ablest of the Socialist traitors, is nothing more than a hopeless scholarly buffoon—a common example of the pedant and a bourgeois shopkeeper in his outlook." On the other side was the menace of the Nazis, whose urgent propaganda, sent in from Germany, was all the more dangerous in form because their Führer was—the Italian read from a third slip of paper—a "pathological liar and megalomaniac." *Benissimo*, the Social Democrats no longer governed; after ruining Austria completely they were now in the opposition. A coalition of Christian Socialists, Peasants, and German Nationalists were running things, but this Government controlled literally one single majority vote in Parliament and therefore could be overthrown at any hour. Moreover, since Monsignor Seipel resigned there had been no real statesman at the head. Consequently there was, in Il Duce's belief, only one alternative: armed self-protection. The Sozis had their "Republican Defence League," which they mobilized and used to terrorize the public with whenever they saw fit. They wished to overthrow the coalition Government and throw in their lot with democratic Germany, which was daily giving fresh proof of its ineptness. The Nazis, on the other hand, who had only a small following in Austria but who were all the more generous in their distribution of arms and spick-and-span new uniforms, wished to join Austria with a National Socialist Germany which would, according to Il Duce, do away with the ridiculous Weimar republic. There was just one point.

Here the Italian looked carefully around him on all sides and drew from his briefcase, not a slip, but a large sheet, unfolded it, and then read it with such reverence as if he were inwardly bowing before each word. They were Il Duce's words, and he had been allowed on the spot in Palazzo Venezia to commit them to paper. Il Duce had said: "*Io racommanderei, e racommanderei persino vivamente, l'organizzazione immediata a traverso l'Austria, di una milizia armata all'esempio fascista, per proteggere la popolazione contro il terrore communista e l'ancor piugrave minaccia del Nazismo. Al momento propizio e quando la milizia, sarà organizzata, le armi e l'appoggio necessario verranno provisti.*" That meant, if Signore Alt did not understand Italian sufficiently well: "I recommend, and recommend urgently, the formation of an armed militia, on the fascist pattern, in Austria, to protect the population from communist terror and the still more dangerous threat of Nazism. Help and arms will be placed in readiness at the right moment as soon as the militia is formed."

The gentleman just arrived from Rome paused. "*Ecco!* What do you say to such magnanimity?" was his next question.

When he had begun to tell about things familiar to every Austrian schoolboy Hans's thoughts again had strayed to his impending evening appointment. "You mean about the militia?" he replied absentmindedly.

"That is what Il Duce means," the Italian corrected him. "That was why he wanted me go to Rome. You will perhaps find it too easy-going of me that it is only now I ask you to be completely discreet about this. But I knew I was dealing with a gentleman."

"I don't grasp what I have to do with any militia," said Hans. "I'm a maker of pianos."

"But a great Austrian, Signore Alt! A distinguished member of the cultural circle which is of inestimable value to Austrian patriotism. That patriotism, in Il Duce's eyes, must be thoroughly reawakened; people must put themselves at the head of it who politically have no record but who, nevertheless, are representatives of Austrian culture. These are the people who, with their military knowledge, their talent for organization, and their capital, will be the ones to set up the militia."

"Pardon me," said Hans, who was loath to hear about

Austrian patriotism from these lips, "but why do you not address yourself to people who possess those gifts? I have none. I'm a hopeless soldier, a miserable organizer, and no capitalist."

"Modesty, sheer modesty," objected his visitor, flashing his white teeth in the smile which so fascinated Martha Monica. "Confidentially, I've already been in touch with such men. On my return trip I conferred in Innsbruck with Herr Steidle and yesterday in Linz with Prince Starhemberg. Both are enthusiastic and proposed that the already existing Heimatschutz organizations should be reformed into a single Heimwehr on the fascist pattern."

"Fascist, you say?" Hans asked.

The Italian confirmed the obviousness of his remark with a gesture. "Then I am even less your man. I have—forgive my saying so—never had much sympathy for a system that could find nothing better for its symbol than a bundle of rods."

"It's not every one who can have an angel with a trumpet for his emblem," retorted the Italian. And for an instant his urbanity failed him. "Signor Alt, you will continue to make pianos, and you want your profit from them. To that end you will need protection. That protection in turn requires money, and that money must be found!"

"Have you an official authorization from your government to find it?" Hans asked, astonished.

At this his visitor readily produced still another document. It was a list of Austrian industrialists, headed by Apold, general director of the Alpine Montan-Aktiengesellschaft, and wound up with Zweig, proprietor of a textile mill. Hans Alt's name came before Apold, but there was a blank left for the amount he was to contribute. Apold's contribution, on the other hand, was entered as one million Austrian shillings.

"The Italian Government is collecting this?" Hans asked again, with the portrait of the man who would have put the same question before him.

The Italian smiled.

"The Austrian Government, in fullest accord with the Italian, has chosen this method in order to avoid all appearance of interfering with private property, and the Italian Government has loyally offered its services as trustee. You understand, Signore Alt?"

"Not quite," Hans replied. "You'll allow me to make inquiries before I give you my decision?"

"*Naturalmente*," his visitor agreed. "Of anyone on this list. And, by the way, would it not be an excellent idea to interest your brother in this matter? He has a brilliant military record."

"Of course," Hans said. "In comparison with me he's positively a Napoleon."

"Even a Radetzky would suffice," declared his visitor, pushing his own disinterestedness and that of the Italian Government to the chivalrous extreme of thus paying a tribute to the Austrian marshal who inflicted a crushing defeat on Italy. "I trust we shall become more closely associated," he added in taking his leave. "From every point of view that would afford me satisfaction."

On the dot of nine o'clock that evening Hans was standing in his uncle's study. In this large room, with its three windows, nothing had changed—neither the brown wallpaper, darkened by tobacco smoke, nor the comfortable furniture in the Maria Theresa style, nor yet the family portraits on the walls and tables. The shades were drawn, and the globe lamps were lighted on the writing-table and on either side of the bookshelves which were stacked to the ceiling with law books and court rulings.

Hans recalled that he had last discussed with his uncle questions of guilt and innocence, before the war, after a night spent in the police station lock-up, during which the problems of justice had kept him from sleeping. At that time Otto Eberhard had seemed like an aged man to him, far removed from daily life. Today he seemed scarcely more of a human being. It was all but incredible that a heart should beat beneath that high buttoned-up waistcoat. In the first instant the nephew had the impulse to beg his pardon for having disturbed him and to go away again.

"To what do I owe this pleasure?" the old man was already asking.

Accursed house! People can say what they like about Vienna's being the most warmhearted, easy-going, frivolous city, yet could there be in all the world more chilliness, more oppressive formality than here? What destiny had condemned one to belong to this house, the stony embodiment of which sat there in person? Did this man, despite his ninety years, still not know that coldness did not save? That all one needs or wants is warmth, nothing else!

"I have come on account of my mother," Hans answered, burning his bridges behind him.

"Sit down," his uncle suggested. "You smoke, don't you?"

Hans sat down. The round white lamp lighted up every wrinkle and every white hair on the parchment-like face of the aged man. "I don't know, Uncle, exactly how to explain it to you," he began.

"Take your time," the old man said. "You look exhausted. Are you having difficulties in the factory?"

"It's not the factory."

His uncle nodded. "You have some worry in your personal life."

It was only when he heard this icy voice once more that Hans realized how wrong Hermann had been. This was not the most competent man sitting before him, but the most unfit! Uncle Otto Eberhard had always condemned Mother. "It has to do with Selma's death," Hans said. "It's only a suspicion, Uncle. But that in itself is horrible."

"A suspicion against your mother?"

"Yes."

"How long have you had this suspicion?"

"For a long time. But I—"

"Stop. Why didn't you come to me sooner? Did you want to wait until I was dead?"

As always, when he faced Otto Eberhard Hans felt himself to be at a disadvantage. "It doesn't concern you, Uncle," he explained.

"If it has to do with people in this house it does concern me," was his answer. "Now speak. But don't tell me what you feel or what you think; tell me only facts. Feelings and thoughts are not evidence." He crossed his arms as though he were still wearing his red-trimmed court robe.

In the ensuing quarter of an hour he did not alter his attitude. The longer Hans spoke, the more solidly he had to build up the body of guilt against his mother, the more clearly he felt: I have come to the wrong person. This man with his crossed arms is prejudiced. And as the relative of a mortally sick person, who knows exactly how ill the patient is, still asks the hopeless question when the doctor has finished his examination, "What is your opinion, Doctor?" so the nephew, when he had finished his statement, asked the expert in murder cases: "What is your opinion, Uncle?"

Otto Eberhard changed his position only to the extent that he uncrossed his arms. Before his eyes, which still had good vision without glasses, there passed in review the time when this Henriette had come into the house. Her first belated visit, as a fiancée, in the next room. She wore an over-large hat. Her hurrying away to an operetta from the supper that had been prepared for her. Her attachment to an exalted personage. Her audience with the most exalted person in the land. The birth of this son which almost cost her her life. Her frivolous return to life and her affair with a nobleman. Her harshness to little Christine. Her interest in her children, especially in the oldest and the youngest, who was not Franz's daughter. Her attempts to make up to Franz for the things in which she had failed him. Her shortcomings inherited from her mother and, to an even greater degree, from her father. Her coquetry. Her pretence at being more worldly wise than she was. Her quickly aroused and quickly fading sympathy.

Before the eyes of this old prosecutor lay a gray-bound imaginary brief with the inscription: "Record of the Criminal Proceeding against Henriette Alt." On page one was the phrase of the indictment he had seen written in his own handwriting so many hundreds of times: "The Imperial and Royal prosecuting authority of Vienna hereby accuses… of the intention of killing Selma Alt and of acting in such manner as to result in the death of the above-mentioned, thereby committing the crime of murder according to Paragraph 134 of the Penal Code."

And to his nephew, awaiting his reply in a state of anguished expectation, he said, "Your mother is innocent."

It was so unexpected that Hans jumped up with a shout.

"Keep your seat," requested the old man, who had weighed everything and, with an eye which had been unerring in the course of a long career as a prosecuting barrister, had seen that the dotted line in the indictment was not to be filled in with the name of his sister-in-law Henriette but with that of someone else. "Your grounds for suspicion," he said, "are conclusive. I shall change my opinion that it was a case of suicide. It was murder. But your mother is not the murderess. I can see that you believe I want to protect her in order to save the reputation of this house. Once before, a long time ago, you held a similar belief and found it legitimate to remind me of my duty. Young man, I've never consciously neglected my duty, and if I'm soon to follow your dear father to that place where I long to be, let that speak in my favor. You are no jurist; circumstantial evidence confuses you. But there is one thing you should have said to yourself: My mother is of Jewish descent. The Jews—I don't hold with the definition made by the ridiculous new party in Germany, but consider as Jews those who have inherited specific Jewish qualities from their ancestors—never perjure themselves by the life of people dear to them. Jews rarely, if ever, murder, and never relatives. That's something you overlooked."

"Thank you!" Hans said from the bottom of his heart.

"Come here to me," requested the old man. "I know what you've thought of me. The same as nearly all of you think. That a person like me makes life difficult for you. But life is based on respect, and whoever lacks it, as you all do, or does not demand it, as I do, is not free, as you believe, but the least free of all. He is dominated by judgments which are ungrounded or false. Lack of respect makes for lack of freedom. Give me your hand. I too have sometimes misjudged you. You are a decent man. See that you remain one. That's the only human achievement that counts."

"Yes, Uncle," Hans promised, and, deeply moved, bowed over the icy hand held out to him, touching it with his lips.

"Now go," said Otto Eberhard, whose stony face quivered. "The rest is up to me. I can see that, before I finally retire, I have one more case to settle."

"You have a suspicion!"

"A State lawyer always has a suspicion," answered the old man, and his voice, which for a few seconds had sounded human, reverted again into the chilly regions of principles.

"And what should I do?" Hans asked,

"Go up to your mother and humbly ask her pardon," advised the old man. Then he nodded and said, "She hasn't deserved this at your hands. She may have had shortcomings as a wife, but as your mother she has none. Good night."

CHAPTER 40
Two Depositions

The deposition of Police Sergeant Johann Greifeneder read
as follows:

*Police Headquarters, Vienna. Date: July 31, 1934. Present:
Chief of Police Skubel as examiner. Police Sergeant Johann
Greifeneder as witness. Councillor of Police Kunz as recorder.*

Chief of Police: *I summon you to tell the whole truth and to
conceal nothing that you know concerning the murder of the
Chancellor. Your deposition is pursuant to your oath of office. A
false deposition would be perjury. Is that quite clear?*

Sergeant Greifeneder: *Yes, sir.*

Chief of Police: *Bear it in mind. As you are one of the few eye-
witnesses, your deposition is conclusive. On it the verdict to be
handed down by the court may have primarily to be based.
Weigh each word before you speak.*

Sergeant Greifeneder: *Yes, sir.*

Chief of Police: *Your name is Johann Greifeneder; you are
thirty-four years old, born in Tulin in Lower Austria, Catholic,
married, have two children, and live at Number 6
Sonnenuhrgasse, Sixth District. Is that correct?*

Sergeant Greifeneder: *Yes, sir.*

Chief of Police: *What did you witness in your own person on
July twenty-fifth?*

Sergeant Greifeneder: *I was on guard duty in the Chancellor's
office in the fourth story of the Ballhausplatz, near the accoun-
tant's office. My hours were from ten to one. Just before one
o'clock I heard a noise on the stairs, went out and opened the
door to the staircase. Opposite me were five fully armed men in
uniform.*

Chief of Police: *What uniform?*

Sergeant Greifeneder: *The uniform of the regular Austrian*

Army. The men surrounded me and shouted, "Hands up!" I couldn't offer any opposition. They took me down to the third floor of the Chancellery, where I had to wait on the landing. There were eight or nine other men there in uniform and with drawn pistols.

Chief of Police: *Didn't you ask what all these men were up to?*

Sergeant Greifeneder: *I certainly did. But they said I should see in due time. Meanwhile other men in uniform were bringing down all the officials out of the Chancellery in the fourth story, shouting at them, "Hands up!" They waited till everybody was there. I told them it was a bad idea to keep so many people there, for it was too heavy a load for the staircase. One of the men yelled at me: "I do the commanding here; you have nothing to say about it."*

Chief of Police: *Do you know who he was?*

Sergeant Greifeneder: *He wore the uniform of a major. His name was Hermann Alt.*

Chief of Police: *How did you happen to know his name?*

Sergeant Greifeneder: *Because he himself told me. He said, "I am Major Hermann Alt, in case you would like to know who rid you Austrians of that criminal pygmy who stained for ever the honor of this country and betrayed our Führer!"*

Chief of Police: *I see. What happened then?*

Sergeant Greifeneder: *A non-commissioned officer came and ordered us to go down into the courtyard. Here the civilian officials were separated from us policemen. We were left in the first courtyard near the main gate.*

Chief of Police: *How long did you stay there?*

Sergeant Greifeneder: *The whole thing may have taken ten to twelve minutes. Between half-past one and a quarter to two the major came.*

Chief of Police: *Don't call him major. He merely stole and wore a major's uniform.*

Sergeant Greifeneder: *Very well, sir. The man by the name of*

Alt came to us in the courtyard and asked my colleague. District Inspector Jellinek, if toe knew that Chancellor Dollfuss had been wounded. When we said no, he asked if we would like to see him, and we told him yes. But he let only me go up at once.

Chief of Police: *How do you account for that?*

Sergeant Greifeneder: *I don't know. He may have supposed I was a Nazi too.*

Chief of Police: *Proceed, please.*

Sergeant Greifeneder: *Herr Alt and I went up and found His Excellency the Chancellor in the so-called corner salon by the window near the Congress Hall.*

Chief of Police: *Do you recall his position?*

Sergeant Greifeneder: *He was lying on a couch, his hands spread out.*

Chief of Police: *What did you do?*

Sergeant Greifeneder: *I asked the major—pardon me—Herr Alt, whether he was seriously wounded and by whom. He answered he did not know, and it was none of my business. Then I saw blood coming from the Chancellor's lips. I asked whether a doctor had been attending to the patient. He answered no. Then I asked whether a doctor was sent for. He again answered no. "You can attend to him yourself, if you like," he said, sitting at the writing desk and smoking a cigarette. I said, "Yes, I will." Thereupon he opened the window and yelled out of it: "Some of you! Come up with a first-aid kit!" Then he asked me: "Do you know how to put on a bandage?" I said, "Yes." But it was some time before one of the rebels came up with the bandages—*

Chief of Police: *One moment. What did Alt do in the meantime?*

Sergeant Greifeneder: *He kept on sitting at the desk, smoking.*

Chief of Police: *Did he say anything?*

Sergeant Greifeneder: *Not then.*

Chief of Police: *Was the Chancellor conscious or unconscious?*

Sergeant Greifeneder: *Unconscious.*

Chief of Police: *Proceed, please.*

Sergeant Greifeneder: *The rebel who came up with the bandages slit the Chancellor's clothes with a pocketknife and cut away the shirt. There was nothing but blood. I asked the man to hold the Chancellor's head while I tried to apply the bandage. But the man said: "I won't. This man cold-bloodedly murdered scores of my fellow workers. He told every one how good a Catholic he was. Now he shall know what blood for blood means."*

Chief of Police: *Did you succeed in putting on the bandages?*

Sergeant Greifeneder: *I applied them but was unable to check the haemorrhage. Nobody was there to help me. Afterwards I washed the Chancellor's forehead with water from the carafe on the table, and he came to.*

Chief of Police: *Did he speak?*

Sergeant Greifeneder: *Yes. He asked whether the other Ministers who were closeted with him when the rebels started their putsch were all right. I told him so far as I knew they were. For a moment he seemed to think he was free, because he said: "Thank God you reached here in time! Did you catch the lot of them?" Then his eyes fell on Herr Alt, who was laughing. Whereupon the Chancellor said to me, "This major, a captain, and several soldiers shot at me at a distance of four inches."*

Chief of Police: *Did he mention the names of the major or the captain or the soldiers who shot at him? Or did he give you any indication or characteristics by which to identify them?*

Sergeant Greifeneder: *He did not.*

Chief of Police: *Did Alt say anything?*

Sergeant Greifeneder: *He said, "Herr Chancellor. You shot at thousands of innocent German workers. You despised our beloved Führer. We shot at you, and we despise you!"*

Chief of Police: *Did the Chancellor answer?*

Sergeant Greifeneder: *Not for a moment. Later he asked for the Minister of Education, Dr. Schuschnigg. Herr Alt said,*

"Schuschnigg is not here" Then the Chancellor asked for the State Secretary of Police, Karwinsky, but Herr Alt paid no attention. Finally the Chancellor asked for a priest. Herr Alt listened but didn't move. I begged him to send for one. He laughed, said "No," and left the room.

Chief of Police: *Does this mean you were alone with the Chancellor?*

Sergeant Greifeneder: *Yes.*

Chief of Police. *What did you do?*

Sergeant Greifeneder: *I tried to console him. I told him it was only a flesh wound. But he asked me to raise his arms and legs. I did, and he said, "I can't feel anything, I am paralysed." I said, "No, Herr Chancellor. You'll be all right in no time." He looked at me and answered, "You are so kind to me. Why weren't the others kind? God forgive them." Then he said he wanted Dr. Schuschnigg to form a Government. If Schuschnigg was no longer living then you, Herr Chief of Police, should undertake it. These last words were overheard by Herr Alt, who had come back a little while before. He said, "Herr Chancellor, come to the point! All that is of no interest to us. Nobody will form a Government except the people of our choosing. Give the order at once that neither the police nor the executive must take any action concerning the Chancellery until Minister Rintelen has taken over the Government. Phone immediately to the chief of police. I'll connect you." He then brought the portable telephone from the desk to the couch where the Chancellor was lying. The Chancellor murmured, "Yes. No bloodshed." Blood was coming up into his mouth; he tried to wipe it away. Then there was a rattling sound in his throat. He said almost inaudibly, "Tell Mussolini to care for my wife and children." This last was meant for me. Then there was more sound of rattling, and he died. That was about a quarter to four in the afternoon.*

Signed before me: SKUBEL, Chief of Police;

JOHANN GREIFENEDER,

Police Sergeant

On August 4 Police Sergeant Greifeneder deposed further:

In completion of my statement of July thirty-first, and in answer to questions, I have to state that I never left the room while Chancellor Dollfuss was dying and therefore must have heard everything that was said. The Chancellor spoke in a low tone, but his voice was clear, and I never moved farther from the couch than to the writing-desk for fresh bandages and once to the table for the water carafe. The distance may be about three feet.

The record of the hearing of Hermann Alt, held for trial, read as follows:

County Court Criminal Cases, Vienna.
Division of the Examining Magistrate Alois. Osio of the Court of Appeals. Recorder: Dr. Eugen Schick.

Name of the accused:	Hermann Christoph Alt.
Date of birth:	November 3, 1893.
Place of birth:	Vienna.
Religion:	Roman Catholic.
Marital status:	Single.
Profession:	Assistant to Chief of Program at Ravag.
Domicile:	First District, 10 Seilerstätte, Vienna.

After the accused had been brought into court and was informed that the prosecuting authority of Vienna had filed an indictment charging him with the crimes of murder, high treason, and instigation to riot, and that he was to be examined in accordance with Paragraph 38 of the Code of Criminal Procedure, he made the following statements in answer to interrogation.

"I admit that I am guilty according to outmoded Austrian penal law, but innocent in the eyes of the living peoples' law of our beloved Führer."

On being warned by the examining magistrate that he would have to omit such remarks under pain of additional disciplinary punishment, the accused replied:

"Don't be ridiculous. Do you think I do not know that even without this farce I have no chance under your justice?"

Interspersed with frequent vituperative remarks made against the members of the Government, the higher clergy, and officials, despite reprimands from the examining magistrate as to their being inadmissible, the accused gave the following coherent account.

"I knew, from the very day that my uncle personally instituted a house search in our apartment house, that I was finished. For it was then he discovered the spiral staircase which I had had constructed between my ground-floor apartment and the cellar under our house, as well as the printing press, also in the cellar, on which the leaflets of the National Socialist party in Austria were printed. At that time my uncle harboured another suspicion against me, of which I am just as guilty as I am of all the other so-called crimes I am now charged with, and of which I am just as proud today as ever. Your incompetent justice has only now discovered, in relation to the present investigation being held against me, that it was I who liquidated the Jewess Selma Rosner. In this connection I desire the following to be recorded verbatim. For what I have to state here is to be preserved for the day when this Austrian system of government, which fires on working men and Germans, will be swept away by the wrath of the populace and my memory will be reinstated, in all honor, by all true Germans as that of the Austrian Horst Wessel.

"The Brown House in Munich had no need to remind me that I could perform no services for the party as long as I lived with people, and as long as people belong, to my family, who were Jews. This is the one reproach I make to my party comrades. It was absolutely superfluous, and a failure either to appreciate or estimate me, to order me to Munich so that I should be impressed with the necessity of ridding my family of such members as did not meet with the racial requirements of our Führer. For from the very first instant when I was privileged to look the Führer in the eye and to swear blind fealty to him I should never have tolerated breathing the same air and being under the same roof with persons whose every expression was unsympathetic and intolerable. My mother has Jewish blood; my so-called sister-in-law was a full-blooded Jewess. To get rid of both of them was my intention, of which the major part was executed. The one thing that I regret about my otherwise perfect plan is that my mother, thanks to the vacillation of my brother, who was always a pitiable weakling, has for the time being escaped the fate I had prepared for her. I regret this, but at the same time wish to emphasize I have great sympathy for people who condemn a son because he opposes his mother. A mother, for me too, is the highest being on earth. But she must be a mother. My mother was what that philosopher of our times, Alfred Rosenberg, calls Jewish mothers: 'a monstrosity of unmotherliness.' I never considered her to be my mother, never in my life followed her advice, never nourished any feelings for her except those of disgust and shame that she should have borne me. From the very start the blood of my pure Aryan German forbears in me fought against her, and when I came back from a war lost through Jewish treason I knew what I had to do.

"My uncle's death was a definite piece of luck both for me and for the National Socialist party in Austria. And yet, despite the fact that he turned against me through a false interpretation of duty, I cannot refrain from paying the tribute due to a man of such sterling German worth. Under his scrutiny I should no longer have been able to serve our Führer. But he died on the very day when he uncovered our cellar printing press, and so I succeeded, with the help of party comrades, in nipping all suspicion in the bud.

"Since I look upon this examination as an accounting not to this court, which I do not recognize, but to my Führer and my fellow countrymen, I wish to record once more my admiration for the farsightedness and thoroughness with which our party knew how to act even when our Führer, although he was triumphant in the Reich, was barred from Austria, stricken as it was with blindness. It has been the Jews, the so-called artists, writers, and journalists, who have made Austria blind and dumb. To save their profits and their skins they found no insult too low, no calumny too vile. They have trampled in the filth the purest and most heroic party there is and have made the Austrians think that Messrs. Otto Bauer, Seipel, Dollfuss, Schuschnigg, and their like were fit even to breathe the same air as our Führer.

"When I came back from the war I immediately recognized these dangerous vermin for what they were. That was my reason for joining the National Socialist party in Austria, with the express desire of becoming an active and acting member. I have been a party member since the creation of the Austrian Gau. My party number is seventy-one."

To the question of why the accused had joined a party declared illegal, he replied, "Out of disgust for the corruption on all sides, right, left, and center. Out of loathing for clericalism, bolshevism, and Judaism. No one in Austria has the right to declare illegal something which is in itself an embodiment of the principle of right."

To the question of what motive the accused had for murdering the late Chancellor, he declared, "After what I have already said I am astonished at the question. No true German could ask it. Dollfuss, that defender of the Jews and lackey of the Jews, dared to set his pygmy figure in the path of the most gigantic figure of world history and to prevent Austria from being rescued by National Socialism from certain doom. Instead of joining our Führer with flying banners on the very day he became Chancellor of the German Reich, he attempted to maintain the independence of his pygmy state because he wanted to remain in power."

In reply to the admonition not to cast aspersions on the memory of the dead man, the accused said, "Bourgeois morals have been discarded. A pygmy and a criminal remains that even after he has been liquidated."

In answer to the question of why he did not heed the dying man's request for a priest, the accused said, "The only decent priest is Cardinal Innitzer, who believes in our Führer. All the rest are a lot of liars."

When challenged to name those who participated with him in the putsch, and especially to clear up the part played by Minister Rintelen, the accused refused to divulge any information.

To the question of whether the plot to remove the Chancellor and take over the government was promoted by the National Socialist party in Germany or whether it was known to them, the accused gave a negative reply.

When asked if he would tell who it was that acted as go-between in establishing the contact between the Austrian Heimwehr and the illegal National Socialist party in Austria, he named the military attaché of the Italian Legation in Vienna.

The accused asked to have the following supplementary explanation recorded: A further motive on his part for the killing of Chancellor Dollfuss was based on the fact that the murdered Chancellor had undertaken to break the opposition of the Austrian working classes with armed force.

To the question as to what means he used to murder the

actress Selma Rosner-Alt the accused replied, "See the report of the autopsy."

To the question of how long the secret printing press had been in operation in the cellar of the house at 10 Seilerstätte the accused replied, "Since September 1923."

To the question of where the means for running the press came from the accused refused to reply.

To the question of who ran the press the accused declared, "I did it myself."

To the question of how it was that the noise of the press had not led to its discovery sooner the accused said, "National Socialists make no mistakes."

Read Approved Recorded
ALOIS OSIO
HERMANN ALT
DR. SCHICK

Four days after this deposition was signed Hermann Alt was condemned to death by a special court presided over by General von Huelgerth and was shot that same evening.

The bullets which laid him low, together with eight other participants in the putsch of July 25, were fired by a platoon from the Viennese home regiment, the Fourth Hoch-und-Deutschmeister, in the courtyard of the vacant Palais Coburg. The volley was so loud that it could be heard in nearby streets.

On the fourth floor of 10 Seilerstätte, from which one could see the roof of the Coburg Palace, a family sat together in silence.

It was a small family now. It consisted of Henriette, Hans, and Martha Monica. The newspapers and radio broadcasts about the trial of the putsch participants had announced the execution for this evening, without stating the hour or place.

So when the volley rang out every one of the three knew that over there someone who had belonged to them had been executed. Every one of them knew in addition what the executed man had said in court, for they had been called to court to confirm or to refute his statements. It was there that they had seen him for the last time. He had turned his back and not spoken with them. Before he was taken back to his cell he had shouted, "Heil Hitler!"

The radio program was interrupted for the announcement: "The execution of the murderers of Chancellor Dr. Engelbert Dollfuss took place at 8 P.M." The names of the murderers were given, in alphabetical order, and Hermann's name was first. Trembling, Martha Monica held her mother's hand.

Henriette nodded. Her eyes were wide open. "Neglect," she said, looking into space. "Neglect is poison."

Hans said nothing.

He waited until his mother and sister had stopped crying. Then he went down to his own apartment and talked to Selma's picture. "Neglect," he said to her. "It was not that. He was a man who hated. Hatred was his will and his talent. God forgive me, I can't feel sorry for him. Do you remember the formula for the origin of all? Whether it be fear or hatred—it is all one and the same catastrophe. Selma, are you so sure that despite all it might not be love? I am now forty-three years old, and I have seen too little love and too much hate. I have an indescribable, unquenchable yearning for love that grows with every day!" Then he said good night to her as usual.

That night he determined to wipe out the slander to which his brother had subjected Selma in court. This would, he decided, take the form of a memorial tablet. It would be of white marble, so that anyone going by could read it. It would be set beneath the angel with the trumpet and would bear the inscription: "Died in this house the actress beloved of Vienna, Selma Rosner-Alt. She lived for truth."

Part Four
THE YELLOW DRAWING ROOM

CHAPTER 41
Requiem

The lights in the auditorium were dimmed; Arturo Toscanini raised his baton for Verdi's *Requiem*. The thousands of black-clad people who filled the Vienna Opera House did not move. On the stage stood the chorus, dressed in black. On the black curtain behind them hung an over-lifesize death mask of the murdered Dollfuss.

Spreading the thumb of his left hand in a gesture familiar to the Viennese, the conductor demanded absolute silence; with his right hand he rapped his slim baton twice on the stand before him, and the music began. The red, gold, and ivory of the gay opera hall seemed to have disappeared. Not only a stillness, but also the reverential atmosphere of a church, had taken possession of it. With the *Kyrie Eleison* there was sobbing. It increased during the *Dies Irae*, but was suddenly silenced by the breath-taking impetus of the *Libera*.

Three women who were among the audience of this memorial celebration and who were sitting in one of the most secluded boxes also gave rein to their emotions. Henriette felt that the attitude of not play-acting, not being allowed to weep or laugh, was partly responsible for this tragedy, although she took all the blame on herself.

It was the first time she had gone out since the shots echoed at Coburg Palace, three months earlier. In all that time she had not left the fourth story at Number 10, deeply convinced as she was that wherever she went people would point their fingers at her, saying: "There goes the mother of the murderer!" She dreaded to see the postman come, for she feared that he would bring news of the horror Vienna felt for the mother of a murderer. When none of this happened and she was treated with nothing but sympathy, and when she even received letters of condolence from strangers (thanks to the efforts of Otto Eberhard's son Peter, the integrity of the Alt family was reinstated and everything put in the proper light), her fear of being seen in public began to dwindle. Nevertheless, she could not be induced to go out. It was only when Peter, who had had even more qualms about his own career, proved to her in black and white the wish of the Chancellor himself that she appear at the memorial celebration, and thereby finally and publicly seal the breach between her son and his country, that Henriette finally gave in.

Clad in black, she sat with Martha Monica and Franziska in the rear of the box, while Hans and the painter Drauffer occupied the side seats. Liesl, Fritz's wife, was in the artists' box; Fritz was playing in the orchestra, and Peter, together with his wife and Pauline Drauffer, had seats on the floor, while Otto sat in the box of the Christian Socialist Club. The grown-ups of Number 10 were present in force and prepared to parry the blow the reputation of their house had received. Only the widows of Otto Eberhard and Colonel Paskiewicz were absent. Frau Elsa was bedridden, and the Widow Paskiewicz no longer visited public places to take part even in such occasions. One other person connected with Number 10 who was absent, and who would surely not have missed this memorial had he not been in his grave for two years, under a stone recording proudly his tides, dignities, and achievements, was Professor Stein.

My son was the murderer, thought Henriette, who had devoted so little thought to this son and who now, since the shots in the Coburg Palace, thought of no one else. The brusqueness and austerity of the *Libera* overwhelmed her with crushing power. "*Pater in coelis!*" sang the chorus. *Dear God*, she thought, and caught her breath, *how much unhappiness lies at my door!* She abandoned herself to the tumult of her emotions, allowed them to carry her away like a stream which has burst its dams. The austere, agitating music hurled all the guilt of her life at her, magnified it a thousandfold, forced her to listen. She had been 'afraid of conventions,' and she had lacked that pitiful mite of courage that was needed to make a man happy. Otherwise Rudolf would still be alive. Otherwise there would have been no war. Otherwise she would not have borne this son. Otherwise the widow of the murdered man, with her two white-faced children over there, and Hans in the background of this box, would not be gazing with such despairing eyes into the void.

The men who had so often reproached her had disappeared from the dark house on Seilerstätte. In this still darker house she reviled herself. And so frightful was her sense of guilt that she, in a gesture of complete helplessness, dropped her head, her shoulders racked with sobs that did not cease.

Someone laid a hand on her shoulder. It was her brother-in-law Drauffer, who once, long ago, had sat behind her in a box when she had lost control of herself. *Isn't it extraordinary, thought the old painter, this woman cannot grow old! She's as impulsive as she ever was! Number 10 hasn't been able to change her one jot. Nature just does not change.* "Hetti," he whispered to her, "be reasonable!"

That was just what she thought she had finally become—reasonable. This was what counted: to make others happy. And in this she had failed.

While the chorus raised its voice in an upward surge she went over the destinies of those to whom she had failed to give happiness. Rudolf. Franz. Christine. Hermann. Her head sank deeper. Not be happy yourself—give happiness to others! That was the thing.

"Hetti!" admonished her brother-in-law, "do control yourself!"

In the former Imperial box, in the center, sat the members of the Government on either side of the new Chancellor, Dr. Schuschnigg. His narrow and prematurely gray head was also bowed, and the deep emotion with which he was listening was obvious. Again and again he had to wipe the tears under his glasses. Henriette's eyes fell on him, and on the widow of the murdered man, over and over again on that widowed woman staring hopelessly into the void. They did not control themselves either.

That's what comes of it when you do control yourself! thought the widow of the piano-maker Alt. *That's what comes of systematic hiding, minimizing, denying, renouncing. What a mortal fallacy! One cannot be happy if one hides one's feelings. Nor can one make others happy.*

The nearer the requiem, which despite its performance in an opera hall was more like a mass for the dead, approached its reconciling climax, the clearer became Henriette's vision. At her age she could no longer give happiness. But something else was still possible.

She closed her eyes, and her lips fervently framed words which had meaning only to her.

She laid her hand gently on that of her elder daughter Franziska, who had come up from Salzburg, for a few days' visit and rest after the misfortune of losing her first child, born dead. The wife of Dr. Baier shrank back. She thought she was being reproved. When she realized that her mother's gesture was one of tenderness it took her a moment to collect herself. Then she gave a shy, surprised smile that moved her mother even more deeply. *I am sixty-nine*, thought Henriette, *and it has taken all these years to open my eyes*! She wiped them with a tiny lace handkerchief, quickly powdered her face, and rose. The requiem for the man whom her younger son had murdered was at an end.

On the arm of her elder son she walked the short distance home to Annagasse.

"I have something to tell you," Hans said on the way.

"You mean something unpleasant?" she asked, and then caught herself in confusion: *I have just sworn to change my ways and my first word is a reproach!*

"No, nothing unpleasant," Hans answered. "You know that Fritz is going to New York on business for the Salzburg Festival. I'm going with him."

"Really?" Henriette said, catching her breath. "I had no idea."

"He suggested it, and I think he's right. A change of air won't do me any harm. This place is too full of memories."

"Yes," his mother agreed.

"Don't you want me to go?" asked her son. Since he had followed Otto Eberhard's advice, kissed her hand and begged her forgiveness, a coolness—almost a sense of embarrassment—had lain between them. On Hans's side it was the unrealized wish to make her forget. On hers it was the uncertainty of how he felt towards her.

"I think Fritz is right," she said. The thought of his being far away had always been terrifying to her. First during the war, and later when Selma had threatened her with it. Now it seemed harder to bear than ever. Hans was the only one for whom she lived. Franziska had her husband. Mono had consoled herself for the recall of her Italian and did not need her. Hans needed her, even if he did not know it, did not admit it, did not love her as before. Hans, who had always been so good to her except for those dreadful weeks, and that she had long since forgiven him.

"It will only be for two months." He spoke uncertainly, as he did when he was a boy.

"That's no time at all," she replied. Supposing he never comes back? it occurred to her, and she put her hand to her heart, which nowadays was apt to trouble her. "Will two months be enough?" she asked.

"Easily," he asserted. "Our Ministry of Education, which means, of course, our all-powerful Cousin Peter, is sending Fritz over to negotiate with Koussevitzky and Stokowski. You probably don't even know their names. They're American conductors."

"Are Toscanini and Bruno Walter no longer good enough for Salzburg?" Heririette asked, and then reproached herself again for speaking in the old tone she had sworn to give up.

"They want to put Salzburg on as international a basis as possible. I find it very reasonable. It's shameful how little Austria is known abroad."

"Yes," Henriette agreed.

"And I could discuss a branch with Steinway," Hans told her. "You remember that was always a favorite idea of Papa's."

She nodded. They were passing St. Anna's. "And when are you leaving?" she asked casually.

He cleared his throat and answered, "Tonight."

"Really," said Henriette. "Are you packed?"

"I don't need much for such a short trip," he replied.

How often he emphasizes the shortness of the time, she thought. "Perhaps I can help you?" she suggested. "I seem to remember that you're not much of a genius at packing."

"I was going to ask you to lend me Simmerl."

"It will be better for me to do it. Simmerl grows crankier every day. I have always loved to pack. Probably because I have traveled so little."

They had passed through the angel entrance into the house and were going upstairs. Henriette went slowly.

"By the way, tomorrow they'll start to put in a lift," he said.

She was rooted to the spot with amazement.

"It's not good for you to climb so many stairs, Mother."

"Your going-away present to me?" she asked, her breath quite taken away by all the news being sprung on her today.

"To us all. Don't talk so much while you're climbing."

Does he consider me an invalid? she thought. *I was never ill in my life except when I bore him.* As they passed Otto Eberhard's door she could not help thinking: *A lift in Number 10!*

"Foedermayer will make reports to you on everything that goes on in the factory. He's absolutely dependable."

"Your father felt that about him too," she said reflectively. She remembered how she had climbed the stairs with Franz when he came home from the war. She walked now almost as slowly as he did then. "Do you think Papa would have approved of the lift?" she asked.

"As a lift, probably not. But as a convenience for you, yes."

"You're right. He was always thoughtful."

She went straight to Hans's apartment to save time. She did not even inquire when his train left; one could always assume, at least, that it went in the late evening or night and thereby gain a little extra time. She knew nothing about trains. She had once been in Venice for a single day, but otherwise only in Ischl and Abbazia.

She laid aside her crepe-trimmed hat and veil, drew off her gloves, and looked round to see what she should do first. She immediately jumped at conclusions when he brought out a dress suit. "Will you bring a dress suit?" she asked.

"Fritz is taking his. They wear them on board ship."

"I see," was her comment. That wild musician was always putting such erroneous ideas into the heads of people.

Taking the dress suit out of his hands and laying it carefully on the bed to fold it, she inquired, "What's the name of the ship you are taking?"

"The *Île de France*. I didn't want to travel on a German one."

"Why not?"

"But, Mother," he said with a smile, "you really are not politically minded. Haven't you heard that the man who took

the examinations with me at the Art Academy is now governing Germany?"

"That you and he took examinations together and were
failed, I have heard. You certainly told me about it often
enough," she retorted, with a slight spark of her old-time
humor. "Incidentally, your grandfather Stein considered me
quite a politician. I even predicted that you would never make
a name for yourself in the army.

And that your brother—" She stopped short.

He kissed her tenderly.

"Is your train going so soon?" She turned away. If one had
never in all one's life been allowed to play-act one could not
change all in a flash, no matter how firmly one was resolved to
do so. "I need some tissue paper. I wager you haven't any," she
said.

"Over in the drawer. I think Selma put some in there." At
the mention of the name they were both silent. In the drawer
with her things he found the tissue paper Selma had bought.
Her books were also there and the copies of her parts. And
even her silver cuirass.

"She was tremendously tidy," Henriette said, after a pause.
And then, finding that her praise was still too slight, she added,
"I mean it's so unusual in an actress."

He said nothing but watched her as she took his things,
carefully smoothed them out, and packed them with as much
economy of space as possible in the steamer trunk. A layer of
clothing, then a layer of tissue paper, exactly as she had been
taught by her old housekeeper, Theresa. Father Stein had been
a great traveller. The gray streak along her brown parting,
which she had always left gray, was now white, and her beautiful brown hair was gray.

"Mother?"

She looked up.

"Nothing. Except that I'm terribly fond of you!" When she

looked out of the corner of her eyes that way she seemed so incredibly young.

"Even if it isn't true one loves to hear things like that," she said. She had begun to arrange his shirts.

"Do you know something?" he asked suddenly. "I'm going to make a suggestion! Fritz and I are taking the *Île de France* in Le Havre and are spending a few days beforehand in Paris. If it would amuse you won't you come with us to Paris? How's that?"

She put down the shirt she was holding. "Paris?" She spoke the name with the respect and yearning felt by all her generation for the place.

"It would be a bit of recreation for you after all you've been through. Wouldn't it?" he urged.

Her eyes shone. How often she had begged Franz to take her to Paris! How she had always devoured the books that came from there! For a time—and this was something she had never confided to anyone—she had even seen a resemblance between herself and Madame Bovary. And an almost greater one between Franz and the doctor Bovary. "That would be marvellous!" she said.

"Settled!" he said excitedly. "Let me finish packing my own things, and you go up and fix yours. Meanwhile I'll telephone for a sleeping-car reservation for you. Anyhow, you needn't pack many things. We'll buy what you need in Paris!"

She would be buying in Paris. The saleswoman at Spitzer's would no longer have to say to her, "A genuine Paris model, Frau Alt!" She would choose her own genuine Paris models in Paris, in one of those fabulous establishments she knew so well by name. At Poiret's or Lanvin's.

"Hurry, Mother! Look your best!"

Now she was walking down the Champs-Élysées. The Rond Point. The Arc de Triomphe. She was driving in the Bois. All the smart younger set in novels had their *pied-à-terre* in the Rue

St. Honoré. Or was it the Rue de Rivoli? In the great Opera House women wore tiaras in their hair.

"What are you thinking of?"

From St. Augustine it struck two.

"It's very sweet of you," she replied, and the flush in her cheeks gave way to a deep pallor. "Thank you so much, Hans."

"Now I feel really happy about my trip!" he said, delighted.

She took up the shirt and laid it in the trunk. The left cuff was not quite in place, so she straightened it. "Unfortunately it can't be done," she said, talking into the trunk. "Mono heeds me. And there are other reasons."

She knew he would not believe her, but nothing else occurred to her. For she could not tell him that during the requiem she had made a vow. Not such a simple one as when he had left for the war. A real one. There were those who made vows earlier and took the veil. And there were others who came late, very late, to take them and who yet bought Paris models. Henriette sighed and straightened up. She would have to continue to buy her Paris models in Vienna.

"You're old-fashioned," he said, disappointed. "I really never thought that of you."

Nor I of myself, she thought. I always imagined I was so modern. That was probably another of my mistakes.

Then she quickly finished his packing and said good-bye. She did not want to know when his train was leaving, she hated to stand about on station platforms and say, "Write soon. Did you remember to take warm things?" No, perhaps she was old-fashioned, but when someone went away all that was left was a bit of a white handkerchief waving, a little smoke, and much heartache, and she wished to spare herself that. "God keep you," she said, and kissed him. She held him close, as she had done when he went away to war. Then, too, she had thought it was for ever. She believed it again today, but she said, as she had done then, "Come back safe."

"Yes, Mother," he promised. "Take care of yourself."

That was exactly what he had said as he carried his heavily packed knapsack. Selma had stood behind him.

"Good luck," she wished him. At the door she turned round once more. "And thanks for the remarkably easy journey. I was in Paris today for two minutes."

CHAPTER 42
The Statue of Liberty

Fritz had thought it was an excellent occasion to pull Hans out of a state of mind that to him seemed to be growing constantly more critical; the cult of the dead, in which he was indulging, bordered on the abnormal. Every day in the early morning a visit to the far-away cemetery. Every day fresh flowers in front of her picture. Hardly ever seeing anyone.

The musician still had his old feeling of sympathy for Hans, or rather he had gained a fresh one. The longer he "watched him," as he called it, the more respect he had for him. I take my hat off to him, he said to himself. He is one of the very few people of my acquaintance who maintains absolutely the purity of his human standards. To call him an idealist, which they were prone to do in Number 10, he considered mere slackness of thinking. For where was the line of demarcation between a so-called idealist and someone you could not take seriously? Hans was most certainly to be taken seriously. If a word such as 'realidealism' had existed it might have been appropriate for this practical idealist. To be sure, he was no luminary among piano-makers, and he made things easy for Messrs. Ehrbar, Blüthner, and his other competitors. But if he had produced books instead of pianos, or had a chair to teach Austrian history, or maybe even simply a pulpit, he would have been in his proper place.

Paris, which Hans had never seen, disappointed him. Nor did Fritz demur, although he was crazy about the French and everything Parisian, as long as it was not music. But he was tolerant enough to admit that what displeased his cousin about Paris was exactly the same thing they both had objected to in Vienna: an indolent, shortsighted insincerity which at the same time ridiculed and glorified. The two cities were almost alarmingly similar: both were seductive, both voluptuous, both decadent, except that, in their eyes, Vienna possessed more natural charm and Paris more artificial smartness of style. "Do you know what you are suffering from?" Fritz had said to Hans when he was drawing comparisons once more. "An Austria complex. You are a typical case of a man disappointed in love. Except that your unfortunate passion is for a country."

"I thought I was suffering from Selma's death," was Hans's rejoinder. It was the eighth anniversary of her death, and they were just coming out of the Madeleine.

In New York, on their very first evening, Hans went to see a performance of *Saint Joan*. Although Fritz looked upon it as utter madness to keep a memory so painfully alive, he realized that nothing could be done about it. He repeatedly asked himself if Hans had loved the dead woman as passionately while she was alive, and was inclined to doubt it. That was perhaps the very reason. It was a love he was trying to make up.

Hans never allowed himself to be drawn into any conversation about it. Yet when the Broadway actress spoke Joan's lines, "I will deliver you from fear," Fritz saw a look of such unassuaged grief on the face of the man beside him that he took great pains to talk of other things: the theater building which he compared to an automat restaurant; Broadway, which he called a gigantic amusement park; and the public which did not discuss the play but business. He worked himself up into a kind of frenzy, only to divert Hans's thoughts or provoke him into an argument. "This is my second trip to the States," he said, "but I can tell you the institution of the theater is to this day unknown over here. They go to plays in the way they go to restaurants. Can you remember what the theater meant to us when we were young? And even when we were older? *Nora* was the starting point of the emancipation of women. *The Weavers* initiated the legislation to protect sweatshop workers. *Ghosts* did the same for social hygiene. Girardi taught us to see Vienna; Kainz, the world. But over here the theater is a mechanical device. They've driven all experience out of it. The plays are routine. The public is routine. The actors—oh, yes, they are natural enough, but of a naturalness that makes you forget an hour later who played what. At home they were not so confoundedly natural, but in contrast they were personalities pure and simple."

Hans sat there and said nothing. Fritz gave up. Obviously Hans was thinking of the personalities of the theater in Vienna.

From New York they travelled to Philadelphia, Washington, Boston, Cincinnati, and Los Angeles. Hans conducted some business negotiations with little result; when his older cousin gave talks to interest people in the Salzburg Festivals, and Hans was asked, he used his better knowledge of English to correct the mistakes in Fritz's text. His taciturnity grew the farther they went. To the letters he received from home he answered, "I am well." Fritz began to believe it was the silliest thing he had ever done, to bring this incorrigible Austrian over to a country that displeased him so unspeakably. Not for one day did his memories fade; wherever they stayed Selma's picture was set up on a separate, table amid candles and fresh flowers, as on an altar.

When the contracts were signed and the lectures for which the journey had been made were over, they sailed. They had been away two and a half months. The Statue of Liberty, which they were to leave behind them, loomed up, and the ocean, which was to take them home, opened before them.

"Well," Fritz said, "you did survive."

Hans was gazing at the statue with the torch held high.

"There is no uglier monument," commented the musician.

"I find it beautiful," Hans said. This was the first time that he had entered into an argument since Paris.

"Don't make any particular effort on my account," Fritz said with a laugh.

"I mean it," Hans replied. "It's not beautiful as a statue. But it is magnificent in its cry: 'No admittance to this continent to all the Francis Josephs and the Miklaus!'" He watched it until the bronze figure merged with the horizon.

"I'm glad that there was something you liked," Fritz remarked, and, as an old ocean traveller, prepared to make himself comfortable in his deck chair.

"You're under a wrong impression," Hans said. "There was much that pleased me. But that's not the word. There was much that moved me."

Fritz was so nonplussed that he took his cigar out of his mouth.

"Honestly, Fritz, I don't understand how such a fine and intelligent person as you does not feel it too."

"Feel what? The beauty of a country where you have to take a whole day's journey to see a single tree? I want to see trees. Not stony deserts. When I go up or down Madison Avenue I think I am in a mine. I have never liked mines."

Hans shook his head. "We had Vienna Woods in which to build Vienna. They had the desert or a rocky coast. The stones are frightening. But where their lives have taken them away from the city they are better off than we are."

"See here," declared Fritz, and as always, when a conversation began to engross him, he threw back his head with his strongly lensed glasses, "no generalities, please. What do you mean, they are better off? In what way is life made better because it can boast an institution known as the drugstore, where daily seventy million human beings at least eat their midday meal in full view of hair removers, laxatives, and catarrhal jellies? A life amid perpetual noise—man. I'm a musician! A life amid the perpetual stench of petrol—have you no nose? A life where every tenth house is a garage and every twentieth one is a petrol station. A life sacrificing loveliness for comfort, making certain things so easy that people loathe bothering about those other things which are difficult. A life where the radio has to tell me about some lotion or deodorant before it can announce who has been elected president. A life in which the phrases 'Isn't it a fine day?' and 'It certainly is' more than exhaust the potentialities of conversation. A life in which I am overwhelmed by headlines that in the first place I cannot comprehend and in the second place are not true. A life where in churches they advertise strawberry suppers and chicken dinners. A life in which a man is rated by his weekly pay envelope. A standardized life fond of quantity, lacking in imagination, passion, mystery—an assembly line which runs the same in New York as Philadelphia, in Philadelphia as in Cincinnati, in Cincinnati—God save the mark—as in Hollywood. In the morning coffee and rice crispies, or coffee and wheaties; by subway or surface car to the office; thirty minutes off at lunchtime for a sandwich in a drugstore, or the same length of time for a sandwich in a fancy restaurant; back to the office; home during the rush hour by subway, surface car, or private motor; dinner in a cafeteria or fancy restaurant, or at home; tomato juice, steak, French-fried potatoes, apple pie. A life where everyone eats the same thing, reads the same thing, asks the same questions, receives the same answers. Lord save me from such murderous monotony, superficiality, and impersonality!"

His cigar had gone out; he threw it overboard in a pet.

"Strange," Hans said. "How mistakenly an intelligent person can see things. Everything that you say is true. But it's all false because it is not essential. Has it never struck you that the Americans have discovered what is decisive—everyday life?"

"For goodness' sake, don't make jests!"

"I'm establishing a fact. It's only now that I realize how right Papa was to insist on facts. From my first day in America to my last the thing that interested me was that Americans have an everyday life which they enjoy. Does our everyday life give us joy? Why did we come over? Because of the festival. Because of the thing for which we live: the holiday, the exception. They, on the contrary, have found that life consists of every day, and that one must live for that. They rush about in the subways and drugstores, yes. But even at dinner they celebrate. Have you never watched them eat? Every mouthful is a feast. And after dinner they have some little pleasure. Everywhere. Everyone. Every day."

"The little pleasures of a cinema!" Fritz broke in. "The enjoyment of watching some hair-raising nonsense while you hold somebody's hand. I have, to be sure, not watched them eat, but I have seen them in the cinemas. When the story turns serious they laugh. Mistaking the sense of life for 'lots of fun,' they have even less of an idea 'what's all about' death. Has it not reached your attention, since you have been collecting facts, that they laugh when someone dies on the screen? They have no heart!"

"They have no fear," countered Hans, and looked into the waves which were mounting higher. "They have been educated to believe that things will turn out right. Even their everyday has a happy ending."

"But things don't turn out well," Fritz objected, growing constantly more irritated by this utterly unexpected difference of opinion.

"That's a remark which they would dismiss as 'Continental.' They know as well as I do, Fritz, that many things don't turn out right. But they do not say so. They prefer to say—and anyone brought up in Number 10 can well appreciate this—under all circumstances, when they are asked how they are, 'Fine!' They've done away with the habit of self-commiseration along with various other things—the humiliating keys to lock up drawers and lock out trust, for instance. If you ask a European how he is he will answer, 'Not as well as you.' Disaster, sickness, death, the Americans bear as something which belongs to life. They don't rebel against it. Fritz, can't you see why this has moved me so?"

"Don't try to inject occult meanings or motives into things which are lacking in all mystery! They act in that way because they have no imagination! Because they cannot or are not used to picture to themselves as we do either the good or the bad. That's why they are so gullible. You're surely not going to make me believe that it is a philosophy of theirs not to complain. They say, 'I am fine,' mechanically, as they do almost everything mechanically. They have for this purpose, as for every other, a ready-made formula."

"Don't you remember Uncle Otto Eberhard said exactly the same thing when he answered, 'Thank you, well,' when anyone inquired about his health? They have the attitude he demanded of us and that we didn't produce—not because we had too much imagination, but simply because we were not educated for life. Our first lesson was in fear. Our last in irony."

"I'm amazed at the way you contradict yourself! In one breath you dismiss the Francis Josephs and Otto Eberhards and in the next you quote them as examples!"

"No," Hans said reflectively. "I think I should perhaps let Otto Eberhard in." Then he was silent. He appeared to be absorbed in something for which he found no words. He took several turns around the deck, then stopped again beside Fritz's chair. "I think I know what it is," he said. "They have no malice in them. They are guileless."

"Hence the term 'gangster.'"

"You are deliberately misunderstanding me. What we were, or at least what I was, told about this country is wrong from A to Z. They're uneducated. You can't go out at night or you'll be attacked by gangsters. The people have no manners. They're constantly slapping you on the back. The last person who slapped me on the back was your brother Otto. Nowhere is there a more lovely atmosphere or one more readily dedicated to learning than in their public libraries. Nowhere have I seen more correct manners."

"Naturally. In Linz the pharmacist and his wife entertain the hardware merchant from Graz and his wife. All America is just one large provincial town."

"I have not the slightest objection to provincial towns. Life is led on a cleaner basis there. They lead such a life. They keep their word. That's why they keep their marriages clean."

"The orgy of banality you're indulging in! Are you going to tell me that you keep marriages by changing your wife or husband as often and easy as you move from one apartment to the other? Besides, our Reno happens to be Rome, and the Vatican is somewhat more particular about divorces than the judges in Nevada."

"I think it more honest to divorce than to go on with an unhappy marriage only to keep up appearances. At least I thought so as long as I lived on the fourth floor of Number 10. Don't you feel that the Americans are more sincere than we in the old country?"

"Because they are just ridiculously naive?"

"Because they are wonderfully naive! It is because they have something childlike about them that they move me. Because their great men and women think thoughts which are great not out of distrust and complexity but out of simplicity and trust. They call it democracy, but I don't believe that it has to do with a political system. It's just human attitude. They are themselves, they want you to be the same, and they respect you as fellow creatures."

"Who produce the Al Capones and the ladies and gentlemen who daily drink themselves into a stupor because of their inner vacuity, and the governors who kills the Saccos and Vanzettis!"

"Since when is a people judged by its shortcomings? What is their saying? Give them a chance! Tell me, Fritz, what do we ladies and gentlemen without any 'inner vacuity' do when someone tells us a story? We cast doubts on it and criticize. They, on the contrary, are inclined not only to believe but also to appreciate it. What do we do when we go into society? We speak slightingly of the ladies and gentlemen who are not there. In all the time over here I hardly heard a single sarcastic, ironical, or wounding remark!"

"Because they lack the necessary intellectual superiority for it."

"No, Fritz, because for that you need a certain courtesy of the heart, which they possess. And the will to have it. And the training for it. I'll trade every witticism and sharp-tongued facility for it."

"Why didn't you simply settle down over here?" Fritz asked, his patience now reaching its limit.

"It's strange that you should say that. Once I was on the verge of deciding to do that very thing. The day you were speaking about Austria in a high school in Philadelphia. Remember?"

"Where the old ladies knitted and the young ones asked if Salzburg is in Hungary."

"Have you always known where Cincinnati is? I can recall Aunt Hegéssy's telling us that Boston is in England. In any case, that school in Philadelphia made an unforgettable impression on me. The boys and girls together. No sex shams. No fear. Fritz! Have you any idea what that means? No fear in high school! We were obliged to go for eight years to the prison of Messrs. Miklau and Rusetter, to lose our youth and optimism there! And these American boys and girls told me they loved their school! Let me emigrate, I said to myself. Let me get away from the place where school children fear their teachers, where subjects fear their overlords, where every one fears life!"

"However, you came aboard the ship. Why?"

Hans smiled. It was the saddest smile in the world. "Over there lies a grave," he said.

The waves had risen, and it promised to be a rather stormy crossing.

"Forgive me," Fritz said.

Even after night had fallen the two cousins were still sitting out on deck.

"And besides," Hans concluded, as though there had been no extended silence since his last words, "the Americans are mistaken on one cardinal point."

"The Americans can be mistaken?"

"Oh, Fritz, why the irony? The Americans believe that Europe is a continent whose role is played out."

"Even though you blame me for irony, that's the one thing in which I agree with them. We have grown old. They are young. We no longer need to prove that the world could not have done without us. They still have to. They have to show that they possess a music of their own, a national literature, an American philosophy. Even an American love life. We have not had to do that for a thousand years."

"I believe firmly in the future of Europe," Hans said, without answering his remarks. "America will never be able to give up Europe!"

"You contradict yourself chronically," was the comment of the musician.

"In what does the contradiction lie? I now know what Europe needs."

The sea grew so rough that the travellers could not remain on deck.

"I recall a book by a Viennese," Fritz said. "His name was Ferdinand Kürnberger, and the title of the book was *Weary of America*. Perhaps you will write the counterpart?"

"I know the book," Hans told him. "It makes the error all Austrians make. They apply the Austrian standard of measurement on the world."

"And what do you intend to do?" Fritz asked, struggling in the storm to open the door to his cabin.

"To apply the standard of the world to Austria. It would be an undertaking."

The door withstood his efforts. "I am afraid I have overestimated you," Fritz declared when he finally opened it. "What they said about you at Number 10 is right. You are an idealist."

CHAPTER 43
Last Will

As always on Tuesdays when Peter, now Chief of Division, invited the inhabitants of Number 10 and his friends to hear chamber music, there was a lavish buffet supper. He himself played the viola; Annemarie, his wife, the violin; Fritz was at the piano, and Mr. Foedermaycr performed on the cello. Fritz, who was charged with planning the programs and conducting rehearsals, found that, according to his scorn for every form of amateurishness, the whole business was a "gross impropriety." The former Annemarie von Stumm, especially, had to swallow many biting remarks about people who "can't tell the difference between a musical key and a door key" and who derive from barbaric lands where Prussian military barks are held to be music. But since Peter was a lover of chamber music and fiddled quite acceptably, and Mr. Foedermayer, chief clerk of the C. Alt piano firm, was almost a virtuoso on the cello, the critical cousin put up with the family foible. His own second symphony had been conducted with extraordinary success by Furtwaengler, for the Philharmonic's last concert; and even Julius Korngold, the all-powerful music critic, had given the stamp of his approval in the *Neue Freie Presse* with his words "a new Austrian composer of the first rank."

Hans noticed that his mother had not made her appearance, so he inquired of his sister about her. Martha Monica, who had taken advantage of his absence in America to lose her heart to another angel, found her mother's delay quite natural; Mother always took so much time to make herself beautiful. As for Martha Monica's new flame, he had gazed at her rapturously all during the music and now was at the buffet recovering from the strenuousness of the last sonata. He was the young Baron Waldstetten, aide-de-camp to the Vice-Chancellor Prince Starhemberg, a little younger than Martha Monica but just as much in love. The green uniform he wore was that of the Heimwehr. "You know how vain Mother is!" was the reason given by his sister to Hans.

To look at her was still a pure pleasure. With her joyousness, infecting even the most impervious, she formed a focal point in the gathering, which irked her hostess. After all, one did not take so much trouble, first with rehearsals, then with playing, and afterwards with all the supper, to see that girl from the fourth floor come down and carry off the honors. Yet one could not hold it against her, she was so enchanting. Rushing over to Annemarie and putting her arm round her, she now said, "You played simply brilliantly. I enjoyed it so much!"

"Simply or brilliantly? Make up your mind," Fritz demanded severely.

Although in Martha Monica's domain there was no room

for cares, Hans was concerned over his mother's continued absence and went up to the fourth floor to find out about her. Madam was still at home, Hanni informed him, and Dr. Einried too.

"Who?" asked Hans, who heard only the title of "Dr." and thought it was a physician.

Whereupon Henriette called from the living room, "Let the young master come in, Hanni!"

At the Maria Theresa desk Hans found an unknown gentleman. His mother, all dressed in her evening clothes, was seated in an armchair beside him.

"You know each other," she said.

In the gray-haired gentleman with a pince-nez Hans recognized his former schoolmate, Eugenie's son.

"Very pleased to renew the acquaintance," said Dr. Einried, embarrassed. "I hear you have been in America? Was it interesting over there?"

"Yes. How are—your parents?"

"Papa has been dead some time. Mother is celebrating her seventieth birthday next Monday. Won't you come and see us? Mother is sure to be very pleased."

"I'd be glad to, if I may," said Hans, embarrassed. Then, glancing at the papers spread out over the desk, "Forgive me for interrupting, if I've disturbed you. I only wanted to know what was keeping you so long, Mother."

"You see!" exclaimed Henriette. "Didn't I tell you what kind of a son he is? He even came back from America!" Then, looking at this son with tenderness, "It is probably a good idea that you came up. I'm making my will and in any case wanted to ask you several things. Did you not know that Dr. Einried is my lawyer?"

"No," Hans said.

Now it was her turn to be embarrassed. "As it happens, I made a will while you were away. Our old Dr. Schultz drew it up. But dear old Schultz received, in the course of his life, too many directions from your late father and your late uncle. In dealing with him I felt like a ward. That's not right if one is to make one's will—isn't that so, Doctor?" she inquired with all the charm she still possessed.

"Not necessarily," replied the man, who as a schoolboy had been first in crystallography, and coughed slightly behind his raised hand. He too felt ill at ease since Hans appeared.

"Consequently I've emancipated myself and turned to Dr. Einried," Henriette explained. "To him Number 10 is, thank God, an unknown quantity. Besides, I did think that you wouldn't be coming back."

"How so?" Hans asked, with increased bewilderment.

"Well, you're here now," Henriette answered, nodding to him, "and that's the main thing. Now listen. The only point still to be discussed is this house. As you know, I'm residuary legatee under your father's will, and he had a one-third interest in the house. A second third was Otto Eberhard's property, inherited by Elsa after his death. The third is the joint property of your Aunts Drauffer and Paskiewicz. When I am no longer here the house will have not four owners, as previously, but six. I think that is correct, isn't it, Doctor? Property problems are Chinese puzzles to me!"

"That was the position also when Fraulein Sophie Alt and Frau Betty Alt, formerly Kubelka, were still alive," said Dr. Einried, immediately establishing a fact. He was ever a prime scholar.

Downstairs at Cousin Peter's someone must have sat down at the piano; you could hear the playing and, following it, the sound of singing:

Way out in Schönbrunner Park,
Way out in Schönbrunner Park,
Sits an ancient man full of woe.

Dear old, good old, ancient man,
Do not let your heart ache so.
Dear old, good old, ancient man In Schönbrunn …

"Quite right," confirmed Henriette. "And that's exactly how it would be again. One third would go to my three children; the second will remain the property of the old ladies, and the third would be Elsa's and go, after her death, to Peter. Is that correct?"

"Quite so, Frau Alt."

"Mother, I think you're bothering your head quite unnecessarily," Hans said. "They're waiting downstairs for you before serving the punch; you have such a lovely dress on and are still delaying. I can't understand, Einried, how you can back Mother up in these dismal interests!"

The former bright boy coughed slightly. If rich people wanted to indulge their vagaries he was not one to forgo drawing his own advantage from it.

"But they're not dismal," Henriette explained gaily. "Don't bother Dr. Einried. The poor man is so busy that I can see him only after office hours, and besides, he is charming enough to come to see an old lady who is terrified of any kind of office and look after her foibles. Young men who will come to see old ladies are scarce!"

"Thank goodness you're so well that such conferences are not necessary," asserted Hans, to whom, as a matter of fact, the successor to the old family physician had recently painted a far less rosy picture.

"You don't understand me. It's just because I feel so well that I've decided to rid myself of all cares," said his mother, fingering her pearls, which were not so beautiful as Martha Monica's. "Since you have come back I feel as though I were on a holiday. To tell the truth, Dr. Einried, we have not had many holidays in this house—holidays from care, I mean."

"I understand," agreed the lawyer, obviously wishing to bring the over-long conversation to an end.

This did not affect Henriette. "I feel like the pensioned officials who move to Graz to enjoy their retirement there," she went on. "I'm not moving to Graz, because I should find it too tame, but I've firmly decided to move away from all cares. I want to grow to a ripe old age. Older than, or at least as old as, Aunt Sophie—who, incidentally, at eighty still looked passably attractive. In this house, Dr. Einried, people grow to be as old as Methuselah. I've never been insured for anything, although my late husband was always urging me to take out some life insurance. But I always hated to pay monthly instalments. Now I should like to be insured, as it were, against care, without premiums. When this will is out of the way, and Hans and Mono are with me, I shall not have a care left in the world. I shall live the life of a lotus-eater!" She hummed a line from the song they were singing downstairs. "I think I shall allow myself a glass of champagne every day. Not punch. Besides, it's good for the heart."

Did Mother mean what she was saying? Hans could not tell why it all sounded so forced to him.

She seemed to mean it, and insisted on his hearing Paragraph 3 of her will and expressing his views about it.

Dr. Einried read, "Paragraph 3. 'My third interest in the house at 10 Seilerstätte I bequeath in equal shares to my children Hans, Franziska Baier, and Martha Monica. It is my wish that after my death my children dispose of their shares by sale to the other owners of the house and take up their residence elsewhere. For it cannot have been the intention of the builder of the house to stand in the way of the well-being of his descendants. And I trust I shall be forgiven if I venture the remark that I do not consider the house of 10 Seilerstätte as conducive to well-being.'"

This made Hans think of a postscript in a letter he received while in his prison camp and what at that time had seemed revolutionary to him.

"What do you say to it?" Henriette asked. When the opposition she feared was not forthcoming, she beamed. "This is how I look at it. Franziska lives in Salzburg anyway and, thank goodness, is contented to be there. Mono will marry. And perhaps you will too?" Seeing the shadow that fell on his face, she hastened to add, "I mean, it would not be, a source of unhappiness to you to be rid of your share."

"On condition that the other co-owners are unanimously in favor of it. According to the will of your respected spouse, you, Frau Alt, may dispose of your interest only within the limits prescribed by the testament of the founder, Christopher Alt. And that testament made certain explicit stipulations," said the lawyer firmly.

Hans was surprised that his mother should think this was something new, since he himself had been aware of it since childhood.

"Old Christopher's will is crazy, and it cannot be valid forever! Time has broken many another will!" Henriette exclaimed.

That was exactly what Selma had written to him in his prison camp.

"Quite right," the lawyer agreed. "Except that you are thinking of it in terms of laws affecting public bodies or constitutional changes brought about by circumstances. On the other hand, in civil law—and this is exclusively a matter of civil law—we are for better or for worse obliged to abide by the civil code, which has not been changed by the revolution, I am tempted to add, thank God!"

Henriette had grown nervous. In her eyes all lawyers were manipulators of law, and this one should prove no exception. That is why she had had him come!

"We shall find a solution. A thousand thanks in any case for the time you have spent on me outside your office hours." With that she concluded the interview in the grand manner she had had a taste of in her youth.

The lawyer kissed his client's hand, the two former schoolmates shook hands, and they all left the fourth floor together.

Henriette let the outsider go first and then followed slowly with her son. The utterly unexpected remark of the prime scholar had ruined her whole plan. For she had not taken such a firm stand behind the bulwark of her will for the purpose of having the children leave the house after her death, but because she herself wished to leave it at last. Not another night in this haunted house! But she could not possibly tell Hans what had been happening here since the night he went away.

She had lain awake on that night as on many others. And between the two windows the dead woman had stood. She wore a doublet of silver mail, whose sheen glinted through the dark. Henriette was so frightened that she was incapable of any movement.

She tried to say to herself, I am dreaming, she is not standing there. But there she stood looking at her with wide-open eyes. Henriette had waited in an agony of suspense. She had heard the clock on her bureau strike the quarter-hour twice. For that length of time, at least, the dead woman had stood there and looked at her with anguish. Twice Henriette attempted to speak to her, but her throat produced no sound. When she finally succeeded in drawing herself up, the dead woman had vanished.

The apparition had come again three times. Clad in silver mail, she had stood between the windows. The night before was the last time.

It was impossible for Henriette to tell Hans that his murdered wife found no peace in her grave. She knew, of course, that his thoughts were still not freed from her. He would have believed her, and it would have robbed him of his reason.

Rudolf too had firmly believed in the White Lady, who appeared to the Empress in the castle whenever she wanted to warn her about anything. What warning was Selma trying to convey to her? Henriette slept even less than she did before the apparition came. She was afraid of falling asleep ever since. Away from this house!

"You know," she said when the lawyer was no longer in sight, "I have even thought that we needn't wait so long. Of course it's ungracious of me, now that you have just had a lift installed for me, but I think it would be enchanting if we all moved away from here together—you, Mono, and I."

"Why not?" he asked.

With her training in the Otto Eberhard school, she never expected such an easy victory. It had been ground into her that to arrive at legal results one must prepare a scaffolding of paragraphs, foolscap with lawyers' writings, so that she asked with an infinite sense of relief, "Do you really mean that?"

"Why not, if you wish it?" he told her. "I certainly do not cling particularly to this house. Nor does Mono. Besides, there is nothing we would rather do than give you pleasure." Under the impression of Dr. Herz's successor's diagnosis he almost said, "One last pleasure."

"Splendid!" she said. "That's wonderful! Now all we have to do is get the others to agree. I mean, the other coowners."

"That will be the simplest thing in the world," Hans said. "They never loved us overmuch, you know."

In front of the door to Peter's apartment, which had been Otto Eberhard's, she asked him, "Will you handle it? But please do it as quickly as possible! Will you?"

"I shall speak to Peter at once," he promised. And mother and son joined the Tuesday evening guests.

Their host was in magnificent humor. The wife of his chief, the Minister, had assured him that these evenings of chamber music were a sheer delight. The von Kagenecks of Brünn, leading figures of society there, could not say enough in praise of Fritz's second symphony, and complimented him on his cousin. They called Fritz "our maestro," and, according to them, one would hardly recognize Vienna. It had become once more the irresistible city of enchantment that it used to be under Francis Joseph. The performances at the opera under Bruno Walter! The theater in the Josefstadt, that jewel of the speaking stage, under that genius Max Reinhardt! The matchless Philharmonic concerts!

"You've performed miracles," said Frau von Kageneck, in praising the achievements of her host. "There's nothing to be seen of the Reds and even less of the Browns!"

"You are all too amiable, Baroness," was the rejoinder of her host, with the duelling scar on his cheek, who had so rapidly climbed the ladder of officialdom to reach his present position of chief of the Department of Art and Culture. "That is due only in a very modest degree to my efforts. I shall not deny that I make the cultural mission of our little state my particular affair, but the credit must lie with"—here he bowed in the direction of the wife of his exalted superior—"His Excellency, the Minister, and in the very first instance with our highly revered Chancellor!"

"Of course," agreed Herr von Kageneck, who owned a sugar refinery and a publishing house in Brünn. He had had the honor of being received the day before by Dr. Schuschnigg. He had scarcely ever, he averred, in all his career met a more significant statesman nor one with so fine a mind.

At this point the aide to the vice-chancellor felt it incumbent to put in a word of praise for his own chief. Prince Starhemberg had had, according to him, the smartness necessary to root out the Red and the Brown mobs.

"But, Baron Kari, wasn't Ernstl at one time associated with Hitler?" inquired Frau von Kageneck (née Baroness Eichhorn), who was informed about everything. The young man in the Heimwehr uniform indignantly objected. "Baroness Maud! How can you say such a thing? Ernstl is beyond himself with rage when he so much as sees a picture of that house painter!"

"He does look repulsive," was the opinion of the lady from Brünn, who had recently had an opportunity to observe the German Chancellor at close range from a specially favorable seat at the Olympics in Berlin. She was prepared to admit that "Ernstl" (under which name Prince Ernst Ruediger von Starhemberg was meant) had, in the course of years, developed into a statesman.

Martha Monica found that amount of praise all too niggardly. Her interest in politics derived only from the particular angel she was in love with. And since, at the moment, her heart was set on the aide to the vice-chancellor, she preferred the vice-chancellor to all other statesmen of history. "And he is marvellously handsome," was her judgment. Whereas Chancellor Schuschnigg looked "more like a scholar."

"One might do worse," remarked Hans.

Henriette, however, begged them "not to speak of politics."

Since she had appeared she dominated the scene. The rumors about her past had crystallized into a kind of saga, and the generation who knew about it only from hearsay, judging by the beauty of her daughter, considered her the most seductive woman of an epoch grown legendary. Henriette was now accorded a position analogous to the one Frau Schratt had held in Vienna in her day, a kind of social extra-territoriality.

"She's still dazzling to look at," remarked Captain Kunsti, program director at the Vienna broadcasting station, to the playwright Vogl, a compatriot. "Between you and me, Captain," Vogl replied very discreetly, "I find her still a hundred times more attractive than her daughter. That woman certainly has a fascination about her."

She unquestionably had, on this evening. It was as though

the release from decades of severe control had restored her to herself and she blossomed out in the atmosphere that was hers. Music, brilliance, admiration, smartly dressed people, who brought her neither cares nor reproaches—this was her element. Anyone who knew her well would have noticed the glint in her eyes.

She took some Waldmeister punch offered her by Annemarie, who, despite all efforts to be stylish, still looked "Prussian," emptied her glass, and asked for a second. "No champagne?" she inquired

"No," answered the former Fraulein von Stumm emphatically. This was just a superior bourgeois establishment.

"Why do you say that so despotically?" Henriette asked with a laugh. "Sometimes you need champagne. Incidentally, your punch is excellent."

Hans wondered whether he should warn his mother against the punch, but decided not to. He was touched to see her make up the small pleasures which had been denied her. He could understand so well what went on in people who were trying to make up for things they had missed. They were lucky to be able to do it!

A moment ago the actor who played the archbishop in *Saint Joan* had come up to him and resonantly declared, "She was a remarkable little woman. In time she would surely have accomplished things." It was the revenge for the memorial tablet which the Burgtheater had never forgiven the murdered woman.

Henriette was dancing!

Young Waldstetten had invited her to dance. When Fritz saw that, he replaced the man at the piano, who was playing Viennese songs, and began to play a waltz. He had inherited the velvety touch of his master, Alfred Grünfeld. The *Schönbrunner Waltz*, which was so ravishing under the fingers of that waltz magician of other days, now sounded as much so under his, and the old lady in the arms of the Heimwehr officer whirled with a fire and an enjoyment of life too long repressed. Her year of mourning was long since over. Her self-reproach had waned. Time had robbed her terrifying memories of their terror. Once she could move away from this haunted house—anywhere where it was friendly and bright and cheerful—then she could be rid of her memories too. Friendly, bright, and cheerful. That is how she had longed to have her life. And it could still be that!

"You dance divinely," said the young baron.

"You think so?" she replied. There had never been much dancing at Number 10, but she still managed well enough. If her breath were not so short perhaps no one would have even noticed the difference between the old days and now. The girls of today really had no idea of how to waltz! The horrible jazz music had quite ruined it.

"Better than anyone I know. Even better than Miss Mono," asserted her partner.

Fritz smiled to his aunt as she danced by him. "Thank you," she smiled back. "You play enchantingly!"

"May I ask you something?" inquired the Heimwehr officer when the other couples had stopped in order to make room for the two to dance, and stood watching them admiringly.

Can he be going to make me a declaration of love? thought Henriette, who began to feel the effects of her two glasses of punch.

"I want to ask you for Miss Mono's hand," he said softly.

Her head swam with the punch and with joy. Leaning a little more heavily on the arm of her partner, she signalled to Fritz that she wanted to dance another waltz right away, so he began the beautiful *Blue Danube.* Past Frau von Kageneck, whom she heard say, "That is the most charming pair of dancers I ever saw," past Captain Kunsti, who laid his hand on his heart in a gesture of homage, past friendly, admiring, delighted eyes she danced her favorite waltz.

I am play-acting, she thought to herself in a moment of embarrassment.

"Are you displeased with me?" asked Baron Waldstetten when she gave him no reply.

This young man held you well. He was good-looking. "Why, son-in-law?" she said. "What is your first name?"

"Kari," he answered excitedly.

"Kari," she repeated. They will have good-looking children. She had no grandchildren. "I am delighted, Kari," she said. "Will you make her happy?"

"I—" he began, overwhelmed, but she interrupted.

"Don't make any promise. Even when you make a promise you don't always keep it. Promise nothing, but make her happy. It's the making happy that counts. Not the promising."

"Of course," agreed her partner enthusiastically.

"It's not quite such a matter of course," was her opinion. "And it's very difficult." Her head was swimming again.

"Would you care to stop, Frau Alt?"

"Of course." It was her turn to say it. "But it's sweet of you, Kari, not to betray that I'm an old woman."

CHAPTER 44
Old Scores

The family discussion of Henriette's wish to move out of Number 10 Seilerstätte took the form of a regular session. Peter, who called the meeting and represented his invalid mother, Elsa, presided. He led the negotiations in the first-floor apartment, just as he did those in his office at the Ministry in the Minoritenplatz, suavely but also objectively, with all the little side remarks calculated, when it was a case of ministerial councils, to arouse the applause of ministerial councillors.

He sat at the head of the dining room table, extended for the occasion, and had before him the certified copies of the wills of Christopher Alt and Franz Alt, in addition to the extract from the files of the Registry, which Franz had had to produce for the same purpose as that now pursued by his widow: to bring Number 10 to a unanimous decision.

On the right of the chairman sat Henriette. The dancing, the punch, and the pleasure of the day before did not seem to have harmed her in the least. Quite the contrary. She wore a two-piece beige dress with a brown leather belt and large brown leather buttons. Much too young for her, was the opinion of one of the other ladies present. Her face was rested; the wrinkles around her eyes and mouth were skilfully hidden. Her full lips shone red against her markedly pale complexion; her hair, now turning white, was so luxuriant that it was dressed with difficulty but perfectly, and the fragrance of Chanel No. 5, which she diffused, appealed to the aesthetic sense of the departmental chief.

On his left (the order of precedence followed the bureaucratic protocol) sat the doyenne of the house, the widow of Colonel Paskiewicz. Despite her ninety-four years, she did not wear glasses, nor was her hearing impaired. But she had grown remarkably small, almost tiny, although in the colonel's day she was looked upon as tall. Now her expressionless, peaked, birdlike face did not reach even the rim of her high-backed chair. Next to her sat her younger sister, Pauline Drauffer, recently turned eighty-six, the same who had been so hungry at Francis Joseph's wedding ceremony. Although she no lodger possessed her round apple cheeks, her face still beamed with good humor. She too was elegantly gowned in bottle green with a jabot of real lace which her husband (out of atonement for goodness knows what pangs of conscience, so she thought) had brought her once upon a time from Brussels. Her eyes rested on him, her aged painter husband whom she, where women were concerned, still did not trust round the corner, and she smiled at him with the indulgence she had always shown for whatever he did. She would not have given up a minute, no, not a single minute, of her life, thanks to this husband who, although he looked like St. Peter, was yet the biggest rascal in Christendom. She had always found his every word interesting, and life at his side had been an unbroken joy, provided one did not expect the impossible of a rascal—that he should be a moralist. A man who all his life had painted half-naked women!

An exception had been made to allow him to come to the meeting, for he was only the husband of a co-owner (even so, the co-owner of only a one-sixth interest). It was made because Aunt Pauline was hard of hearing. So there sat old Herr Drauffer at the narrow end of the table opposite his nephew Peter, having scornfully refused, as always, to subject his open collar to the restraint of a necktie, and using the ministerial foolscap laid at each place to draw a cartoon of the chairman, which made his wife, who kept looking at it out of the corner of her eye, laugh.

"I open this consultation and greet those present," Peter had said in true official style. Checking over those present in turn, he satisfied himself that the owners of Number 10 were represented in full, either in person or, as in the case of his mother, by an authorized agent, and, as in the case of dear Aunt Pauline, by an authorized assistant.

"Allow me to introduce myself. I am the authorized assistant," remarked the old painter. Pauline laughed heartily, and Henriette, nodding to the couple, said, "And the best there is!"

She was determined to bring her heaviest artillery into play. Inclined, as always, to form her judgments instantly, she now made her calculations: the Drauffers would make no difficulties. Peter, perhaps, but I'll bring him round. Old lady Paskiewicz doesn't count.

"The purpose of our gathering, as you all know, is the desire, or shall we say the request, of Aunt Henriette to: *(a)* dispose of her one-third interest in the house by sale to the other members, and *(b)* to obtain the consent of the family council to move out of the house and take up her abode in—Is it Vienna?" the chairman asked, interrupting himself.

"Yes, in Vienna," Henriette replied with a smile.

"In some other part of Vienna. Have I reproduced your chain of thought correctly, Aunt?"

"Perfectly. You are a master of conciseness."

"And you a model of amiability. Has anyone any question?" When none was forthcoming Henriette's good humor increased. "We can perhaps take up at once the question of the money," she suggested, in accordance with the advice given her by Dr. Einried, who was not allowed to be present at the meeting. "I am ready either to sell my third to you share and share alike or, if you prefer, sell it in its entirety to one of you. I should be grateful if you would set the price on it which would meet with your ideas." She had learned this by heart. Now she congratulated herself on having handled things pertaining to law and to finance correctly.

"Set the price which would meet with your ideas," repeated the chairman, who was also taking down the minutes. "Does anyone care to take the floor?"

The old painter wished to do so. "I am, to be sure, only an authorized assistant, which in plain language means a fifth wheel to the coach," he told them, and as he spoke he filled in the hatching in his caricature with sharper strokes. "Nevertheless, I think it is superfluous that we should be sitting here like a star-chamber court because someone wants to move out of the house. Actually, if I didn't see it with my own eyes, I wouldn't believe it. I have heard of the family statutes of crowned heads, which are ceremoniously confirmed or amended on family occasions. I have even heard tell of the 'Pragmatic Sanction' of the House of Hapsburg, which was supposed to protect it from disintegration. But in our case it's nothing short of a farce! Old Christopher, who, as we would say today, had a family complex and who, like me, must have heard of the pragmatic sanction, will forgive me if I say—incidentally, I'll tell him this to his face when I meet him up there shortly—there's no reasonable human being in the world today who can prevent another civilized human being from living where he chooses! If it suits Henriette today to move to Dobling then to Dobling she shall move; if she prefers Grinzing—all right, she shall live in Grinzing. I move we close the debate!"

"Forgive me, Uncle," said Peter. "What you are bringing forward is not germane to the discussion. It's a matter of course that heirs, who have accepted and entered into a heritage, are not only justified in but obliged to obtain the fulfilment in every particular of the will of the testator in so far as this same—to quote our civil code—does not conflict with good morals or the penal code. I submit that neither of these points come into consideration in relation to my great-grandfather's last will. The founder of a family, who for good reasons—"

"Which?" interrupted the painter.

"I am speaking, Uncle; pray excuse me."

"Spare us the monkey business!" exclaimed the man with the St. Peter beard.

His wife Pauline, who had not heard everything, said, "Drauffer, behave yourself!"

Whereupon the old painter assumed an expression of resignation and went on drawing furiously.

"The reasons—if I were to answer Uncle's interpolation—were undoubtedly the best that exist," said Otto Eberhard's son in defence of the very letter of the testament. "They consist of forging among the members and descendants of a family a bond so firm that it assures the continuation of the principles for which the founder of the family lived and died, namely those of an Austrian citizen devoted to the State, to the Church, and to art."

"Rats!" exclaimed the painter, but this time in a lower voice. "In the first place, principles in themselves are nonsense, and in the second place, a family offers the best of all fields in which to ride them to death. To try to inject some metaphysical interpretation into the childishness of this will is absurd. It is—let us be polite about it—a misunderstood imitation of the 'Pragmatic Sanction.' The piano-maker Christopher Alt lays down an Austrian house law! Comment is superfluous."

The departmental chief rapped on the table with his sharply pointed pencil. "It strikes me as somewhat strange that you should at this particular juncture be speaking, Uncle, as though absolute freedom of choice of domicile were a foregone conclusion," he remarked (in the tone of voice he was accustomed to use with a little air of superiority when in the Ministry he said, "My dear councillor, I regret to state that you are unfortunately misinformed on that point"). "Has it escaped your notice that at the present time in all Germany there is no one who is allowed to change his domicile or even his apartment without the authorization of his municipality?"

"I see," remarked the painter, drawing a comical little moustache on his nephew's portrait. "You ascribe prophetic gifts to old Christopher! He foreshadowed my great colleague from Braunau on the Inn!"

"That is beside the point," the nephew answered shortly. "I come back to the original proposition: Does anyone wish to speak on the subject of the sale price?"

The widow of Colonel Paskiewicz said, "I didn't know that Henriette wanted to move."

"That is not under discussion now, Aunt," Peter explained.

"You said that we knew it," contradicted the little old lady, who had grown even more wizened than the former Miss Kubelka had in her day. "I, in any case, knew nothing about it."

"Very well, you know it now, Gretl," said Henriette, growing impatient.

"Why do you want to move out?" asked the old lady.

"Because she doesn't like it here any longer!" exploded the painter. "She's a highly eccentric person who does not like a house that is, as previously, eternally damp, eternally cold, eternally dark, and eternally sour!"

"Yes," agreed the colonel's widow. "You're quite right, brother-in-law. She's eccentric. She always has been."

"I was not aware of having inconvenienced you," countered Henriette, who was beginning to lose her self-control. What did this old mummy want? No one even knew that she was still about. "You have inconvenienced me. And many others in the house."

"If it had not been for you my Christl would have become a happy wife and I should have had grandchildren. You were the one that hindered that! With your eccentric ways! With your impious conduct! You squeezed people like lemons and then discarded them when they could no longer give you anything. Do you think we have been blind? You never went to mass! You deceived your husband. Not once –"

"Please, Aunt! I beg of you!" pleaded the departmental chief.

But the colonel's widow was not to be checked. "But often," she concluded, "we have had cause to be ashamed of you indeed. Not only I. The whole house. Ask them! If they have any vestige of decency they will tell you to your face!"

Henriette pressed the tips of her fingers to her temples. Her heart had begun to throb uncomfortably again. "Then you should be all the more glad to be rid of an unworthy fellow inhabitant!" she answered, having grown deathly pale under her white powder.

The wizened old lady with the thin lips nodded and went on, her eyes intent on the table top in front of her. "That would suit you! Now that you think you have become your own mistress you want to move out and lead a riotous life! You demanded champagne!"

The departmental chief had reached the point of delivering a reprimand. Insults being hurled while he was in the chair! "For the last time," he said, "I beg all those present to moderate their language. Please!" He had the same displeased, turned-down corners of the mouth as Otto Eberhard. Even his voice had grown to resemble that of the late Public Prosecutor. "We must look on Aunt Henriette as the widow of Uncle Franz. Don't let us forget that."

"And the mother of Martha Monica!" added the wizened old lady.

"If the discussion is going to be continued on that basis I regret to state I cannot participate in it," Peter declared, and laid down his pencil.

"It is superfluous anyhow," was the rejoinder of Paskiewicz' widow as she rose. Standing beside her seated nephew, she barely came up to his shoulder. "The vote of the family council must be unanimous; that I know from the time when I had to obtain permission for Christl to take the veil. I refuse to give my consent," and she turned to go.

"For heaven's sake, Gretl," cried the painter, who felt that his earlier cantankerous remarks had caused all the trouble and who reproached himself for having harmed Henriette's cause. "Do consider things in a reasonable light. There is no logic in what you say. If you are against Henriette you should be in favor of her leaving the house!"

The old lady, who had already reached the door, looking straight ahead, said, "It's just because I consider how those who have had a hard time of it still stuck it out here. Why shouldn't she, who has had an easy time of it, stick it out? And if she cannot stick it out let it be her punishment. My sainted brother Franz hears me. She deserves it!" Then she refused to be detained any longer and left the room.

An embarrassed silence fell.

"With all due respect, she is simply no longer normal," exclaimed the painter. "You will just have to act against her veto, Hetti, and the rest of us will give you our blessing."

"Of course," Pauline agreed comfortingly. This was the first part she had taken in the debate.

"I'm afraid that won't do. There is something more involved here this time than the construction of a lift," said the departmental chief slowly.

"Then Henriette will have to have the old harpy's mental condition examined! That woman has a religious mania despite the twaddle about Christl's supposed tragedy. She's insanely proud of her holy daughter! She spends all her days on her knees at St. Anna's!"

"That would be a bad reflection on the house," was the opinion of the departmental chief, finishing the minutes with a few nastily jotted down lines. "As a matter of fact, I regret to say I too am against Aunt Henriette's proposal. If she moved out, and thereby broke the will of the founder of the family, I should be compelled to restrain her by instituting a suit in confirmation of the will and obtaining a so-called temporary decree. That would be done, I repeat, in the name of my mother, whom I represent here, not against Aunt Henriette, obviously not. But it is just as obvious that our attitude is dictated by a desire not to allow a testament sacred to us to be profaned into a scrap of paper. Surely you would not wish to have my mental condition investigated, would you, Uncle?"

"You can go to the devil!" the old man retorted angrily. He left the cartoon on the table, jumped up, and said, "Come, Pauline; a wax-figure cabinet is no place for us," and to his sister-in-law, to whom he had always been partial, "I give you my word of honor no one here will sue you! Don't worry about anything and do exactly as you please!"

Henriette felt her heart pound hard. "That's something I fear I've lost the knack of doing here in this house," she said. Then she left the room and walked slowly up to die fourth door, like a schoolgirl bringing home a bad report. It was only when she had reached the second door that she remembered the lift. But she did not use it.

The force of habit had triumphed.

CHAPTER 45
Brother Mozart

It is probably correct to say that world history is city history. By that, however, one is implying not only that world history is made in the cities, but also that the city has displaced the land; in other words, intellect has displaced nature. Apologists for the cities maintain that they are the centers of progress. In the cities, so they say, the inventions are made which lift mankind to a constantly higher level.

"To those who say that, I say: No. There are types of progress which do not advance man but, on the contrary, throw him back to his original point of departure in evolution, and it is to such types of progress that the city civilization of our epoch has come. I have no authority for my remarks, and I have no proof for my conviction except that it is my conviction. Yet, having been invited by you, brother masters, to share with you impressions gained in America, I feel that I am speaking to men who will admit such meagre proof and will even forgive me if I speak less in terms of facts about my journey than I shall in unfounded feelings about the future.

"I came back from America imbued with admiration for the Americans. For their achievements, for many of their institutions, and above all for their originality. For the very reason, however, that I believe in the boundless future for America, I am convinced that Europe is an irreplaceable factor for America. Consider, if you will, what I have to say as an *oratio pro domo Europee.* It is that. The indisputable fact which you can establish over there, the opinion that Europe is definitely finished, or, as they say, 'done for,' was a challenge to me, and also, I admit, it wounded me. Yet the longer I thought of it, the surer I became that their opinion is a mistaken one. As far as I could judge, in the ridiculously brief time at my disposal, America's emancipation from Europe is an idea which has come to the fore in the general train of a tendency towards isolationism. To my mind it is a fundamentally erroneous idea … Am I going too fast, Fraulein Hübner?"

As he walked up and down in his office on the Wiedner Hauptstrasse, dictating the address he was to give that evening in the "Futura" Lodge of Freemasons, Hans looked inquiringly at the secretary, whom Mr. Foedermayer had recently engaged to take English and French correspondence. Foreign contracts were increasing.

"Perhaps a little," answered the girl. "But it doesn't matter, Herr Alt. What you are dictating is so interesting."

"Really?" he said. "I thought it was dry as dust." As she made no reply but busied herself with her notebook, he went on, "America has, so to speak, written Europe off as an asset and put it on the debit side of the ledger. Let us, as Europeans striking a balance, establish the just fact that this happened after they were saturated with Europe and had absorbed all that was desirable. No European can deny that our continent today is not an asset or anything like it, but a bankrupt estate being criminally managed. What the managers Hitler and Mussolini do they do against the credit of Europe. But they and the desperadoes who conduct the business for them, as well as the dupes who put their faith in such business methods, will all be bankrupt in the instant when the spell of gain is broken and the net loss becomes apparent. After them and despite them Europe will recover her mind, pathologically clouded for a few seconds of world history. It will then possess that for which America for the time being has no use, but which one day it will need as much as a body needs a heart.

"Our epoch, in addition to other destructive devices, has produced two nullifying things bound up but indirectly with politics and systems of power: it has taught men to forget how to marvel and it has taken the word 'impossible' out of their vocabulary. Everything is possible and nothing is marvelous. The blame for this is primarily to be laid on the progress deriving from cities, which has put machines in the place of men and has robbed the man who serves the machine—for the machine has for long not been the servant of man but the man the slave of the machine—of the last shred of faith remaining to the cities in anything supernatural. It was for the sake of the machine that human life assumed importance, rather than the other way round. And it is a bitter piece of irony on the part of fate that the machine, an invention of the middle class, should be the first instrument to strike a mortal blow at its inventors through the aggravation of social questions it has brought about. The engineer hoist with his own petard.

"'Miracle' and 'to marvel' mean the same. The world which no longer believes in supernatural miracles because it strives to make them natural by the machine; the petrified world of cities, which with every aeroplane usurps God's handiwork, in return for which God's revenge on them is the aeroplane—that world no longer marvels. It believes in superman, but not in the force superior to man. A phenomenon like Hitler is the logical consequence of it, for he asks of man's inability to marvel the unbelievable, thereby making it possible to achieve it.

"It is because the rootless, self-seeking spirit of the city predominates much more deeply over that of the soil in America than in Europe that the danger from the machine is increased a thousandfold. What distinguishes a village from New York is not its size but its spirit. The spirit of the city is the intellect, even the sterile intellect. The spirit of the village is the soul, it is cosmic, hence ever fertile. The country of America, and this to me is the most beautiful and moving part about it, has by nature the spirit of the village, although everything you read or hear about it would lead you to expect the opposite. But the spirit of the city is dictatorship, whereas the spirit of the village is freedom.

"A village is free even if Hitler and Mussolini dominate it; but the American city is eternally unfree, for its dictators are the machine and money.

"It is this dictatorial spirit of the city, which together with the word 'impossible' eliminated man's power to marvel, having undermined respect and humility by means of a false—because it is mechanical—concept of equality: it is this spirit which America underestimates. At the same time it so grossly overestimates the achievement of the city—looking upon it as the ocean and the land behind it merely as tribute-bearing rivers—that it has drained dry the springs of inner growth. Thereby it exhausts its last possibility of warding off the coming Stone Age, which is bound to be an era of inner turning to stone if no help comes.

"In the continent of dictators, in this degenerate, outworn continent of Europe, those springs still rise unchecked. As the new continent in an earlier day drew its forces from the old, so it will again, if it is to evade its inevitable inner turning to stone and be regenerated. Here in Europe, not to say Vienna, for Vienna is the heart of Europe, lies the healing power which one day will be vitally needed in New York and in Chicago. There and in the other stony dictatorships material achievements, on which America bases its attitude of the outworn and superfluous quality of Europe, will have reached their full development: their machines will be incomparably better than ours; their chemicals, their serums, their precision instruments, their highways, their system of education, their newspapers, their cinemas. Nevertheless, they will never have a Mozart. Never a Schubert. Never anyone who can write: 'Ober allen Gipfeln ist Ruh.' The gentle outline of enchantment with which the houses of Salzburg stand at the foot of the mountains, as though they were an integral part of them, is not theirs. Nor yet the charm of the Vienna Woods, which protect Vienna from turning to stone. It is not a matter of chance that Mozart was born in Salzburg and Schubert in Vienna. It is rather an organic expression of those cities which have not turned to stone but have remained part of a living landscape. One can live, you may say, without Mozart and Schubert. Yet one must needs have the symbol for which they stand and will ever stand for men to live and die by.

"This symbol is Europe and will remain that: the village, the land, the continent, the world of beauty which was not willfully produced but was created and grew. Not of relative beauty, whose purpose and conditions one must know in order to see it, but of absolute beauty, which convinces at first sight, and therefore is a measure and filter to separate the real from the apparent. The economists among you may prefer the expression 'a clearing-house of standards,' although for my part I should be reluctant to define what I mean in such terms. For what I have in mind is God-given beauty, in which man does not share at all—or else only as its happy recipient. The beauty which has survived intact the despotisms of man, machines, and money. If the mechanized world has doomed itself to sterility then it is only the world of our lodge brother Mozart which can redeem it. That will be Europe's eternal mission, even if for the time being America looks upon it as nothing but the mass burial-ground of her sons. For Europe's spirit is Goethe and Mozart, not Napoleon and Hitler. And since power yields only to power, it will be the power of Goethe and Mozart that in the end will rob the power of the machine of its inhumanity."

Hans stood still. "There. That's all," he said.

"Too bad!" commented Fraulein Hübner. She realized she had overstepped the limits set a shorthand-typist, so she added, "One or two carbon copies, Herr Alt?"

"None. I shall need only this product of my volubility for tonight."

Fraulein Hübner obviously would have liked to say "Too bad," but she took her notebook and left.

"Thanks!" he called after her through the felt-covered door. Immediately afterwards the tapping of her typewriter rose above the persistent sound of the piano-tuning. When Hans, a few hours later, walked up the steps of the Futura Lodge at Number 5 Annagasse, which he had recently joined and where he was to make his apprentice speech, he could not rid himself of a certain sense of mystery. That might, it occurred to him, have been part of his theme. The lack of mystery in our time. It was another consequence of the spirit of the city, whose mechanized sport had unveiled the mystery of the sexes and whose sterile brain had disclosed the mystery of creation to all eyes and thereby done away with its aura. Then his thoughts turned to the mysterious power of which he was now a part. How was this power, which had for centuries given rise to fables among the laity, exercised? From his family history he knew that the founder of Number 10 was suspected of being a Freemason, one of those dangerous people who threatened Pope and Emperor and who formed secret cells which brought about or did away with revolutions.

Arriving at a door on the second floor, he gave, as the preparatory master had instructed him to do, two short knocks and one long one, and it was instantly opened to him. As this was his first regular 'work' since his initiation, he was rather taken aback to see how his lodge brothers garbed themselves for the occasion. They fastened on leather aprons; for the apprentices they were white; for journeymen they had a blue border; for masters they were trimmed with blue circles. They also decorated themselves with medals, hung on blue silk ribbons around their necks. To the newcomer it was almost comic to see how these more or less portly gentlemen tied the little aprons around their middles with such lack of self-consciousness, and he could barely keep his face straight when later he saw their entrance into the so-called temple, two by two, during which, with their right hands on their throats, they marched, taking two short steps and one longer. An organ accompanied their progress.

In the long, rectangular room where the masters occupied the back rows on the long side, the journeymen sat on chairs in front of them, and the apprentices sat out in front, he recognized many faces he had overlooked during his initiation ceremony. The master beside the speaker's table was the pharmacist from Karntnerring; beside him sat an optician. There was also present among the masters the stationer from Number 10, with whom Hans had never discussed anything except exercise books and pens, and later, when he was no longer a schoolboy, the cold in Number 10. He also recognized an opera singer of the third magnitude and, of course, Ebeseder, who had overcome his instinctive opposition and brought him here. "A man like you belongs to us at this particular time," he had patiently explained to him. "We can make use of you and you of us." During the long-drawn-out procession he could not help thinking what Selma would have thought of it. It really was not easy to keep a solemn expression on one's face at the sight of these costumed opticians and stationers gravely treading a strange dance step as they entered the room. But Ebeseder gave the new apprentice a pregnant look admonishing him to please postpone his judgment until later. Besides, the tablet with the roster of lodge members happened to be directly in front of his eyes. Member number 7 was "Wolfgang Am. Mozart, musician from Salzburg." On the other hand, no one by the name of Alt, except himself, appeared on the framed tablet under glass, from 1759 to the present. They suspected my great-grandfather without grounds, thought the great-grandson. Above the tablet hung a portrait of the musician from Salzburg. In a white wig, a long chestnut-colored coat, black satin knee-breeches, pumps, his Mason's apron fastened in front, he stood at an open window through which the fortress of Hohen-Salzburg could be glimpsed. In the middle of the wall, and covering almost all of it, was the portrait of Emperor Joseph. He too wore the apron of a Mason.

After the customary ceremonies had been completed the Apprentice Brother Alt was asked to give his address.

Hans went over to the speaker's desk. Saluting the master in the way he had been taught to do (with a rectangular movement of the right hand beginning from the left shoulder and then stretching the right arm stiffly downward), he felt the embarrassment that overcame him in any kind of exhibition; it was the reason why it had been so difficult to reconcile himself to Selma's decision to become an actress; "Brother Masters! My beloved brothers!" The word "beloved" was hard for him. But then he read what he had dictated, concentrating exclusively on that, adding to it what thoughts had come to him in the meantime. His subject carried him away. When he looked up he caught Ebeseder's encouraging look.

"I thank you, dear Brother," said the master when the apprentice had finished, and Hans went back to his chair. "Very nice," commented the brother next to him, whom he did not know. Behind him too he heard, "Yes indeed. Nicely done."

Other subjects were discussed. Two hundred and seventy shillings were needed for the home for the blind in Dobling. Brothers Jellinek, Schmidt, and Anton Singer had not paid their monthly dues and were requested please to see the Brother Treasurer. On the following Saturday there would be a Sisters' Evening. Brother artists were asked to get in touch concerning the musical program for it with the Brother Preparatory

Master. After the fifteenth of the month the Wednesday meetings would no longer be held in Café Fetzer but in Café Siller. On the seventeenth Sister Freundlich, wife of our beloved Brother Freundlich of the Lessing Lodge, was to sing at the Volksoper. All beloved brothers were urged to attend the appearance of Sister Freundlich, tickets at reduced prices to be obtained from Brother Second Overseer.

When the 'work' was concluded with a collection for the 'widow's sack' and some organ music, the brothers laid aside their aprons and lodge insignia and gathered together on the first floor at the "Weisse Tafel."

Here they enjoyed their *gulyas*, Linz cakes, and lager beer. There was gossip to the effect that Brother Mandl and Sister Zerkowitz had again been seen together. Brother Slezak had produced a wonderful witticism. Iron shares were to be avoided; if one were going into the market public utilities were favored. After they had eaten they discussed the lecture of Brother Alt.

The lodge brother who bore the title Brother Speaker characterized it as a very worthwhile maiden speech. The Brother Lecturer had perhaps offered them too many personal reflections and too little data. What are the population statistics of American cities? What the birth rate? How do they compare with the European figures? It might also have been instructive to hear something about an industry which one might call a purely American one, the films. What did the Brother Lecturer think on that subject? Might one look upon them as trail-blazing, or did they incline to devote themselves too one-sidedly to optical rather than educational effects?

Whereupon a brother who wrote reviews for the Sunday book supplement of the *Neue Freie Presse* expressed himself as disappointed in Brother Alt's remarks. To tell the truth—and among brothers one was pledged to tell it—he had been unable to find any real continuity in his conglomeration of ideas, which he attributed to undigested reading of Marx,

Houston Stewart Chamberlain, Taine, and Spengler. Also he misinterpreted the problems of the day. America was no problem to Europe. The problem of Europe was Europe.

Ebeseder jumped up. "They say of us Masons that we are a power factor," he declared irritably. "But if they listened to us here they would think we are a social club. Why the devil don't we at last make use of the power we are supposed to possess? Five hours' journey from here there have long since ceased to be any lodges, and a free expression leads to the concentration camp. But we sit here and work on Sisters' Nights!" He went on to say that it was only through such lodge members as Brother Alt that Freemasonry could recover the significance it once had had and which it needed more urgently now than ever before. "Who will help us, brothers? Parliament no longer exists. The Government of Messrs. Schuschnigg, Starhemberg, Fey, Miklas, and whatever the rest of the professors, Parlour Fascists, and black shirts are called, is insanely amateurish, not to say criminally insane. Who will help us Austrians if we do not help ourselves?"

"Your party colleague, Monsieur Leon Blum in Paris!" someone answered, and there was laughter.

"My party colleague Blum has his hands full dealing with un-teachable people like you!" retorted Ebeseder with the sharpness characteristic of Austrians of the opposition in Parliament.

"Bravo!" cried four or five people. The majority of the rest had not been listening.

Then Hans was asked to make a concluding comment. He explained that he had nothing more to say, which appeared to suit most of the members. Did he play bridge or tarot? As he did not the bridge and tarot players went about their games. A moment later the green-topped tables in the next room were filled with players and onlookers and one heard nothing but bidding.

It was all wrong, Hans thought, directing the concluding comment to himself as he fled from the complacent gathering at the first opportune moment.

When he left the building to walk the few steps over to Number 10 he was stopped by someone. It was pitch-dark, and he could only see that it was a woman. Since the rendezvous hotel, Romischer Kaiser, happened to be in the same narrow street, this was no uncommon occurrence and he paid no attention.

"Good evening, Herr Alt," he heard a voice say behind him. On turning round he recognized his shorthand-typist.

"What are you doing here?" he asked in amazement.

The girl stammered in her hurried reply. An express letter had come, and she thought it might be important. She handed him the letter. By the light of the single streetlamp on the corner he saw that it was of no consequence. The new shorthand-typist could not, of course, have known that.

"Thank you, that was very kind of you," he said. "Only I am sorry that you took the trouble so late in the evening."

"It wasn't any trouble," she replied.

"How did you know where I was?" it occurred to him to ask.

"You said you were going to make a speech in the Lodge. Was your talk successful?"

"I don't think so. Good night, Fraulein Hübner."

"May I say something, Herr Alt?"

"Of course. What is it?"

"I know I've no right to say this. But I have seen you every day since you came back from America—and I don't think I have once seen you look happy."

"I'm afraid these are not times in which one can very well be happy," he replied without arguing the point. He had had more than enough discussion upstairs.

"To be happy is a silly expression. I mean something else," she said. "Forgive me, I'm detaining you."

"What else did you mean?"

It took her a moment to answer. Then she said, "That you give the impression of being a very unhappy man."

"And I made such an effort to dictate glowing letters in English to you! You see what a bad actor I am! Besides I'm a bad speaker too."

"You do everything well," the girl said in a tone of absolute conviction.

In the poor light of the streetlamp he looked at her. Until now he had scarcely given her more than a cursory glance when she came in with his letters or to take dictation. She was very young.

"Thank you," he replied shyly. "I'm afraid you are mistaken again."

"No," she said. "I feel so sorry for you."

"There is really no occasion for that," he said with growing embarrassment.

"But there is. Good night." She stepped out of the lamplight and walked off.

"Thank you, Fraulein Hübner," he called after her for the second time that day.

CHAPTER 46
Aimless beneath the Stars

How long did you really wait for me last night?"

"Have you been thinking about that?"

"To tell the truth, I have. In any case, I preferred thinking about that to other things."

"Then I'm glad I came. I too have thought about it, and I reproached myself. I suppose you have made up your mind about me?"

"To tell the truth again—no. Tell me a little about yourself."

She was standing in front of his desk, on which she had laid his morning mail.

"I'm afraid Herr Foedermayer would not approve. He will not tolerate private conversations in office hours," she said.

"But I will. And I'm the boss."

"Forgive me. I had momentarily forgotten that." It came out so naturally that he had to laugh.

"You look upon Foedermayer as your boss, don't you?" Then, without giving her time to answer, he went on, "You're probably right. I've never been the head here and never shall be."

"See here, Herr Alt: that is something I really can't understand about you," the girl began. Then she evidently thought she had once more gone too far and checked herself.

"Since you don't in any case look upon me as the boss, you mustn't speak to me as though I were the boss. What is it you don't understand about me?"

"That you get so little joy out of your work here. So much that is beautiful is produced here. So much that will give joy to an untold number of people!"

"Won't you sit down? I'll have some dictation for you later."

"Thanks," she said, and seated herself at the narrow table where she was in the habit of taking dictation.

She could not have been much over twenty. She had the face of a real Viennese girl, soft and unaffected. No makeup to be seen; her eyebrows were not plucked; her mouth was barely colored with lipstick. The maturity early in evidence in Viennese girls was obvious in her too.

"I admit it," he said. "But there are reasons for it. They lie far in the past. Allow me, as an older man, to tell you this much: the impressions you receive when you're young remain with you for life."

She had to laugh. As she did it her cheeks dimpled. "It was because you called yourself an 'older man.' Excuse me."

"How old do you take me for, Fraulein Hübner?"

"Not for an older man."

"Thanks. I hope you're more exact in other matters." Nevertheless he did not tell her his age but began to dictate to the Pleyel firm in Paris. "*Cher confrère …*" he began. Now and then he glanced at his shorthand-typist. She was leaning over her notebook and did not look up, She had lovely blonde hair.

Nonsense, he thought. I am not going to be impressed because a young girl who wants to curry favor with her boss makes friendly eyes at me. Then he dismissed the favor of the boss. That did not apply in this case. On the other hand, it was true that she had made an impression. And what had not happened for an inconceivable space of time now occurred: he began to be interested in a girl.

"Etc., etc., *veuillez agreer, monsieur, l'expressiori de mes compliments les plus sincères*—You know the rigmarole."

"Anything else?"

"No, thank you."

She stood up, ready to go.

"Have you something special to do today, Fräulein Hübner?"

"I beg your pardon?"

"I meant after office hours. Or could we have dinner somewhere together? It's nice and warm. We could sit out of doors."

She blushed fiery red. "Thank you," she said. "I'd love to." At the door she turned to ask, "When the office closes could I run home and change my clothes?"

"Be sure you make yourself beautiful!"

All day he was in a humor no one had seen him in for a long time. Mr. Foedermayer was so struck by it that he cautiously put the question to his boss, over whom he still watched as though he were his apprentice, "Good news, Hans?"

"I rather think so, Herr Foedermayer. Tell me—when do you think a man should call himself an older man?"

"At sixty-five?" suggested Foedermayer. He was over seventy himself. And then, coming back to more essential problems, "We are, of course, not going to have that exhibition of our pianos in the Mozarteum?"

"Of course we're going to have it," Hans told him decidedly. "It would be an excellent idea to have some prominent pianist playing for us every afternoon during the exhibition, don't you think?"

"It would cost a fortune and not sell a single piano," said his old mentor, rejecting the suggestion. "Fuss," was what the real head, the father of this young man, would have said.

"Horowitz will, in any case, be in Salzburg with his father-in-law. Fritz is spending the whole summer there, for his symphony is to be produced. Arthur Schnabel would be glad to do a favor for us. I shall write immediately to Rosenthal and Johanna Harris. Send Fraulein Hübner in to me."

Without a word the old man left the room, from the walls of which the portraits of the heads, the real heads of the firm, looked down disapprovingly. Immediately afterwards the girl appeared.

"It's all off for tonight?" she questioned in a tone of disappointment.

"On the contrary. Please take this: 'Dear Mrs. Harris: At the Salzburg Festival this summer there will be an exhibition of our pianos at the Mozarteum. As Mr. Harris' Third Symphony is to be on the program for August seventh I trust you will be coming over. I should like to ask you'—But why am I dictating that to you!" he interrupted himself. "Write her one of your flawless letters and invite her to play some Schubert for us on one of the afternoons. Don't forget to tell her she is an outstanding player of Schubert."

"Is she that, really?" asked the shorthand-typist.

"There is no sense in lying. Remember that."

"Advice from an older man?"

"From a man. I have done some research meanwhile."

"I shall not forget it, Herr Alt."

The incredible happened when later that afternoon Mr. Foedermayer heard Hans singing in his office. It was Schubert, to be sure, and only the ballet music from *Rosamunde*. But he was singing.

Still later Hans was waiting at the Karlskirche. From where he stood he could see the coppery patina on the cupola of the cathedral, the green roof of the Technical Institute, and in front of it the hawthorn in pink bloom, laburnum, lilacs, and the acacias in Roessel Park. The air had the mildness and fragrance of springtime in Vienna. When he suddenly saw her coming his heart chopped a beat and then began to pound so that he could scarcely speak. "My, but you have made yourself pretty!" he said after she had been standing in front of him for a while.

"I had too little time," she said deprecatingly. "But you have a new tie on, haven't you, Herr Alt?"

He was pleased that she had noticed it. "Well, where shall it be? The Prater? Kobenzl? Grinzing? Sievering?" he suggested.

She chose Grinzing, and they took a taxi. "Wouldn't the tram have done?" she asked, falling easily into the Viennese dialect which she evidently tried to suppress in her business hours. They drove past the Opera House and along the Ring. The sun was setting and lavishing its splendour on the old trees of the wide boulevard, the public parks to the right of it, on the facades of the baroque houses and monuments on either side. As far as the eye could reach were the airy outlines of the castle, the museums, the Parliament, the City Hall, and the University, all magnificent and all lovely. And above them rose the green heights of Kahlenberg and the Vienna Woods.

"Is there anything more beautiful?" he asked.

"I've never been out of Vienna. Isn't there anything more beautiful abroad?"

He did not answer.

"But you have been in Berlin and Paris and in America."

"Yes. That's why I say it."

She reflected. "Do you mind if I ask you many questions? I know so frightfully little."

She had blushed. One must be on one's guard with her, he thought. "You went through four years of the Realschule; that much I know from your record. What did you do after that? I, too, like to ask questions."

"Are you interested in that? I have not much to tell." Nevertheless, she told it as they were sitting in the garden of a small Grinzing inn where new wine was served. Actually it was a courtyard with a few linden trees, a few bare tables and benches. On the tables there were lighted candles in globes. On the benches couples were sitting. On a wooden platform, at a table lighted by two candles in globes, two men fiddled and another played a mouth-organ. Above this courtyard one could see the houses of the ascending village, which used to be the independent community of Grinzing and later had been incorporated in Vienna. Simple, yellow, friendly houses on the gently rising slope of the vineyards leading to wooded Kobenzl, with a parish church between and vineyard hills beyond.

She told him about her girlhood, which was that of a poor Viennese girl. Her father had been in the World War, then an official in a bank, then 'let out,' and unemployed. Her mother did typing for a Government office. There were three children; she was the eldest. How old did he think she was? she asked him. "Twenty?" he ventured.

That made her proud. She was only nineteen.

"How often in love?" he asked.

"Twice. You said there was no sense in lying."

"Was it wonderful?"

She nodded. "But nothing came of it."

He asked why.

She shrugged her shoulders. "Probably because they didn't care enough." The fried chicken with cucumber salad which he had ordered was brought, and she ate it with relish. The new wine came in a bulging, open carafe and was placed on the table before her. After drinking it and trying some of it on her tongue she said, "This is an old one!"

"You are a connoisseur!"

She took that seriously. "In local wines I'm an expert. And in French and English correspondence. And in nothing else."

"And in giving pleasure."

She laid her hand shyly on his. "*Prosit*, Herr Alt!"

"*Prosit*, Fräulein Hübner!"

The musicians had returned from an intermission. Now they began to play: "*Ich möcht' wieder einmal in Grinzing sein ...*"

"*Beside a glass of wine*," she joined in the refrain of the popular song. "Lovely here, isn't it, Herr Alt?"

He nodded.

"Now I have told you about myself. Suppose you tell me about yourself. Will you?"

"There's nothing to tell."

"Oh, yes, there is. Why are you so unhappy?"

The wine made the question easy and the answer not hard. "I have had little happiness in my life. I have never accomplished much in life either," he said.

"Do you know what I wish?" asked the girl, moving closer to him, almost as close as the other girls who were sitting with the men they loved. "I wish you were happy. I'm a bit tipsy now, so I dare say it. But if you think I shouldn't say it I'd better not."

"Go on and say it!"

"I liked you from the first moment. I even think I understood you. I am uneducated, but I understand people well."

He drew her to him.

"You I understand," she said. Then she was silent and clung to him. After a while she looked up at him and asked, "There are lots of things you can't stand, aren't there?"

"For example?"

"Injustice, for example."

"Who told you that?"

"Do you know that you have a great friend in one of our workmen?"

"Czerny?"

"Bochner. I am not even sure you know him."

He recalled Bochner, the metal-caster. He was the man who shot at a police lieutenant. "I have known him twenty-five years. Or even longer than that."

"You haven't changed since then. You undoubtedly looked just the same as a boy!"

"It's good to have you here, Fräulein Hübner."

"Please say that again!"

He repeated it.

Arm in arm they sat there. The musicians at the table with the candles played other songs. The sky was full of stars. From all sides, from the inn gardens on the right and on the left, from the courtyards above and below, the whole length of the gentle slopes, came the sound of foolish little songs. They sang of happiness. The linden trees in the courtyards shielded the couples sitting under them from other eyes and from the present.

When it was time to go she wanted to walk a little way up the hill before they took a taxi at the foot of it. It was so beautiful to climb arm in arm, aimless beneath the stars, and listening to the foolish little songs. Suddenly he stood still. Then he changed their direction.

"Are we lost?"

"No," he said. His voice had changed, and when she could see his face that too had changed.

In the dark they came to a high gateway. He let go of her arm. She did not know where they were.

"Please wait here for me," he requested in his altered voice.

He went through the gateway alone. By the light of the stars he could distinguish the name and the flowers on the graves of the dead in the Grinzing cemetery. Lying amid the vineyards, the Grinzing cemetery sloped uphill to the Vienna Woods.

He stopped before a white marble slab. A name was inscribed on it in letters of gold. Lower down in one corner were the words: "You live—until I die." The stars lighted up the letters. He stood before it and was ashamed.

In the main square they took a taxi back to town.

"Forgive me," she said as they drove along.

"It was just that you had a wrong idea of me, Fräulein Hübner," he answered. "I'm like all the rest. Just as selfish. Grief is selfishness."

"Can't you get over her death?" she asked after a long interval of silence.

He answered softly, as though he were begging both the living and the dead woman for forgiveness, "No. Death ends nothing."

CHAPTER 47
Everyman

Where did the cry come from? First it sounded near by and earthly: "Everyman!"—then farther away, but still earthly: "Everyman!" And finally from a distance and no longer as if it were a human voice. Yet ever from the same direction, from above the Salzburg Cathedral Square. Did it come from the cathedral? Or from the fortress Hohen-Salzburg, which towered in proud and jagged lines against the reddening evening sky? Then all at once, while the mortal Everyman, the main character of the play, sank to his knees on the high wooden stage built in front of the cathedral, and implored God for help in his desperate distress, the cry came from every side. From the terrace of the palace, from the fortress, from Capuzinerberg, from Mönchsberg; high, near, far, everywhere, with its terrifying warning: "Everyman!"

It sounded like the call to Judgment Day, and the bells pealed in reply. The bells of the cathedral, of St. Francis, of St. Peter. Henriette, who was seeing the play for the first time, was frightened. Would the clangour of bells pursue her everywhere? She had fled from the haunted house, for Hans had insisted that she spend the summer here with her daughter Franziska and enjoy the Festival, with which two members of the family were connected: Fritz, whose symphony was being given, and Hans, who had organized an exhibition of Alt pianos.

"Everyman! Everyman! E—very—man!" Mournfully, accusingly. And the bells which called back memories and remorse.

The longer the stirring cries continued, the greater the uneasiness which began to spread among the spectators in the Cathedral Square, formed by the cathedral itself and the palace of the Prince Archbishop. The priest in the front row, who wore the violet biretta of a cardinal, looked smilingly round and then whispered to his neighbor, a man in the dark gray peasant costume of Salzburg. The priest was the Prince-Archbishop of Salzburg. In the years since the morality play of *Everyman* had been given here, he had never missed a performance, despite the bitter accusations levelled against him of sacrilege as well as for having allowed the Salzburg Cathedral to serve the wicked purposes of a mundane play. His neighbor was the Chancellor of Austria.

It is only a worldly sound, was the indication of the expert's smile.

But with the appearance of faith, embodied in the actress

Helene Thimig, coming from the cathedral doors and floating down to the despairing Everyman by means of steps invisible from below, the sense of the otherworldliness of the action deepened. The floating movement, the averted, pregnant look, the attitude of one fleeing the world as she drew her sky-blue veil protectingly close around her—all was unearthly. Nevertheless, and perhaps even because of it, she gave the impression of infinite protection. The weird cries ceased; the sun went down; the pigeons, returning to their nests in the crannies of the cathedral, fluttered overhead as though, like messengers from above, they were taking part in the play. And Everyman, at last aware of his lifelong sins, sank to his knees to say the Lord's Prayer, which he had forgotten how to speak.

Then came a shrill cry.

At first it was barely perceptible, then one could distinguish two words. They came from the Residence Square, bordering on the Cathedral Square into which one could see through a flying-buttress archway.

Yet no one could see the man crying, "Heil Hitler!"

On the stage Everyman was fervently reciting his prayer. As he said, "Hallowed be Thy name," there resounded: "Heil Hitler!"

"Thy kingdom come …"

"Heil Hitler!"

"Thy will be done …"

"Heil Hitler!"

When the prayer came to an end: "… but deliver us from evil …" like the whistling of bullets came the words, "Hitler! Hitler! Hitler!"

The cardinal in the first row had risen to his feet. His fine old face was glowing with anger.

But the play went on, with the angels appearing from the cathedral, and it ended in harmony with the powerfully resonant organ.

"What were they yelling?" inquired an elderly lady of another elderly lady. For the challenging cry had not been indicated in the French text of the play from which she had scarcely raised her eyes during the whole performance. The lady of whom the inquiry had been made answered in French that she supposed it was one of Monsieur Reinhardt's production tricks. Nor did she recognize the name that was shouted.

After the performance Hans waited for his mother by the stone archway.

"To think that such things are allowed!" Henriette said.

"They will not be allowed for long, *gnädige Frau*" put in the gentleman in the Salzburg costume, who was on the point of entering his car.

"It's about time!" exclaimed Henriette, and noticed too late that she was speaking to the Chancellor. Moreover, the fact that he was the successor of Dollfuss upset her so that she did not say another word all the way home.

Later that evening she sat in the hall of the famous Hotel d'Europe and drank a cocktail to change the current of her thoughts. During the summer Number 10 was being renovated, freshly painted, and provided with a heating system which it had needed for generations, Henriette had laid all this down as counter-conditions to the relatives, who had insisted on observing the literal interpretation of that absurd will. Yet all this renovation would not drive away the spirit of the house. Henriette did not dare to say: the ghosts.

She sat ensconced in a deep, comfortable chair covered in a gaily flowered chintz, a sample of which she had in mind to get from the manager before she left: she wanted to use it on the fourth floor. Slowly she sipped the enlivening drink. All she had needed was the advice of her freckled son-in-law Dr. Baier! No coffee, no alcohol, no cigarettes! As often as possible she slipped away to the hotel. In the morning a cup of coffee; that made you feel fresh and gave you a sense of curiosity about the day. Before dinner a cocktail; that drove away fatigue and gave you an interest in the evening. And cigarettes were good for your health at any hour. What do doctors know!

"How about another cocktail?" asked Martha Monica.

"Excellent idea," agreed Henriette, but did not order one. "Is my face flushed?"

"You look wonderful! Like the Empress!" answered Martha Monica, who meanwhile had become Baroness Waldstetten and had come over from nearby St. Gilgen, where she was spending the summer, to see *Everyman*.

An entirely superfluous remark, and too loud as well, thought Henriette. "How are you these days?" she asked, leaning back in her bright-colored armchair.

She learned that Mono was in splendid health. If her eye did not deceive her a baby was on the way. "Are you happy?" she asked her beautiful daughter once more.

"Blissfully," replied Martha Monica. From a distance, like a minuet, came the sound of the baroque chimes in the Residence Square. At any rate, those were bells which one could enjoy.

Henriette wished that Hans had had something of Mono's temperament. Of course it was fine of him to be so exclusively absorbed in serious and important things, and in the course of time he had become something of a politician. Like Father Stein, she thought. In any case, the Chancellor seemed to think well of him, didn't he? But unfortunately he was another man who did not know how to live his life. He too had lost his wife and mourned her exactly as Hans did. No one could convince Henriette that the whole trouble with Hans was anything but this abnormal mourning! She too mourned her dead, only God knew how deeply. But what was it that that woman had said to her in St. Augustine's? "It hurts the dead for you to cry." It was so wrong to live in the shadow of the dead and to live their life instead of your own; your own life is much too short for that, even if you live to be a hundred, which is to be hoped.

She got Martha Monica to tell her who the people were who came and went, filling the hotel hall with all the languages of the world. Did she know who that ancient lady in black was? Of course she knew her; that was the daughter of Meyerbeer. The gentleman with the silk-lined cape was Sacha Guitry. Did Americans always go in bunches and make so much noise over their cocktails?

"It's just that they are jolly," Martha Monica said.

Then they were right, Henriette decided, and was on the point of saying so. But she did not say it. Looking at the flowery material, which pleased her so, and at the jolly people who seemed to her to be so right, she recalled something which had made an impression on her that afternoon during the performance, and which had been driven out of her mind by the shouts from the Residence Square. It was the Lord's question to Everyman: "What have you accomplished and done down here?" She had felt that had the question been put to her she would have had to make the same reply as Everyman: "Nothing, Lord. Or at least so little." What had she accomplished or done? How could she give advice to Hans on how to live his own life? To him it consisted of being concerned with the life of others, not of some four or five people. With many, with all. Was that the right way? She had sat all her life in armchairs like these. They had scarcely ever had such a jolly look to them, but they were upholstered, comfortable armchairs. When you sat in one you acquired a sense of importance to yourself. So did four or five other people. That was all.

Henriette recognized the Chancellor quickly enough this time, as he passed by, to say, "Forgive me, Excellency, for not having recognized you earlier today."

He answered, "Of course, Frau Alt. In any case, I knew who you were. Your son had pointed you out to me."

"Hans is an admirer of yours," Henriette said. Under other circumstances she would not have said that to this man who did not know how to live his life.

"I have a high regard for your son," was Dr. Schuschnigg's rejoinder. Henriette had the impression that, like Hans, he too was struggling with shyness. He took his leave of the two ladies and left the lobby. Two men who had been standing behind him followed him out.

"To the Archbishop's residence!" one of them was heard to say.

"That's the life for you!" someone behind Henriette said with envy. She turned round and remarked in a loud tone to Martha Monica, "He makes the impression of a human being who knows what one should live for."

"Yes," said Martha Monica, without knowing what was in her mother's mind.

From the windows of the main hall of the Prince-Archbishop's palace, which the man just discussed was shortly to enter, one could see the baroque courtyard illuminated with the red glare of torches; a serenade was in progress there. Inside, round an oval table, sat six persons awaiting him. The Archbishop, the Governor of Salzburg, the president of the Festival, Peter Alt, chief of division in the Ministry of Education, Max Reinhardt, the director of the Festival plays, and the piano-maker Hans Alt. Peter had brought his cousin with him. The agenda of the day was: Promotion for the Salzburg Festival.

No one paid any attention to the agenda. The cries on the Cathedral Square were still resounding in all their ears. Some of them considered that it would be necessary to triple the police guard.

"It's incomprehensible to me how anyone can take a ridiculous person so seriously!" said Peter.

"You think so?" asked the Chancellor, and turned to the chief of division.

"Would Your Eminence and the Chancellor allow me to speak freely what has been in my mind a long time? I find it's absolutely wrong to waste our strength on taking Hitler seriously. May I state my reasons?"

The cardinal smiled in anticipation of a welcome diversion. "You may speak," the Chancellor said.

"Our federated state," Peter explained, "does not recognize its enemies. I don't say that Hitler isn't a mortal enemy. But he's a ridiculous enemy, and we should take advantage of that fact. If we strip the man of the mysticism that surrounds him—what remains? A ridiculous person. He looks ridiculous; his teeth are false; his martial gait is false; his martial speech is false. He chose a style of moustache without knowing it was that of a Jewish comedian, He shies away from every foreign word, and if he ever uses one he mispronounces it. He says '*status ko,*' and to this day is incapable of pronouncing the name of me very party he himself founded. His suits bag as though he had hired them from a secondhand dealer. When he receives diplomats he waits to see what they do and then imitates them. When he eats in society he looks to see how the others eat and copies them. All that is ridiculous or at least pitiful.

"At the same time he is an example of a person who knows precisely how ridiculous he is, and he is more surprised than the rest of the world at being taken seriously.

"When this man started out he was the most cowardly creature there was. Therefore he made no bones of doing in public the most cowardly thing a man can possibly do: during the Munich Putsch, when the police fired, he held children in front of himself in order not to be wounded. In the World War, in the course of those four years, all he achieved was the rank of corporal.

"This most ridiculous and cowardly of men, by being taken seriously, was encouraged to become significant and martial. Since he is a hysterical neurasthenic and gambler, this was possible. For both reasons he thrives on extremes and takes extreme risks. With the mentality of a beer-hall politician, he evolves his attitude towards the world not from knowledge but from private revenge. Because a Jew treated him ironically at an Academy examination he hates the Jews. Because Trotsky said of him, 'No Bolshevik would trust him to shine his shoes,' he is against Bolshevism.

"This primitive man hit upon the primitive idea that immediately after a four-year war no one would be willing to make war again and would do anything rather than that. As a gambler he staked all or nothing on that idea, and he had the luck to break the bank; people took his bluff seriously. When he set fire to the Reichstag building in Berlin the world, instead of unanimously saying, 'Hitler burned it,' talked about and printed 'The Case of the Reichstag Fire'; when we accepted the vote he blackmailed in the Saar as a bona fide plebiscite, instead of blackmail, something happened which never before occurred in history: a zero, who knew that he was one, an Everyman—to quote our Festival play—or even a sub-Everyman, promoted himself to a billion. And the astronomical figures grew, the more seriously he was taken.

"I have heard this man speak in Munich. He gives the impression of a clown. But instead of giving him the only answer he deserves—to laugh him loudly out of court and prick the bubble of his inflatedness, thereby reducing it to the nonentity it is—we systematically enlarge it and call out the police to combat it. I ask the indulgence of you gentlemen if I have trespassed on your patience."

"It was very interesting," remarked the Chancellor, who was sitting where he could look across to the Berchtesgaden mountains. "I regret only that I can't agree with you. In the first place, I wouldn't call a man a coward who was awarded the Iron Cross, First Class. Besides, even if it is a clown who sets fire to the world, I don't think that laughter is the right reaction. Scorn is wrong in any case. As for Hitler, he may be setting the world on fire, or at least may want to do so, but he is less of a clown than I am. All of us here—for we are, after all, Austrians—honor religion, education, culture. Yet the lack of it, in my estimation, is not a cause for ridicule but at most for pity. And our own Metternich has told us that a person who thinks himself a Napoleon, without being one, can be more dangerous than Napoleon. Megalomania, whatever its derivation, should be dealt with by strait jackets and insane asylums. As long as madmen are unconfined we must protect ourselves against them as best we may."

Whereupon they went back to the agenda. Various participants, including Hans, made proposals which were accepted: a competition for symphonic compositions, followed by the world premiere of the prize-winning work at the next festival, in the summer of 1938; guest performances of the Paris Opera and the New York Metropolitan Opera in exchange for the Salzburg production of Mozart's *Così Fan Tutte.*

When the Chancellor left the archbishop's palace Hans walked down the stairs with him.

"I was so pleased to meet your mother," the Chancellor said.

"She's a wonderful woman," said the son. "I'm beginning to see that she's been underestimated in our family."

The other man nodded. "That's Austrian. Your cousin is right in one respect. We do the opposite from the Nazis. We make a business of underestimating ourselves. But perhaps we're obliged to do it when we are at home here and see constantly before our eyes the standards of real greatness." He looked up to the Untersberg rising in the moonlight like a silver block out of the dark green surface of the night.

They fell into a conversation which continued as they walked along the Salzach quay. "You too are a widower?" said the Chancellor, and stood still. The two men following him also stopped.

Hans nodded.

"We understand each other," said the Chancellor, and walked on. "I should like to have a talk with you, unofficially and without the shadow I cast." As he said it he looked back at the two men behind him. "You're a good Austrian, Herr Alt."

"That is perhaps all I am, Herr Bundeskanzler," was Hans's answer.

"That is not a small thing. But I know how little it is appreciated. I shall look forward to seeing you again!"

In the night Hans was awakened in his hotel room by the conversation of a couple who, returning late and being under the influence of alcohol, did not care whether others slept. Apparently they had been at the Festival play that afternoon and were attempting to imitate the disturbing shouts. They seemed to have found them extraordinarily comic, for they could scarcely go on, they were laughing so. They kept mixing up their cues and argued (in a Prussian dialect) as to whether the "Heil Hider" came after "Thy kingdom come" or not until after "Thy will be done."

As he could not go to sleep again, Hans did what he had done so often before when he was trying to get at the meaning of things. He stood at the open window and let the night air cool his brow. Over there, beyond the Staats-Bridge, was Mozart's birthplace. One could see the house and the golden letters which proclaimed it. Beyond the frontier half an hour away, lived Hitler. One could see the constant searchlight coming from his house as it pierced the sky ...

Thanks for your friendly letter [Hans wrote later that same night on a postcard of Mozart's birthplace]. Our exhibition has been a great success. The pianists whom I, or rather you, invited all came. Salzburg is now crammed with enthusiastic foreigners horn all over the world. For next summer they are going to construct a new Festival building in the park of Schloss Mirabell. One sees what an attraction Austria can have when it remembers Mozart. Cordial greetings and good wishes.

Yours,
HANS ALT

As he was addressing it he realized he did not know Fraulein Hübner's first name. He had to look it up in her letter. Mitzi.

Then he read, until it grew light, in Hofmannsthal's posthumous writings. One passage moved him almost to tears:

Every one sees himself in the figure of Everyman. The foreigners, who come to see the old play revived, the English, the French, the Americans, the Germans. Perhaps they do not believe their hour has struck, but they sense that it will strike and they see themselves in a mirror. Only we Austrians do not see ourselves. Why is that so? Is it because we are so pious we have no further reason for remorse? Or are we still like that old ditty singer of the time of the plague, good old Augustine, the most Austrian of all figures and the incarnation of divine cheerfulness, who staggered drunkenly into a pestilential grave, slept off his stupor there, and awoke next day unharmed, to continue uninterrupted his song from the depths of the plague-infested tomb? Or are we more akin to that neglected, poor stonecutter in Anzengruber's play to whom nothing could ever happen and who is just as much of an Austrian character? Happy the people to whom the omens do not speak …

CHAPTER 48
Invitation from a Friend

Hans was in the small group of people waiting for the Austrian Chancellor early in the morning of February 14 at the West Station in Vienna. The man who stepped from the train was not the same who had driven away two nights before. He held his hand out to those standing there as though he did not see them, greeted the guard of honor drawn up before the station with a listless "Long live Austria," and drove with his two escorts to his apartment in a small building, formerly the head clerk's residence at Belvedere Castle. It was Sunday. Although he regularly went to mass every morning at seven, he missed it today. Nor did that seem to concern him.

All this time he had been holding a leather briefcase tightly under his arm. Now he laid it on his desk, opened it, and said in his even voice, reminiscent of Monsignor Seipel's speech, but underneath which there was a feeling of intense excitement, "Before I go to the president to make my report I should like to reconstruct the notes I made on my return journey, of hay conversation of yesterday at Obersalzberg. Will you be good enough, Guido, to take it down? And you, Hans, will see that it is put in final form. I don't care to take anyone else into my confidence."

The leader of the Fatherland Front, Guido Zernatto, prepared to take dictation. Hans nodded his agreement. For many months he had been a constant evening guest in this long, narrow, red-and-white room, as soon as the man who lived there had his day's work behind him and was free to talk. These conversations had usually begun with music and nearly always ended with Austria. The two men had come to have the deepest confidence in one another. The Chancellor was glad to be able to talk frankly with someone who possessed a mind of his own but who had neither an official position nor ambition and therefore was completely above suspicion when he used him to get information or convey it. Hans, on the other hand, found that this man whom he visited in the late evenings was one of the most sincere men he knew. He had never met anyone who loved Austria more passionately and selflessly.

"On February the ninth the German Minister von Papen called on me," he began his dictation, not looking at anything except his papers, and smoking cigarettes at intervals. "I must state in the beginning that on February the fourth the Supreme German Army Command was changed and the Generals Fritsch and Blomberg, who had given their pledge to our Chief of General Staff Jansa to respect Austrian independence, were removed. On February the sixth von Papen saw Hitler in Berlin, of which fact I was aware. When Papen called on me on the ninth he declared that he had splendid news for me, which would, by a single stroke of the pen, remove all the outstanding difficulties between Austria and Germany. The Chancellor of the German Reich had invited me to visit him at the Obersalzberg near Berchtesgaden.

"When I inquired as to the nature of the stroke of a pen Papen explained that the stroke of a pen was merely a metaphor and not to be taken literally. As far as Hitler was concerned, his sole intention was to have a friendly talk with me. He himself knew no further particulars, but he had been entrusted to deliver to me the invitation of a friend. I replied that I was well satisfied to hear of this sudden change of attitude but that, as he would easily understand, I desired to be acquainted with the subjects that would come under discussion during our conversation; up to the present the attitude of the German Chancellor towards Austria and myself had in any case not aroused an impression of friendship. Von Papen countered with the question of whether I insisted on being informed in advance of the subject of negotiation, which in his private opinion could not be anything but a treaty of friendship with Austria. I said that I did, and he promised to obtain further information.

"That very afternoon he returned with the statement that he had spoken to Hitler on the telephone and was authorized to say: 'Tell Schuschnigg I am waiting for him with outstretched hands. He cannot possibly refuse the hand of a friend!' I replied evasively and addressed myself through the Italian Minister Salata to Mussolini, who, in the Pact of Rome, guaranteed our independence and that of Hungary. Minister Salata that same evening said that he had communicated with Mussolini and Ciano and that Mussolini had declared: 'Schuschnigg is enough of a statesman to know what he must do.' Count Ciano, the Italian Foreign Minister, had said, 'By all means accept the invitation.'

"After I had reported to the President and the Cabinet and the decision had been reached that we could not turn down an offer from Germany to settle our far-reaching differences by peaceful means, I informed von Papen that I accepted the invitation and left on the night of the twelfth for Berchtesgaden. Accompanying me were our Foreign Minister Guido Schmidt; my personal adjutant, Major Bartl; my secretary, von Fröhlichsthal; six detectives; and a personal bodyguard of six men."

He interrupted his dictation to say, without looking up, "That was your wish, Guido!"

"At Freilassing on the frontier," the Chancellor went on, "three gentlemen from the Gestapo, in civilian dress, entered my compartment. They identified themselves as Chief Commissar Dittrich, Chief Commissar Holz, and Commissar Fischer, and produced a typewritten order according to which I was to cross the frontier accompanied only by Minister Schmidt and Major Bartl. All the other Austrian functionaries were obliged to remain behind in Austria.

"I declared that this was not in accordance with international law with respect to the representatives of a sovereign state. The gentlemen expressed regret and said that was their order. When I inquired who had signed the order, since the signature on the bottom of the typewritten slip was illegible, the only answer was that no information could be given on that score.

"Under those circumstances I refused to continue my journey and went out into the corridor for the purpose of leaving the train. But at this moment the train was already moving and I saw my escort, except for Minister Schmidt and Major Bartl, left behind on the platform. They were taken off the train while I was talking to the Gestapo men. Immediately after the train left the border station a captain of S.S. by the name of Spitze introduced himself as a 'guard of honor' sent by Hitler and prevented me from executing my intention of pulling the emergency signal cord. Later I discovered that this Spitze was an Austrian who had been banned from Austria by Chancellor Seipel for his Nazi propaganda and had been commissioned as a captain by the Nazis.

"From Berchtesgaden I was taken in a closed car to Obersalzberg. In the car Herr Spitze sat beside me. I wished to open the window, but Herr Spitze prevented me from doing so with the words that it would be against his orders. It was five minutes past nine when we entered Hitler's house.

"Herr Spitze announced me at once, but it was at least twenty minutes before I could go in. During those twenty minutes I waited in an antechamber filled with officers. I recall that it was nine-thirty by the clock on Hitler's desk when I stood before him. He did not rise to greet me, but remained seated at his desk, and yelled at me vehemently as I entered, 'It's a filthy mess you have in Austria!'

"'Good morning, Herr Reichskanzler,' was my greeting to him.

"Without returning it, giving me his hand, or offering me a

chair, he jumped up and paced around the room while I remained standing near his desk.

"'Of all the unheard-of baseness! An infamous breach of trust and faith such as history has never known! Pure Austrian ways!' he said in an ever louder voice as he paced round the room. 'That is something you have on your conscience! You and no one else! But let me tell you that from today it is going to stop! Even my patience has a limit! I will not tolerate it any longer! Do you understand? I will not tolerate it!' This last he screamed.

"I was literally speechless in the face of such treatment. As I learned later, Hitler's outbreak of anger was due to the arrest of the Viennese Nazi propagandist, Captain Leopold, which I had ordered in the latter part of January.

"'Are you dumb?' Hitler stormed at me. 'You can open your mouth all right if it's a case of slandering or when you make your Catholic genuflections before the heads of the so-called democracies. You're in the wrong pew now! I am no incense swinger and no weakling like the French and English gentlemen. With me it's a case of looking facts in the face!' He rushed back to his desk and handed me the memorandum attached to these notes.

"'Herr Reichskanzler,' I said, 'I had not believed such treatment possible. There is now standing before you not a person who chances to bear the name of Schuschnigg but the representative of a sovereign state. Even if you believe that you are not called upon to respect a man of my name I do demand that respect from you for Austria, where you were born!' After a fleeting glance at his list of demands, and realizing what was at stake, I decided not to give him any occasion for further outbreaks.

"'You could have sat down by yourself,' was his rejoinder. 'I am a man of the people. I don't bother about ceremony. But I save my people. You stick to ceremony and let your people go under!' He had seated himself at his desk and telephoned the order to have von Papen and Minister Schmidt sent in.

"In their presence we discussed the memorandum with the demands point by point, against point 5 of which, containing the principal demand—the naming of Dr. Seyss-Inquart to the Ministry of the Interior—I remonstrated especially, because this would have delivered the Austrian police into the hands of the Nazis. My actual words to Hitler were, 'Herr Reichskanzler, with the nomination of Seyss-Inquart you are asking for something which actually runs counter to conditions in Austria. Austria has, at most, twenty-seven to twenty-nine percent, of National Socialists. The turning over of the portfolios of the Interior, War, Justice, and Education to the National Socialists, as you require in your memorandum, would be in gross disproportion to the actual distribution of parties—that is to say, the will of the people, which you on many occasions have indicated as the basis for your own Government.'

"'One moment!' Hitler interrupted, and again by telephone gave an order to have a general sent for, who, when he came, was introduced to me as von Reichenau.

"'How long would you need to occupy Austria, General von Reichenau?' he asked him.

"'Twelve days if we were held up, otherwise three, my Führer!' the general replied with a laugh.

"And Hitler laughed too, for the first time. 'You see, Herr Schuschnigg,' he said, 'those are the actual proportions.'

"Up to this moment I had firmly suppressed the thought that Austria might be attacked by a German army. In the World War I had fought beside the Germans and formed an opinion of the spirit of the German Army. I had believed that an ally's army cannot fall on an ally—and still believe it. There is one card in the game which is being played against us. I admit it is a trump card but neither is Hitler in a position to play it. The honor of the German Army could not submit to the shame of attacking an unarmed ally, not even if its supreme command has been changed. Under Blomberg and Fritsch not even the threat of such a thing would have been possible. On that belief I based my refusal which I justified point by point.

"The negotiations were interrupted by a brief midday meal, the only meal which was offered me during my stay of eleven hours. My seat was between General von Reichenau and the chief of the German General Staff, von Keitel. Opposite me sat two other generals and a colonel, whose names have slipped my memory. During the meal there was talk of nothing except the armed invasion of Austria. 'And what do you think about it?' Hitler asked one general after another. Sometimes he added, 'Did you hear that, Herr Schuschnigg?'

"After luncheon I lighted one of my own cigarettes, as I need to smoke to help concentrate my thoughts. Hitler stopped me with the words, 'No one is allowed to smoke in my presence! 'If you want to smoke go outside!'

"In the course of the afternoon he modified his manner noticeably. He said, 'I know you too are temperamental. You will not hold my outbreak of temperament of this morning against me?' I assured him I should not.

"When we separated towards nine o'clock in the evening we had not made any actual progress whatsoever. I had positively declared that under the Constitution I was not authorized to make the required agreements, because they lay in the jurisdiction of the President. I promised to report to the constitutional authorities and meanwhile to take the memorandum with me for purposes of reference. As I went to put it in my pocket Hitler attempted to prevent me from so doing; it was only due to the interference of General von Keitel that I was able to keep the document.

"Herr von Papen was present at both parts of the discussion. Minister Schmidt was present only in the morning."

When the speaker, still in an even voice struggling for self-control, had finished his dictation, the State Secretary, Zernatto, said, "You should never have gone! One doesn't trust people like Papen!"

"Yes," agreed the man who showed the bitter insults he had suffered, "it was a mistake. But, so help me God, I shall make up for it! Hitler's argument is that the will of the people is decisive. Very well! I shall let the will of our people decide! We shall hold a plebiscite on whether the Austrian people want Hitler or Austria. At least seventy percent will be against Hitler. In that way he will be downed with his own weapon!"

Zernatto was silent. Hans would have liked to say something encouraging. He was so infinitely sorry for this gray, tired man. The trust which he placed in him was as boundless as his trust in human decency. Not by a single syllable or thought had he ever made him feel that he was Hermann's brother. Anyone else in his stead would not have allowed him to come near him. He not only had him around but allowed him to come humanly close to him. But when Hans now saw his questioning look resting on him, all he could answer was, "A plebiscite without the working men is impossible!" This was a point on which they had tried to agree an untold number of times before. Hans had explained again and again that Austria was suffering more from February 1934, when the workers' resistance to Dollfuss was broken by murderous force, than from St. Germain. Now he said it again.

"Shots were fired on both sides," declared Zernatto. "The Government and the workers lost an almost equal number of dead and wounded. You forget that. And you forget too that shots were fired only because the workers were about to cut off our light, our current, and our water."

"Then we should have just gone for two or four days without light and water," said Hans. "You cannot fire on workers!" he repeated, desperate that he had to say so obvious a thing again and again and that no one wanted to listen.

The Chancellor had locked up his papers in his leather briefcase. He went up to Hans. "I have a request to make of you," he said. "I know you're friendly with Ebeseder. Help me to make peace with the Austrian workers. Will you do that? As far as I'm concerned, I honestly wish it."

"I'd like nothing better!" Hans answered with passion. "Now Austria is saved!"

The State Secretary shrugged his shoulders. "Saving Austria has been the order of the day since the Turkish wars! Come along, you optimist. I shall dictate to you the saving plan of our friend Hitler."

CHAPTER 49
The Masks Fall

Hans had hade an appointment to meet his mother in the Three Hussars restaurant in Weihburggasse. As often as he could he gave her the pleasure of being 'taken out.' She was so pleased to be rid of housekeeping cares. But he was late again on this evening, as on nearly every evening since he had begun roaming about town.

Henriette was at first inclined to suspect a woman. She was concerned about the boy, as she still called her forty-seven-year-old son. The dark shadow which he had piled up between them had long since vanished, and all her love come back. Only a woman could bring him help, yet she, his mother, felt herself incapable of it. What had she still to offer him except tenderness and the bit of experience she had gleaned from life? But on closer observation it did not look to her as though Hans's absences were connected with a woman. When he went out he wore his oldest clothes. When he telephoned it was to that man Ebeseder whom he seemed to be in really unbroken communication with day and night. Always politics. Even in her father she had never been able to understand it. Yet in Professor Stein's day Austria had been a Great Power, whereas now …? God save us!

Waiting for her son, she was seated at a table on the raised platform in the restaurant then favored by Vienna Society. When Hans was over an hour late she began to be uneasy.

At the next table sat the von Kageneck couple from Brünn. Had they not seen Henriette? So much the better! Otherwise they would be smothering her with attentions. The wife was so expansive, one could never extricate oneself from her flattery. Opposite sat the Italian Minister with his flirtatious daughter. Henriette waved to the daughter. She wore an incredible hat! A large velvet pansy plastered at an angle on her head was literally all there was to it. Was this the Paris style in spring hats?

The young Italian returned her greeting. Now she would probably call out through the whole place, "*Buona sera, Mammina!*" which annoyed Henriette so. The older she grew the less she enjoyed public show. But the Italian said nothing.

Captain Kunsti of the Ravag broadcasting station came in. He too was an admirer of hers. The nicest people came here. After that evening of chamber music at Peter's he had presented her with a record from the Ravag record files of Selma's "I will deliver you from fear" speech. He had thought this would greatly please her, for of course he could not know how things really stood. Anyhow, the letter he sent with it was one of the most charming Henriette had ever received: "To the best dancer of Viennese waltzes; to the most enchanting young Viennese lady!" It was no empty dream—Austrians did have charm! "Good evening, Captain," Henriette said to the delightful man. But he was talking to someone else and did not hear her.

The meat was inexcusably tough. Henriette told the waiter so, as considerately as she knew how. This otherwise so attentive person, however, cast a critical look at her.

"There's nothing wrong with that filet," he remarked, and disappeared.

All right. Perhaps she just had no appetite. It was inconceivable what could be keeping Hans. And who would thank him for what he was doing? He worked day and night, hardly slept any more. The Chancellor (the latest gossip said he was interested in a beautiful woman) would not thank him. If a woman was absorbing the interest of the man there would be little left over for others.

She did not know the people who were talking in such monotonous voices behind her. What was it they were saying? Poor dear Papa had so often been annoyed with her when she did not know big words. I see. A plebiscite meant a popular vote. What was to be voted on? She listened with half an ear and learned that on the following Sunday all Austrians were to vote on whether they wished an independent Austria or a union with Germany. Why should one have to vote on anything as obvious as that? Could it be that anyone here wanted to have things as they were in Germany? Over there they apparently had to ask for permission for every breath they drew!

"What do you say to the poll?" she inquired of the writer Vogl, who was also sitting on the raised platform in the restaurant. People said he wrote interesting books. She, unfortunately, had no longer the leisure to ascertain this for herself. She had begun to reread all her old favorites: *Madame Bovary*, Schnitzer's *Therese*, Tolstoy's *War and Peace*. But naturally one could not say that sort of thing to a modern writer. And they say women are vain. No one is so vain as a writer. When you spoke to them you had to put in at once, "Your last book was another magnificent achievement." It was lucky that they did not question you further. Vogl replied, "We shall have to await the results."

The Rothschilds came in. She hadn't changed much—

Clarice; still very attractive. Now all heads would be turning and every one would be tumbling over themselves to bow to them, showing off how intimate they were with the Rothschilds. Baron Rothschild bowed and she returned his greeting with a smile.

What were the Kagenecks of Brünn discussing in such an absorbed way? Usually they hardly said a word to each other. "How are you?" Henriette called over to the adjoining table. Her nervousness over Hans had reached a degree where she could not eat anything.

"Thanks, very well," was the Moravian gentleman's brief response.

"You're a newspaperman. What do you say to the election on Sunday?"

"According to my opinion, we shall have to see what the Führer's attitude towards it will be," declared the gentleman from Briinn. "In any case, we're not concerned. We're Sudeten Germans."

Henriette regretted her question. Of course they were not voting. Besides, people from a small city like Brünn used not to like to admit they came from such a place. Was it suddenly the fashion to come from there?

"As good old Edi says quite rightly," joined in the wife of the sugar refiner and publisher, speaking in a voice that carried beyond Henriette's table, "it's up to Berlin. I really can't see that this plebiscite is a stroke of genius on the part of Dr. Schuschnigg."

Was Henriette mistaken, or weren't these two only recently raving about Schuschnigg?

"Quite of your opinion, Baroness Maud!" cried Captain Kunsti over Henriette's head. "I subscribe to every word."

And Vogl, who had published that morning a leading article in the Catholic *Reichspost* entitled "All Austrians behind Schuschnigg," said, "Count me in absolutely too."

With whom does he want to be counted in? thought Henriette, more bewildered than ever. It was a shame how untutored she was in political matters. Since all these people were in agreement, must she not have misunderstood the purpose of the plebiscite? She decided to ask Hans.

The Rothschilds appeared to have a rendezvous with Princess Colalto, who had just come in and who, together with the Van der Straatens was on the point of joining them when a yell was heard, "Out with the Jews!" It came either from the Stephansplatz or the Kartnerstrasse; one could hear it plainly.

"Not such a bad idea!" remarked Captain Kunsti loudly. Frau von Kageneck laughed too and said, "Splendid."

Henriette grew still more bewildered. The captain's remark was, of course, aimed at the Rothschilds, and nothing sillier could possibly be imagined. You could not find less typical Jews than the Rothschilds anywhere.

"Sieg! Heil! Sieg! Heil! Smash the Jews! *Juda verrecke!*" The people behind Henriette called it a speaking chorus.

So many new inventions, and none of them amounting to anything. I almost make myself think I am like Franz, she thought. I used to be all for the new things and he was not. It seems to me I am getting old.

What the next table had called a speaking chorus came nearer, and suddenly Hans burst in, his hat on, his coat buttoned askew. He rushed straight over to her, without seeing or bowing to anyone, and said, "Mother, come quickly!"

"Life-saving crew!" Henriette heard the delightful captain remark. The amiable Italian Minister called, "*Cameriere*, my bill!"

Hans did not even give her time to put on her coat. Moreover, her Sacher cake and coffee were standing, still untouched, on the table. Why make such a scene in public? Because of a few shouters?

Hans would not wait a single instant. "Don't you want at

least to say good evening to the Kagenecks?" she asked in an attempt to delay him. There had always been mobs and always would be. One ignored them; that was what one should do with mobs.

But Hans took her out into the raucous street and put her into a taxi he had waiting in a side alley. "I don't want you to leave the house until Sunday," he said as they drove along.

"How absurd!"

"We must wait until Sunday," he insisted.

She was familiar with this feverish expression of his.

"What for?"

"Look, Mother, there is no sense in asking. All I know is that the Nazis are raising heaven and hell to prevent Sunday's plebiscite from taking place."

"They have shouted for years and distributed the leaflets Hermann printed," said Henriette, "and what have they accomplished with all the clamor? Nothing. I often think they should have taken Hermann less seriously, and then he would have caused less tragedy and had less of it himself."

"Hermann!"

She had never heard Hans speak in such an implacable tone.

The taxi could not drive into Annagasse, it was so full of people, so the chauffeur let his fares get out at the church. "There must be something going on down at Number 5," he volunteered. "These damned Nazis!"

"That's the first sensible thing I've heard this evening," declared Henriette, and pushed her way through the crowd who were yelling "Sieg! Heil!" as though they were so many machines.

"I implore you, don't make any remarks!" begged Hans.

"Don't be ridiculous. For so long I was not allowed to say what I wanted to. You're not going to rob me any longer of that pleasure."

The mob made way before the lady with the uncovered white hair, the regal necklace of pearls, and the commanding manner. "What are you after here?" asked a woman with a Berlin accent, who was leading the shouting.

"I'm going home. I live here," answered Henriette contemptuously.

"Attention! The Empress of Annagasse!" came the cry from a handful of Viennese, half in earnest. But they let her pass.

It became apparent that the demonstration had been directed against the Freemason Lodge at Number 5. Every window on the front had been smashed, and the mob was still throwing stones.

As mother and son had almost reached Number 10 a cry was heard, "Over there is something Jewish too!" A hail of stones was the reply. It shattered Selma's memorial tablet. The stones also struck the angel with the trumpet overhead.

The body of the angel broke and crashed to the ground. Only the arm, which held the trumpet, remained intact. As ever, since the house was built, it rose above the door.

CHAPTER 50
Homecoming to an Alien Land

On Friday evening two days before the plebiscite, the saddest voice Hans had ever heard said over the radio, "Austrians! Chancellor Hitler has threatened that German troops will occupy our land if I do not cancel the plebiscite within one hour's time and withdraw from the Government. In order to avoid the shedding of blood, I bow to force. I take my farewell of you. God protect Austria!"

Hans had recognized the voice and heard the sobbing that accompanied it. Nevertheless, he was not willing to believe that it spoke the truth. But a few minutes later another voice came over the air which made long, embarrassed pauses between the words: "German fellow countrymen! I, Dr. Arthur Seyss-Inquart, have succeeded Dr. Schuschnigg as Chancellor and am happy to announce to you that German troops have crossed our frontier and taken over the defence of our land."

Now there was no longer any doubt.

Day and night, night and day, without ceasing, roaring bombers flew low over Vienna. The sound of their motors was unrelenting; it deafened the ears and tore; the nerves to such an extent that one gave up. Anything—but no more of that penetrating, grinding roar! Loudspeakers were set up everywhere. They bellowed forth a speech of Hitler, who had reached the Danube. Night and day, day and night, German troops tramped down Mariahilferstrasse. Their greenish uniforms were unfamiliar to the Viennese, also their helmets, their boots, their marching steps. They set up their camps in the public squares; their field kitchens smoked before the castle; their cannon stood in front of the statue of Mozart; their stacks of arms were polished bright beside the Beethoven monument. On Ring Boulevard you could not see the trees for the red flags with the sprawling black swastikas. On all the advertisement pillars one gigantic placard was displayed. It was an over-life-size picture of Hitler's face. Wherever you went it was looking at you. Under it were the words, "One people! One country! One Führer!" Inside of a single day and night the aspect of Vienna had changed beyond recognition. Early spring had no glow. Blossoms no space. Lightness no voice. Loveliness no breath.

When the roar of the bombers, the bellowing of the loudspeakers, the goose-stepping tramp of marching soldiers was smothered by a deafening hurricane of shouts of "Heil!" Hitler had come. He stood in an open car which was driven at a snail's pace down Mariahilferstrasse and the Ring. Hans saw what his eyes refused to look upon. The tears flooding them veiled what he did not want to see. As never before, he prayed for a miracle. Would it be given to this man, whose ugliness could not be mitigated even by a smile, to ride in triumph past that academy which had rejected him because of his absolute lack of talent? Hans stood on the steps of that academy and saw the gaze of the defeated candidate burn with hatred as it fell on the scene of his defeat. He stretched his hand out at an angle; a contemptuous expression made his vulgar mouth even more vulgar as he cried, "I greet my Viennese!"

Did no one see the hideous vulgarity of this man?

It cannot be that I am the only one to see it! thought Hans. *Among these thousands there must be thousands who see it as I do! Haven't the Viennese for hundreds of years lived by their eyes? Isn't this man too hideous for them?* And he listened anxiously to hear the crowd say the manifest thing.

But the crowd did not say it. Their eyes followed the repulsive, triumphant man as if enthralled; their arms were stretched out to him in friendly greeting, and even after he had passed they stood there for a while, motionless. The miracle, which in Hans's eyes would have been natural, did not occur. No shot was fired; not one of the tens of thousands who only the day before yesterday were crying, "Heil Schuschnigg!" now cried anything but, "Heil Hitler!"

I did not fire a shot either, said Hans to himself, attempting to defend the Viennese. But he gave it up at once, when he thought that they had not, like him, wondered all their lives whether men were allowed to shoot at each other. Only the man whose name they were still shouting the day before yesterday, and which today they had already forgotten, had not been willing to shoot. He was not willing to face the reproaches again which he had made to himself because of shooting at the working men. That was why he was now a prisoner and this other man was riding in triumph.

The procession had reached the Opera House; the acclamation of the crowds grew more tempestuous. Shortly thereafter a voice made even more metallic by the loud-speaker was heard: "People of Vienna! This is the proudest day of my life! For I, an Austrian, was chosen by Providence to fulfil your century-old longing and to lead you home into the German Reich!"

Home in the German Reich. Home in a most bitterly alien land. Never, whether they cried "Heil Hitler!" or not, whether, enthralled, they turned their eyes and arms to him or not, did any of these people here ever have the desire to become German. They had laughed at things German, or hated them, or tolerated them, with resistance. Hans had seen this too often during the war and afterwards not to know that. Whatever had come over them to make them stand there now and shout for joy, they had never for a single hour looked upon Germany as their homeland. For their home and that of their ancestors had for a thousand years been here; it was this Austrian city of Vienna, which had been made to mask its springtime trees under garish red banners, and through the beautiful streets of which goose-stepping feet tramped in a way to pierce one's very heart.

The miracle did not happen. The thing which should have been manifest failed to materialize. Hans stood on the steps of the Academy of Arts, opposite which the Goethe monument was now covered by three gigantic swastikas. Behind him stood Christopher Alt, his great-grandfather, who had to thank Maria Theresa for his start in life; his grandfather, Emil Alt, who was responsible for making the product of the C. Alt Firm achieve the distinction of being named the "melody of Vienna"; his father, Franz Alt, whom Francis Joseph made Purveyor to the Court; his uncle, Otto Eberhard, who had served Francis Joseph. These dead Austrians of the house of Number 10 Seilerstätte stood behind the living one who had to live through the agony of seeing Vienna no longer Austrian. He and those cheering were strangers in their homeland. The one thing to which he had still clung with passion was now lost to him. And when he admitted that his last hope was being buried under all the triumphant shouting he was so overwhelmed by despair that he no longer attempted to conceal it. He wept openly.

"Have you lost someone, mister?" a man asked with typical Viennese curiosity and sentimentality.

He did not see who it was. He saw nothing; everything was opaque. "Yes," he answered.

Then he began to walk without knowing where he was going. He had lost someone. After losing the one human being with whom he wanted to live, he had lost the one land in which he could live. For him there was no other.

CHAPTER 51
The Cry to Heaven

"Come back for me about ten," Henriette had said to Simmerl.

Age was one of the best excuses. You could say your hearing was poor if you wanted to avoid the nuisance of the eternal radio, broadcasting absurdities anyway. You could say that your eyesight was not good if you were forced to go to the cinema, where the metallic voices and gray shadows had never been a cause for enthusiasm and where nowadays much less enjoyable fare was to be had. And you could say you were tired as soon as you could no longer stand the endless chatter about politics, which began whenever two people came together.

Simmerl, at whom you had to yell (his age was not an

excuse), had replied, "Very good, Your Ladyship," and Henriette had gone down to her nephew Peter's, where there was a Tuesday gathering. No chamber music was being played today, and only a few of the regular attendants were present. Henriette found it little to her taste to go into Society just now, but she realized that she must show herself there. It was only people like Hans, determined to butt their heads through the wall, who refused to admit this. People eat even on the day of a funeral, and they laugh again at some time or other afterwards. Life was the most illogical thing there was. It went on.

Henriette wore her old champagne-colored dress; why have anything new made now? For whom? The ladies from Berlin and Breslau, who were flooding Vienna these days, dressed so that you could not even look at them; for them her champagne-colored dress, worn so often, was still too stylish.

She sat for a while with Liesl Drauffer and Fritz, whom she began to like because they did not keep their mouths buttoned up, and later with Pauline, who was almost more hard of hearing than Simmerl. It was a cross to bear with these old people. With Pauline you literally had to shout at her. Moreover, the subject matter of the conversation was not interesting: they were discussing Gretl's grave. For the colonel's widow in her will had expressed the wish not to be buried in the Alt family vault but with her Paskiewicz where she now actually lay. Here was another example of what attention should be paid to principles! In death Gretl had ignored the family will which in her lifetime she had insisted should be respected to such a degree, and why? Because this time it was a case of her own well-being.

That Joachim, Peter's eldest son, was a funny boy. He was constantly hovering around Henriette. She had never bothered her head much about these offspring of Peter's, but when she saw them she was at a loss to make them out. Adelheid was pretty, even if she was the absolute image of her Prussian mother, and the youngest appeared to take after his father. Anyhow he was just as plump. As she looked at him Henriette could not help remembering the fat little boy who, the day she came to pall on the family when she became engaged, was led into the room by a corseted Frenchwoman, and Franz gave him a candy. How many years lay between? Better not count them up—it makes one even older. But to think that they had named the fat young-ster Otto Adolf! Otto Eberhard had sounded stiff enough and, God knows, had been it too! Incidentally, it must be a new fash-ion to let children take part in receptions nowadays.

"Well, Joachim, how are things with you?" she asked, hav-ing made up her mind to speak to the youth who did not leave her side. But he did not answer.

I probably spoke too low because a moment ago I was yelling so at Pauline, thought Henriette, and repeated her question in a louder tone to the young man. He wore one of those new uni-forms, cropping up every day which one could never really rec-ognize.

But again Joachim did not answer. He merely stared at his great-aunt.

"Tell me," said Henriette, taking it for social inexperi-ence—and what could one expect with a mother who was wearing a blouse and skirt to an evening reception!—"have you lost your tongue?"

Then the young person in the black uniform opened his mouth and said, "I don't speak to Jewesses!"

At first she was not sure of his sanity.

Pauline had heard nothing. Fritz said, "Hold your tongue, you! We don't want to hear anything of that sort! Either today or on any other day!"

"Don't tell me," Henriette asked the composer, "that he really meant what he said?"

"What does he know!" Fritz answered, vexed. "He blabs

what he hears others prating. Haven't you had any tea yet, Aunt Hetti? May I get you some?"

"Wait a moment," said Henriette, calling him back. "In the first place. I'm not taking any tea. And in the second, I want to know what that young man has in his mind. He's no longer so young that he can say such stupid things!" She had raised her voice slightly.

"Grand-aunt is insulting Joachim," Joachim's sister Adelheid was heard to say to her mother, who was busy pouring tea.

"What I have in my mind is: Jews and Jewesses are to get out!" was the young man's reply to Henriette's question.

Again Henriette hesitated to believe he meant her. When, however, there was no longer any room for doubt she rose and slapped the young man in the face.

He shrank back, but his mother came up to Henriette.

"Frau Stein," she said, still holding the teapot in one hand as she addressed her, "this German house is no longer a place for the encroachments of your race!"

The host also left a group of fellow functionaries to come to his wife's side. "I should have thought," he said in an undertone, "that you yourself would have had the tact to stay away from our gathering. And when I saw you appear I hoped that at least you would be aware of the limits now drawn in German Society. I shall excuse the regrettable incident which has just occurred by attributing it to your age and ignore for this once the conclusions I should otherwise draw. But I must ask you to leave this company at once."

But this is not possible, thought Henriette. *To whom is he speaking?*

Yet he was addressing her, and the guests were gaping at her, some of them disconcerted, others concurring, when Fritz, throwing back his now gray head, said, "Come, Aunt Hetti. Although I have not the honor to belong to your race. I'm so fed up with my own that I'm glad to leave this tea-party company for good." He offered his arm to the old lady, while his wife Liesl, who for long had not been slim enough to dance moonbeams but who could still take the parts of ballet mothers, walked on her other side.

"Bravo!" cried someone from the other end of the room. It was long-bearded Otto, and although no one could remember when the twins, since they were grown up, had been of one opinion, they acted in unison on this evening as decades ago they used to do when they took such pleasure in teasing their cousin Peter.

"Exodus from Egypt," commented the youth who was slapped. Now Henriette saw Simmerl arrive. You could say what you liked about that old man but he was punctual to the minute. "Thank you, Fritz," she said to the composer. "Thank you, Liesl." To Otto she said nothing. The man with the long beard had never been a favorite with her.

As always, when he came to fetch her, Simmerl announced with a bow, "It is ten o'clock, Your Grace."

Henriette acknowledged the announcement. She nodded to Pauline, who sat there open-mouthed, not knowing what she should do. She nodded also to old painter Drauffer, who had been rambling around Heaven knows where, and had just arrived all out of breath. He showed by a grimace what he thought of the whole thing. Then she let Simmerl open the door for her and left. Today she again forgot the lift.

The renovating had not helped much. To be sure, it was electricity instead of gas which now binned in the staircase, but the patches of dampness were almost more evident under the gleaming fresh white calcimine than they used to be under the dull gray finish. It was a good thing that one should not talk while climbing the stairs. Or else one should have been compelled to say the one word over add over: incomprehensible.

Arriving at the fourth floor, Henriette made an effort to grasp what had happened. She was glad that Hans was not at home. He was so worked up about everything anyway, the poor boy.

The old lady could not settle down. She had been deeply upset, and immediately afterwards the annoying palpitation in her heart had begun again. She took ten drops of baldrian on a lump of sugar.

Mono's time must be close at hand, she thought, trying to force her mind on to other subjects. *I believe it will be a girl. I hope she will not call her Henriette, as she wrote to me she would. She is always so sweet and wants to give me pleasure. But Henriette is too old-fashioned a name. I really underestimated Franziska. It is very decent of her to have Mono to stay at her house at this time. In Salzburg it is much better than here. Down there Mono, with her Heimwehr husbahd, won't have any such difficulties.* Then she was thinking of the unborn child, who would be her first grandchild, when she noticed that Simmerl was still in the room.

"Thanks, I don't need anything more."

"Good night, Your Grace," he wished her.

"Good night, Herr Simmer!" she replied, whereupon he withdrew with his usual evening bow. Would he perhaps now turn against her too? If what had happened downstairs was possible anything was possible.

For her throbbing heart it was best to walk round the apartment a little. This she did, and everywhere she turned on the lights. In the light everything seemed more bearable, and that was something which had been lacking long enough in this house.

As she went from room to room the old lady tried to find an explanation. Downstairs, the society was German. Apparently she should have known that. And she had no place in German society.

And why had she no place in a society where she had always had her place, which, indeed, she had forced to belong to her?

The part about the Jews could not possibly be the reason, because that would be too stupid even to be considered. Anyone who was good enough for the Austrian Crown Prince should not be too bad for Frau Annemarie.

She paused in front of the photograph on the bureau. The picture had been taken in Agram. Franz had sent it to her from a business trip of several days in that city. She had had it framed and set it there ever since. "In memory of your Franz," was what he had written under it. In those days there had been another picture before her eyes. Perhaps that was why he had sent her his. She studied his face, which had always been so easy to read. His mouth was still straight, and his eyes had that straight, trustworthy look which never changed and which nothing could change. Was it because of my sin? she asked the picture. You know, it never, seemed like a sin to me, and for so long I even looked upon it as my right. I have known now, this long time, that it was a sin on my part. Is it because of that?

They had stood together at the window, and music had floated up from below. Alfred Grünfeld had played waltzes at her wedding. She could hear herself asking, "Do you remember, Franz, what you promised me up in the Giant Wheel?"

She kept coming back to the picture, was that the reason?

Restless, she wandered from room to room. To have such a thing happen to you in your old age as happened down there tonight you must have been very wicked, she said to herself. And she attempted to add up the debit side of her ledger. Since she was born she had been a Catholic. She had seldom gone to confession. She had lacked piety. She had deceived. She had been selfish.

Then she wished to look at the credit side, but she saw nothing. The page was blank.

That cannot be so, she said in despair to the picture. She

gazed at it until the face in it began to live. No, she now read. On the debit side there are many things. But for the credit side there are things too. The scales were balanced.

But was that enough? she kept asking, more and more filled with the sense of strange uneasiness she had always felt before the apparition came which she so feared and which, thank God, had not appeared for months. Was that enough for a life-time?

There was noise in the staircase. The gathering downstairs was apparently breaking up. Immediately following, knocks echoed from the door on the fourth floor and the shout "Open!" When it was opened voices became audible in the vestibule.

Was it Joachim, who had wanted to turn her out of her own house, coming up in the middle of the night? Earlier she had been too dumbfounded. Now? she would give him the answer he deserved!

There was a light knock at her bedroom door. Simmerl, in his dressing gown, stood before it and said, "Three gentlemen are here, Your Grace. Or rather—three men. They say they are from the police. I did my best to make them understand that Your Ladyship had withdrawn for the night. But they say it is urgent. Would Your Grace care to see them?"

In the vestibule stood three men in a uniform she did not recognize. "Secret State Police," said one of them.

"There must be some mistake," suggested Henriette.

"It's no mistake."

"What should the police be after in my home?"

"Where's your son?"

"Not at home."

"Doesn't he live here?"

"Yes."

"At a quarter before midnight he is not at home?"

"He often comes home later than that."

"What does he do with himself?"

"He goes for walks. He loves Vienna."

"You mean the Vienna Schuschnigg System? Wasn't he a great friend of Schuschnigg? With him every evening? What?"

"I mean Vienna. I am somewhat tired, gentlemen. I'd like to go to bed."

"How dare you speak like that to us! Don't you know who we are?"

"You told me."

"And you have the impertinence to talk down to us? Do you know what you are?"

"I have known it for seventy-three years and never had occasion to forget it."

"You're a filthy Jewess! That's what you can know you are!"

Henriette nodded. "I have already heard that once today. I have never felt myself to be a Jewess, although my sainted father was a Jew. But the difference between my father and people like you is so immeasurable that it makes me proud to think of my father."

The three looked at each other nonplussed. Then they looked at the aged servant, with his hand to his ear so that he could hear better, nodding at nearly every word his mistress said. Then they looked at her, in her champagne-colored gown, her hair perfectly dressed, standing erect.

"Give us the keys to your son's desk," the young man who was the spokesman said with a Saxon inflection. The Saxon dialect had always seemed comic to the Viennese, and the comedian Girardi had shown them how laughable it was by his imitations.

"I haven't got the keys," Henriette said. "My son keeps them."

"And where are the keys to your own desk?"

Now she was mortally alarmed. In her desk were three letters from Rudolf, two from Count Traun, innumerable letters and cards from Franz. Henriette belonged to the women who keep their letters.

"No," she said, and looked at Simmerl, who was shaking his head. Good, thought Henriette, that's clear. Not even a foolish old creature like Simmerl, who after all was twelve years her senior, would give them the keys.

"Hand over the keys!" ordered the spokesman, and came a step nearer. "We have a house search to execute here! Understand?" This last he bellowed.

Is he going to strike me? thought Henriette, looking again to Simmerl for counsel. The old man was shaking his head wildly.

"No!" repeated Henriette. It was really remarkable what courage the old man had.

"You know the consequences of this?" asked the Saxon.

Of course she knew them. They would arrest her. Perhaps they would kill her? For an instant Henriette grew cold with fear.

"There's nothing in my desk which could be of interest to you," she forced herself to say.

"Break it open!" the Saxon ordered the other two.

By then Simmerl was already in the boudoir, where Henriette's little Biedermaier writing desk stood. He threw himself in front of it, stretching both his hands behind him to protect the lock; a second later he was lying on the floor, stabbed. "It would be better for Your Grace—" he was still able to say, but Henriette did not learn what would have been better for her.

Leaning over him and stroking his paling cheeks, she said, "Thank you, Herr Simmerl." Perhaps he still heard it. Blood flowed from his lips.

Henriette stood up. "To get into this desk you will have to do the same to me," she said, and followed the old man's example. With both hands blocking the top of her desk, she stood guard over her past.

"Whether one or more croaks is all the same to us," the young Saxon said in a matter-of-fact tone.

Henriette nodded. "That is the second thing I have learned today. I am a Jewess. I was not aware of it. And you are pitifully poor people who are not even aware of what compassion is."

Then the other two, at a signal from the Saxon, had hurled themselves on her and seized her by the throat. She screamed.

She still heard something confusedly. She still saw something in a daze. It was the voice and habit of Christl, and she was calling, "Aunt Hetti!"

Aunt Hetti is no longer here, she thought to herself. *It is pleasant not to be here any longer.*

When Hans came home from his aimless wandering Christl was waiting for him. She said that she had been asleep but was awakened in the middle of the night by a piercing scream. It had left her no peace until she could come over from her convent. She had come just in time, she said, and held his hand firmly in hers, to close his mother's eyes. It was a gentle death, without any struggle. He would see for himself when she took him in to her.

She, who had always been with him when the irrevocable happened, led him into the bedroom. On the bed, where she had borne him, lay Henriette. She had on her champagne-colored dress, her gleaming pearls, which hid her bruised neck; her hair was perfectly dressed, and she was beautiful.

CHAPTER 52
A Simple Viennese Girl

After the two funerals Hans returned to the factory. Following his mother's burial a service was held for Simmerl, who was interred not far from the Alt family vault. It was

Simmerl's widow Hanni who had dressed her mistress and prepared her for her last rest. It was Hanni's words, too, at the graveside which stirred Hans most deeply. "She was a woman who wanted to be happy. And, seeing she couldn't, she wanted to make others happy." Whether or not she succeeded, Hanni did not say. About her husband she said, "He was a simple man. But true he was, as gold." The two funerals passed almost unnoticed. Not even all the relatives took part in them.

For that evening Hans made an appointment with Dr. Einried to go through his mother's last will. She had left exact instructions; from the heirs she named and the legacies she left one could see again whom she had liked and whom not. Her pearls she bequeathed, in a codicil to her original will, to Franziska. Her whole wardrobe went to Hanni. Sister Agatha was to have the letters in her desk "so that she will understand why I sinned and because she, of all the people I know, is best fitted to hold her tongue." The direction to her children to move out of the Seilerstätte house after her death remained unaltered. As Martha Monica was living in Salzburg, in order to protect her compromised husband from the concentration camp, this direction affected only Hans, and he was determined to act in accordance with it. Since he had learned the facts which Christl had concealed from him, the house was unbearable.

The chief clerk Foedermayer, Fräulein Hübner, foreman Czerny, and Bochner, the metal-caster, as spokesmen for the workers, came into the office. They were dressed in black, had taken part in the funeral, and now came as a delegation to express their condolences to their boss.

"Herr Alt," said the metal-caster Bochner, "we know how you feel. You've been with us since you were a boy. We want to tell you, Herr Alt, that we're all fond of you. Every one of us. And not just the workers and the staff in your business. If there are people who can disprove and overcome prejudices and class conflicts you are one of them."

Bochner seemed to have prepared a longer speech, for he was obviously on the point of saying more. Then he either would not or could not go on, for he cleared his throat, went over to Hans, and thrust out his hand.

In silence Hans took his hand and shook it. Then he did the same to all the others. But when he took Fräulein Hübner's hand it was even colder than his own.

The delegation was still in Hans's office when some S.A. men walked in unannounced.

Bochner cried, "Watch out!"

There were seven of them, under the command of a superior officer who introduced himself, "Sturmbandführer Esk. I believe you knew my father. Or your mother knew him. My father's pen name was Jarescu."

"My mother was buried an hour ago," Hans said stonily, as he had said and done everything until now.

"We have come in that very connection," explained Sturmbandführer Esk. He had the same blue-black oiled hair of the man who had borne the name of Jarescu the writer.

"You won't expect me to have any use for the condolences of murderers. Excuse me," Hans said.

"It is not a case of condolences. I'm here on behalf of Gauleiter Bürckel to take over your firm in the course of the Aryanization of Vienna business enterprise."

"What did you say?" exploded Foedermayer, usually so reticent.

Foreman Czerny, whose head, like that of the chief clerk, had grown white in the service of the firm, turned as though he suddenly wished to leave the room.

"You remain here!" Esk ordered. Three S.A. men barred the way to the felt-covered door.

The metal-caster Bochner, who years ago had fired on a

police lieutenant, did not stir. His hair was gray now. His glance hair was gray how. His glance went back and forth between the Sturmbandführer and Hans. His hands remained in his trousers pokets.

"Our interview will perhaps be lengthy," said the son of the publisher of the *Vienna Signals*, and he pushed a chair for himself into the middle of the room.

"There is nothing to discuss here," Hans said. "The firm of Christopher Alt is Aryan and has been since it was founded it was founded. It has existed in this same place for one hundred and seventy-eight years."

"I regret to state it has not been Aryan since your father was at the head of it. Your grandmother, you may recall, was born a Bergheimstein. You yourself are of Jewish descent on your father's and on your mother's sides. You don't meet with the requirements of the Nuremberg laws."

Before the eyes of the man saying this hung the paintings of Christopher and Emil Alt, Hans's great-grandfather and grandfather.

Hans too could see the portraits of these Viennese who were not only the founders of a Viennese firm but who were the very embodiment of Vienna life itself. They had never meant much more to him than a dead past. In this instant that past began to live.

"My co-workers," he said, "will confirm the fact that I've never cut the figure of a head here. I came into the firm, at the request of my father, as he had done at the request of my grandfather. My grandfather did it at the request of my great-grandfather. The Alt firm, Herr Esk—I believe you come from Romania and therefore may not know it—has not only been a Christian firm since its founding, but—and this to my mind is much more decisive—has been a truly Viennese firm. It is unbecoming to me to emphasize the merits of the firm, to the reputation of which I personally have contributed so little.

But every Viennese, by which I mean every true Viennese, will be of the opinion that the pianos on which Mozart, Beethoven, and Brahms composed have more significance for Vienna than Herr Gauleiter Bürckel can ever have. Now please leave me. As I said before. I've just come from a funeral."

"You will turn over to me whatever is requisite to the co-ordination and further conduct of the firm," Jarescu's son said. "Understand?"

Hans's eyes fell on Bochner, the metal-caster. In one bound he was at his side and holding him tightly, by the hand. "Yes," he said, pressing the hand which was gripping a revolver. "But first I should like to say good-bye to my fellow workers." Shaking the metal-caster's hand, he said to him, "Adieu, Bochner. We'll go on helping each other as before, shan't we?"

"Yes, Herr Alt," the man said, bringing the words out with difficulty.

"Adieu, Herr Foedermayer," Hans said to the chief clerk. "I think you're not losing much of a boss. I never did anything except what you taught me. But I hope you'll carry on in the same way to the best interests of the arm under my pure Aryan successor." Then he stretched out his hand to Czerny, but the old man kissed him on both cheeks. "I've never called you Hans," he said. "It wouldn't have been proper between boss and workman. But now it is—good-bye, Hans. Much luck to you, and may we meet soon!"

Now only Fräulein Hübner was left. She was so pale that even Hans noticed it. "I'm going with you," she said as he put out his hand to say good-bye. "I'm not going to leave you alone now."

"Look after him, Fraulein Mitzi," said Bochner, "so that he doesn't do anything rash. People do, sometimes."

"I give you my word," the girl answered.

"Is this touching private interview at an end? I shall expect your lawyer at the earliest possible moment to arrange for an absolutely legal transfer," said the new boss.

Hans laid the keys on the desk and left.

The noise of dip cabinet-makers, the metal-casters, the tuners faded. Then it was gone entirely.

"I don't care. I know you don't love me. You don't need me. But you need some human being. You cannot drive me away," said the girl who had followed him.

You cannot possibly refuse the hand of a friend. Who had said that? In Hans everything had turned to stone. He was so frozen, so rigid, that he could not speak.

"Things are not as bad as they seem to you now," the girl went on desperately. And since she could not think of any other words she repeated, "They really aren't!"

She loved the man beside her with a power which to her was stronger than his unhappiness. She knew nothing of accounting for her actions, nor had she any plan. If this man had said to her, "Let us, go and jump into the Danube," she would have gone with him unquestioningly.

"If Czerny was allowed to call you Hans may I too call you Hans?" she asked.

She had already called him that. Was it in Grinzing?

She had wiped that evening out of her life, although it was the most beautiful one of all, she said. And also the saddest. But at the time, and since then, he had not noticed this. He had not noticed her much at all. She found that only natural.

His dislike of exaggeration was roused. She was making of him a man he had never been. "Fräulein Hübner," he said, "you couldn't find anyone who is more bankrupt more shattered in every respect, than I am."

"Would it be quite impossible for you to call me Mitzi?" she said. "I've been for long—I'd better not say for how long—in love with you. But every time you call me 'Fräulein Hübner' it goes right through me like a knife."

"All right, Mitzi," he said.

She stopped still in Wiedner Hauptstrasse, as though he had made her a present. "I'm very silly," she said in excusing herself. "And I know you had a wife who was a genius—forgive me for speaking of it. I think it's magnificent of you not to forget her. But between not forgetting and not even seeing anyone else—isn't there a difference?"

The shadow of a smile lurked around his lips. "What do you think you could do with a boss who has been fired?"

"If I only dared to say! But I don't dare," she said.

He did not want to go back to the house of death. He did not want to look people in the face who had shouted "Heil Hitler!" Every face he looked into was an insult to him. As though every one of them had betrayed him.

She hesitated before she made the suggestion. She had a tiny apartment over in Karolinengasse. "You see, I've moved away from my parents."

His mother had lived in Karolinengasse when she was a girl.

"It's an awfully little apartment," she told him. "When I took it I thought to myself: 'I wonder if he'll ever come to see it?' When was that?"

That day they went to Grinzing—did he remember?—she had asked him if she could go home before she met him. She wanted to change her dress; that was the reason she gave. He had never noticed that she did not change it. But she had dashed over and taken an apartment.

He did not seem to object to her going on with her story. The apartment had belonged to a friend who had moved and who had intended it for someone else, she said. But this friend had told her that if you were in love with a great gentleman you should have a little apartment. That is why she took the apartment in Karolinengasse at the time. Now he would naturally think ill of her?

His thinking was not functioning well. Thoughts came but did not stick. But even when they did hot stick they hurt.

"Would you perhaps like to see the apartment now?" she asked. And when he said "Yes," she added, overjoyed: "It will be a great honor for me."

She was a simple Viennese girl.

CHAPTER 53
"I Will Deliver You from Fear"

Since he had been dismissed Hans was, so to speak, a free man. He had all the time he wished to convince himself of the state of things in Vienna.

Spring had come with unheard-of beauty and with a sudden, premature, eruptive power, as though it were intent on burying the swastikas under a flood of blossoms. The Prater chestnut trees paraded an unwonted wealth of foliage; the violets smothered the meadows with their fragrance; the lilac bushes between the equestrian statues of Prince Eugene and Archduke Charles were as luxuriant as if they had never graced Hitler's entry. The more Hans saw of the city on which spring was lavishing her Maytime splendor, the more clearly he came to realize that that entry was an illusion.

Hitler had made his entry. Since then someone had ruled in his name—a man called Burckel, who was born in the Saar and who had never been in Vienna before. The name Austria had been wiped off the map by the Austrian who had freed it. The country, a thousand years old, was now called Ostmark. All this was no illusion.

But Hans was after the truth, and he found it. He had wanted to talk with people, and he did talk with them. "Perhaps you are right; things are not what they seem," he said to Mitzi, who as usual went to the factory in Wiedner Hauptstrasse every morning and, when she came back towards evening, waited for him to come to her. And when he came her joy was so great that it warmed him in his benumbed state. Slowly, little by little, she helped him back to life.

Not one of the Viennese whom he had seen and with whom he had spoken had been in the cheering crowds which to him, as to all the world, had lent an aspect of jubilation and conclusiveness to the entry of the liberator. This too helped him back to life.

It was people from South Germany who had lined the way of the triumphant march into Vienna, he learned from Ebeseder. Together with Mitzi and Fritz, Ebeseder stood by him. When he was unwilling to believe this, his old friend—he outwardly had reverted to being once more a painter of still life—showed him an order of the Ministry of Propaganda and Public Instruction under the date line of Berlin, March 13, 1938, and signed "Goebbels." The order read:

> To Gauleiters in Bavaria, Baden, and Württemberg. It will be the responsibility of the propaganda chiefs to see that, in connection with the entry of our Führer into Vienna on March 14, 1938, district contingents of party comrades are to be dispatched to Vienna. Each district is to provide fifteen thousand party comrades who are to participate in the entry celebration and produce an overwhelming demonstration. The propaganda chiefs must see to it that the Viennese populace, as well as the foreign observers, receive the impression that it is not tourists but native Viennese who are cheering our Führer. Consequently the propaganda chiefs will make it their duty to place in the first three rows of all lanes lining the entrance procession exclusively party comrades from South Germany, whose dialect resembles the Viennese mode of speech. All matters pursuant to the above to be carried out in concert with the leader of the Gestapo in Vienna, party comrade Heydrich. Transportation costs to and from Vienna, as well as maintenance charges while there, to be undertaken by

the Ministry. They are not to exceed thirty reichsmarks per person.

No government order had ever delighted Hans so much. He read it over until he knew it by heart. Under the Prater trees, in the Volksgarten, in the City Park of his childhood years, where the benches now bore little plates reading "For Aryans only," he kept repeating to himself: "Must see to it that the Viennese populace receives the impression …"

The longer he looked in the face of the city he knew so well, the more distinct the gigantic hoax to which he and it had fallen victims became to him. A few well-timed special trains and a few thousand paid shouters had overridden them and stopped their mouths.

"I'm not sure that it is wise for you to be seen about so much," Cousin Peter had said to him. "It reaches my ears that you have been seen in districts where you have no business to go. You talk with people you don't even know. You ask questions which for a piano manufacturer are, to put it mildly, far off the mark. Credit me with my old sympathy for you if I caution you. People like you must be particularly prudent. You not only stood in closest contact with Herr Schuschnigg, but also you maintain strange relationships with Bolshevik circles. It would not be surprising if one day it will be found necessary to secure your person." This conversation took place before the angel entrance of Number 10; the smashed stone figure was supposed to be repaired, but there were yet no workers to be had for such inessential things.

Hans had let his cousin have his say. Then he asked with a quiet irony, which he was constantly developing these days (together with another even more surprising quality—an almost obsessed straightforwardness): "Tell me, Peter, how about human memory?"

The chief of division, who was on his way to the Ministry

carrying his brief-case in his gloved hands, made an inquiring gesture.

"Do people have such miserably poor memories?" Hans went on. "Or do they merely count on the miserable memories of their fellow humans? I myself have a fairly good one and remember a speech you made about taking a ridiculous man seriously. Do you too recall it?"

Peter produced a smile worthy of the Metternich tradition. "Not that I know of."

"Your father would not have said that."

"My father was a great man. But he lacked a certain realistic sense, or what we now call 'flexibility.'"

"Your father was as great or as small as decency," Hans said. He was holding in his hand the object for which he had gone to his apartment one last time: the gramophone record of Selma's speech from *Saint Joan* which she had recited for Captain Kunsti's program division.

"Are we not going to see you in the house any more?" asked his cousin.

"Oh, yes," declared Hans, to the other's obvious discomfiture. "I am, of course, no longer a piano manufacturer—you overlooked that unimportant fact in the pressure of your affairs. Nevertheless, we have plans for playing the piano a little."

The high official inquired who was meant by "we." He discovered it was Fritz and Hans.

"Fritz?" he said icily.

"We want to get up a little musical celebration in the party rooms. They are empty anyhow. You have no objections, I take it?"

"What kind of celebration?"

"Fritz's boy Raimund is going to be twelve. He sings quite well. We thought it would be nice to give *Bastien and Bastienne*, with children, to celebrate his confirmation. Would your Adelheid care to join in?"

Peter reflected. "When would it be?" he asked.

"In four weeks or so. When we have finished rehearsing."

The chief of division weighed the considerations. "Although I fear that your, shall we say, predilection for Mozart and aversion to—others is the principal motive in this production, still it really is a nice idea. Perhaps we could invite a few people in to see if you'll hear from me."

With that they parted.

Their Conversation was the outcome of Hans's long walks in districts where he had no business to go. Ebeseder and Fritz had worked out the plan together. Since Hans had won back Vienna for himself, his desire to restore it to the Viennese had grown into a passion.

Consequently, for the next few weeks the children were rehearsing, in the yellow drawing-room, a one-act opera written by Mozart in his youth. It was the same six-sided, somber room where the housewarming of the newly constructed building had taken place and where the court composer Mozart, mortally ill, had played *The Magic Flute.* The same pearwood piano still stood in the same place; its ivory keys had taken on the yellowed hue of the wood. The yellow damask curtains were still hanging at the windows which were drawn in thick folds when Henriette and Franz were married and Alfred Grünfeld sat at the pearwood piano to play dances for the bridal couple.

Now Fritz and Hans sat at it, attempting to tune the historic instrument themselves rather than entrust it to the hands of strangers. However, they found that they were inadequate to the task, for no one had played on Christopher Alt's first product for a generation, and neglect, coupled with cold and dampness, had, in the course of more than one hundred and seventy years, bereft it of its fine, clear tone. Hans was obliged to call in experts from the factory, several of his former tuners and Bochner, the metal-caster; even they took several days to accomplish their delicate task. Number 10 made no objection to the disturbance. After all, it was the instrument at which Mozart had sat.

Yet in the end the enterprise came to nothing. During the rehearsals Fritz's son Raimund went down with the measles and Aunt Annemarie strictly forbade all contact with him. Sure enough, since the birthday child could not participate in the event, his father, Fritz, cheerfully abandoned the whole party.

After further consideration, and after having talked the matter over with Annemarie, the chief of division looked upon little Raimund's measles as extremely opportune. That time in front of the angel entrance, under the impact of Hans's uncomfortable questions, he had allowed himself to be pushed to a too-hasty agreement. Annemarie of Potsdam, near Berlin, to whom he owed the possibility of continuing in his position, had made it quite clear to him that—with Hans and Fritz as the moving spirits in the affair—one could in any case not have invited anyone of rank or influence to the house. On the contrary, it was pure luck that the whole thing had fallen through. As for little Raimund, with the measles, he recovered with surprising speed and, as soon as he was allowed to appear in public again, looked as blooming as if he had not been sick at all.

The only result of the unsuccessful preparations was that since that time Hans had formed the habit of coming to the second floor and playing the piano for a while. He did not play for long, always the loveliest things which sounded pleasantly to the ears, and anyhow, Number 10 found them far less disturbing than the dissonant modern compositions of the constantly more unbearable Fritz. Nor could they in any case object, since Hans was no longer living in the house and had no piano in his own apartment. After all he, until Henriette's inheritance was settled, was still a co-owner. His new apartment, so Number had heard, lay in the Fourth District near to that of that simpleton, the little secretary, with whom, however, according to reliable information he was not living. As far as women were concerned, Henriette's son had never given evidence of discriminating taste. It was his mother's blood in him, was the verdict of Peter's household.

During the half-hour or so that Hans was in the habit of playing in the yellow drawing room he broadcast the news gathered by Ebeseder and edited by himself. The microphone built into the keyboard of the piano took advantage of the aerials of the Vienna broadcasting station Ravag, only a street away. Whereas Hermann had attempted in vain to establish a contact with it through the cellar of the house, Hans's workmen proved able to do it. It was also to the advantage of the authors of the plan, and they had considered this factor, that no one would guess that in a house where forbidden propaganda had already once been produced, anything similar would again be undertaken.

At first daily, and later on at intervals of two or three days (according to how much or how little caution had to be exercised), the Viennese heard over their radios a voice which called itself "Austrian Freedom Station" and to which they grew accustomed to listening. The broadcast began each time with a woman's inspiring voice. Then a man's voice followed. It, too, was heartening. In the first weeks it quoted over and over again the order which had been the cause of making the Viennese first doubt and then despair of themselves. By means of that order and an untold number of other documentary proofs it destroyed the assumption that Hitler had been welcomed by anyone outside the mercenary partisans and a number of old party adherents. It also made clear that even most of these old Austrian adherents of Hitler had been disillusioned and bitterly disappointed since the Anschluss.

Over and over again the voice spoke of Austria. That she must be free, and would be free. It did not depreciate the Germans. But, it said, the great qualities of the Germans had never been those of the Austrians. Nor would the innate, rooted aversion disappear between these two people, who had a common language only to understand the more how different they were. Austria the middle, Germany the extreme. Austria the compromise, Germany the challenge. For, said the voice, Austria is more than a land. It is an idea. The idea of a super-nationalism where once twelve different nations lived together under one roof, the United Nations of Europe, united neither through language nor geography, policy nor constitution, only by the will to live together. The speaker himself had never been a politician, had never belonged to any party. Nevertheless, his own life was a proof that the Austrian idea brought classes nearer together, let races develop, and respected minds. When he was a boy and young man imperialism, compulsion, and narrow-minded rigidity had done much to compromise that Austrian idea to a dangerous degree. But in the years of his manhood, when everything was being done to destroy it, it had been restored for all time.

Of all the monuments he had ever seen, the speaker told the Austrians, the American Statue of Liberty had seemed to him the most significant. Yet for centuries it could have and should have served as the symbol of Austria, because the Austrian idea, without ever using or even understanding the word democracy, had anticipated its underlying elements. For the Austrian idea is the recognition of the fact that the only nationality which man unrelentingly may defend is humanity.

Therefore, and in the inevitable nature of things, the voice went on, the Austrian idea was first made manifest in music. In that form it had conquered the world. But for the new, free, future Austria, whose part is to make Europe European again, a universality of spirit must be the goal and the word. Hofmannsthal coined it. Where universality of spirit will prevail, the anti-European spirit of Prussia—to wit, of the Nazis—

is doomed to lasting impotence, and out of the destructive one a creative Europe will arise again.

"If she but wills, our Austria is always the land of the deepest respect for man. 'She wills! She wills!' was what German Beethoven wrote and composed. It was more than an accident, it was an omen, that those words were discovered in Austrian, archives and published in the year 1933, coincident with the rise of the Austrian Hitler, who longed to become a German and destroy respect for man.

When the voice had expressed these or similar thoughts it changed. In it enthusiasm and emotionalism were replaced by tremendous determination. One might, almost think it was another person speaking with such precision and persistence, giving dates and technical information, offering methods of resistance, calling for courage and sacrifice. It was only the light, soft music accompanying also this part of the broadcast that supplied the continuity.

The broadcast ended as it began. A woman's voice spoke, permeated with a deep and penetrating faith. For several seconds, perhaps longer, those who had been listening had not a vestige of doubt about the future.

The woman's voice said, "I will deliver you from fear …"

PREFACE AS EPILOGUE

I used to buy the exercise books prescribed by the curriculum of the Vienna Francis Joseph Gymnasium at the stationer's in Seilerstätte. My daily way took me past the corner house of Number 10, where one of my classmates lived, the son of the best-known piano-maker in Vienna. In this book that schoolmate is called Hans Alt.

I recall how he came into class with bare legs on the first day of school and was admonished by Professor Rusetter, later to become our tormentor, for being "improperly clad." His pained blushes at that time stuck in my memory. Not long afterwards another schoolmate, von Blaas, told me about an extraordinary early-morning expedition to the Prater, the exciting circumstances of which offered food for conversation among us schoolboys for weeks. Only young Alt, who knew most about it, did not take part in them. More than that, he cut himself off from the rest of us in a way which we considered arrogant. Consequently, on our side we paid little or no attention to him, and when our chief tormentor, Professor Miklau, held him up to scorn we enjoyed his discomfiture. His exclusiveness and sensitiveness were too much for us.

In the seventh of our eight years in the Gymnasium Hans made friends with kindly, tall Ebeseder, and that we liked even less. A spoiled little patrician and a proletarian? Meanwhile fantastic rumors about this patrician boy's mother, which were confirmed by our parents, had reached our ears. Our interest in them was boundless. Frau Henriette Alt, so we learned, was a historic personage of sorts.

I saw her first in Hans's small study, with its single window, on the fourth floor of the old house. He had invited a group of us—Einried, Ebeseder, von Blaas, and me—to some kind of party, for the first time in eight years and presumably because it was also the last time. For all of us—except Ebeseder, who had become a painter—had graduated, and our years of forced labour were at an end.

The old house, which from the outside made an impression of such stateliness, and which to me had always been the embodiment of a wealthy, comfortable town house, on the inside was surprisingly severe and sombre. I was as surprised that the gorgeous facade could be so deceptive as that the lady who greeted us could be the mother of our classmate. Instead of the middle-aged motherly woman whom I had expected to see, I met a fascinating young woman. Hans, who obviously was devoted to her, noticed my admiration. Perhaps the relationship which later on developed between us had its starting-point there.

It was not a close relationship—at least, not in the beginning. At the University, where I started out to become a jurist, while Hans studied philosophy, our courses and our ways led us apart. It was only during the war that we came nearer to each other. It was then that I began to realize I had been as mistaken in what I thought of Hans as I had been in the facade of the house in which he lived. Except that with him it was the other way round. Behind his shyness and reticence, his sensitiveness and quiet, there appeared a likeable human being with the typically Austrian qualities of inner tenderness and the typically un-Austrian gift of an almost fanatical power of being convinced and of convincing others.

It was when he had the tragic misfortune to lose his wife, who in these pages is called Selma Rosner, that our friendship began. At that time I was dramatic critic on a Vienna paper and wrote an obituary attempting to do justice to the extraordinary gifts of the dead; it seemed to be of some solace to the widower. From then on we became attached to one another. Our common work on the Salzburg festivals, in which we both had faith, a feeling and a love for Austria, which we both shared, strengthened our friendship. When Hans came back from his trip to America, made on behalf of the Salzburg festival, he was changed. His timidity had abated somewhat, and he seemed to have overcome the shock of Selma's death. In other ways, too, this journey had a surprising result. It had given him a belief at one and the same time in America and in Europe. The revival of Austria in the years before Hitler had proved him to be right and me wrong. I had always believed in Austria, but never put my faith in her being understood by the rest of the world.

When, under Hitler, Austria vanished from the world and flight was all that remained to us, we lost track of each other. I had been in Paris for some time. In an hour of darkest despair, I, without hope, renewed my daily attempts to get short-wave broadcasts on the wireless which some Paris friends allowed me to use. Out of the babel of voices screaming into the ether about Hitler's thousand years of power, one day after Munich, there came a voice I knew. It said, "I will deliver you from fear." And the voice that followed I also recognized. I heard its message, and it moved me as nothing else had done. To me, bereft of everything which was my existence, painfully torn from all attachments which were my very life's blood, this familiar voice sounded the first note of hope.

Since then I, and others who felt as I did, have heard it countless times. Those were the good moments in the inferno of the first months of exile. It was the voice of a submerged world, the resurrection of which it presaged. I had to be very grateful to that voice. More grateful than to any other.

One day it was silent, replaced by a woman's voice. It too spoke courage and truth, but it was no longer the familiar voice. I tried in every way to discover what had happened to that voice, although its fate was all too easy to surmise. Had it been stifled like thousands before it.

After I had been in the United States for some time, and was happy here, I received a letter from my classmate Hans Alt. It was written in Vienna and sent abroad through a friend in a neutral country. It said that Hans was well. And did I still remember the arithmetical progression of our mathematics teacher? In the same ratio as things grew worse for others, they were growing better for him, and one day things would be going extraordinarily well for all of us. "Everything is as it was," said the letter, "even Number 10. I myself arranged a change of air, but in general it is the same air. Don't you find that Mitzi speaks better than I do? She is more convincing and avoids my old mistake of being theoretical. And don't you think also that the two women's voices supplement each other?" So it was that I learned that he was well and who was speaking in his stead. That is the last I have heard from him.

Then came a statement in the New York papers. It told of an announcement in the *Volkischer Beobachter* to the effect that the Austrian Freedom Station had been discovered in a house in the First District in Vienna. I had long before learned which house that was. The news was included with other items printed in much larger type and undoubtedly of much greater importance. Yet, in my eyes, this one was the most important one in the world. Constantly my thoughts returned to that house with the misleading exterior. Was it still standing? What had become of those discovered there? Had they paid with their lives for not having been willing to become fugitives and deserters from the cause in which we believed but which they defended more heroically than Spartans at Thermopylae? Or had an immanent justice, in which we also believed, saved and preserved them for that time when they would reap the fruits of their unutterable torture?

To the feeling of deep concern aroused in me by these thoughts there was now added one of unsurmountable shame. People of the caliber of my classmate Hans Alt were the nameless heroes beside whose heroism military exploits pale. They had stuck it out and raised their voices, preachers in Hitler's wilderness.

I do not know what has become of Hans Alt. A feeling I cannot buttress with logic tells me that he is alive. Meanwhile, until the truth concerning his fate can be learned, I have attempted to fulfil a duty and to render his story up to the point it is known to me. There should at least be a memorial in words. When Hans some day sees it, as I hope he may, he will approve the fact that he does not appear in it as a 'hero.' Nevertheless, I am convinced that some day a real monument will be erected to him. It should stand in the Heldenplatz in Vienna, between the equestrian statues of Prince Eugene and Archduke Charles, the most warlike, aristocratic fighters of the House of Austria, and be the figure of a completely unwarlike, simple, democratic pedestrian. If it bears the features of Hans Alt it will bear the features of all true Austrians, whatever house they were born in.

And so the words of this picture paper of a century apply as much to him as to the almost symbolic house with the misleading facade. We have looked too long on their kind with eyes perceiving only an exterior which we took for granted. Hence the facade of Vienna was the violin of Johann Strauss, a light blue sky above vineyards, the legend of princes and sweet girls, a dance continuing into eternity. And accordingly the façade of the Viennese themselves was the lighthearted philanderer Anatol.

That is why I have tried to see beyond this facade. Behind it things have a dual aspect, are more sombre, austere, perhaps even greater than we are wont to see. Yet, despite all, that is the true, the imperishable, the indispensable Vienna. Despite all, that is the immortal Austria for whose sake a disillusioned Grillparzer passionately lived and a deaf Beethoven, adoring, died.

ERNST LOTHAR
Colorado Springs

About the Author

Ernst Lothar was born in Brünn, Austria-Hungary (now Brno in the Czech Republic) in 1890 and died in Vienna in 1974. He was a writer, theatre director, and producer. In addition to *The Vienna Melody*, first published in the US in 1944 as *The Angel with the Trumpet*, his best-known works are *The Prisoner* and *Beneath Another Sun*. He was married to the Austrian actress Adrienne Gessner.